WITHDRAWN

SMALLER SISTER

MAGGIE EDKINS WILLIS

Roaring Brook Press
New York

For Katie

Published by Roaring Brook Press. Roaring Brook Press is a division
of Holtzbrinck Publishing Holdings Limited Partnership.
120 Broadway, New York, NY 10271 · mackids.com
Text and illustrations copyright © 2022 by Maggie Edkins Willis.
All rights reserved.
Our books may be purchased in bulk for promotional, educational,
or business use. Please contact your local bookseller or the Macmillan
Corporate and Premium Sales Department at (800) 221-7945 ext.
5442 or by email at MacmillanSpecialMarkets@macmillan.com.
Library of Congress Cataloging-in-Publication Data is available.
First edition, 2022. Cover design by Kirk Benshoff.
Interior book design by Molly Johanson and Maggie Edkins Willis.
The illustrations for this book were painted digitally.
Printed in China by Toppan Leefung Printing Ltd.,
Dongguan City, Guangdong Province.
ISBN 978-1-250-76741-7 (hardcover)
1 3 5 7 9 10 8 6 4 2
ISBN 978-1-250-76742-4 (paperback)
1 3 5 7 9 10 8 6 4 2

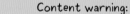

Content warning:
This book contains eating disorder thoughts and behaviors

CHAPTER 1

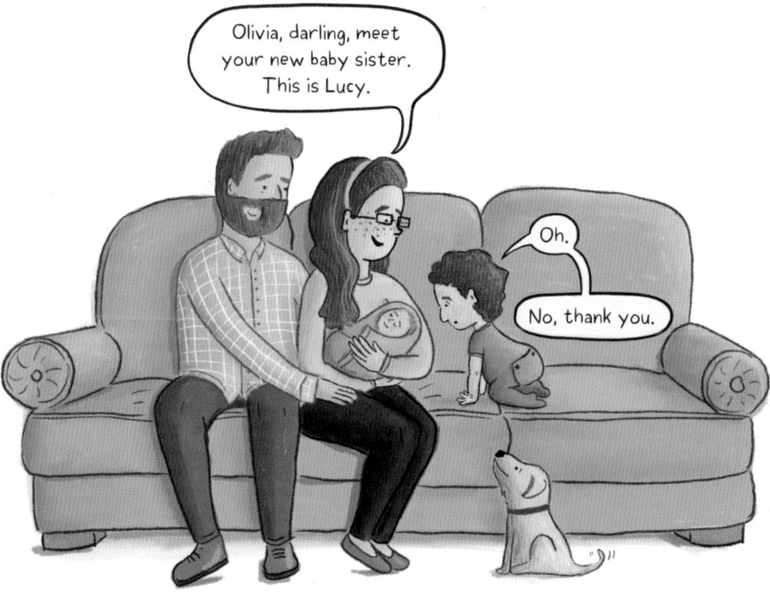
Olivia, darling, meet your new baby sister. This is Lucy.
Oh.
No, thank you.

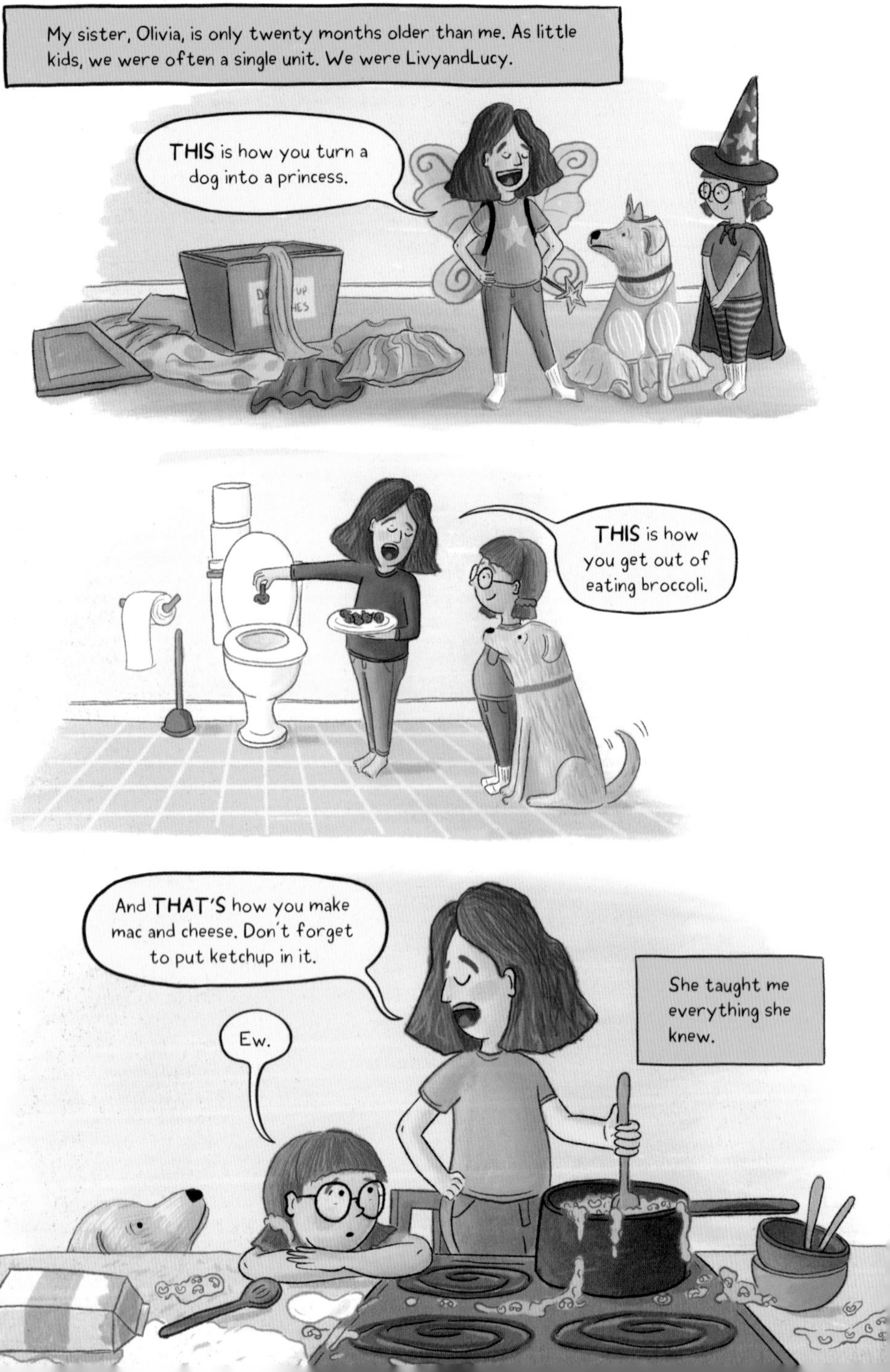
My sister, Olivia, is only twenty months older than me. As little kids, we were often a single unit. We were LivyandLucy.
THIS is how you turn a dog into a princess.
THIS is how you get out of eating broccoli.
And THAT'S how you make mac and cheese. Don't forget to put ketchup in it.
Ew.
She taught me everything she knew.

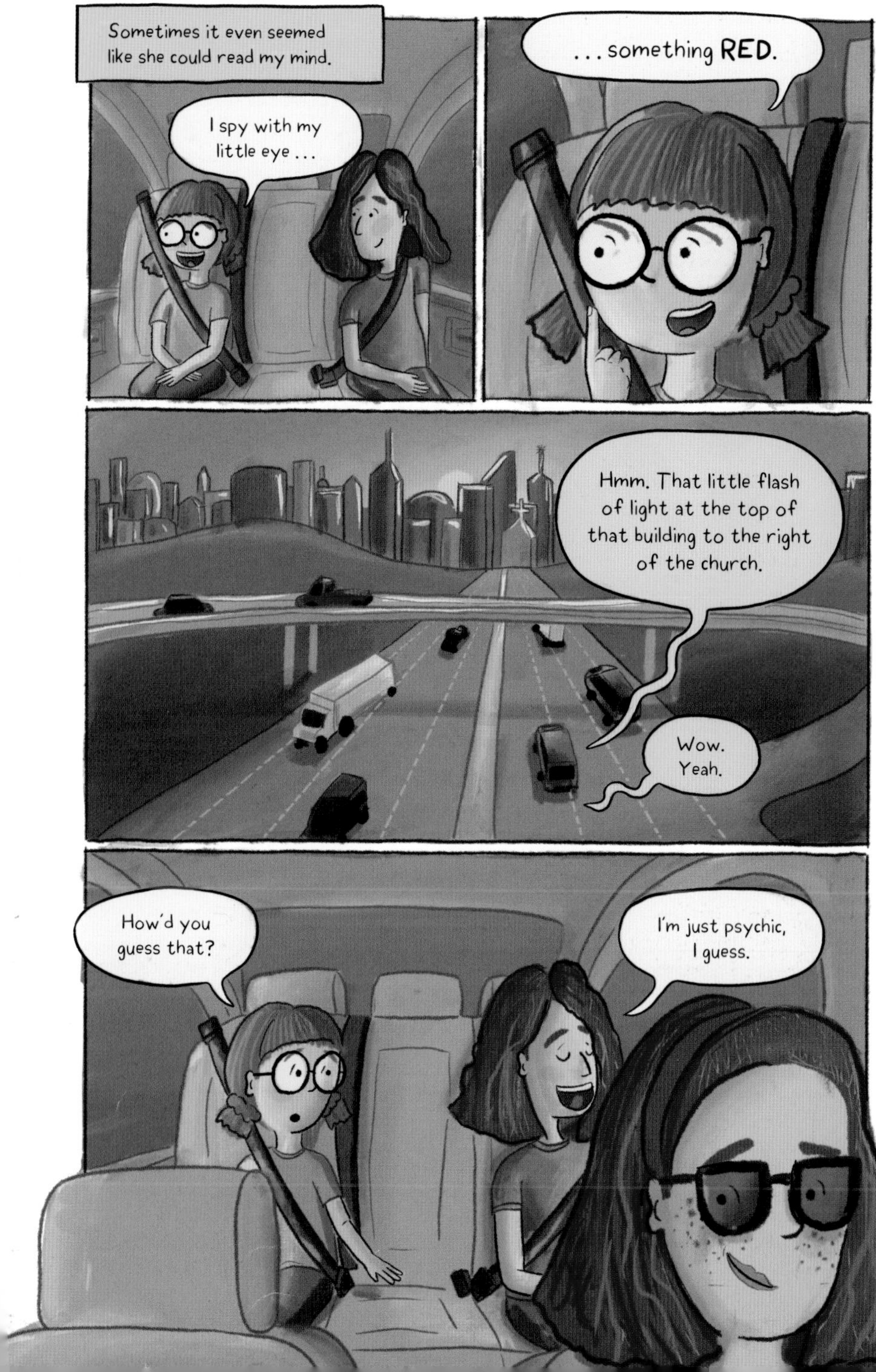
Sometimes it even seemed like she could read my mind.
I spy with my little eye . . .
. . . something RED.
Hmm. That little flash of light at the top of that building to the right of the church.
Wow. Yeah.
How'd you guess that?
I'm just psychic, I guess.

Of course, our relationship wasn't perfect.

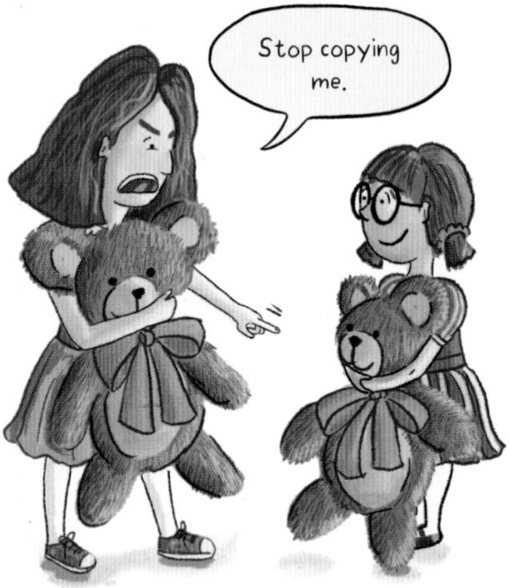
Stop copying me.

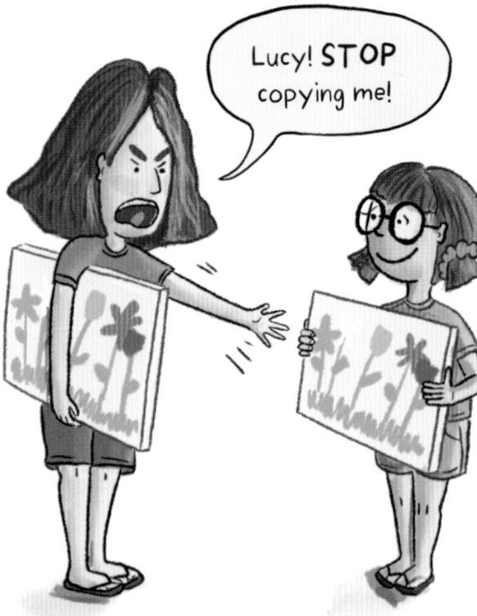
Lucy! STOP copying me!

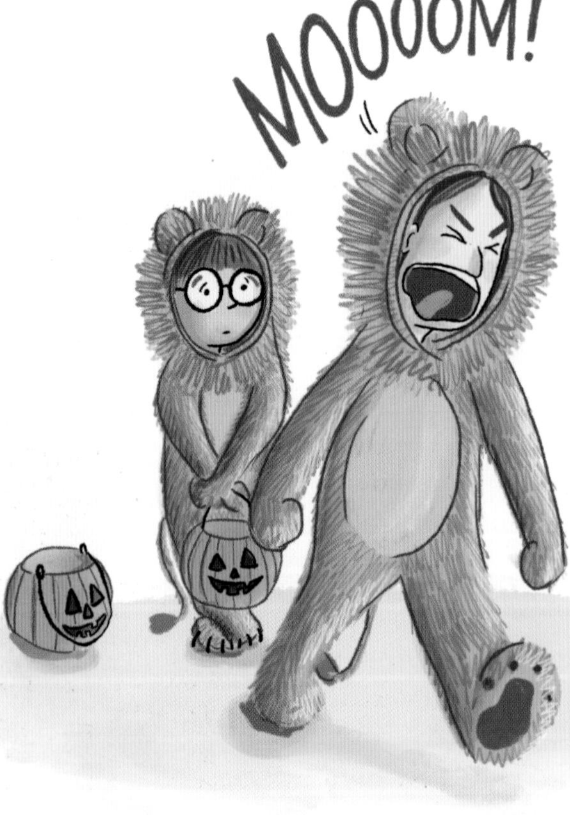
MOOOOM!

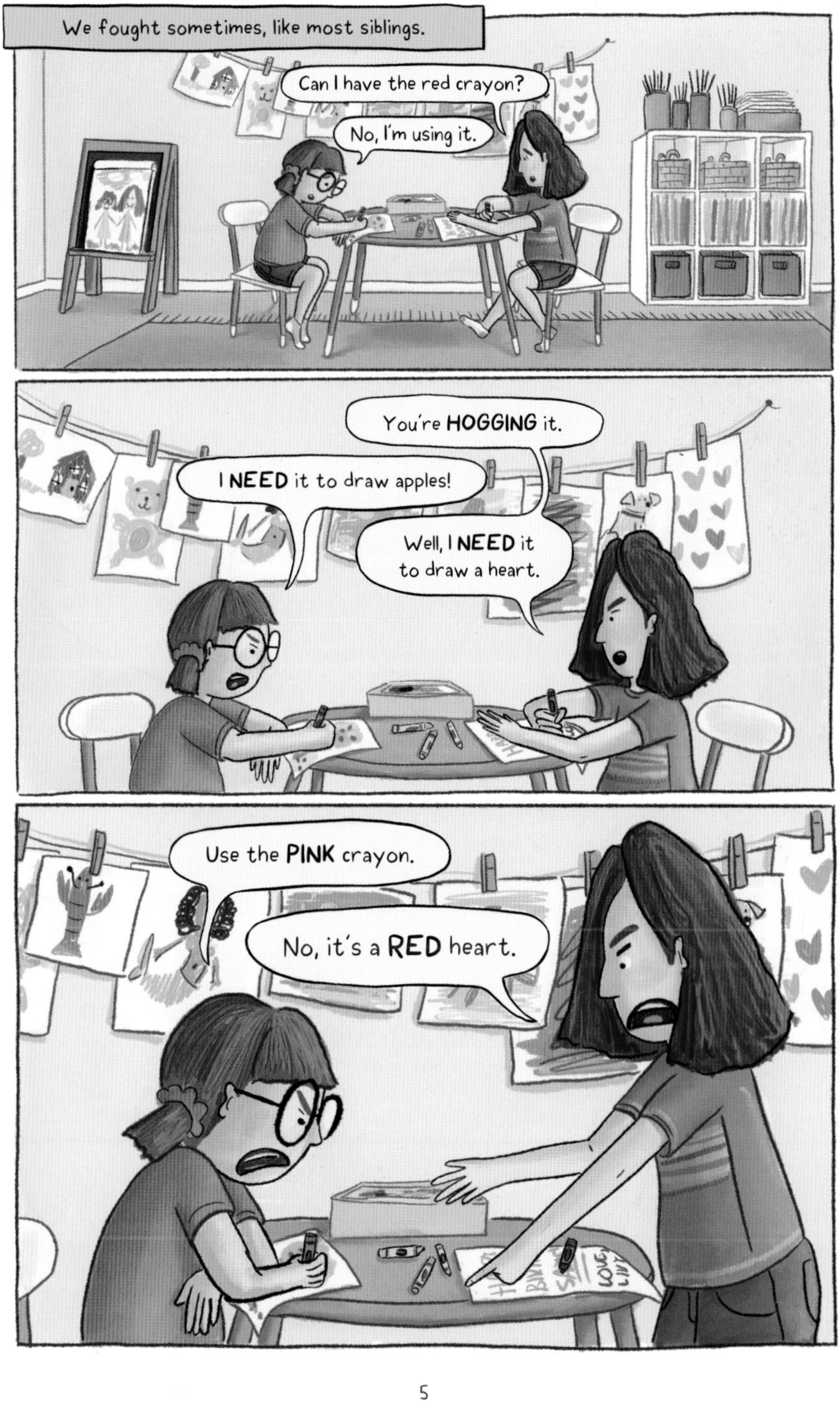
We fought sometimes, like most siblings.
Can I have the red crayon?
No, I'm using it.
You're HOGGING it.
I NEED it to draw apples!
Well, I NEED it to draw a heart.
Use the PINK crayon.
No, it's a RED heart.

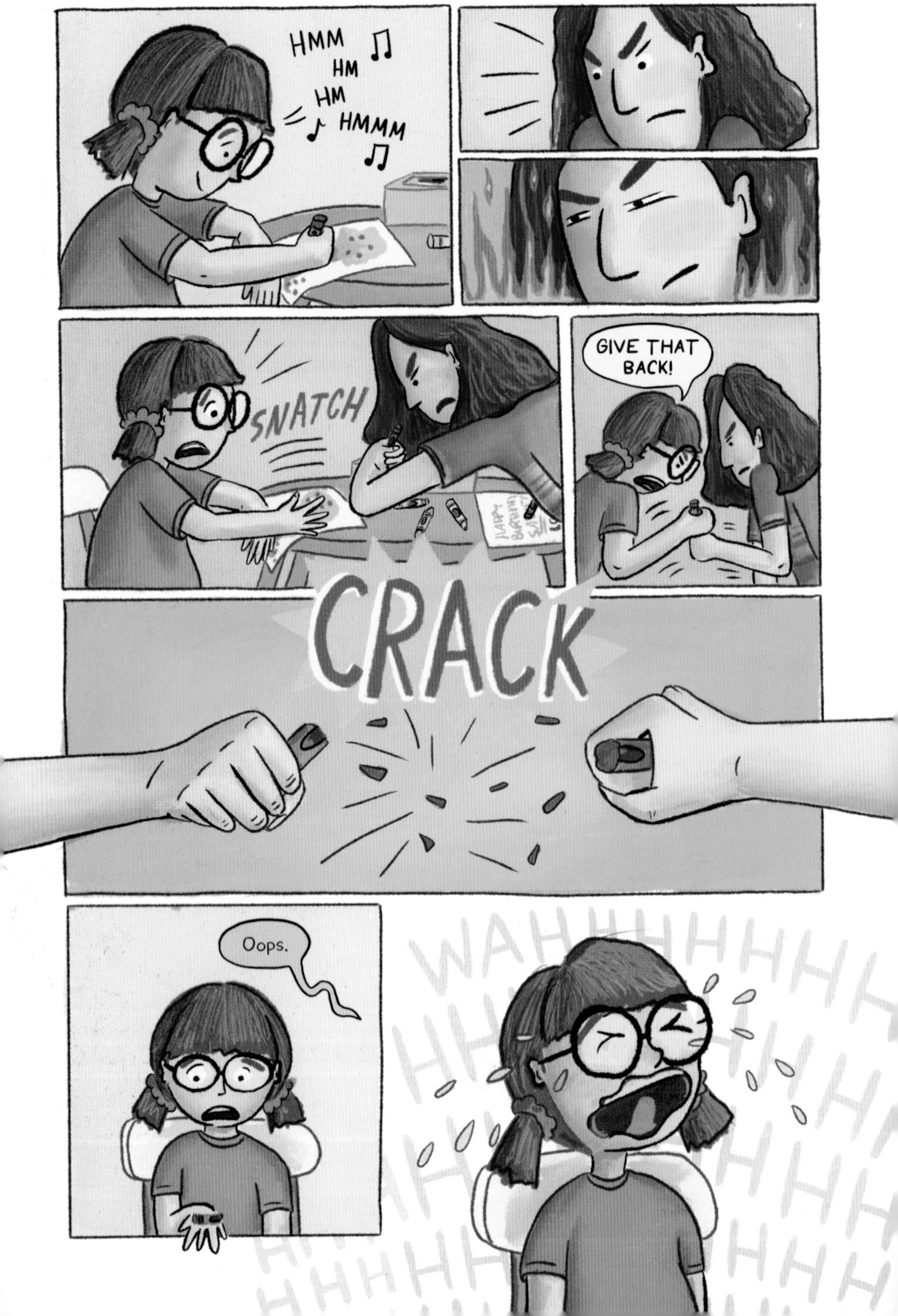
HMM HM HM HMMM
SNATCH
GIVE THAT BACK!
CRACK
Oops.
WAHHHHHHHHH

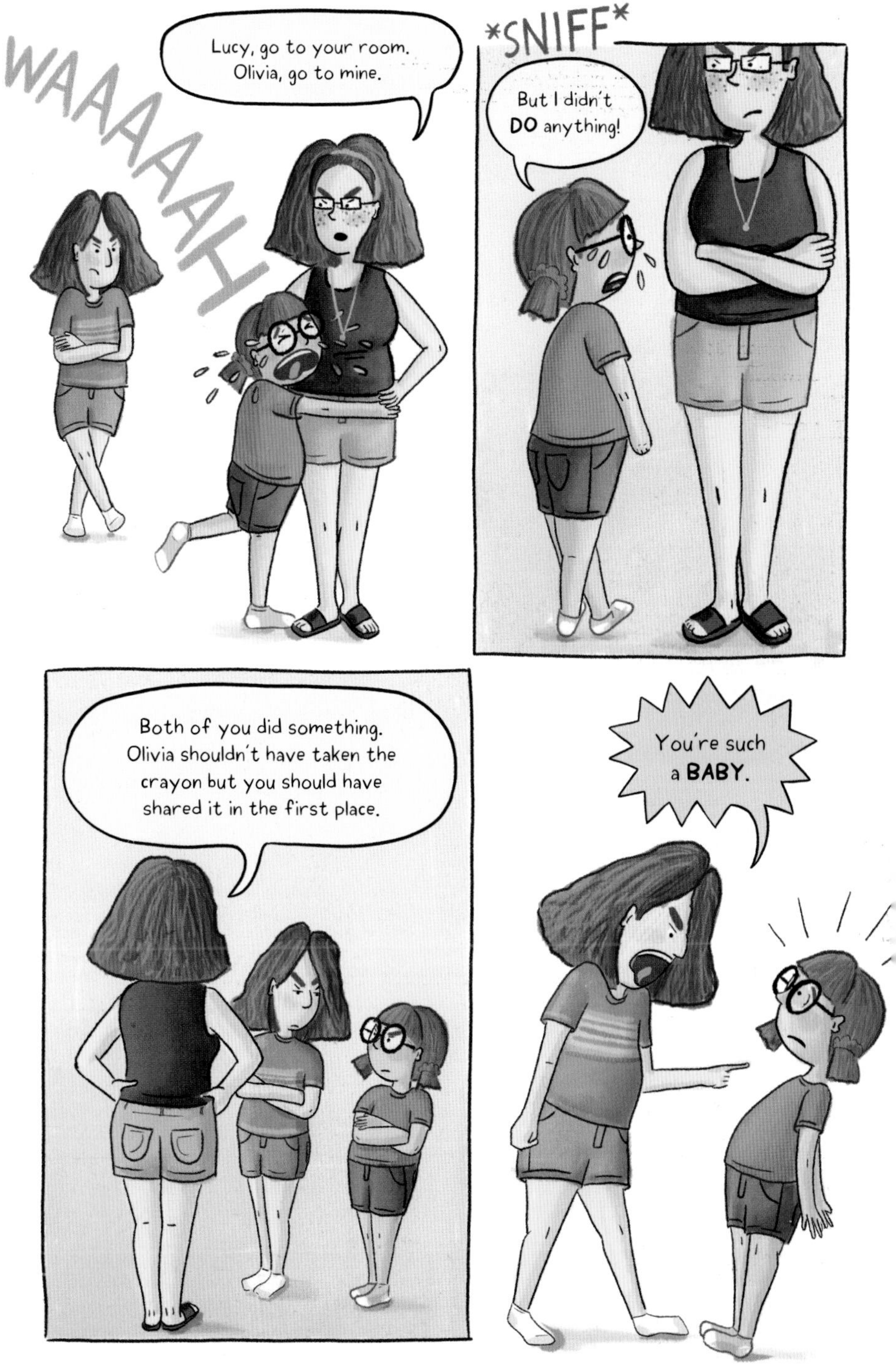
WAAAAAAH
Lucy, go to your room. Olivia, go to mine.
SNIFF
But I didn't DO anything!
Both of you did something. Olivia shouldn't have taken the crayon but you should have shared it in the first place.
You're such a BABY.

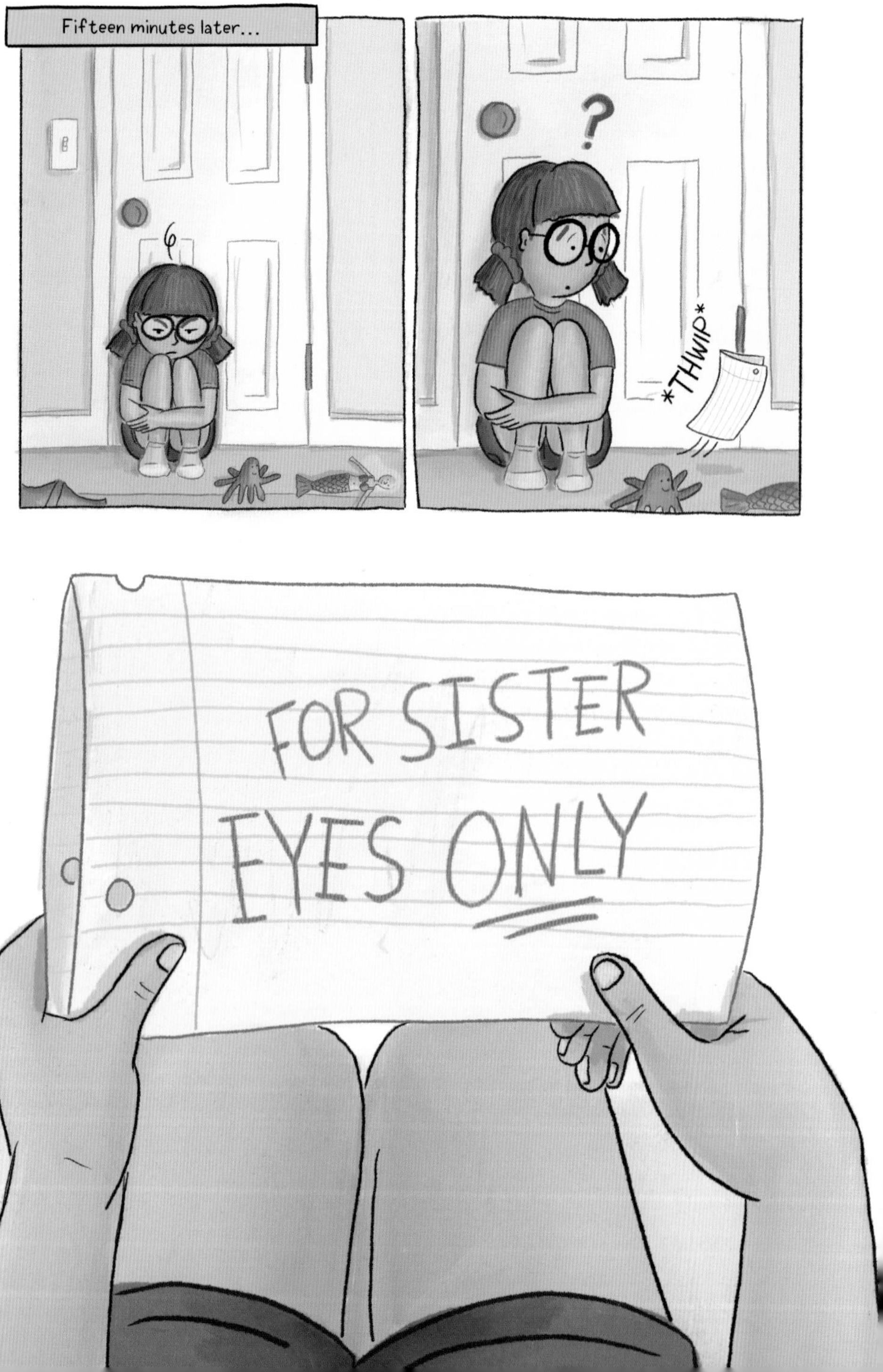
Fifteen minutes later...
?
THWIP
FOR SISTER
EYES ONLY

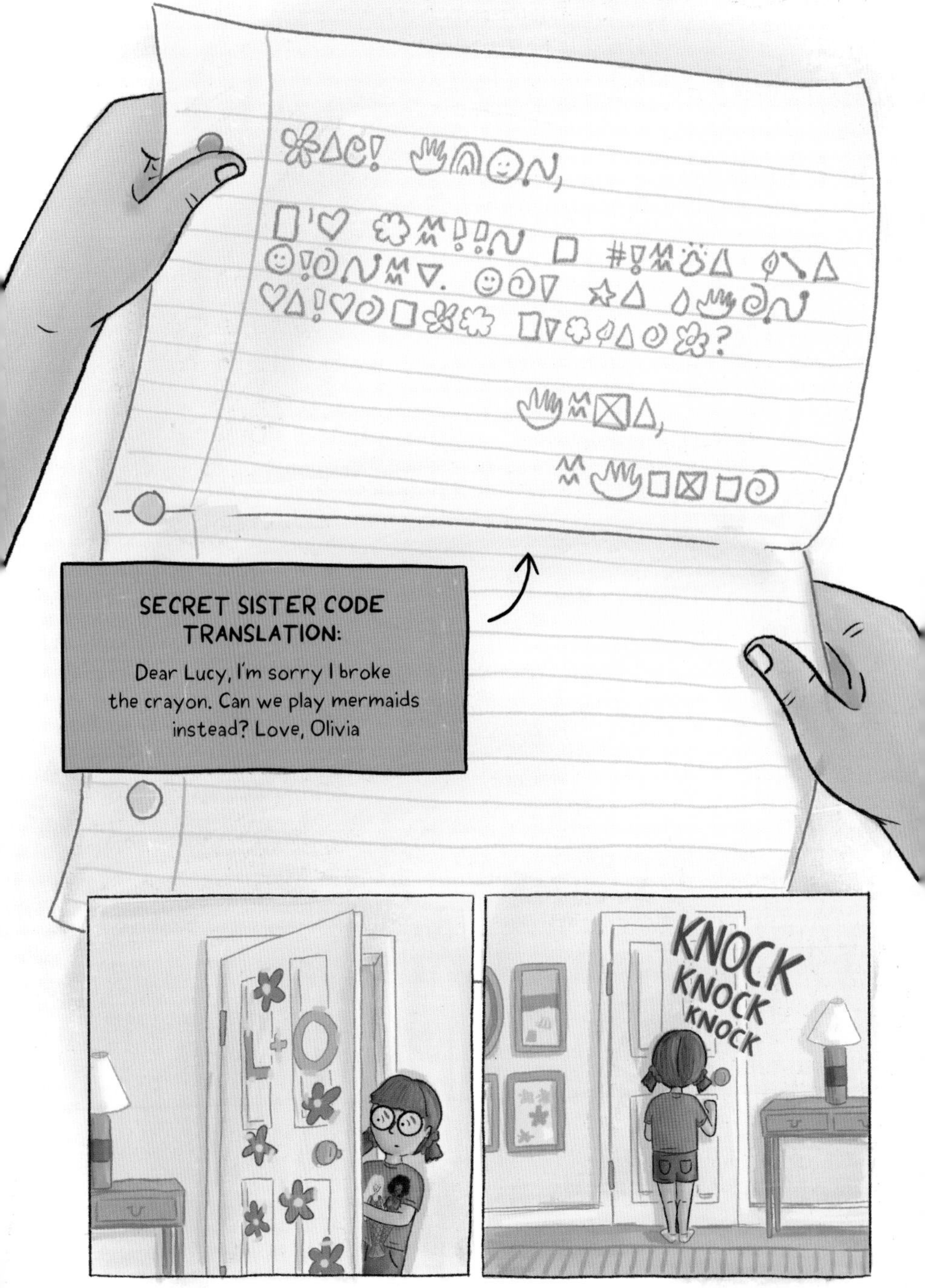
SECRET SISTER CODE TRANSLATION:
Dear Lucy, I'm sorry I broke the crayon. Can we play mermaids instead? Love, Olivia
L+O
KNOCK
KNOCK
KNOCK

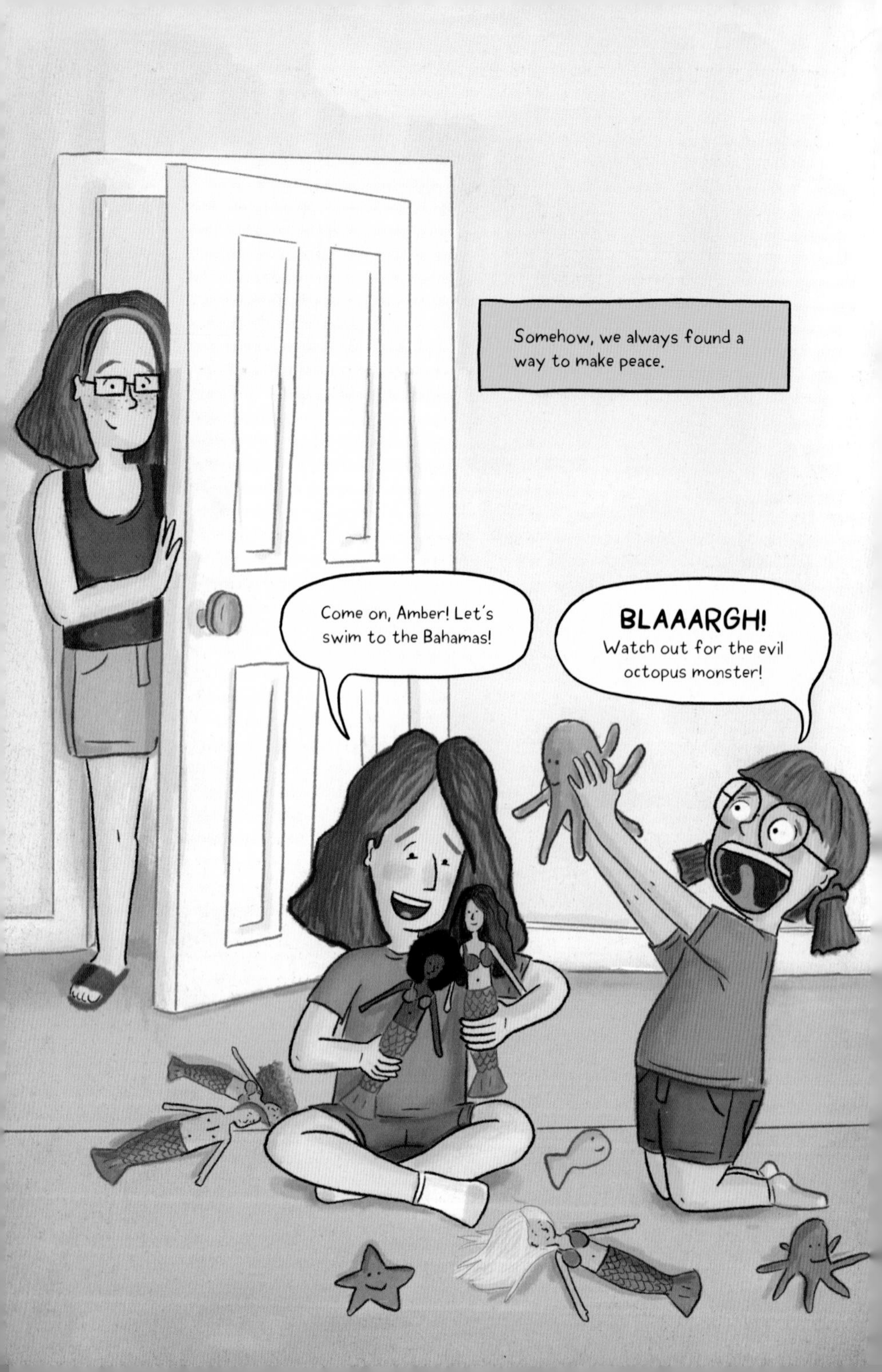
Somehow, we always found a way to make peace.
Come on, Amber! Let's swim to the Bahamas!
BLAAARGH! Watch out for the evil octopus monster!

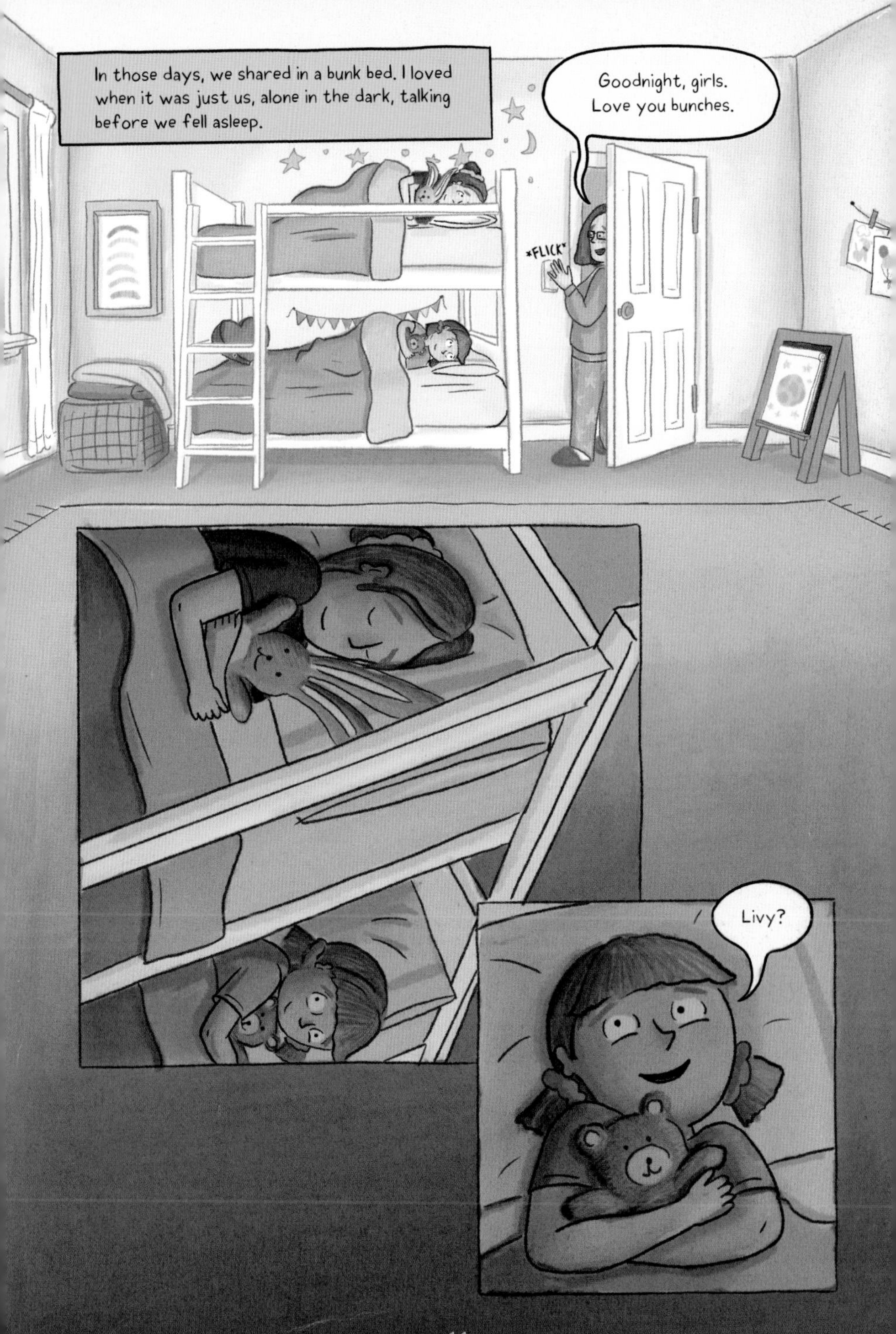
In those days, we shared in a bunk bed. I loved when it was just us, alone in the dark, talking before we fell asleep.
Goodnight, girls. Love you bunches.
FLICK
Livy?

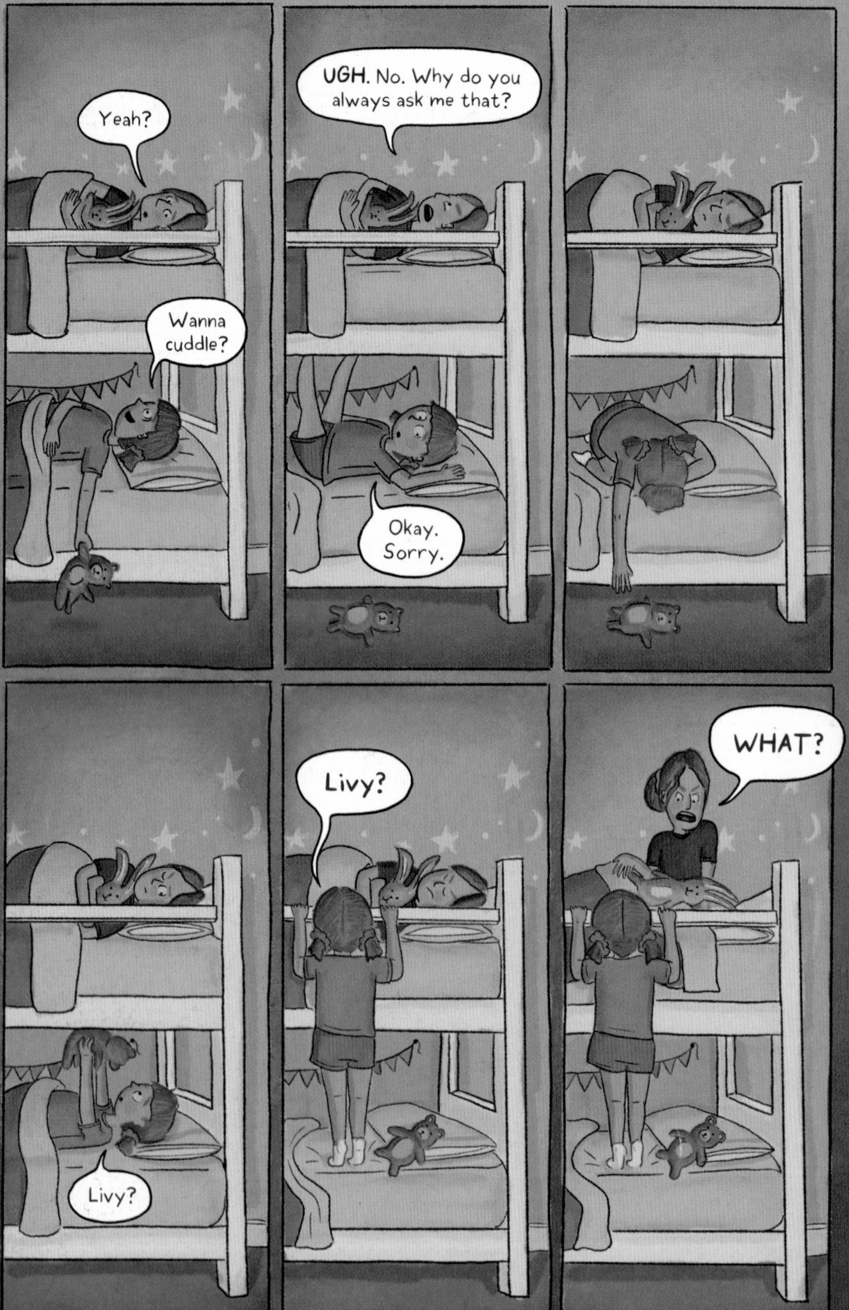
Yeah?
Wanna cuddle?
UGH. No. Why do you always ask me that?
Okay. Sorry.
Livy?
Livy?
WHAT?

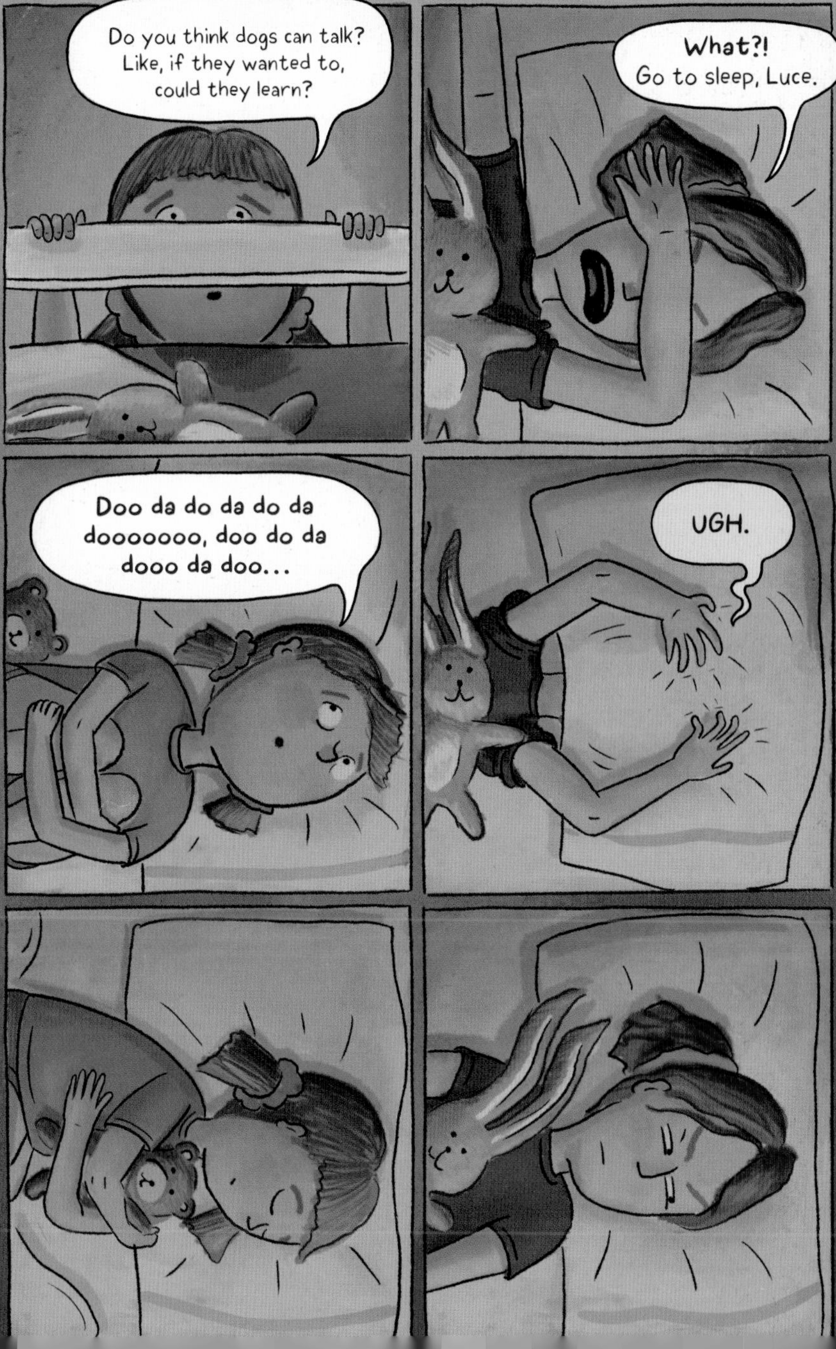
Do you think dogs can talk? Like, if they wanted to, could they learn?
What?! Go to sleep, Luce.
Doo da do da do da dooooooo, doo do da dooo da doo...
UGH.

Are mermaids fish or are they people?

PLEASE go to sleep.

Okay.

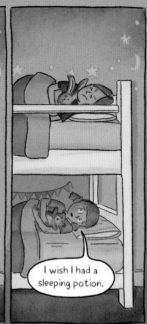

I wish I had a sleeping potion.

AARRGH!!!

Olivia **REALLY** wanted her own room.

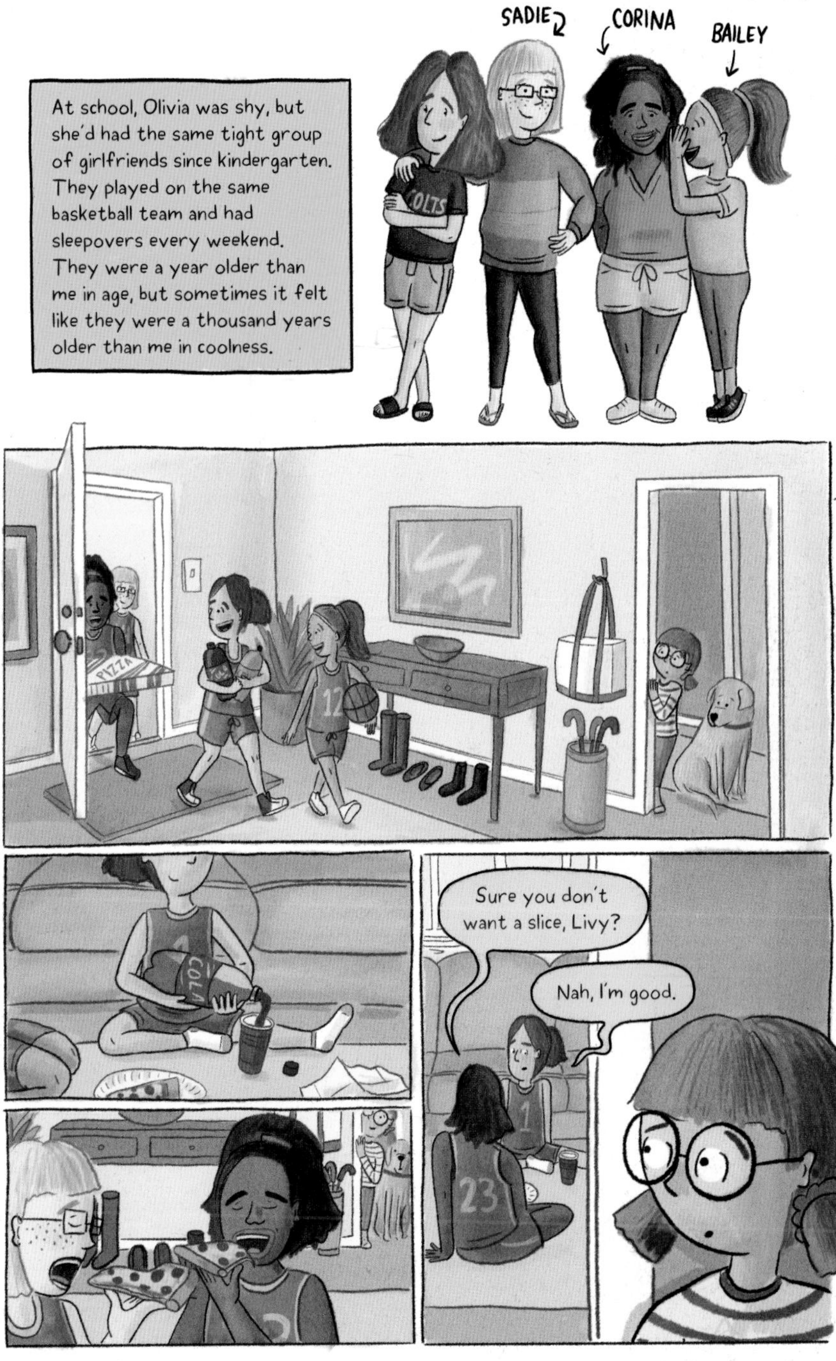
At school, Olivia was shy, but she'd had the same tight group of girlfriends since kindergarten. They played on the same basketball team and had sleepovers every weekend. They were a year older than me in age, but sometimes it felt like they were a thousand years older than me in coolness.
SADIE
CORINA
BAILEY
COLTS
PIZZA
COLA
Sure you don't want a slice, Livy?
Nah, I'm good.

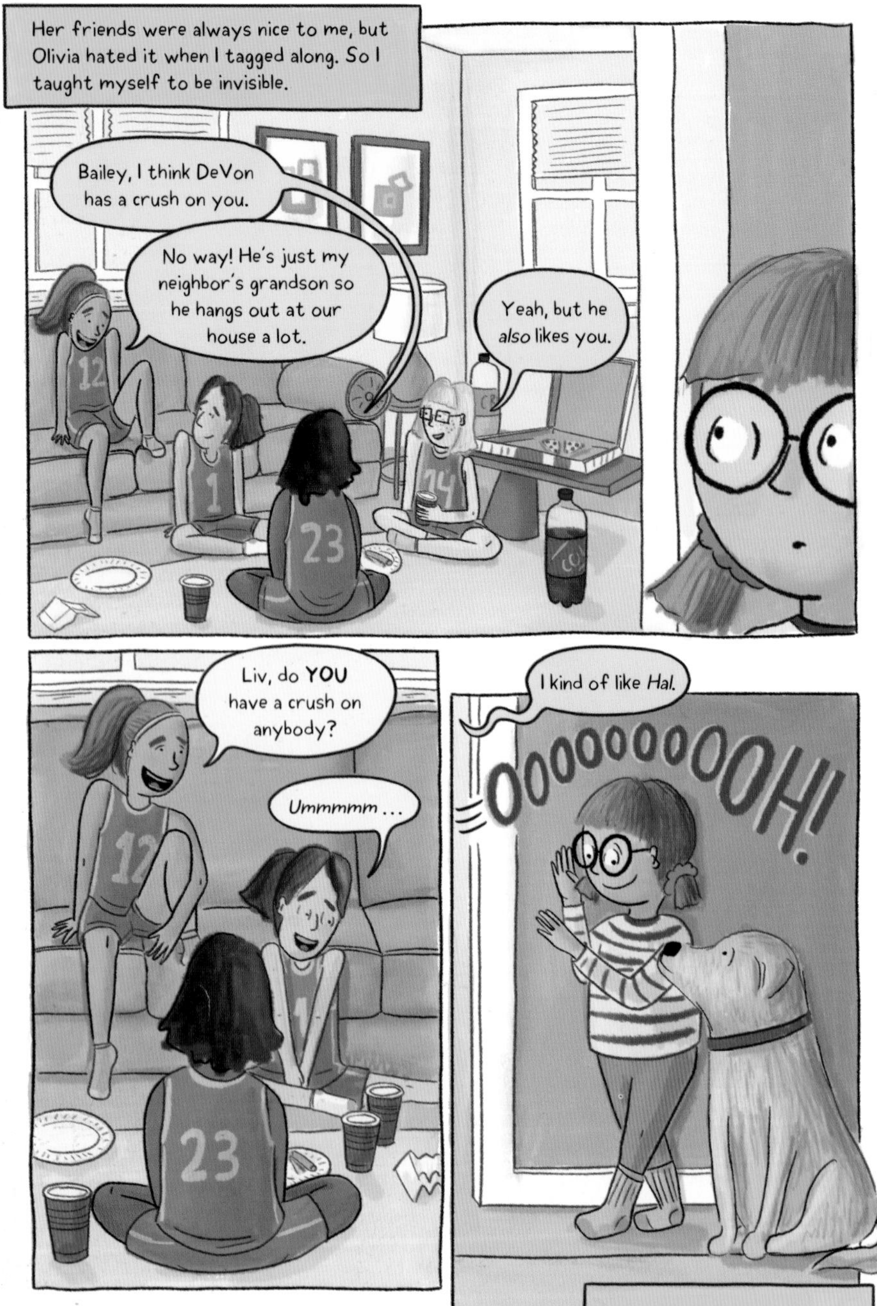
Her friends were always nice to me, but Olivia hated it when I tagged along. So I taught myself to be invisible.
Bailey, I think DeVon has a crush on you.
No way! He's just my neighbor's grandson so he hangs out at our house a lot.
Yeah, but he *also* likes you.
Liv, do **YOU** have a crush on anybody?
Ummmmm ...
I kind of like *Hal*.
OOOOOOOOOH!
I learned **ALL** the best dirt on my sister that way.

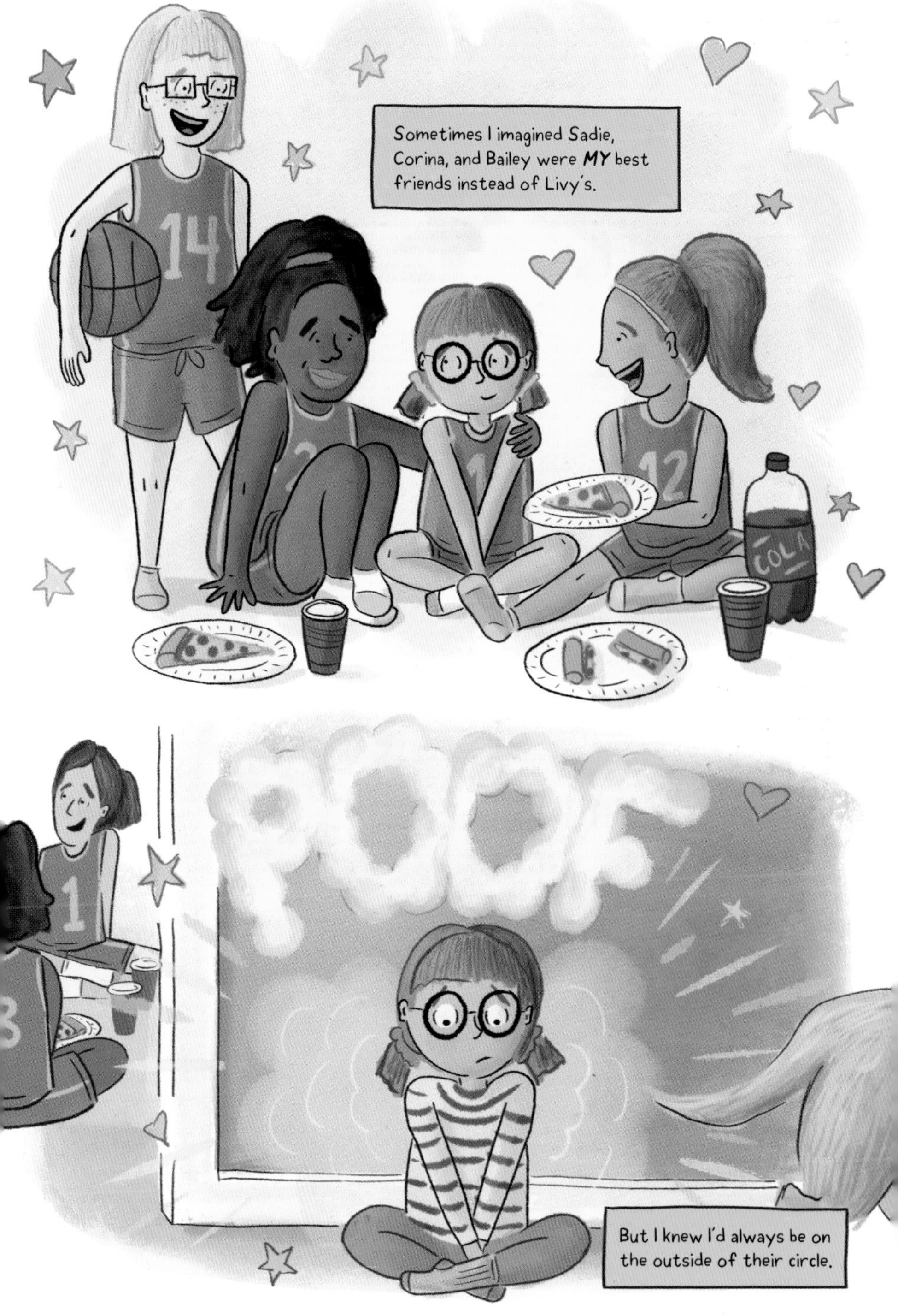
Sometimes I imagined Sadie, Corina, and Bailey were **MY** best friends instead of Livy's.
14
12
COLA
POOF
1
But I knew I'd always be on the outside of their circle.

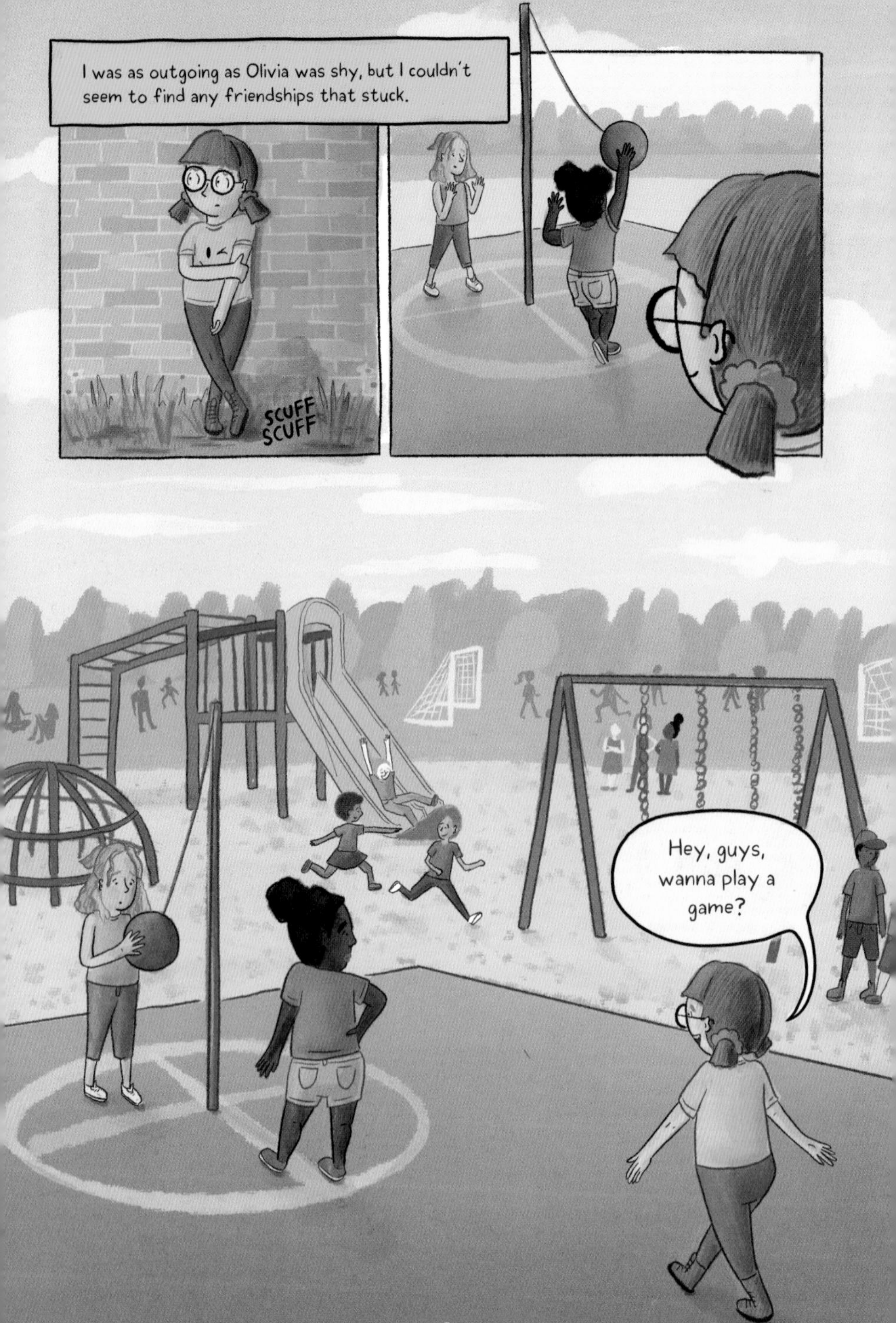
I was as outgoing as Olivia was shy, but I couldn't seem to find any friendships that stuck.
SCUFF SCUFF
Hey, guys, wanna play a game?

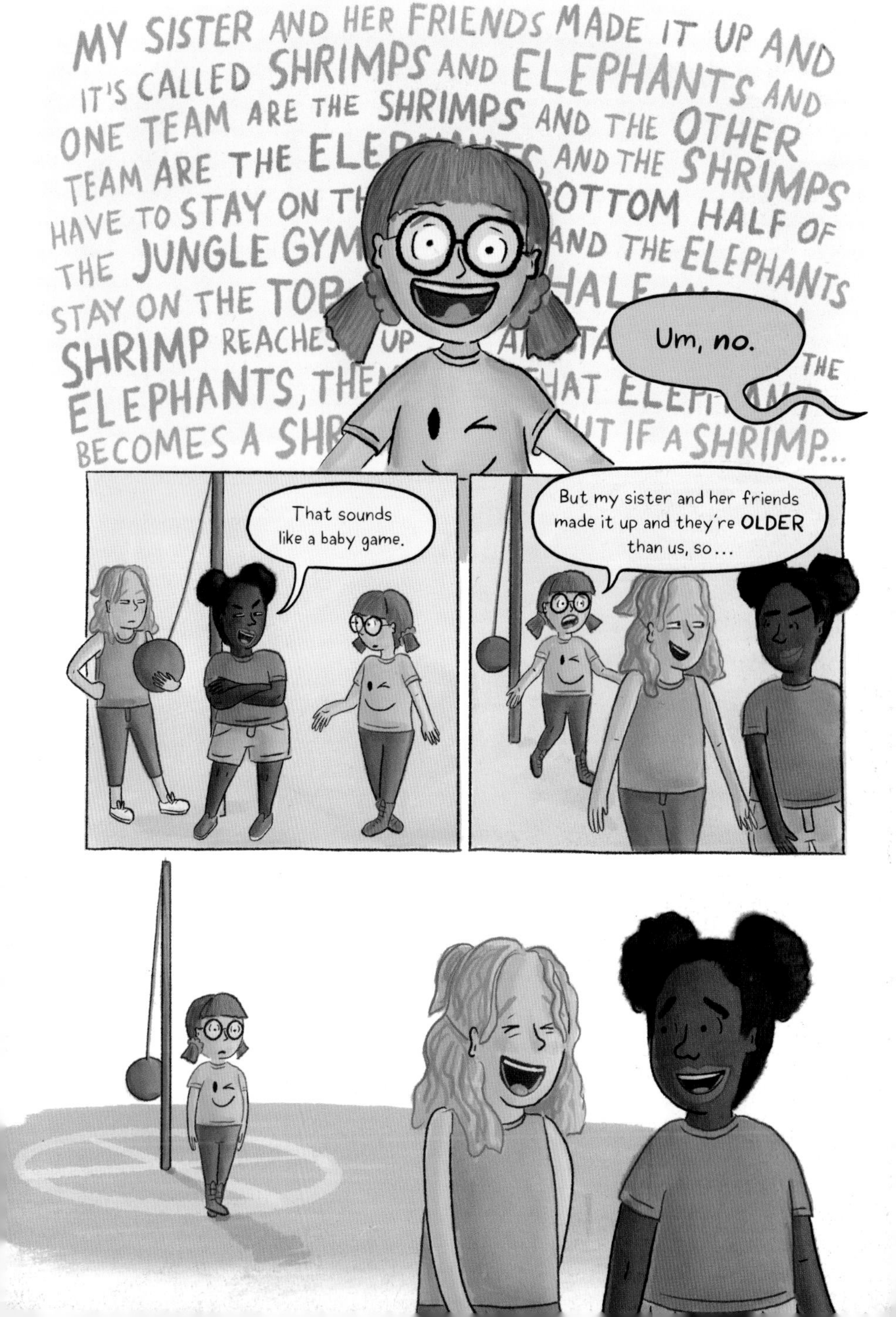
MY SISTER AND HER FRIENDS MADE IT UP AND
IT'S CALLED SHRIMPS AND ELEPHANTS AND
ONE TEAM ARE THE SHRIMPS AND THE OTHER
TEAM ARE THE ELE
AND THE SHRIMPS
HAVE TO STAY ON TH
BOTTOM HALF OF
THE JUNGLE GYM
AND THE ELEPHANTS
STAY ON THE TOP
SHRIMP REACHES
UP
THE
ELEPHANTS, THE
HAT
BECOMES A SH
IT IF A SHRIMP...
Um, no.
That sounds like a baby game.
But my sister and her friends made it up and they're OLDER than us, so...

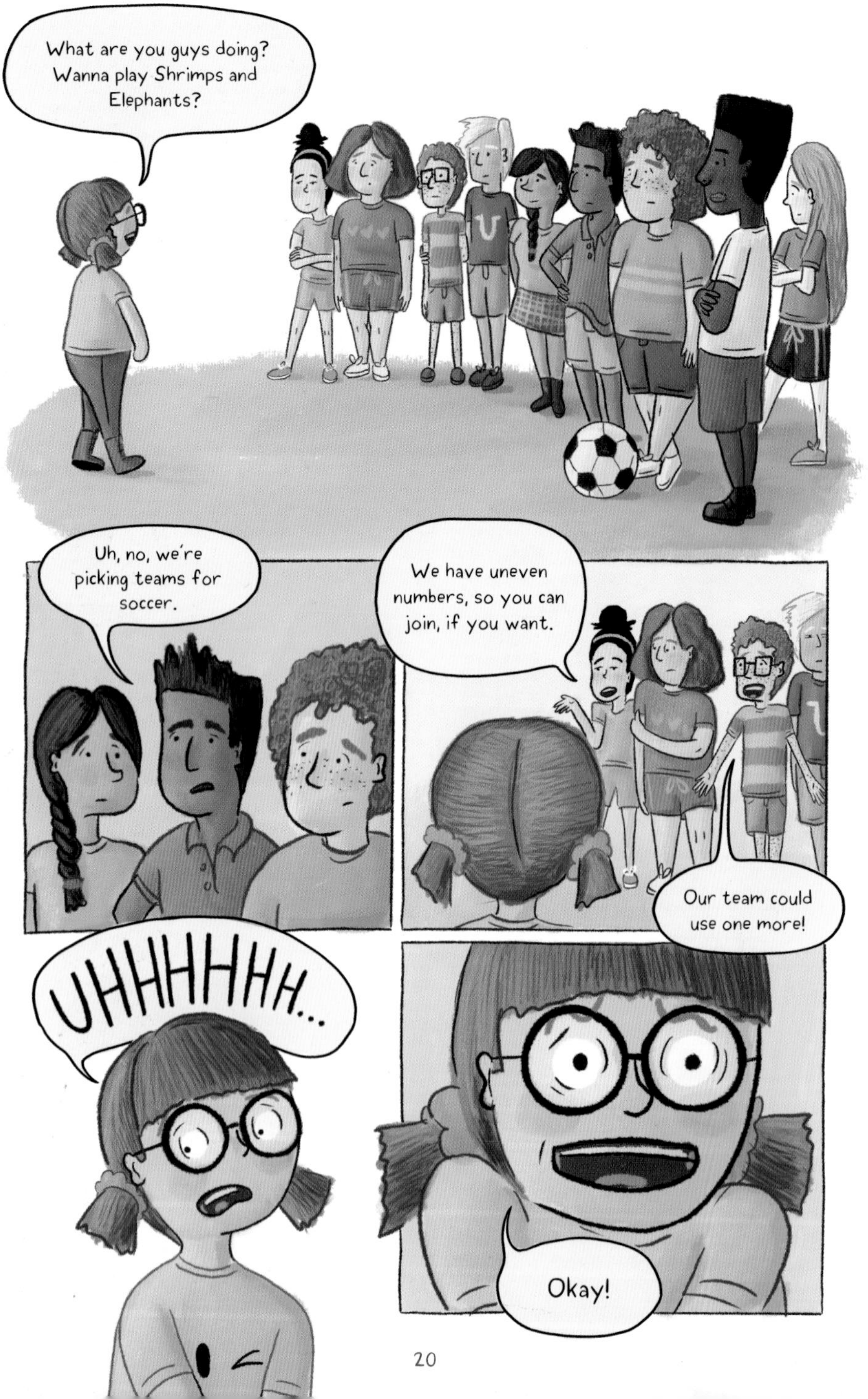
What are you guys doing? Wanna play Shrimps and Elephants?
Uh, no, we're picking teams for soccer.
We have uneven numbers, so you can join, if you want.
Our team could use one more!
UHHHHHH...
Okay!

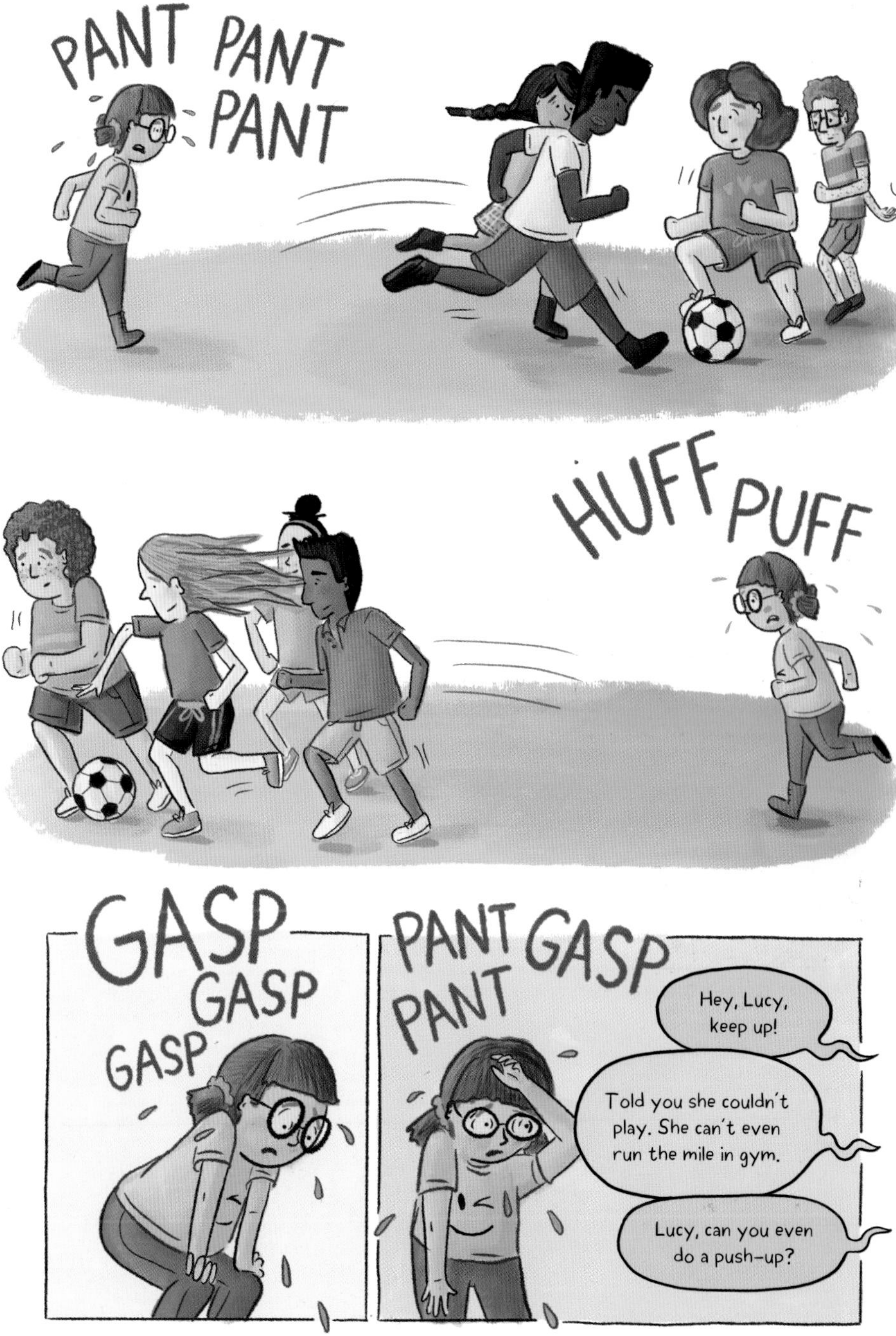
PANT PANT
PANT
HUFF PUFF
GASP
GASP
GASP
PANT GASP
PANT
Hey, Lucy, keep up!
Told you she couldn't play. She can't even run the mile in gym.
Lucy, can you even do a push-up?

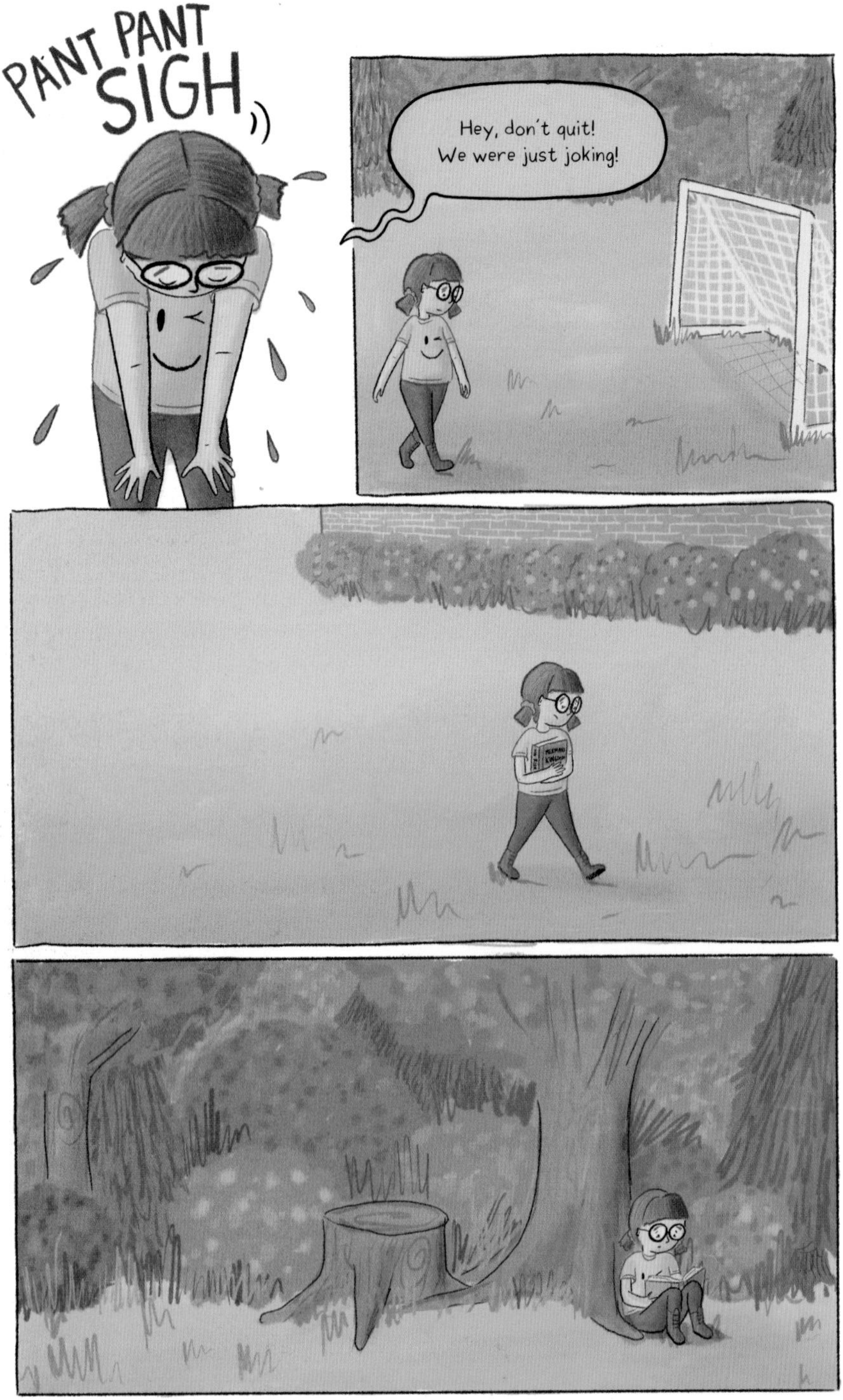
PANT PANT SIGH
Hey, don't quit! We were just joking!

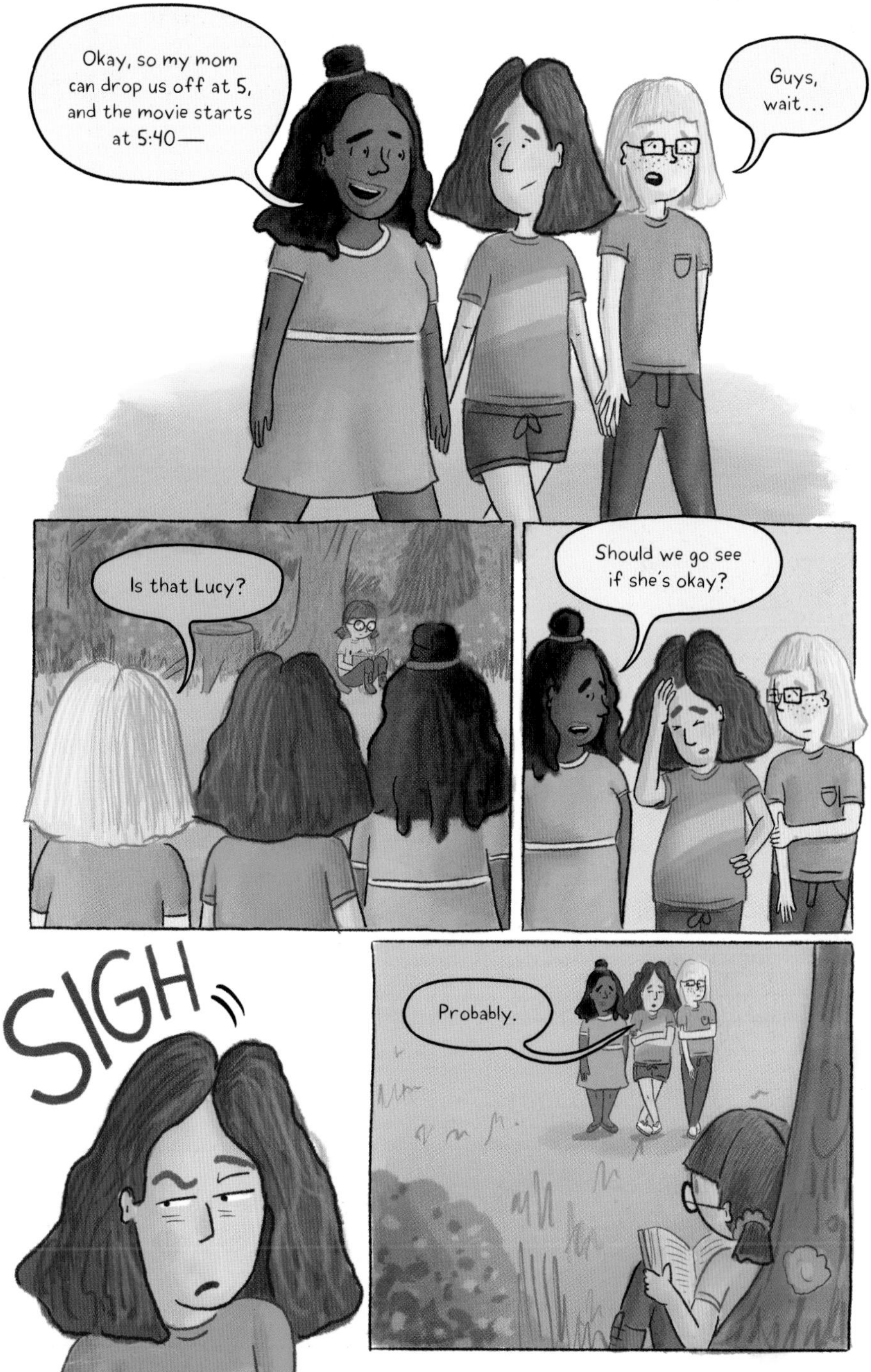
Okay, so my mom can drop us off at 5, and the movie starts at 5:40—
Guys, wait...
Is that Lucy?
Should we go see if she's okay?
SIGH
Probably.

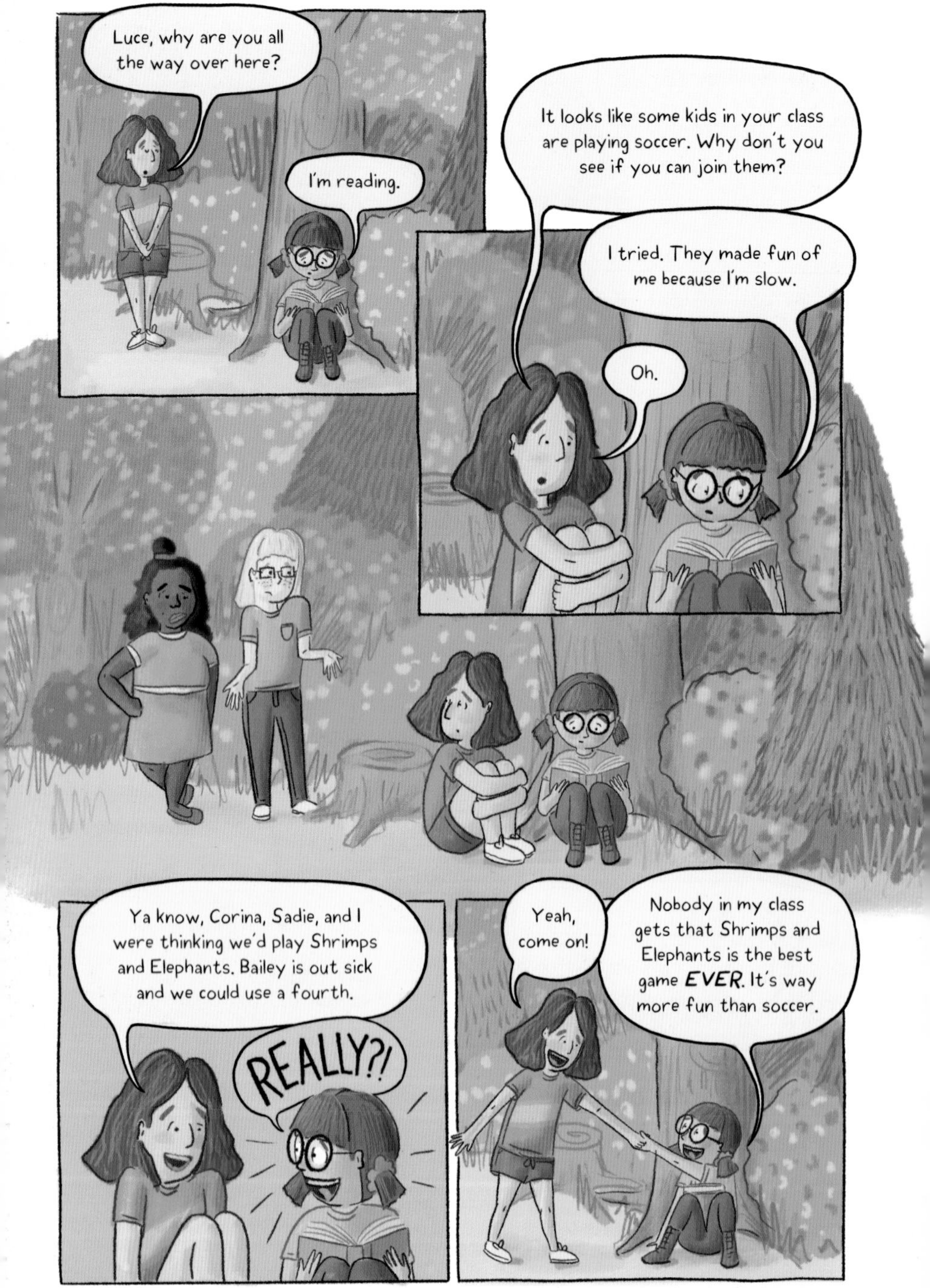
Luce, why are you all the way over here?
I'm reading.
It looks like some kids in your class are playing soccer. Why don't you see if you can join them?
I tried. They made fun of me because I'm slow.
Oh.
Ya know, Corina, Sadie, and I were thinking we'd play Shrimps and Elephants. Bailey is out sick and we could use a fourth.
REALLY?!
Yeah, come on!
Nobody in my class gets that Shrimps and Elephants is the best game EVER. It's way more fun than soccer.

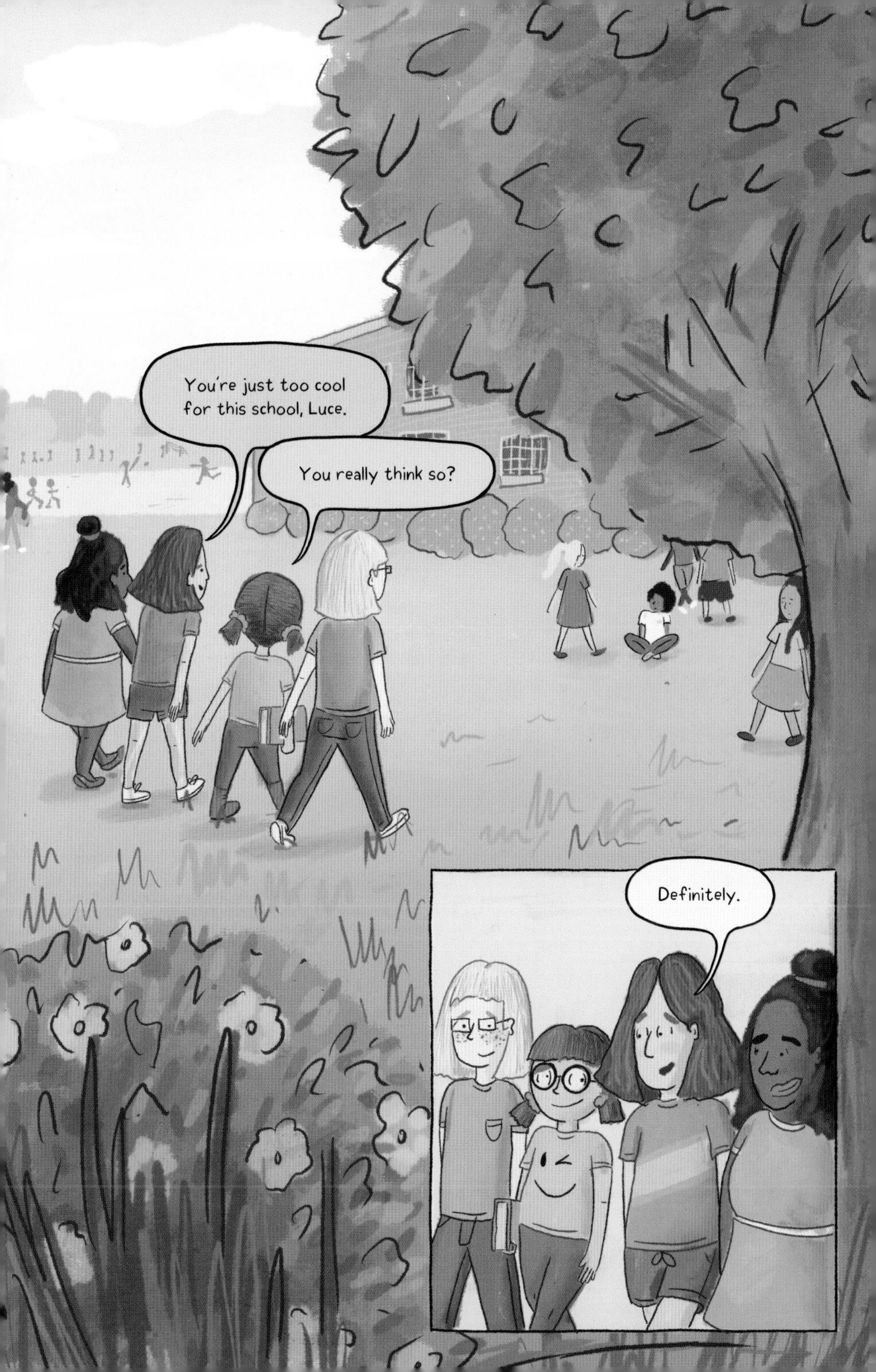
You're just too cool for this school, Luce.
You really think so?
Definitely.

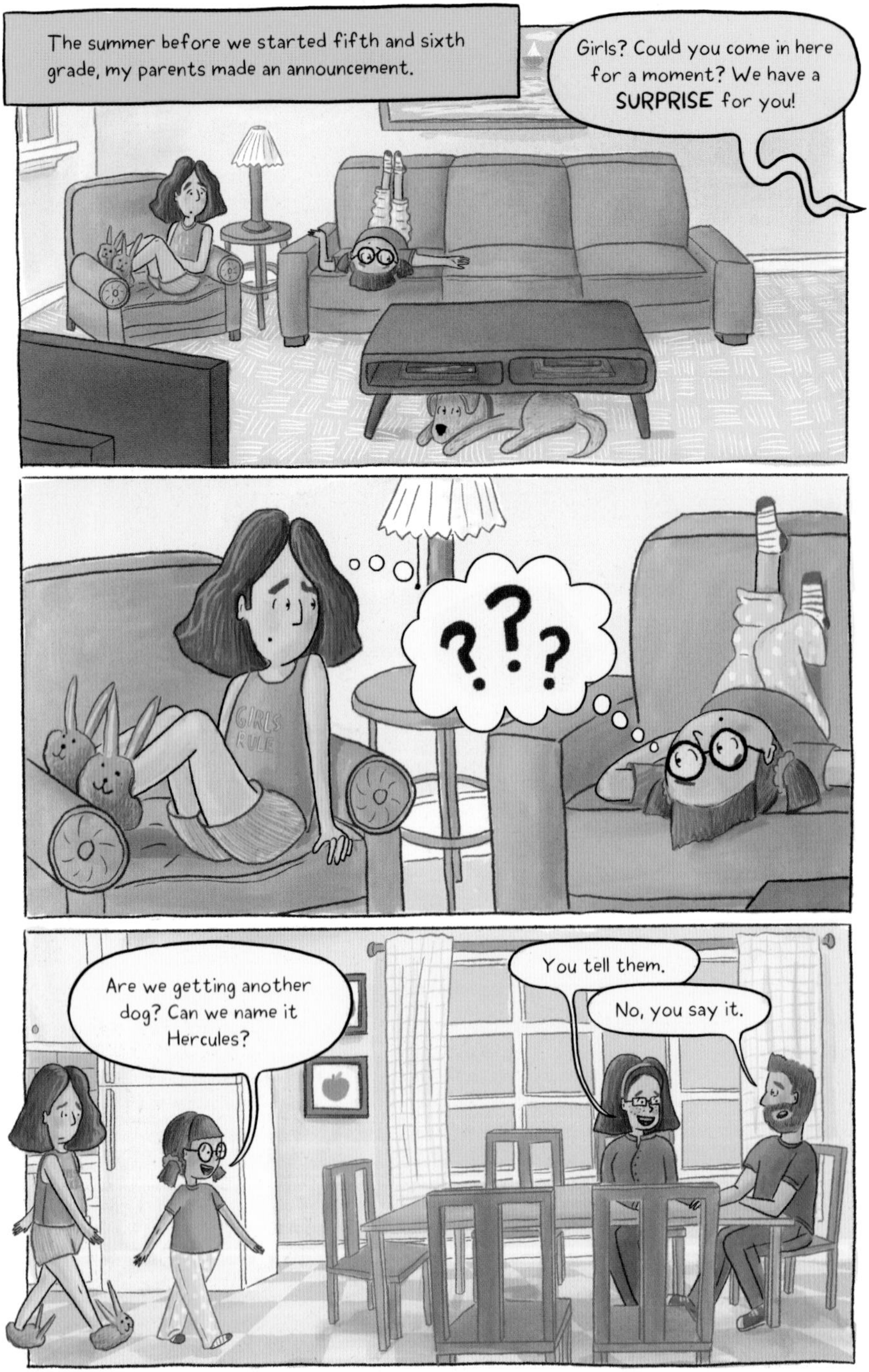
The summer before we started fifth and sixth grade, my parents made an announcement.
Girls? Could you come in here for a moment? We have a **SURPRISE** for you!
???
GIRLS RULE
Are we getting another dog? Can we name it Hercules?
You tell them.
No, you say it.

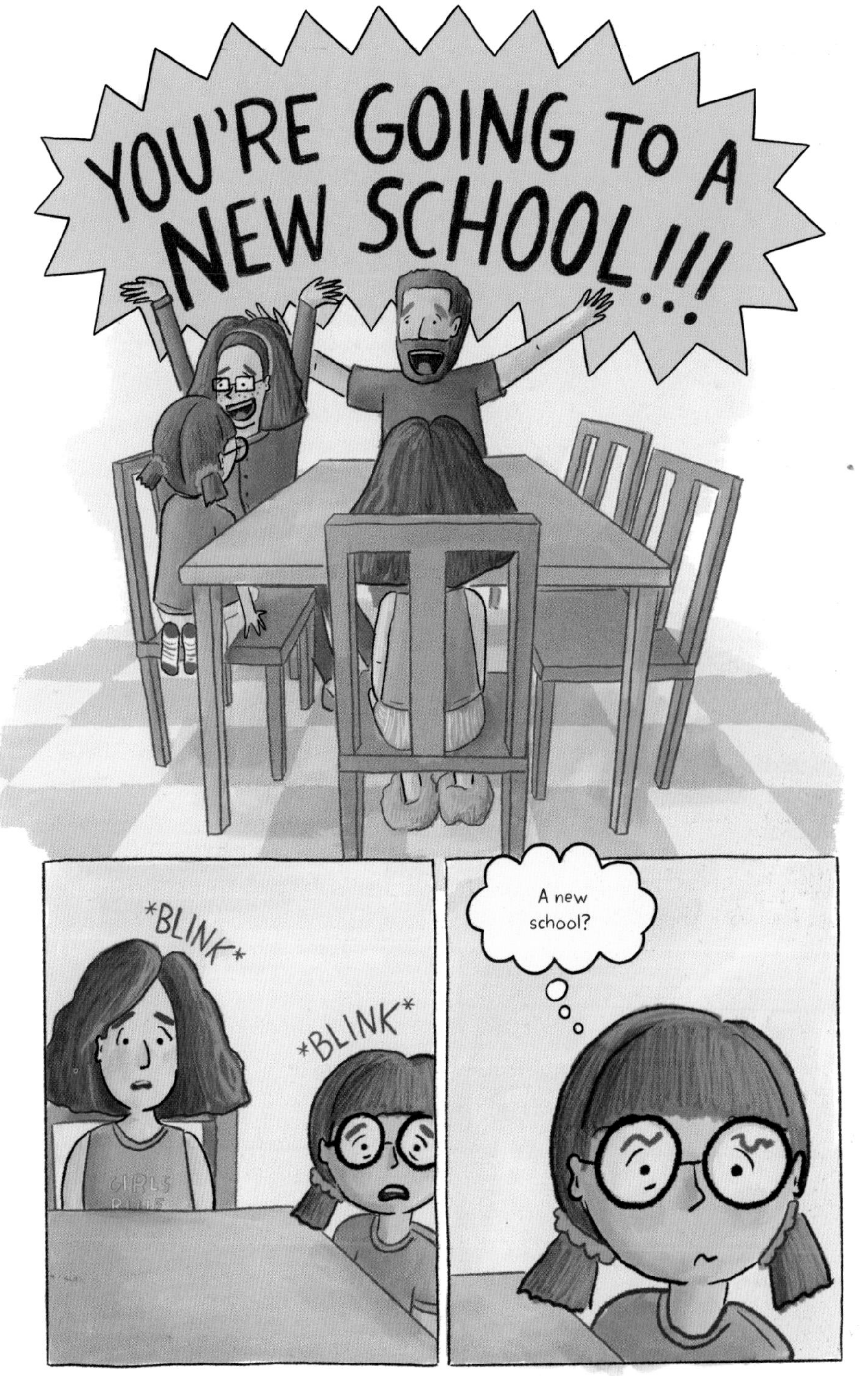
YOU'RE GOING TO A NEW SCHOOL!!!
BLINK
BLINK
A new school?

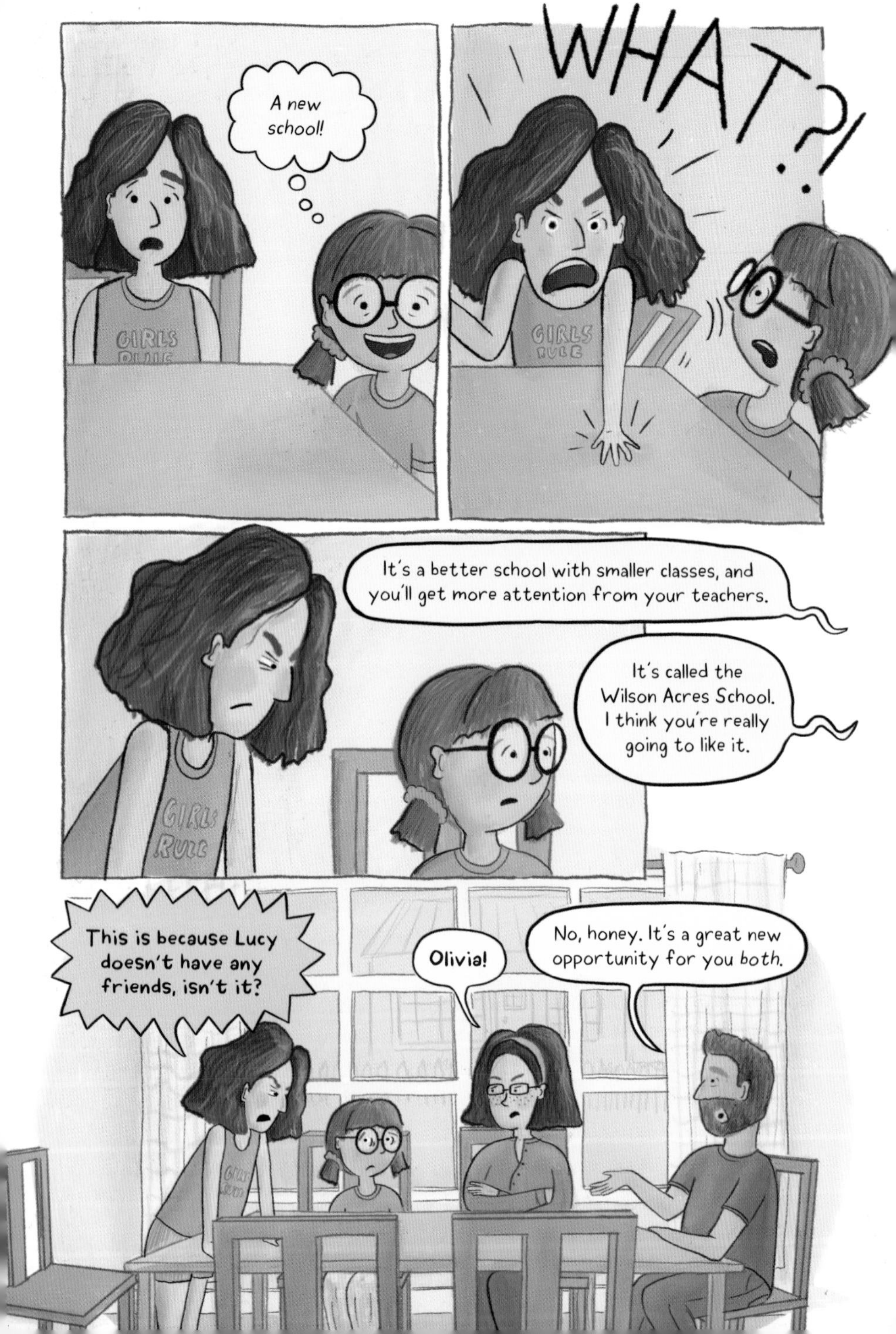
A new school!
WHAT?!
GIRLS RULE
It's a better school with smaller classes, and you'll get more attention from your teachers.
It's called the Wilson Acres School. I think you're really going to like it.
This is because Lucy doesn't have any friends, isn't it?
Olivia!
No, honey. It's a great new opportunity for you *both*.

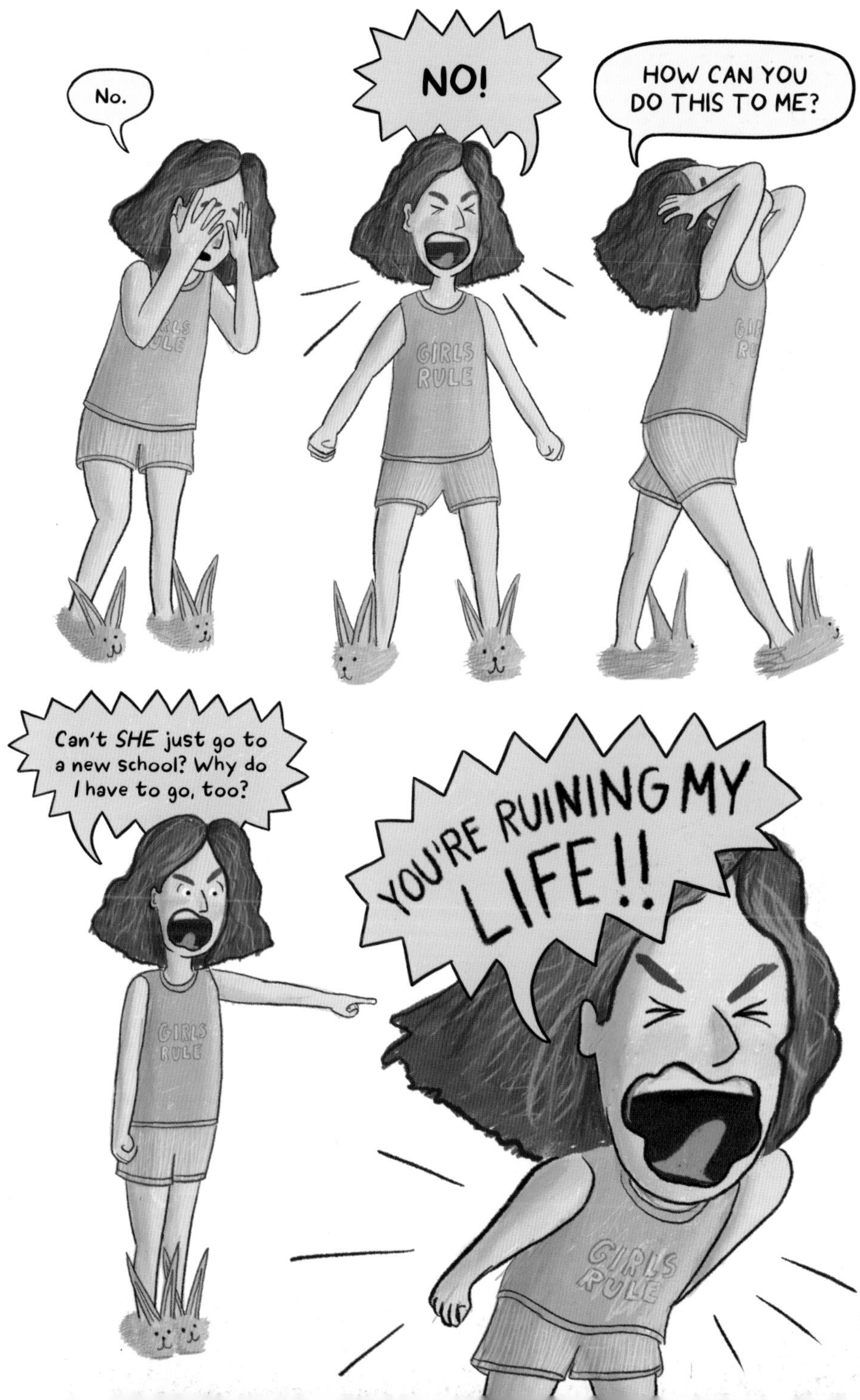
No.
NO!
HOW CAN YOU DO THIS TO ME?
GIRLS RULE
Can't SHE just go to a new school? Why do I have to go, too?
YOU'RE RUINING MY LIFE!!

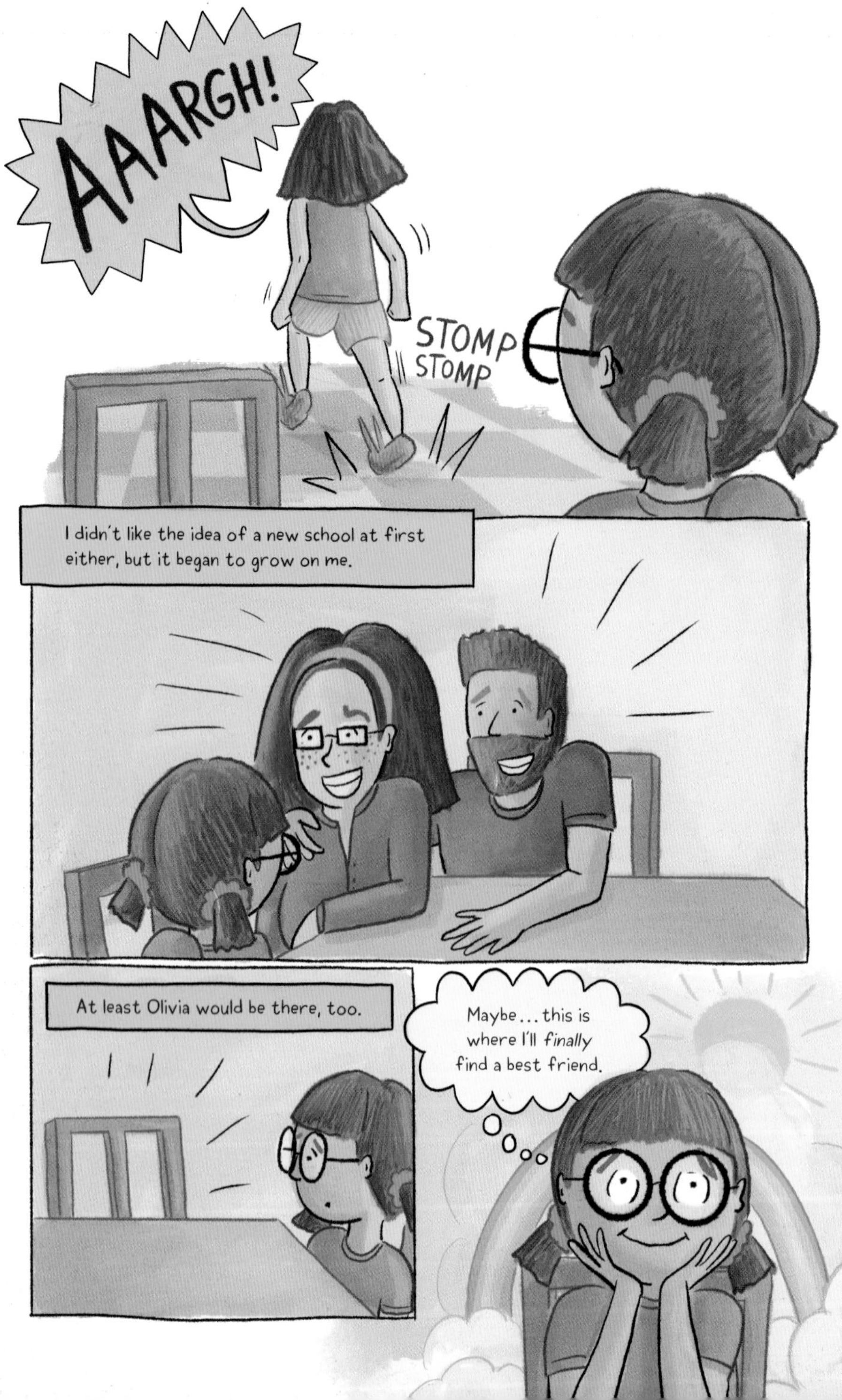
AAARGH!
STOMP
STOMP
I didn't like the idea of a new school at first either, but it began to grow on me.
At least Olivia would be there, too.
Maybe... this is where I'll *finally* find a best friend.

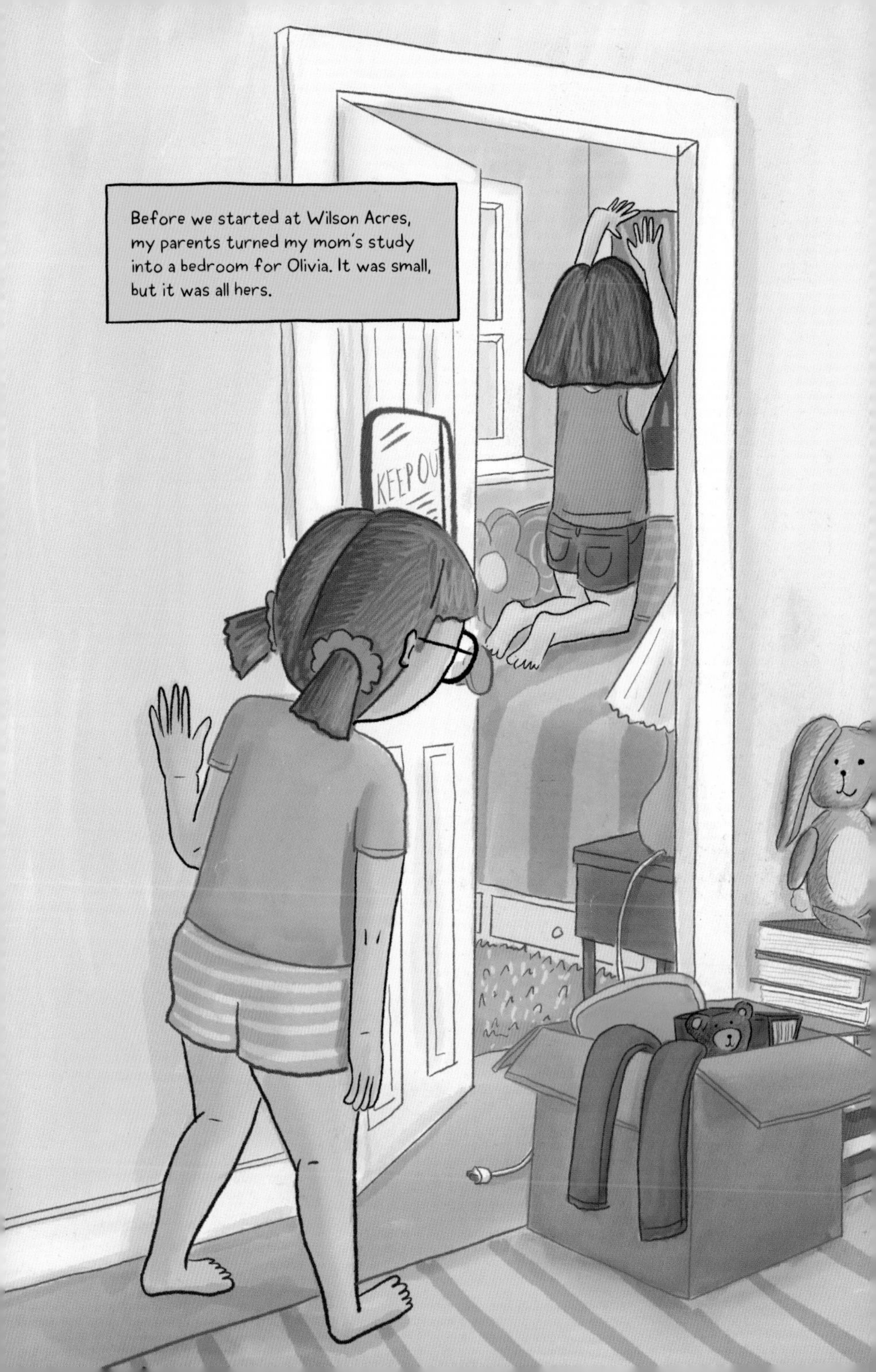
Before we started at Wilson Acres, my parents turned my mom's study into a bedroom for Olivia. It was small, but it was all hers.
KEEP OUT

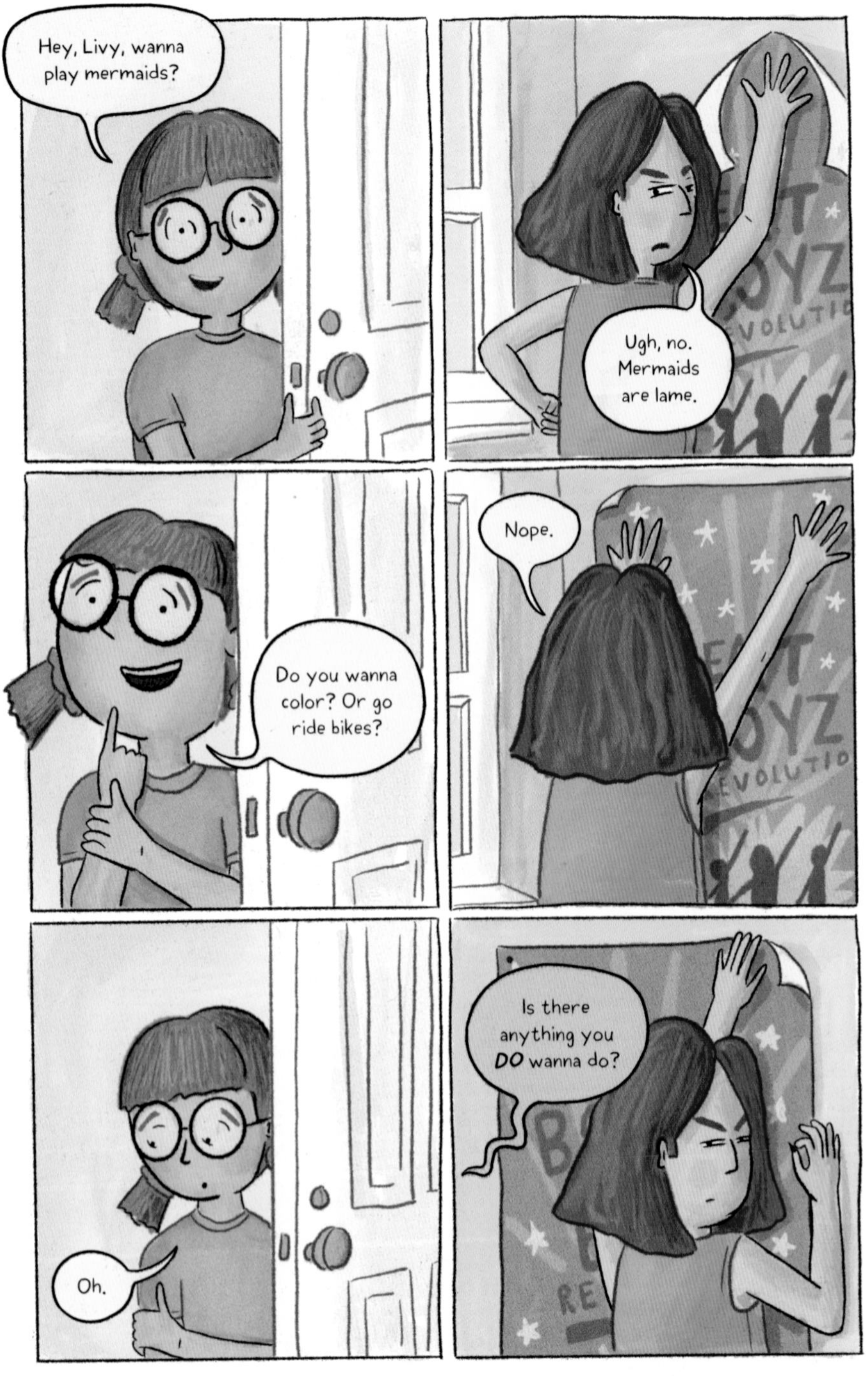
Hey, Livy, wanna play mermaids?
Ugh, no. Mermaids are lame.
Do you wanna color? Or go ride bikes?
Nope.
Oh.
Is there anything you *DO* wanna do?

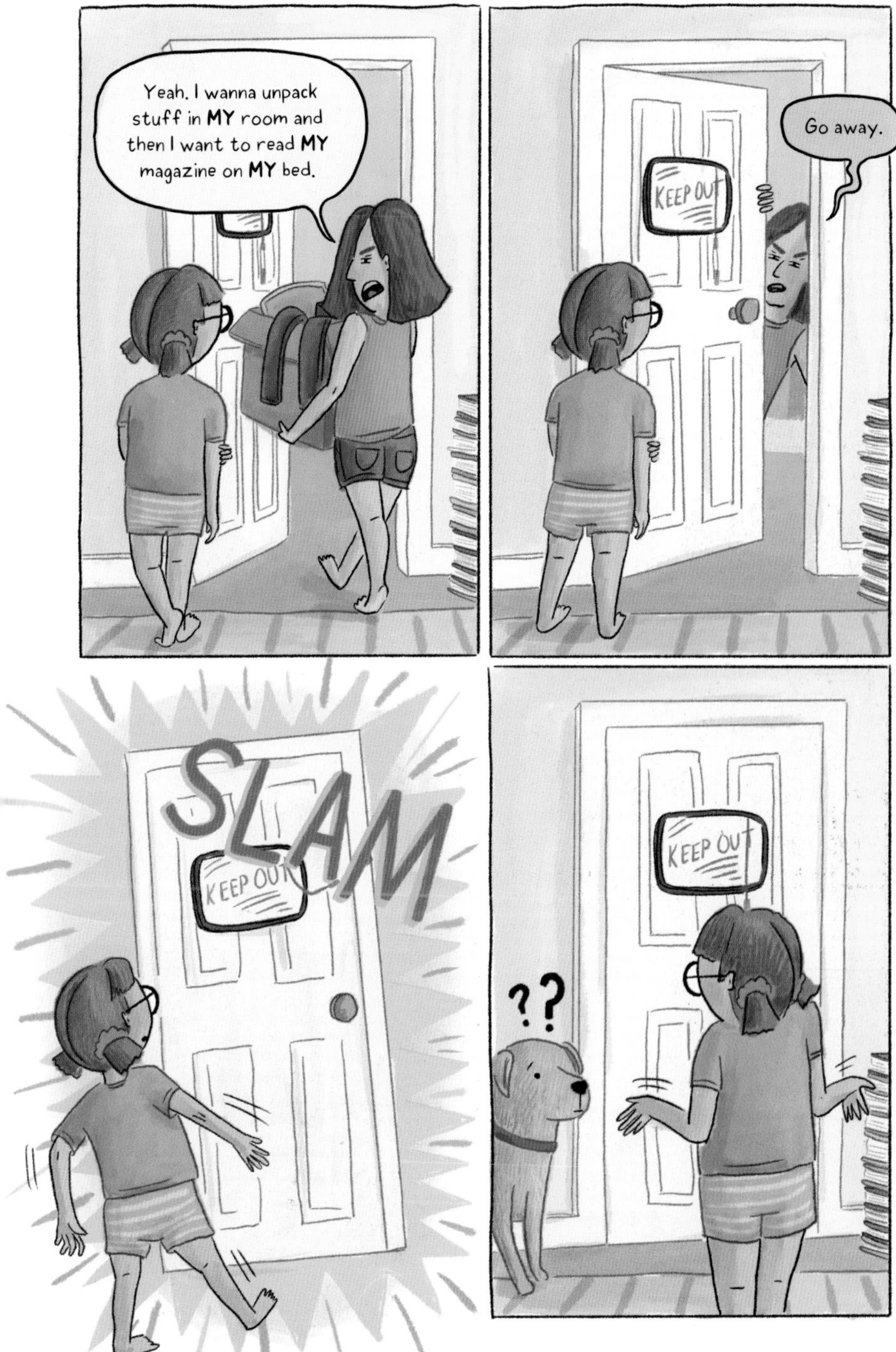
Yeah. I wanna unpack stuff in **MY** room and then I want to read **MY** magazine on **MY** bed.
KEEP OUT
Go away.
SLAM
KEEP OUT
KEEP OUT
??

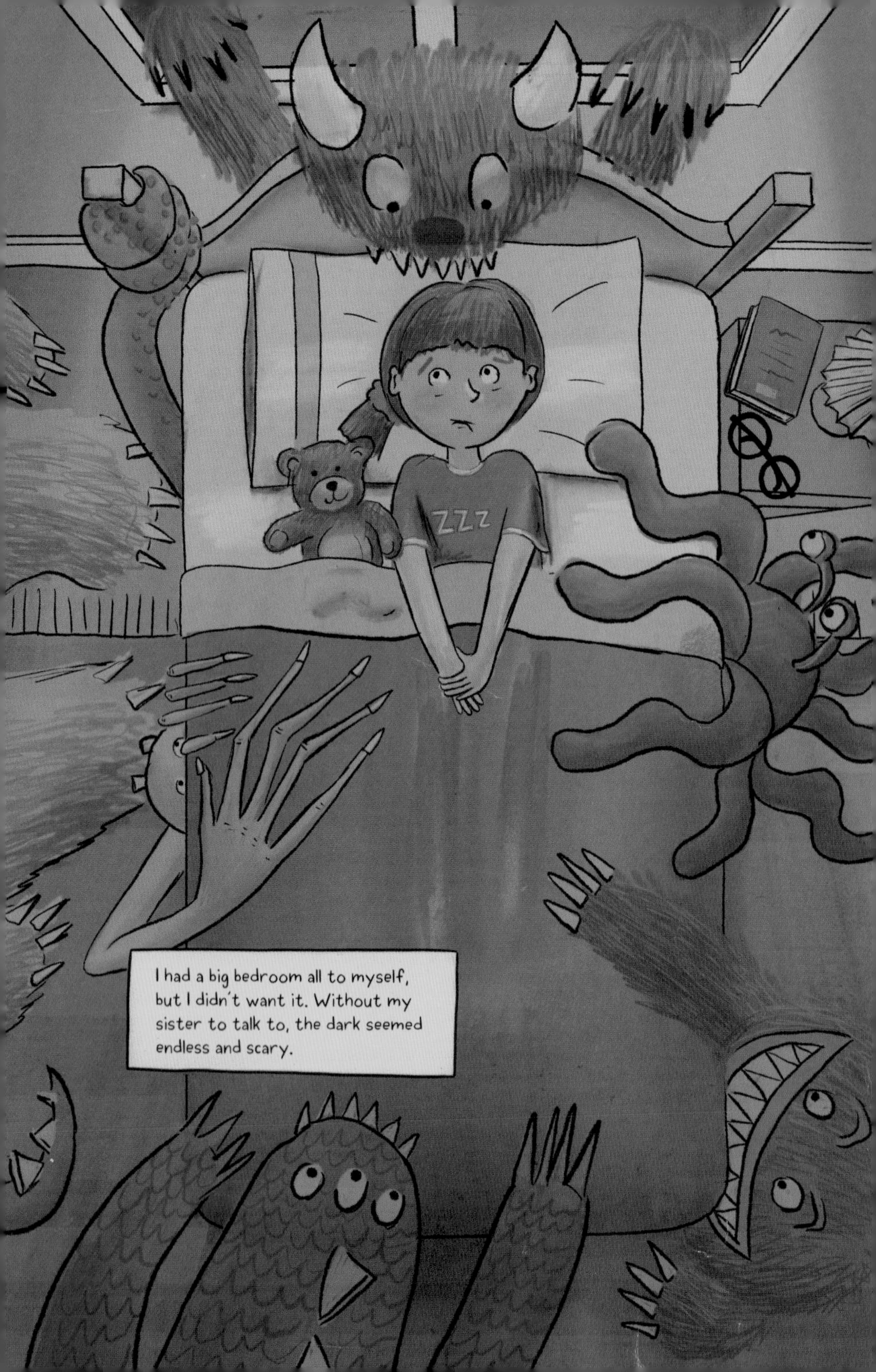
I had a big bedroom all to myself, but I didn't want it. Without my sister to talk to, the dark seemed endless and scary.
ZZZ

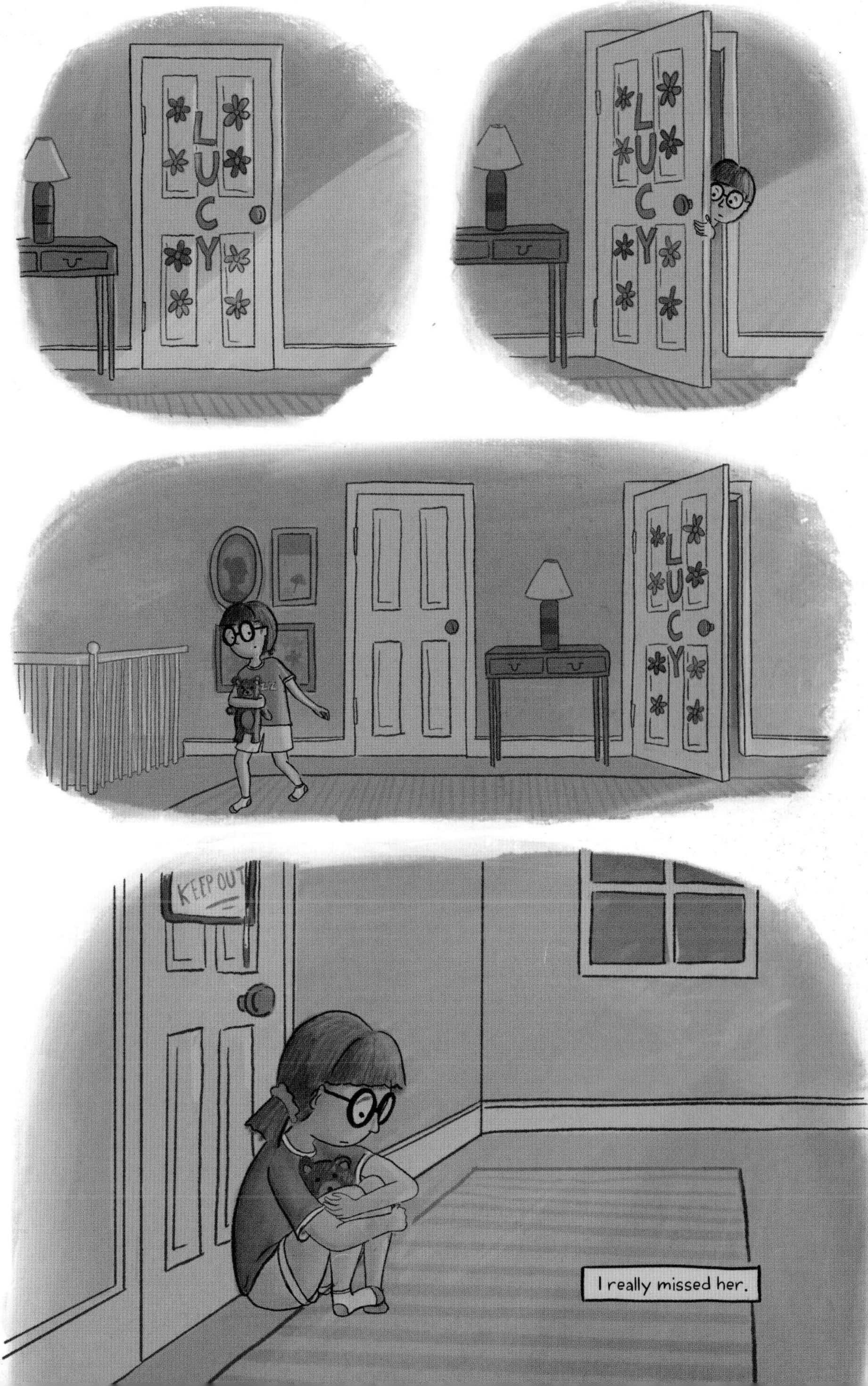
LUCY
LUCY
LUCY
KEEP OUT
I really missed her.

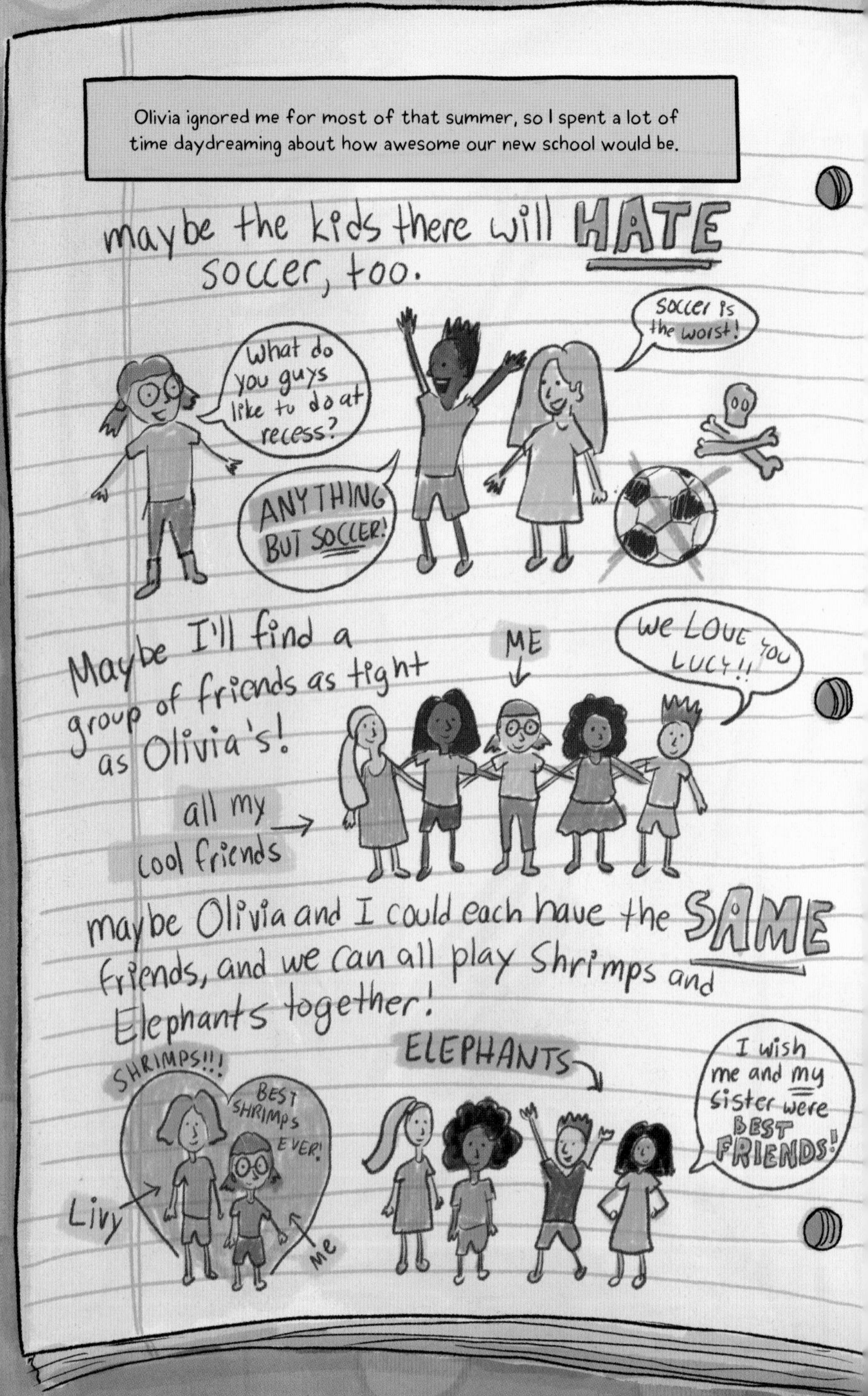

Olivia ignored me for most of that summer, so I spent a lot of time daydreaming about how awesome our new school would be.
maybe the kids there will HATE soccer, too.
What do you guys like to do at recess?
ANYTHING BUT SOCCER!
soccer is the worst!
Maybe I'll find a group of friends as tight as Olivia's!
ME
we LOVE you LUCY!!
all my cool friends
maybe Olivia and I could each have the SAME friends, and we can all play Shrimps and Elephants together!
SHRIMPS!!!
BEST SHRIMPS EVER!
Livy
me
ELEPHANTS
I wish me and my sister were BEST FRIENDS!

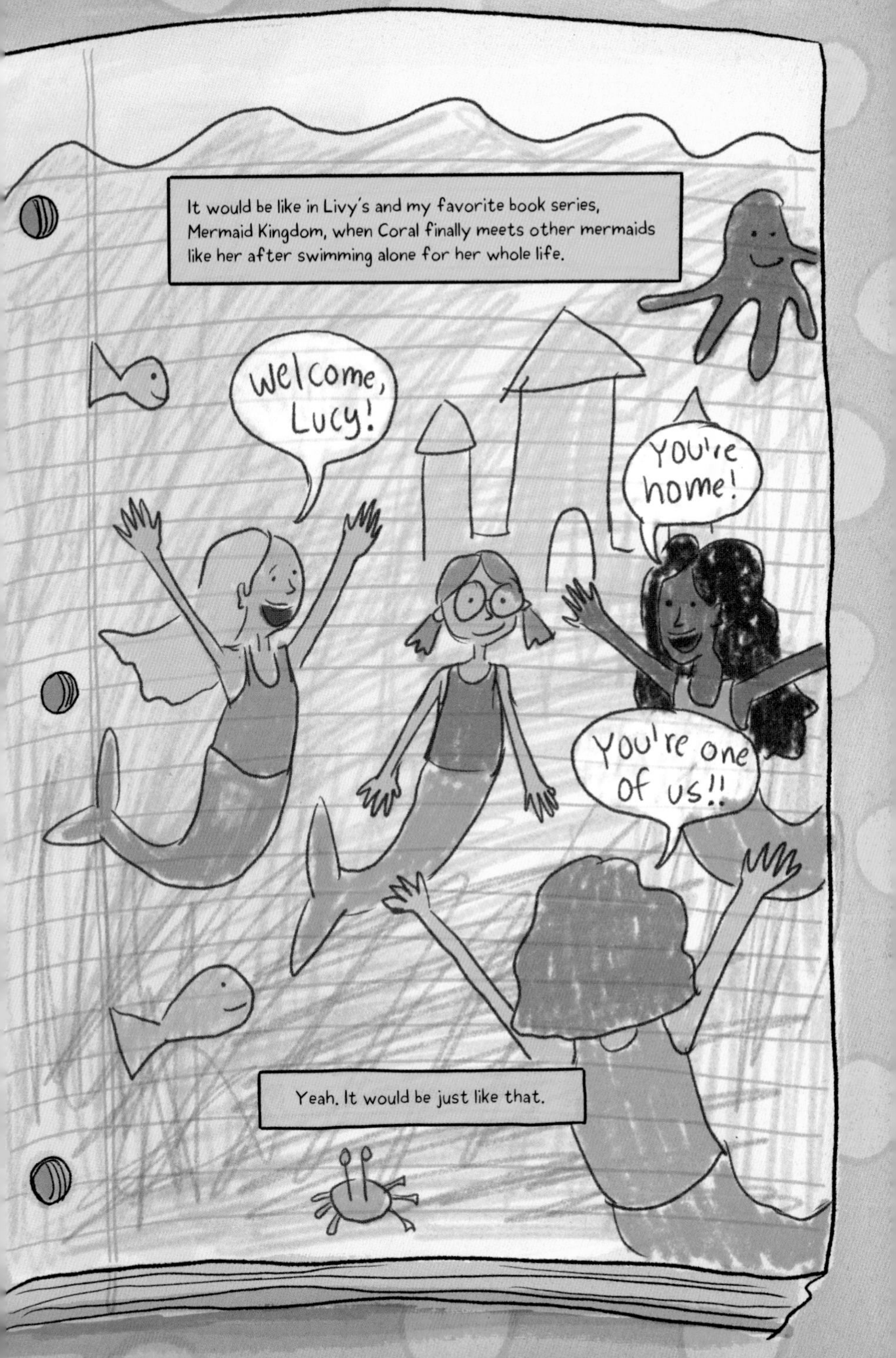
It would be like in Livy's and my favorite book series, Mermaid Kingdom, when Coral finally meets other mermaids like her after swimming alone for her whole life.
Welcome, Lucy!
You're home!
You're one of us!!
Yeah. It would be just like that.

CHAPTER 2

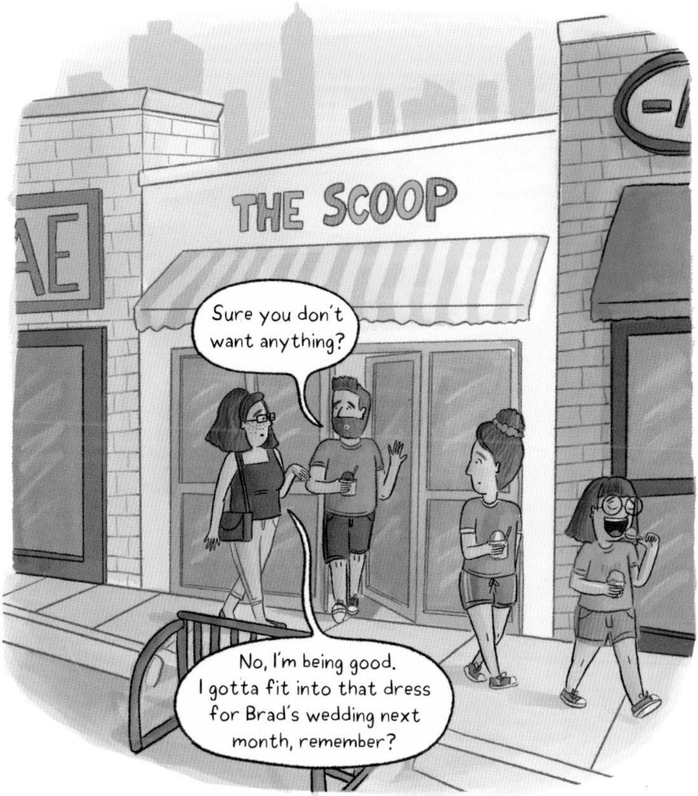
THE SCOOP
Sure you don't want anything?
No, I'm being good. I gotta fit into that dress for Brad's wedding next month, remember?

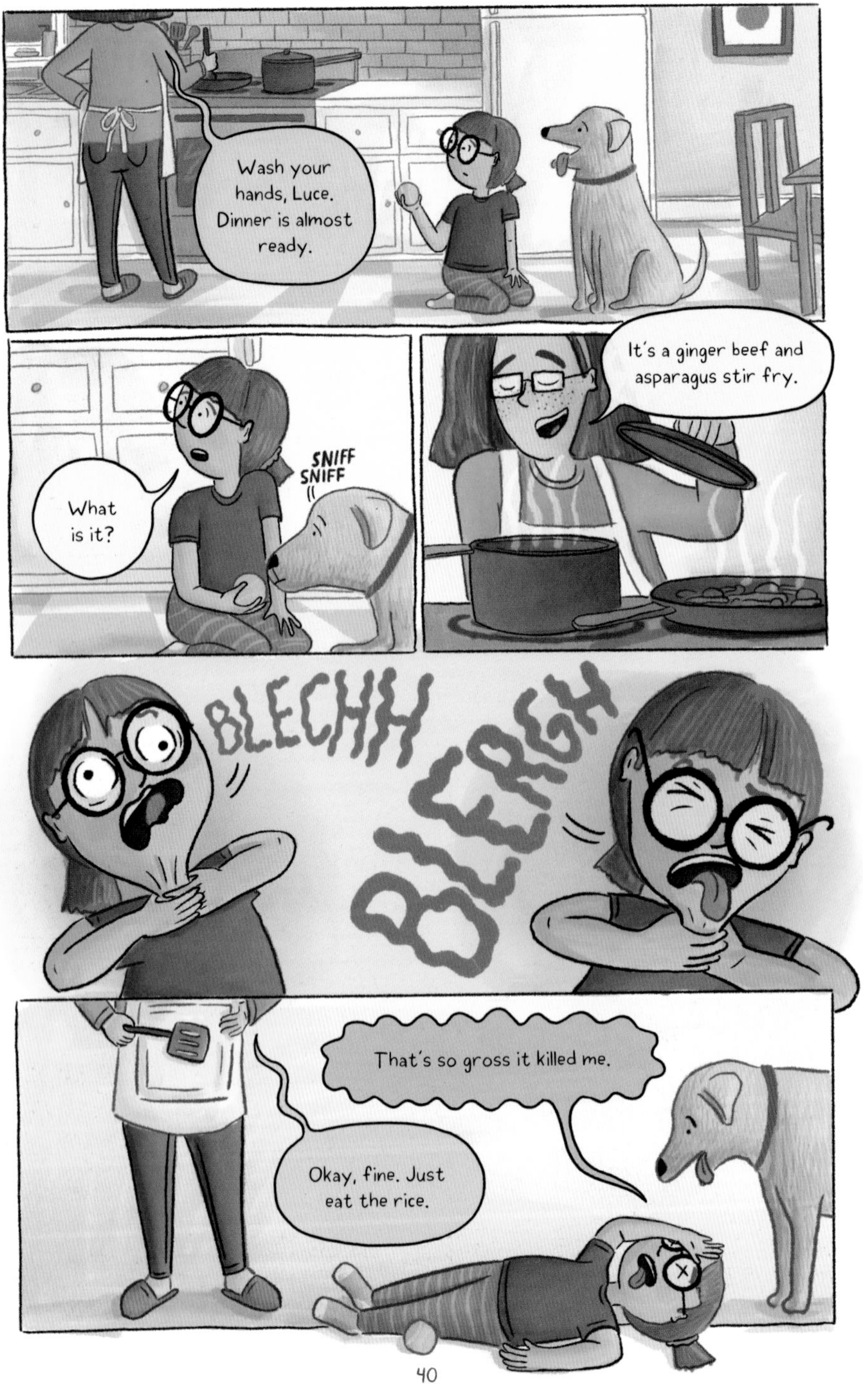
Wash your hands, Luce. Dinner is almost ready.
What is it?
SNIFF SNIFF
It's a ginger beef and asparagus stir fry.
BLECHH
BLERGH
That's so gross it killed me.
Okay, fine. Just eat the rice.

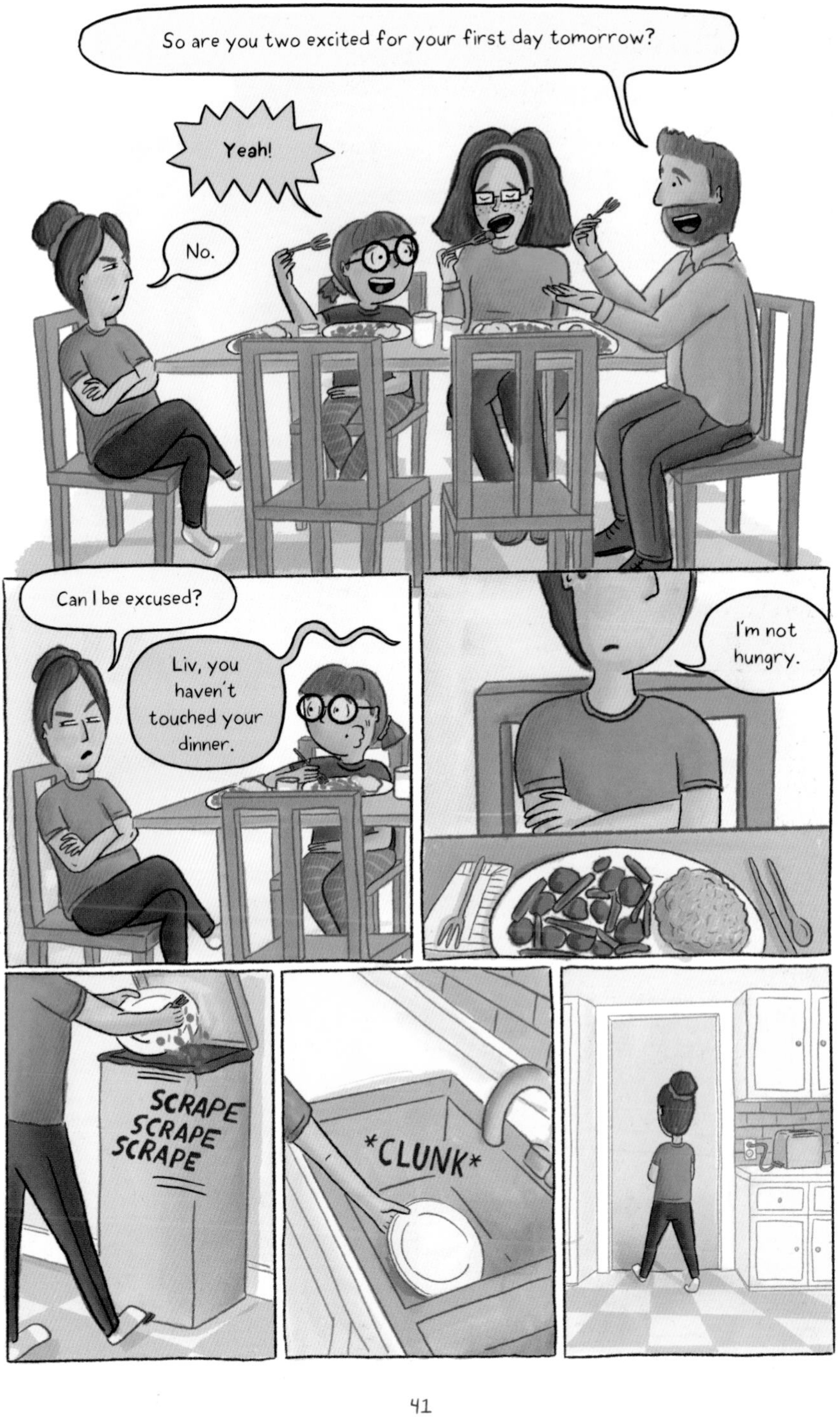
So are you two excited for your first day tomorrow?
Yeah!
No.
Can I be excused?
Liv, you haven't touched your dinner.
I'm not hungry.
SCRAPE SCRAPE SCRAPE
CLUNK

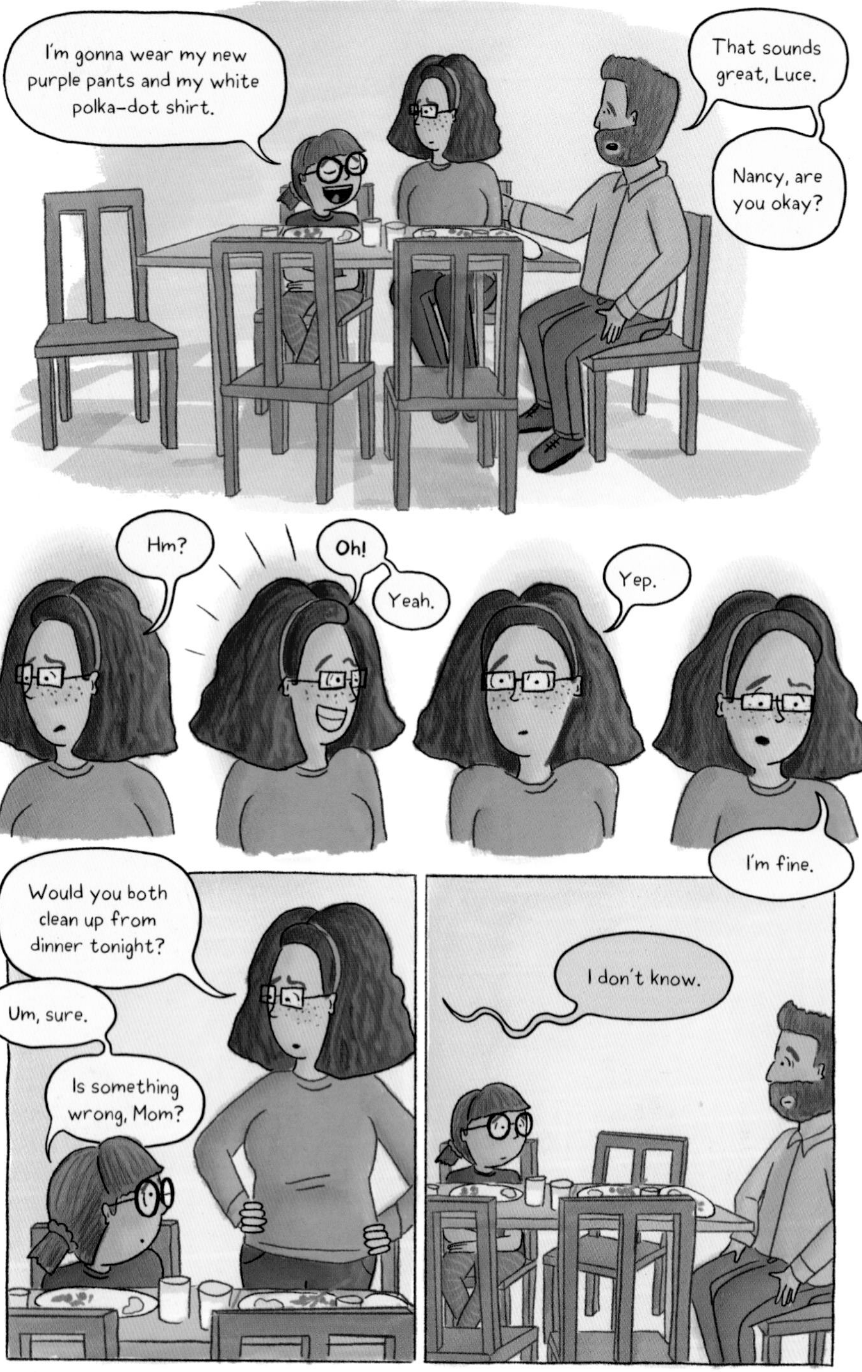
I'm gonna wear my new purple pants and my white polka-dot shirt.
That sounds great, Luce.
Nancy, are you okay?
Hm?
Oh!
Yeah.
Yep.
I'm fine.
Would you both clean up from dinner tonight?
Um, sure.
Is something wrong, Mom?
I don't know.

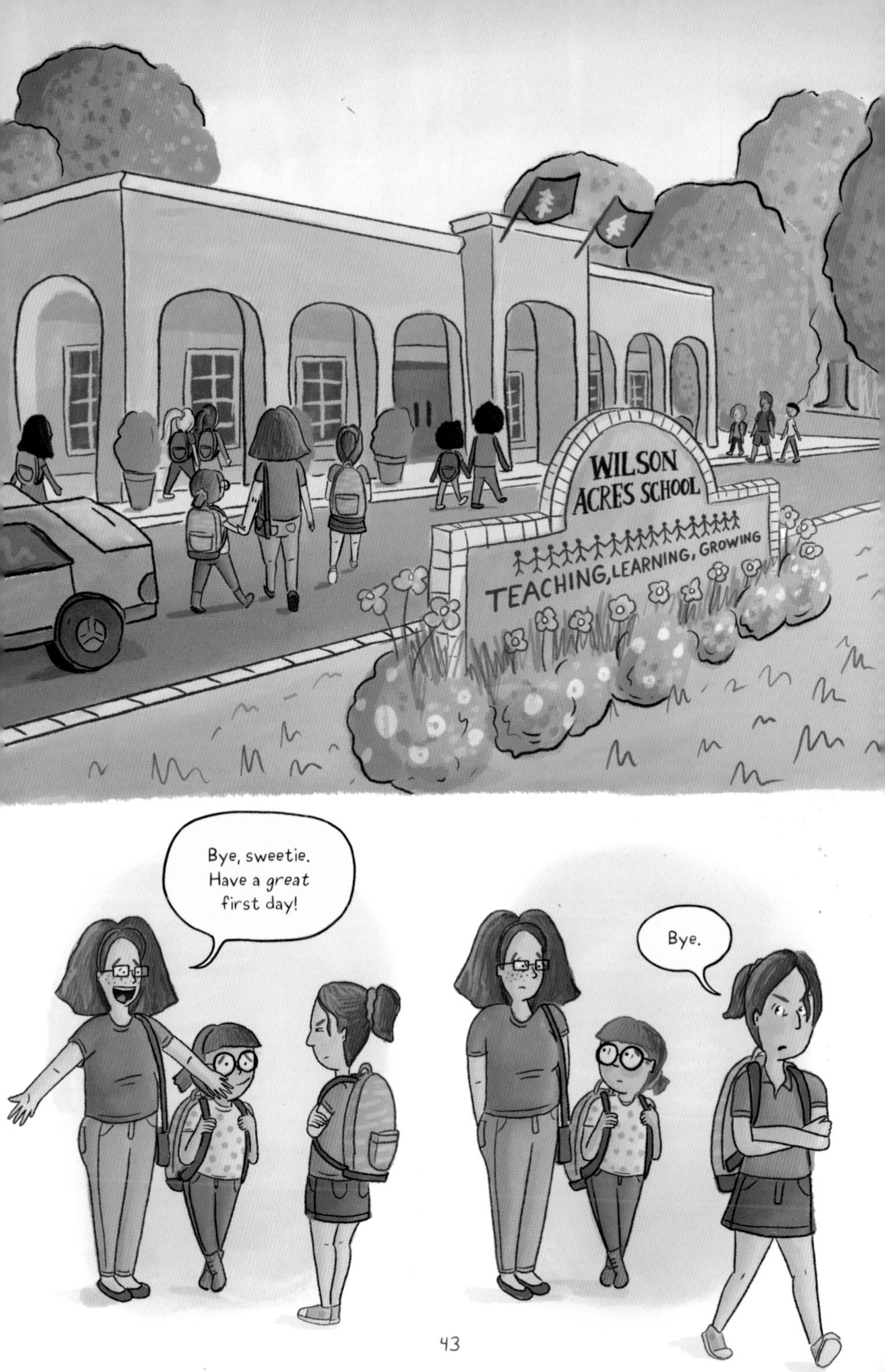
WILSON
ACRES SCHOOL
TEACHING, LEARNING, GROWING
Bye, sweetie.
Have a *great*
first day!
Bye.

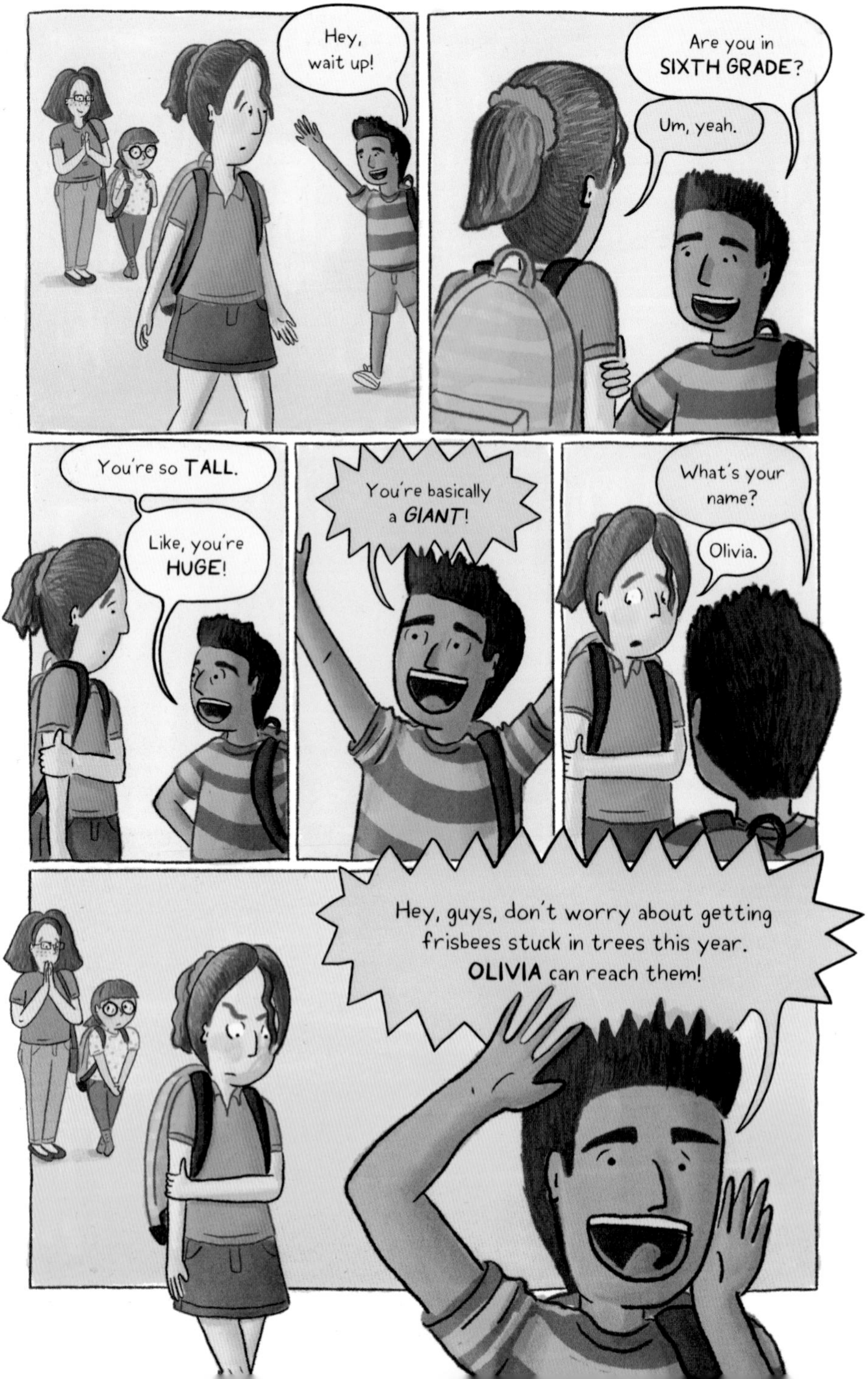

Hey, wait up!
Are you in SIXTH GRADE?
Um, yeah.
You're so TALL.
Like, you're HUGE!
You're basically a GIANT!
What's your name?
Olivia.
Hey, guys, don't worry about getting frisbees stuck in trees this year. OLIVIA can reach them!

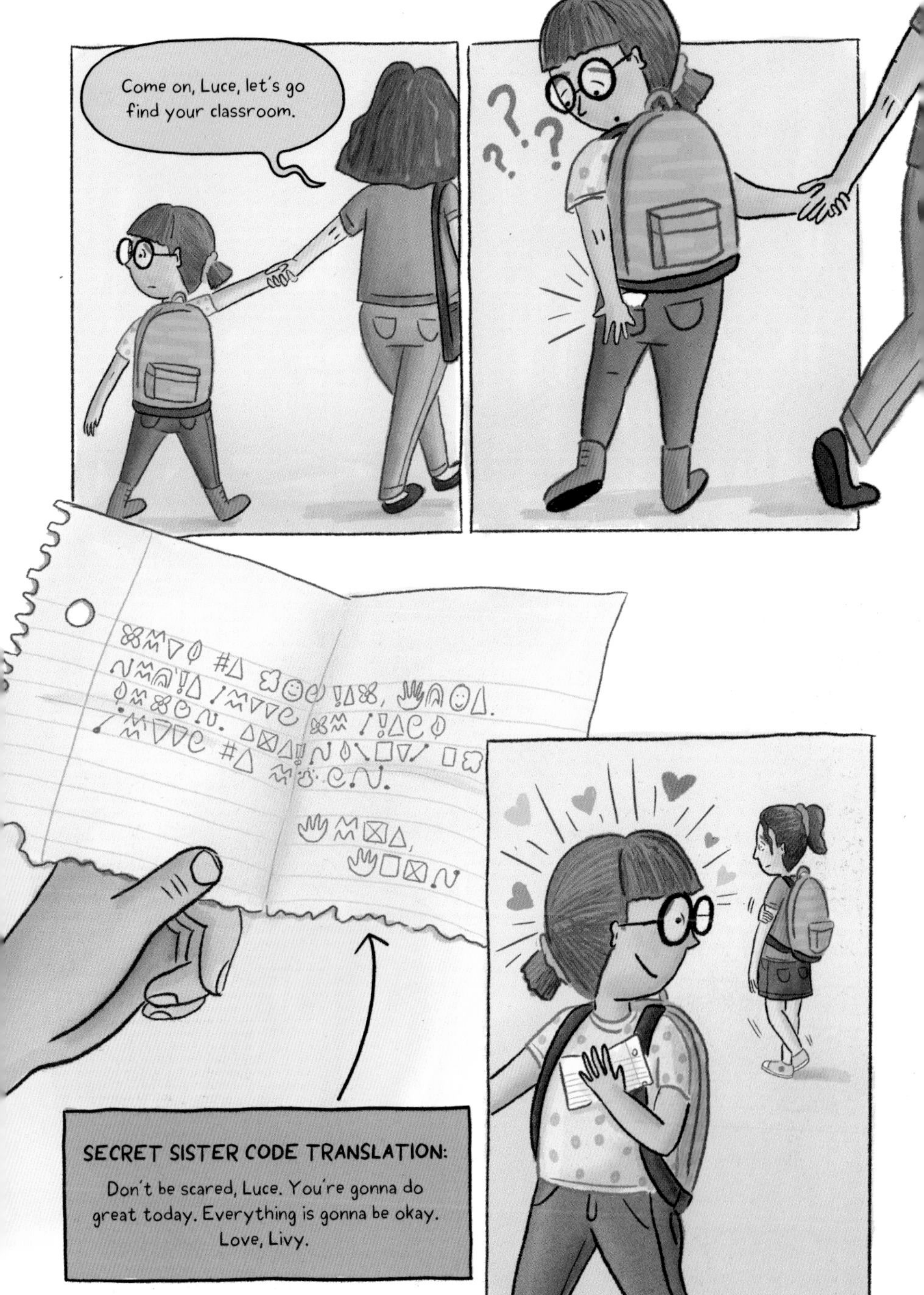
Come on, Luce, let's go find your classroom.
SECRET SISTER CODE TRANSLATION:
Don't be scared, Luce. You're gonna do great today. Everything is gonna be okay. Love, Livy.

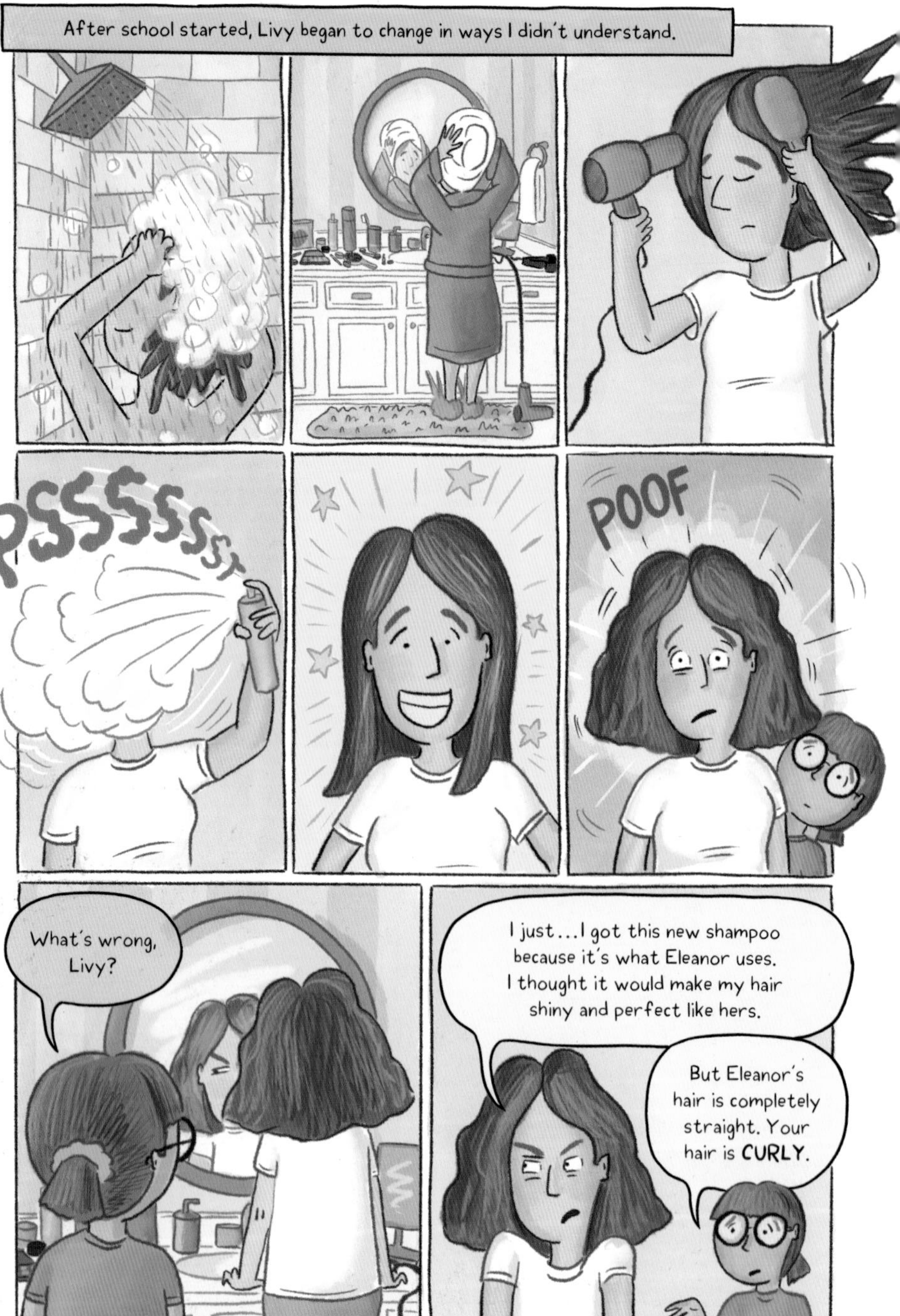
After school started, Livy began to change in ways I didn't understand.
PSSSSSSST
POOF
What's wrong, Livy?
I just... I got this new shampoo because it's what Eleanor uses. I thought it would make my hair shiny and perfect like hers.
But Eleanor's hair is completely straight. Your hair is **CURLY**.

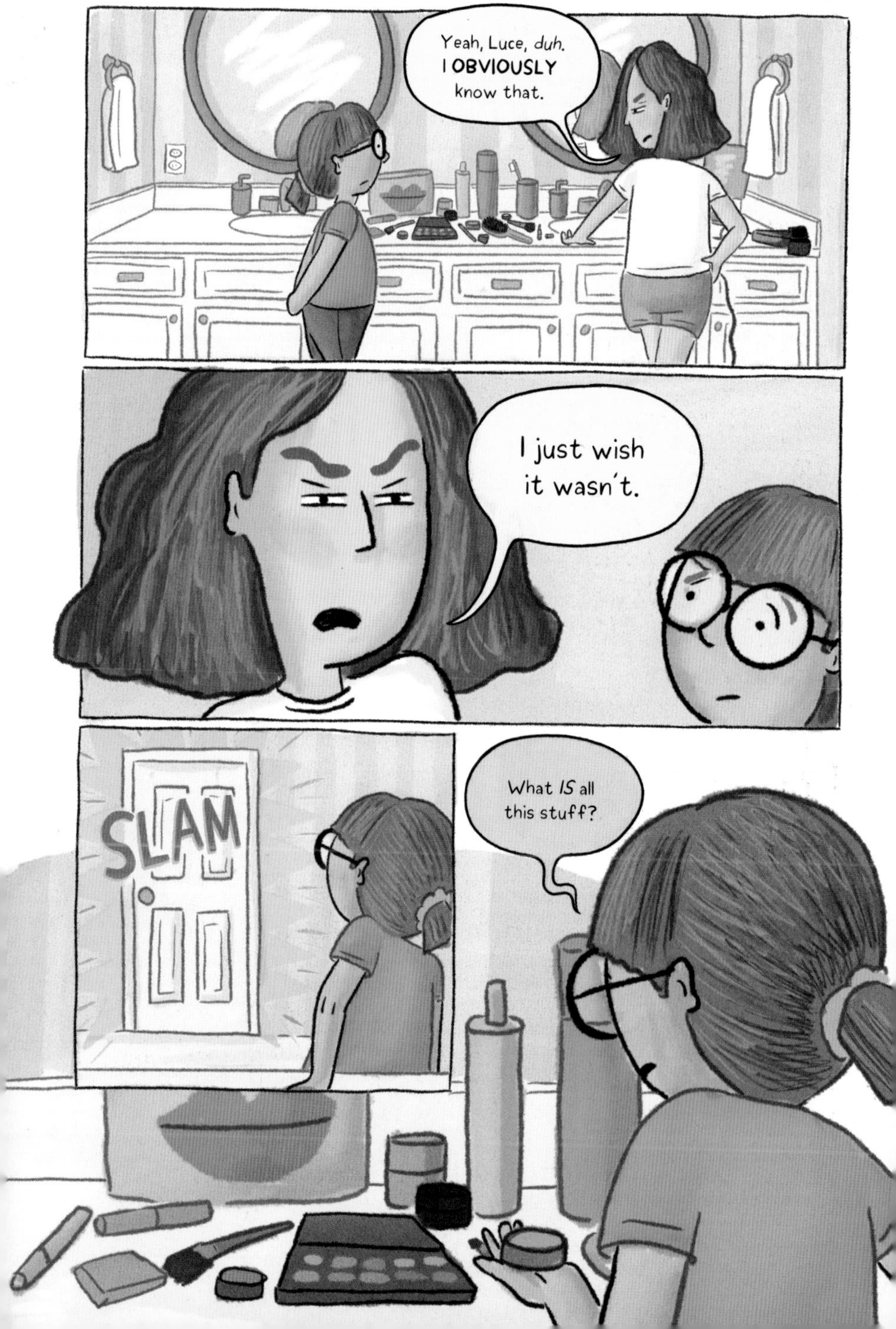
Yeah, Luce, *duh.* I **OBVIOUSLY** know that.
I just wish it wasn't.
SLAM
What *IS* all this stuff?

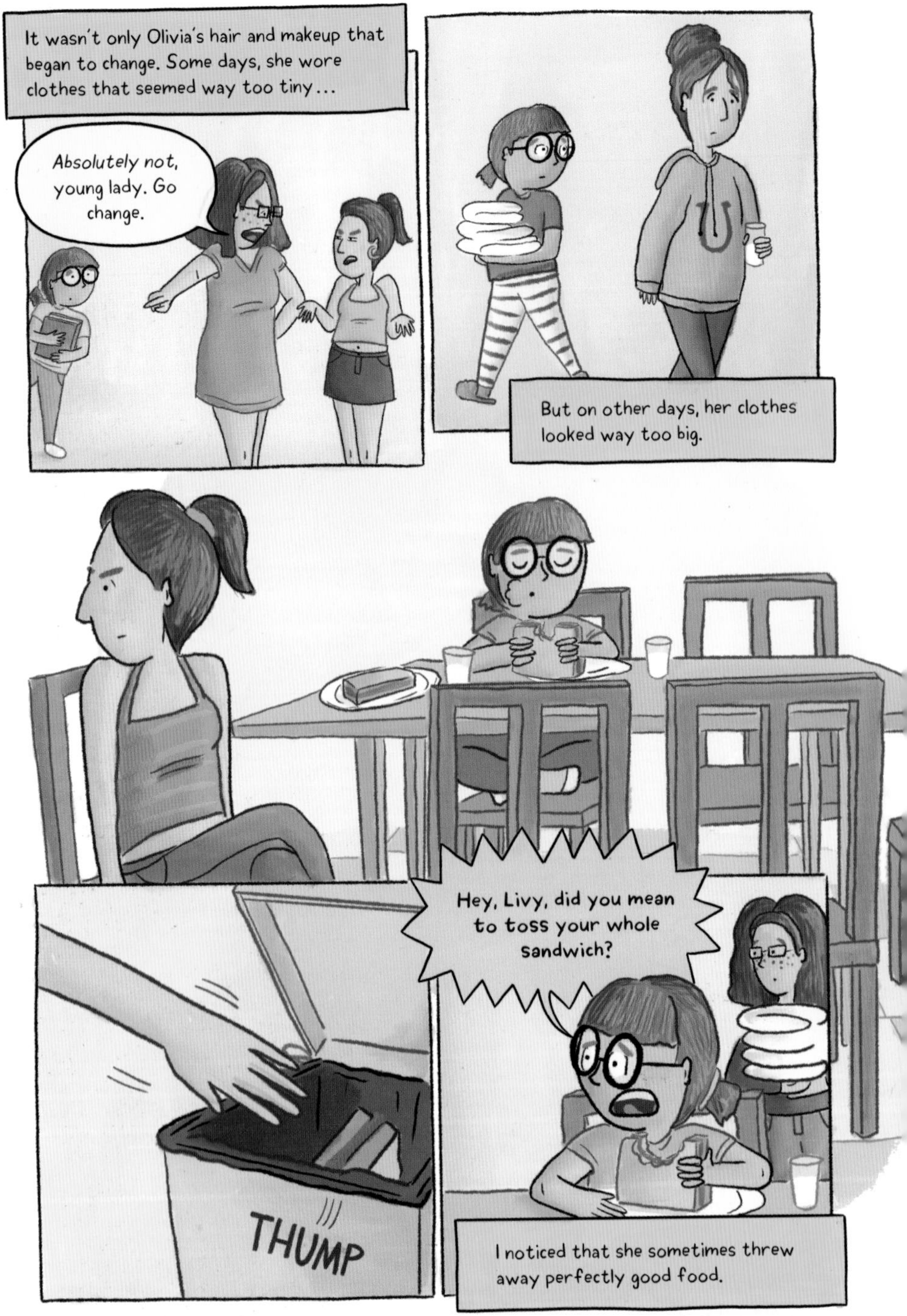
It wasn't only Olivia's hair and makeup that began to change. Some days, she wore clothes that seemed way too tiny...
Absolutely not, young lady. Go change.
But on other days, her clothes looked way too big.
THUMP
Hey, Livy, did you mean to toss your whole sandwich?
I noticed that she sometimes threw away perfectly good food.

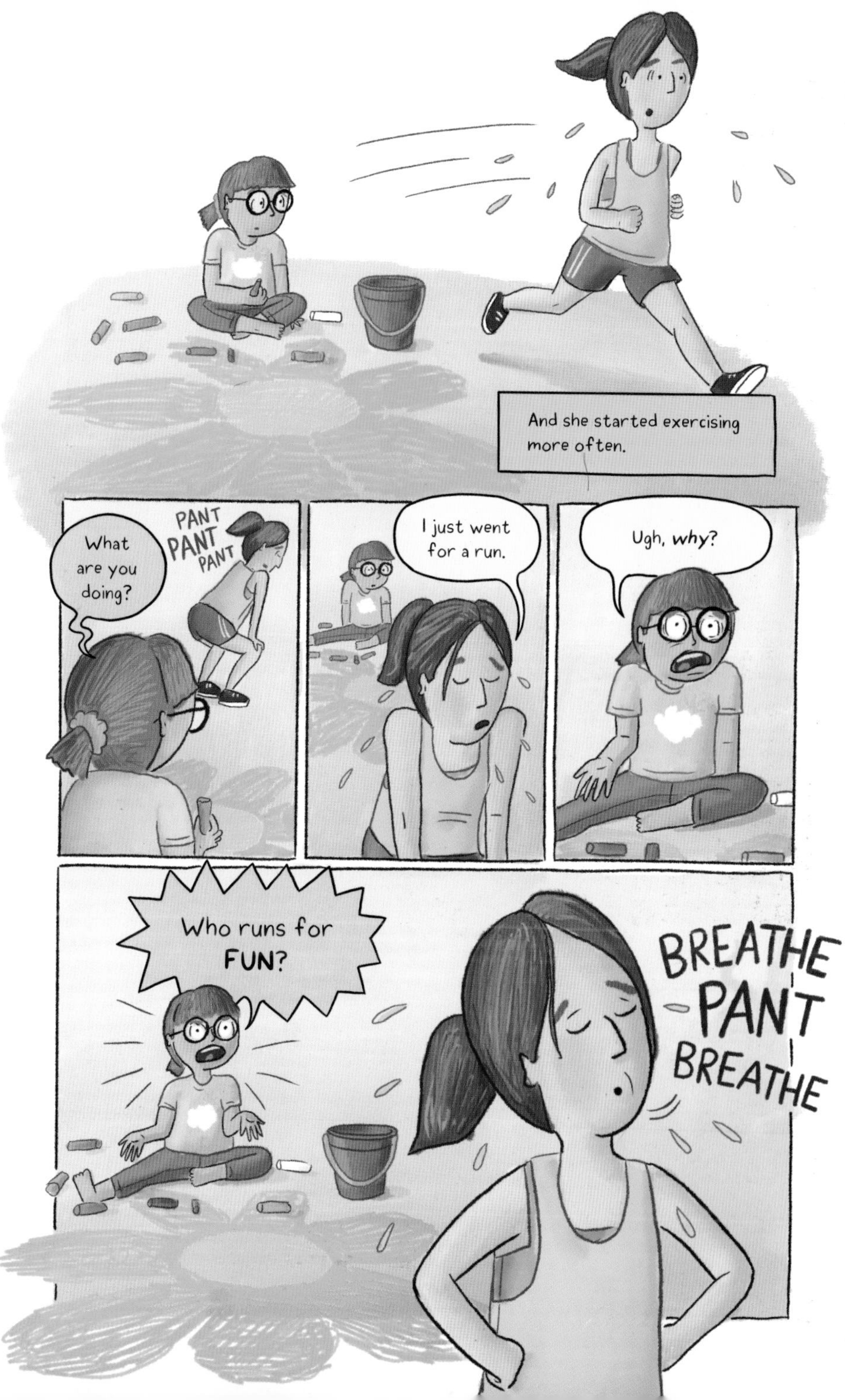
And she started exercising more often.
What are you doing?
PANT PANT PANT
I just went for a run.
Ugh, *why*?
Who runs for **FUN**?
BREATHE PANT BREATHE

I turned eleven a few months into the school year, and Mom took me to our pediatrician for my annual physical.

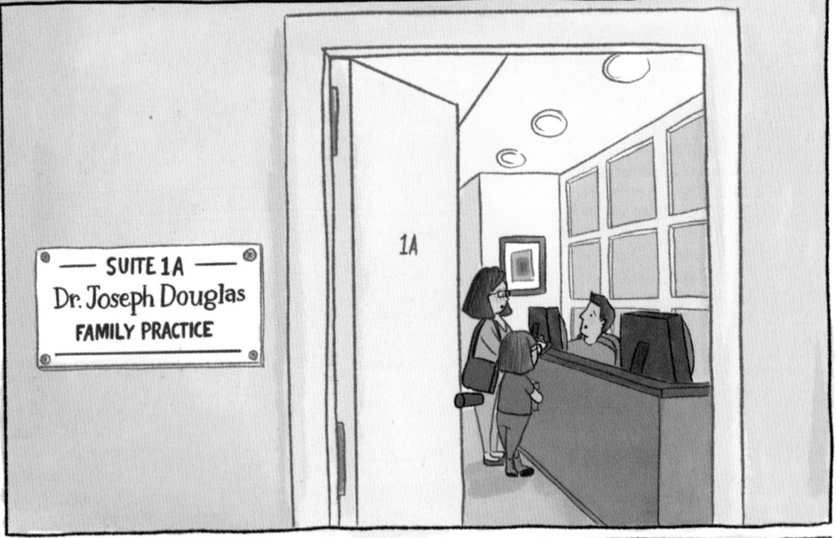
SUITE 1A
Dr. Joseph Douglas
FAMILY PRACTICE
1A

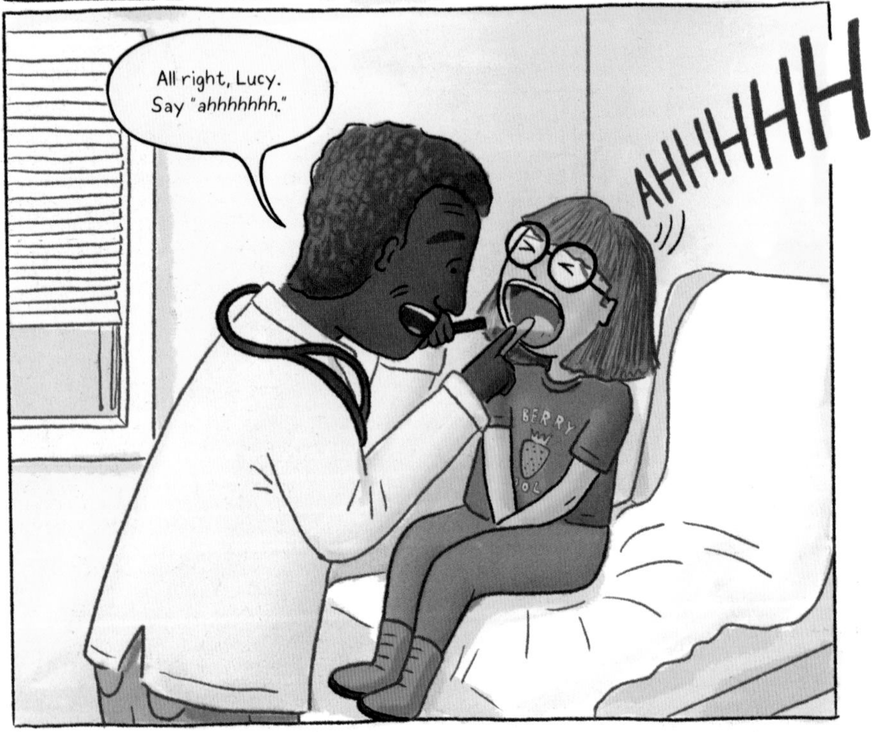
All right, Lucy. Say "ahhhhhhh."
AHHHHHH
BERRY

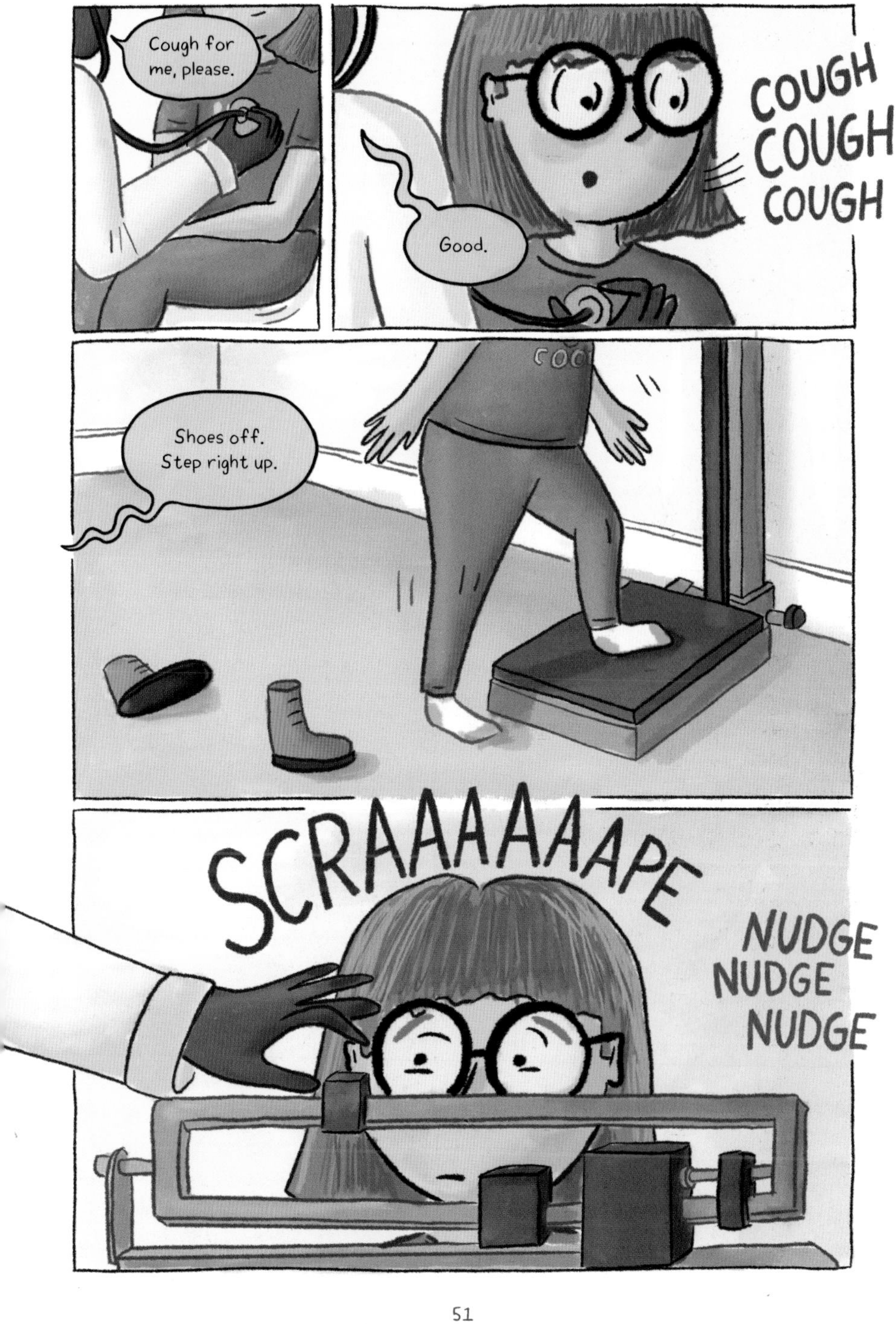
Cough for me, please.
Good.
COUGH
COUGH
COUGH
COOL
Shoes off. Step right up.
SCRAAAAAAPE
NUDGE
NUDGE
NUDGE

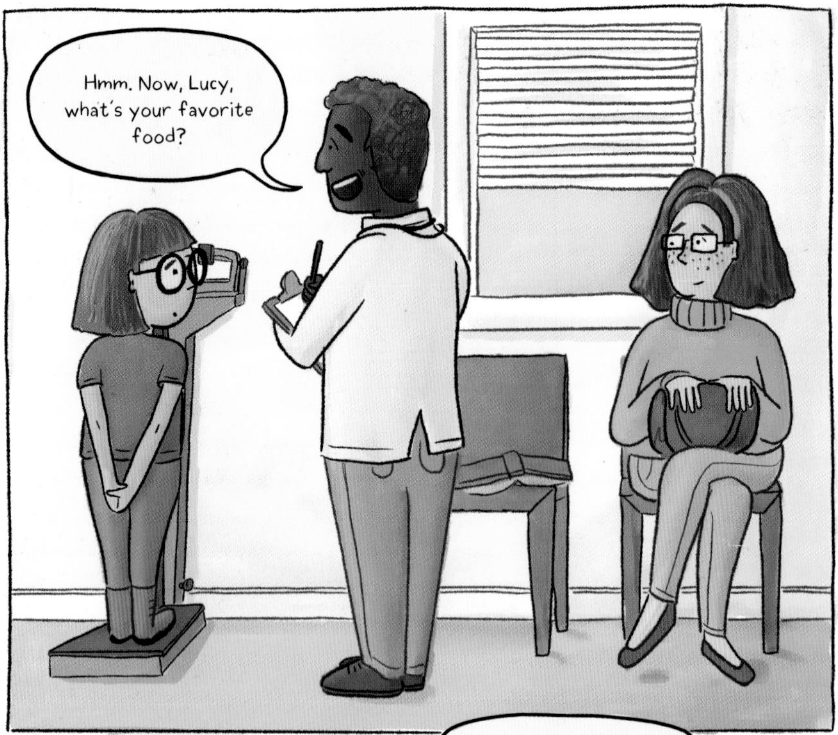
Hmm. Now, Lucy, what's your favorite food?

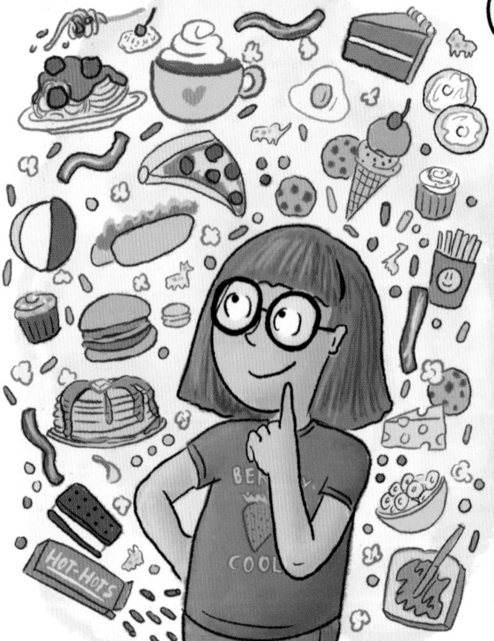
HOT-HOTS

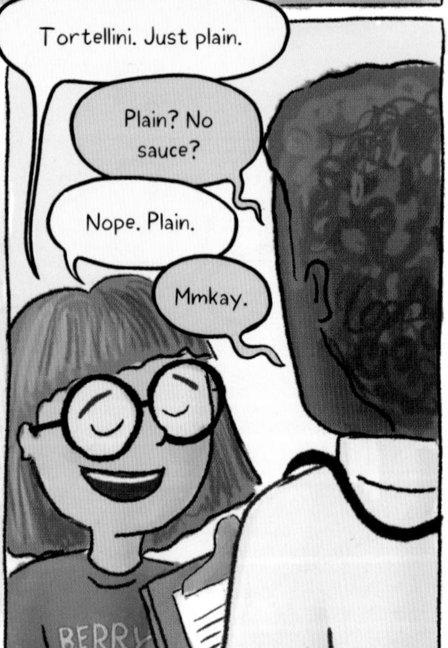
Tortellini. Just plain.
Plain? No sauce?
Nope. Plain.
Mmkay.

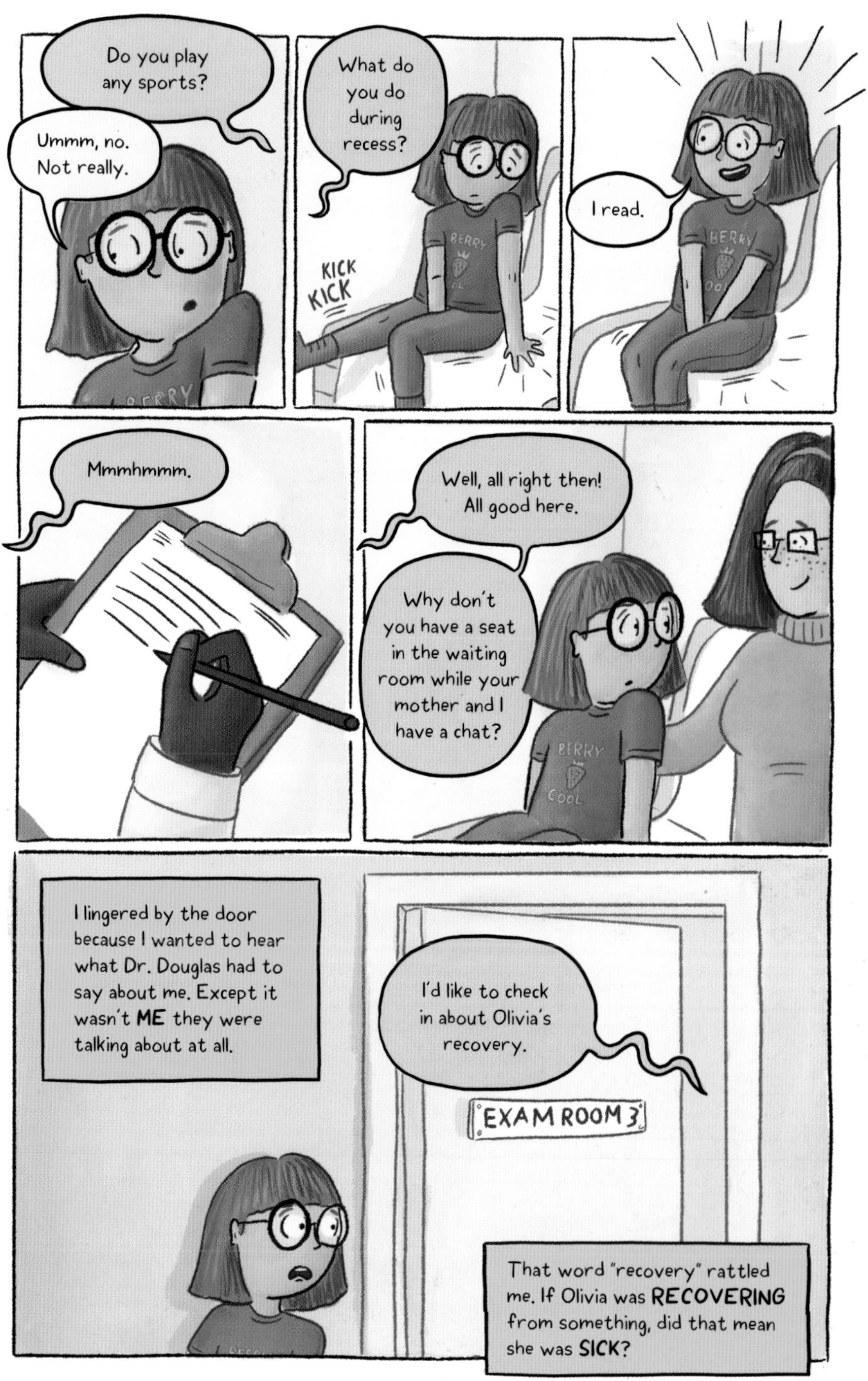
Do you play any sports?
Ummm, no. Not really.
What do you do during recess?
KICK KICK
I read.
Mmmhmmm.
Well, all right then! All good here.
Why don't you have a seat in the waiting room while your mother and I have a chat?
BERRY COOL
I lingered by the door because I wanted to hear what Dr. Douglas had to say about me. Except it wasn't ME they were talking about at all.
I'd like to check in about Olivia's recovery.
EXAM ROOM 3
That word "recovery" rattled me. If Olivia was RECOVERING from something, did that mean she was SICK?

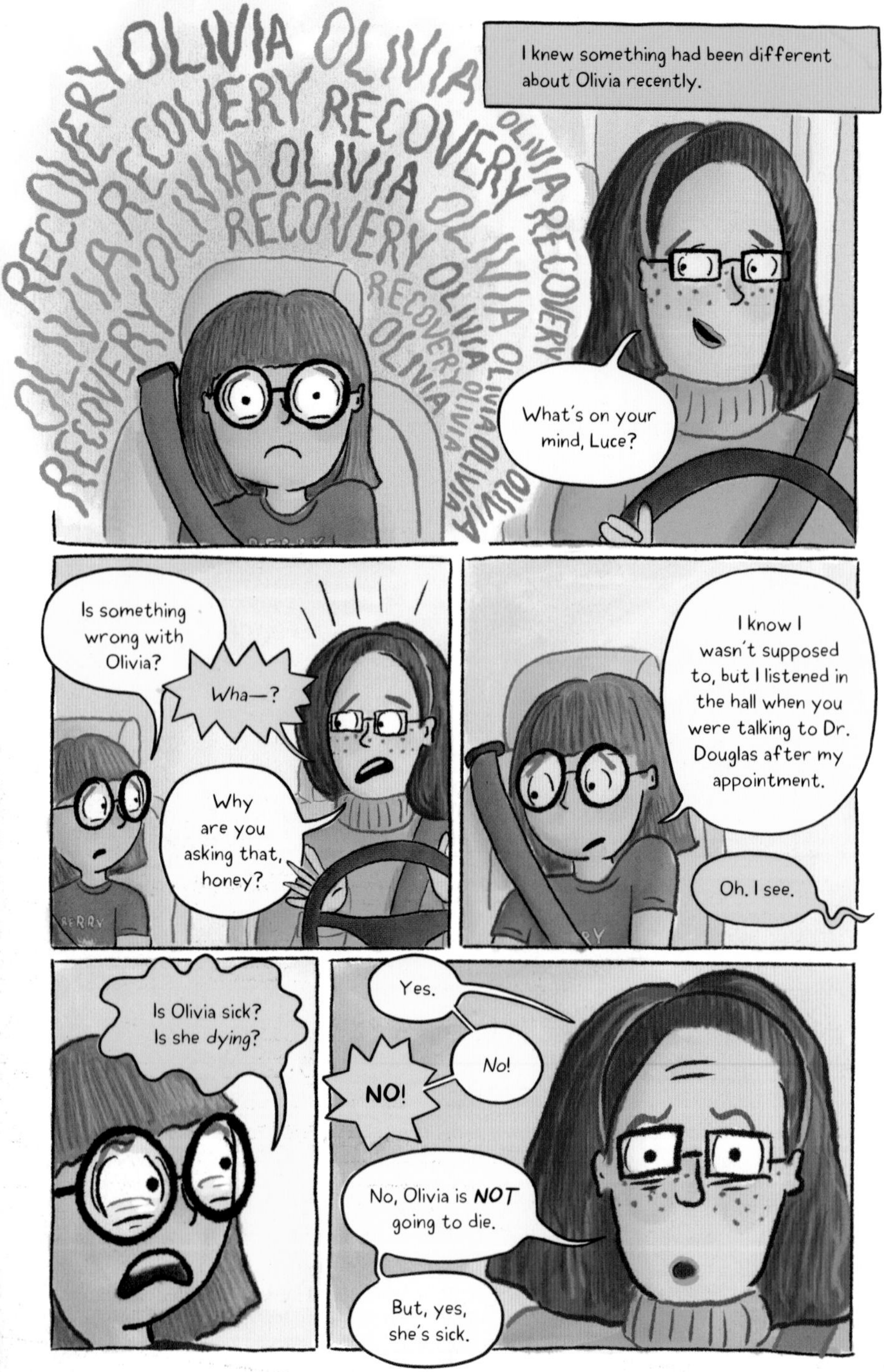
RECOVERY OLIVIA OLIVIA
RECOVERY RECOVERY RECOVERY
OLIVIA RECOVERY OLIVIA OLIVIA
I knew something had been different about Olivia recently.
What's on your mind, Luce?
Is something wrong with Olivia?
Wha—?
Why are you asking that, honey?
I know I wasn't supposed to, but I listened in the hall when you were talking to Dr. Douglas after my appointment.
Oh. I see.
Is Olivia sick? Is she dying?
Yes.
No!
NO!
No, Olivia is ***NOT*** going to die.
But, yes, she's sick.

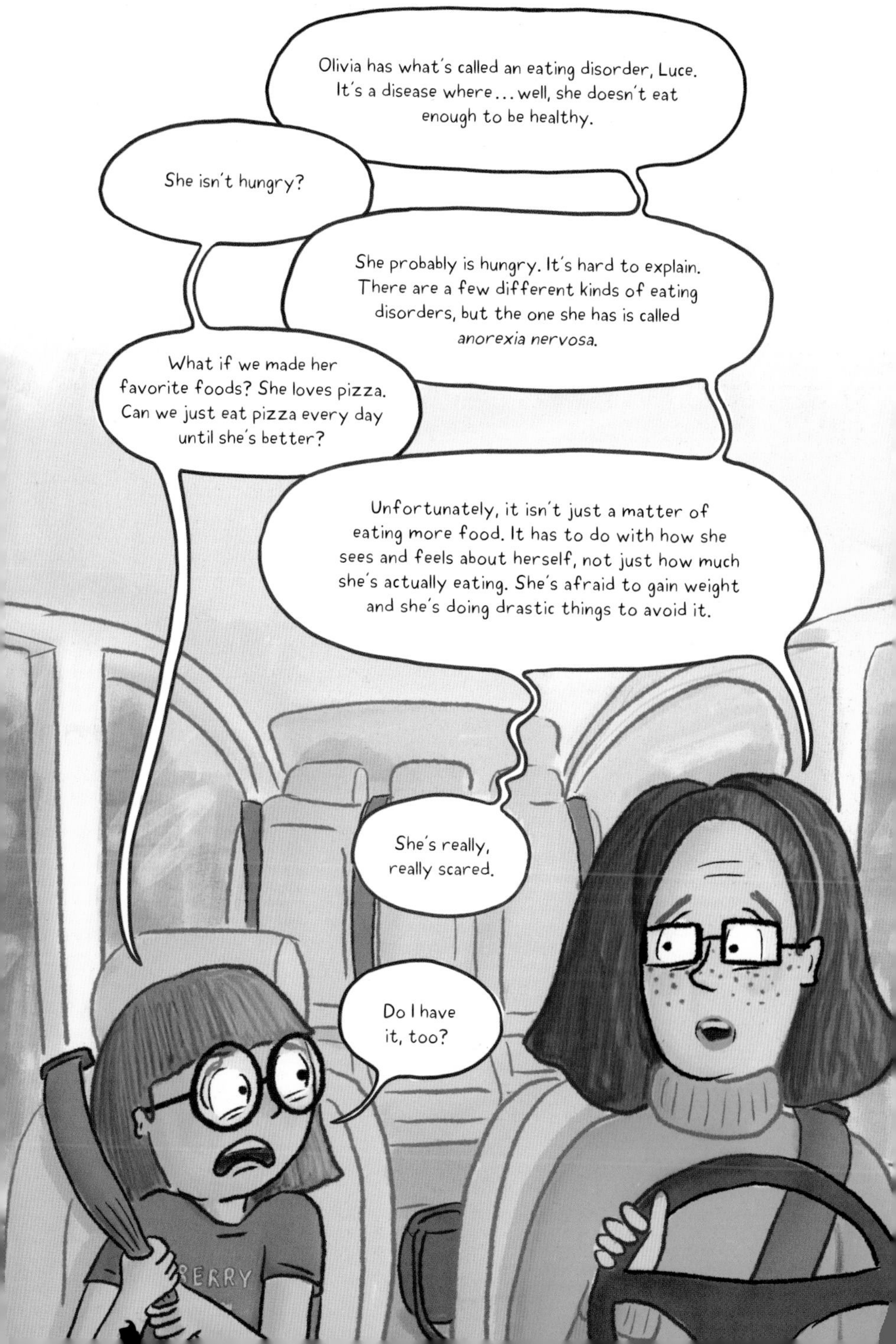
Olivia has what's called an eating disorder, Luce. It's a disease where... well, she doesn't eat enough to be healthy.
She isn't hungry?
She probably is hungry. It's hard to explain. There are a few different kinds of eating disorders, but the one she has is called *anorexia nervosa*.
What if we made her favorite foods? She loves pizza. Can we just eat pizza every day until she's better?
Unfortunately, it isn't just a matter of eating more food. It has to do with how she sees and feels about herself, not just how much she's actually eating. She's afraid to gain weight and she's doing drastic things to avoid it.
She's really, really scared.
Do I have it, too?

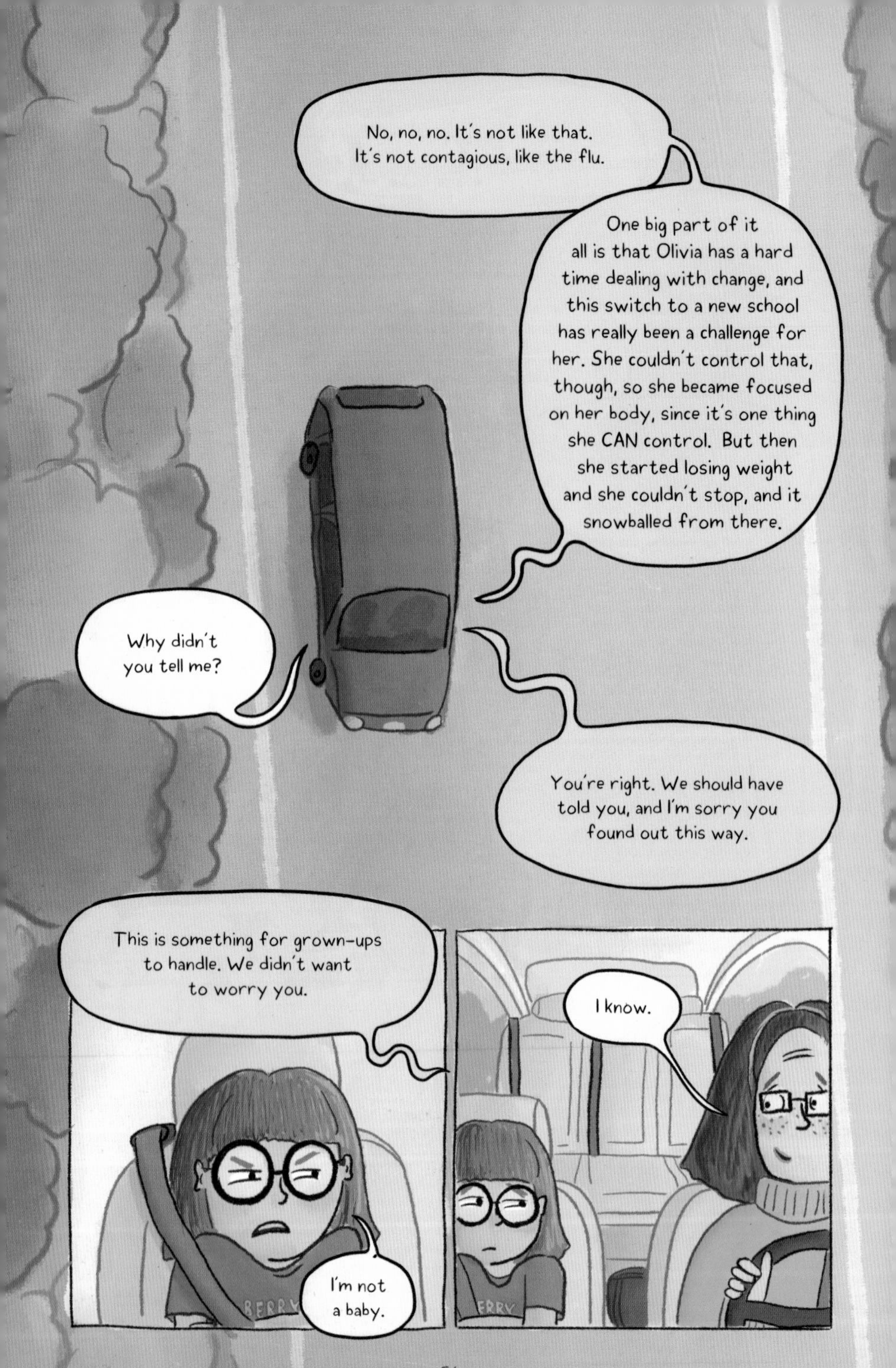
No, no, no. It's not like that. It's not contagious, like the flu.
One big part of it all is that Olivia has a hard time dealing with change, and this switch to a new school has really been a challenge for her. She couldn't control that, though, so she became focused on her body, since it's one thing she CAN control. But then she started losing weight and she couldn't stop, and it snowballed from there.
Why didn't you tell me?
You're right. We should have told you, and I'm sorry you found out this way.
This is something for grown-ups to handle. We didn't want to worry you.
I'm not a baby.
I know.

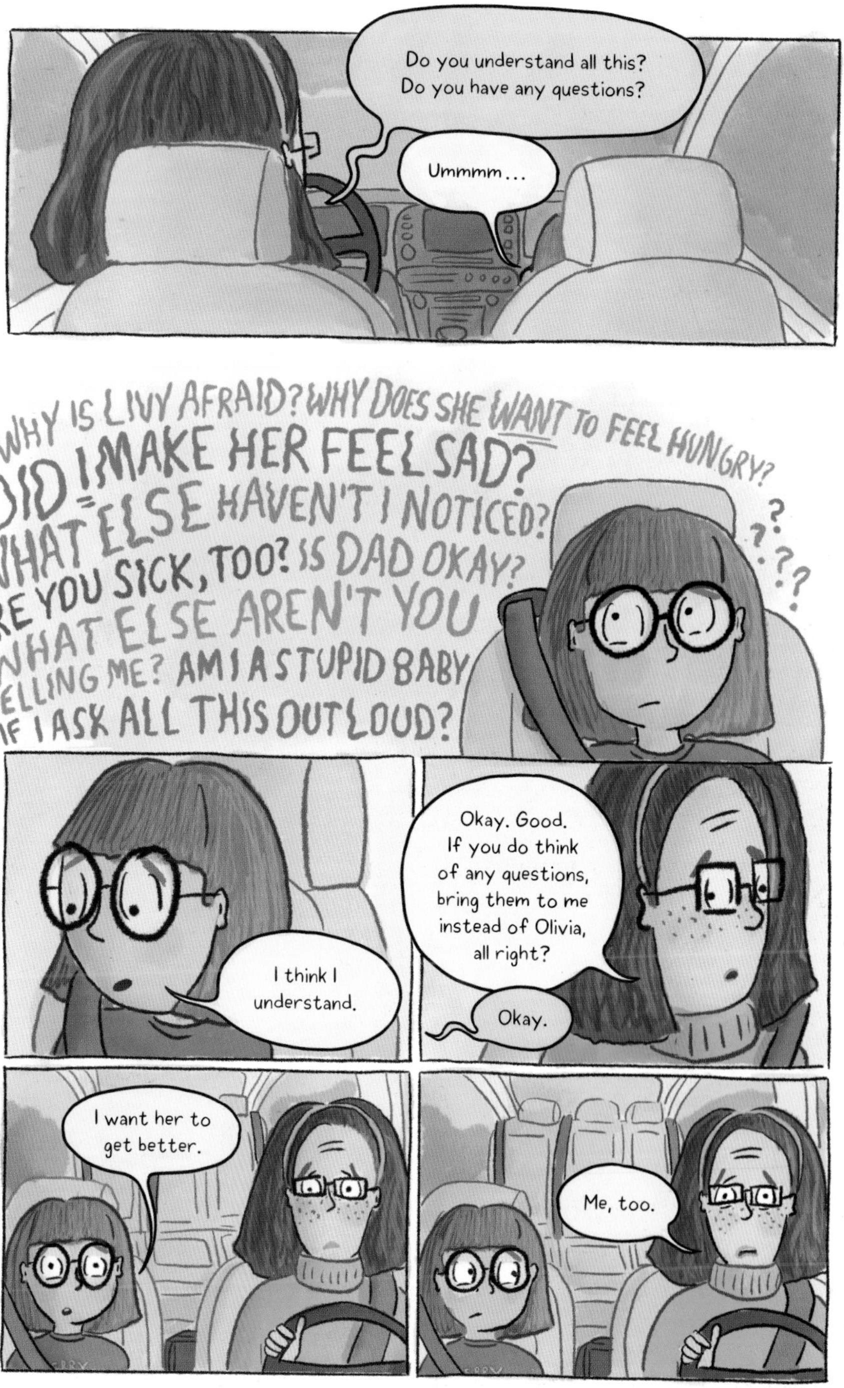
Do you understand all this? Do you have any questions?
Ummmm...
WHY IS LIVY AFRAID? WHY DOES SHE WANT TO FEEL HUNGRY?
DID I MAKE HER FEEL SAD?
WHAT ELSE HAVEN'T I NOTICED?
ARE YOU SICK, TOO? IS DAD OKAY?
WHAT ELSE AREN'T YOU TELLING ME? AM I A STUPID BABY IF I ASK ALL THIS OUT LOUD?
? ? ? ?
I think I understand.
Okay. Good. If you do think of any questions, bring them to me instead of Olivia, all right?
Okay.
I want her to get better.
Me, too.

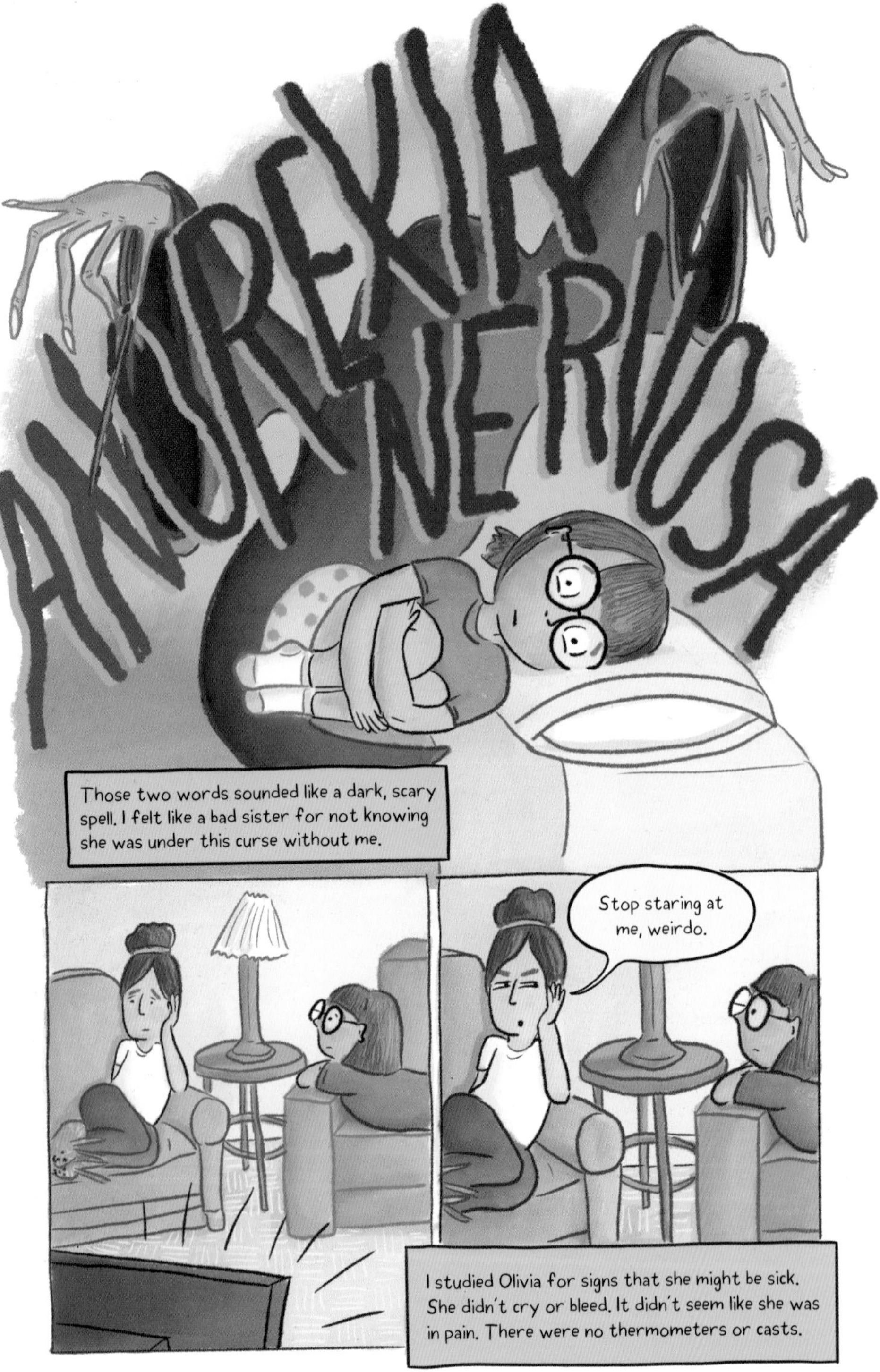
ANOREXIA NERVOSA
Those two words sounded like a dark, scary spell. I felt like a bad sister for not knowing she was under this curse without me.
Stop staring at me, weirdo.
I studied Olivia for signs that she might be sick. She didn't cry or bleed. It didn't seem like she was in pain. There were no thermometers or casts.

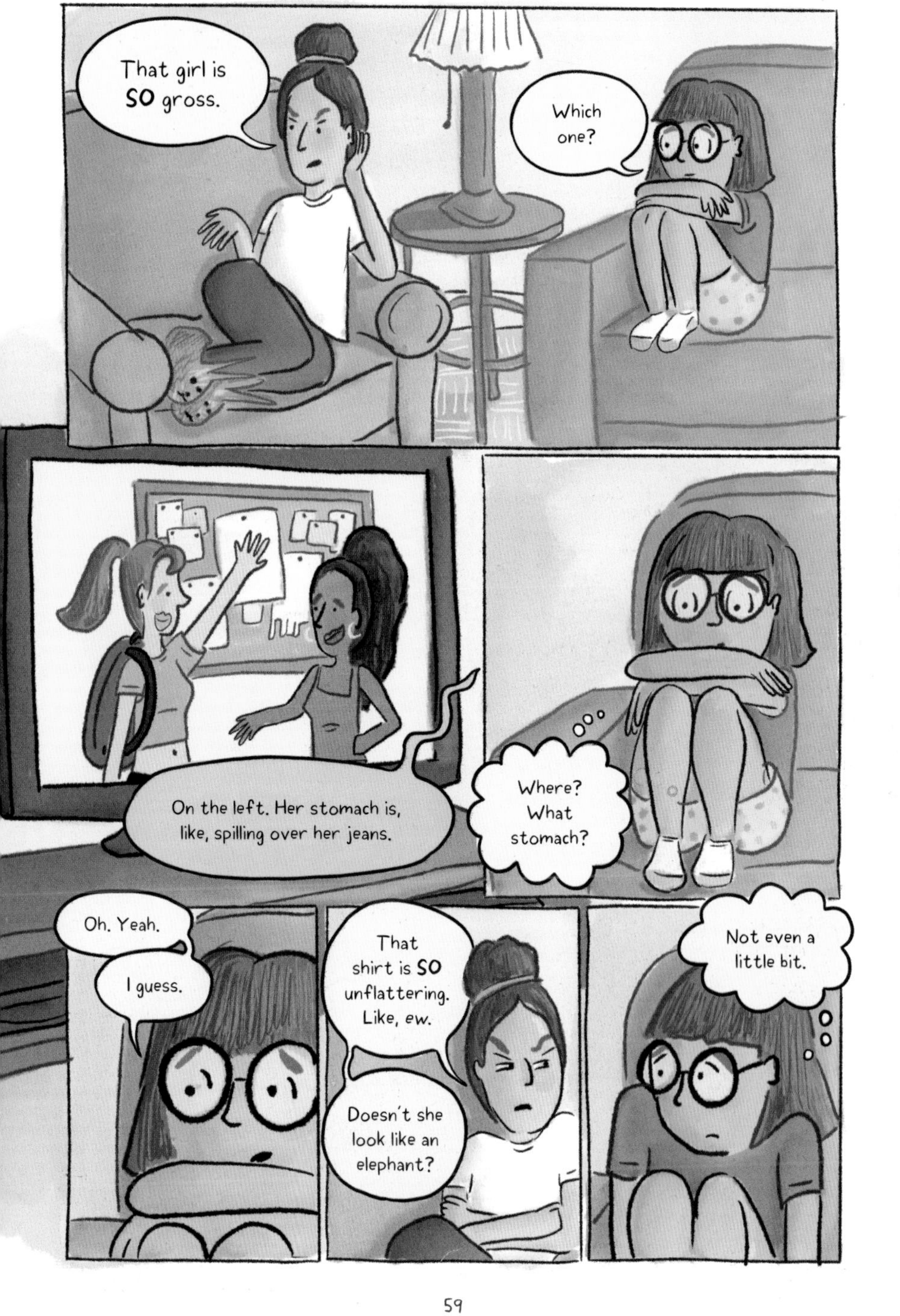
That girl is SO gross.
Which one?
On the left. Her stomach is, like, spilling over her jeans.
Where? What stomach?
Oh. Yeah.
I guess.
That shirt is SO unflattering. Like, *ew.*
Doesn't she look like an elephant?
Not even a little bit.

Once I started paying attention, I realized sixth-grade Olivia dressed a lot differently than fifth-grade Olivia. Old Olivia was confident, but New Olivia just seemed like she wanted to disappear.

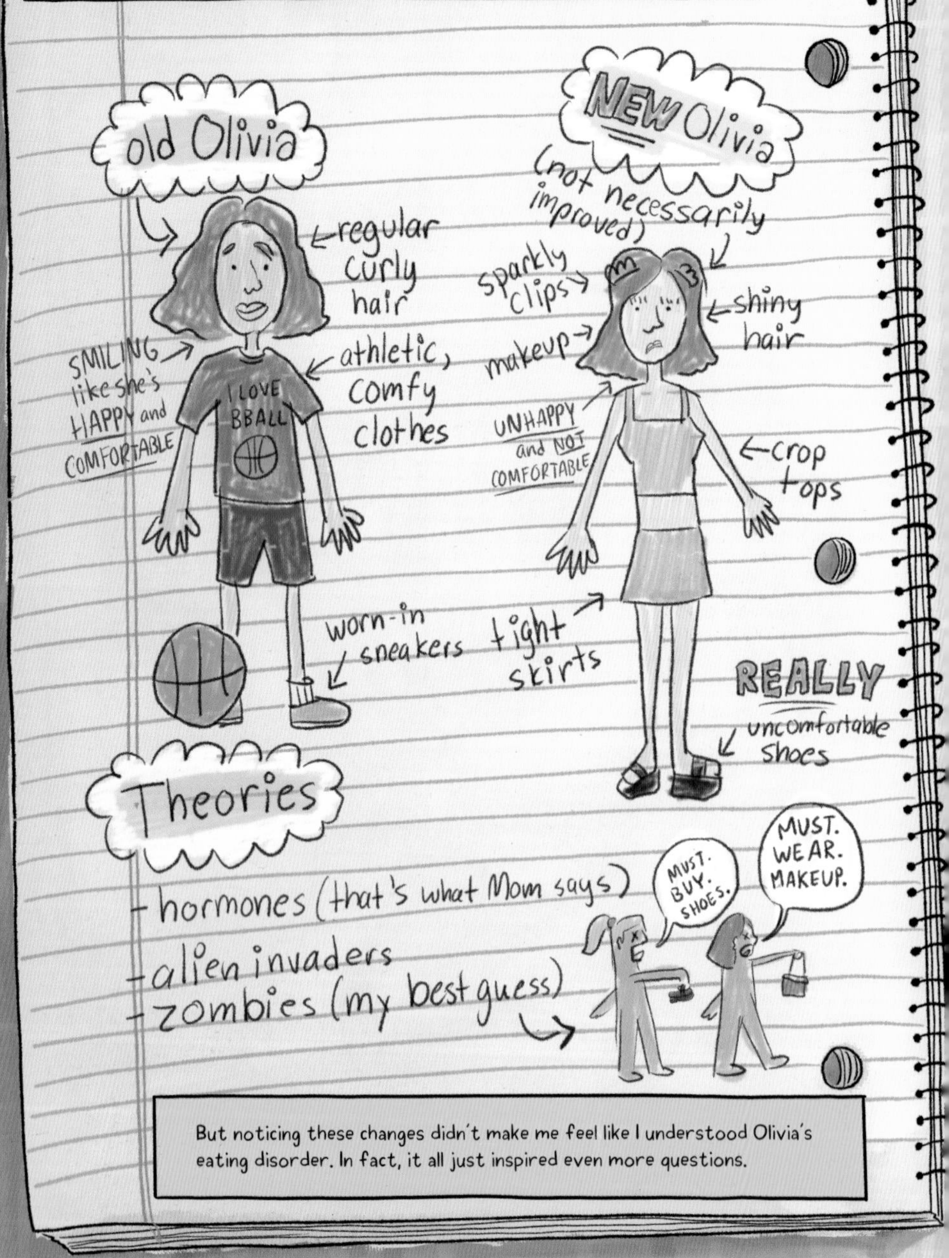

old Olivia
regular curly hair
SMILING like she's HAPPY and COMFORTABLE
athletic, comfy clothes
I LOVE BBALL
worn-in sneakers
NEW Olivia
(not necessarily improved)
sparkly clips
shiny hair
makeup
UNHAPPY and NOT COMFORTABLE
crop tops
tight skirts
REALLY uncomfortable shoes
Theories
- hormones (that's what Mom says)
- alien invaders
- zombies (my best guess)
MUST. BUY. SHOES.
MUST. WEAR. MAKEUP.

But noticing these changes didn't make me feel like I understood Olivia's eating disorder. In fact, it all just inspired even more questions.

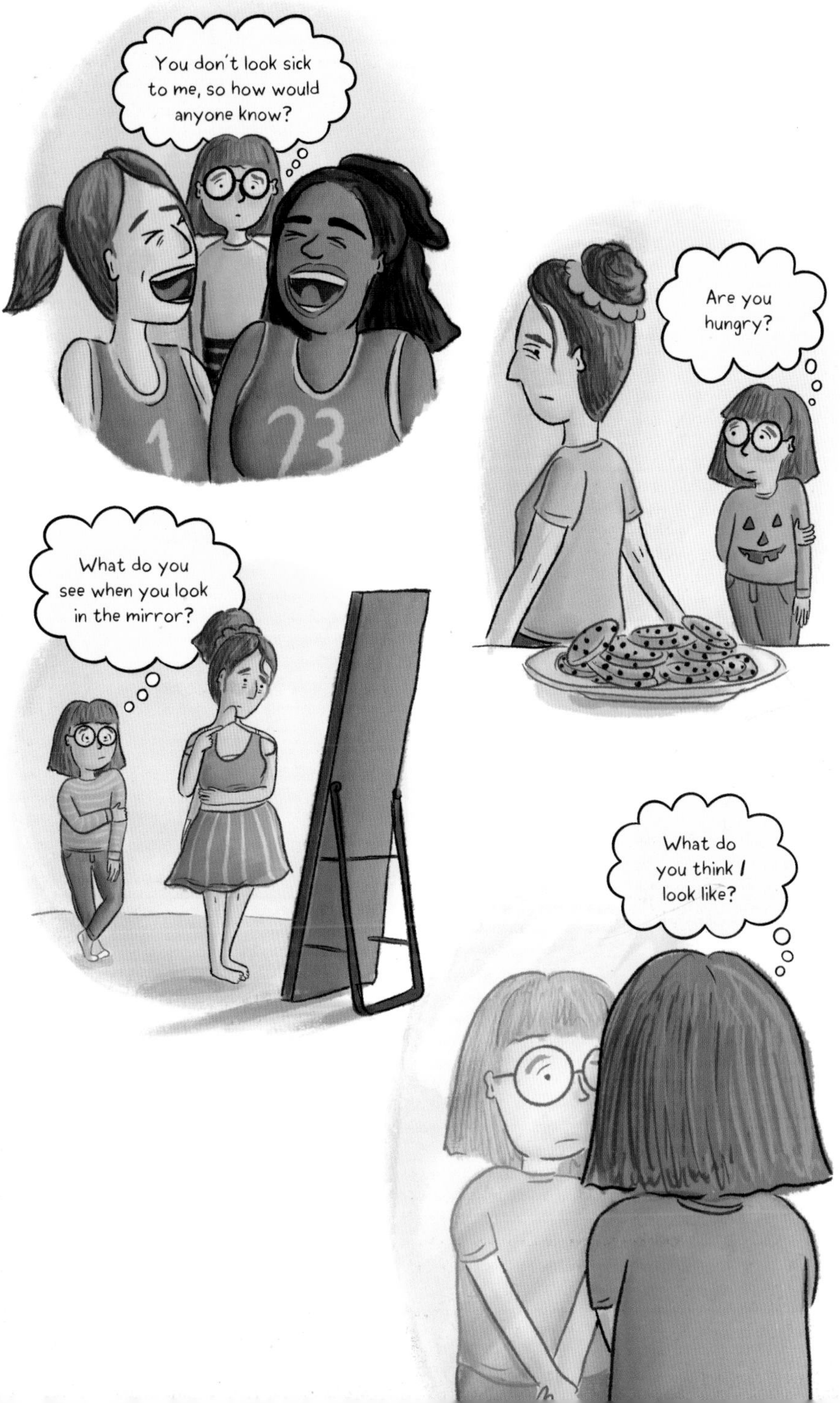
You don't look sick to me, so how would anyone know?
Are you hungry?
What do you see when you look in the mirror?
What do you think I look like?

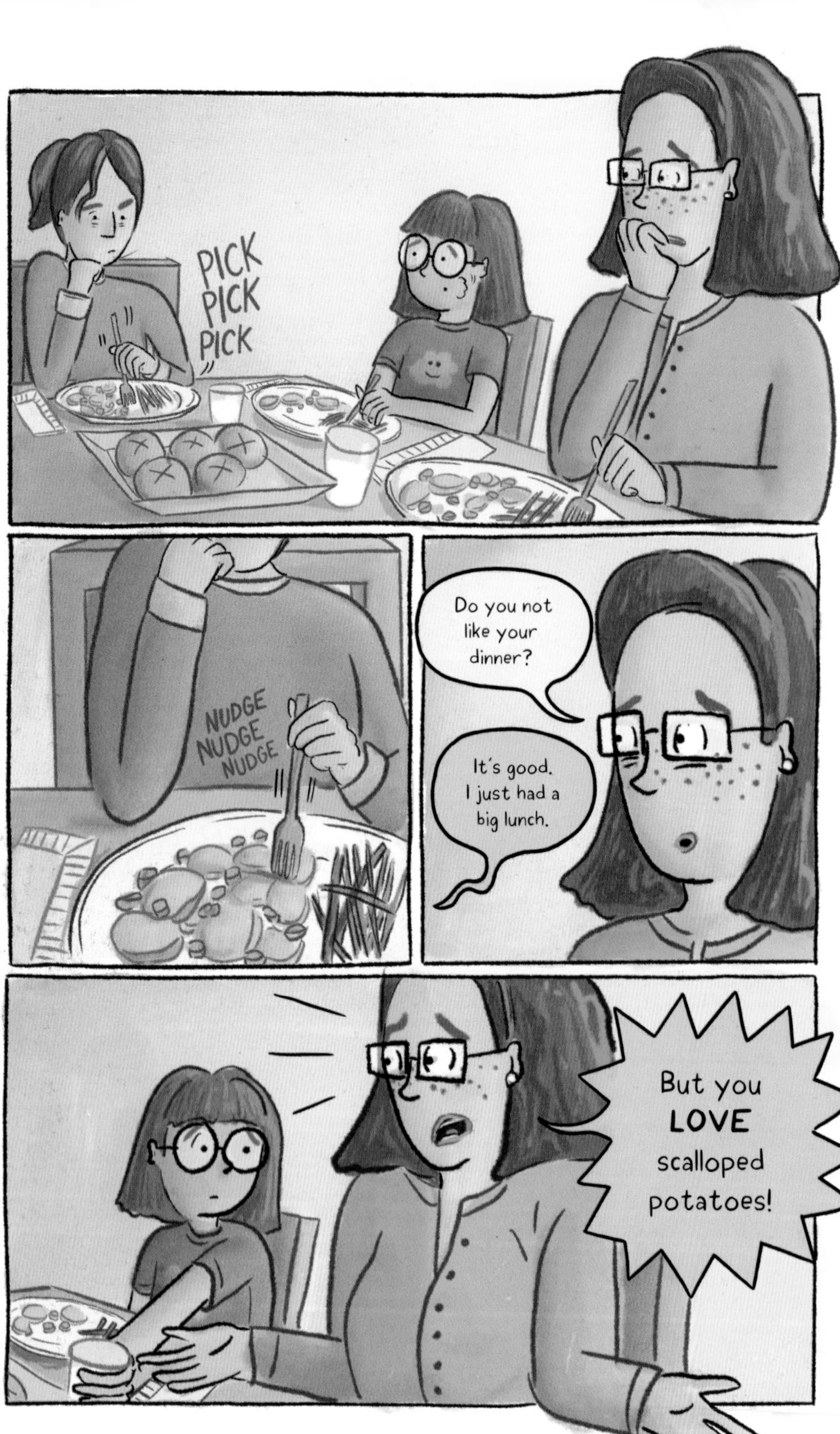
PICK
PICK
PICK
NUDGE
NUDGE
NUDGE
Do you not like your dinner?
It's good. I just had a big lunch.
But you **LOVE** scalloped potatoes!

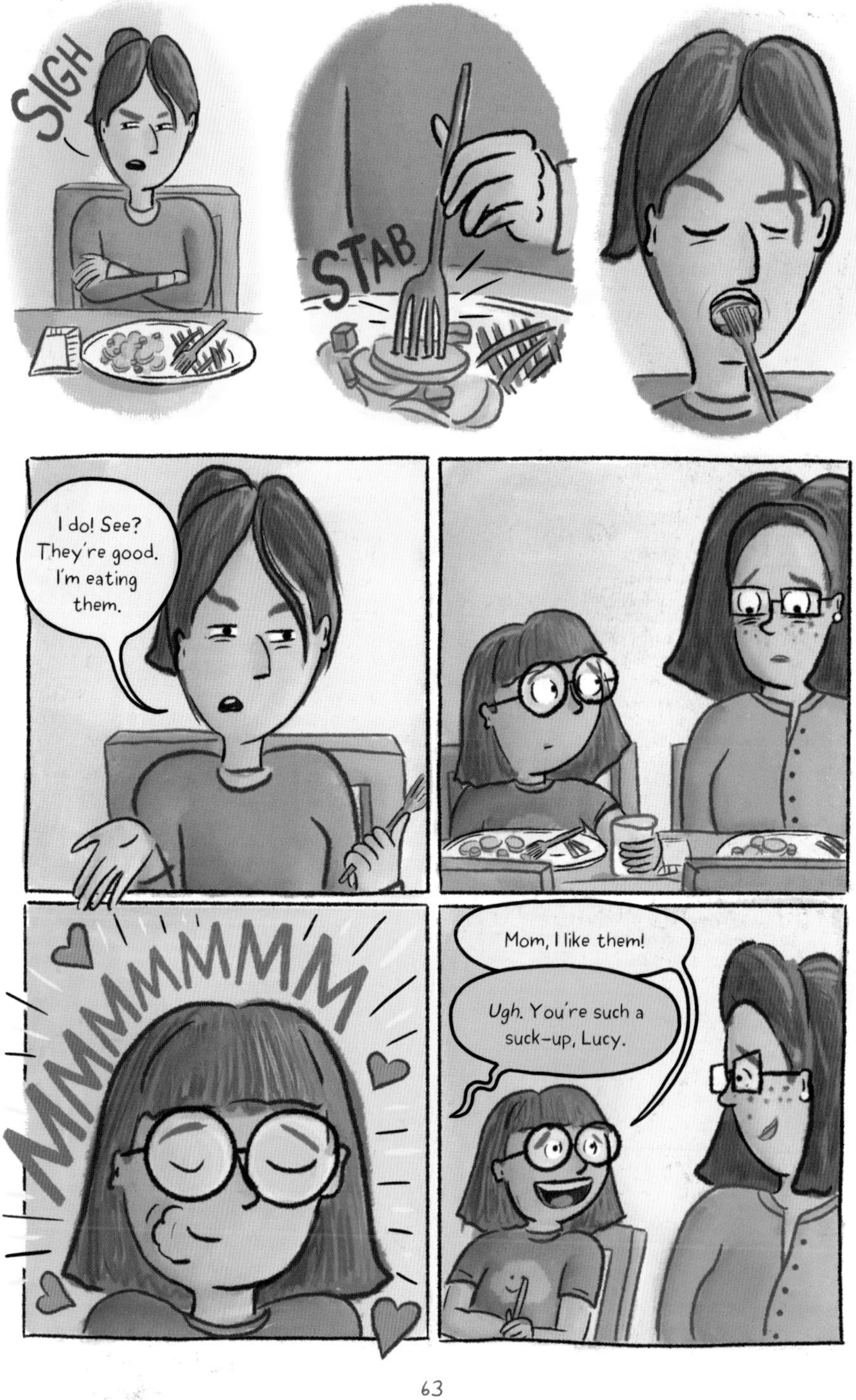
SIGH
STAB
I do! See? They're good. I'm eating them.
MMMMMMMM
Mom, I like them!
Ugh. You're such a suck-up, Lucy.

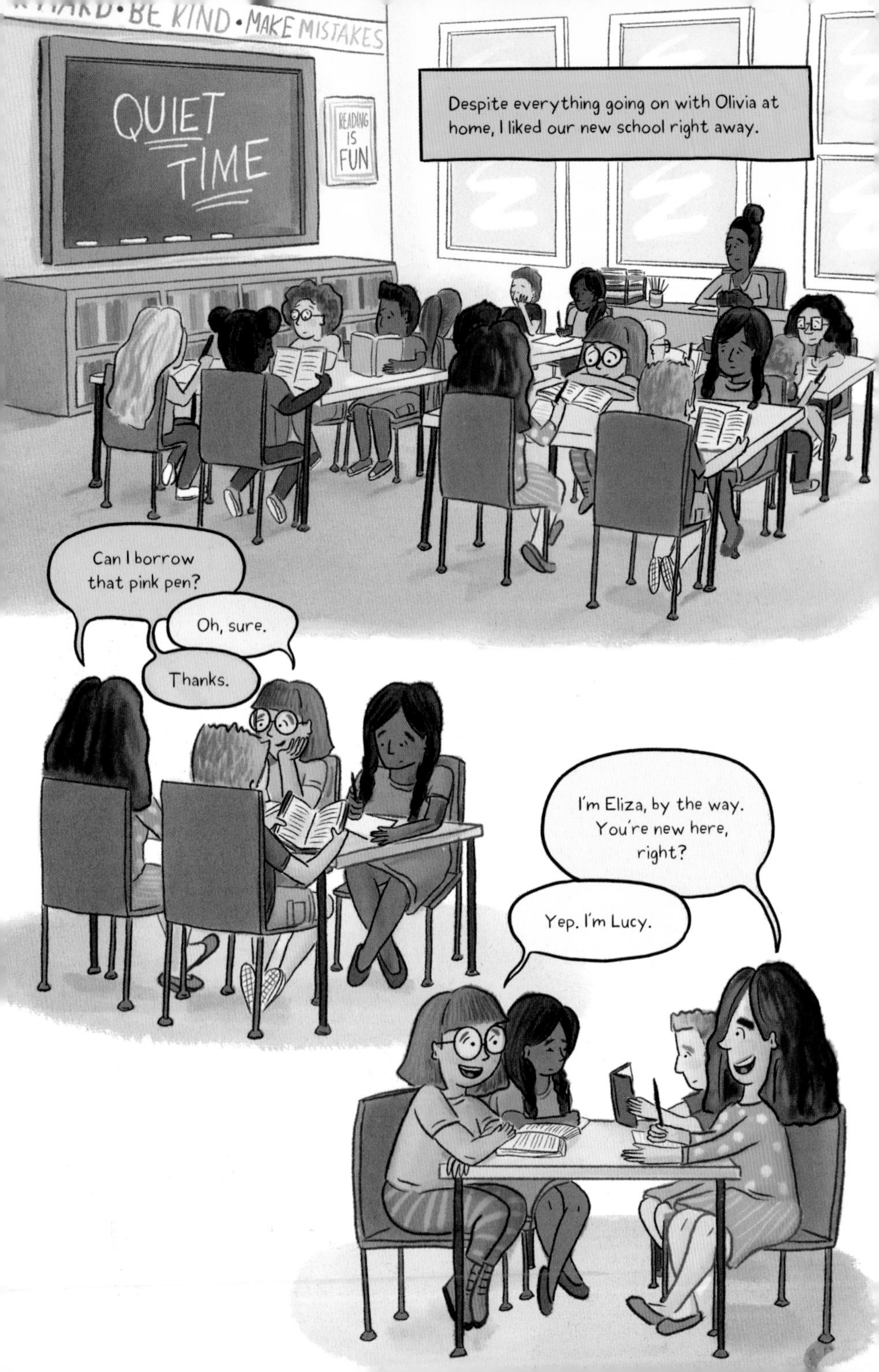
…ARD • BE KIND • MAKE MISTAKES
QUIET TIME
READING IS FUN
Despite everything going on with Olivia at home, I liked our new school right away.
Can I borrow that pink pen?
Oh, sure.
Thanks.
I'm Eliza, by the way. You're new here, right?
Yep. I'm Lucy.

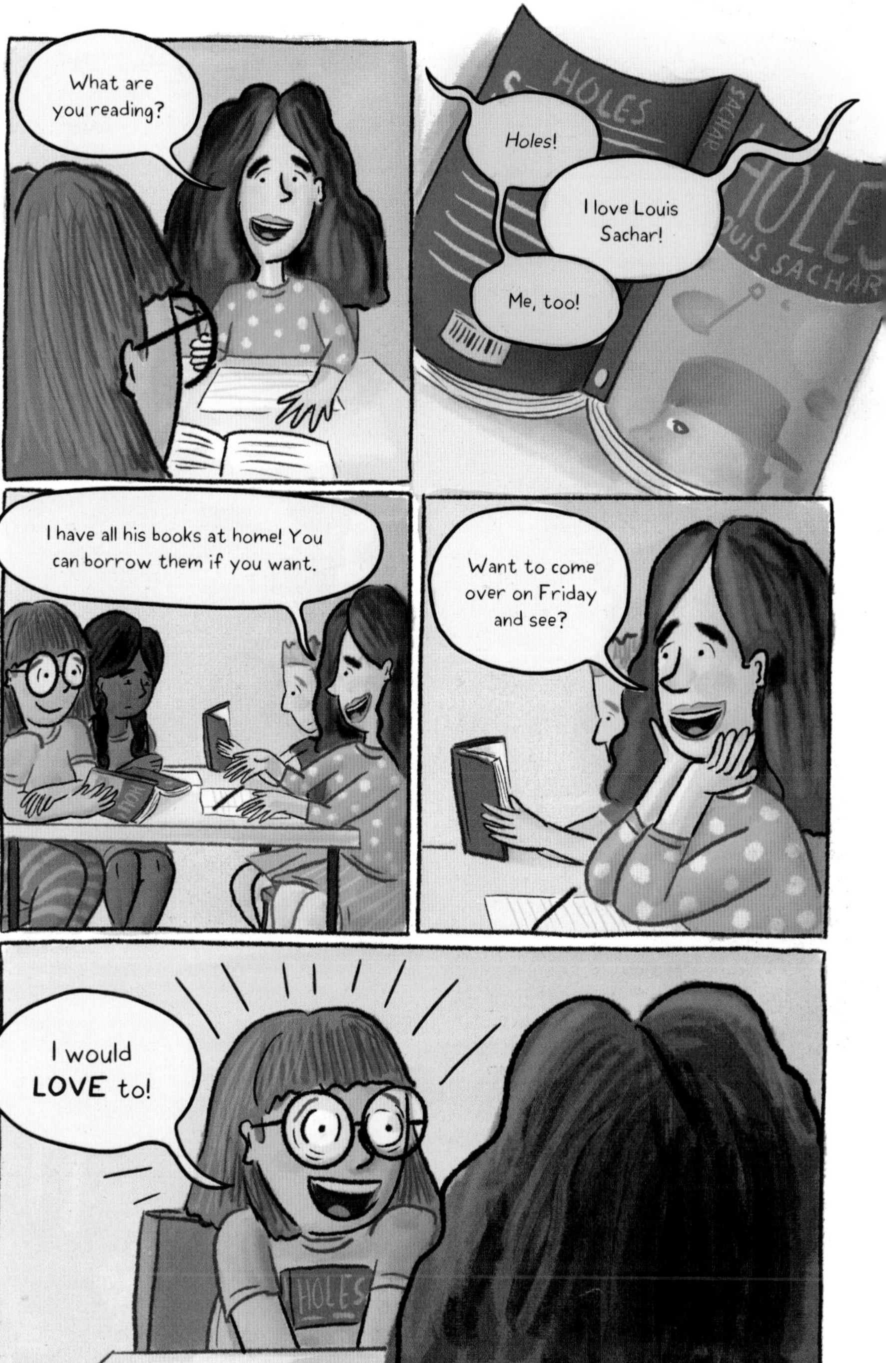
What are you reading?
HOLES
SACHAR
Holes!
I love Louis Sachar!
Me, too!
HOLES
LOUIS SACHAR
I have all his books at home! You can borrow them if you want.
Want to come over on Friday and see?
I would **LOVE** to!
HOLES

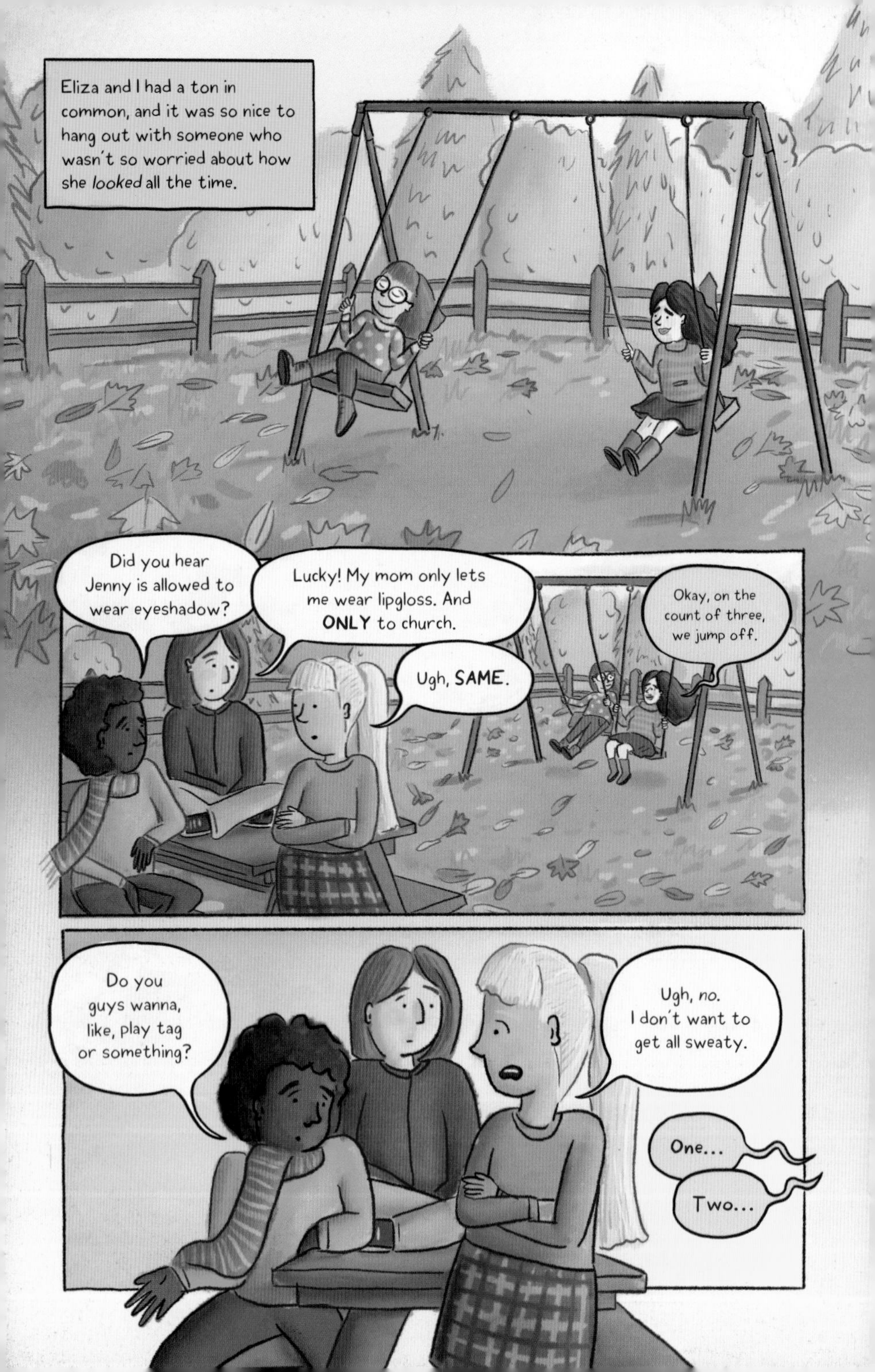
Eliza and I had a ton in common, and it was so nice to hang out with someone who wasn't so worried about how she *looked* all the time.
Did you hear Jenny is allowed to wear eyeshadow?
Lucky! My mom only lets me wear lipgloss. And **ONLY** to church.
Ugh, **SAME**.
Okay, on the count of three, we jump off.
Do you guys wanna, like, play tag or something?
Ugh, *no*. I don't want to get all sweaty.
One...
Two...

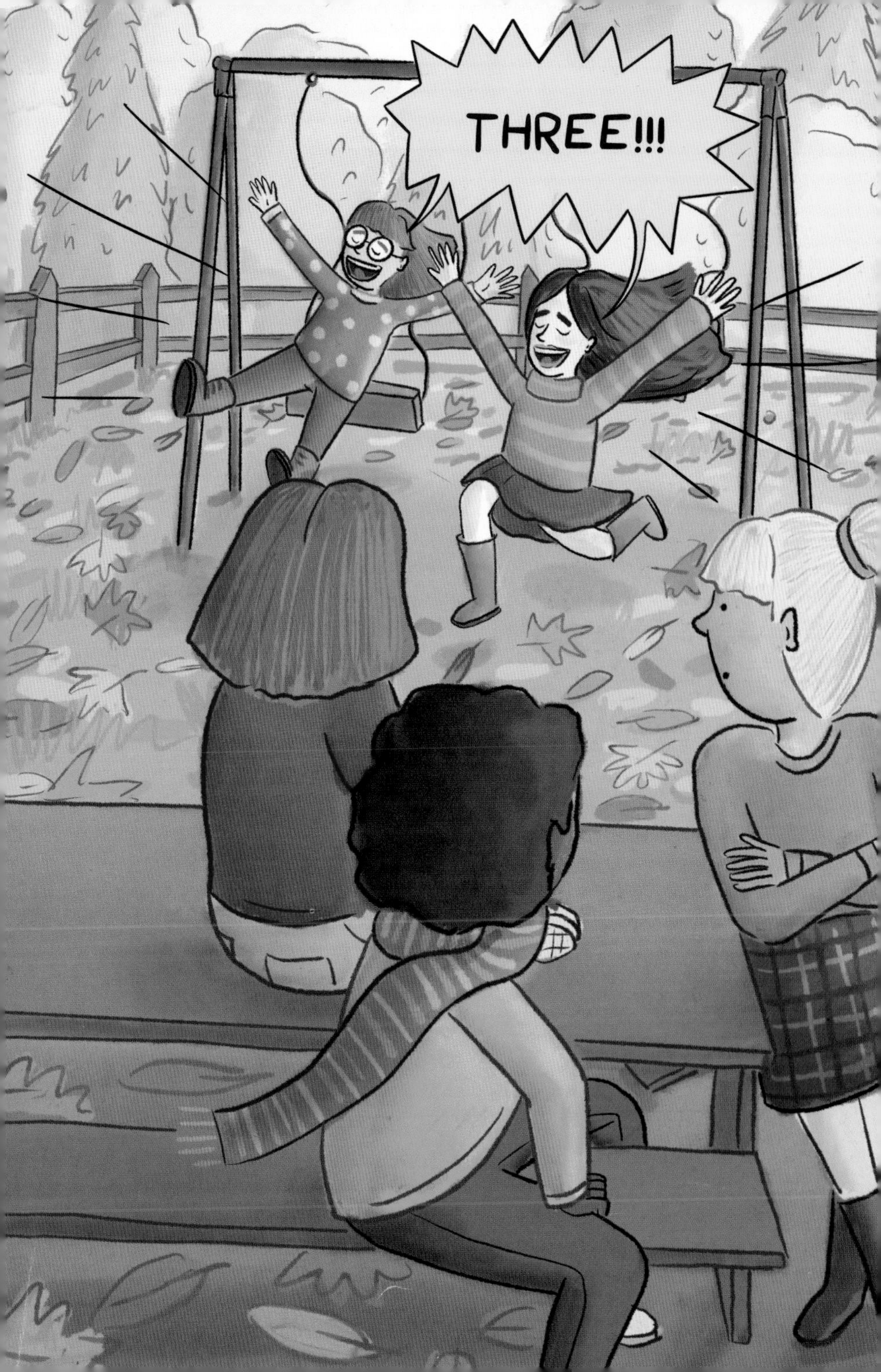
THREE!!!

I missed Livy, though. She made a few new friends in her class, and they spent most of their time walking around the mall and buying silly stuff like *lipgloss*.

Olivia & her new friends conquering lip gloss mountain

SECRET SISTER CODE TRANSLATION:

Test, test, this is a test! Can you read this sentence?

I thought about teaching Eliza our secret sister code.

But if Eliza knew the code, then it wouldn't be a secret for sisters anymore.

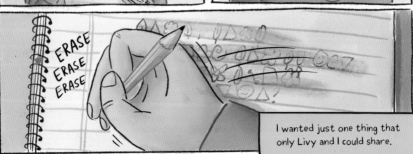

ERASE ERASE ERASE

I wanted just one thing that only Livy and I could share.

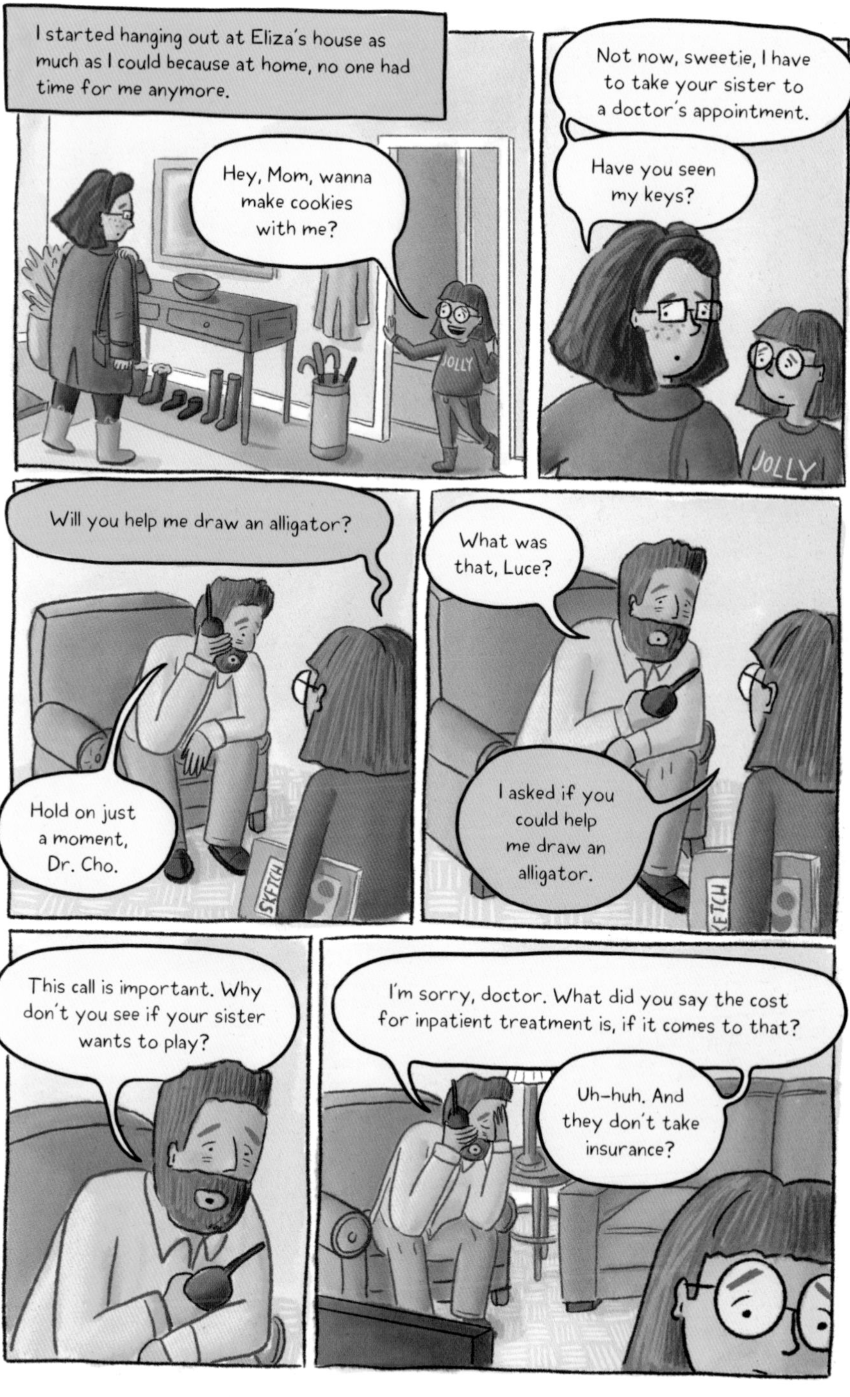
I started hanging out at Eliza's house as much as I could because at home, no one had time for me anymore.
Hey, Mom, wanna make cookies with me?
JOLLY
Not now, sweetie, I have to take your sister to a doctor's appointment.
Have you seen my keys?
JOLLY
Will you help me draw an alligator?
Hold on just a moment, Dr. Cho.
SKETCH
What was that, Luce?
I asked if you could help me draw an alligator.
SKETCH
This call is important. Why don't you see if your sister wants to play?
I'm sorry, doctor. What did you say the cost for inpatient treatment is, if it comes to that?
Uh-huh. And they don't take insurance?

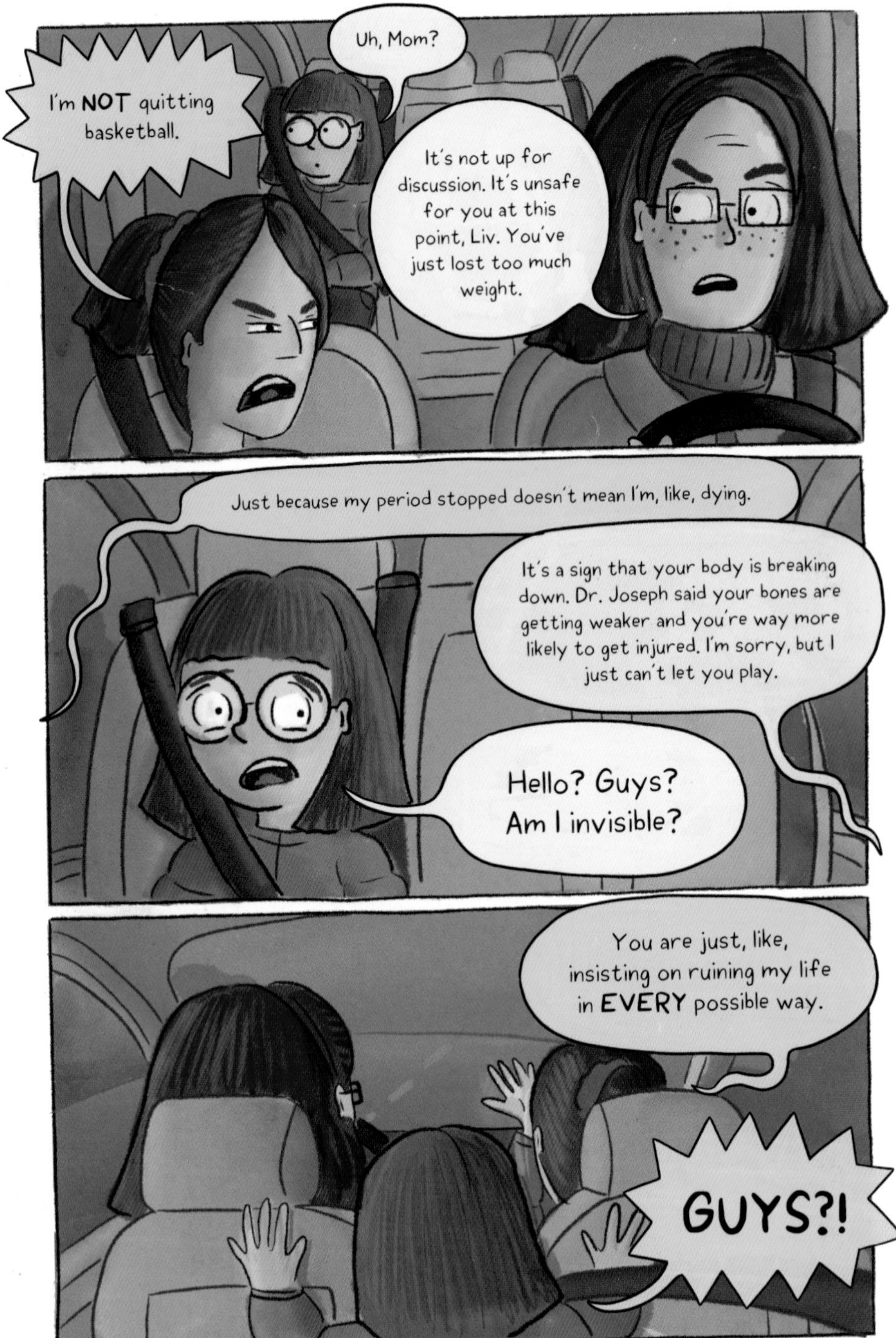
I'm NOT quitting basketball.
Uh, Mom?
It's not up for discussion. It's unsafe for you at this point, Liv. You've just lost too much weight.
Just because my period stopped doesn't mean I'm, like, dying.
It's a sign that your body is breaking down. Dr. Joseph said your bones are getting weaker and you're way more likely to get injured. I'm sorry, but I just can't let you play.
Hello? Guys? Am I invisible?
You are just, like, insisting on ruining my life in EVERY possible way.
GUYS?!

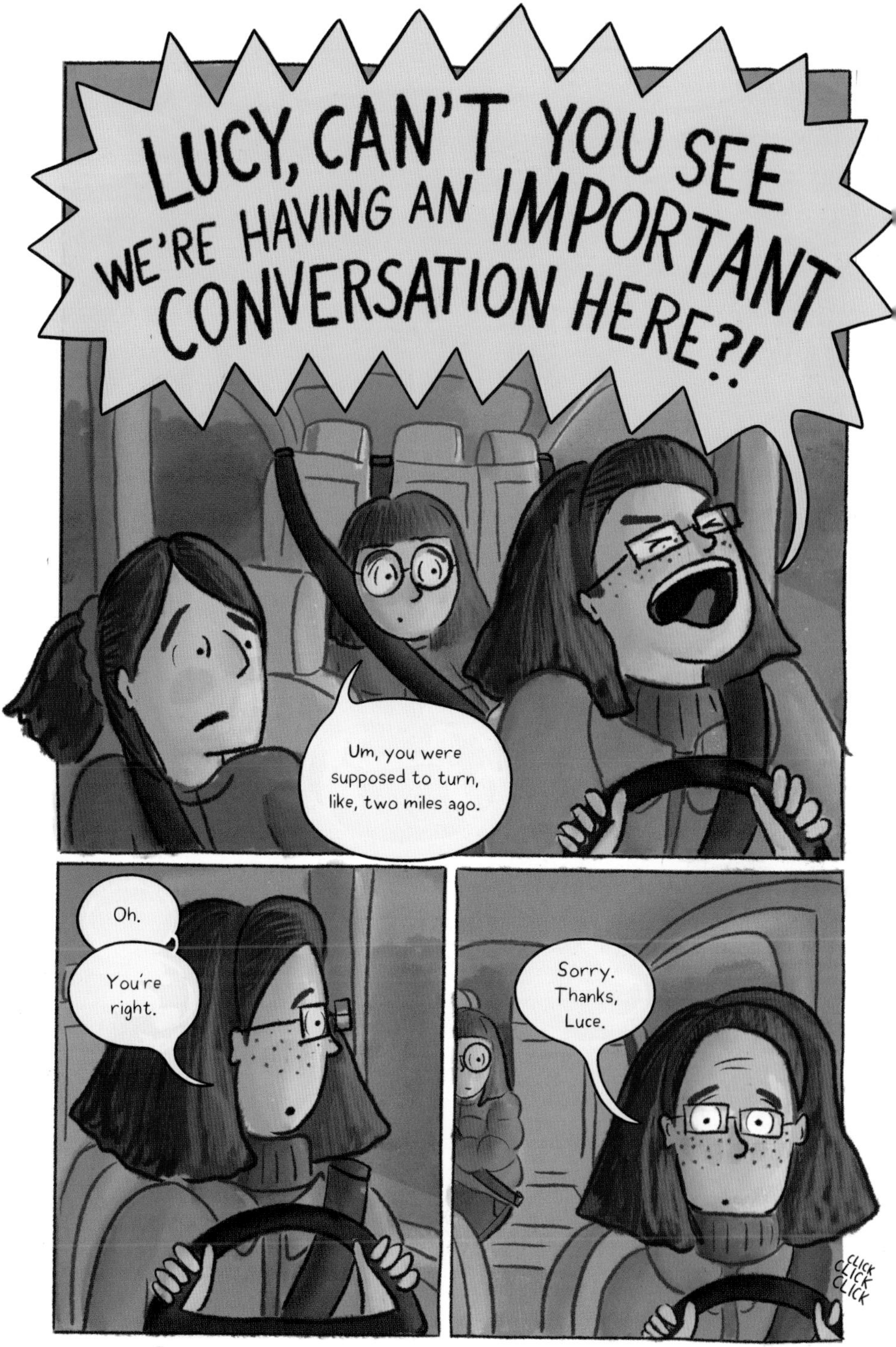
LUCY, CAN'T YOU SEE WE'RE HAVING AN IMPORTANT CONVERSATION HERE?!
Um, you were supposed to turn, like, two miles ago.
Oh.
You're right.
Sorry. Thanks, Luce.
CLICK CLICK CLICK

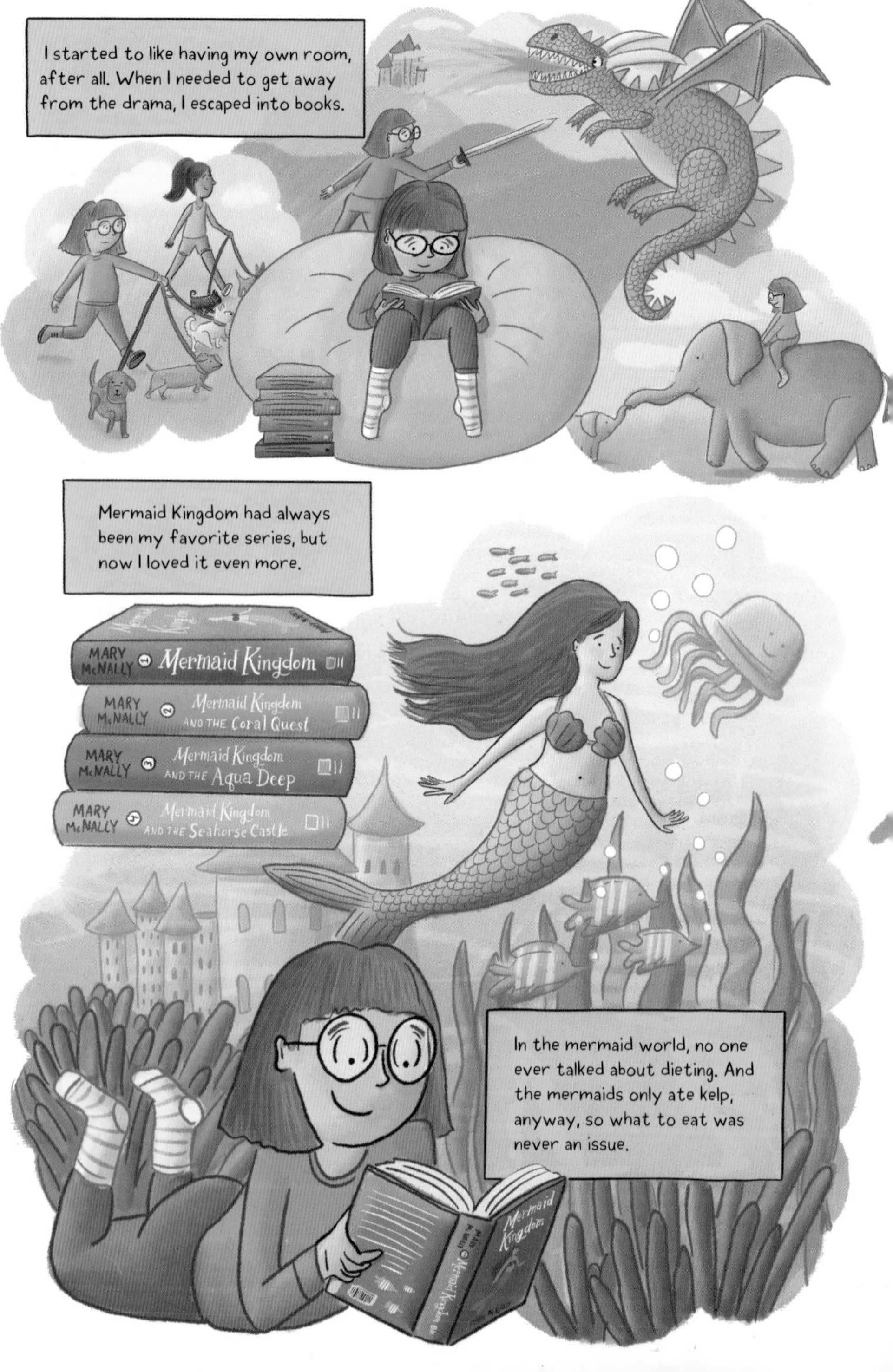
I started to like having my own room, after all. When I needed to get away from the drama, I escaped into books.
Mermaid Kingdom had always been my favorite series, but now I loved it even more.
MARY McNALLY 1 Mermaid Kingdom
MARY McNALLY 2 Mermaid Kingdom AND THE Coral Quest
MARY McNALLY 3 Mermaid Kingdom AND THE Aqua Deep
MARY McNALLY 4 Mermaid Kingdom AND THE Seahorse Castle
In the mermaid world, no one ever talked about dieting. And the mermaids only ate kelp, anyway, so what to eat was never an issue.
Mermaid Kingdom

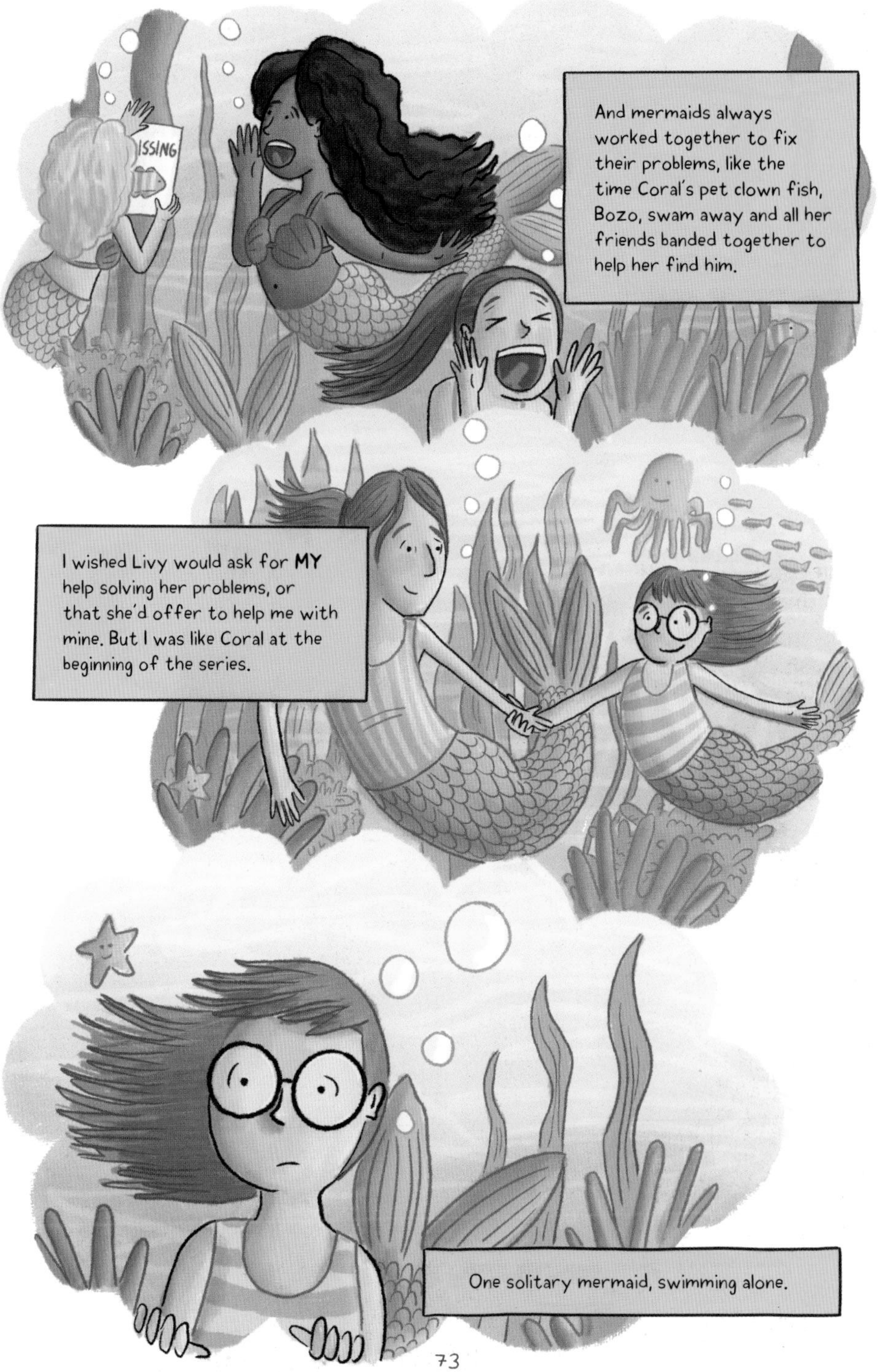
And mermaids always worked together to fix their problems, like the time Coral's pet clown fish, Bozo, swam away and all her friends banded together to help her find him.
I wished Livy would ask for **MY** help solving her problems, or that she'd offer to help me with mine. But I was like Coral at the beginning of the series.
One solitary mermaid, swimming alone.

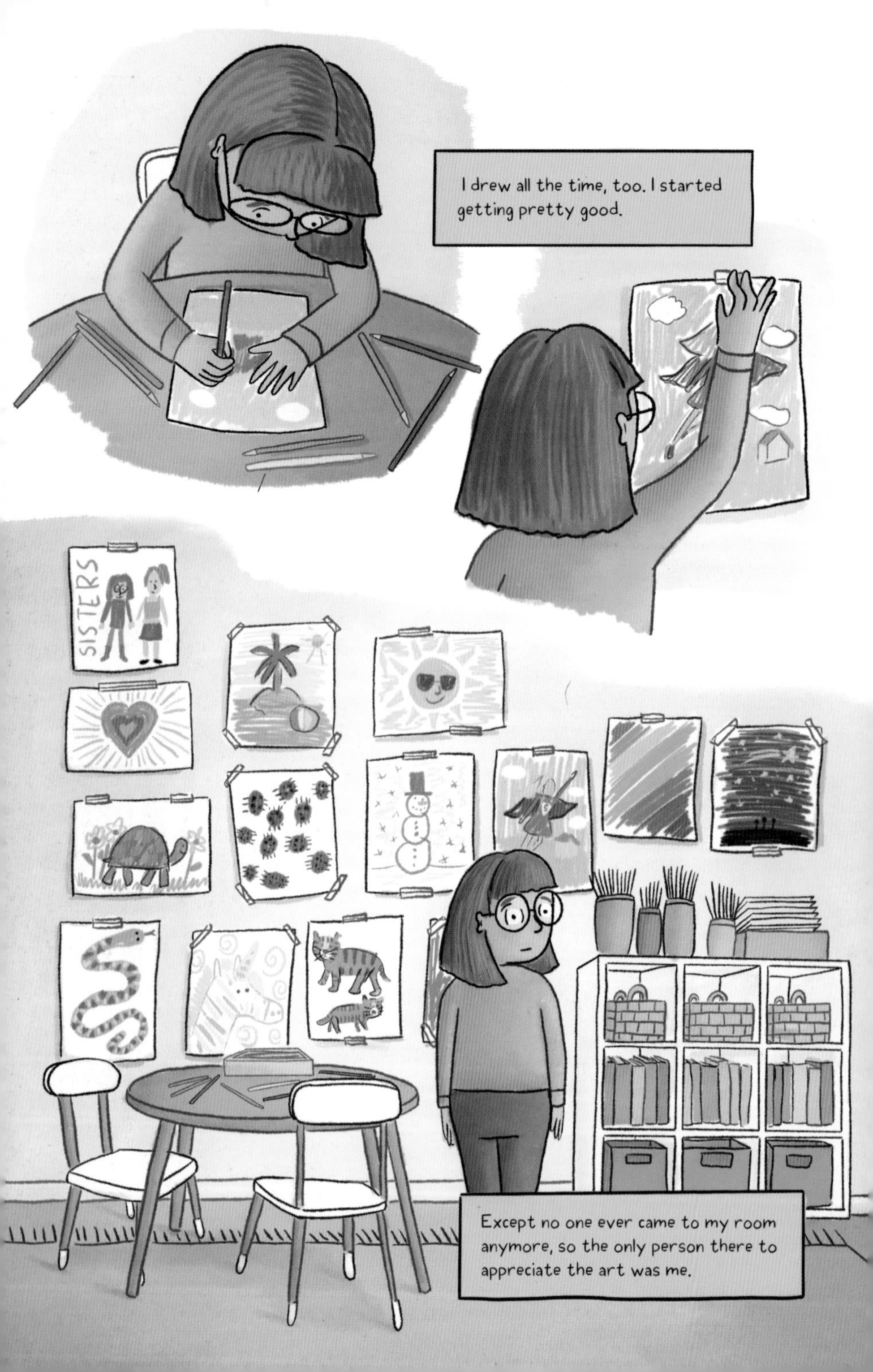
I drew all the time, too. I started getting pretty good.
SISTERS
Except no one ever came to my room anymore, so the only person there to appreciate the art was me.

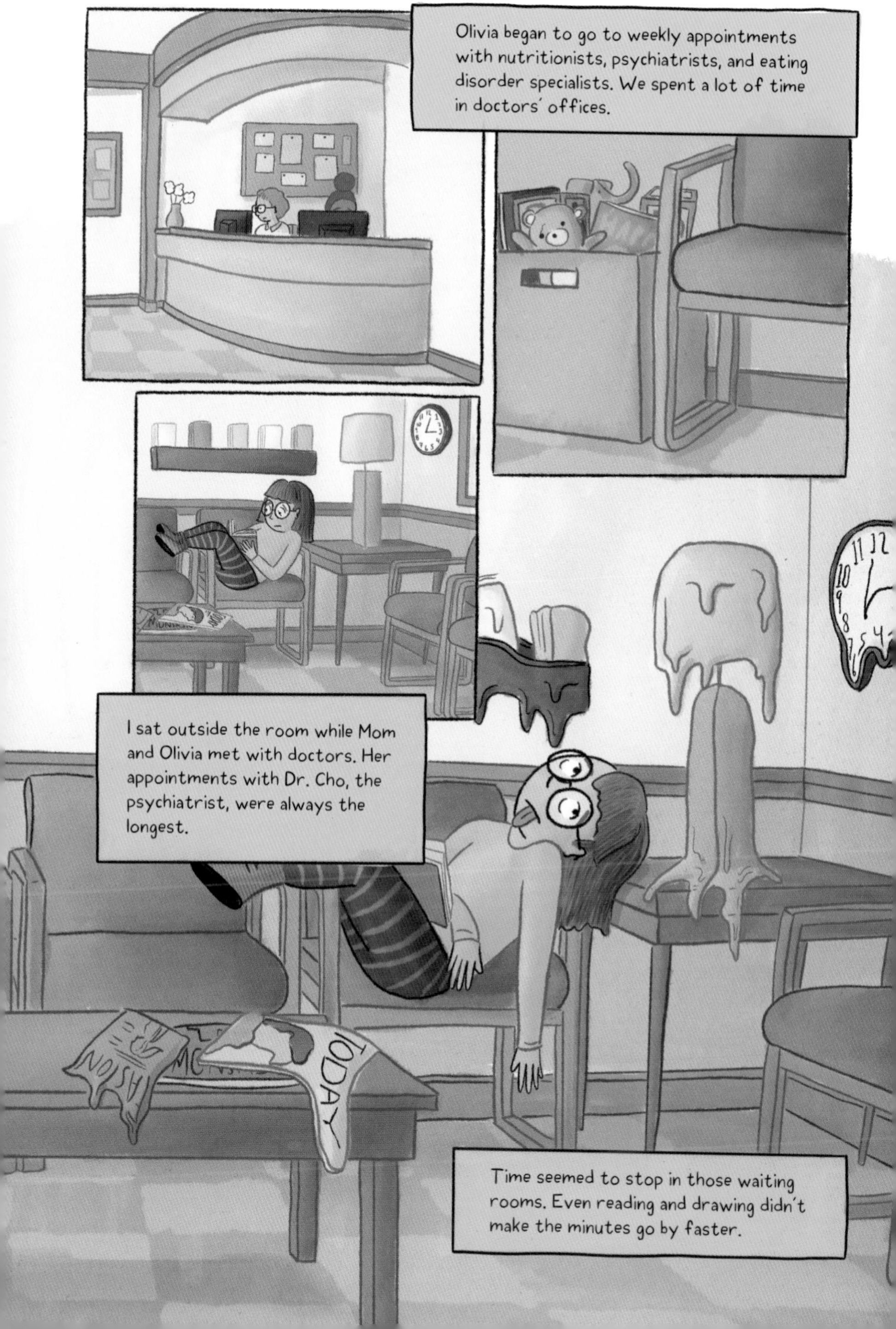
Olivia began to go to weekly appointments with nutritionists, psychiatrists, and eating disorder specialists. We spent a lot of time in doctors' offices.
I sat outside the room while Mom and Olivia met with doctors. Her appointments with Dr. Cho, the psychiatrist, were always the longest.
TODAY
Time seemed to stop in those waiting rooms. Even reading and drawing didn't make the minutes go by faster.

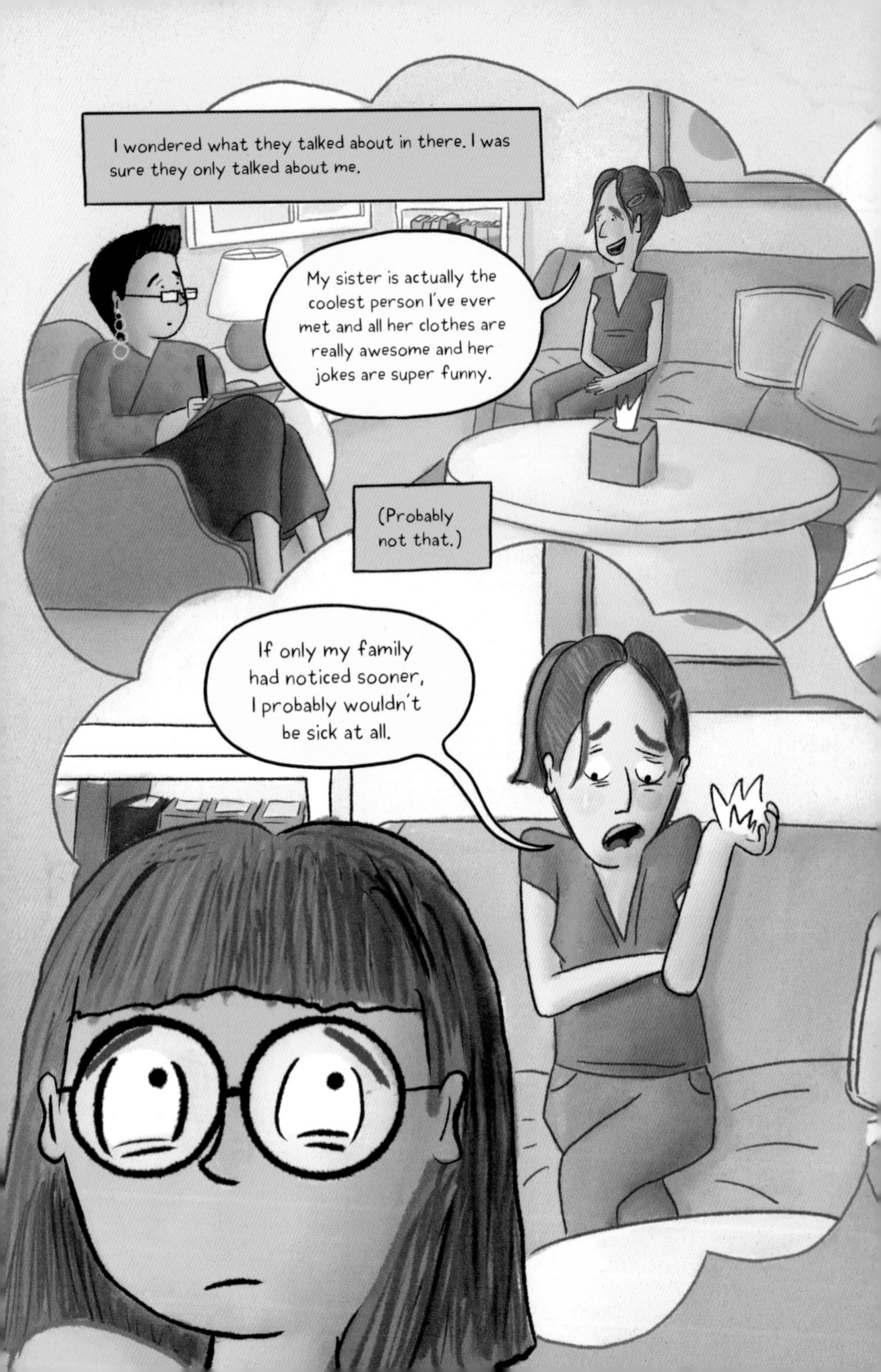
I wondered what they talked about in there. I was sure they only talked about me.
My sister is actually the coolest person I've ever met and all her clothes are really awesome and her jokes are super funny.
(Probably not that.)
If only my family had noticed sooner, I probably wouldn't be sick at all.

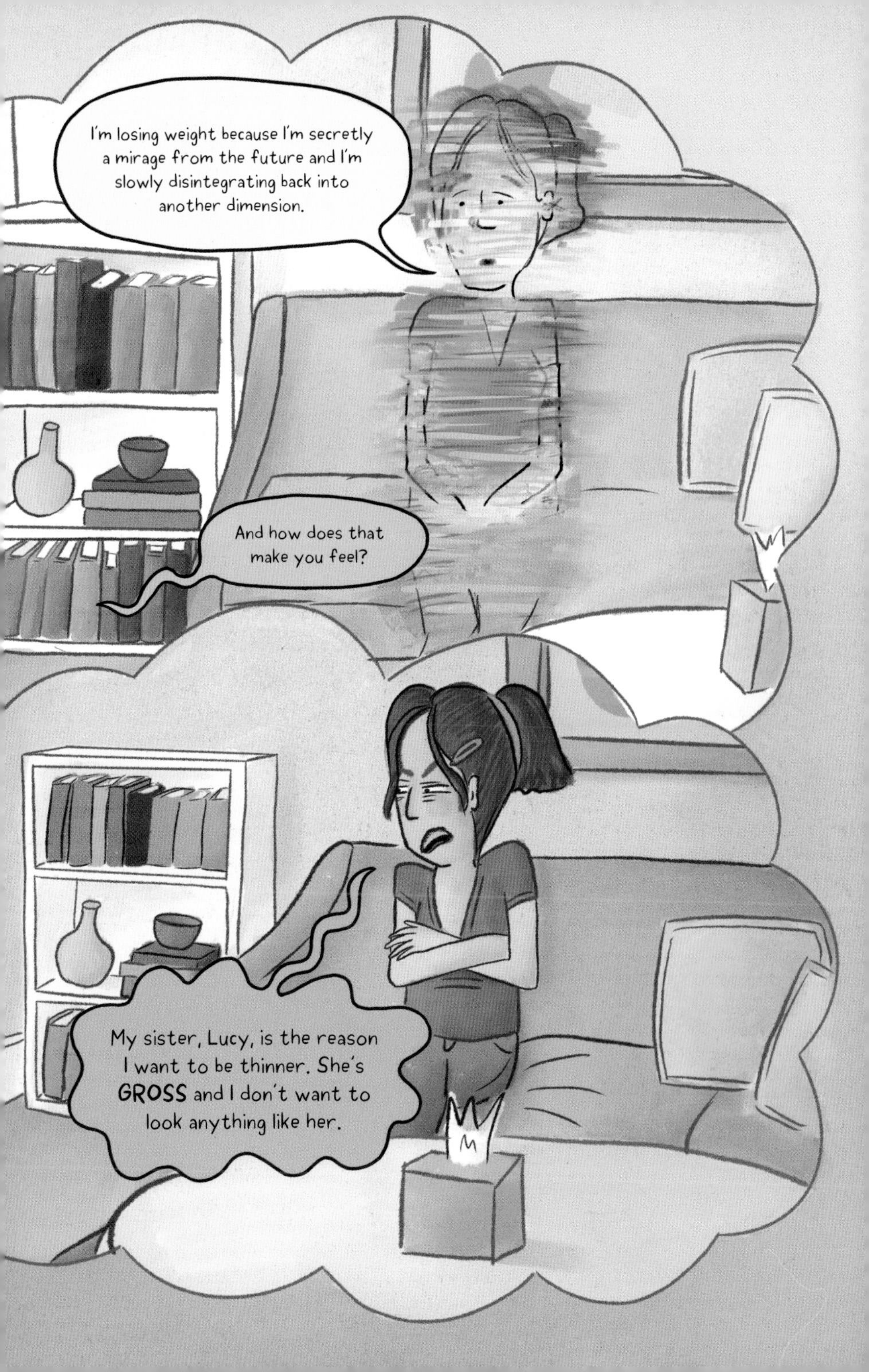
I'm losing weight because I'm secretly a mirage from the future and I'm slowly disintegrating back into another dimension.
And how does that make you feel?
My sister, Lucy, is the reason I want to be thinner. She's **GROSS** and I don't want to look anything like her.

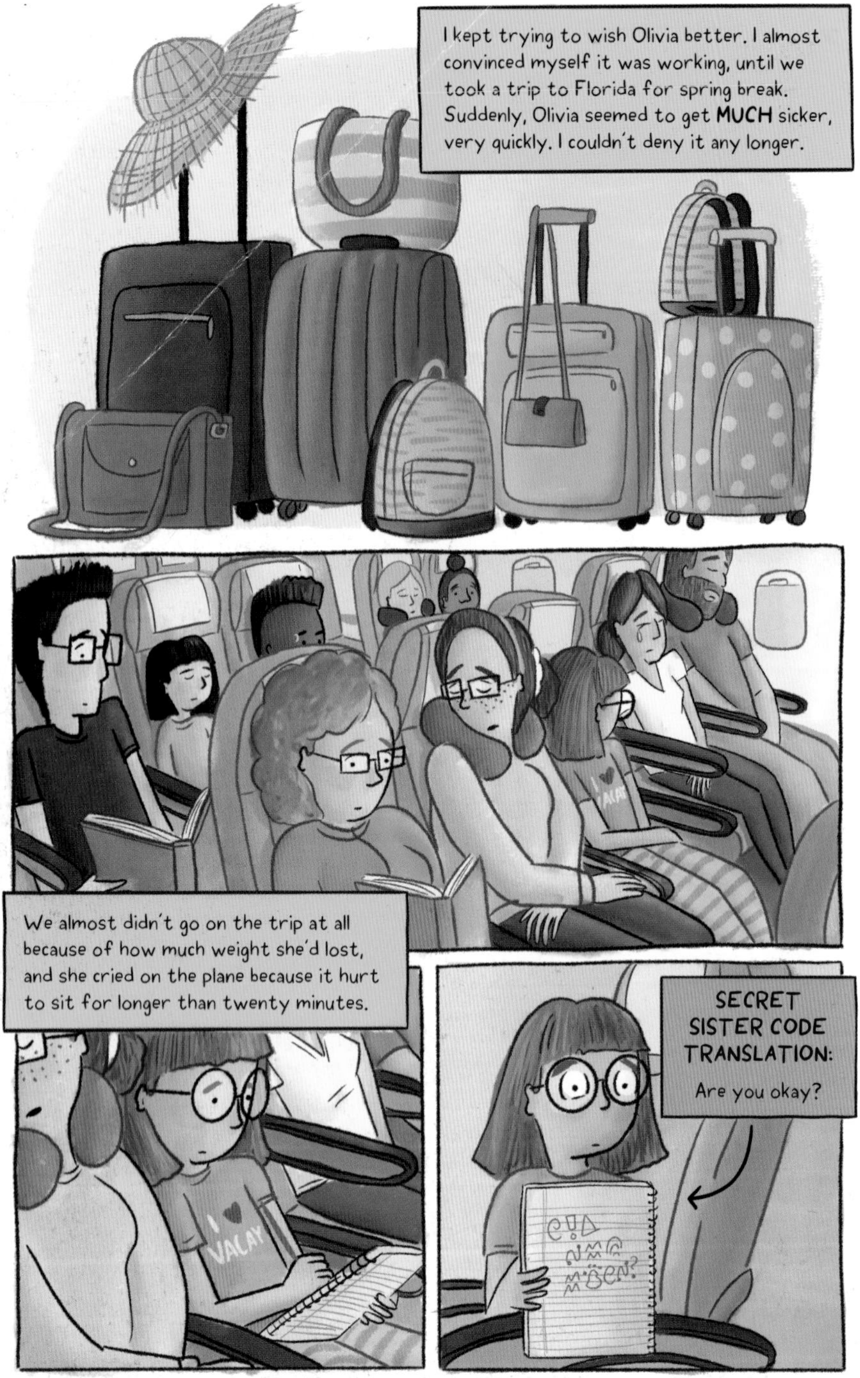
I kept trying to wish Olivia better. I almost convinced myself it was working, until we took a trip to Florida for spring break. Suddenly, Olivia seemed to get **MUCH** sicker, very quickly. I couldn't deny it any longer.
I ♥ VACAY
We almost didn't go on the trip at all because of how much weight she'd lost, and she cried on the plane because it hurt to sit for longer than twenty minutes.
I ♥ VACAY
SECRET SISTER CODE TRANSLATION:
Are you okay?

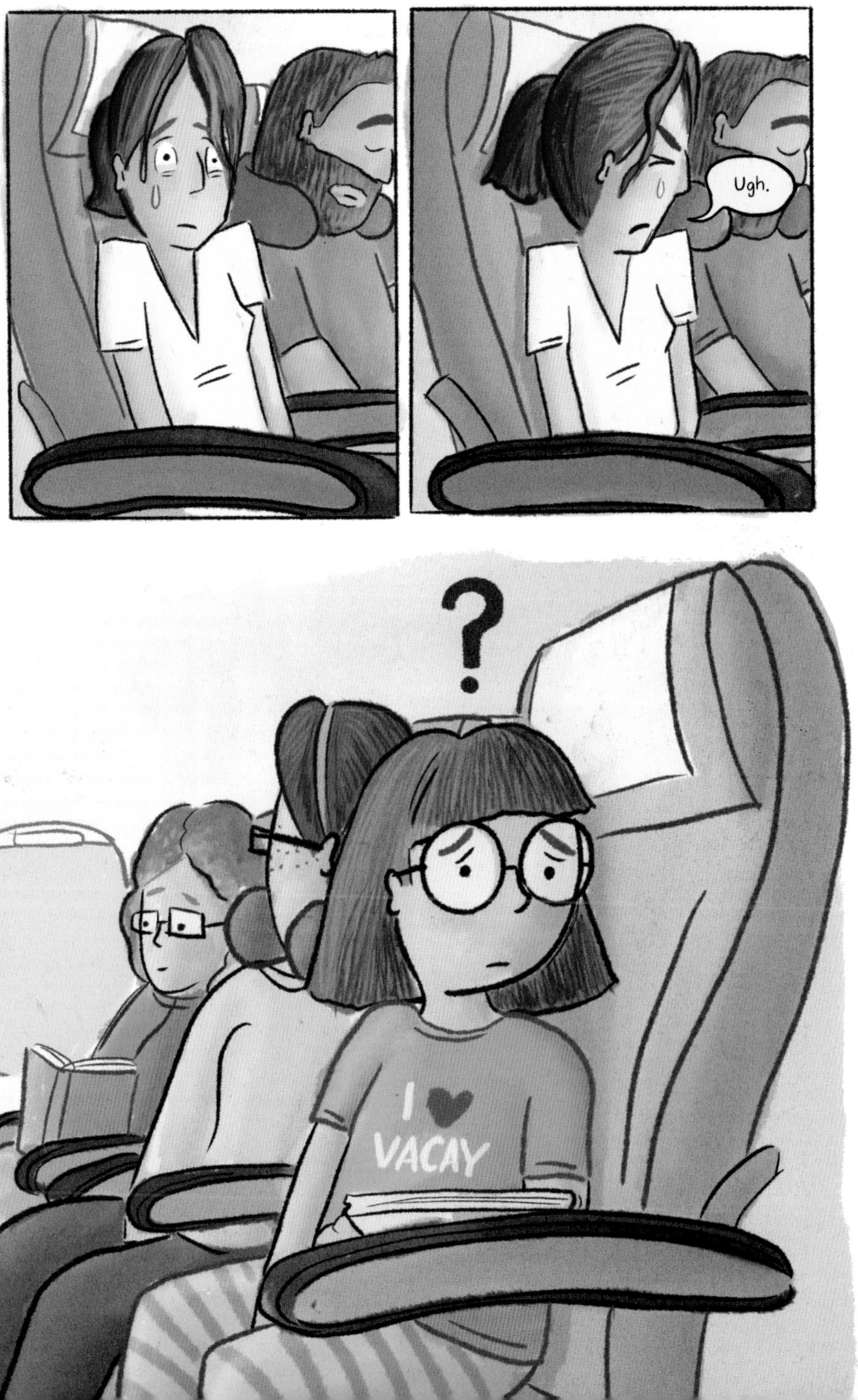
Ugh.
?
I ♥ VACAY

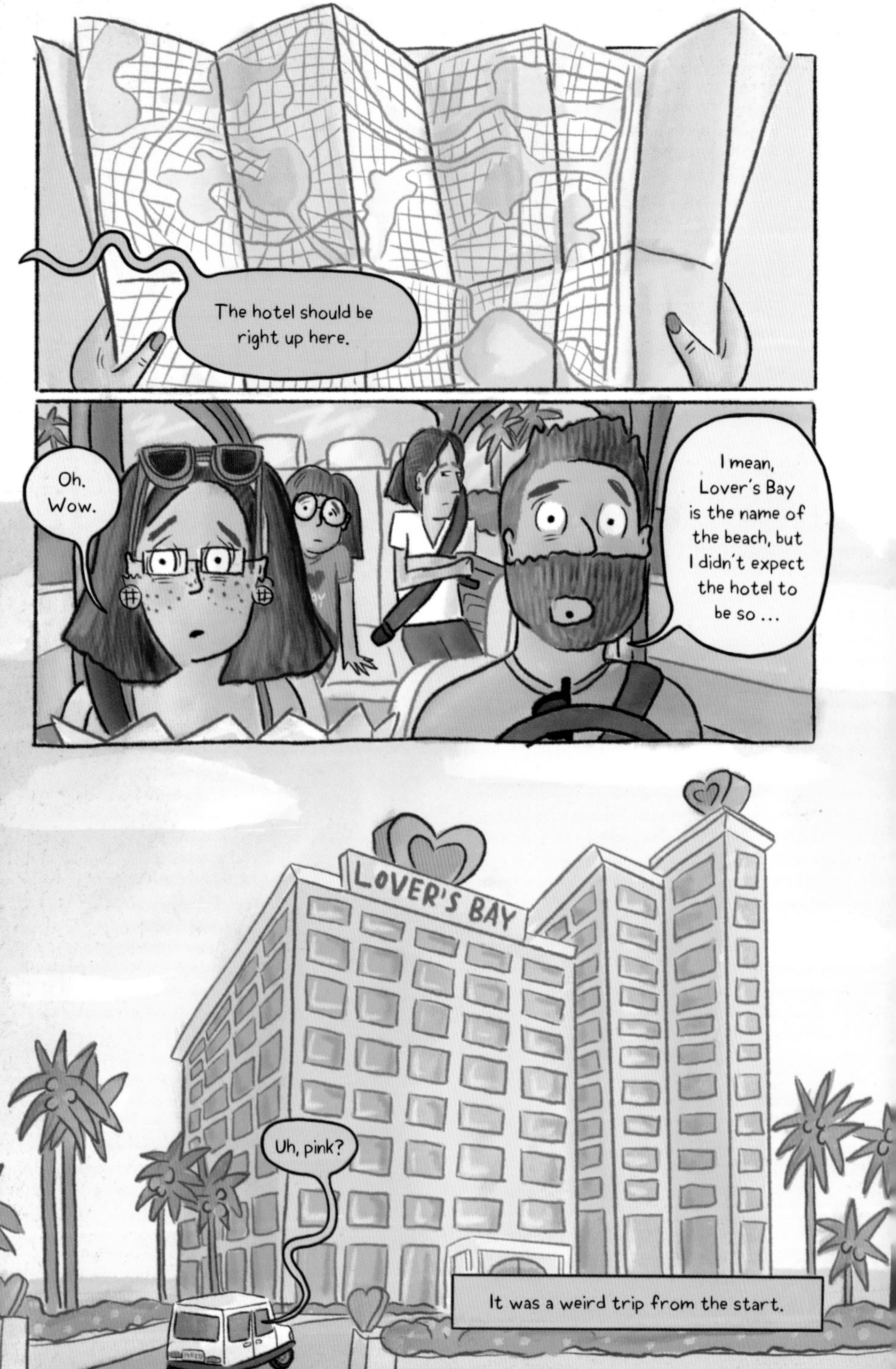
The hotel should be right up here.
Oh. Wow.
I mean, Lover's Bay is the name of the beach, but I didn't expect the hotel to be so . . .
LOVER'S BAY
Uh, pink?
It was a weird trip from the start.

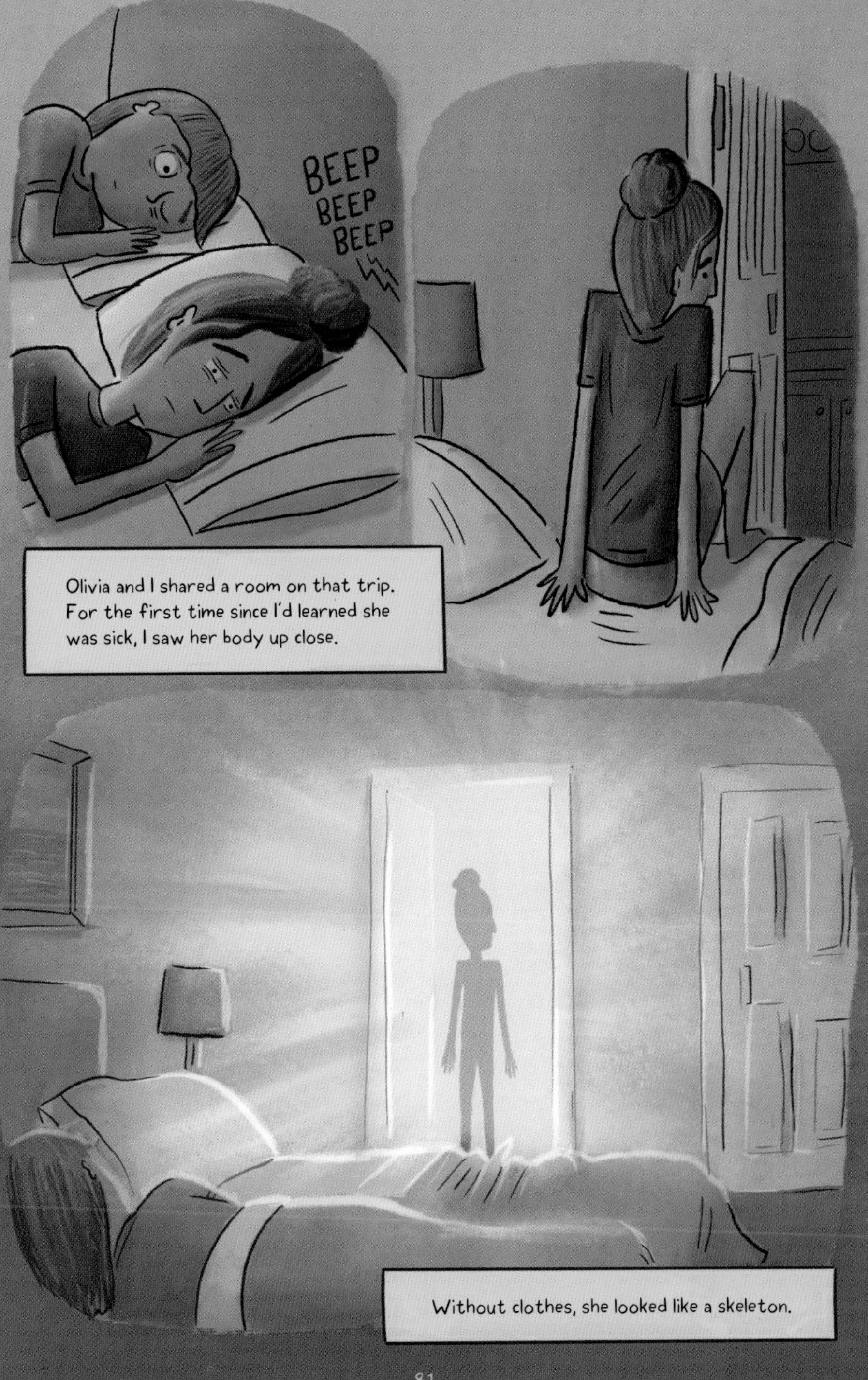

BEEP
BEEP
BEEP
Olivia and I shared a room on that trip. For the first time since I'd learned she was sick, I saw her body up close.
Without clothes, she looked like a skeleton.

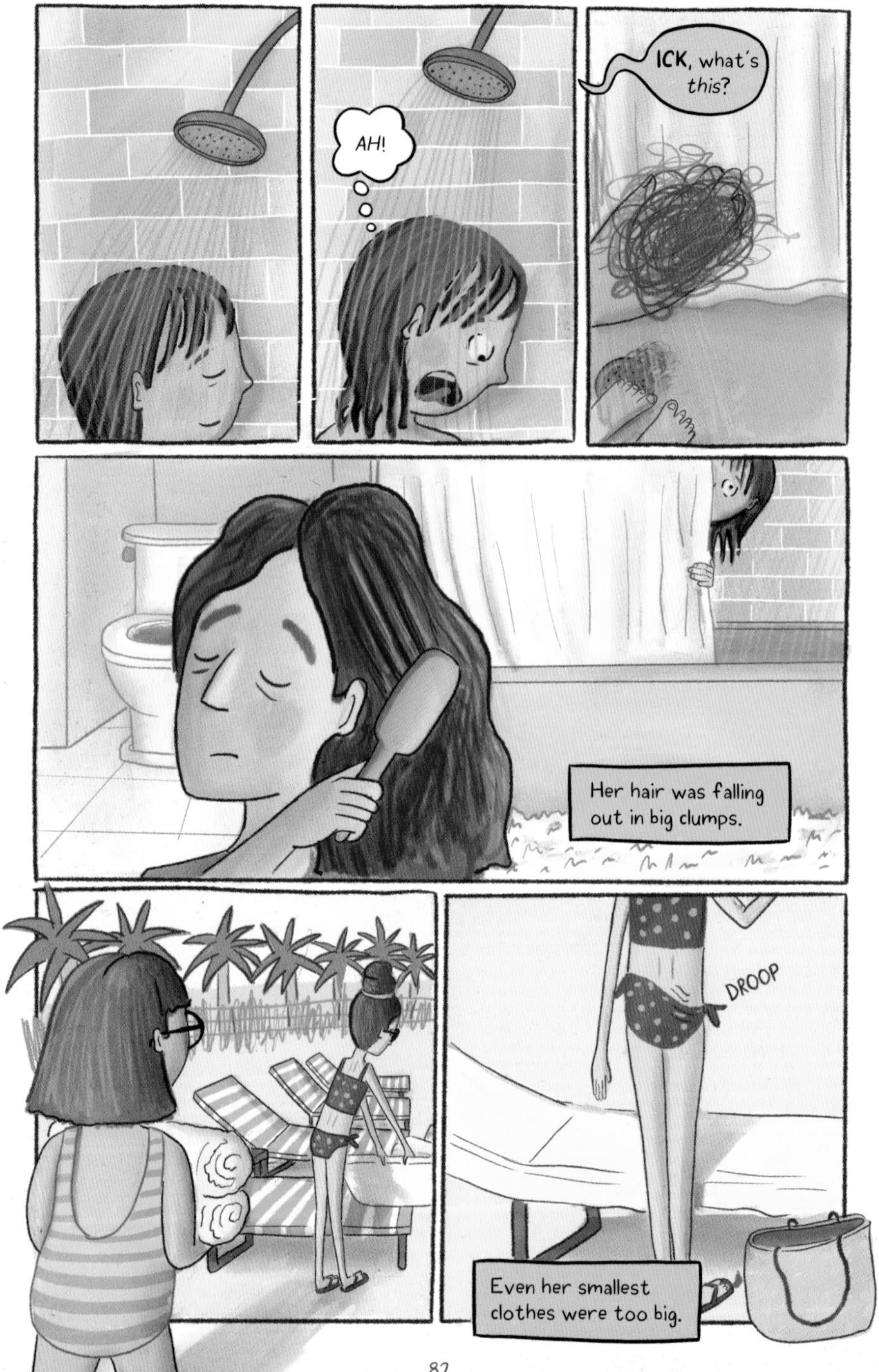
AH!
ICK, what's this?
Her hair was falling out in big clumps.
DROOP
Even her smallest clothes were too big.

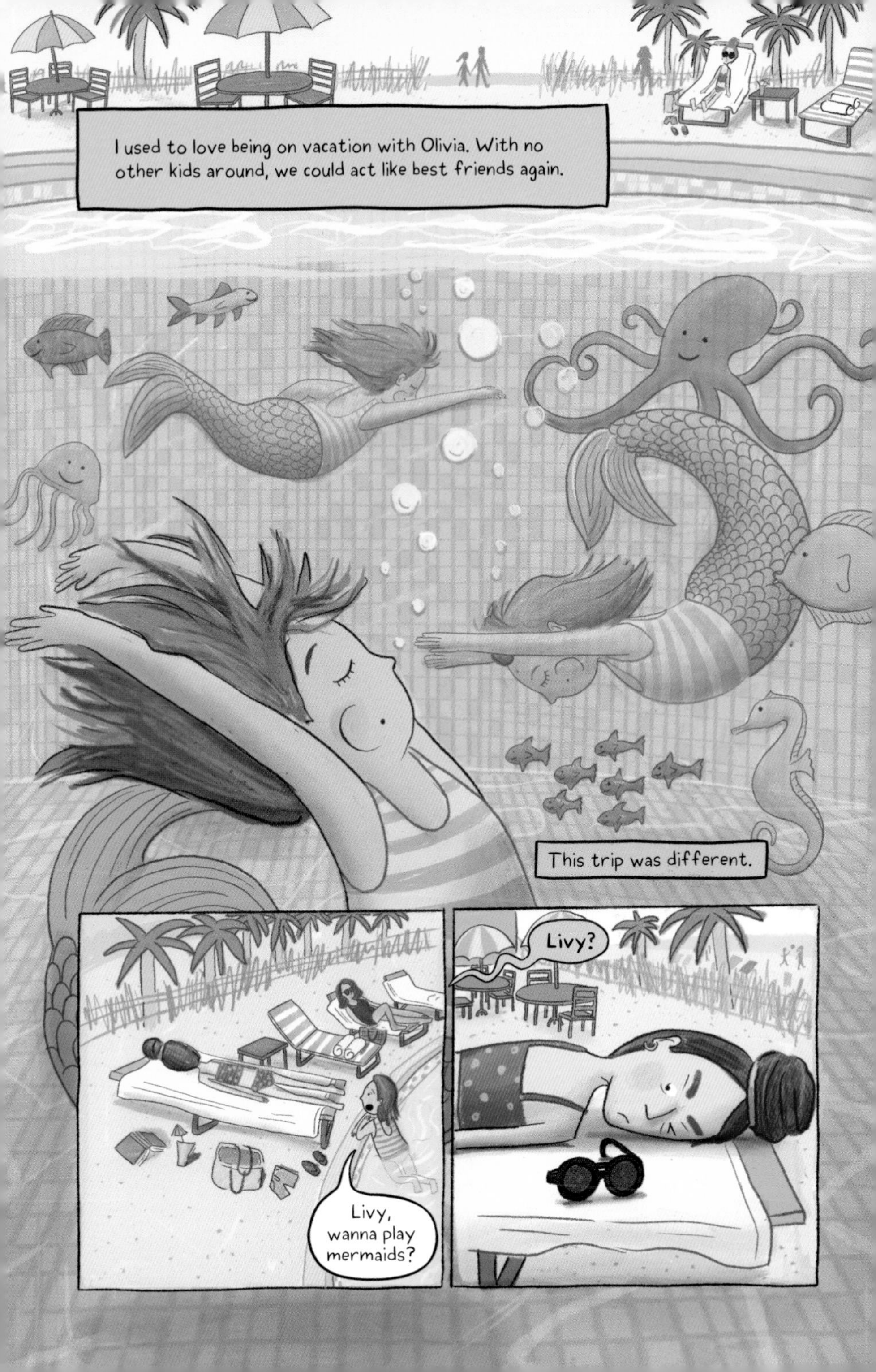
I used to love being on vacation with Olivia. With no other kids around, we could act like best friends again.
This trip was different.
Livy, wanna play mermaids?
Livy?

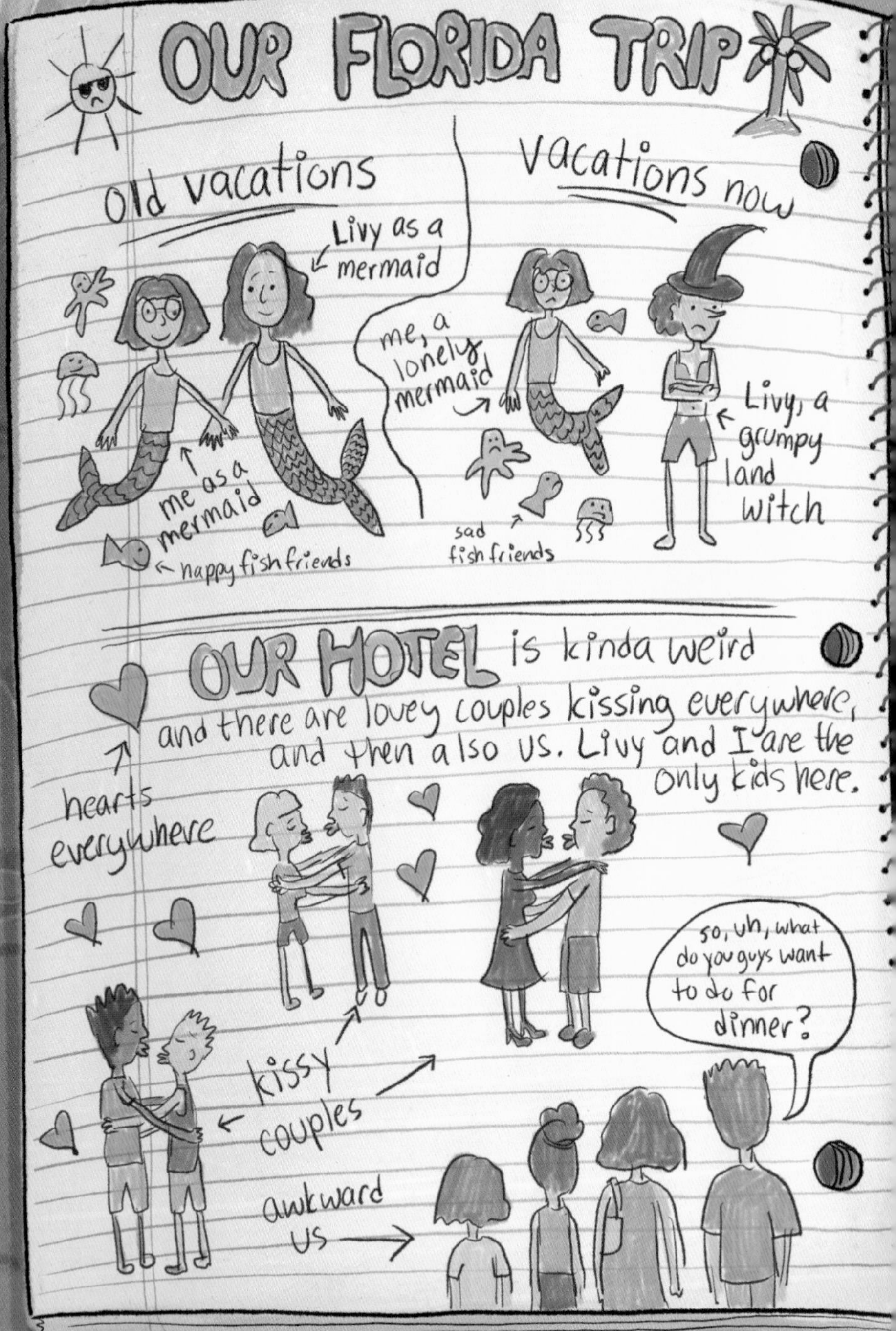
OUR FLORIDA TRIP
Old vacations
Livy as a mermaid
me as a mermaid
happy fish friends
Vacations now
me, a lonely mermaid
Livy, a grumpy land witch
sad fish friends
OUR HOTEL is kinda weird
and there are lovey couples kissing everywhere, and then also us. Livy and I are the only kids here.
hearts everywhere
kissy couples
so, uh, what do you guys want to do for dinner?
awkward us

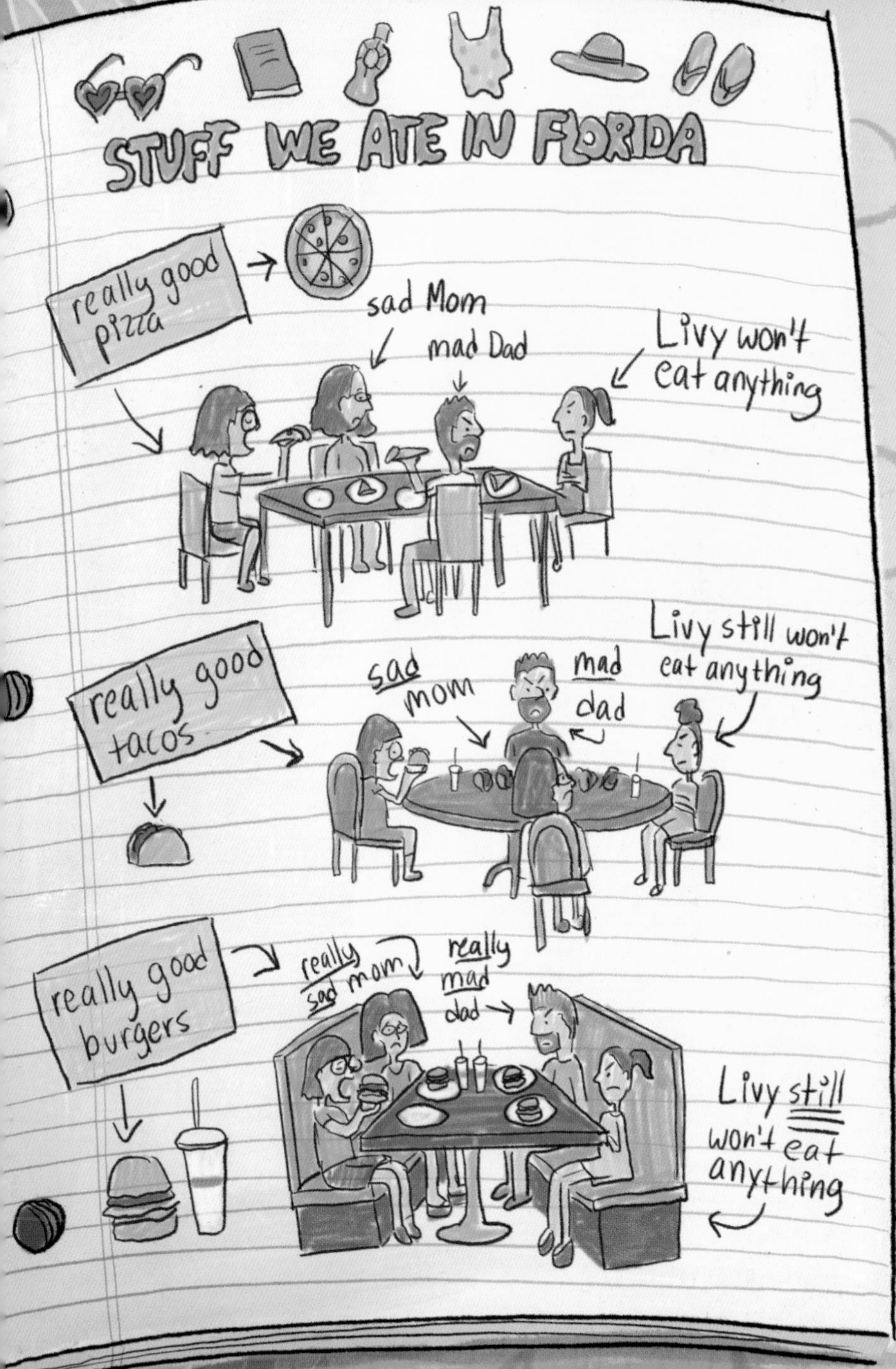
STUFF WE ATE IN FLORIDA
really good pizza
sad Mom
mad Dad
Livy won't eat anything
really good tacos
sad mom
mad dad
Livy still won't eat anything
really good burgers
really sad mom
really mad dad
Livy still won't eat anything

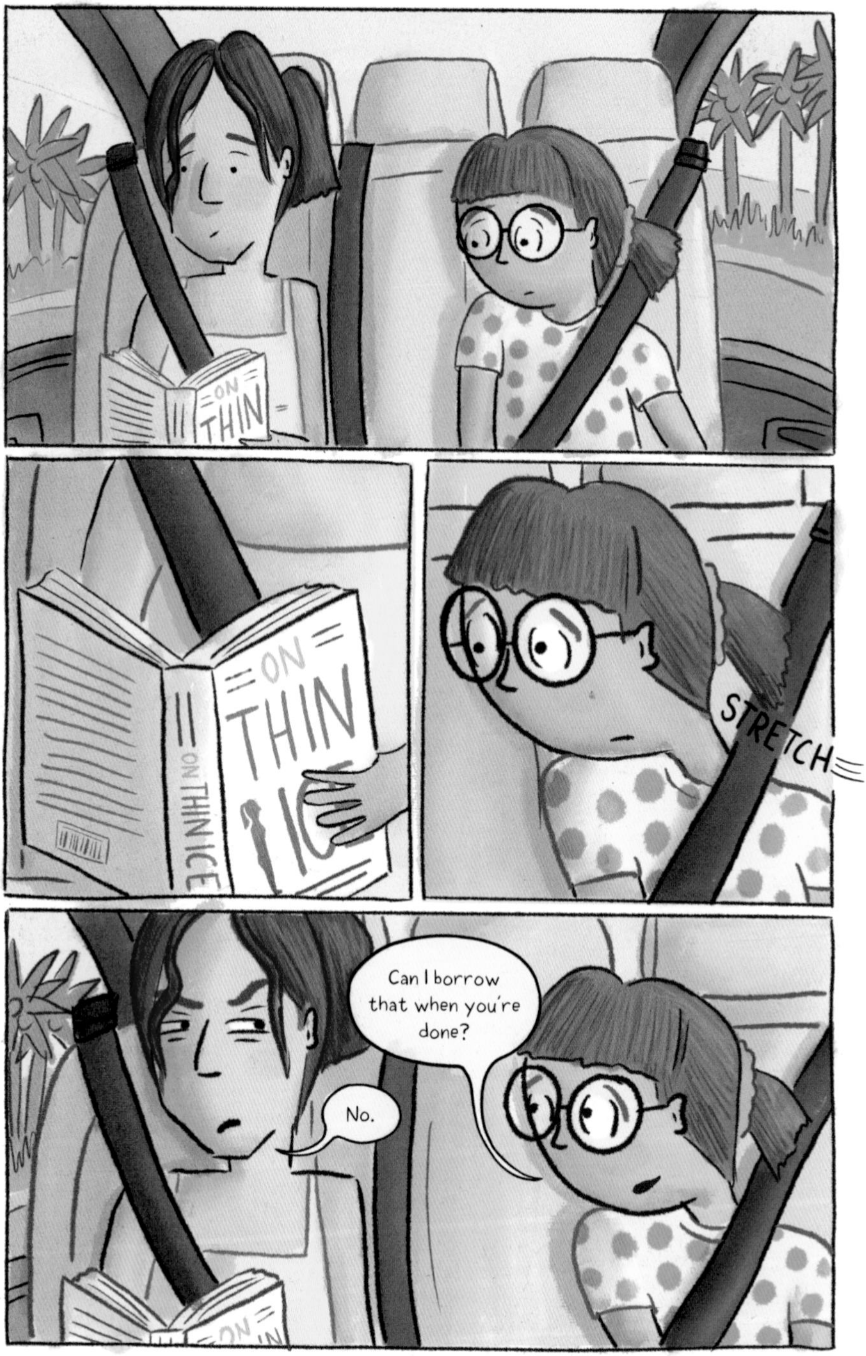
ON THIN
ON THIN ICE
ON THIN ICE
STRETCH
Can I borrow that when you're done?
No.

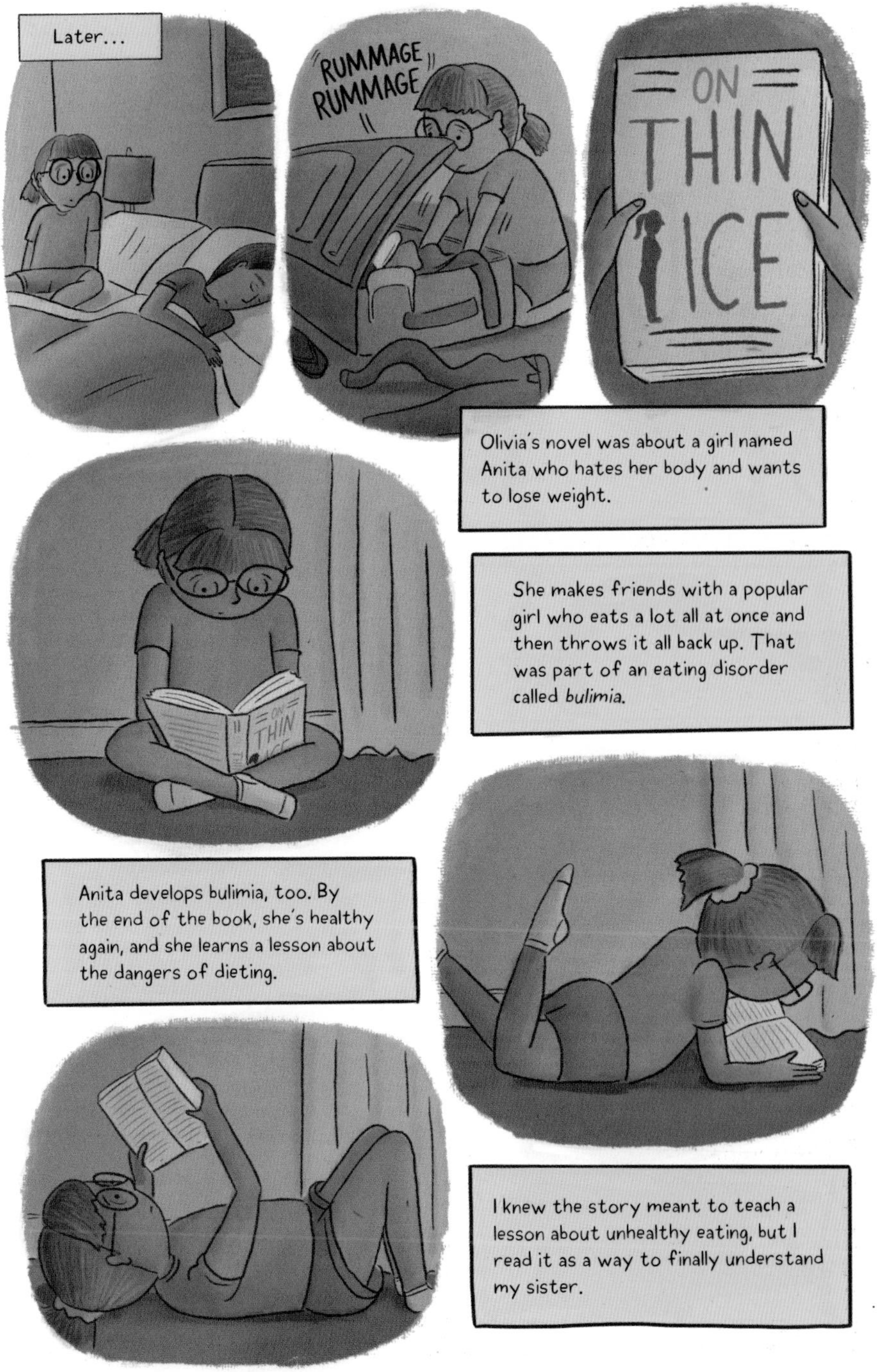

Later...
RUMMAGE RUMMAGE
ON THIN ICE
Olivia's novel was about a girl named Anita who hates her body and wants to lose weight.
ON THIN ICE
She makes friends with a popular girl who eats a lot all at once and then throws it all back up. That was part of an eating disorder called *bulimia*.
Anita develops bulimia, too. By the end of the book, she's healthy again, and she learns a lesson about the dangers of dieting.
I knew the story meant to teach a lesson about unhealthy eating, but I read it as a way to finally understand my sister.

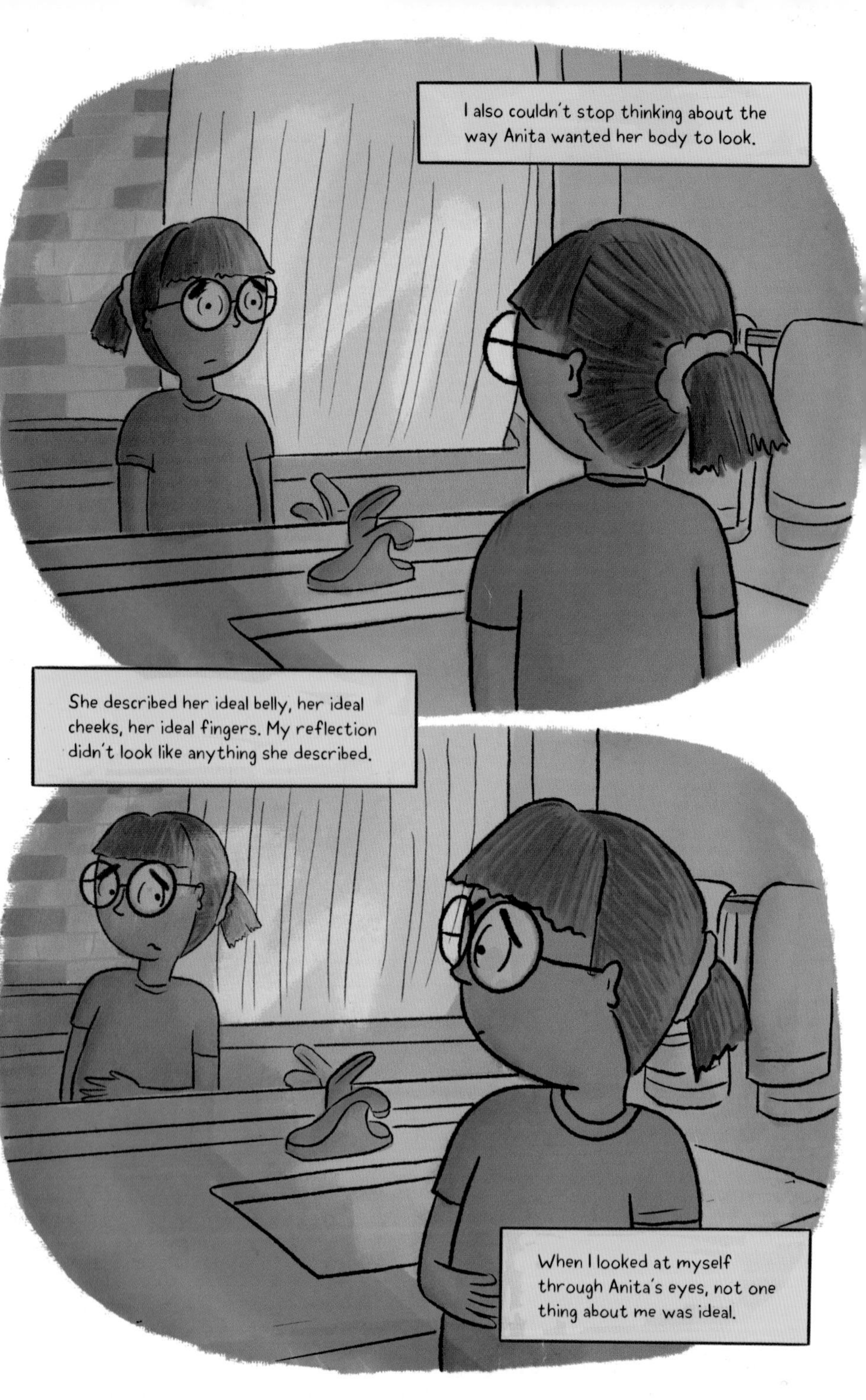
I also couldn't stop thinking about the way Anita wanted her body to look.
She described her ideal belly, her ideal cheeks, her ideal fingers. My reflection didn't look like anything she described.
When I looked at myself through Anita's eyes, not one thing about me was ideal.

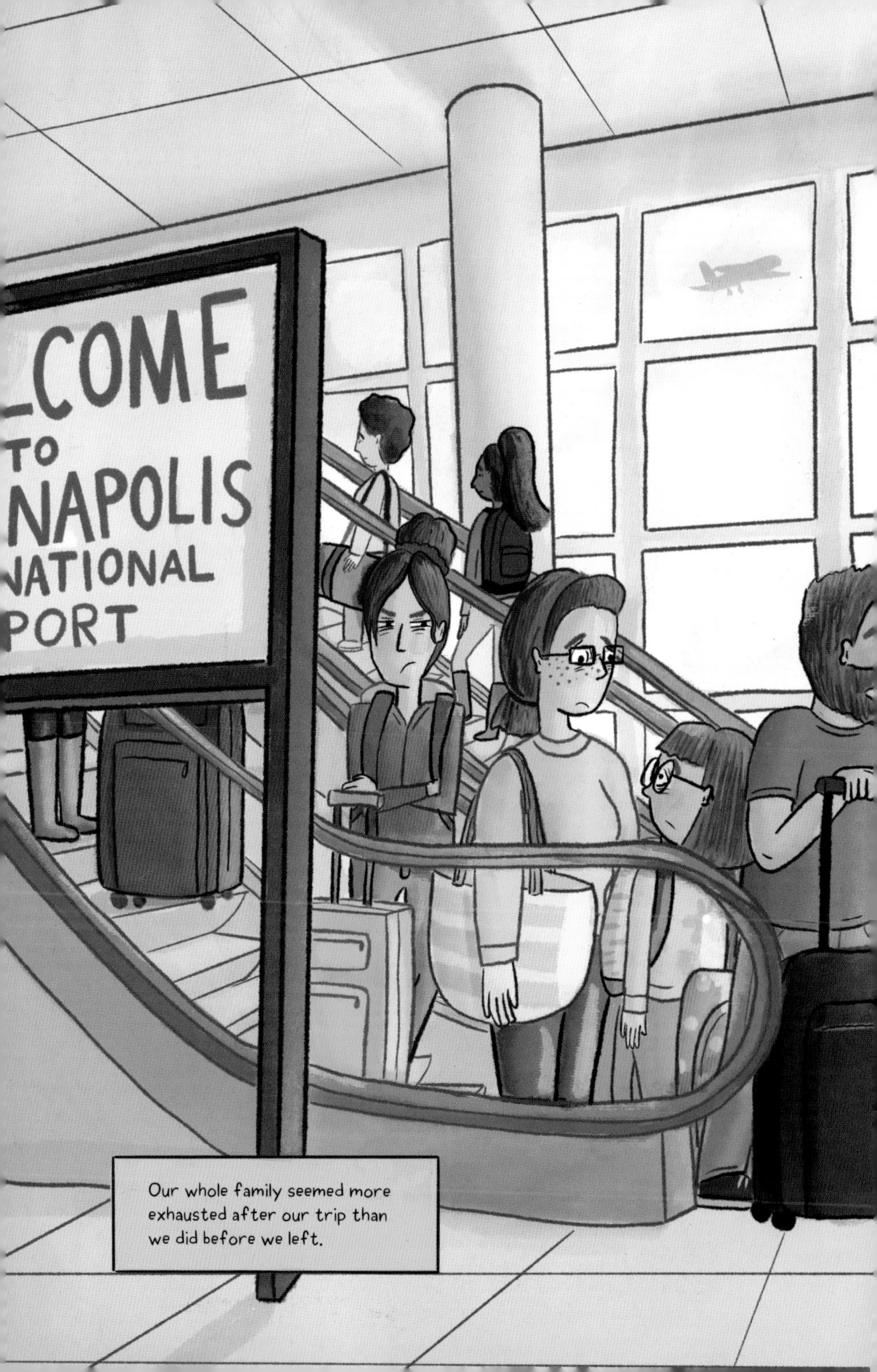

LCOME
TO
NAPOLIS
NATIONAL
PORT
Our whole family seemed more exhausted after our trip than we did before we left.

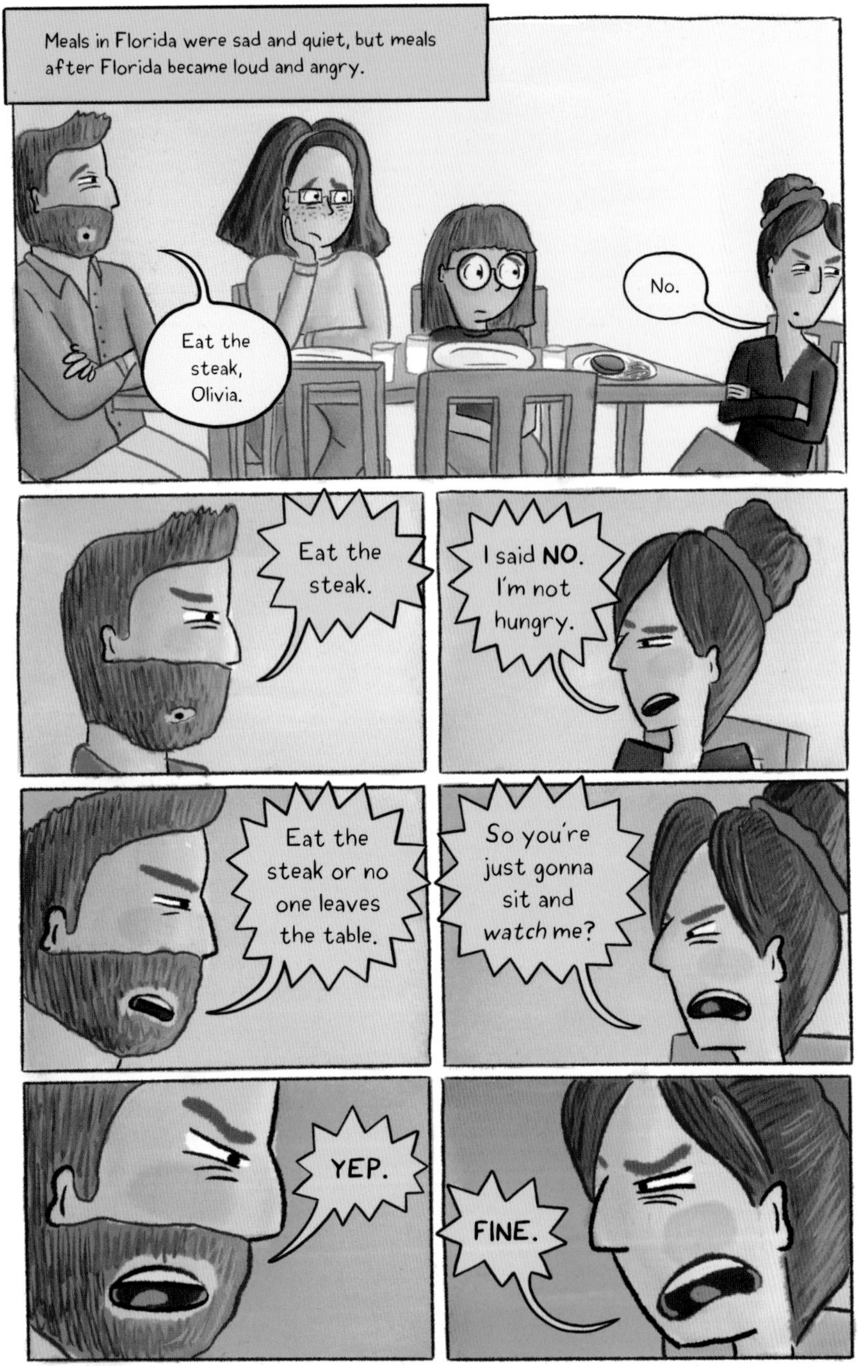
Meals in Florida were sad and quiet, but meals after Florida became loud and angry.
Eat the steak, Olivia.
No.
Eat the steak.
I said **NO.** I'm not hungry.
Eat the steak or no one leaves the table.
So you're just gonna sit and *watch* me?
YEP.
FINE.

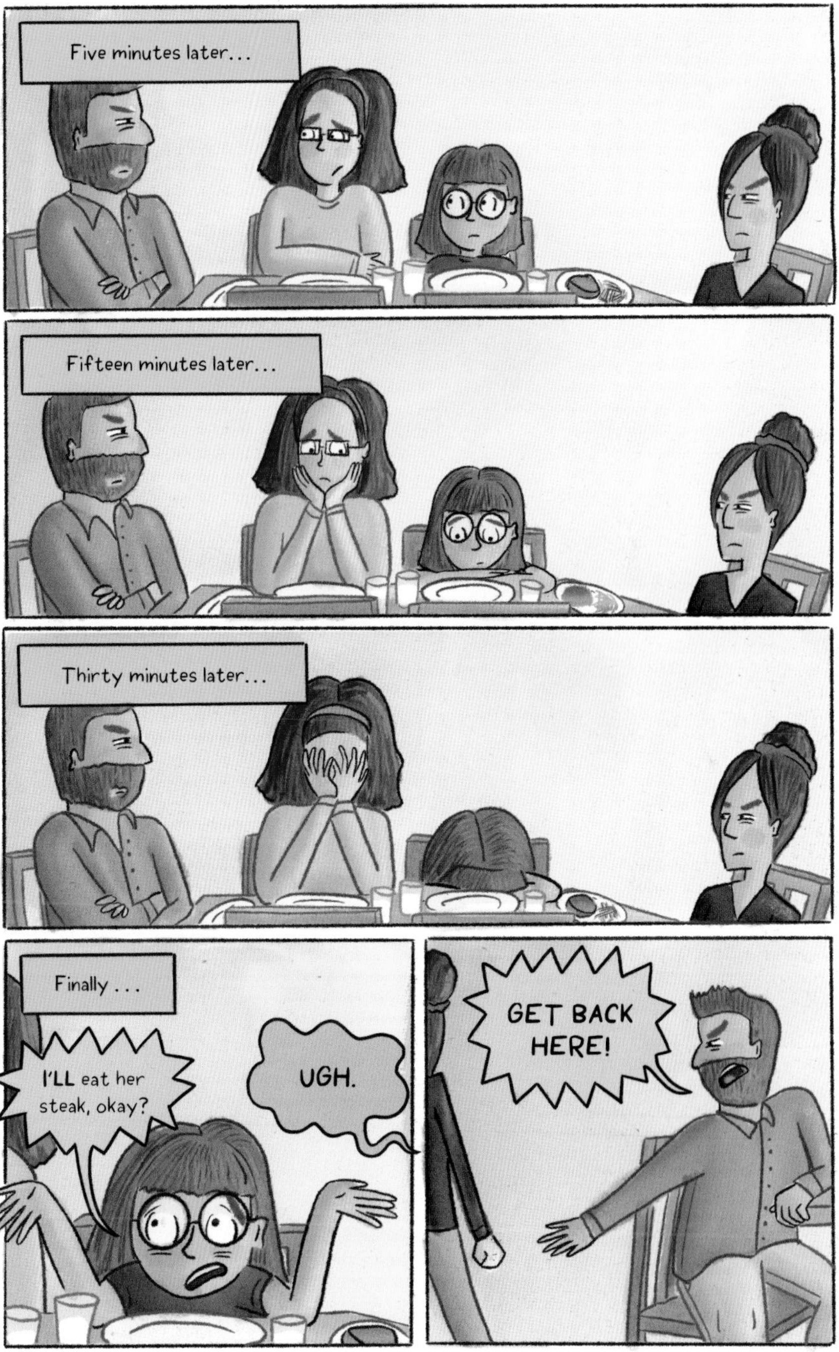

Five minutes later...
Fifteen minutes later...
Thirty minutes later...
Finally . . .
I'LL eat her steak, okay?
UGH.
GET BACK HERE!

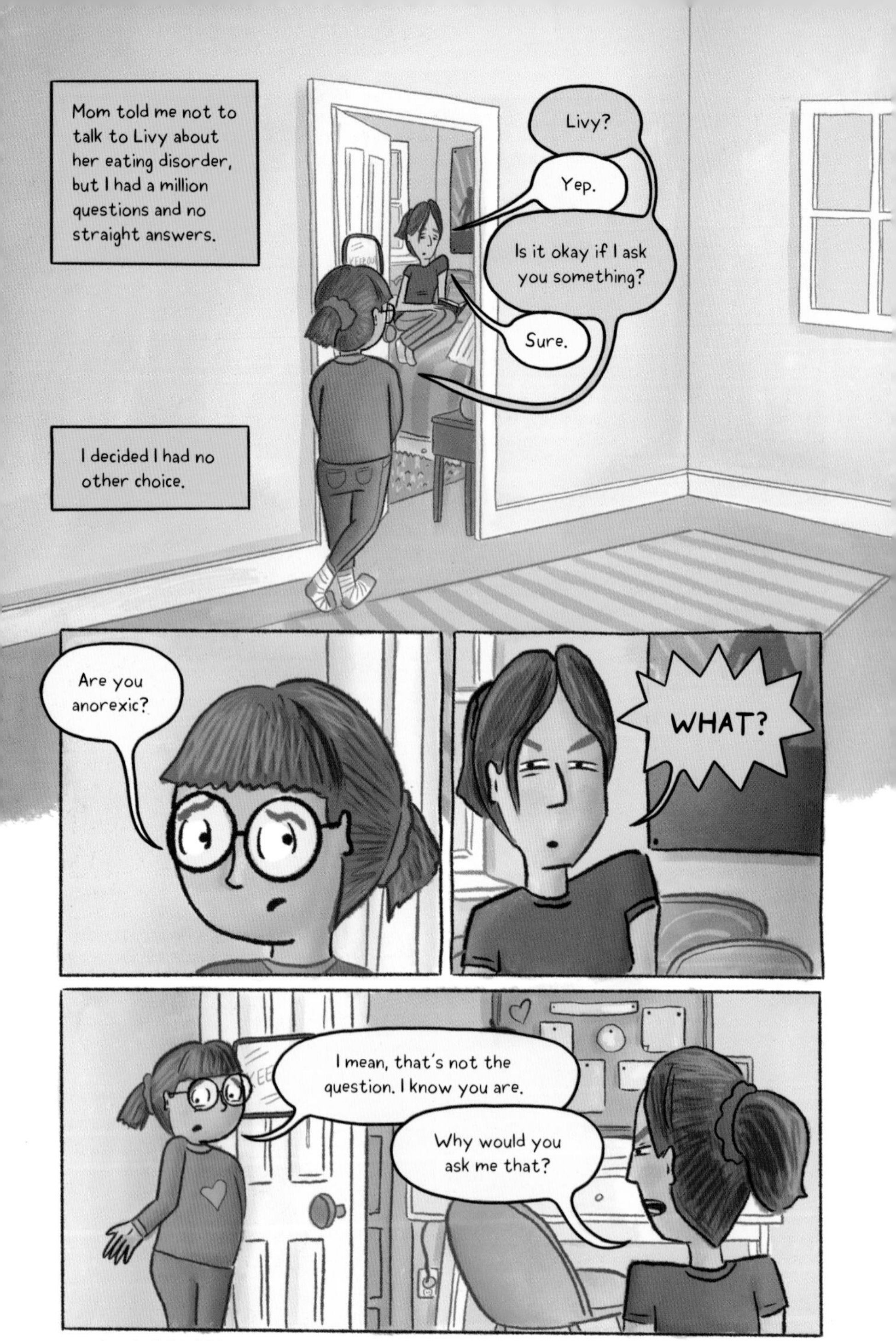
Mom told me not to talk to Livy about her eating disorder, but I had a million questions and no straight answers.
Livy?
Yep.
Is it okay if I ask you something?
Sure.
I decided I had no other choice.
Are you anorexic?
WHAT?
I mean, that's not the question. I know you are.
Why would you ask me that?

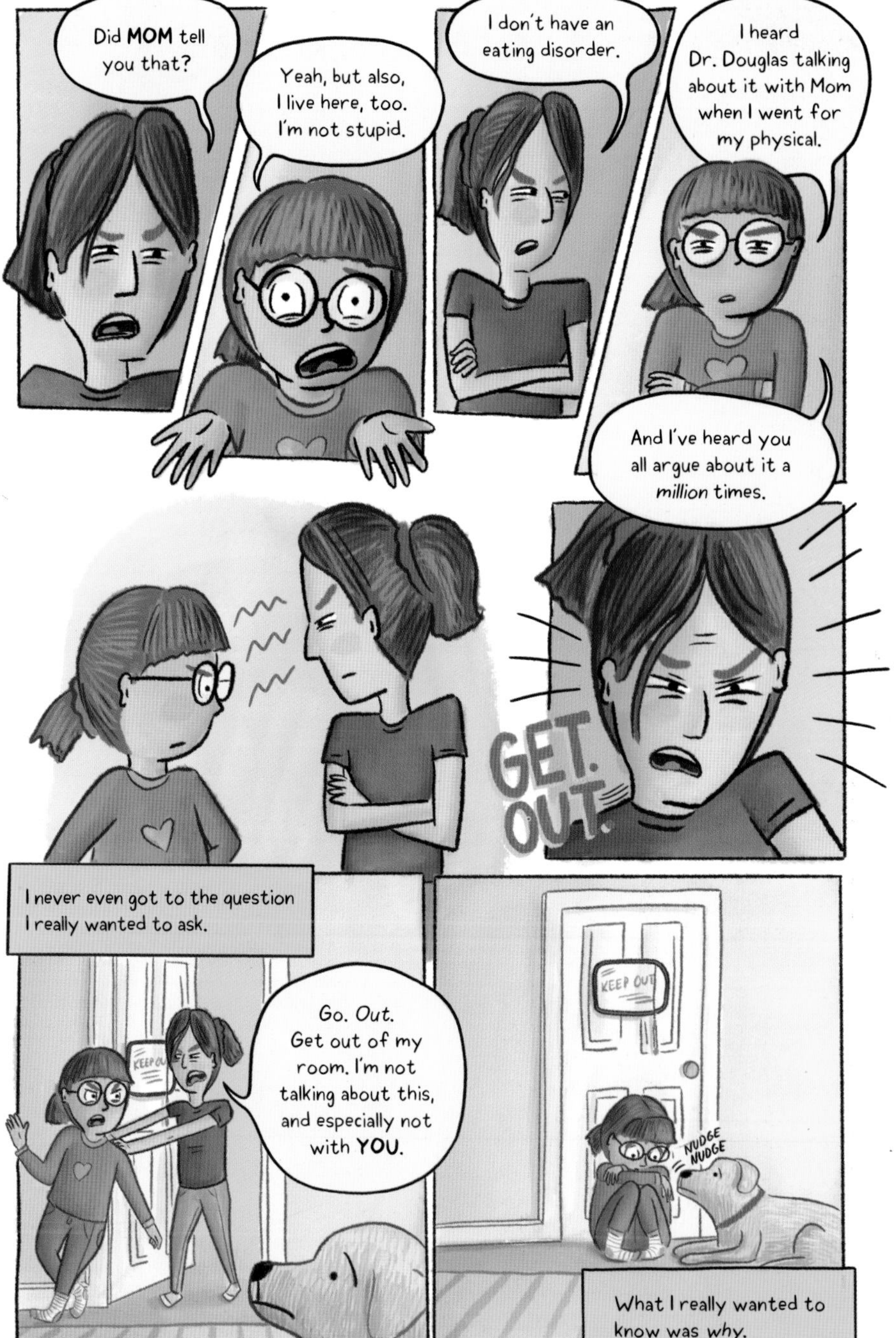
Did **MOM** tell you that?
Yeah, but also, I live here, too. I'm not stupid.
I don't have an eating disorder.
I heard Dr. Douglas talking about it with Mom when I went for my physical.
And I've heard you all argue about it a *million* times.
GET. OUT.
I never even got to the question I really wanted to ask.
KEEP OUT
Go. *Out.* Get out of my room. I'm not talking about this, and especially not with **YOU**.
KEEP OUT
NUDGE NUDGE
What I really wanted to know was *why*.

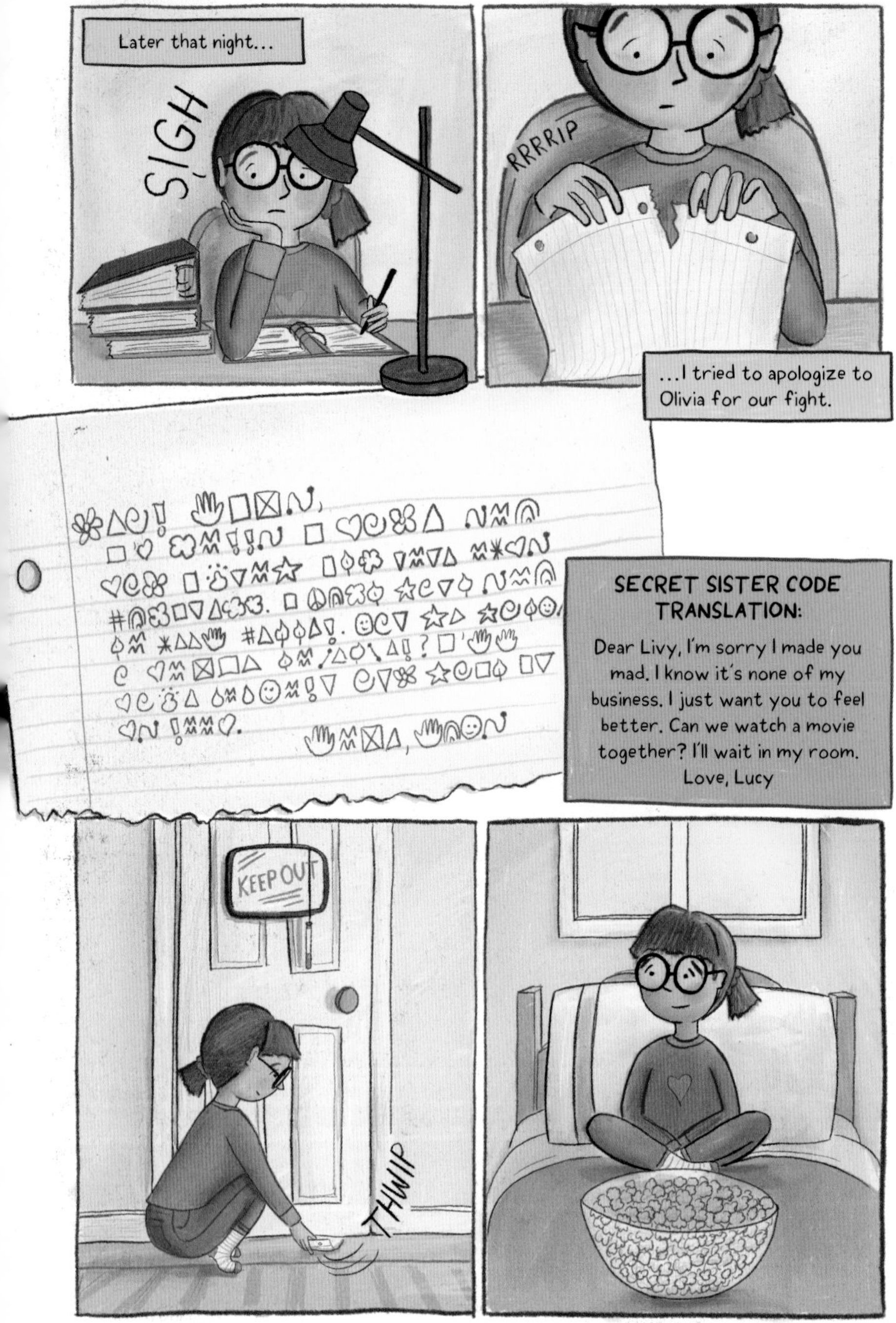

Later that night...
SIGH
RRRRIP
...I tried to apologize to Olivia for our fight.
SECRET SISTER CODE TRANSLATION:
Dear Livy, I'm sorry I made you mad. I know it's none of my business. I just want you to feel better. Can we watch a movie together? I'll wait in my room. Love, Lucy
KEEP OUT
THWIP

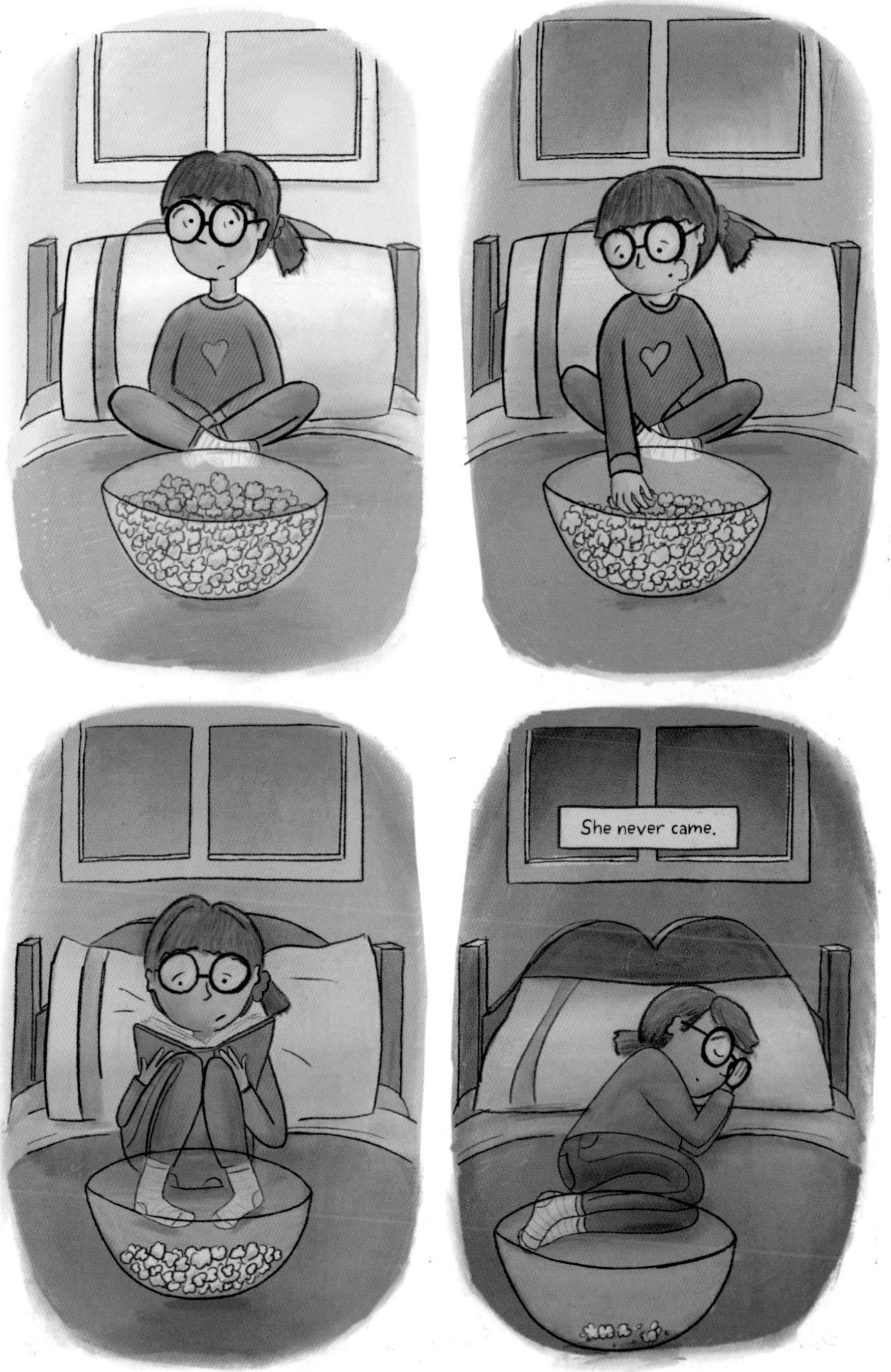
She never came.

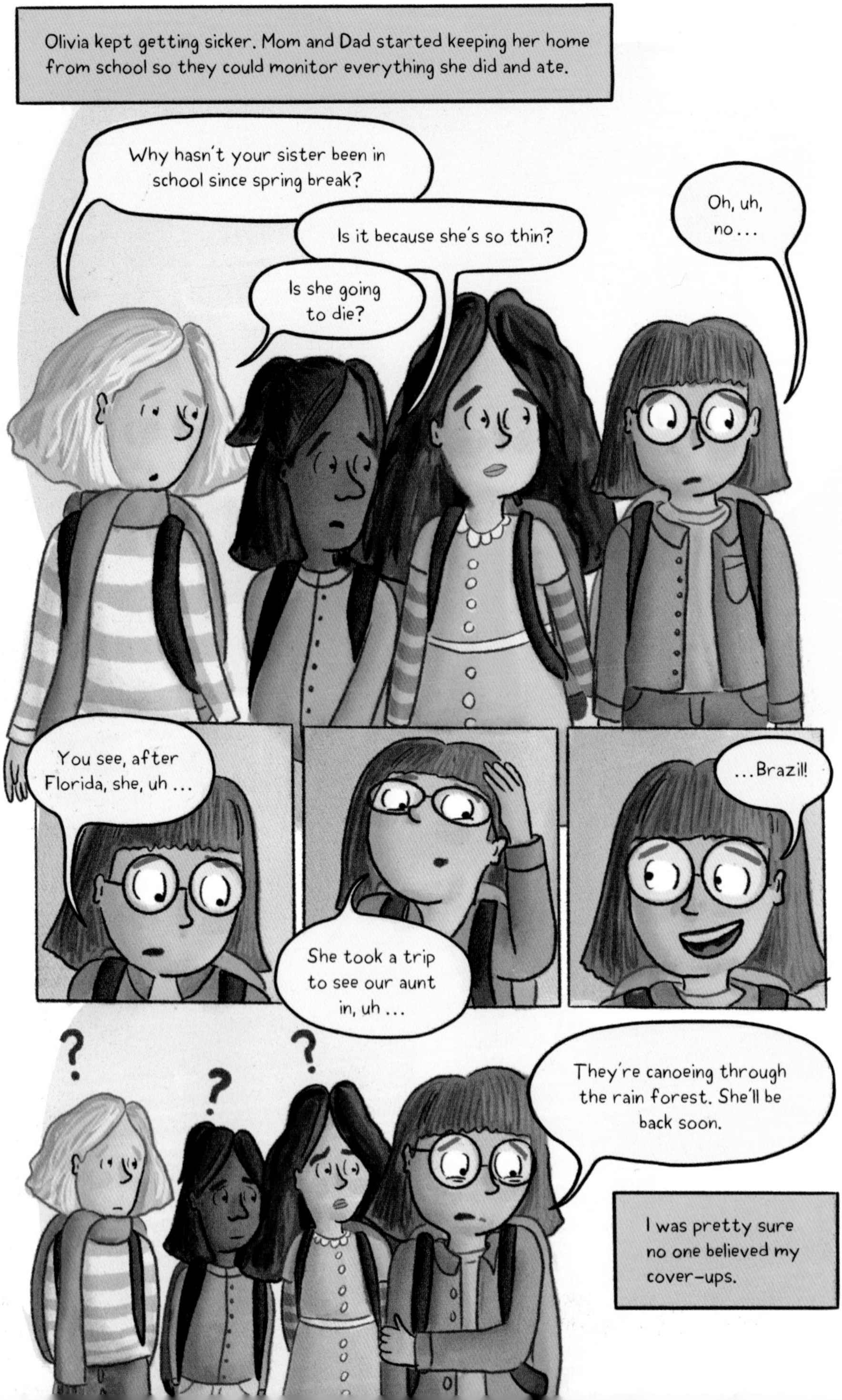

Olivia kept getting sicker. Mom and Dad started keeping her home from school so they could monitor everything she did and ate.
Why hasn't your sister been in school since spring break?
Is it because she's so thin?
Is she going to die?
Oh, uh, no...
You see, after Florida, she, uh ...
She took a trip to see our aunt in, uh ...
...Brazil!
?
?
?
They're canoeing through the rain forest. She'll be back soon.
I was pretty sure no one believed my cover-ups.

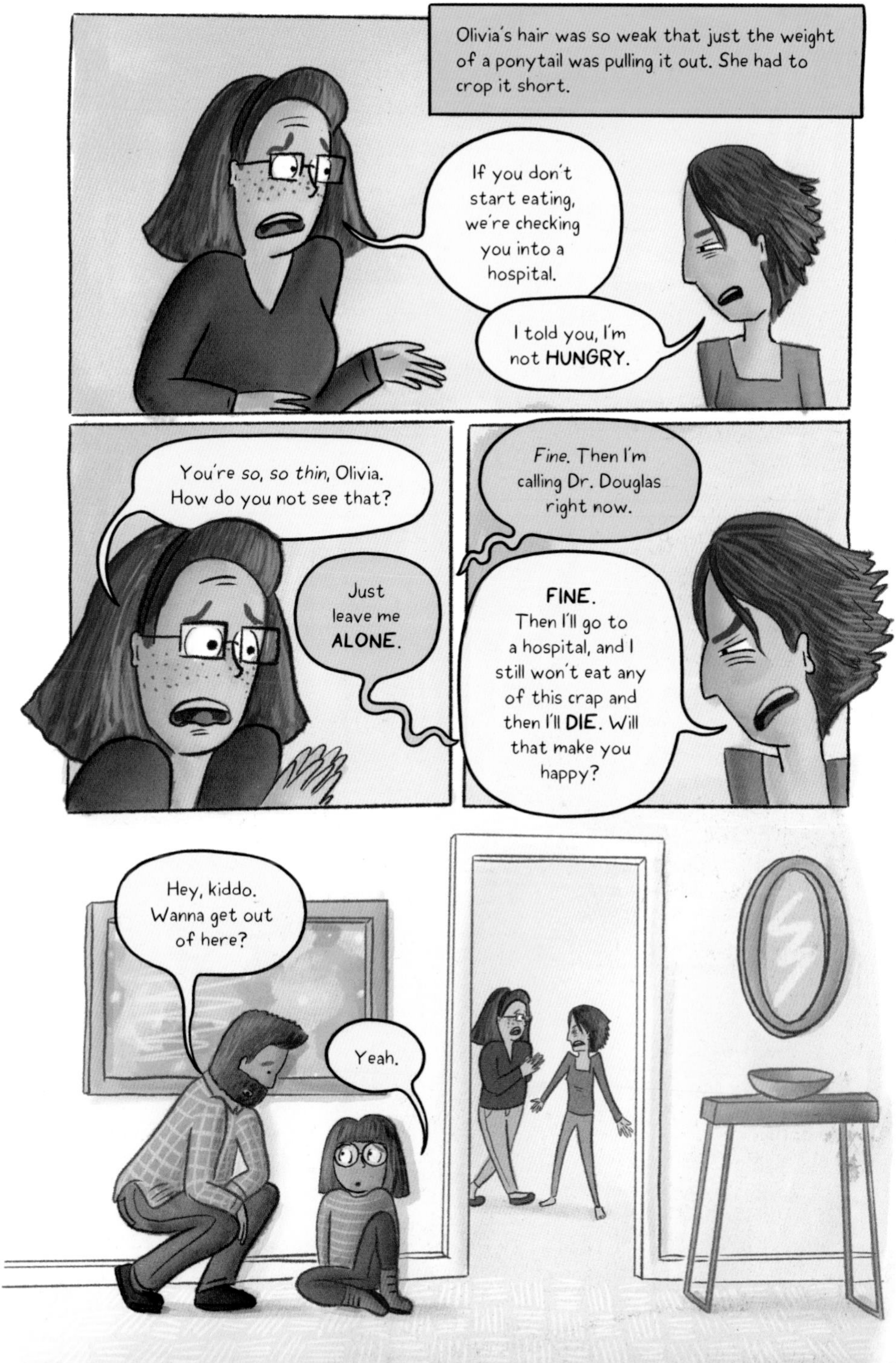
Olivia's hair was so weak that just the weight of a ponytail was pulling it out. She had to crop it short.
If you don't start eating, we're checking you into a hospital.
I told you, I'm not **HUNGRY**.
You're so, so *thin*, Olivia. How do you not see that?
Just leave me **ALONE**.
Fine. Then I'm calling Dr. Douglas right now.
FINE. Then I'll go to a hospital, and I still won't eat any of this crap and then I'll **DIE**. Will that make you happy?
Hey, kiddo. Wanna get out of here?
Yeah.

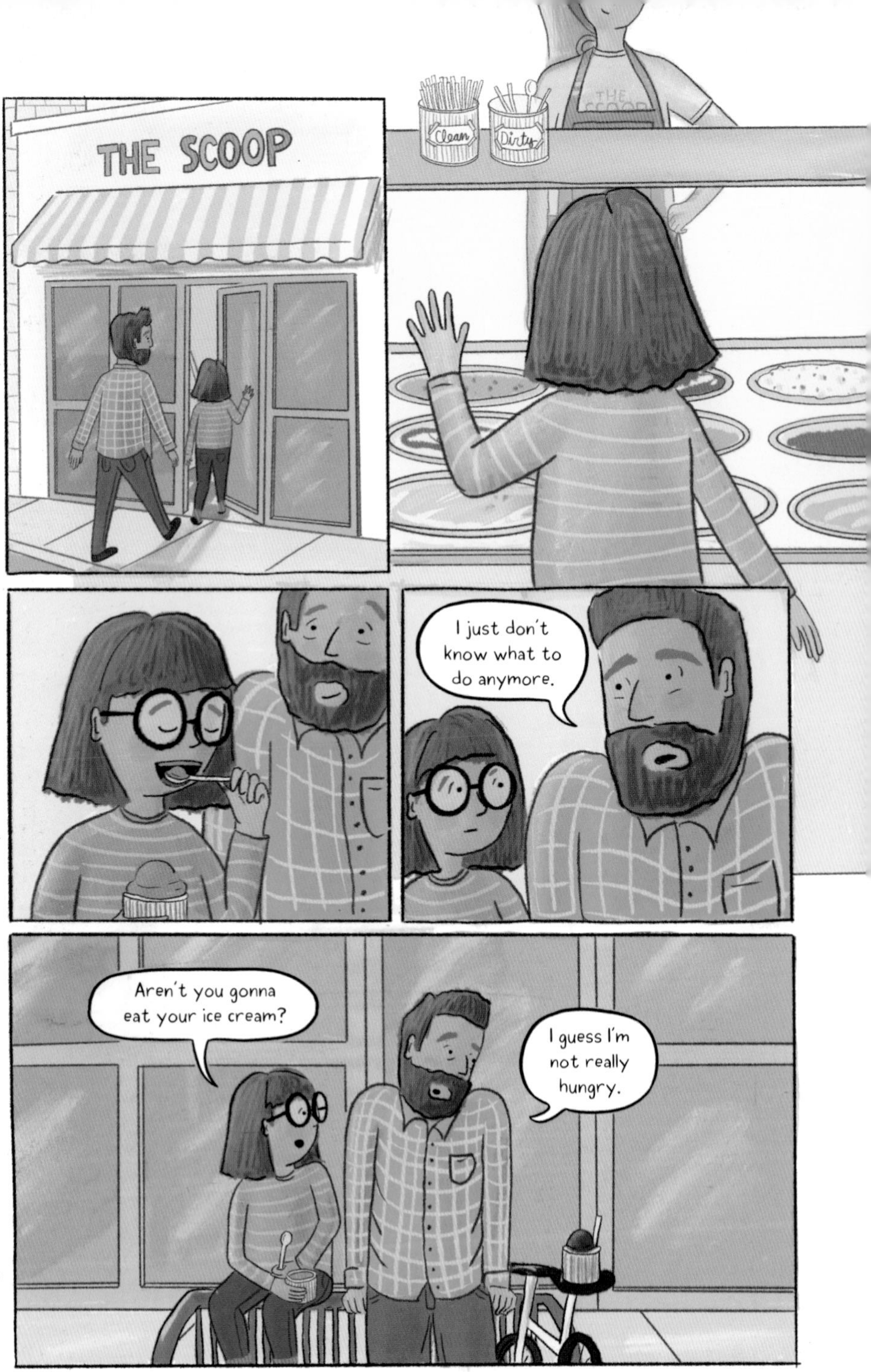
THE SCOOP
Clean
Dirty
THE SCOOP
I just don't know what to do anymore.
Aren't you gonna eat your ice cream?
I guess I'm not really hungry.

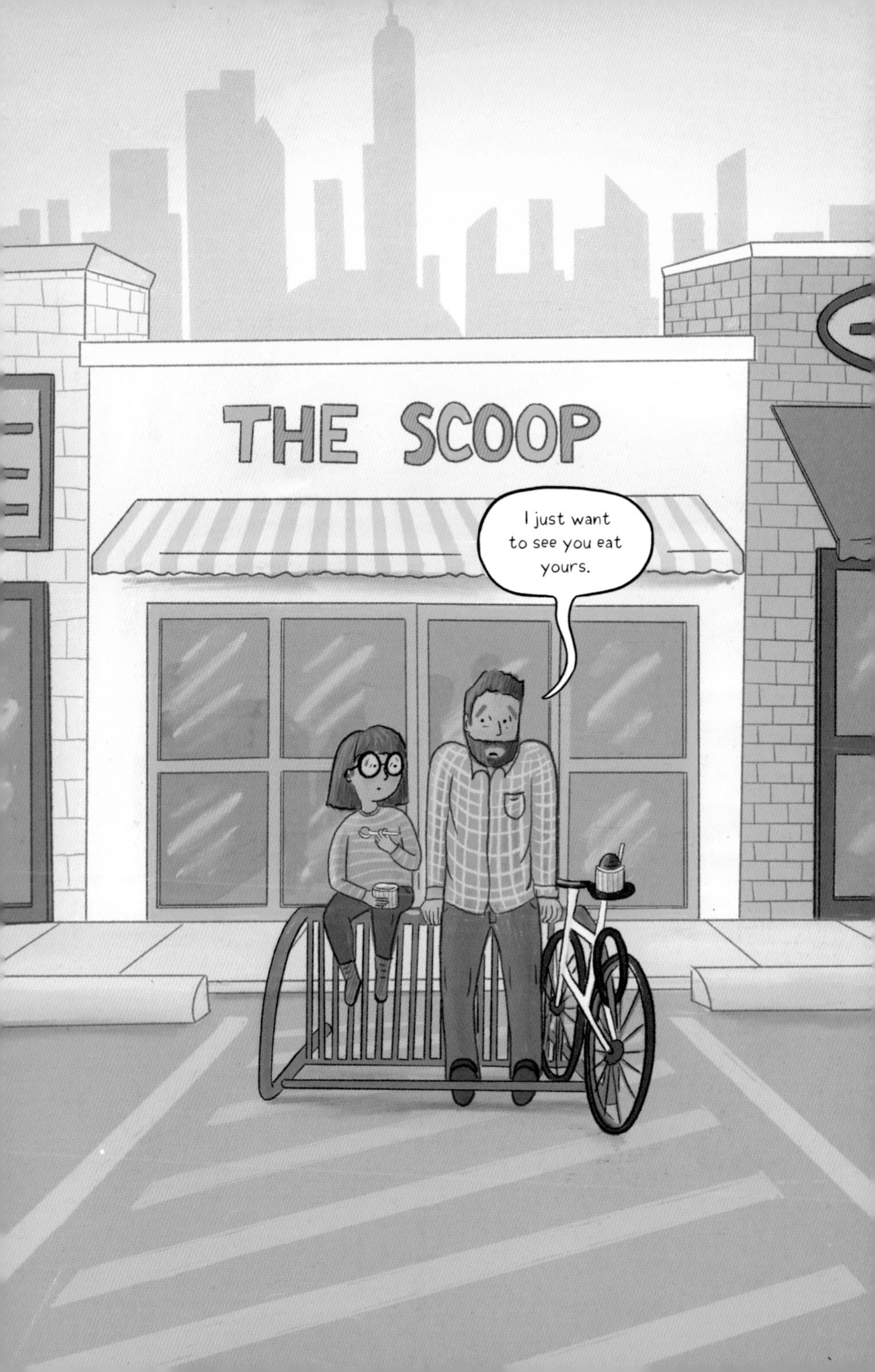
THE SCOOP
I just want to see you eat yours.

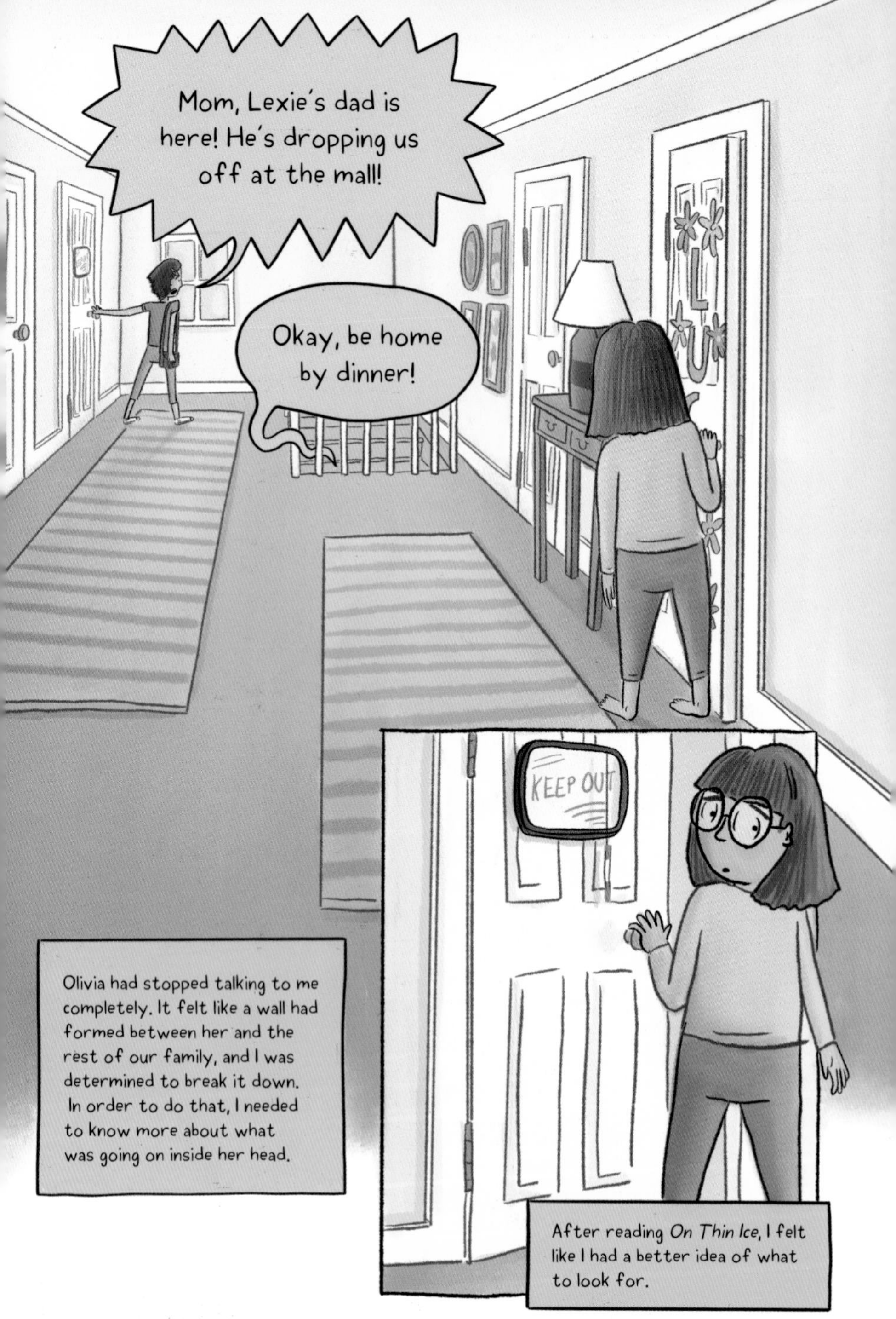
Mom, Lexie's dad is here! He's dropping us off at the mall!
Okay, be home by dinner!
KEEP OUT
Olivia had stopped talking to me completely. It felt like a wall had formed between her and the rest of our family, and I was determined to break it down. In order to do that, I needed to know more about what was going on inside her head.
After reading *On Thin Ice*, I felt like I had a better idea of what to look for.

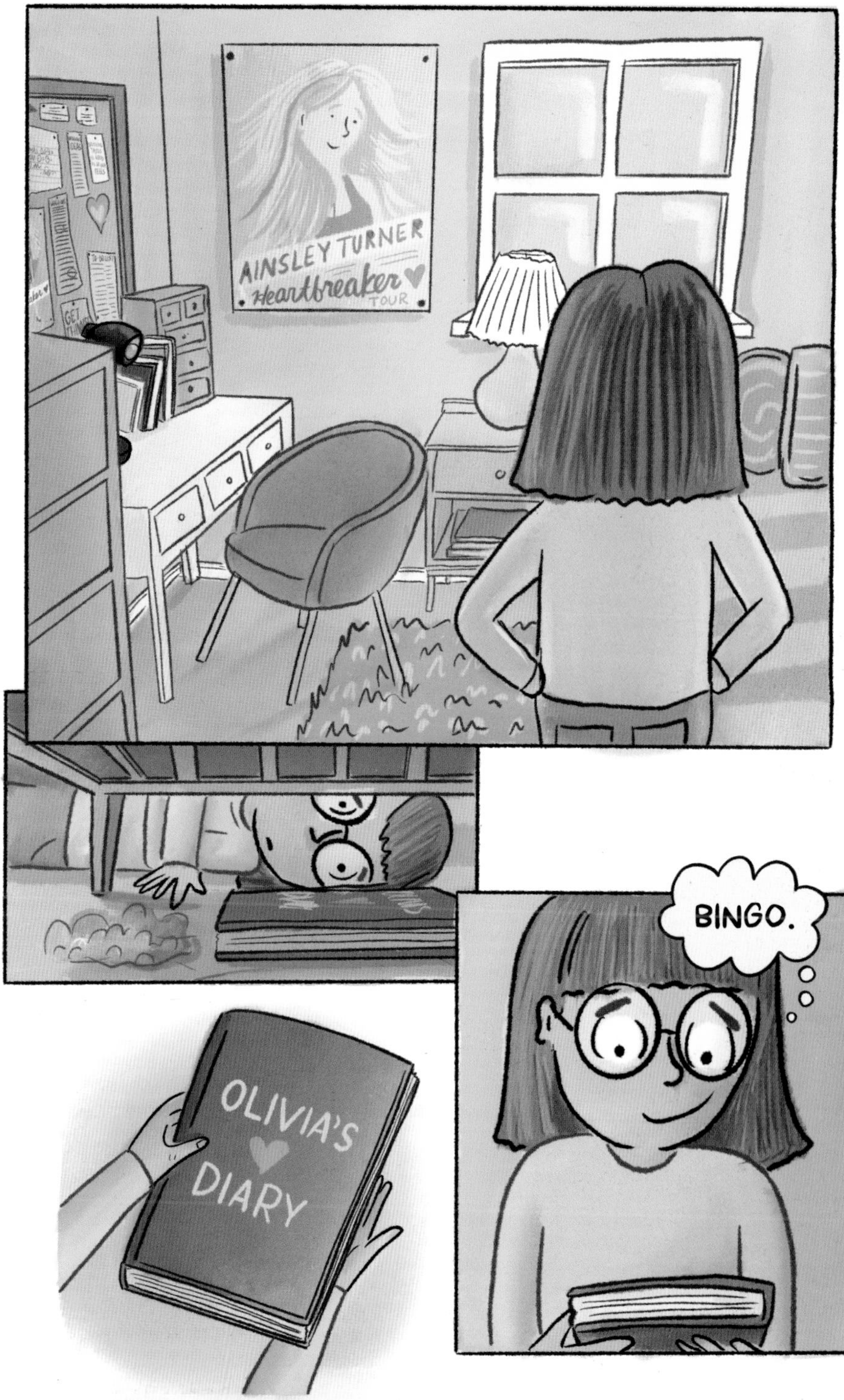
AINSLEY TURNER
Heartbreaker
TOUR
OLIVIA'S
DIARY
BINGO.

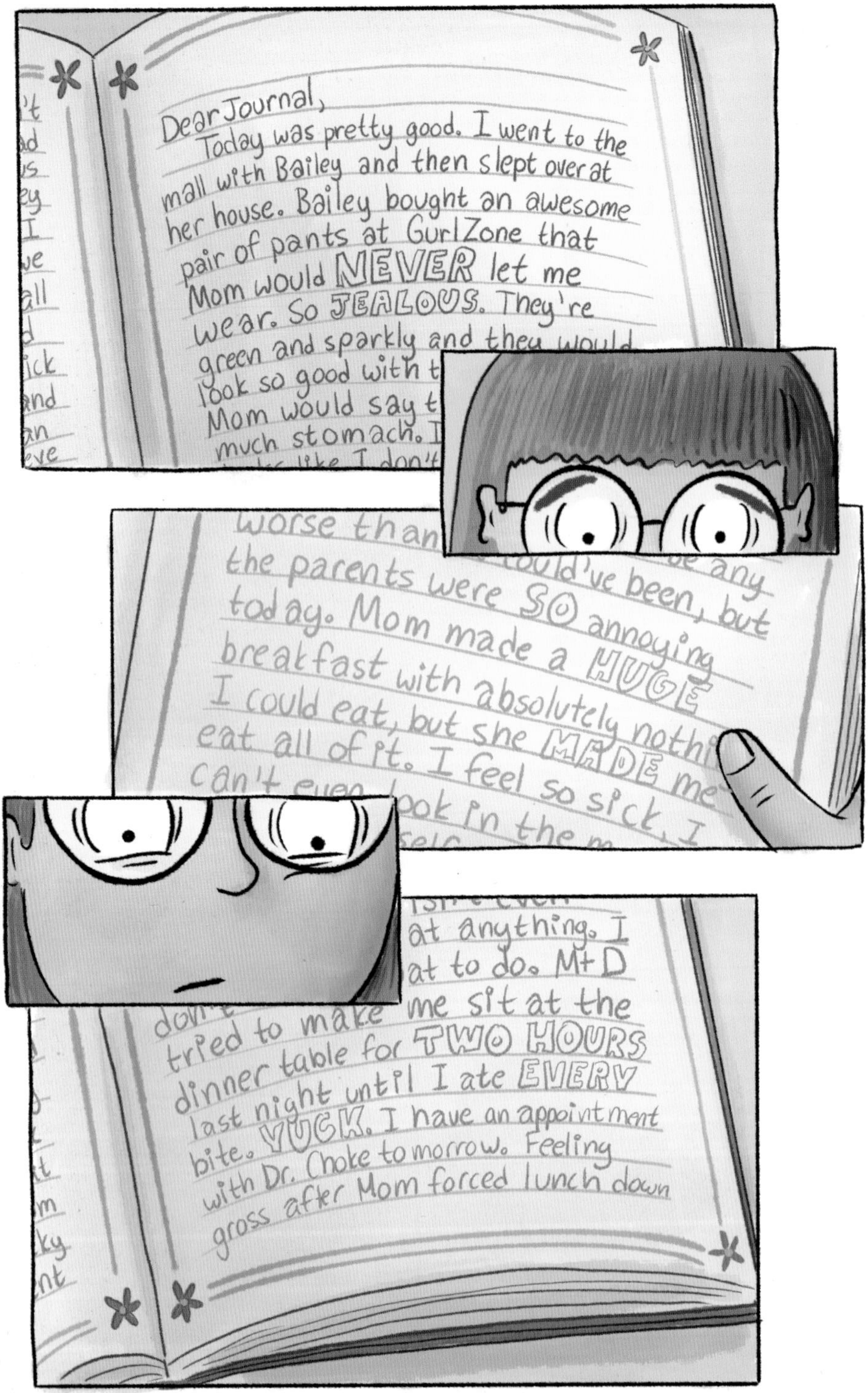

Dear Journal,
Today was pretty good. I went to the mall with Bailey and then slept over at her house. Bailey bought an awesome pair of pants at GurlZone that Mom would NEVER let me wear. So JEALOUS. They're green and sparkly and they would look so good with
Mom would say
much stomach.
worse than could've been, but
the parents were SO annoying
today. Mom made a HUGE
breakfast with absolutely
I could eat, but she MADE me
eat all of it. I feel so sick, I
can't even look in the
at anything. I
at to do. M+D
tried to make me sit at the
dinner table for TWO HOURS
last night until I ate EVERY
bite. YUCK. I have an appointment
with Dr. Choke tomorrow. Feeling
gross after Mom forced lunch down

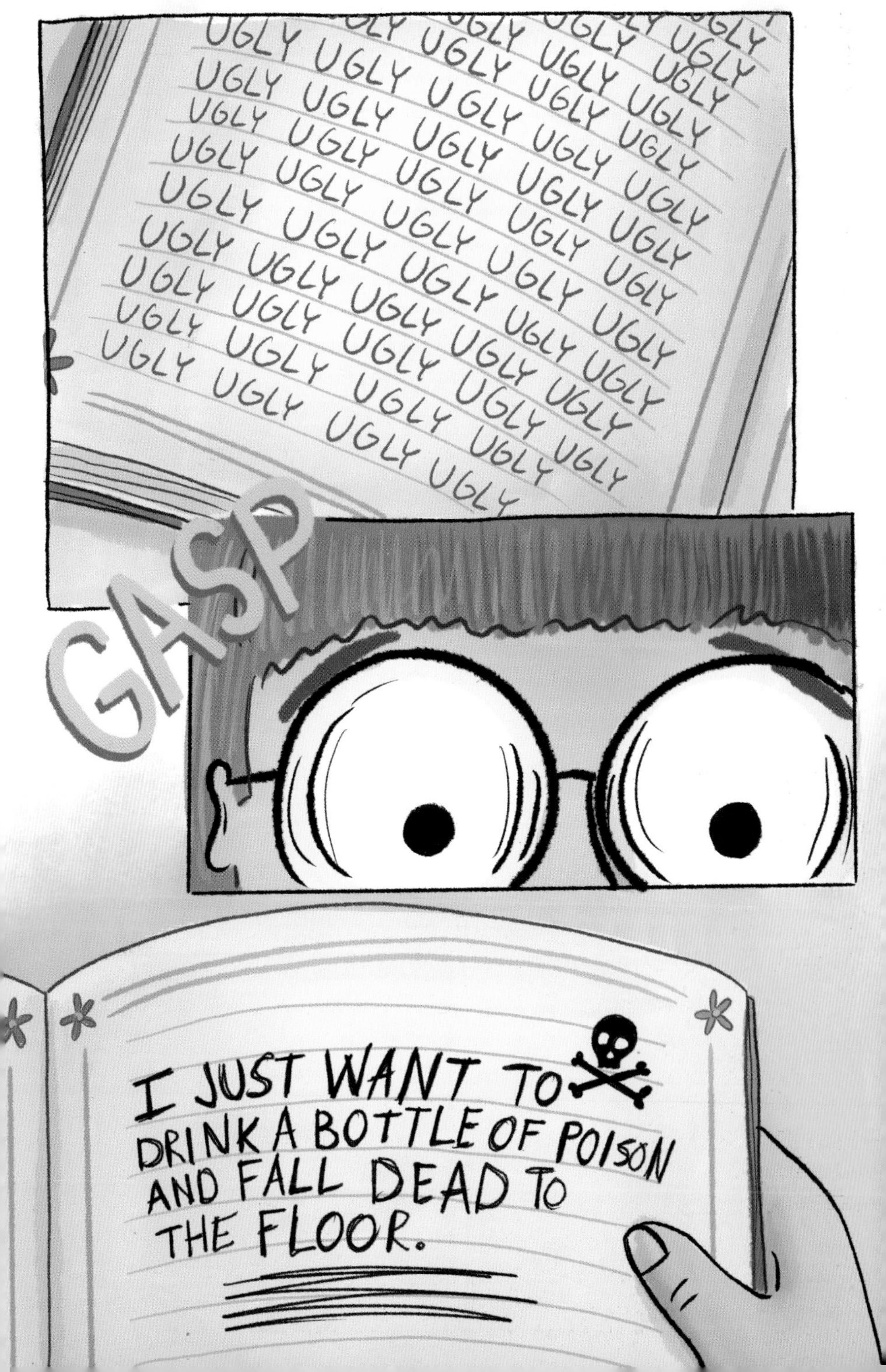
UGLY UGLY UGLY UGLY UGLY
UGLY UGLY UGLY UGLY UGLY
UGLY UGLY UGLY UGLY UGLY
UGLY UGLY UGLY UGLY UGLY
UGLY UGLY UGLY UGLY UGLY
UGLY UGLY UGLY UGLY UGLY
UGLY UGLY UGLY UGLY UGLY
UGLY UGLY UGLY UGLY UGLY
UGLY UGLY UGLY UGLY UGLY
UGLY UGLY UGLY UGLY UGLY
UGLY UGLY UGLY UGLY UGLY
UGLY UGLY UGLY UGLY
GASP
I JUST WANT TO DRINK A BOTTLE OF POISON AND FALL DEAD TO THE FLOOR.

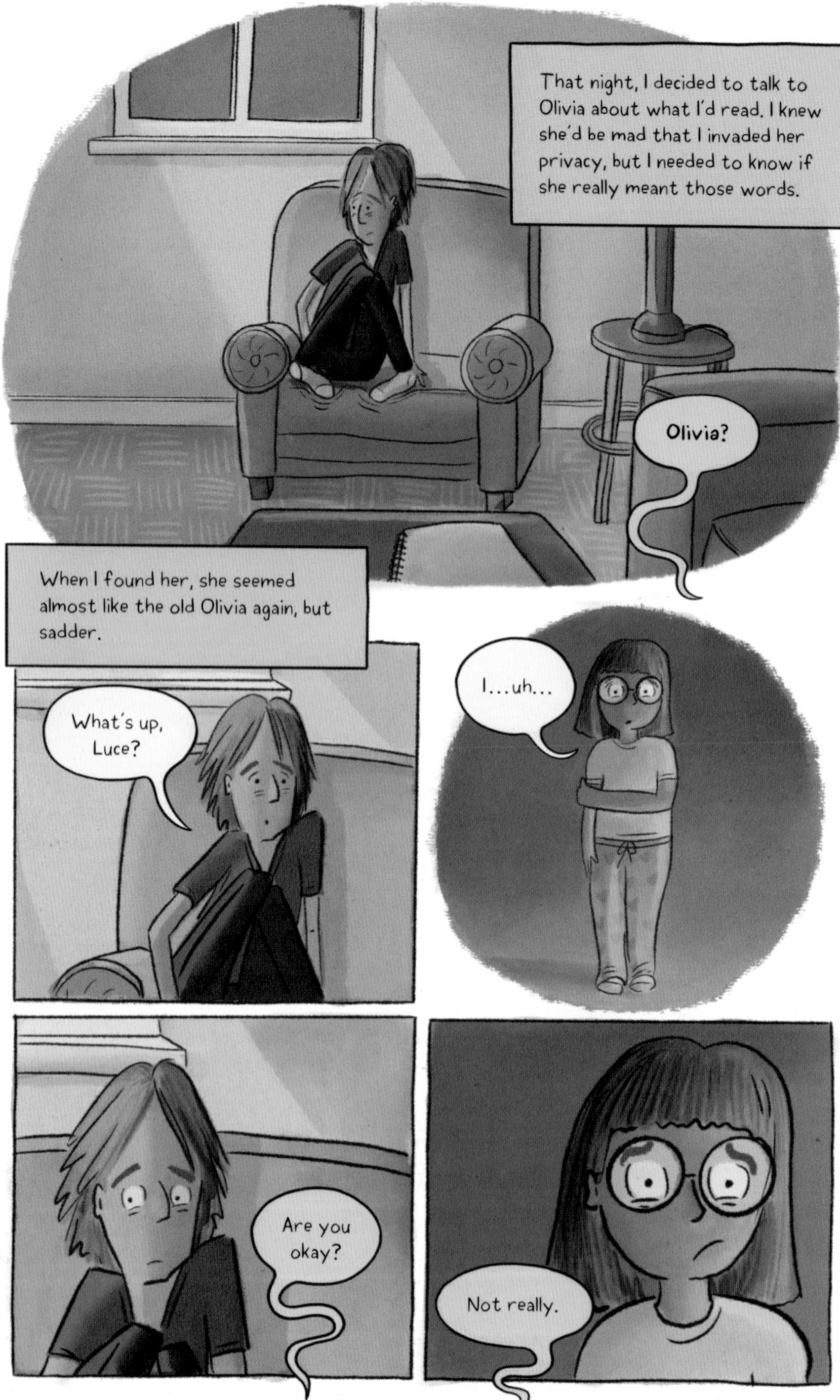

That night, I decided to talk to Olivia about what I'd read. I knew she'd be mad that I invaded her privacy, but I needed to know if she really meant those words.
Olivia?
When I found her, she seemed almost like the old Olivia again, but sadder.
What's up, Luce?
I...uh...
Are you okay?
Not really.

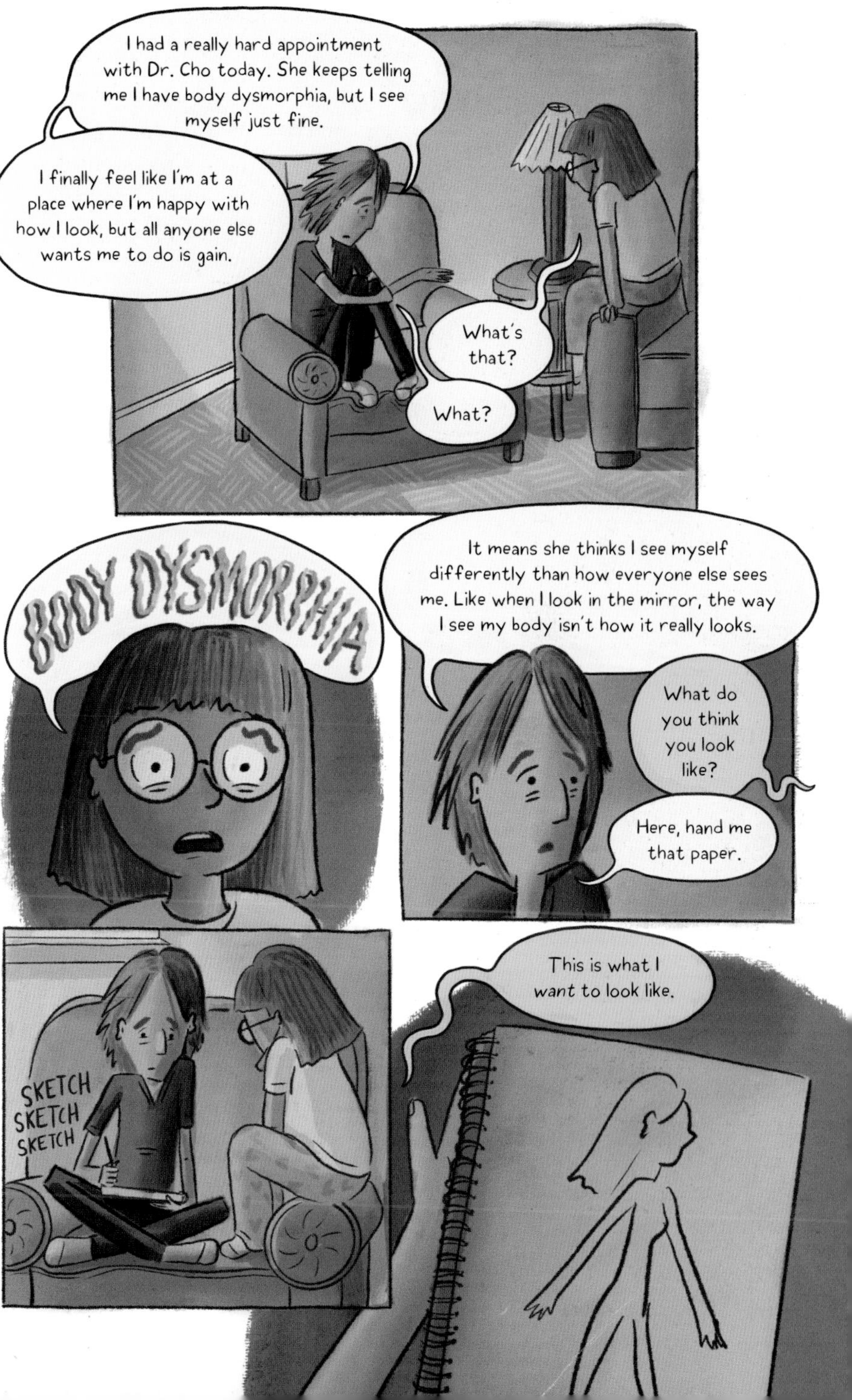
I had a really hard appointment with Dr. Cho today. She keeps telling me I have body dysmorphia, but I see myself just fine.
I finally feel like I'm at a place where I'm happy with how I look, but all anyone else wants me to do is gain.
What's that?
What?
BODY DYSMORPHIA
It means she thinks I see myself differently than how everyone else sees me. Like when I look in the mirror, the way I see my body isn't how it really looks.
What do you think you look like?
Here, hand me that paper.
SKETCH SKETCH SKETCH
This is what I want to look like.

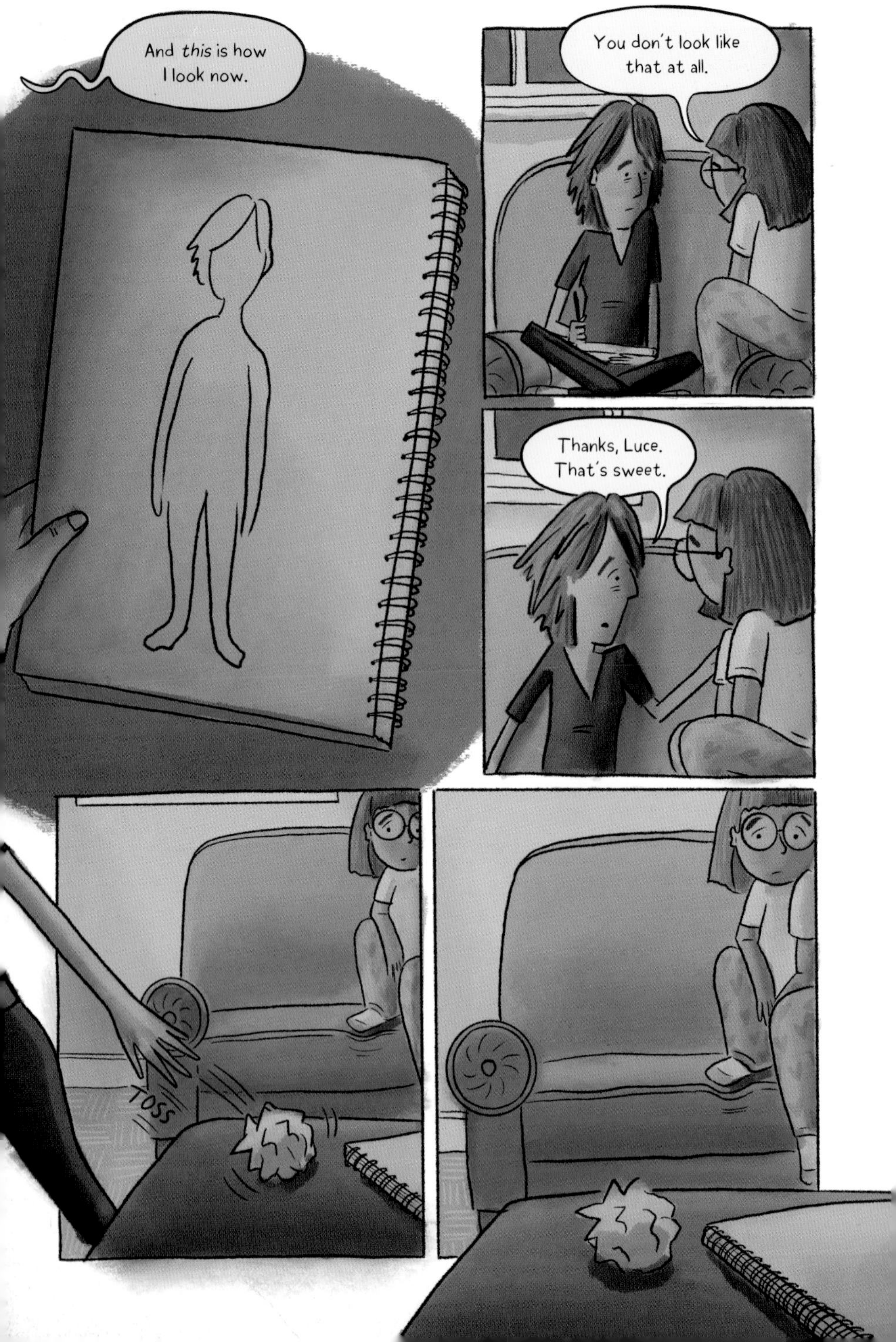

And *this* is how I look now.
You don't look like that at all.
Thanks, Luce. That's sweet.
TOSS

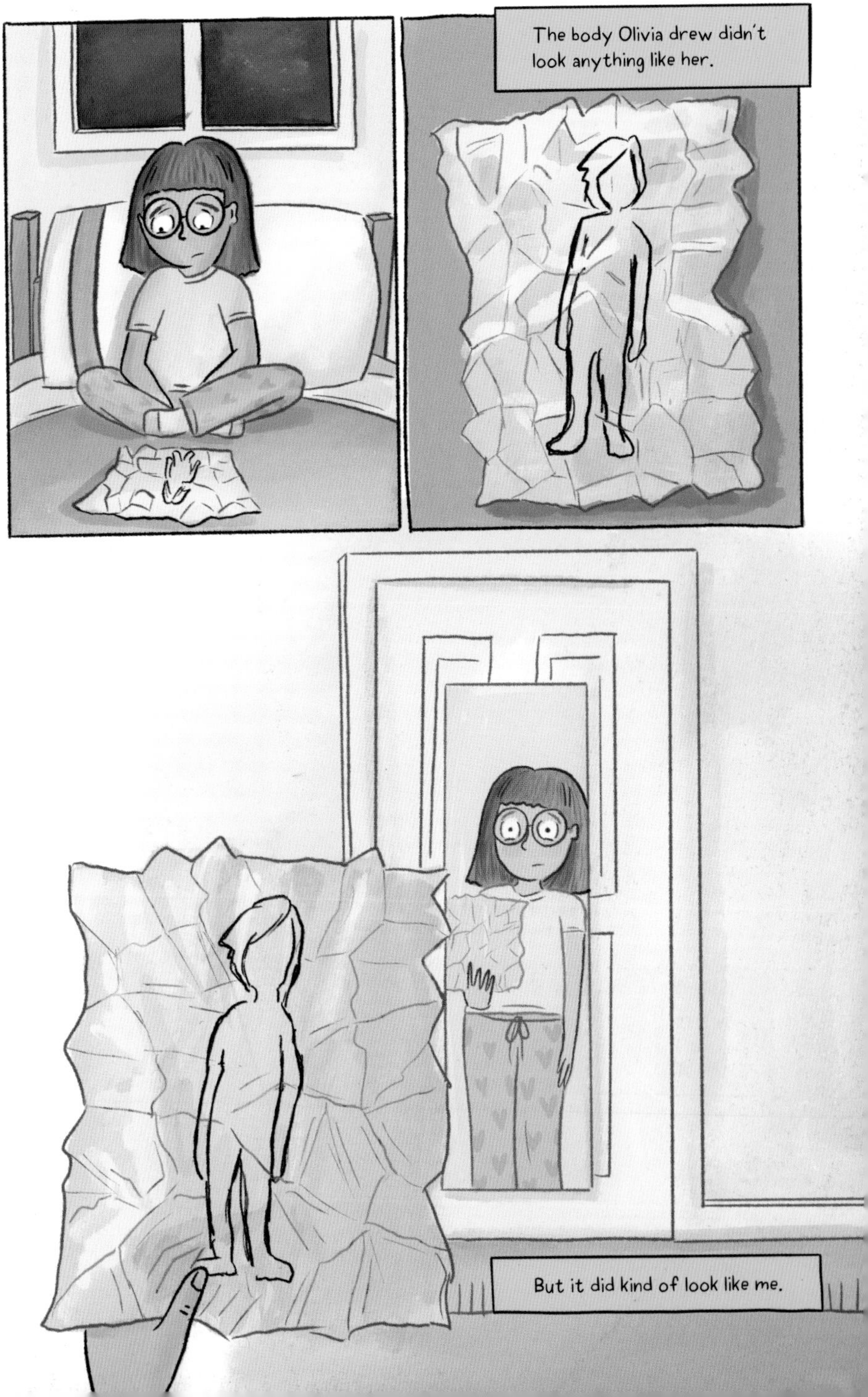
The body Olivia drew didn't look anything like her.
But it did kind of look like me.

CHAPTER 3

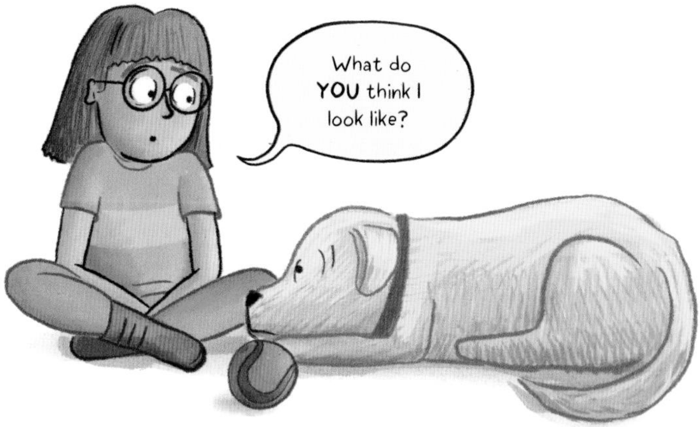
What do
YOU think I
look like?

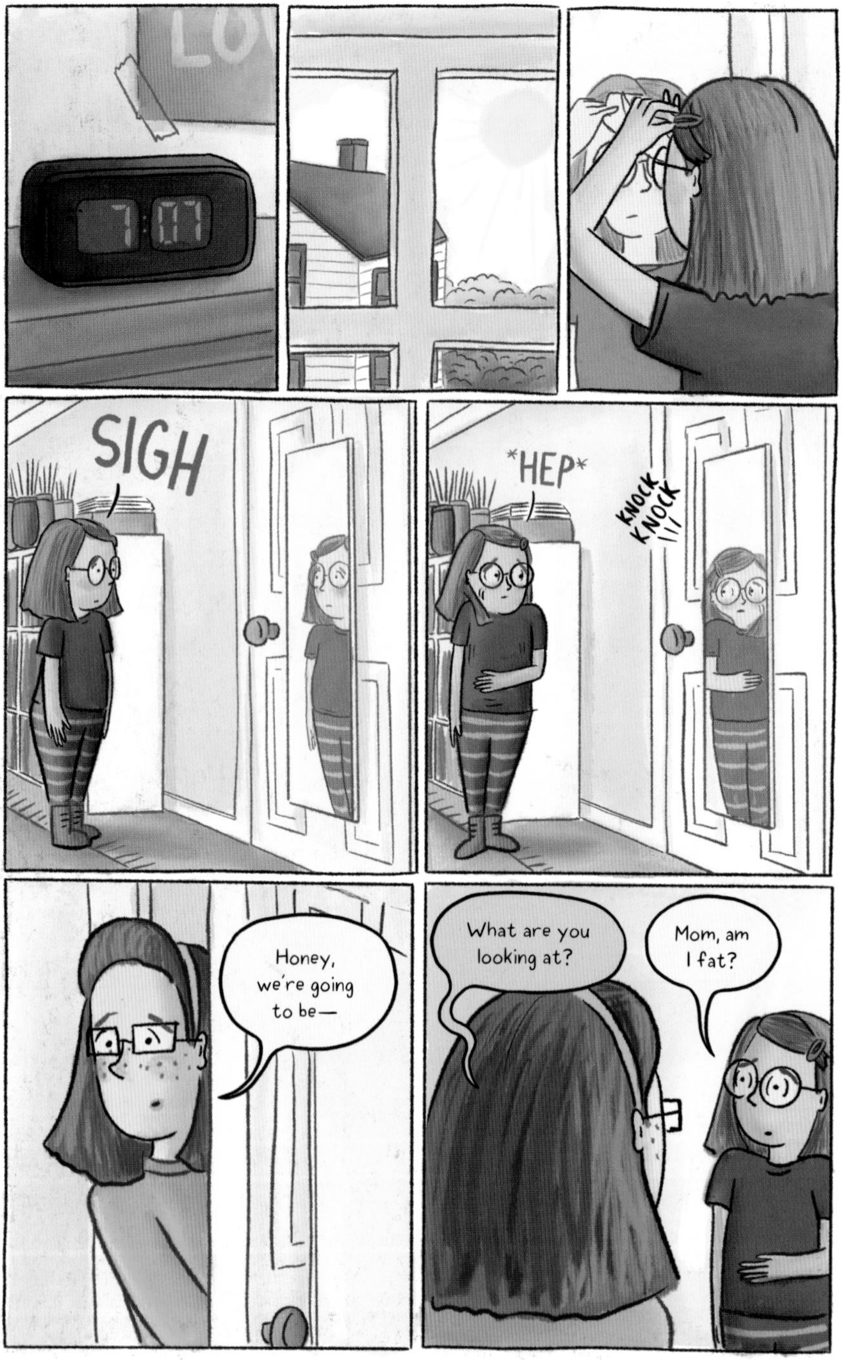
SIGH
HEP
KNOCK KNOCK
Honey, we're going to be—
What are you looking at?
Mom, am I fat?

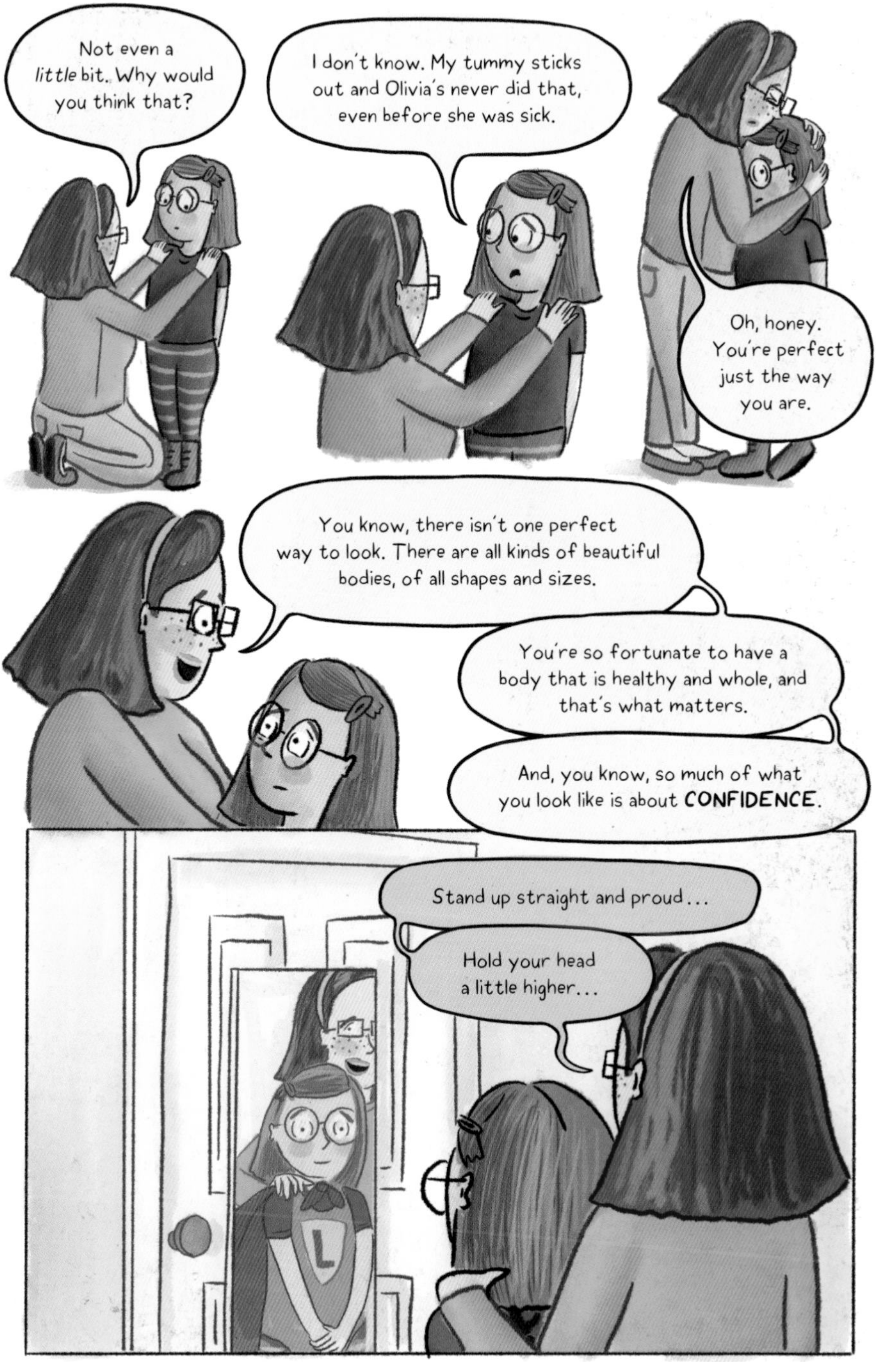
Not even a *little* bit. Why would you think that?
I don't know. My tummy sticks out and Olivia's never did that, even before she was sick.
Oh, honey. You're perfect just the way you are.
You know, there isn't one perfect way to look. There are all kinds of beautiful bodies, of all shapes and sizes.
You're so fortunate to have a body that is healthy and whole, and that's what matters.
And, you know, so much of what you look like is about **CONFIDENCE**.
Stand up straight and proud...
Hold your head a little higher...
L

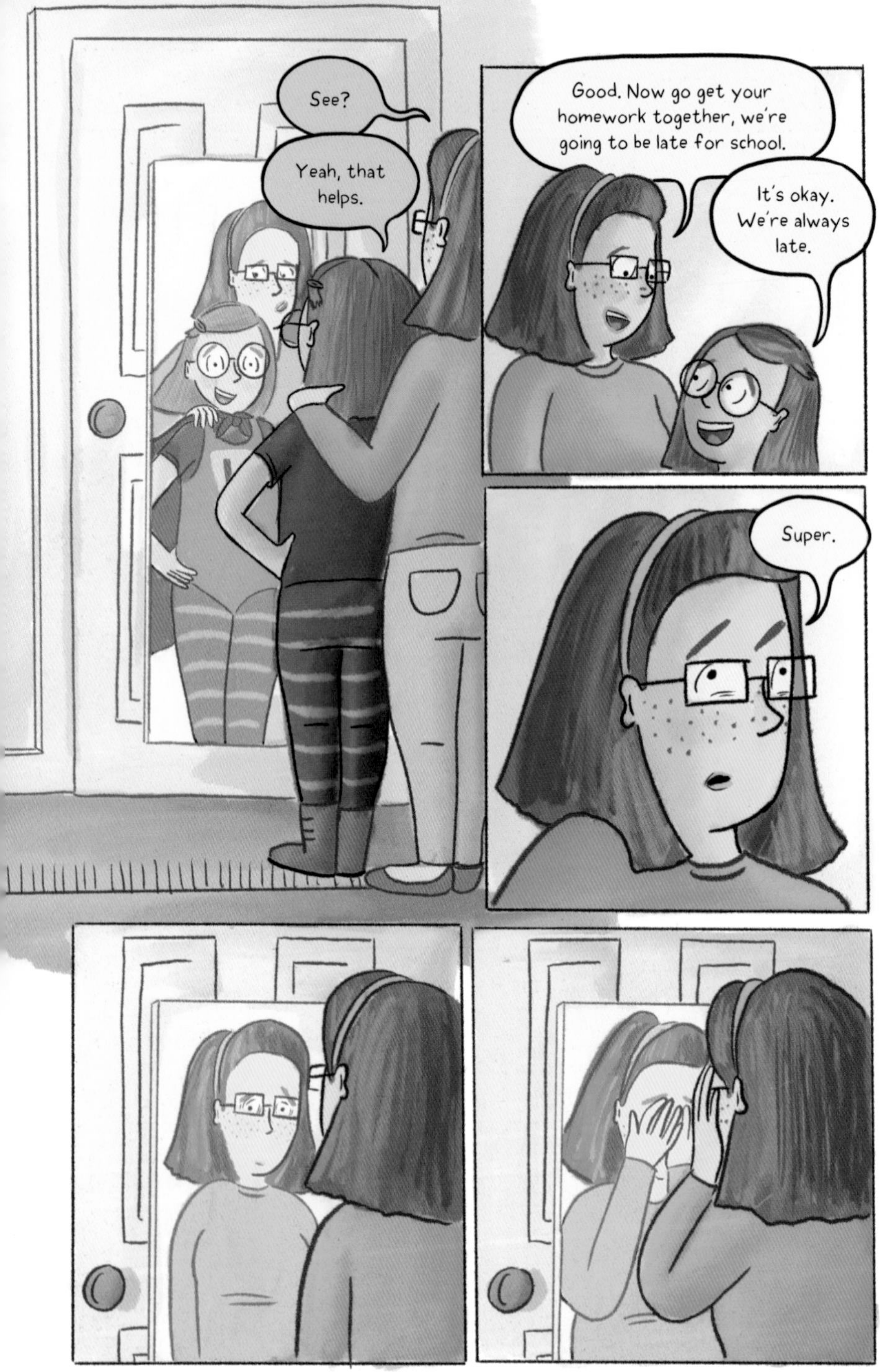
See?
Yeah, that helps.
Good. Now go get your homework together, we're going to be late for school.
It's okay. We're always late.
Super.

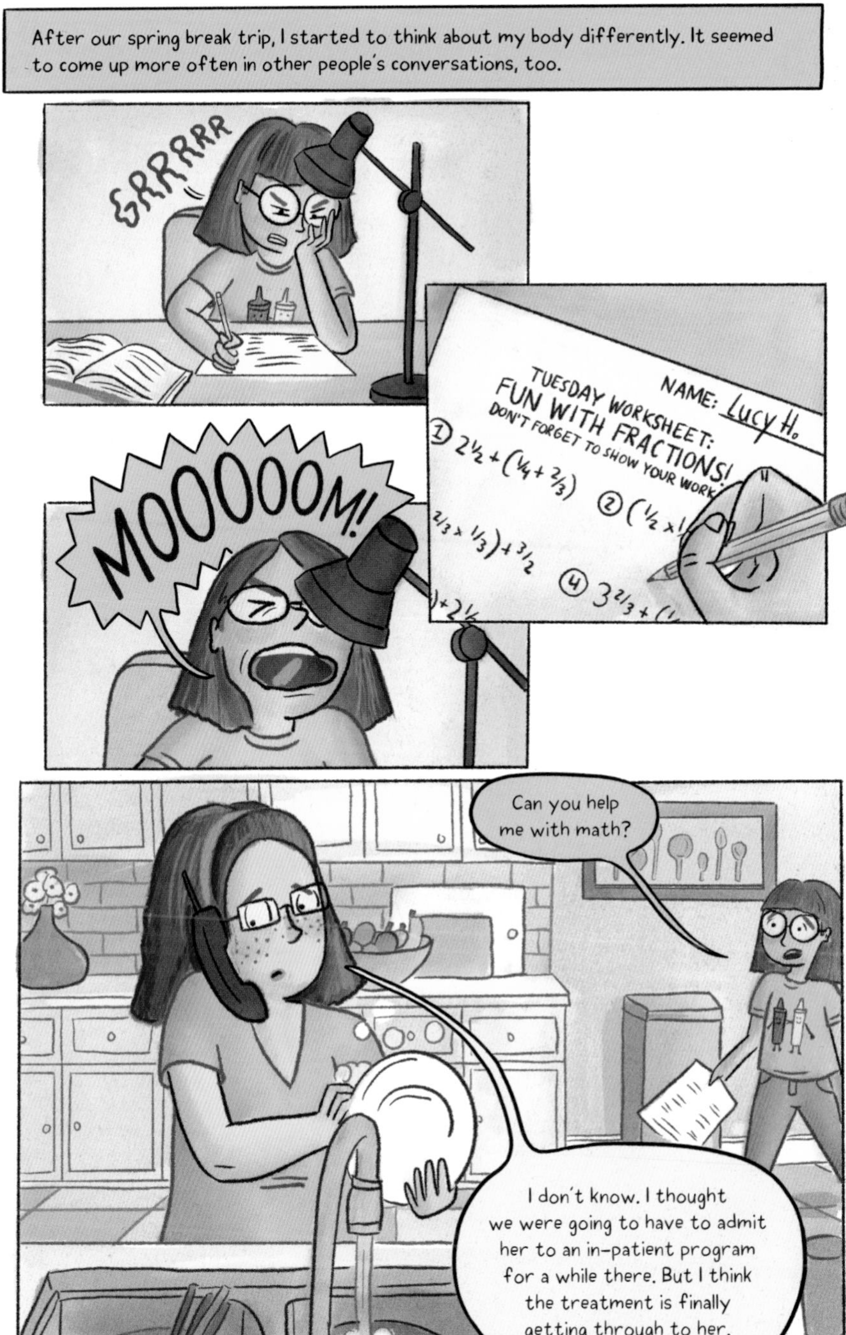
After our spring break trip, I started to think about my body differently. It seemed to come up more often in other people's conversations, too.
GRRRRR
NAME: Lucy H.
TUESDAY WORKSHEET:
FUN WITH FRACTIONS!
DON'T FORGET TO SHOW YOUR WORK
MOOOOOM!
Can you help me with math?
I don't know. I thought we were going to have to admit her to an in-patient program for a while there. But I think the treatment is finally getting through to her.

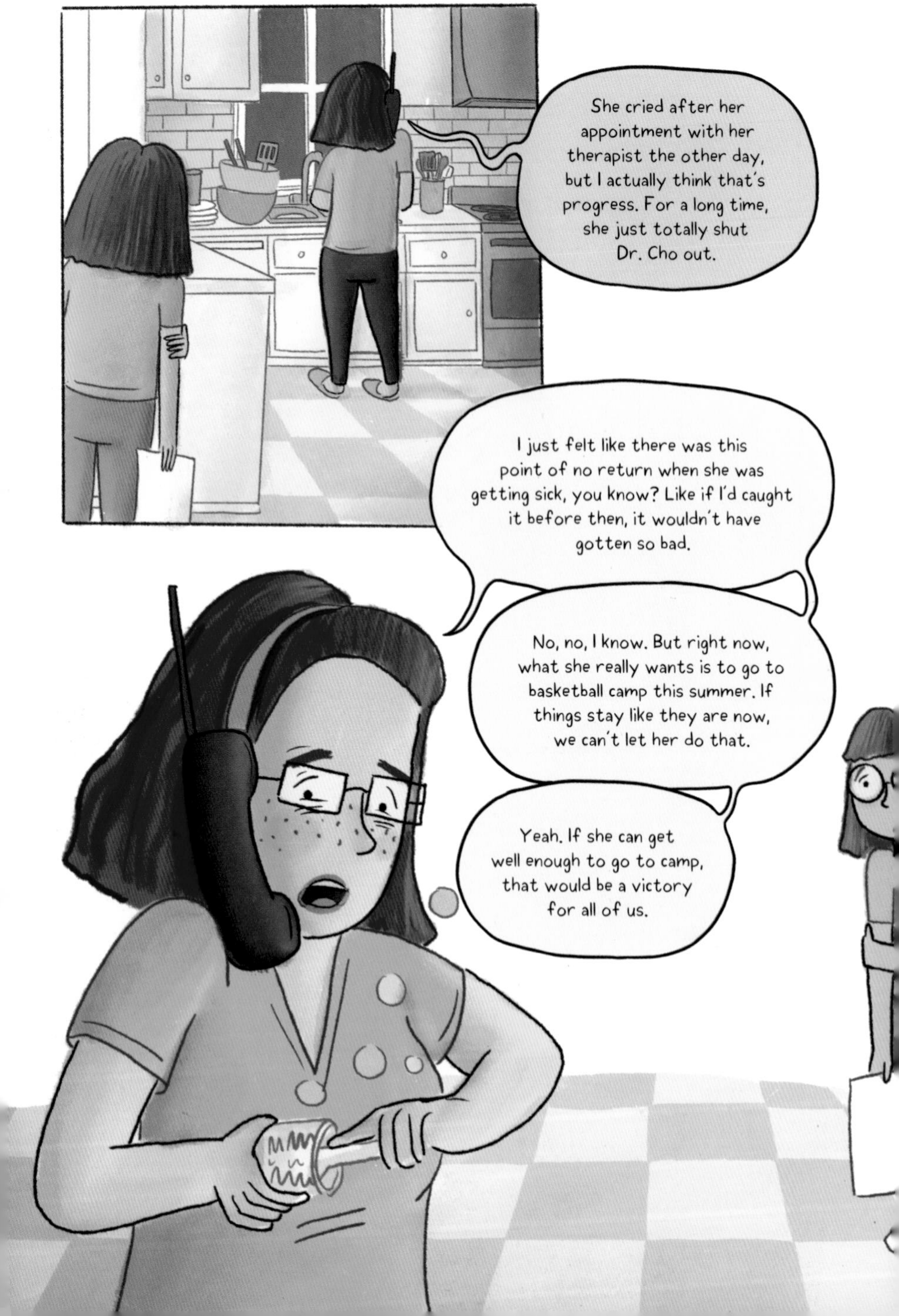
She cried after her appointment with her therapist the other day, but I actually think that's progress. For a long time, she just totally shut Dr. Cho out.
I just felt like there was this point of no return when she was getting sick, you know? Like if I'd caught it before then, it wouldn't have gotten so bad.
No, no, I know. But right now, what she really wants is to go to basketball camp this summer. If things stay like they are now, we can't let her do that.
Yeah. If she can get well enough to go to camp, that would be a victory for all of us.

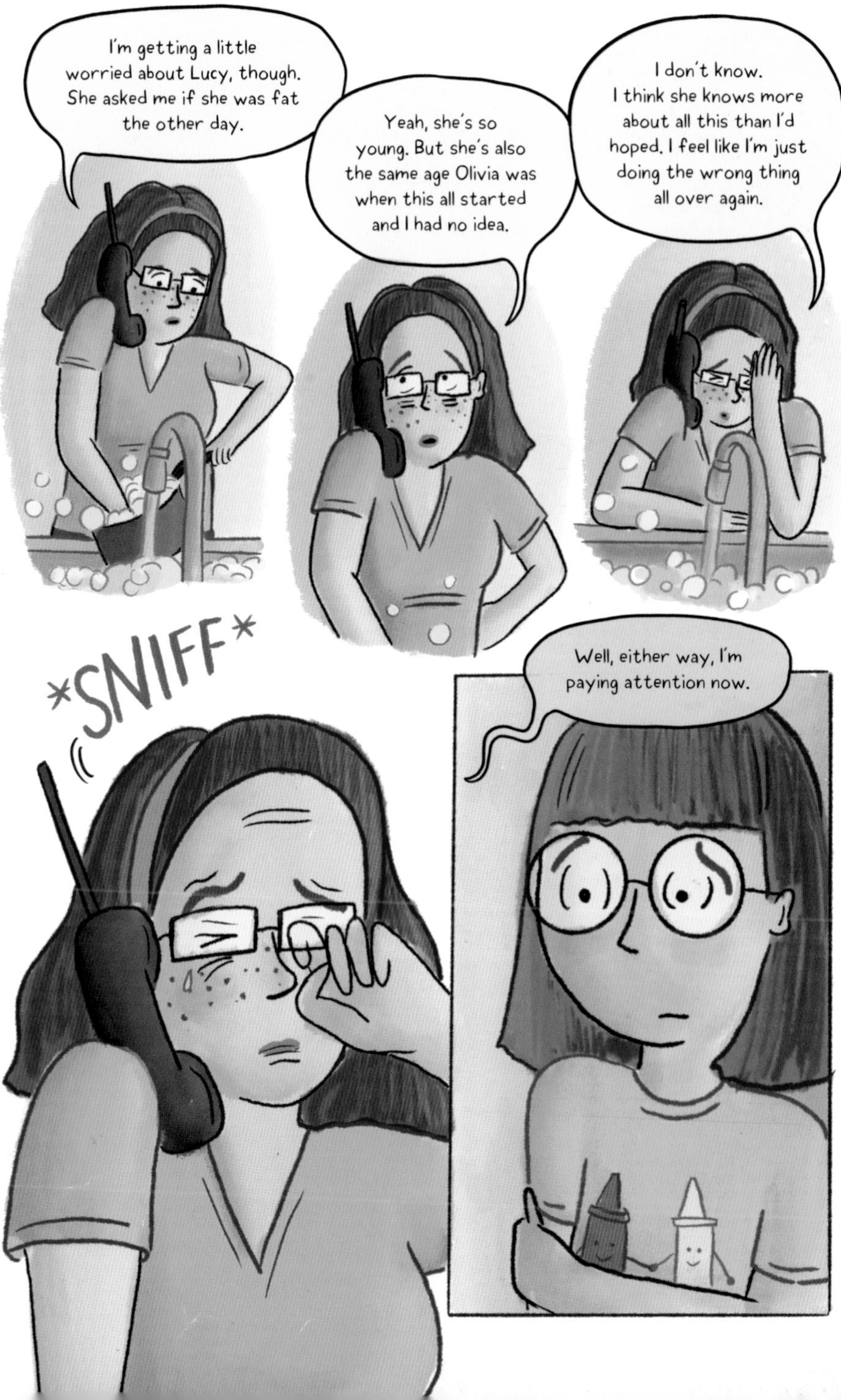

I'm getting a little worried about Lucy, though. She asked me if she was fat the other day.
Yeah, she's so young. But she's also the same age Olivia was when this all started and I had no idea.
I don't know. I think she knows more about all this than I'd hoped. I feel like I'm just doing the wrong thing all over again.
SNIFF
Well, either way, I'm paying attention now.

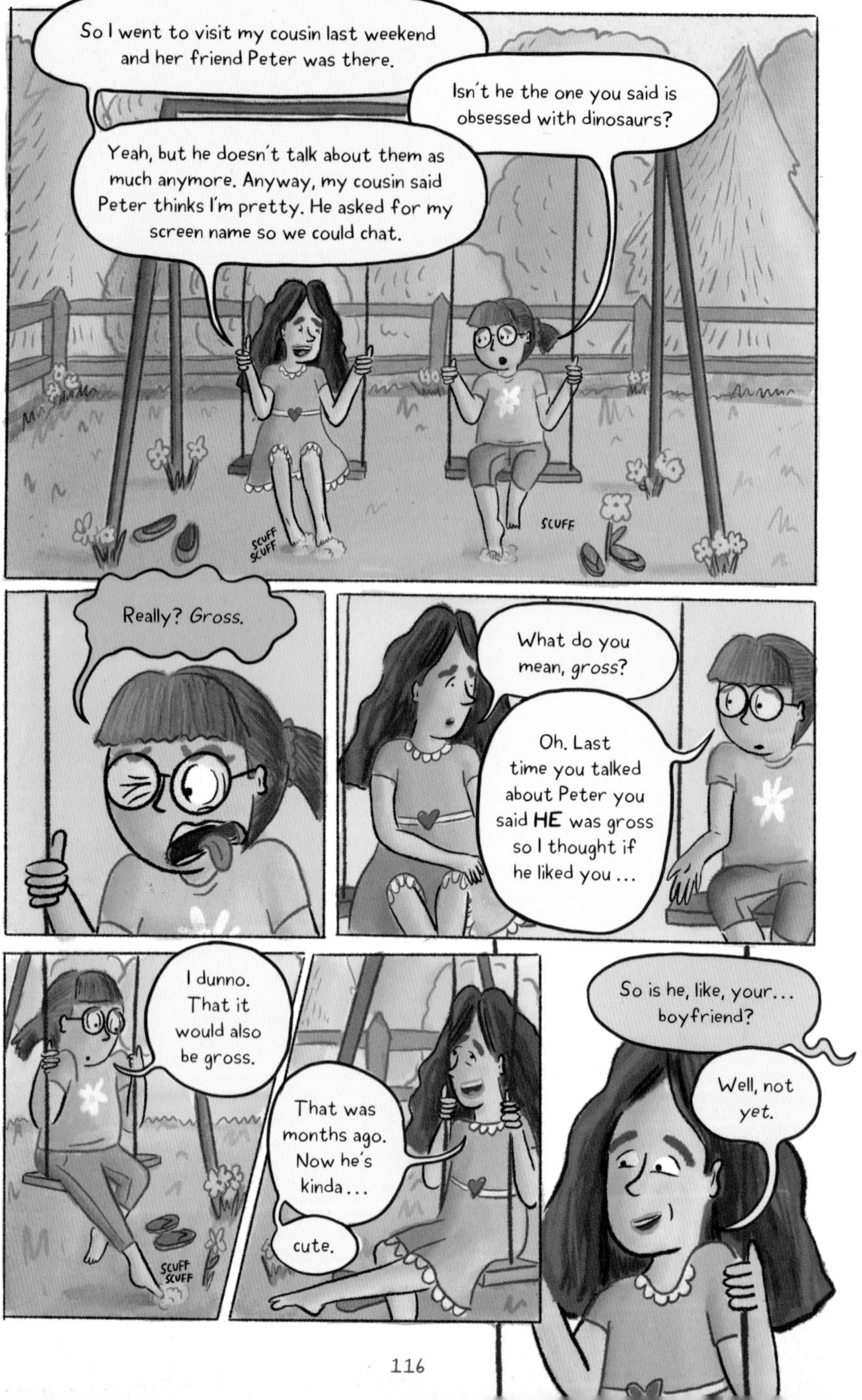
So I went to visit my cousin last weekend and her friend Peter was there.
Isn't he the one you said is obsessed with dinosaurs?
Yeah, but he doesn't talk about them as much anymore. Anyway, my cousin said Peter thinks I'm pretty. He asked for my screen name so we could chat.
SCUFF SCUFF
SCUFF
Really? *Gross.*
What do you mean, *gross*?
Oh. Last time you talked about Peter you said **HE** was gross so I thought if he liked you . . .
I dunno. That it would also be gross.
SCUFF SCUFF
That was months ago. Now he's kinda . . .
cute.
So is he, like, your . . . boyfriend?
Well, not *yet*.

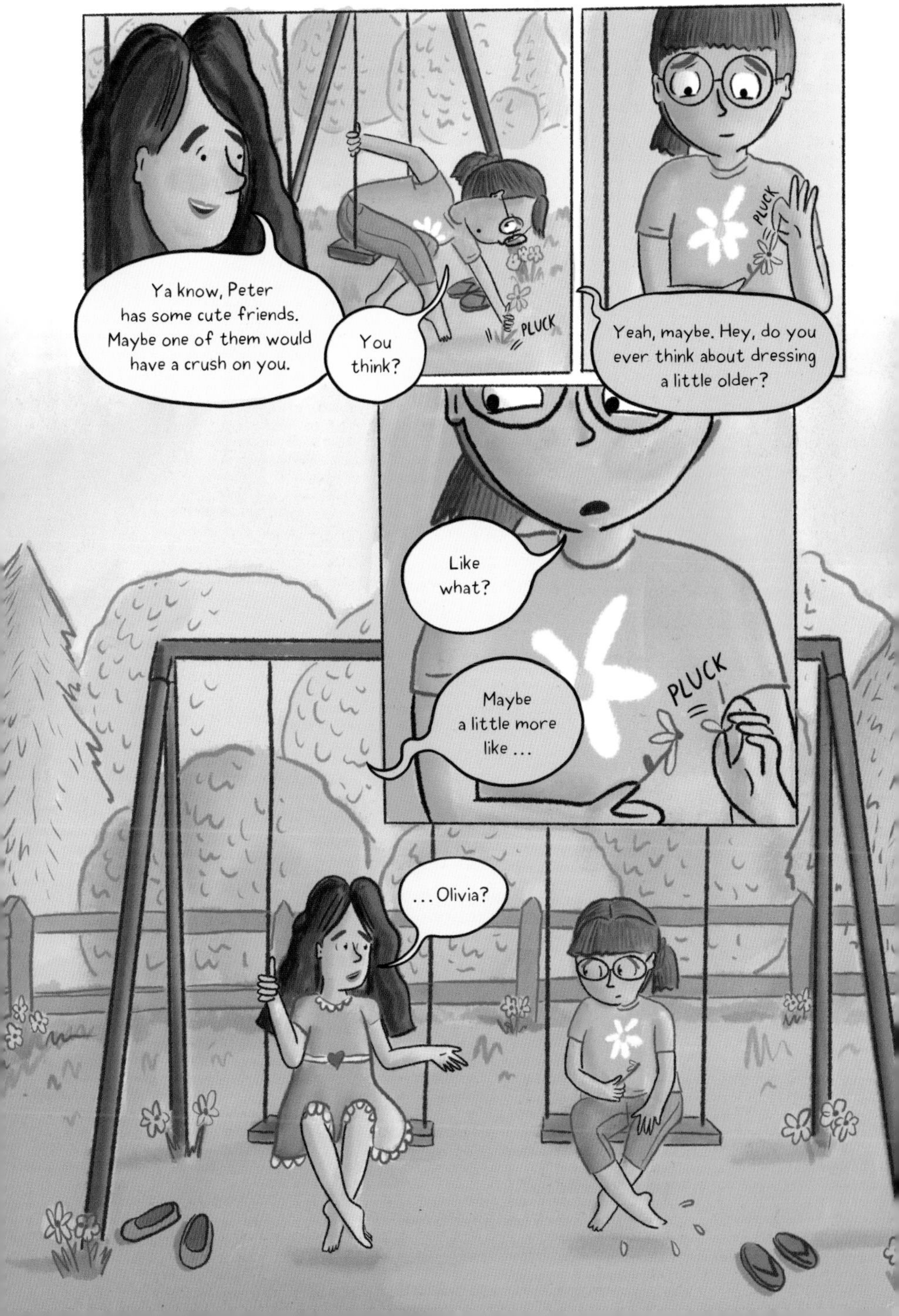

Ya know, Peter has some cute friends. Maybe one of them would have a crush on you.
You think?
PLUCK
PLUCK
Yeah, maybe. Hey, do you ever think about dressing a little older?
Like what?
PLUCK
Maybe a little more like . . .
. . . Olivia?

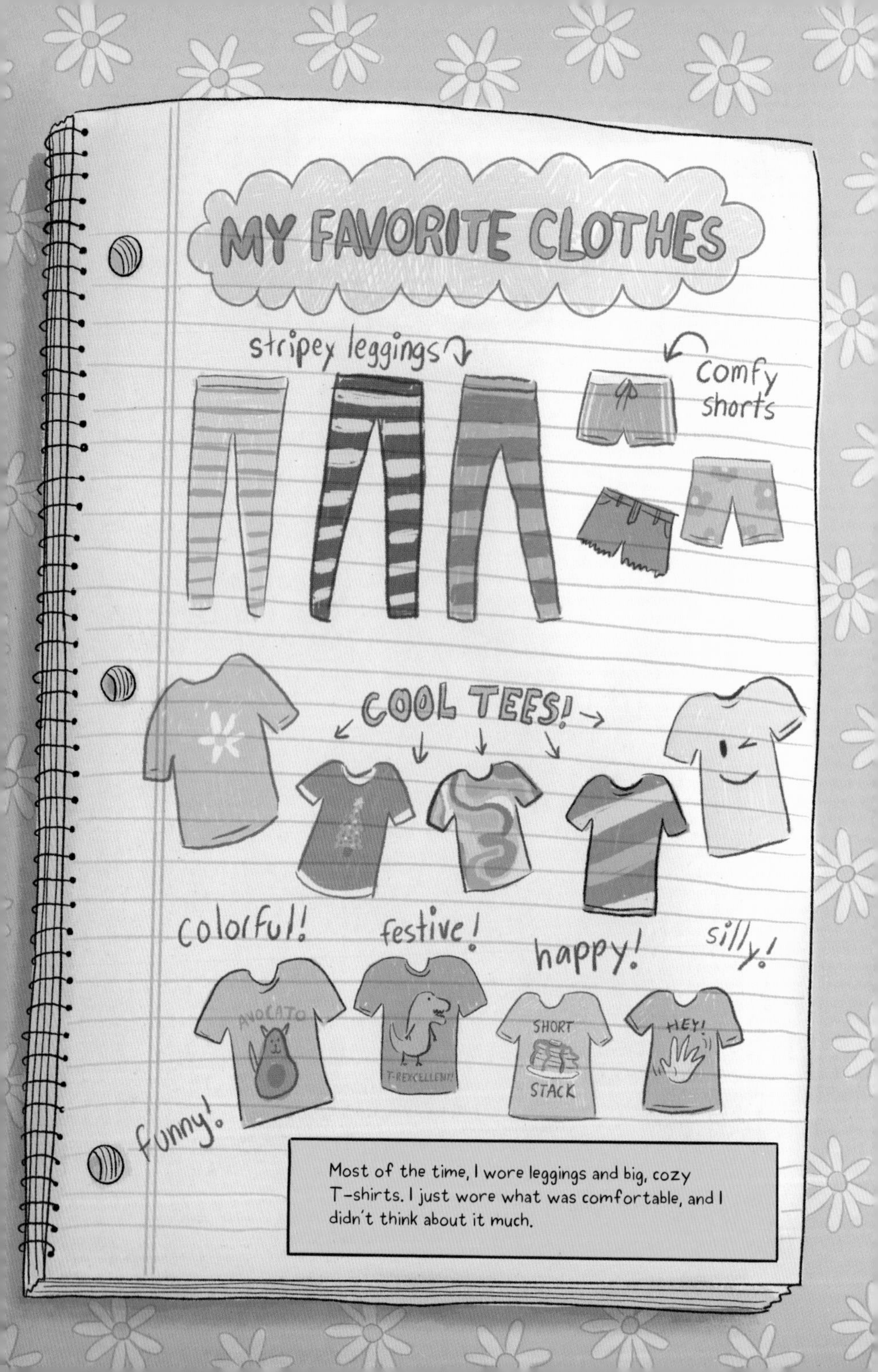
MY FAVORITE CLOTHES
stripey leggings
comfy shorts
COOL TEES!
colorful!
festive!
happy!
silly!
AVOCATO
T-REXCELLENT!
SHORT STACK
HEY!
funny!
Most of the time, I wore leggings and big, cozy T-shirts. I just wore what was comfortable, and I didn't think about it much.

Old Olivia wore all the same stuff as me, but New Olivia's wardrobe was confusing. Before, I borrowed her stuff all the time. But now when I tried on her clothes, nothing fit right. I looked like a little kid playing dress-up.

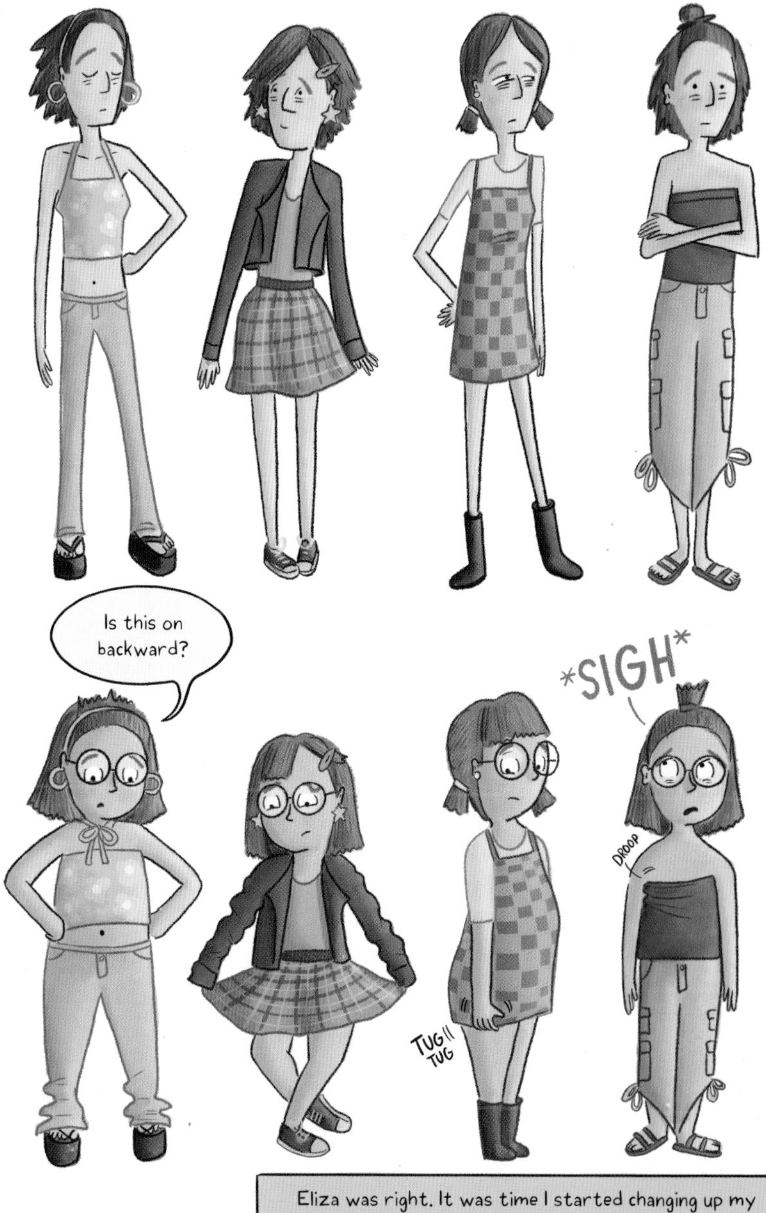
Is this on backward?
SIGH
DROOP
TUG TUG

Eliza was right. It was time I started changing up my look. I just needed to find my own way to do it.

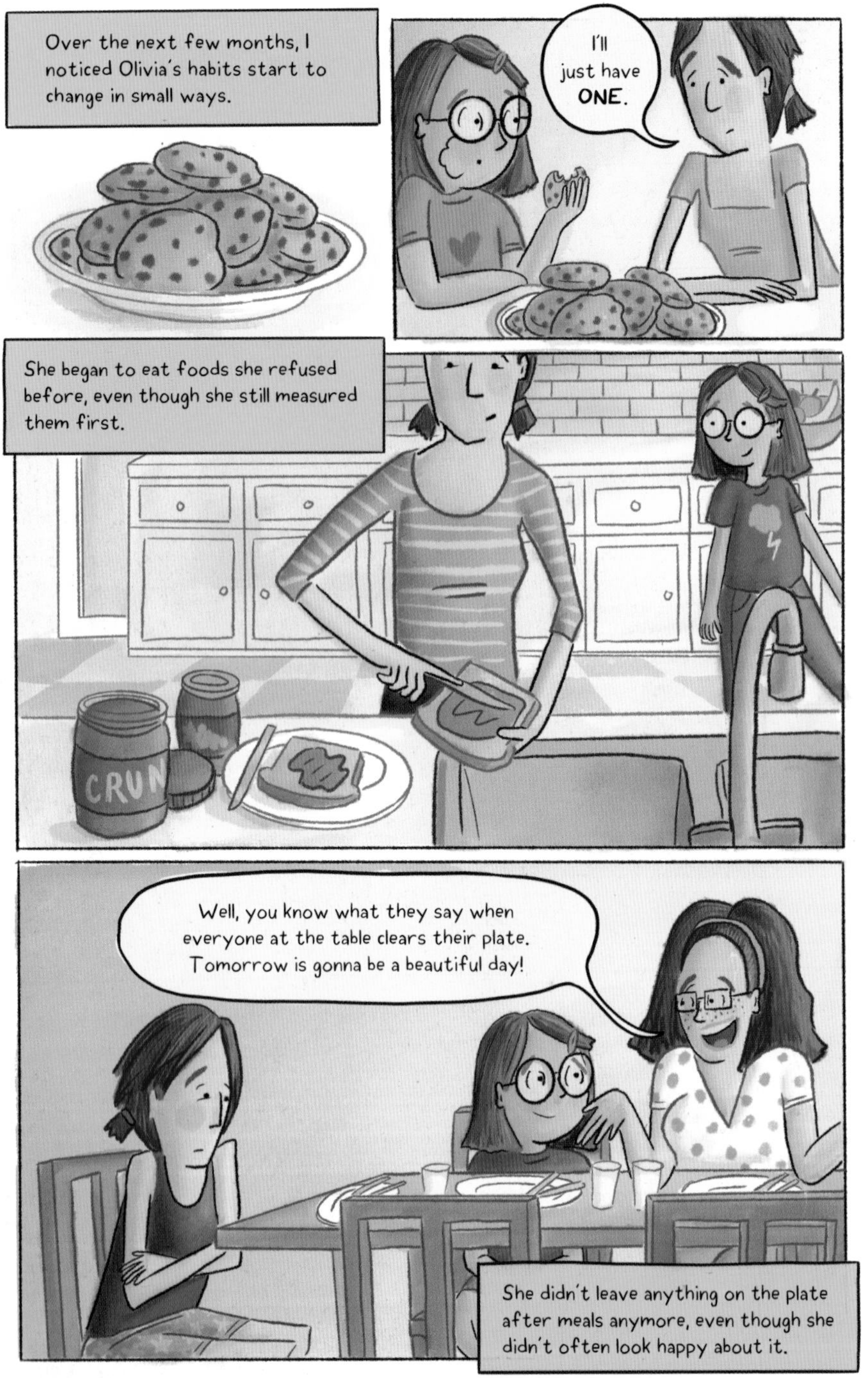
Over the next few months, I noticed Olivia's habits start to change in small ways.
I'll just have ONE.
She began to eat foods she refused before, even though she still measured them first.
CRUN
Well, you know what they say when everyone at the table clears their plate. Tomorrow is gonna be a beautiful day!
She didn't leave anything on the plate after meals anymore, even though she didn't often look happy about it.

HMMMPH

Sometimes, it seemed like she was getting sick all over again, but Mom said Olivia's brain and body each had to get better in their own ways and on their own time, and it wasn't easy.

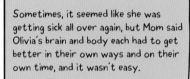

That kind of progress could be frustrating, and we needed to be patient and help her through it.

AAARGHH!

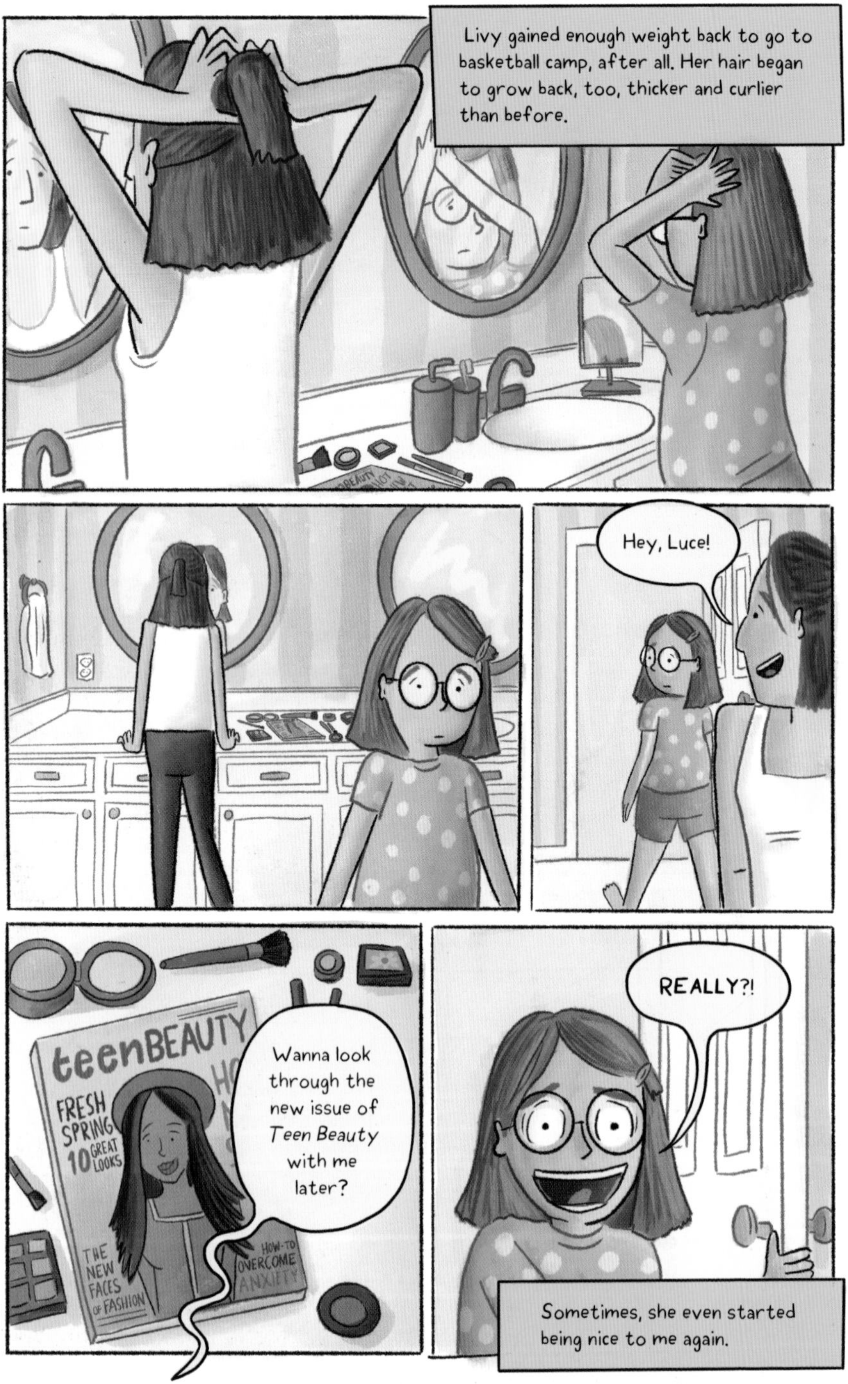
Livy gained enough weight back to go to basketball camp, after all. Her hair began to grow back, too, thicker and curlier than before.
Hey, Luce!
teenBEAUTY
FRESH SPRING 10 GREAT LOOKS
THE NEW FACES OF FASHION
HOW-TO OVERCOME ANXIETY
Wanna look through the new issue of *Teen Beauty* with me later?
REALLY?!
Sometimes, she even started being nice to me again.

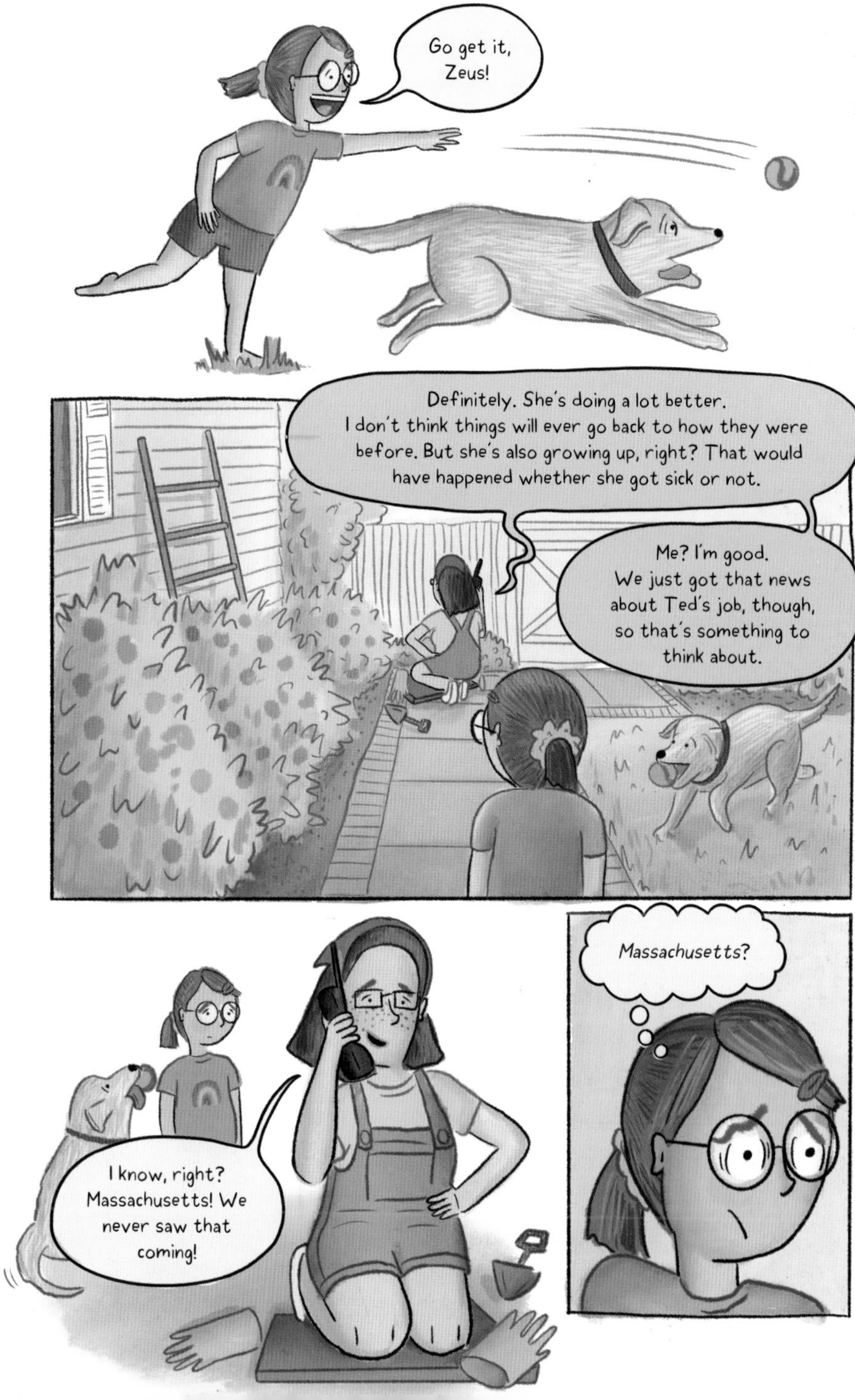
Go get it, Zeus!
Definitely. She's doing a lot better. I don't think things will ever go back to how they were before. But she's also growing up, right? That would have happened whether she got sick or not.
Me? I'm good. We just got that news about Ted's job, though, so that's something to think about.
I know, right? Massachusetts! We never saw that coming!
Massachusetts?

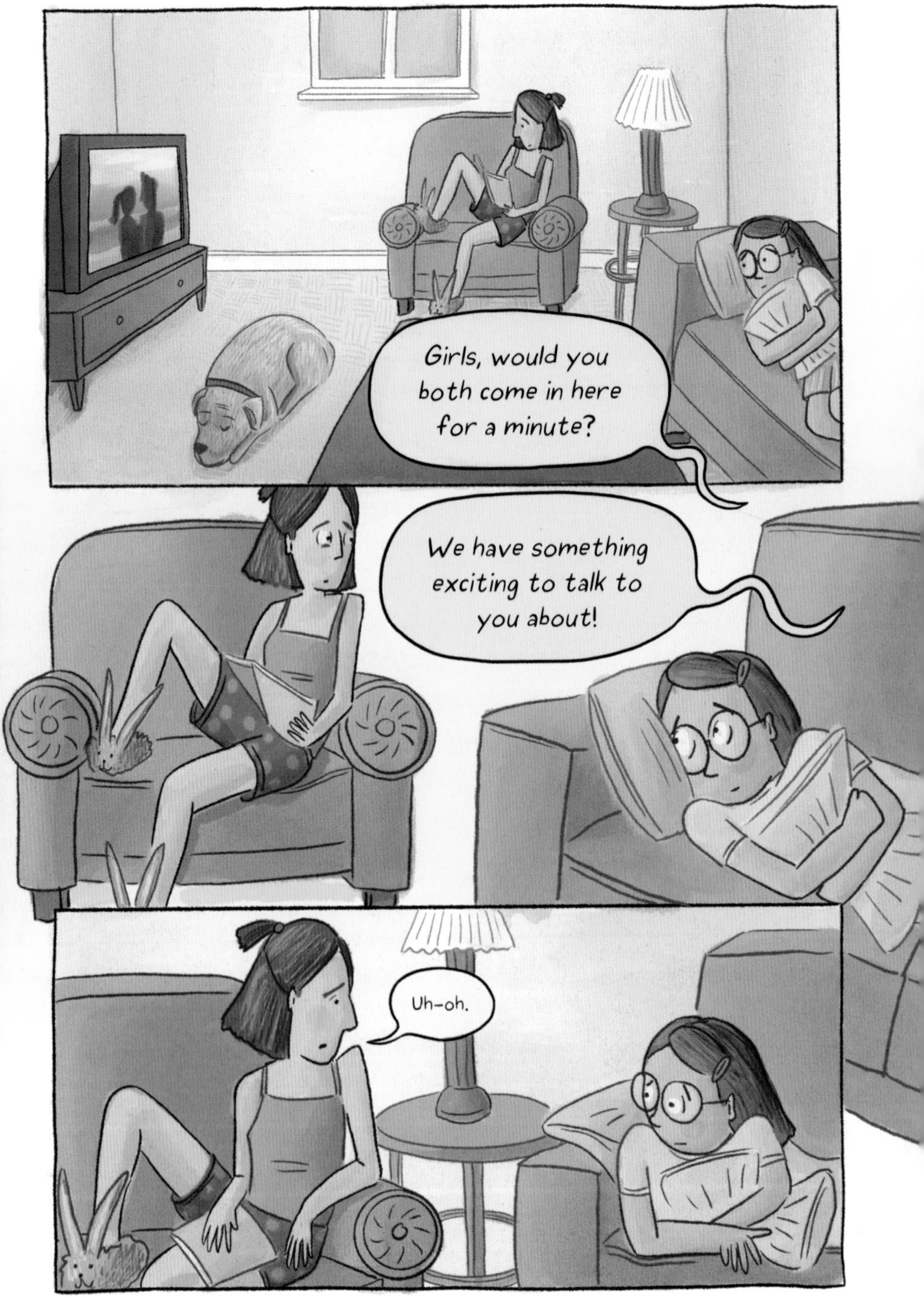
Girls, would you both come in here for a minute?
We have something exciting to talk to you about!
Uh-oh.

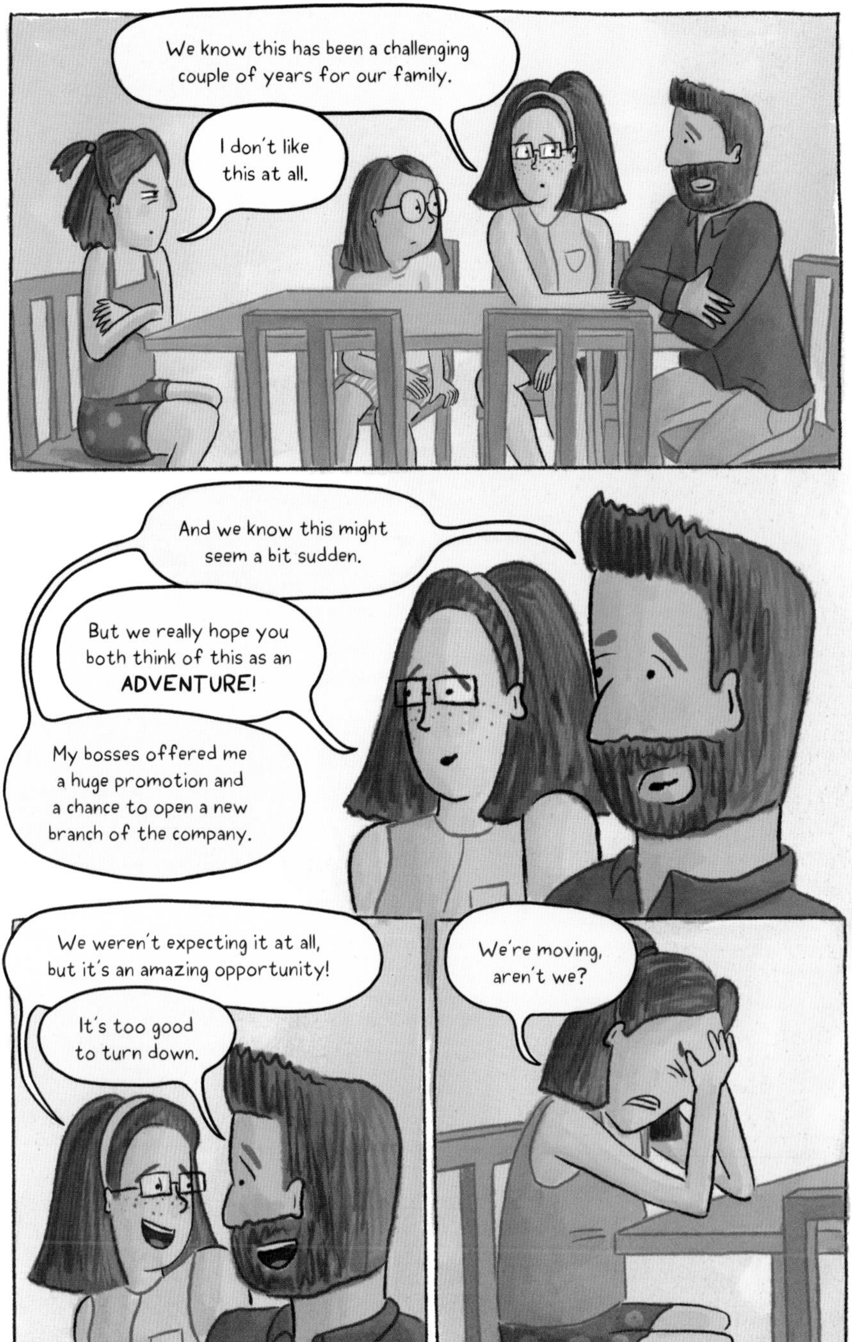
We know this has been a challenging couple of years for our family.
I don't like this at all.
And we know this might seem a bit sudden.
But we really hope you both think of this as an ADVENTURE!
My bosses offered me a huge promotion and a chance to open a new branch of the company.
We weren't expecting it at all, but it's an amazing opportunity!
It's too good to turn down.
We're moving, aren't we?

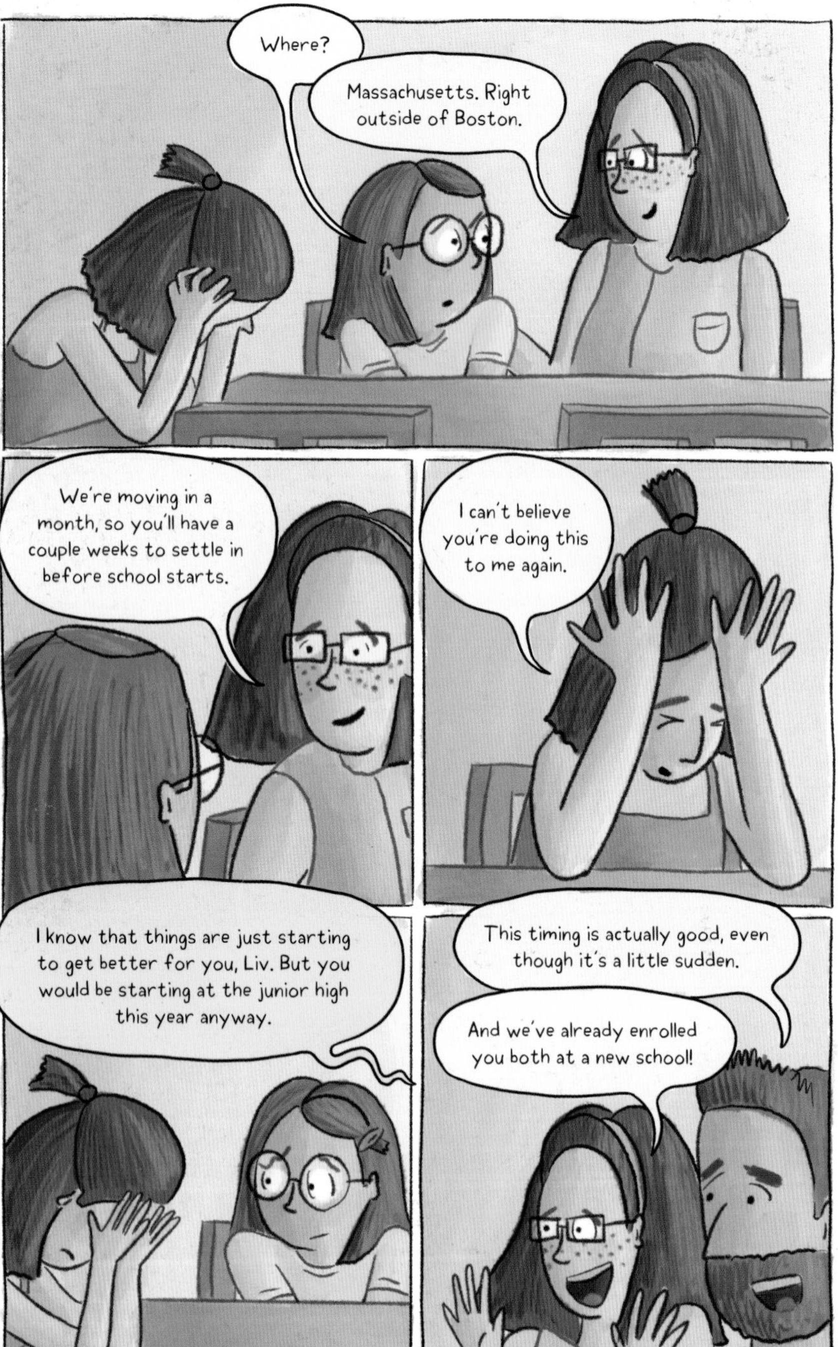
Where?
Massachusetts. Right outside of Boston.
We're moving in a month, so you'll have a couple weeks to settle in before school starts.
I can't believe you're doing this to me again.
I know that things are just starting to get better for you, Liv. But you would be starting at the junior high this year anyway.
This timing is actually good, even though it's a little sudden.
And we've already enrolled you both at a new school!

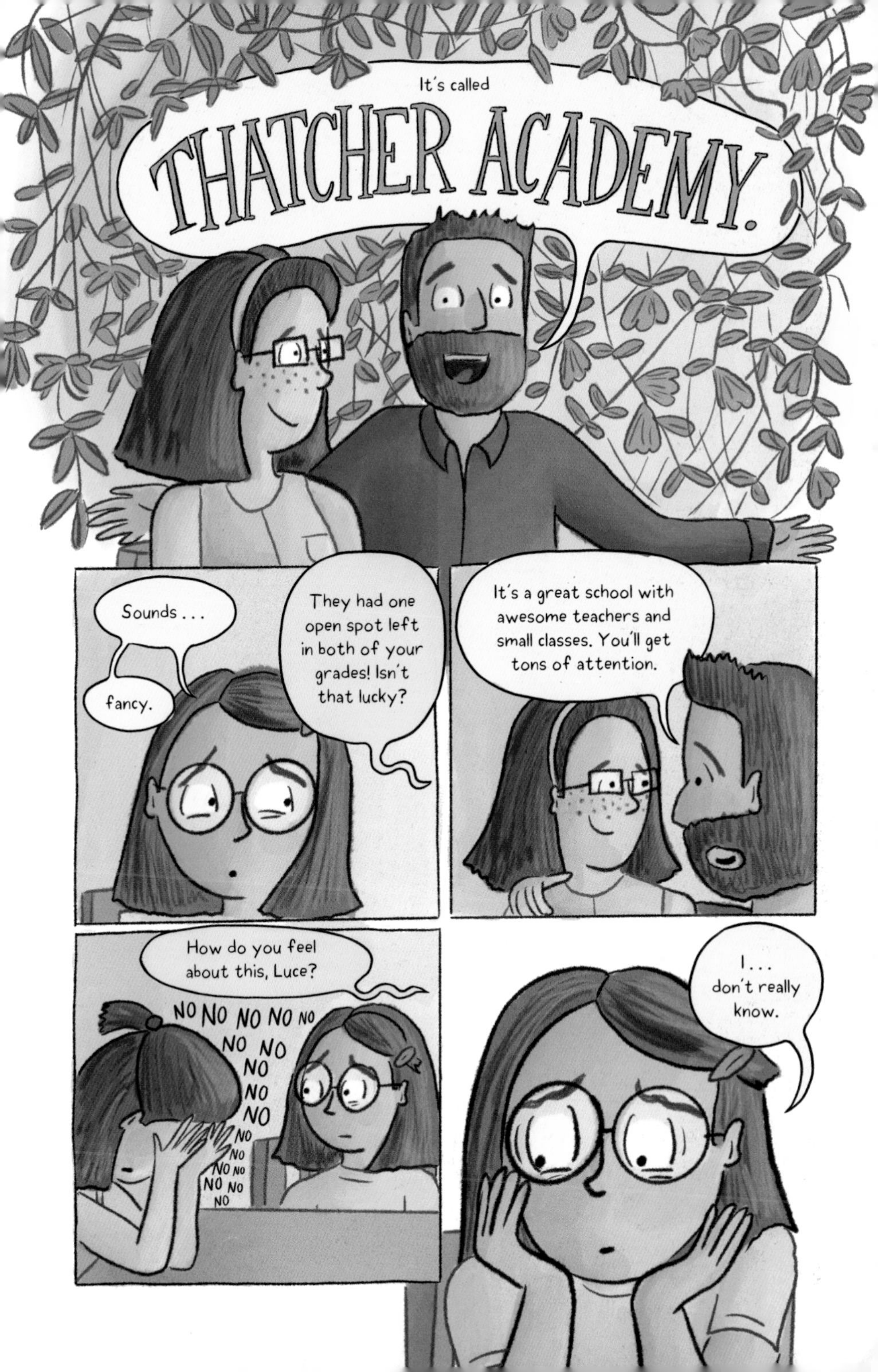
It's called
THATCHER ACADEMY.
Sounds . . .
fancy.
They had one open spot left in both of your grades! Isn't that lucky?
It's a great school with awesome teachers and small classes. You'll get tons of attention.
How do you feel about this, Luce?
NO NO NO NO NO NO NO NO NO NO NO NO NO NO NO NO NO
I . . . don't really know.

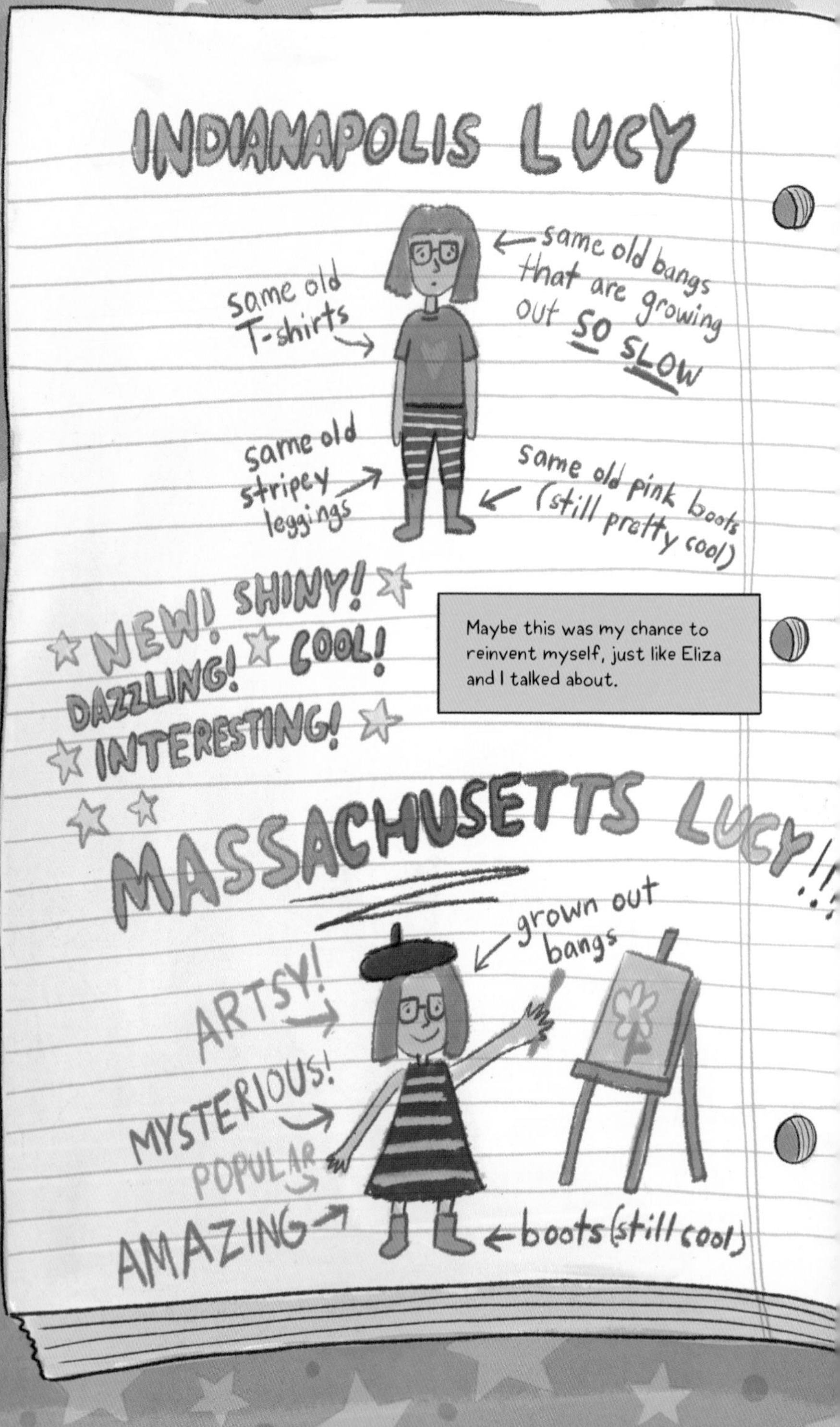
INDIANAPOLIS LUCY
same old bangs that are growing out SO SLOW
same old T-shirts
same old stripey leggings
same old pink boots (still pretty cool)
NEW! SHINY! DAZZLING! COOL! INTERESTING!
Maybe this was my chance to reinvent myself, just like Eliza and I talked about.
MASSACHUSETTS LUCY!!!
grown out bangs
ARTSY!
MYSTERIOUS!
POPULAR
AMAZING
boots (still cool)

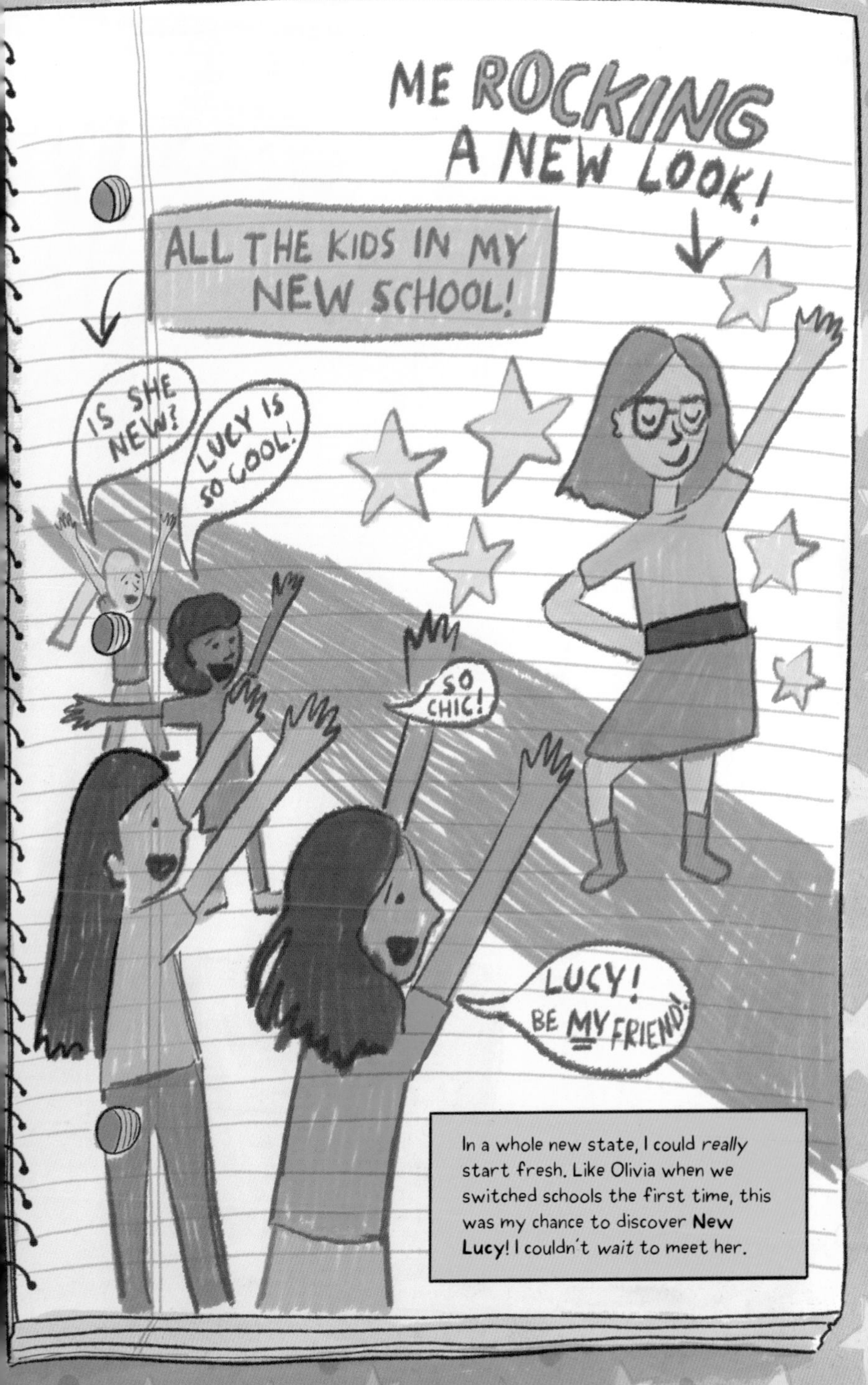
ME ROCKING A NEW LOOK!
ALL THE KIDS IN MY NEW SCHOOL!
IS SHE NEW?
LUCY IS SO COOL!
SO CHIC!
LUCY! BE MY FRIEND!
In a whole new state, I could really start fresh. Like Olivia when we switched schools the first time, this was my chance to discover New Lucy! I couldn't wait to meet her.

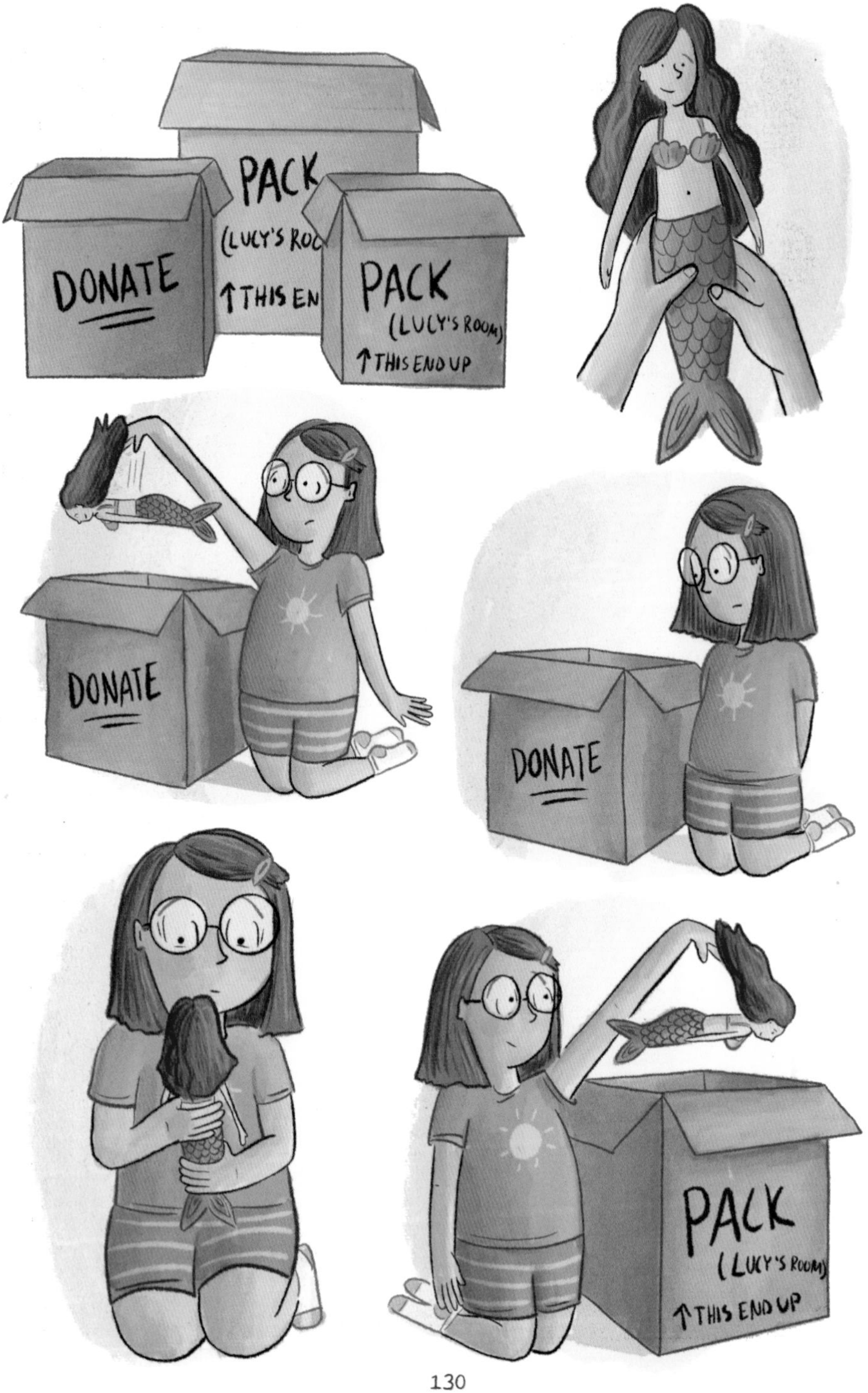
DONATE
PACK
PACK
(LUCY'S ROOM)
↑THIS END UP
DONATE
DONATE
PACK
(LUCY'S ROOM)
↑THIS END UP

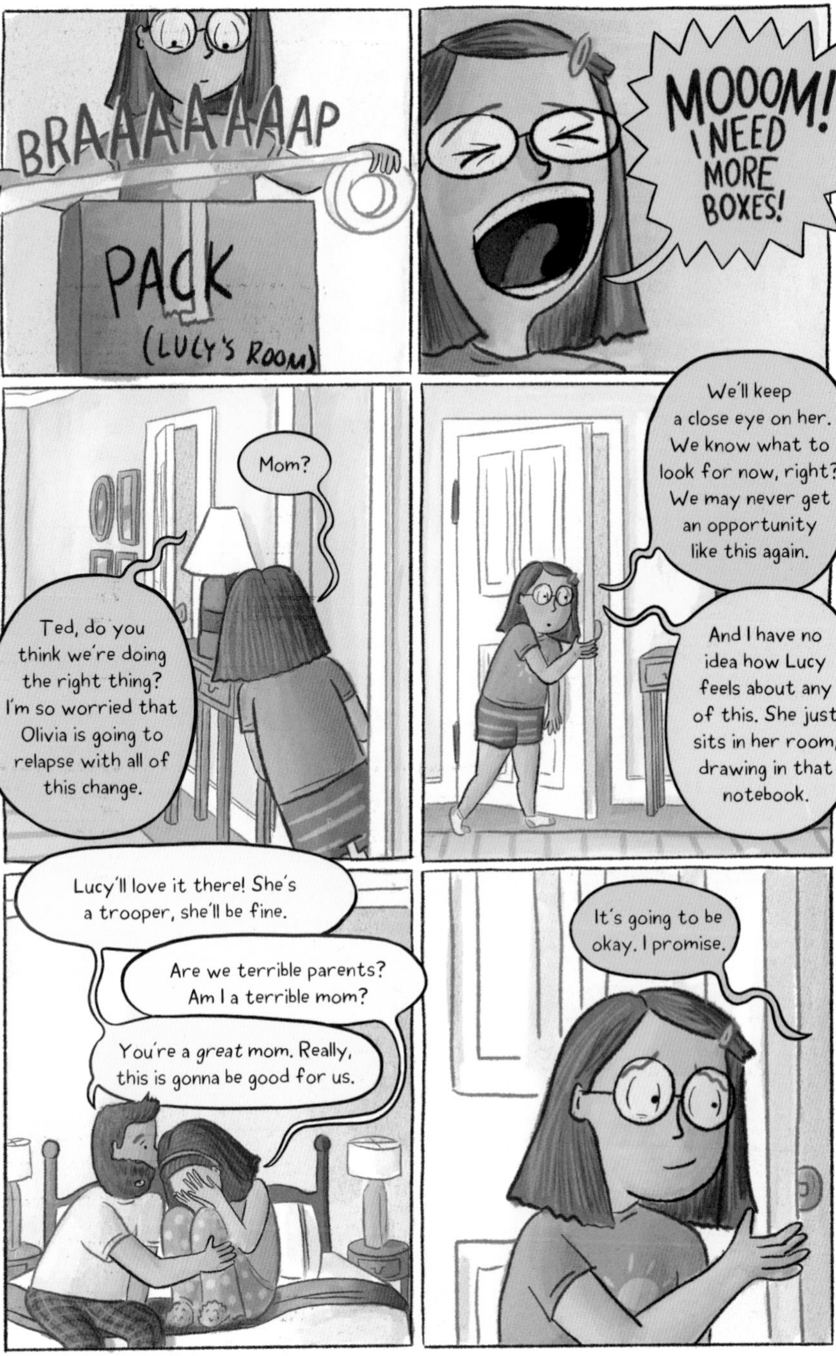
BRAAAAAAAP
PACK
(LUCY'S ROOM)
MOOOM! I NEED MORE BOXES!
Mom?
Ted, do you think we're doing the right thing? I'm so worried that Olivia is going to relapse with all of this change.
We'll keep a close eye on her. We know what to look for now, right? We may never get an opportunity like this again.
And I have no idea how Lucy feels about any of this. She just sits in her room, drawing in that notebook.
Lucy'll love it there! She's a trooper, she'll be fine.
Are we terrible parents? Am I a terrible mom?
You're a *great* mom. Really, this is gonna be good for us.
It's going to be okay. I promise.

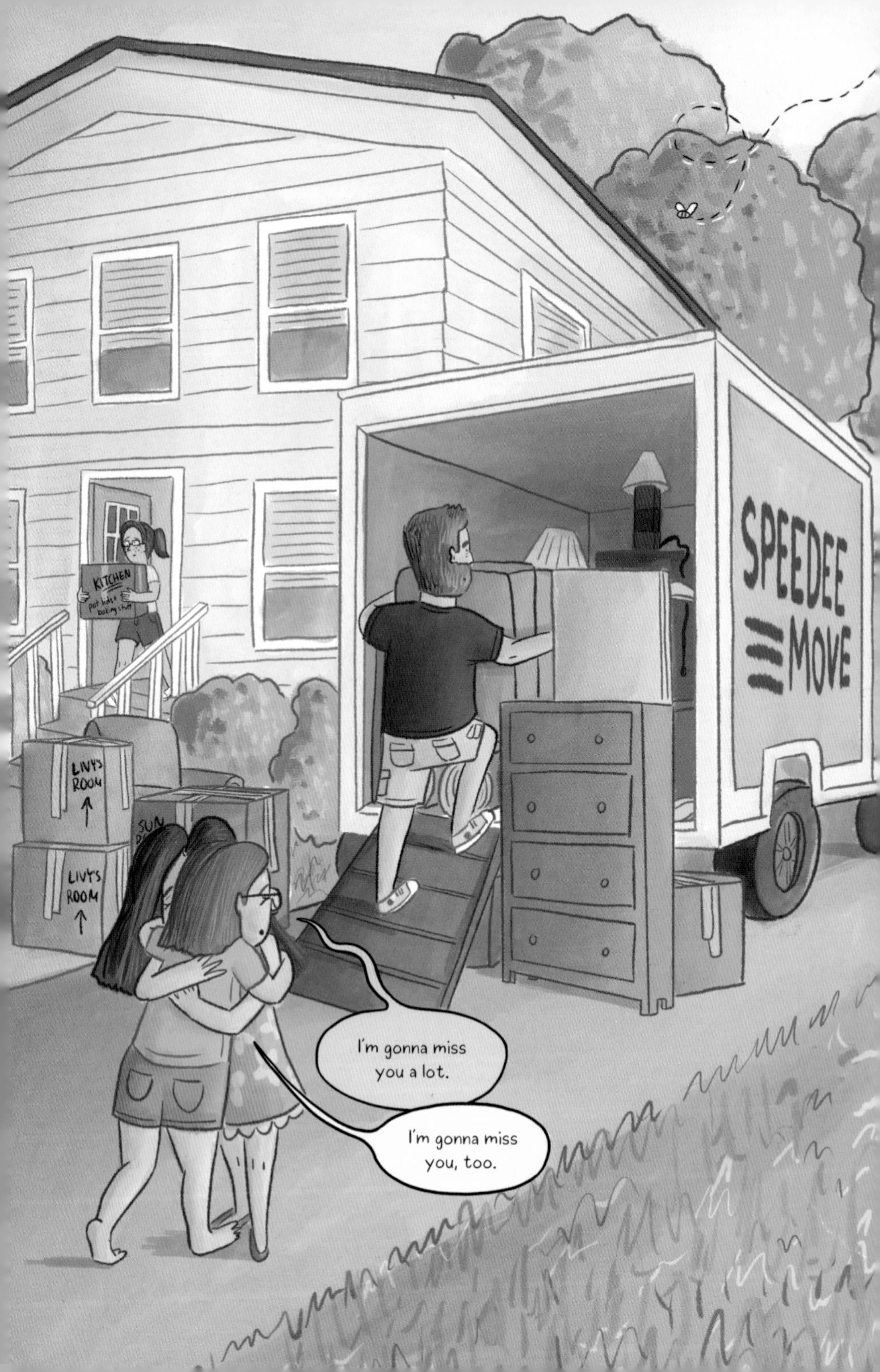
KITCHEN
LIVY'S ROOM
LIVY'S ROOM
SPEEDEE MOVE
I'm gonna miss you a lot.
I'm gonna miss you, too.

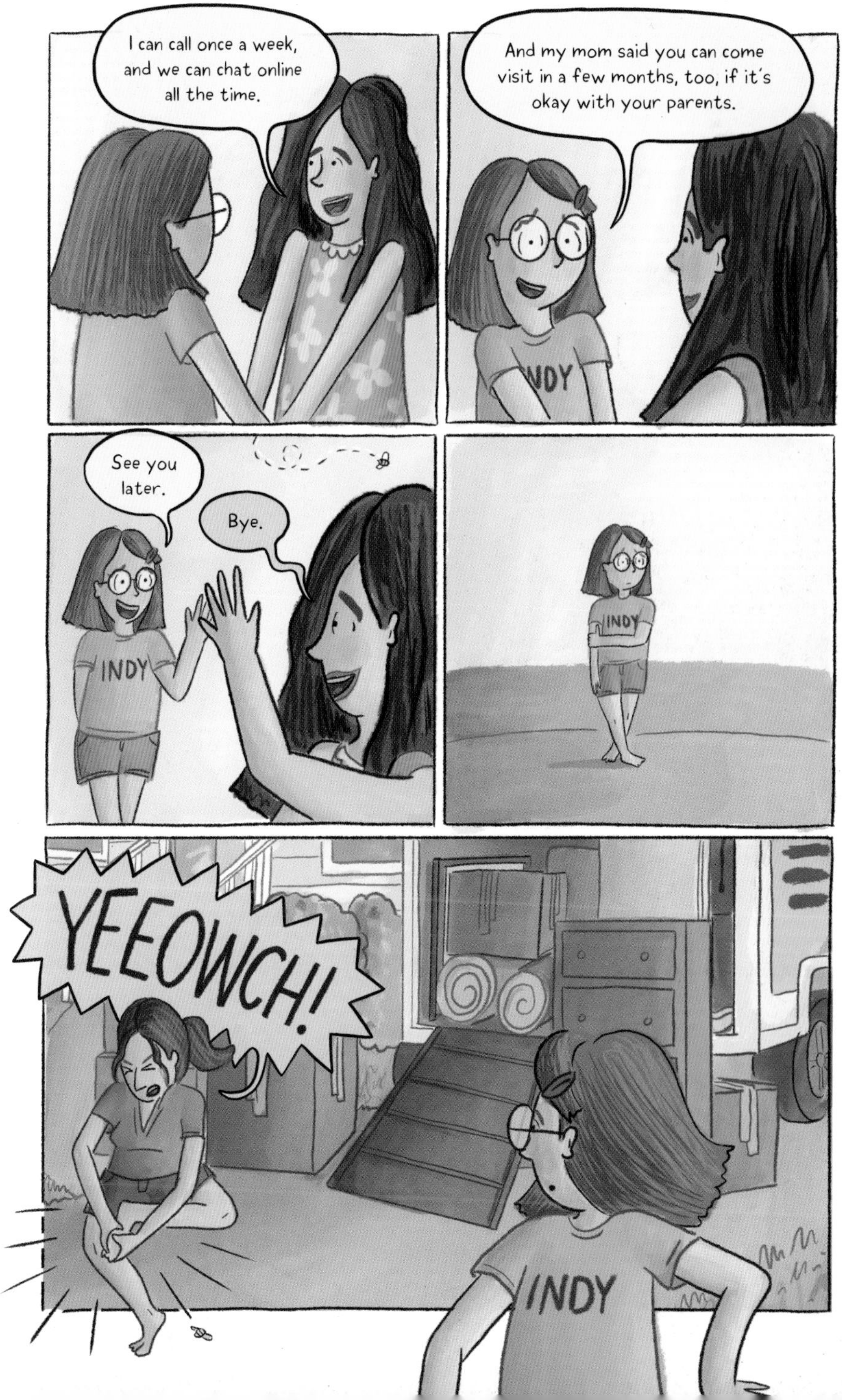
I can call once a week, and we can chat online all the time.
And my mom said you can come visit in a few months, too, if it's okay with your parents.
NDY
See you later.
Bye.
INDY
INDY
YEEOWCH!
INDY

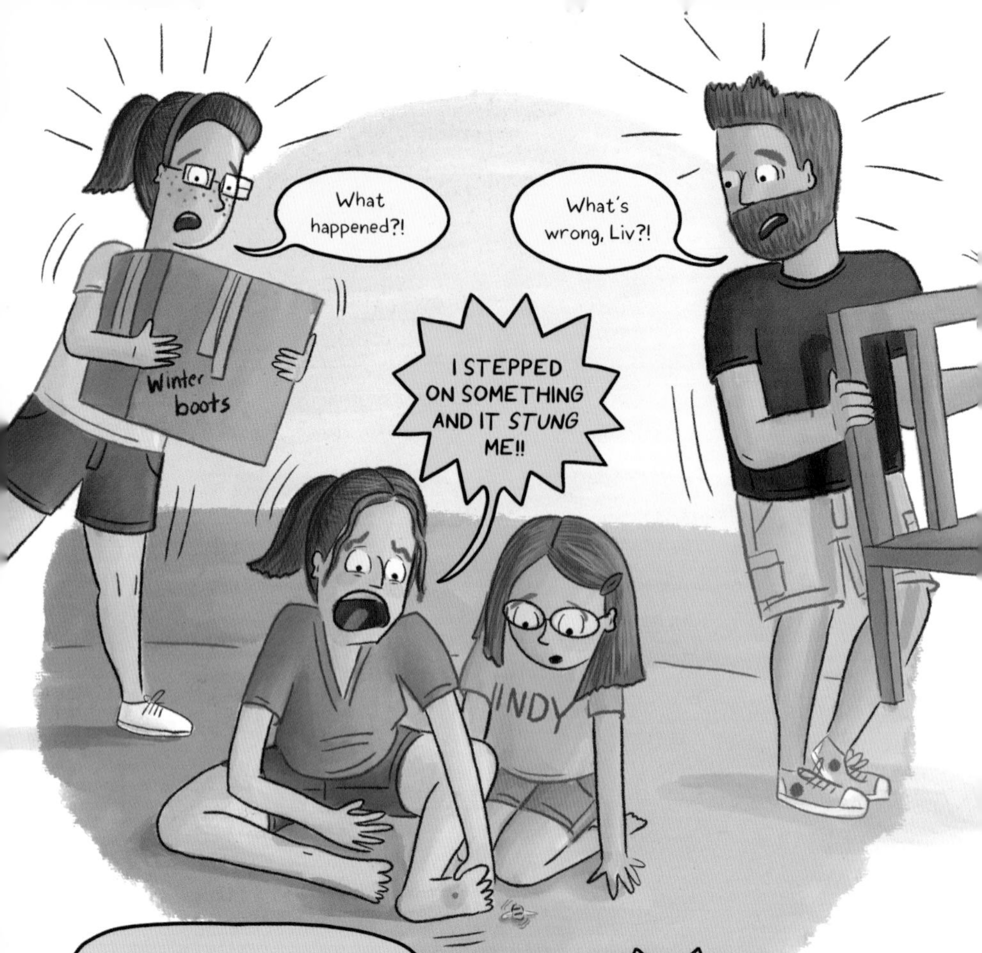
What happened?!
What's wrong, Liv?!
Winter boots
I STEPPED ON SOMETHING AND IT STUNG ME!!
INDY

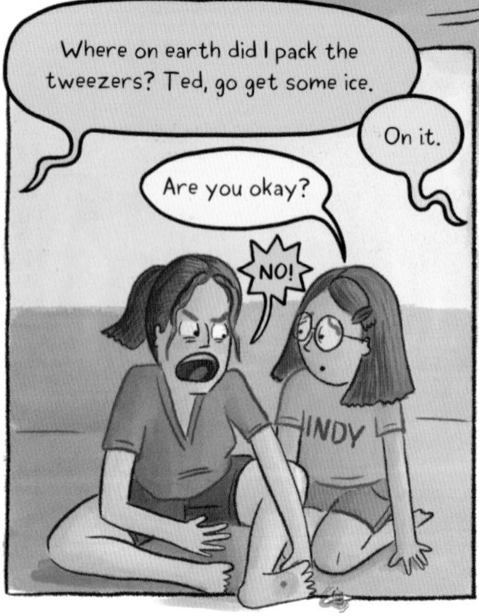
Where on earth did I pack the tweezers? Ted, go get some ice.
On it.
Are you okay?
NO!
INDY

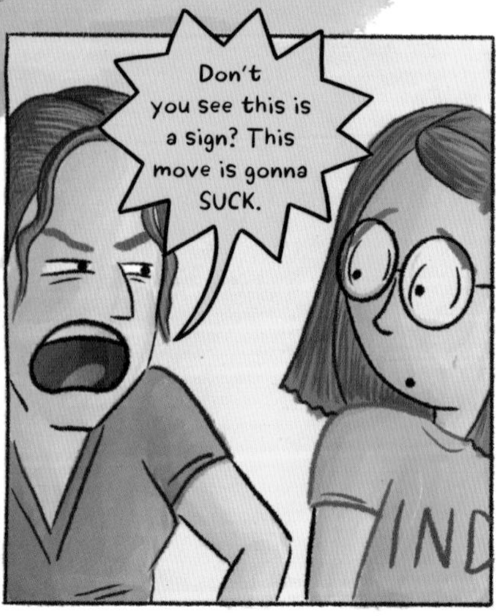
Don't you see this is a sign? This move is gonna SUCK.
IND

CHAPTER 4

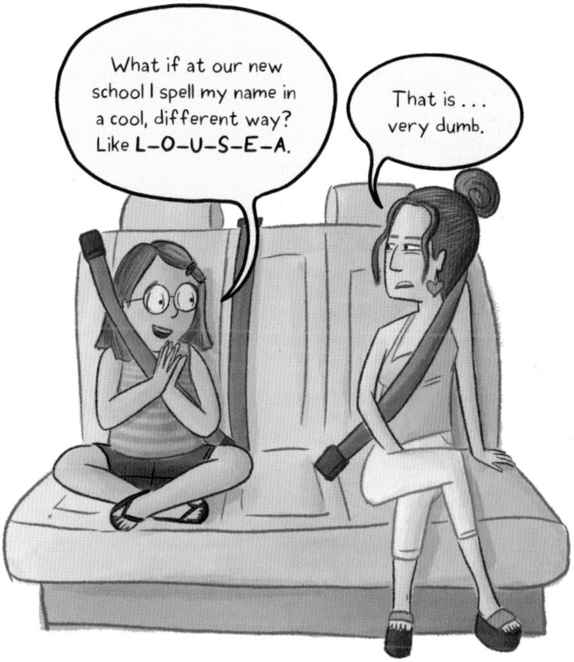
What if at our new school I spell my name in a cool, different way? Like L-O-U-S-E-A.
That is . . . very dumb.

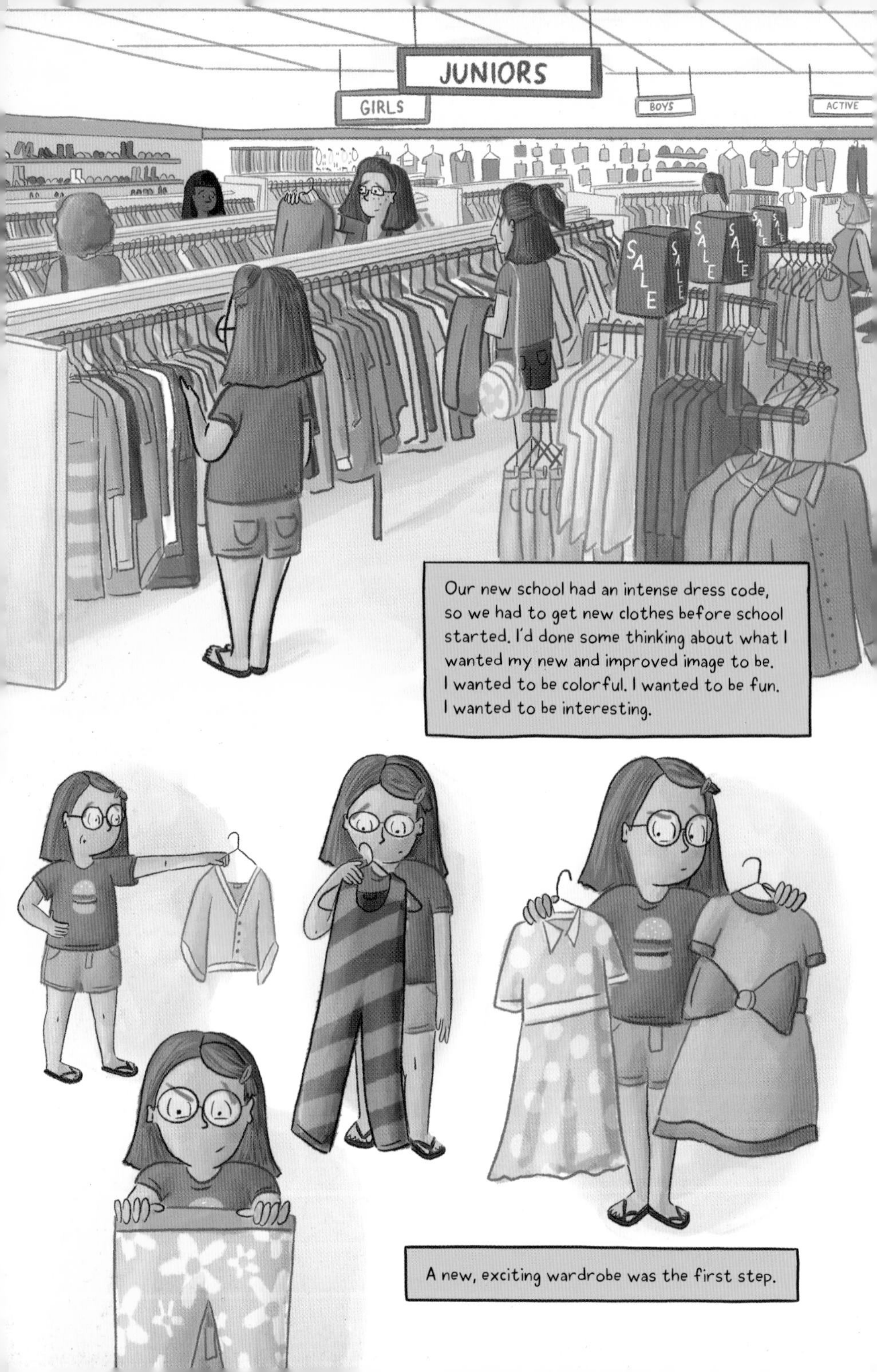
JUNIORS
GIRLS
BOYS
ACTIVE
SALE
SALE
SALE
SALE
SALE
SALE
Our new school had an intense dress code, so we had to get new clothes before school started. I'd done some thinking about what I wanted my new and improved image to be. I wanted to be colorful. I wanted to be fun. I wanted to be interesting.
A new, exciting wardrobe was the first step.

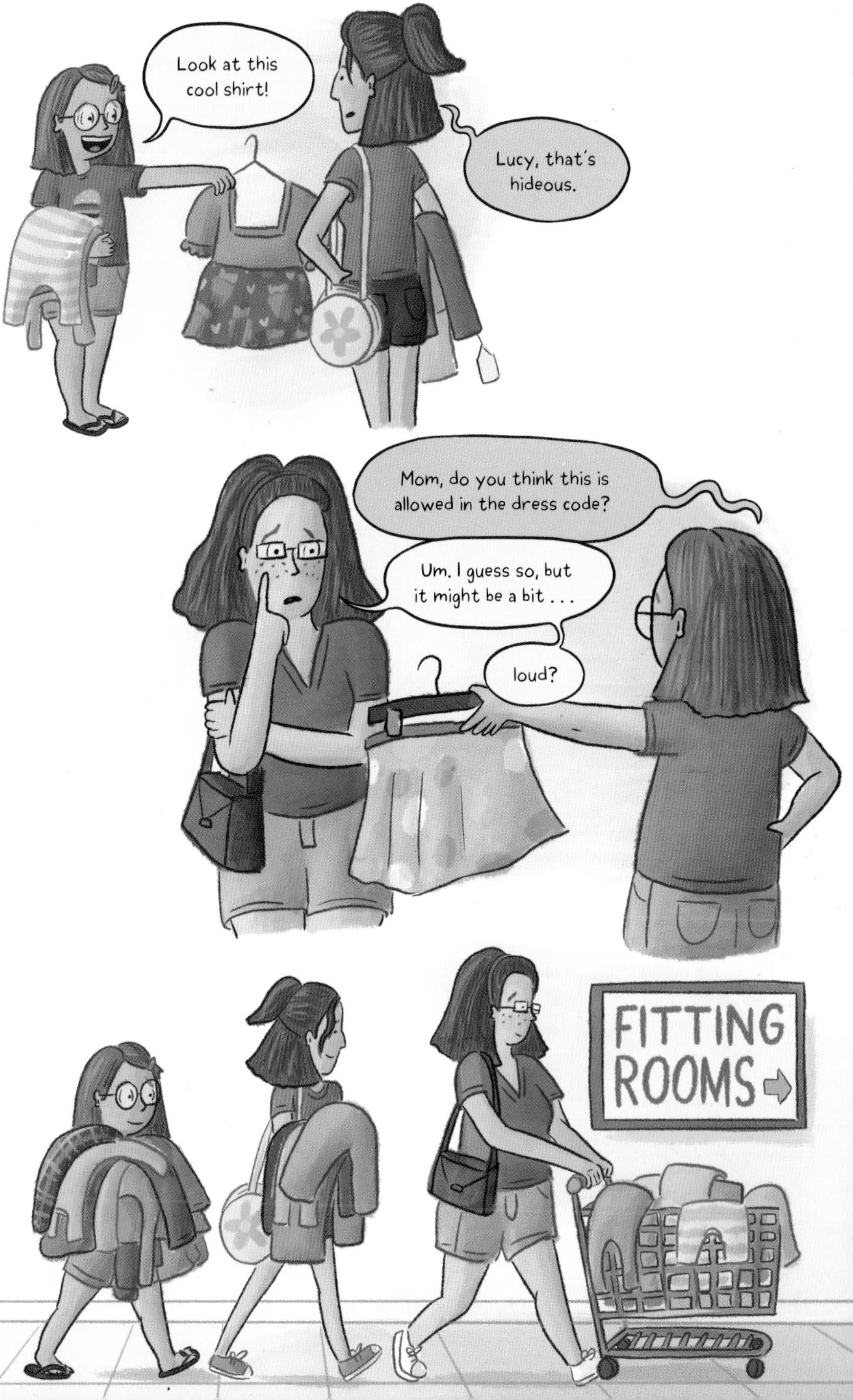
Look at this cool shirt!
Lucy, that's hideous.
Mom, do you think this is allowed in the dress code?
Um. I guess so, but it might be a bit . . .
loud?
FITTING ROOMS

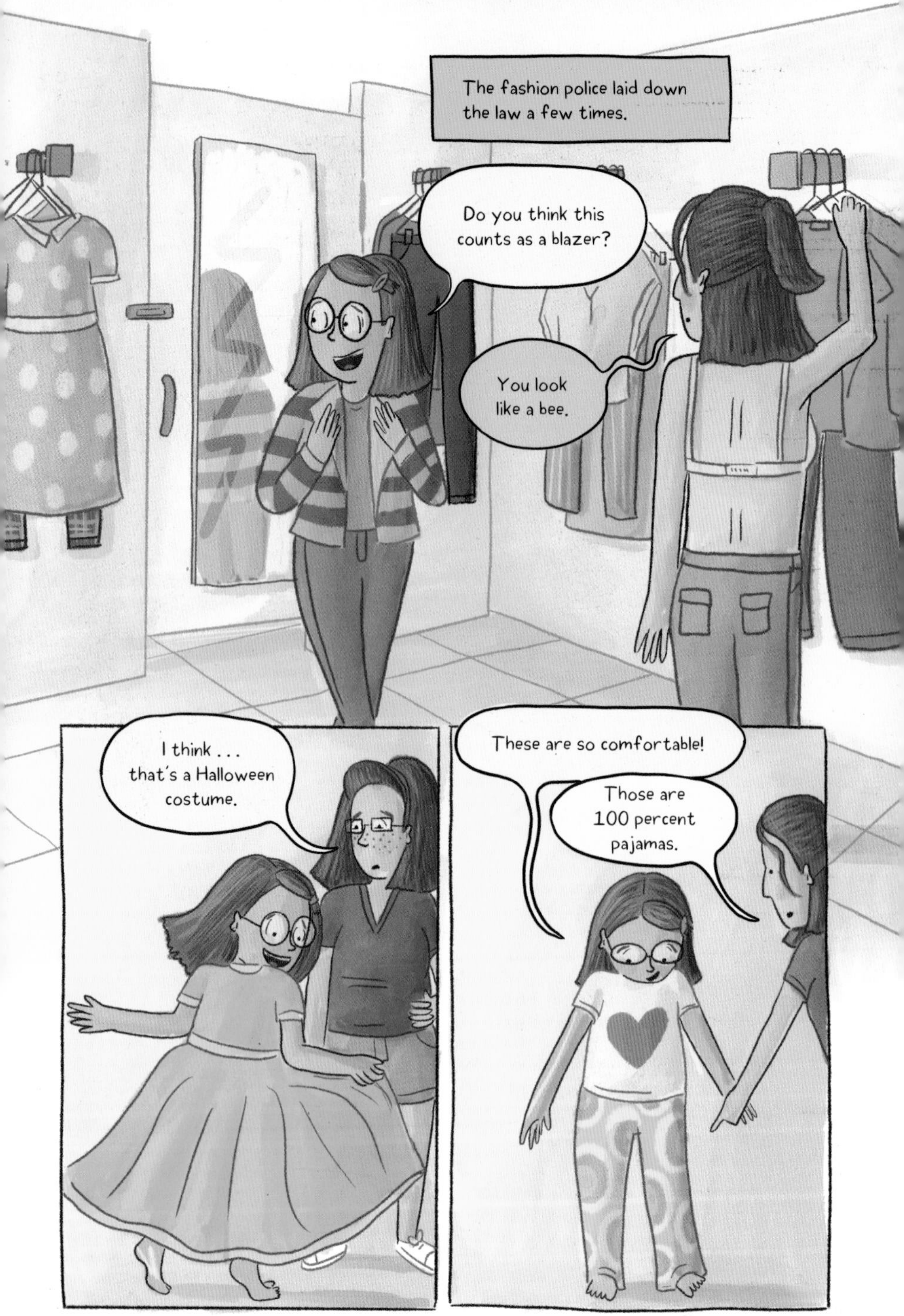

The fashion police laid down the law a few times.
Do you think this counts as a blazer?
You look like a bee.
I think . . . that's a Halloween costume.
These are so comfortable!
Those are 100 percent pajamas.

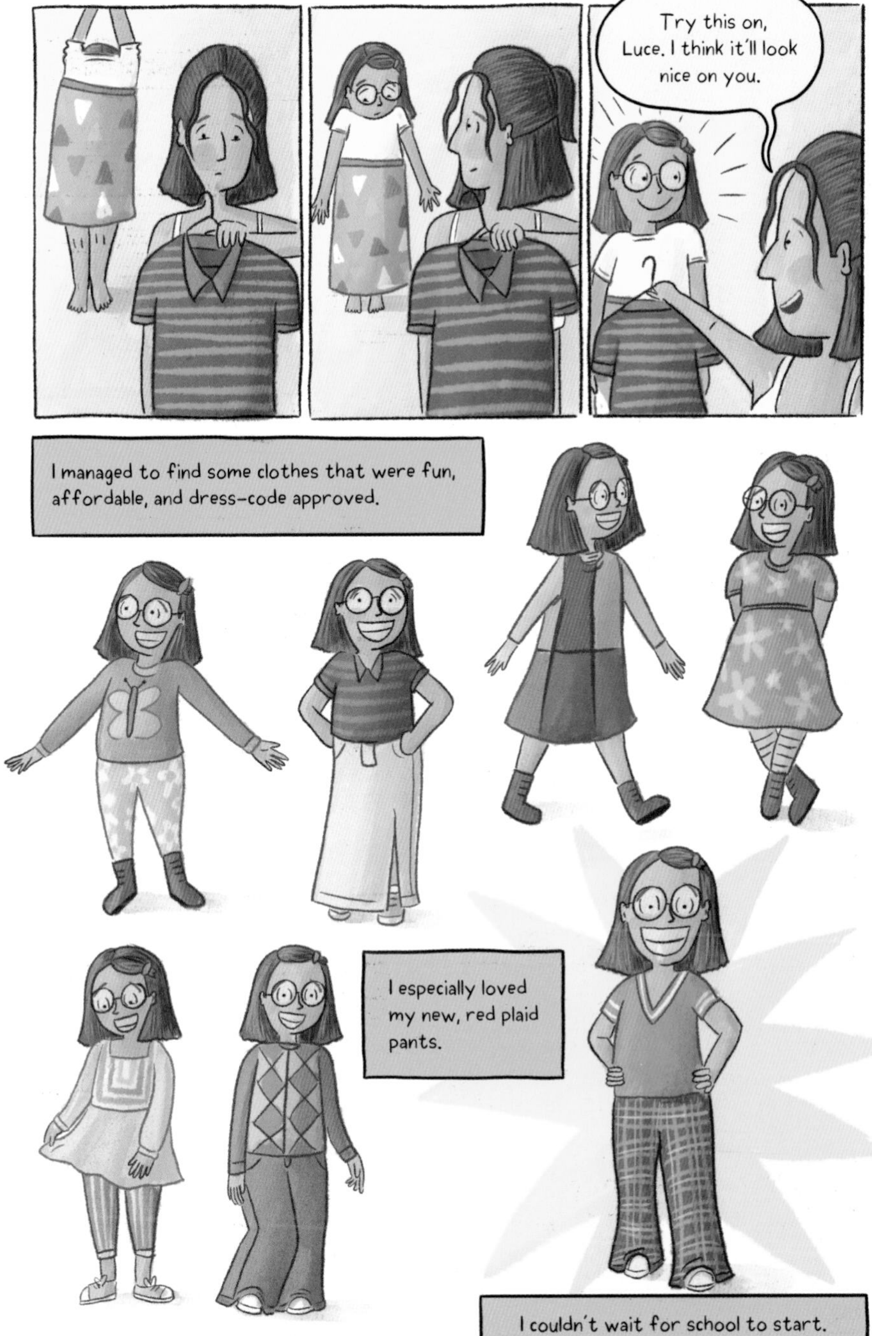
Try this on, Luce. I think it'll look nice on you.
I managed to find some clothes that were fun, affordable, and dress-code approved.
I especially loved my new, red plaid pants.
I couldn't wait for school to start.

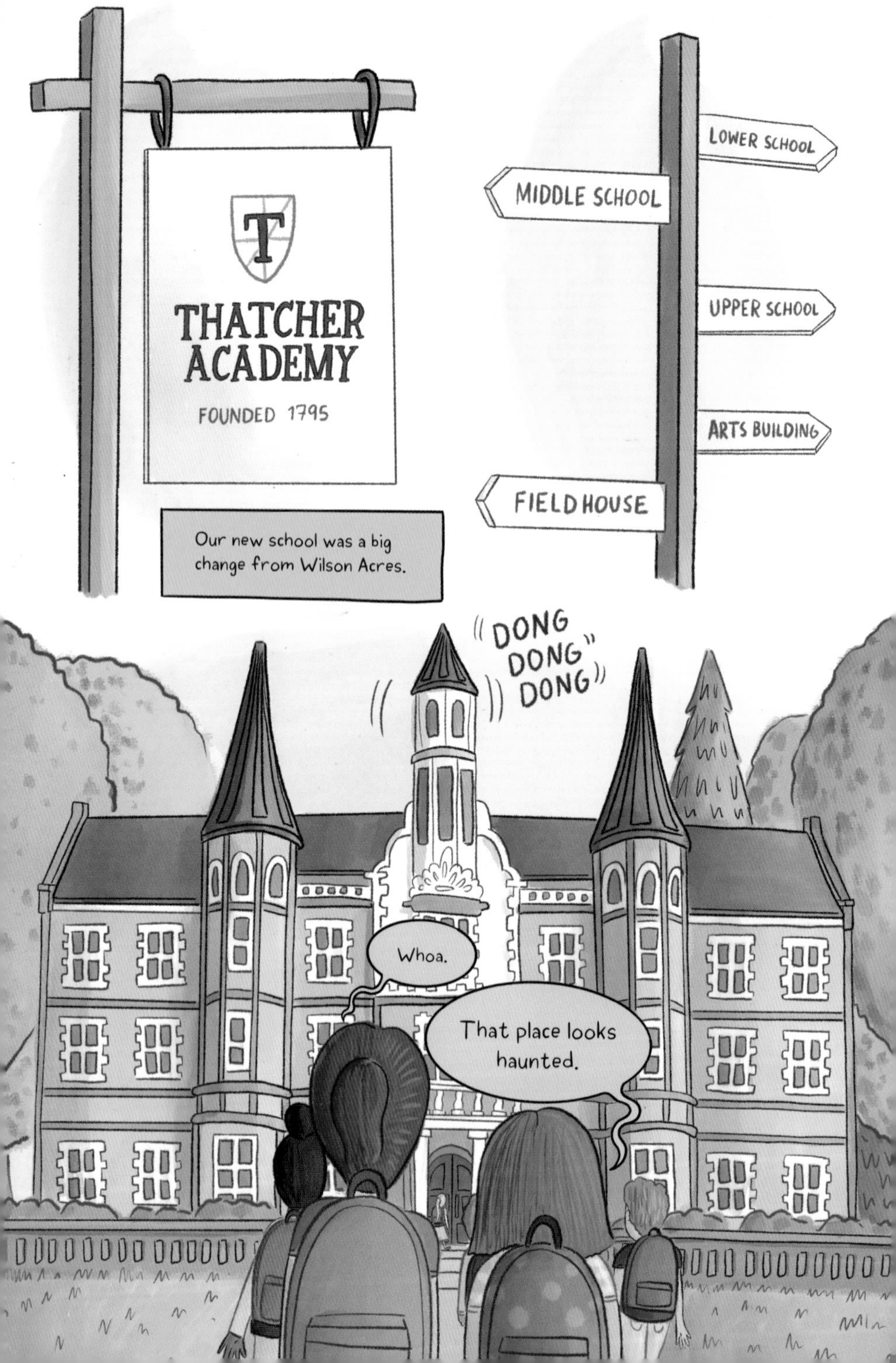
THATCHER ACADEMY
FOUNDED 1795
LOWER SCHOOL
MIDDLE SCHOOL
UPPER SCHOOL
ARTS BUILDING
FIELDHOUSE
Our new school was a big change from Wilson Acres.
DONG DONG DONG
Whoa.
That place looks haunted.

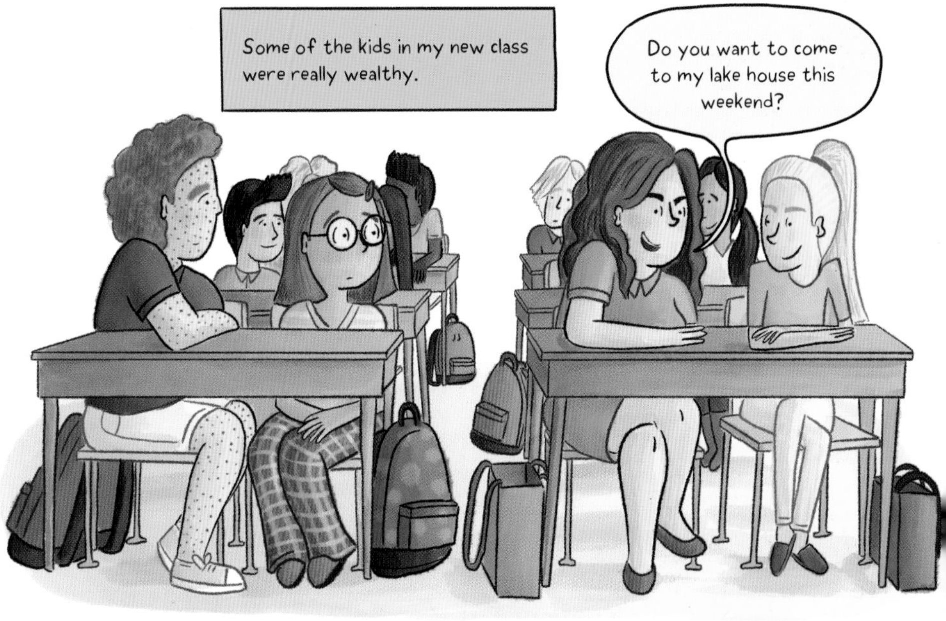
Some of the kids in my new class were really wealthy.
Do you want to come to my lake house this weekend?

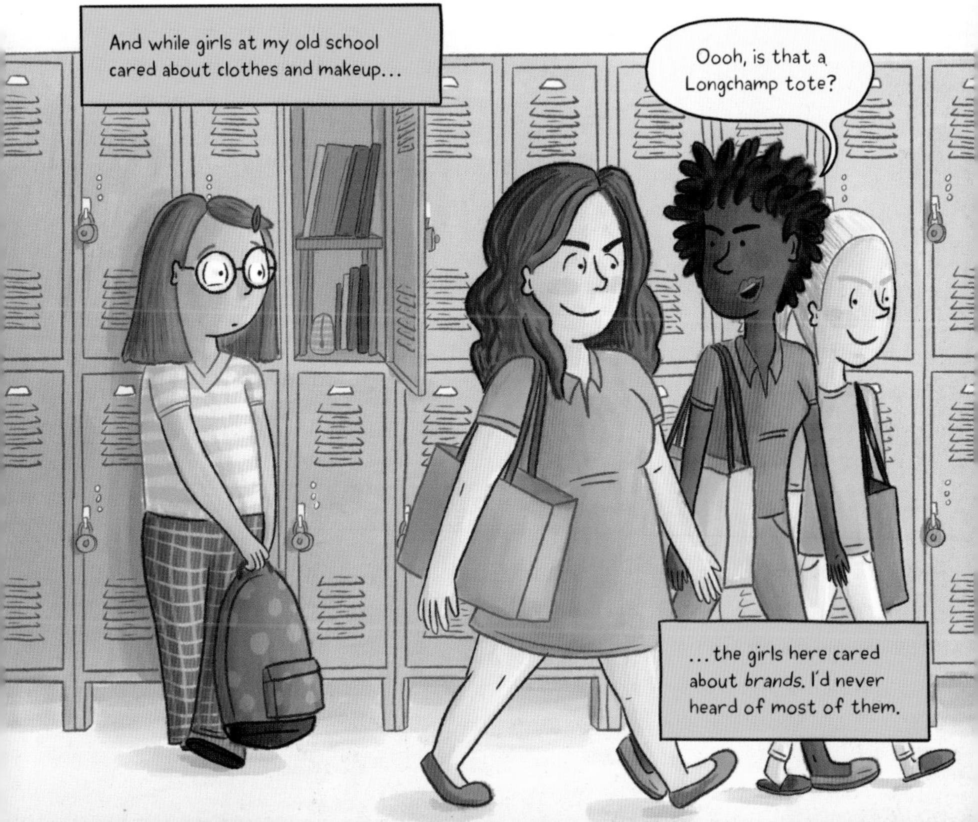
And while girls at my old school cared about clothes and makeup...
Oooh, is that a Longchamp tote?
...the girls here cared about *brands*. I'd never heard of most of them.

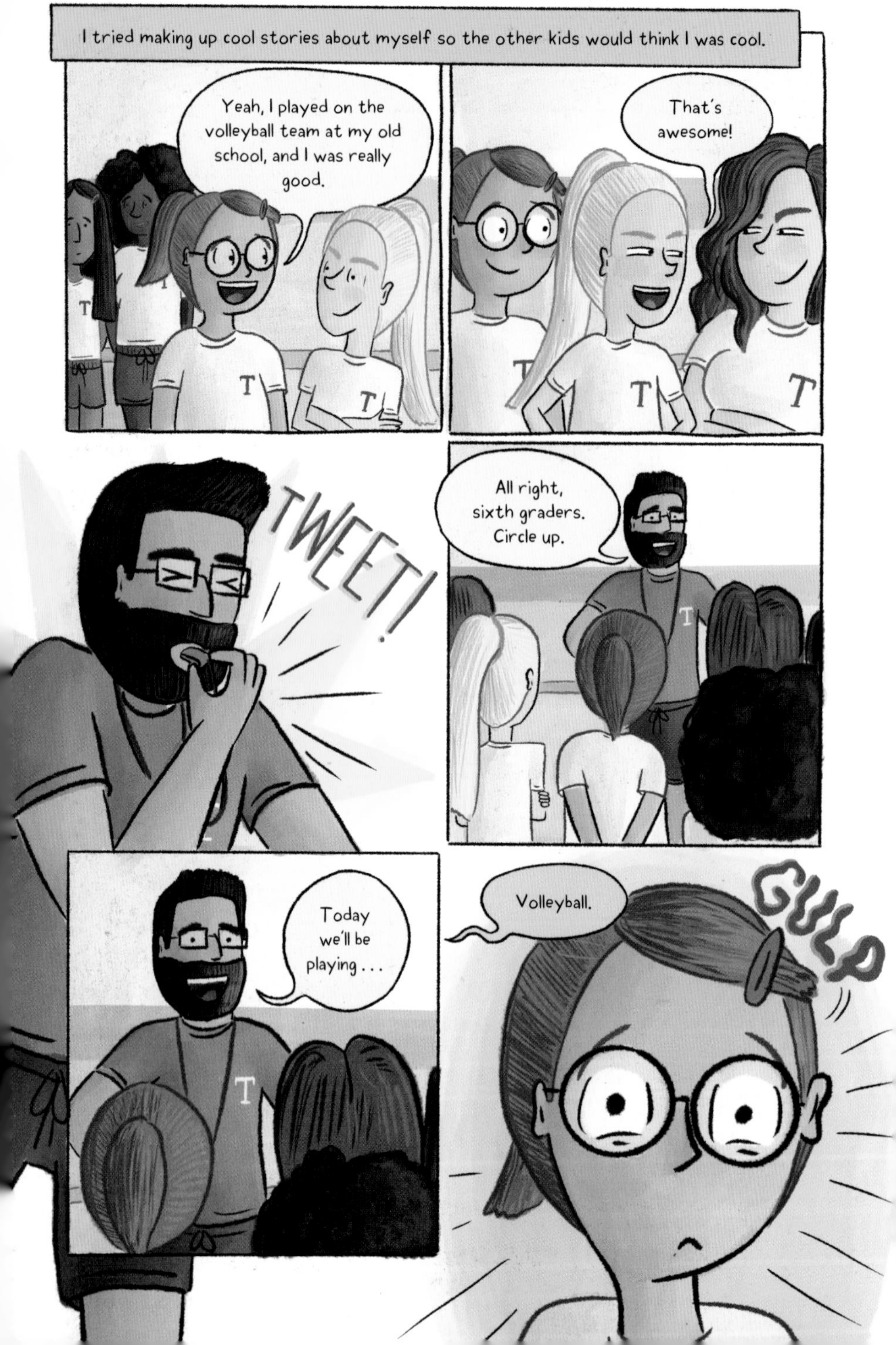

I tried making up cool stories about myself so the other kids would think I was cool.
Yeah, I played on the volleyball team at my old school, and I was really good.
That's awesome!
TWEET!
All right, sixth graders. Circle up.
Today we'll be playing . . .
Volleyball.
GULP

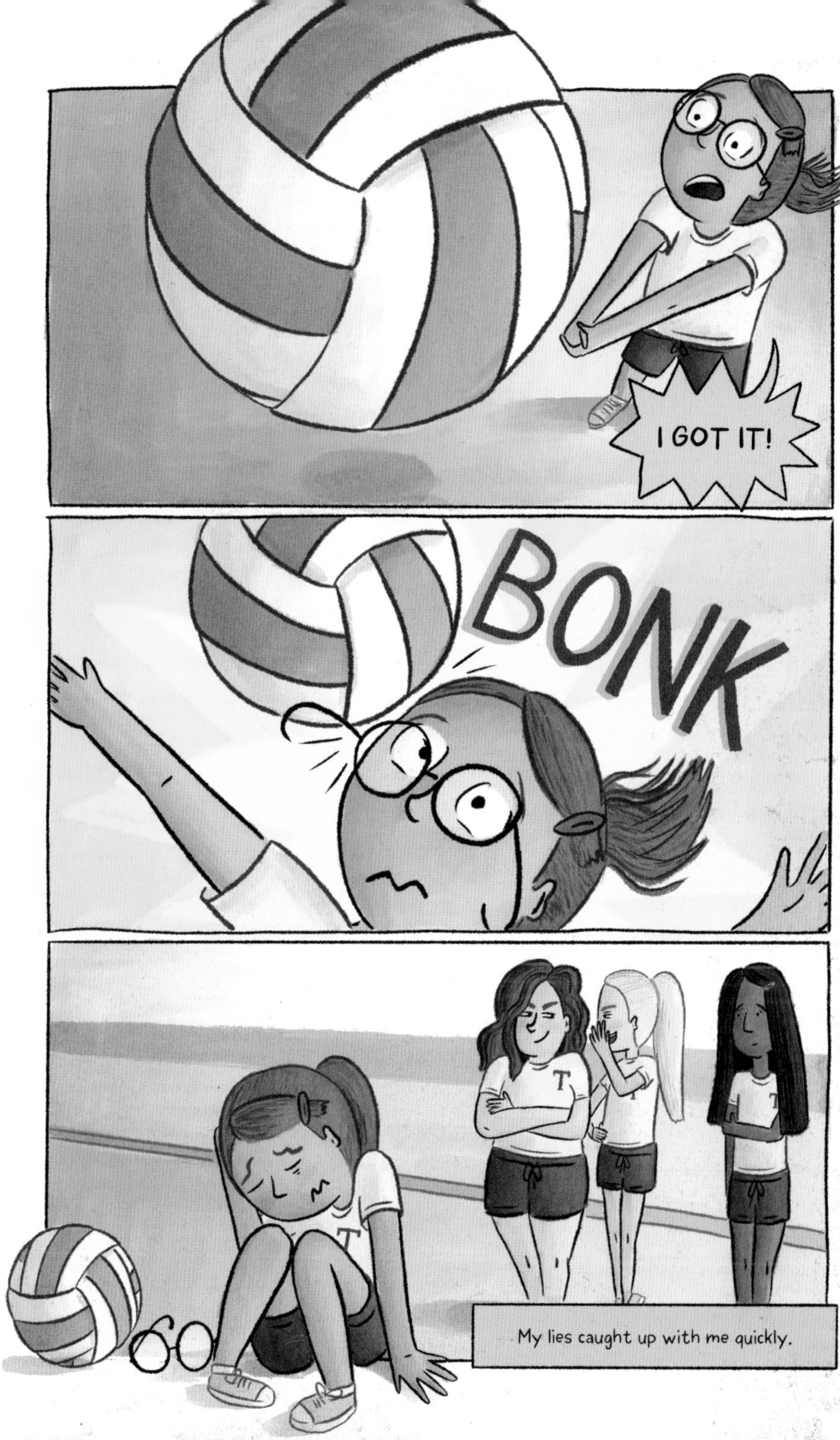
I GOT IT!
BONK
My lies caught up with me quickly.

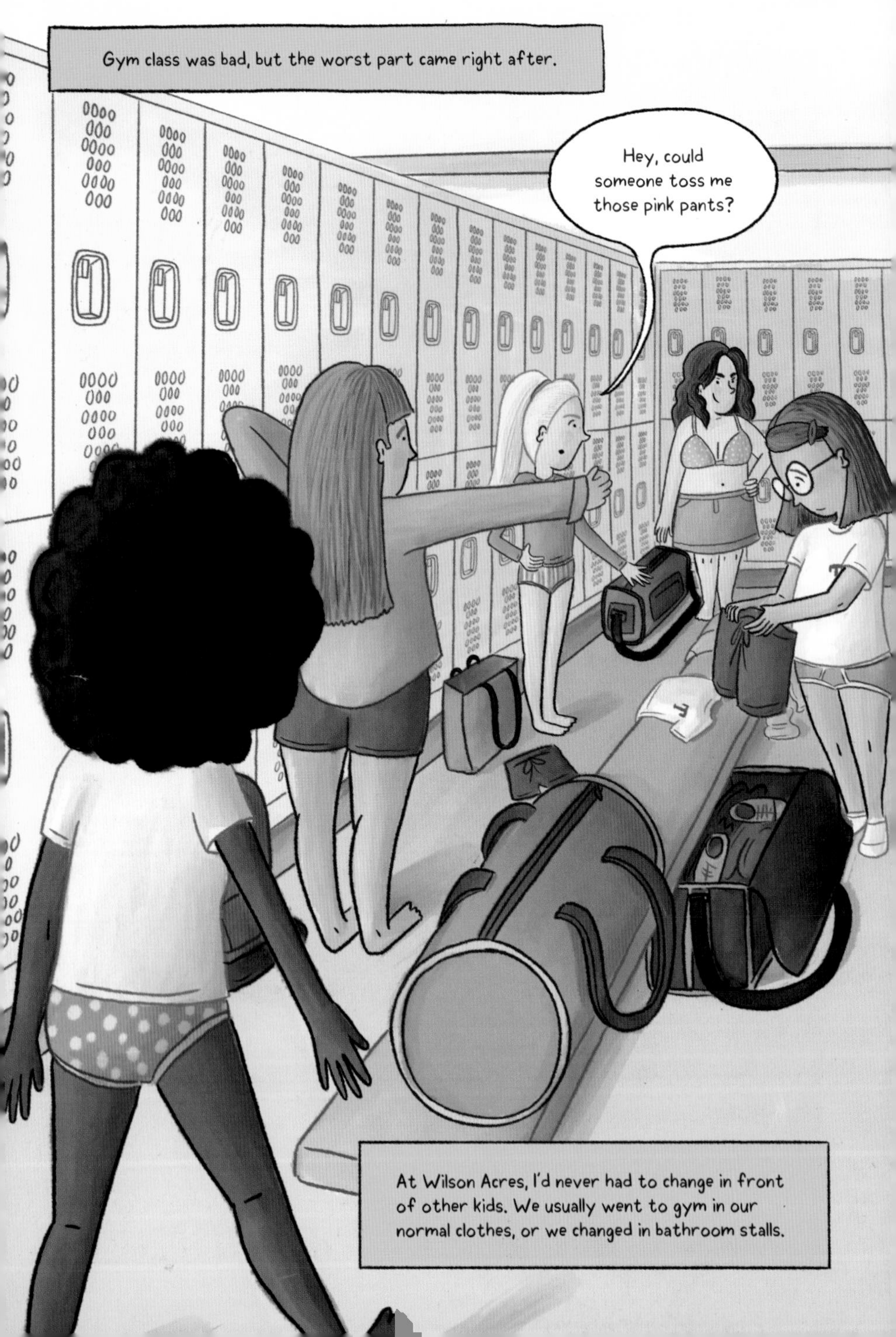
Gym class was bad, but the worst part came right after.
Hey, could someone toss me those pink pants?
At Wilson Acres, I'd never had to change in front of other kids. We usually went to gym in our normal clothes, or we changed in bathroom stalls.

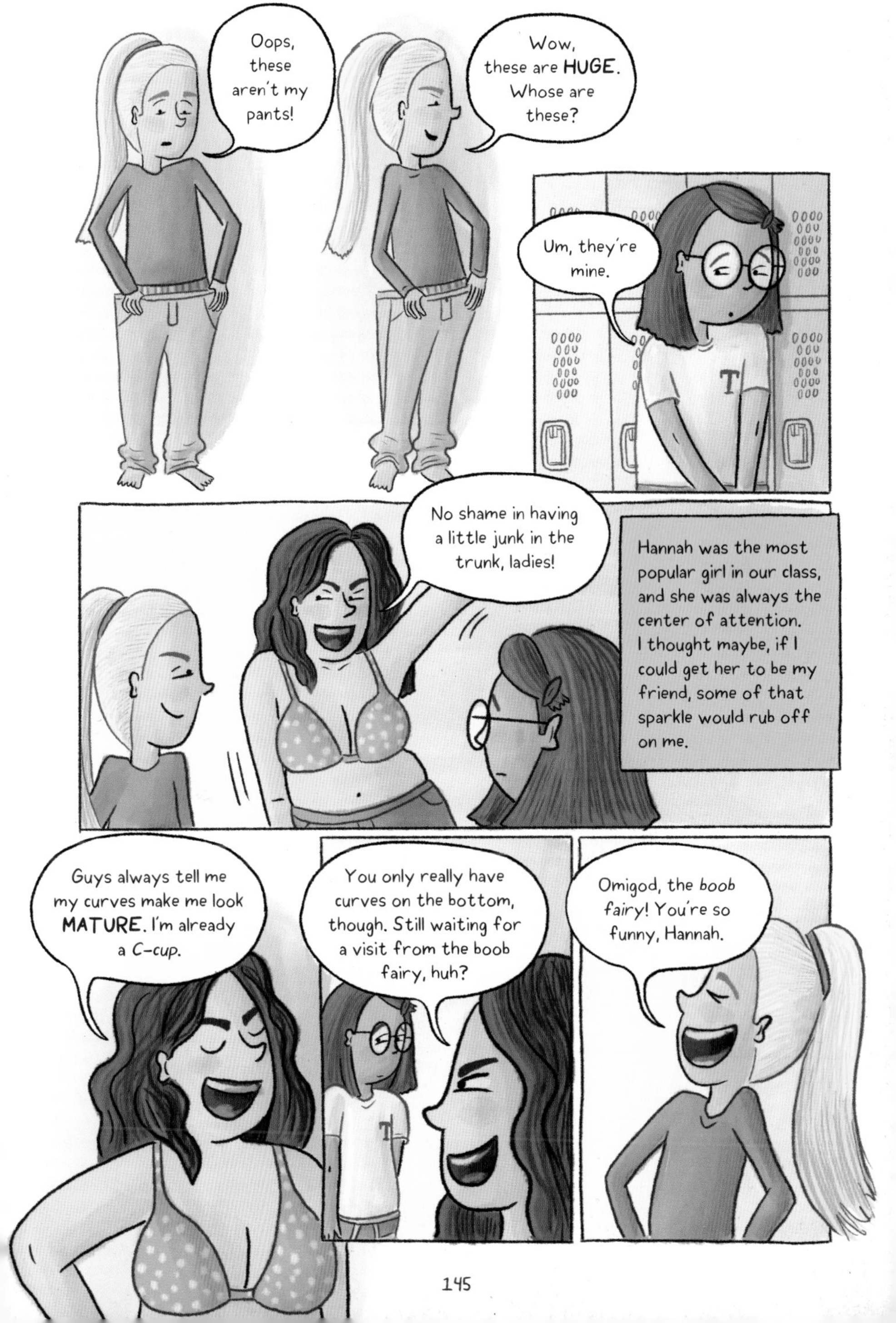
Oops, these aren't my pants!
Wow, these are **HUGE**. Whose are these?
Um, they're mine.
No shame in having a little junk in the trunk, ladies!
Hannah was the most popular girl in our class, and she was always the center of attention. I thought maybe, if I could get her to be my friend, some of that sparkle would rub off on me.
Guys always tell me my curves make me look **MATURE**. I'm already a *C-cup*.
You only really have curves on the bottom, though. Still waiting for a visit from the boob fairy, huh?
Omigod, the *boob* fairy! You're so funny, Hannah.

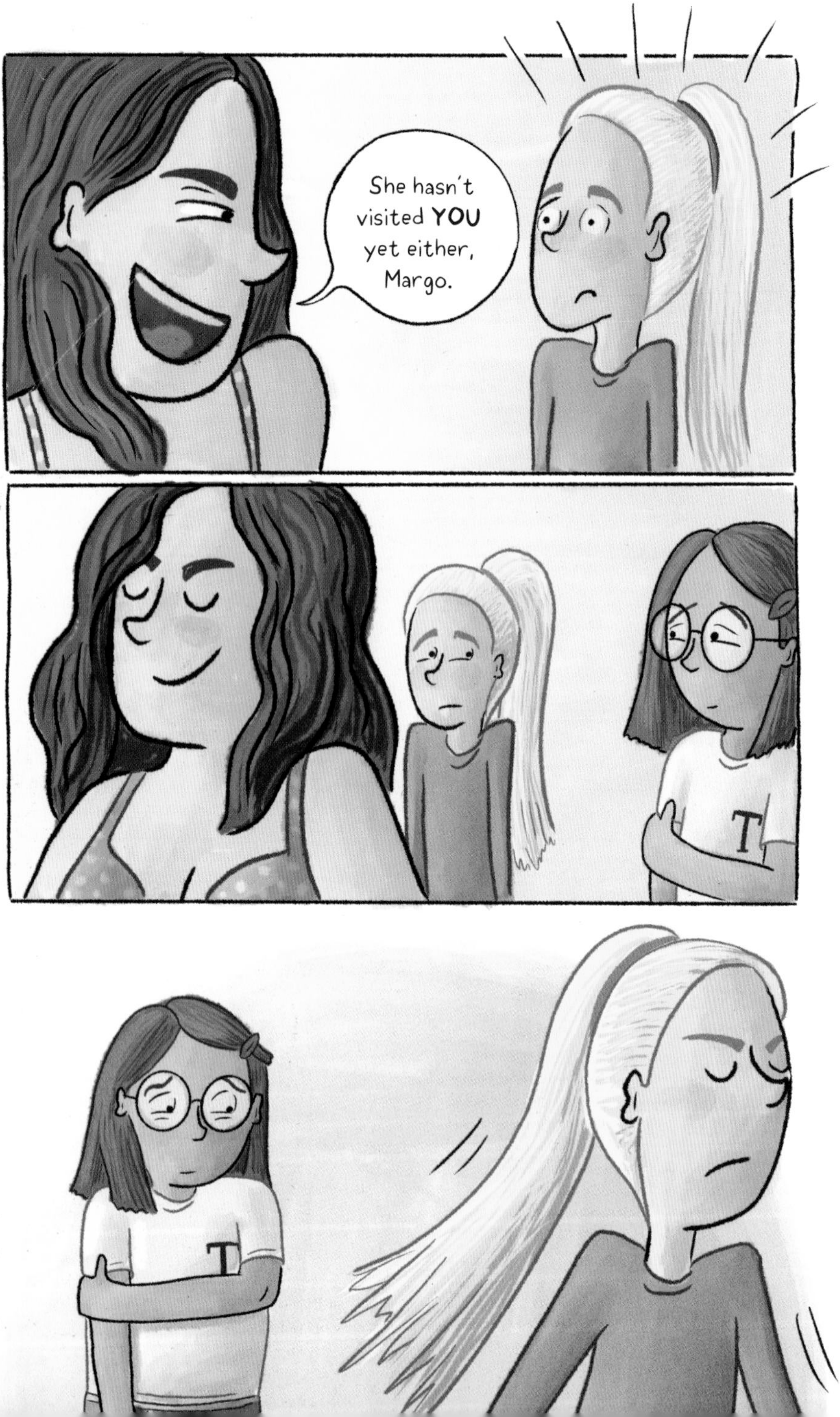
She hasn't visited YOU yet either, Margo.

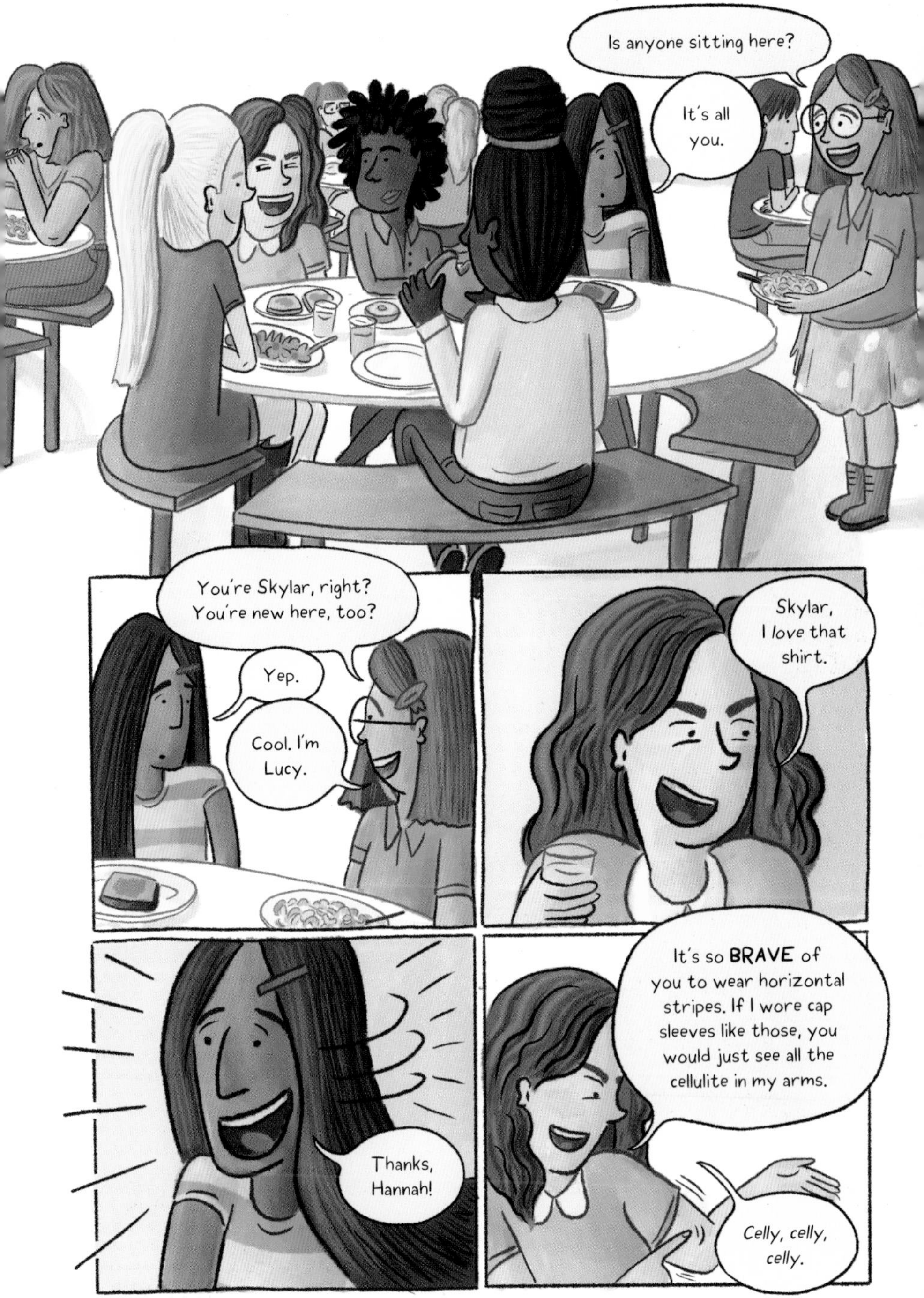

Is anyone sitting here?
It's all you.
You're Skylar, right? You're new here, too?
Yep.
Cool. I'm Lucy.
Skylar, I *love* that shirt.
Thanks, Hannah!
It's so **BRAVE** of you to wear horizontal stripes. If I wore cap sleeves like those, you would just see all the cellulite in my arms.
Celly, celly, celly.

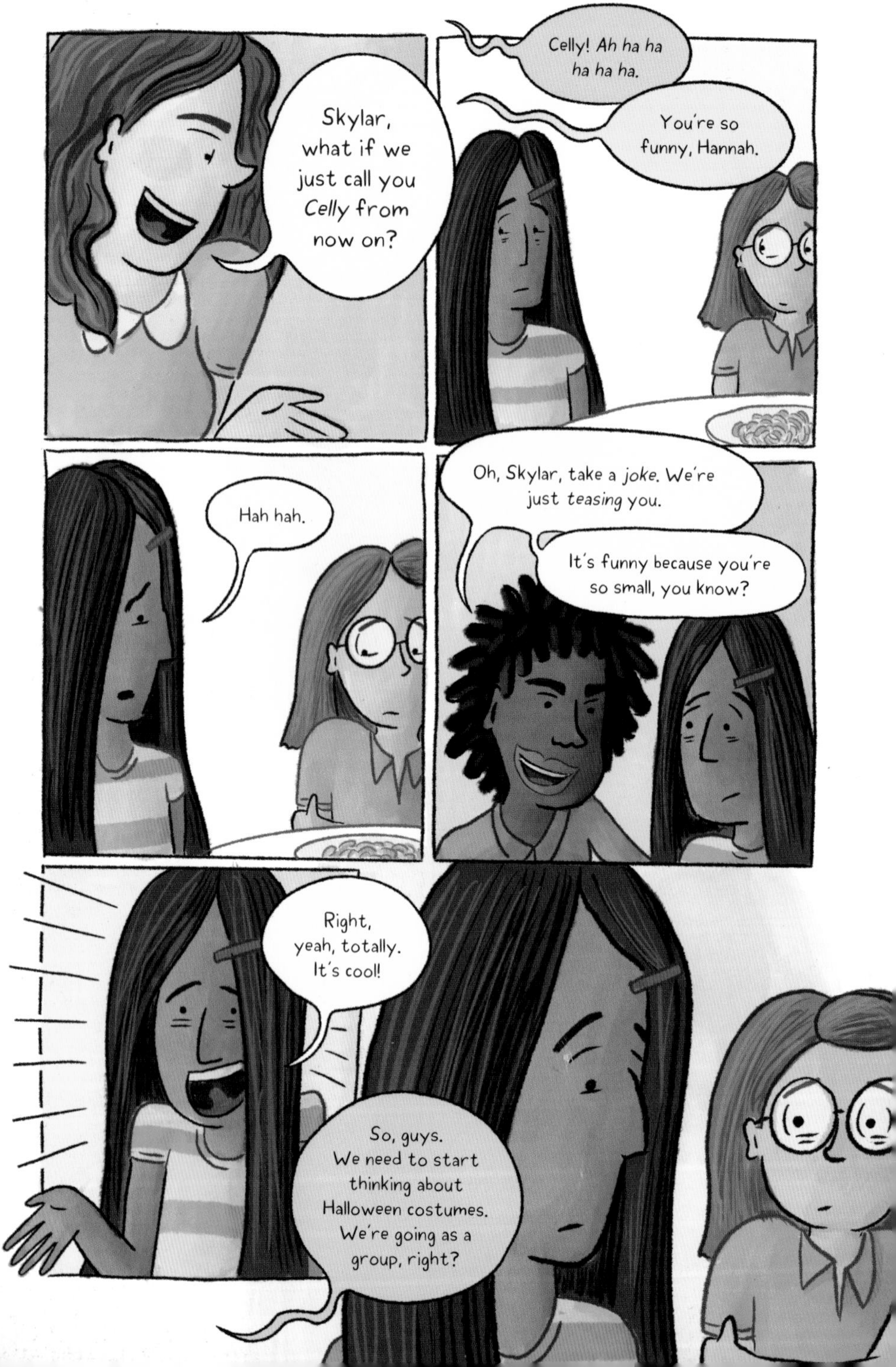
Skylar, what if we just call you *Celly* from now on?
Celly! *Ah ha ha ha ha ha.*
You're so funny, Hannah.
Hah hah.
Oh, Skylar, take a *joke*. We're just *teasing* you.
It's funny because you're so small, you know?
Right, yeah, totally. It's cool!
So, guys. We need to start thinking about Halloween costumes. We're going as a group, right?

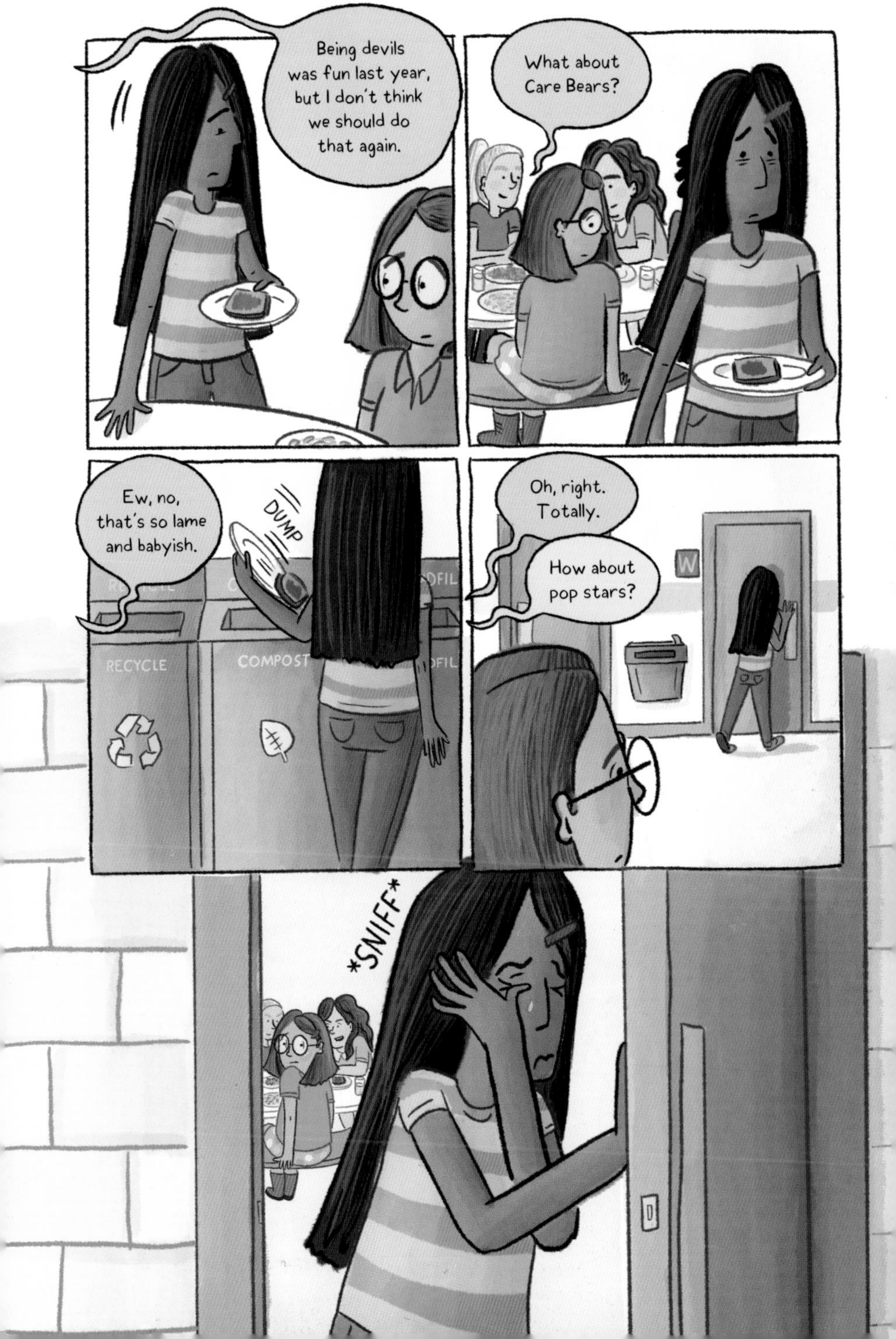

Being devils was fun last year, but I don't think we should do that again.
What about Care Bears?
Ew, no, that's so lame and babyish.
DUMP
RECYCLE
COMPOST
Oh, right. Totally.
How about pop stars?
W
SNIFF

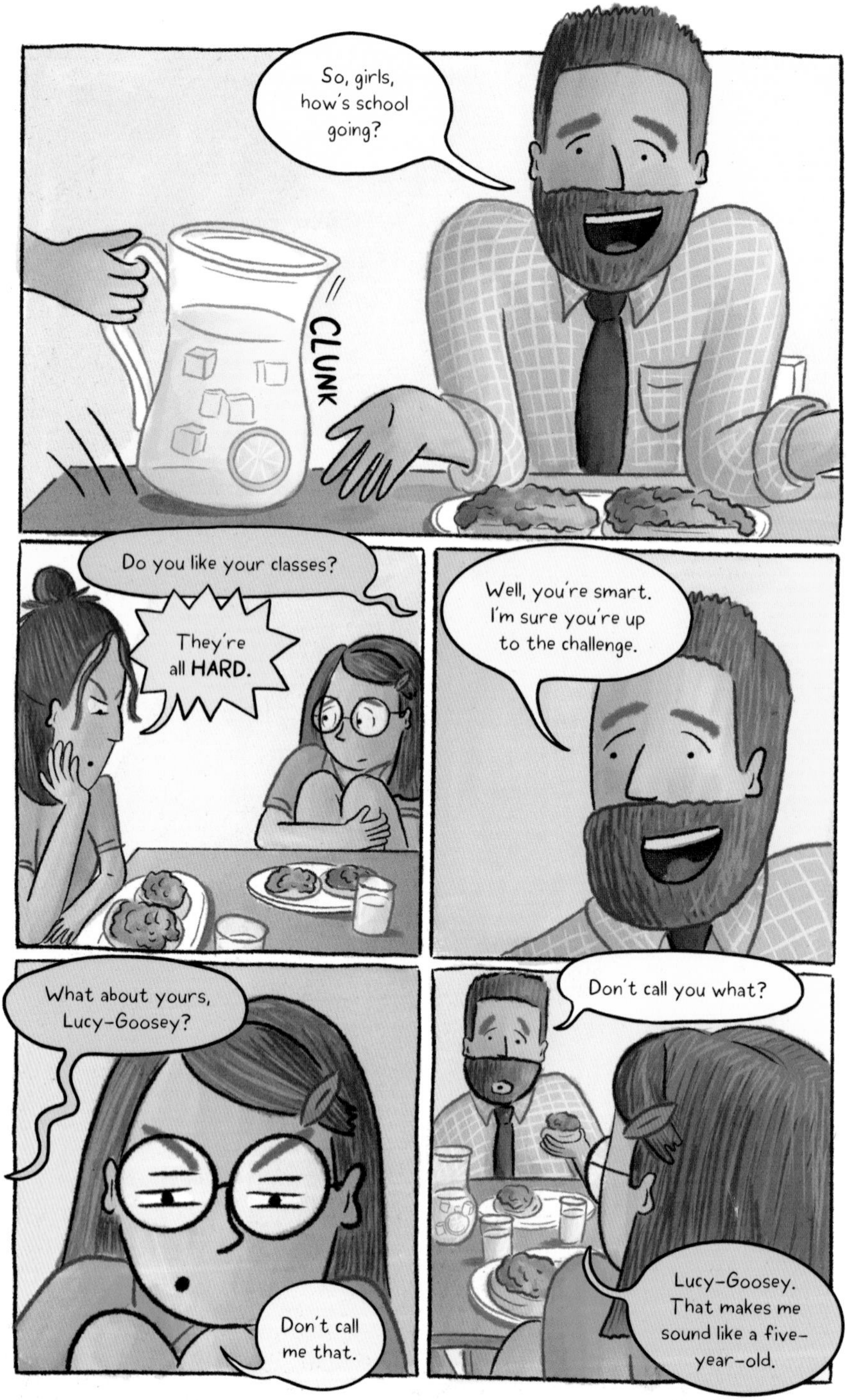
So, girls, how's school going?
CLUNK
Do you like your classes?
They're all HARD.
Well, you're smart. I'm sure you're up to the challenge.
What about yours, Lucy-Goosey?
Don't call me that.
Don't call you what?
Lucy-Goosey. That makes me sound like a five-year-old.

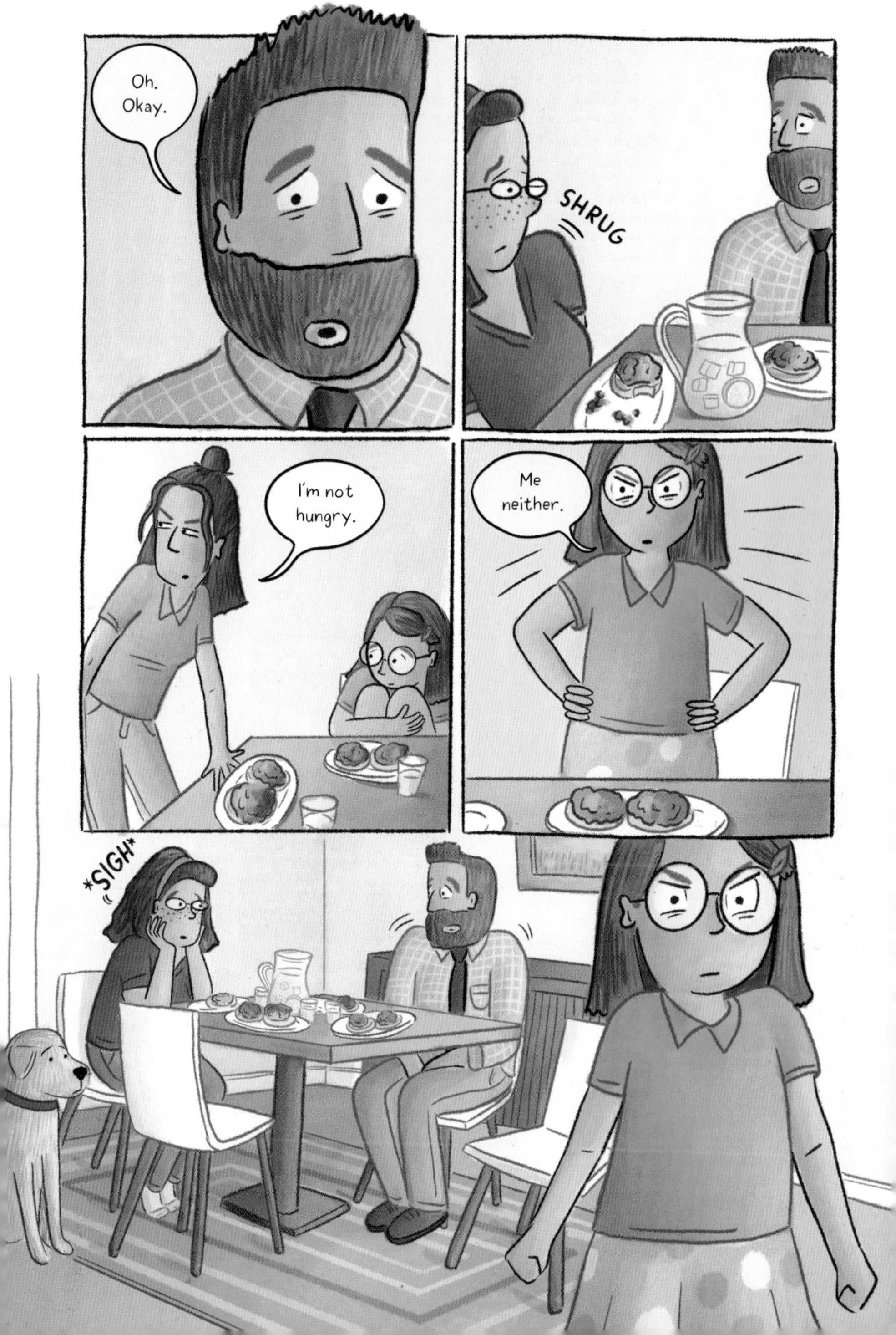
Oh. Okay.
SHRUG
I'm not hungry.
Me neither.
SIGH

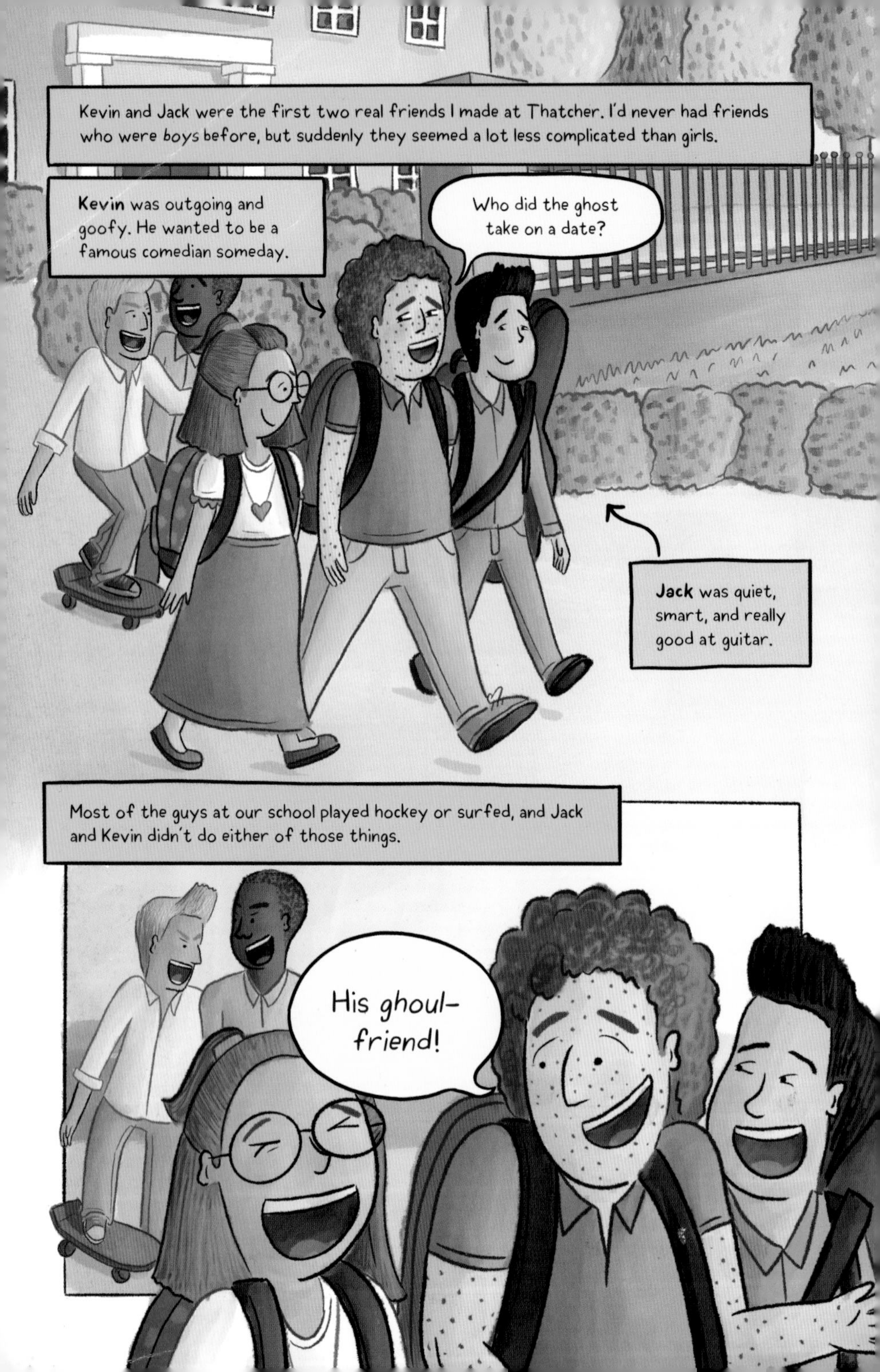
Kevin and Jack were the first two real friends I made at Thatcher. I'd never had friends who were *boys* before, but suddenly they seemed a lot less complicated than girls.
Kevin was outgoing and goofy. He wanted to be a famous comedian someday.
Who did the ghost take on a date?
Jack was quiet, smart, and really good at guitar.
Most of the guys at our school played hockey or surfed, and Jack and Kevin didn't do either of those things.
His ghoul-friend!

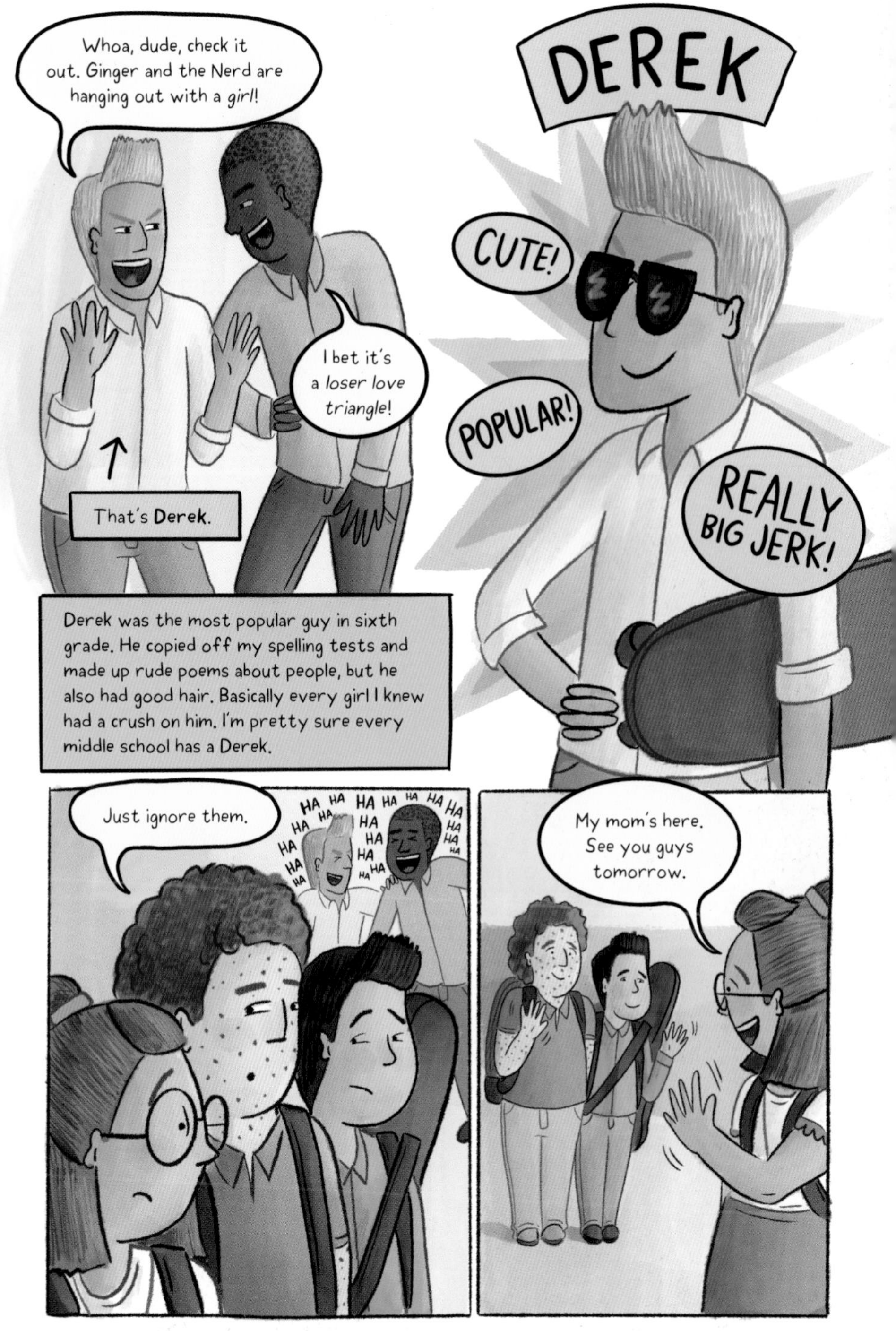

Whoa, dude, check it out. Ginger and the Nerd are hanging out with a *girl*!
I bet it's a *loser love triangle*!
That's **Derek**.
DEREK
CUTE!
POPULAR!
REALLY BIG JERK!
Derek was the most popular guy in sixth grade. He copied off my spelling tests and made up rude poems about people, but he also had good hair. Basically every girl I knew had a crush on him. I'm pretty sure every middle school has a Derek.
Just ignore them.
HA HA HA HA HA HA HA HA HA HA HA HA HA HA HA HA HA HA HA HA HA HA HA HA
My mom's here. See you guys tomorrow.

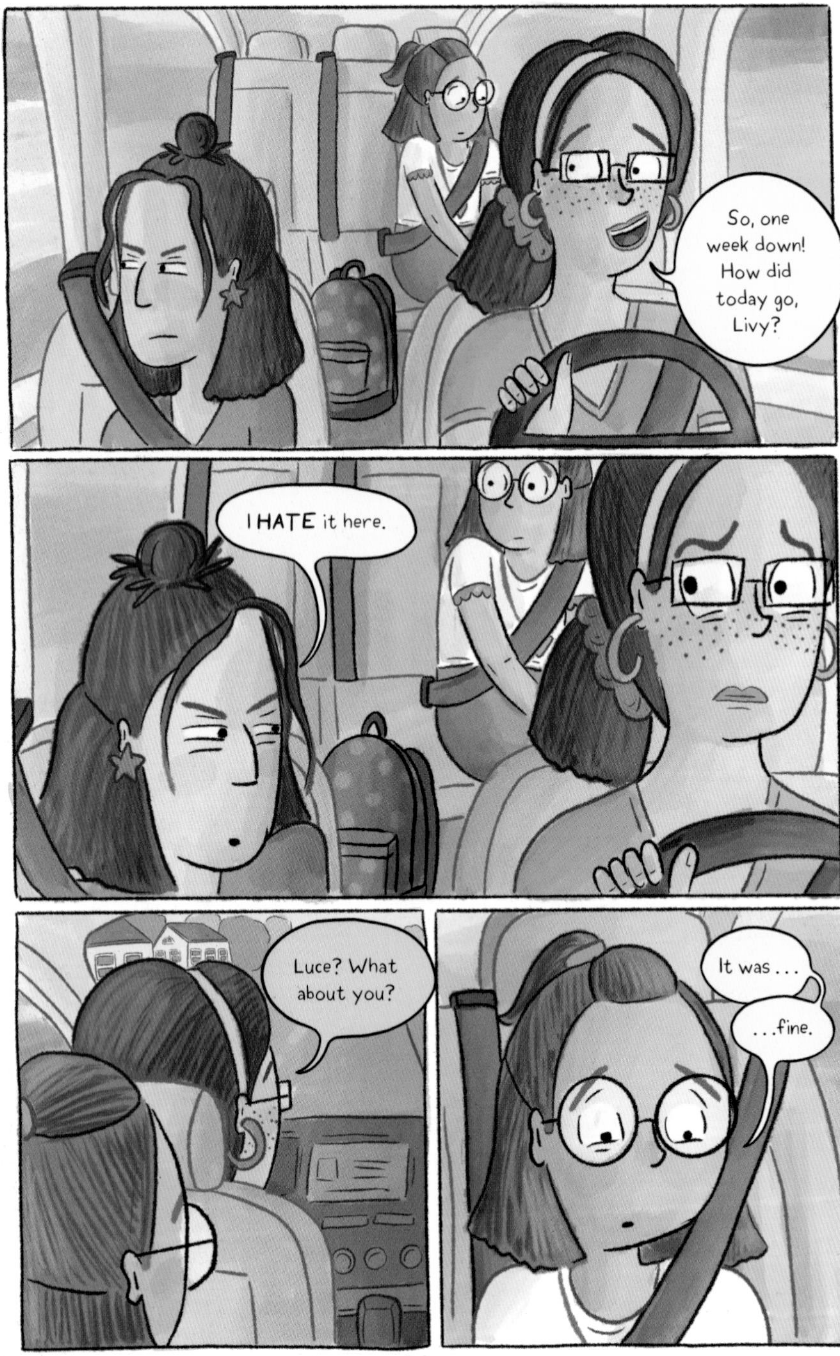
So, one week down! How did today go, Livy?
I HATE it here.
Luce? What about you?
It was . . .
. . . fine.

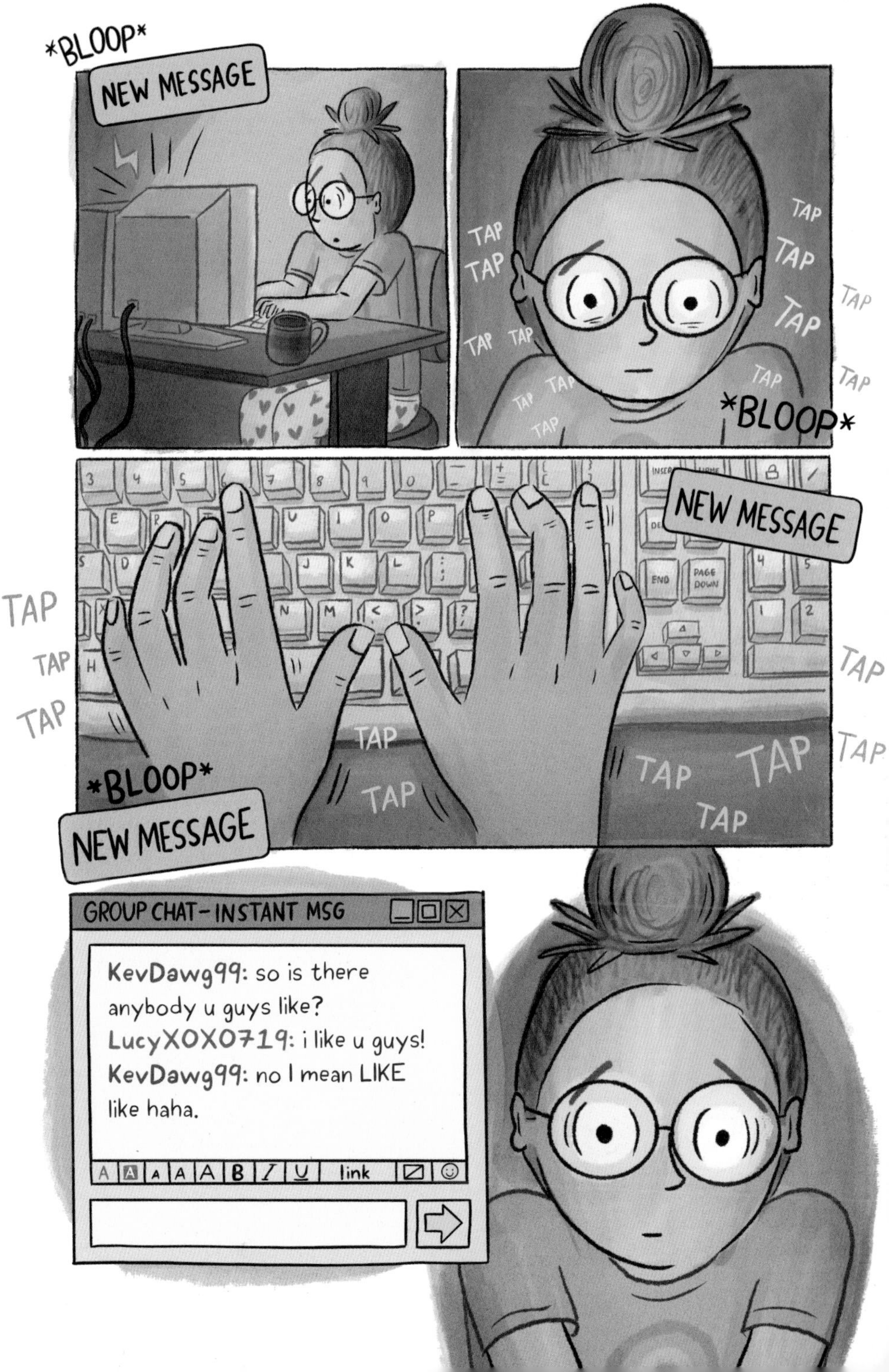
BLOOP
NEW MESSAGE
TAP
TAP
TAP
TAP
TAP
TAP
TAP TAP
TAP TAP
TAP
TAP
TAP
BLOOP
NEW MESSAGE
TAP
TAP
TAP
TAP
TAP
TAP
TAP
TAP
TAP
TAP
BLOOP
NEW MESSAGE
GROUP CHAT-INSTANT MSG
KevDawg99: so is there anybody u guys like?
LucyXOXO719: i like u guys!
KevDawg99: no I mean LIKE like haha.
link

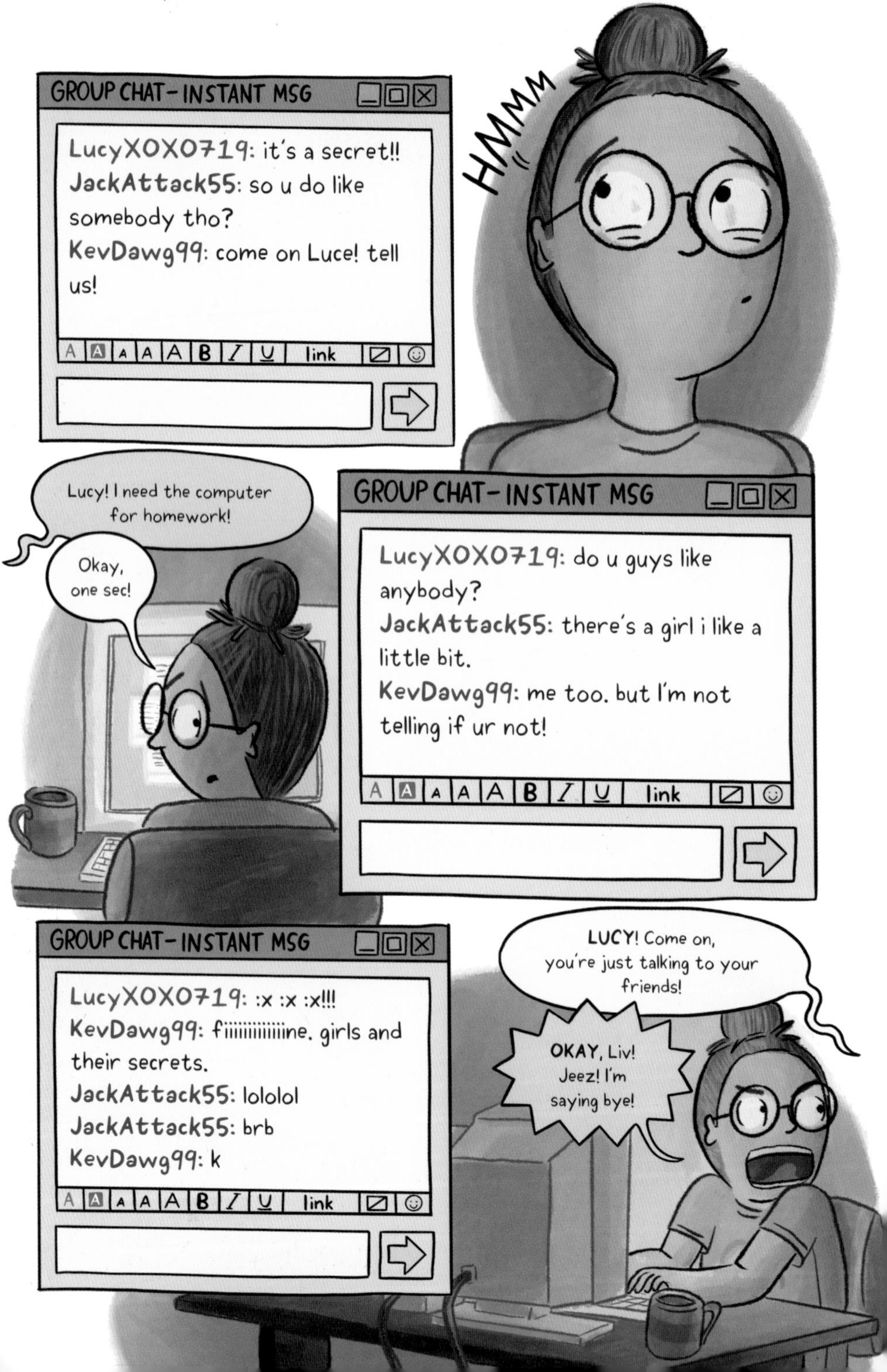
GROUP CHAT-INSTANT MSG
LucyXOXO719: it's a secret!!
JackAttack55: so u do like somebody tho?
KevDawg99: come on Luce! tell us!
link
HMMM
Lucy! I need the computer for homework!
Okay, one sec!
GROUP CHAT-INSTANT MSG
LucyXOXO719: do u guys like anybody?
JackAttack55: there's a girl i like a little bit.
KevDawg99: me too. but I'm not telling if ur not!
link
GROUP CHAT-INSTANT MSG
LucyXOXO719: :x :x :x!!!
KevDawg99: fiiiiiiiiiiiiine. girls and their secrets.
JackAttack55: lololol
JackAttack55: brb
KevDawg99: k
link
LUCY! Come on, you're just talking to your friends!
OKAY, Liv! Jeez! I'm saying bye!

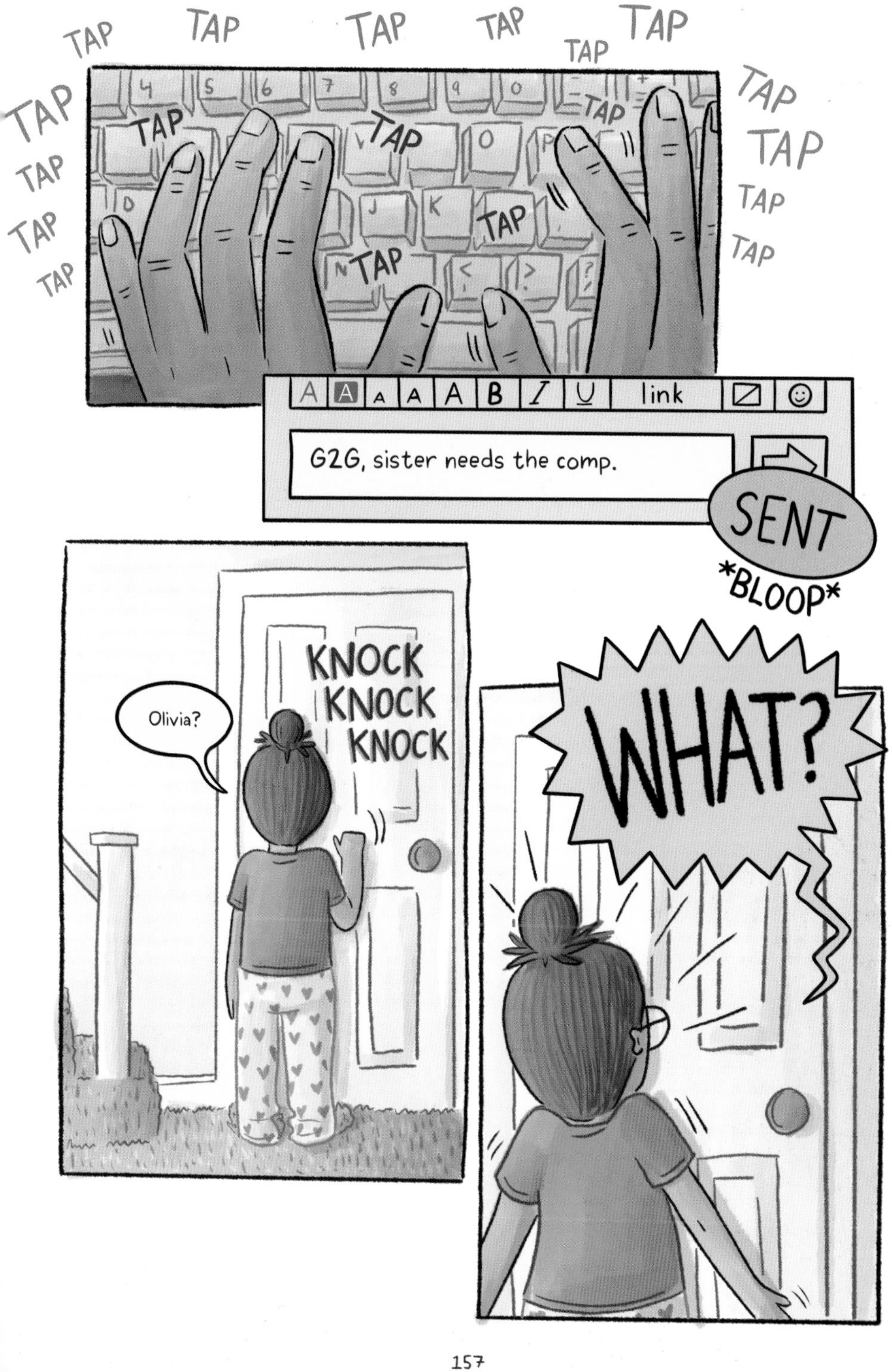
TAP TAP TAP TAP TAP TAP TAP TAP TAP TAP
TAP TAP TAP TAP TAP TAP TAP TAP TAP TAP
A A A A A B I U link
G2G, sister needs the comp.
SENT
BLOOP
KNOCK
KNOCK
KNOCK
Olivia?
WHAT?

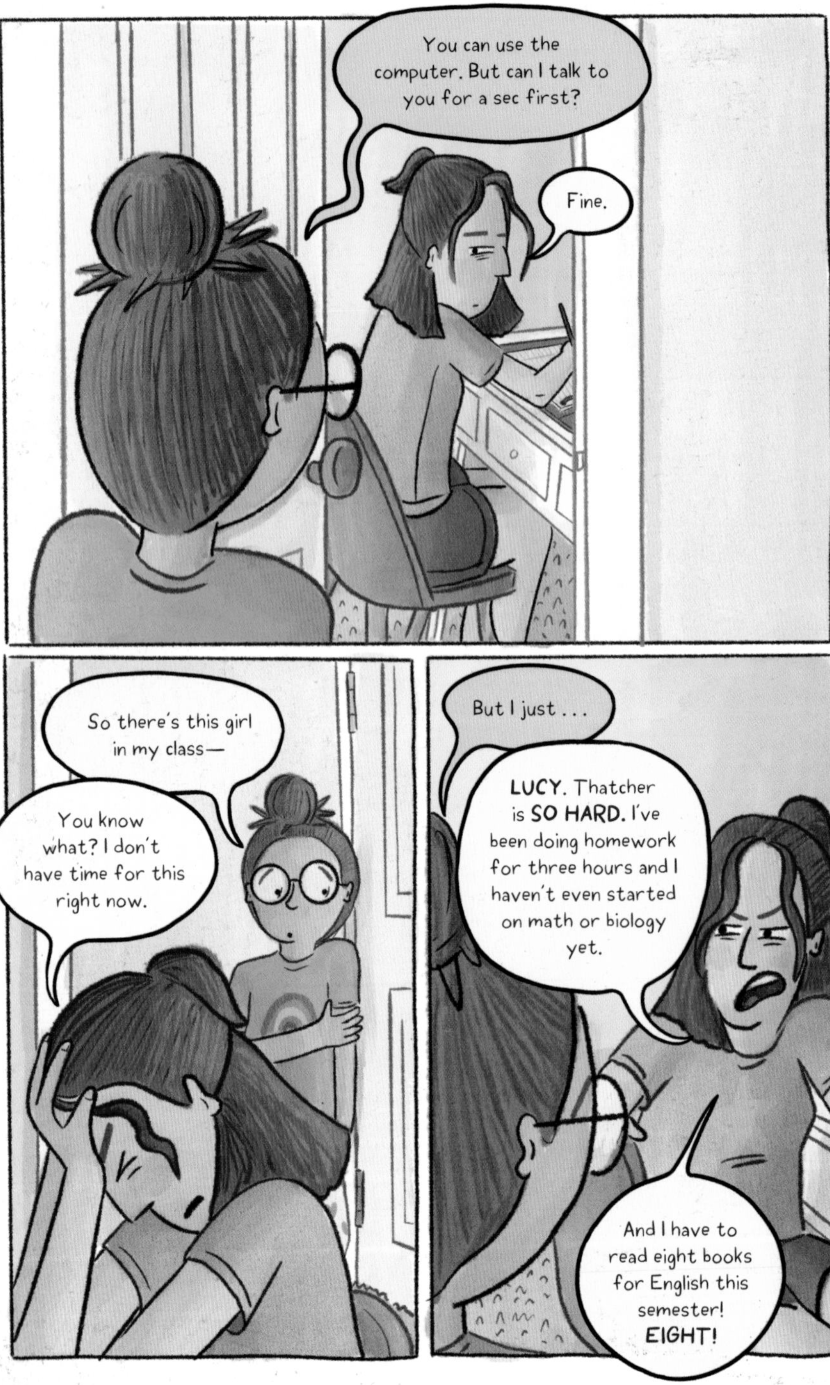
You can use the computer. But can I talk to you for a sec first?
Fine.
So there's this girl in my class—
You know what? I don't have time for this right now.
But I just . . .
LUCY. Thatcher is SO HARD. I've been doing homework for three hours and I haven't even started on math or biology yet.
And I have to read eight books for English this semester! EIGHT!

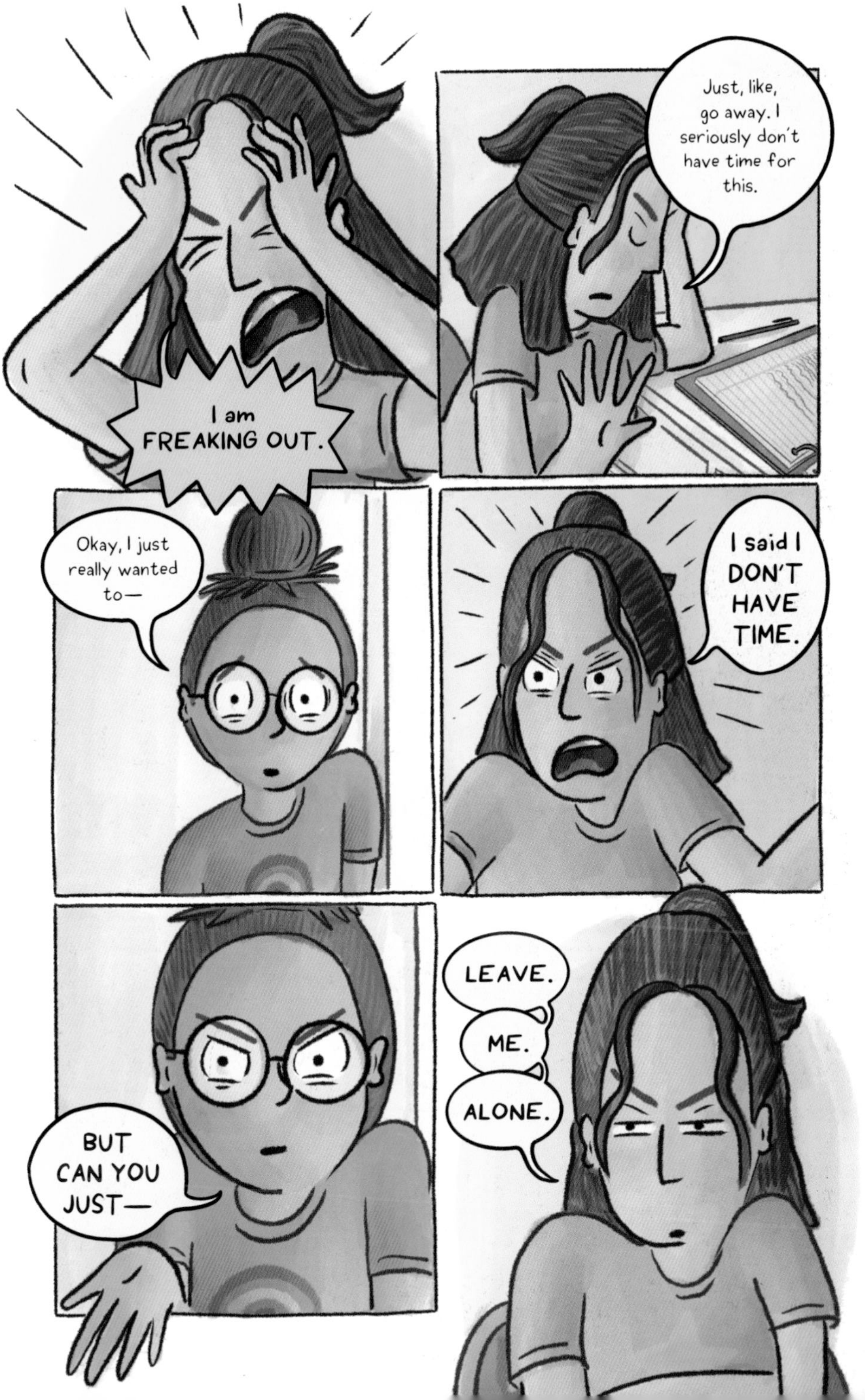
I am FREAKING OUT.
Just, like, go away. I seriously don't have time for this.
Okay, I just really wanted to—
I said I DON'T HAVE TIME.
BUT CAN YOU JUST—
LEAVE.
ME.
ALONE.

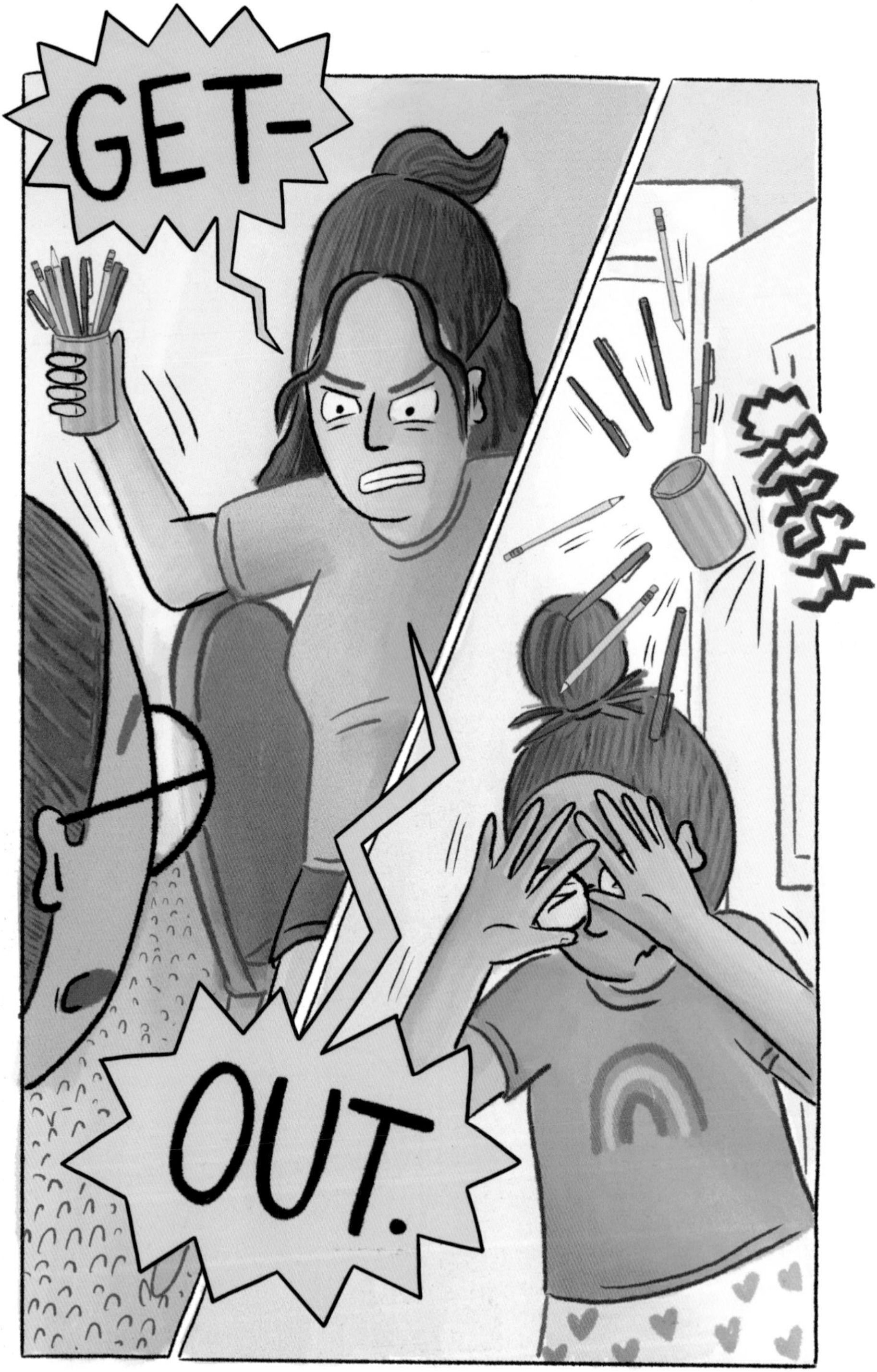
GET-
CRASH
OUT.

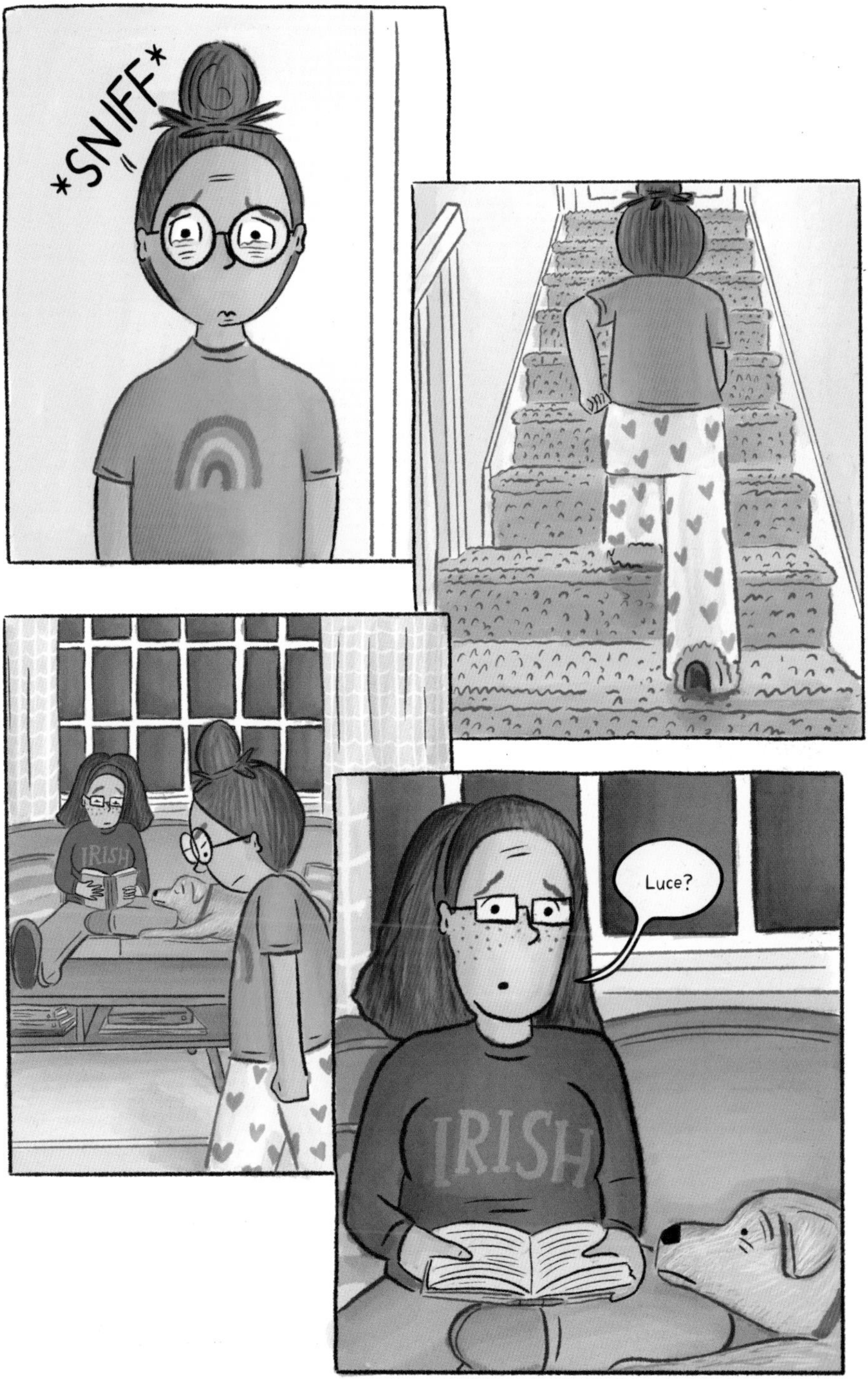
SNIFF
IRISH
IRISH
Luce?

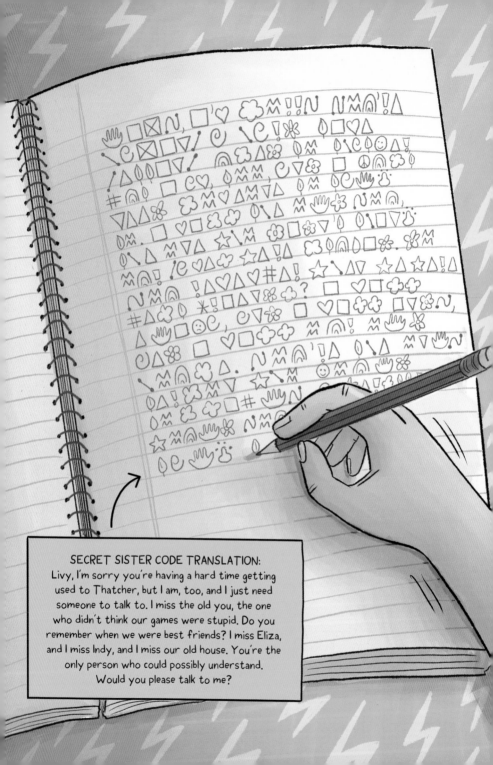

SECRET SISTER CODE TRANSLATION:
Livy, I'm sorry you're having a hard time getting used to Thatcher, but I am, too, and I just need someone to talk to. I miss the old you, the one who didn't think our games were stupid. Do you remember when we were best friends? I miss Eliza, and I miss Indy, and I miss our old house. You're the only person who could possibly understand. Would you please talk to me?

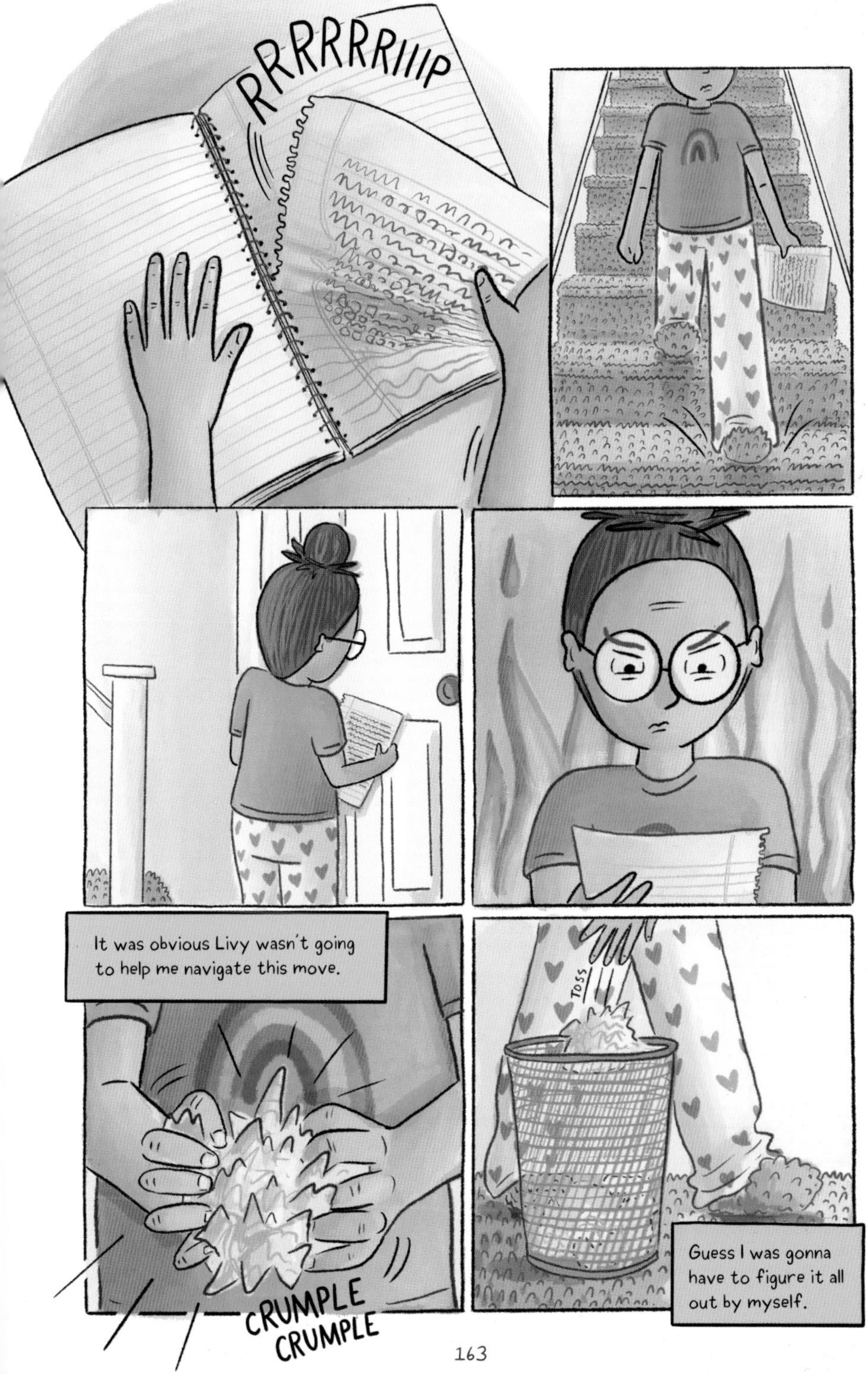
RRRRRRIIIP
It was obvious Livy wasn't going to help me navigate this move.
CRUMPLE
CRUMPLE
TOSS
Guess I was gonna have to figure it all out by myself.

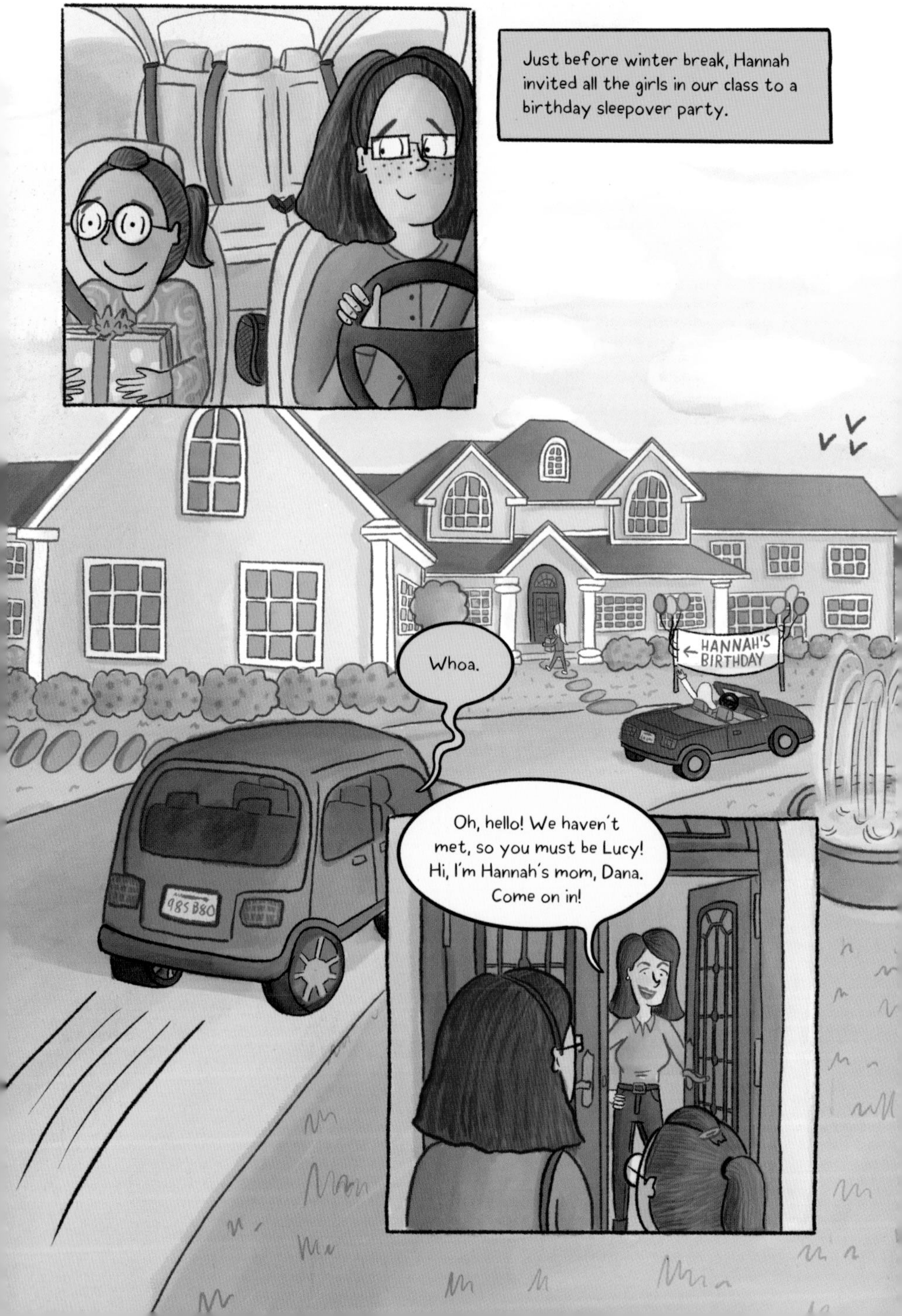
Just before winter break, Hannah invited all the girls in our class to a birthday sleepover party.
← HANNAH'S BIRTHDAY
Whoa.
985 B80
Oh, hello! We haven't met, so you must be Lucy! Hi, I'm Hannah's mom, Dana. Come on in!

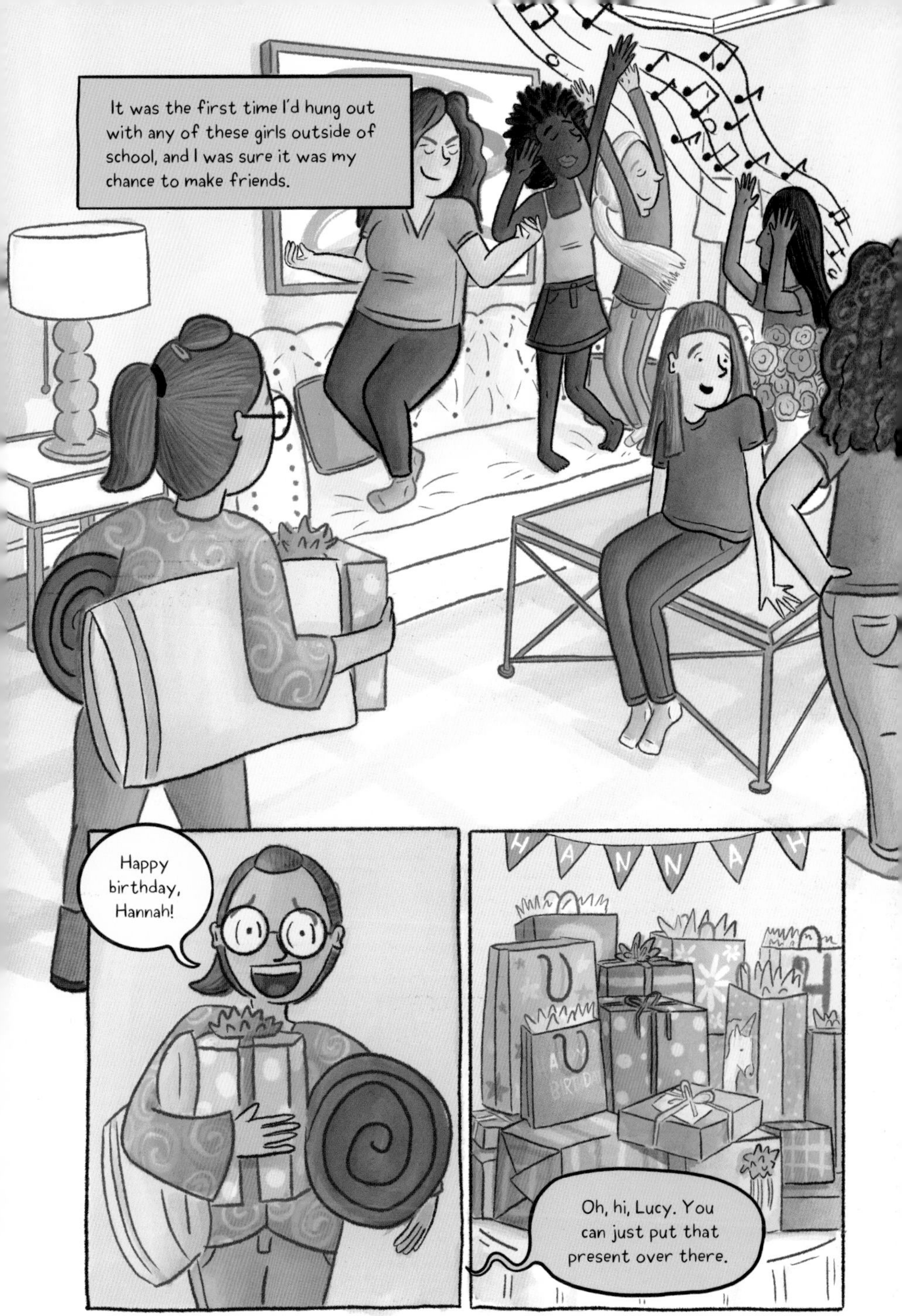
It was the first time I'd hung out with any of these girls outside of school, and I was sure it was my chance to make friends.
Happy birthday, Hannah!
HANNAH
Oh, hi, Lucy. You can just put that present over there.

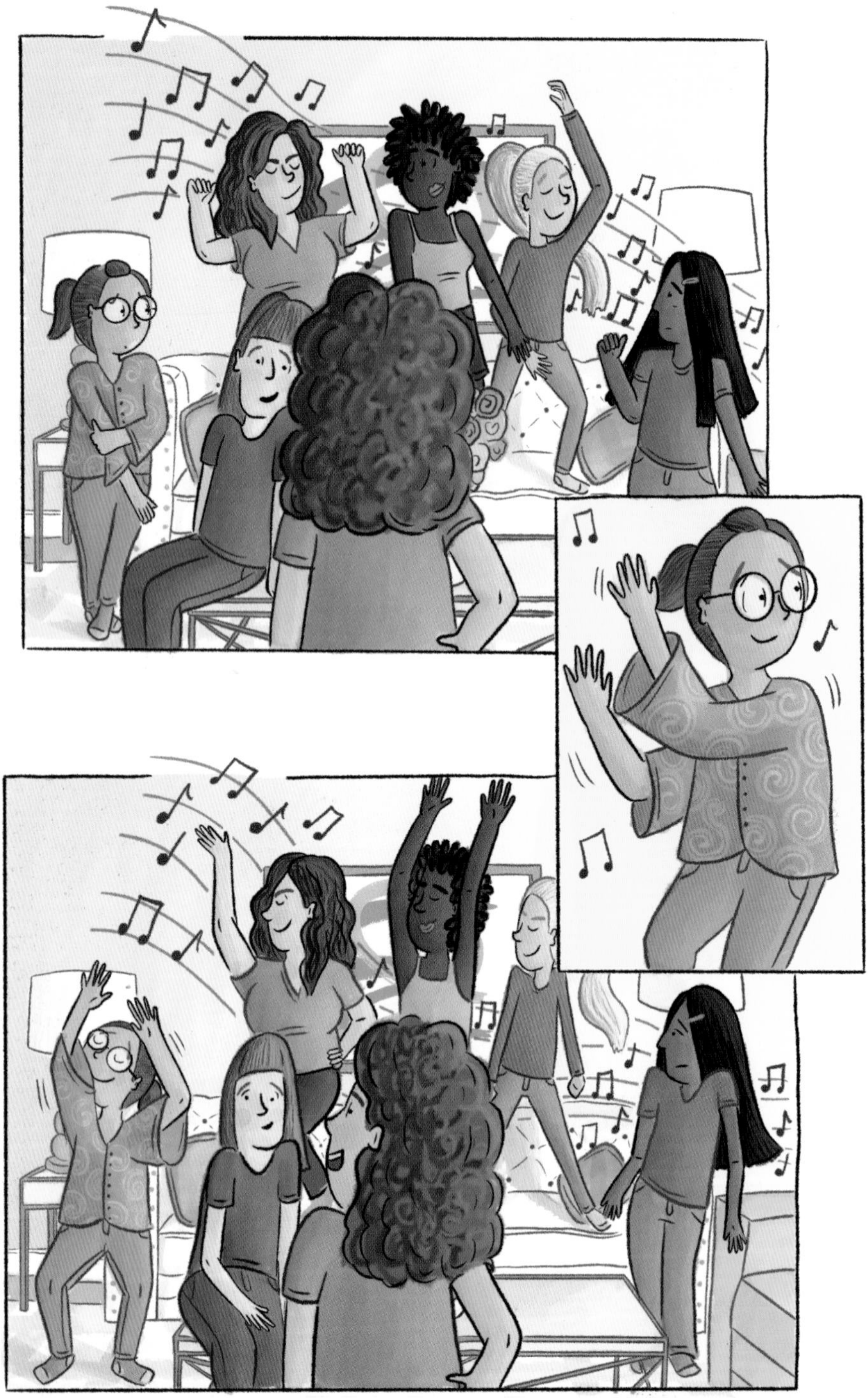

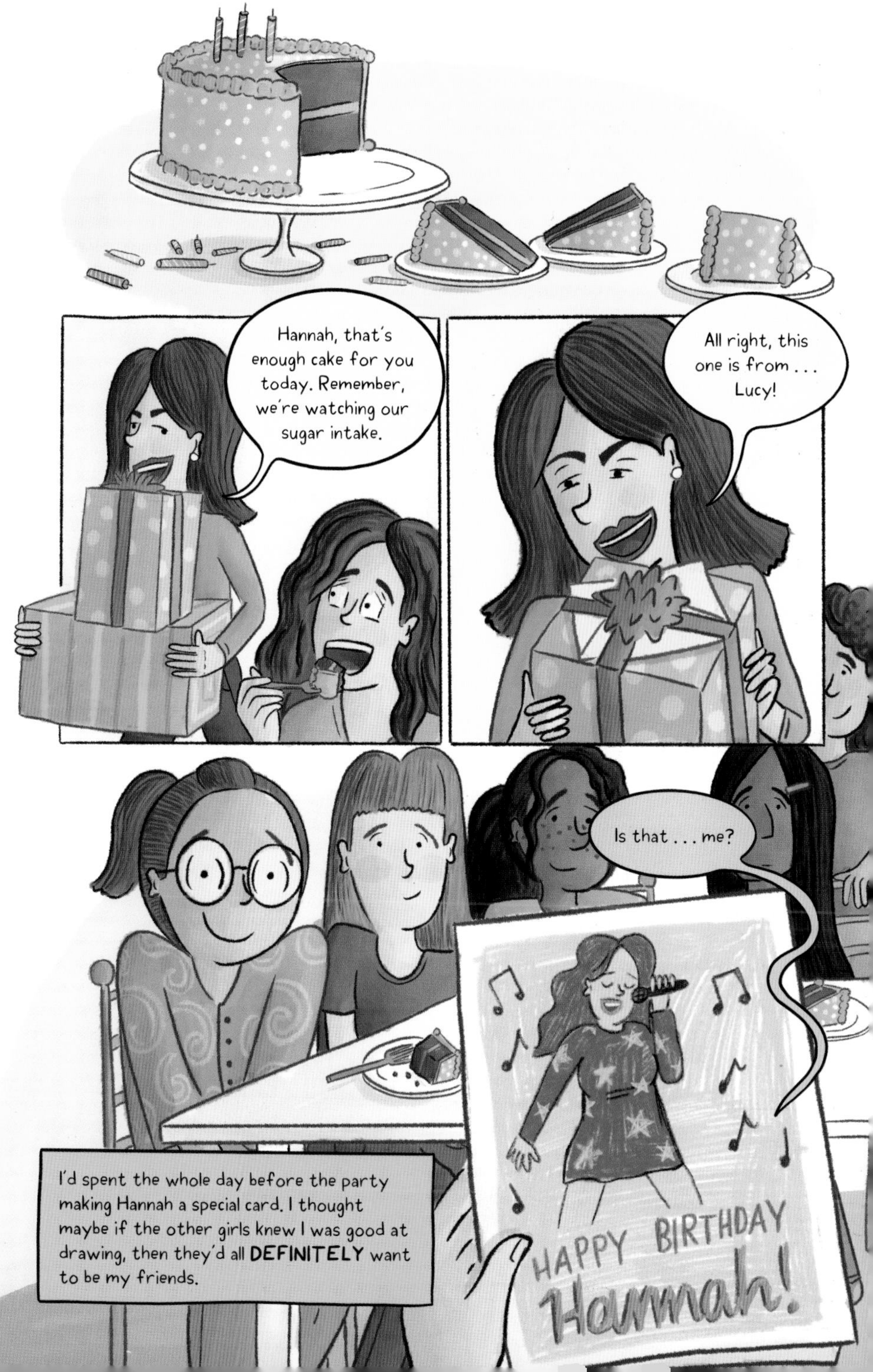

Hannah, that's enough cake for you today. Remember, we're watching our sugar intake.
All right, this one is from . . . Lucy!
Is that . . . me?
I'd spent the whole day before the party making Hannah a special card. I thought maybe if the other girls knew I was good at drawing, then they'd all **DEFINITELY** want to be my friends.
HAPPY BIRTHDAY
Hannah!

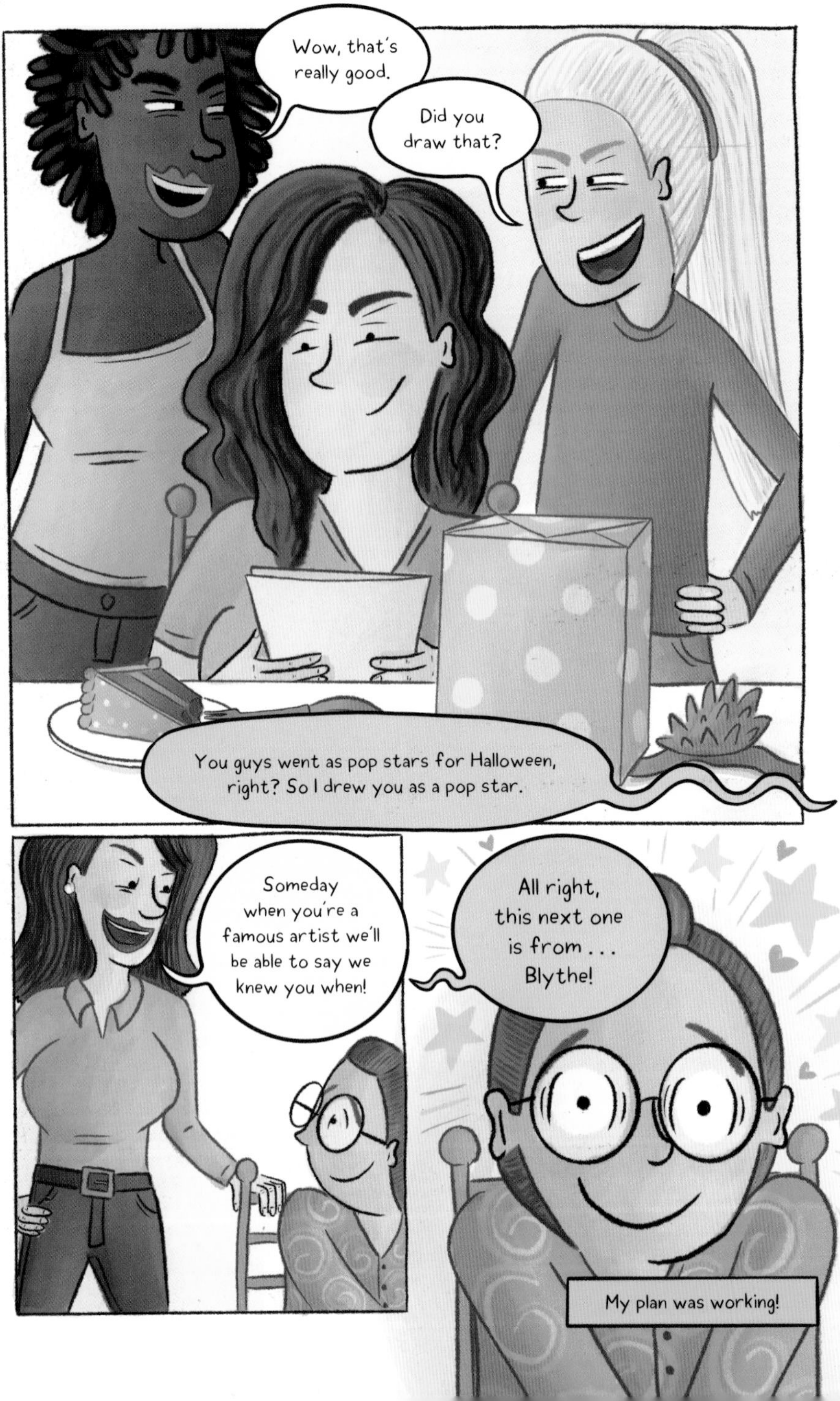
Wow, that's really good.
Did you draw that?
You guys went as pop stars for Halloween, right? So I drew you as a pop star.
Someday when you're a famous artist we'll be able to say we knew you when!
All right, this next one is from . . . Blythe!
My plan was working!

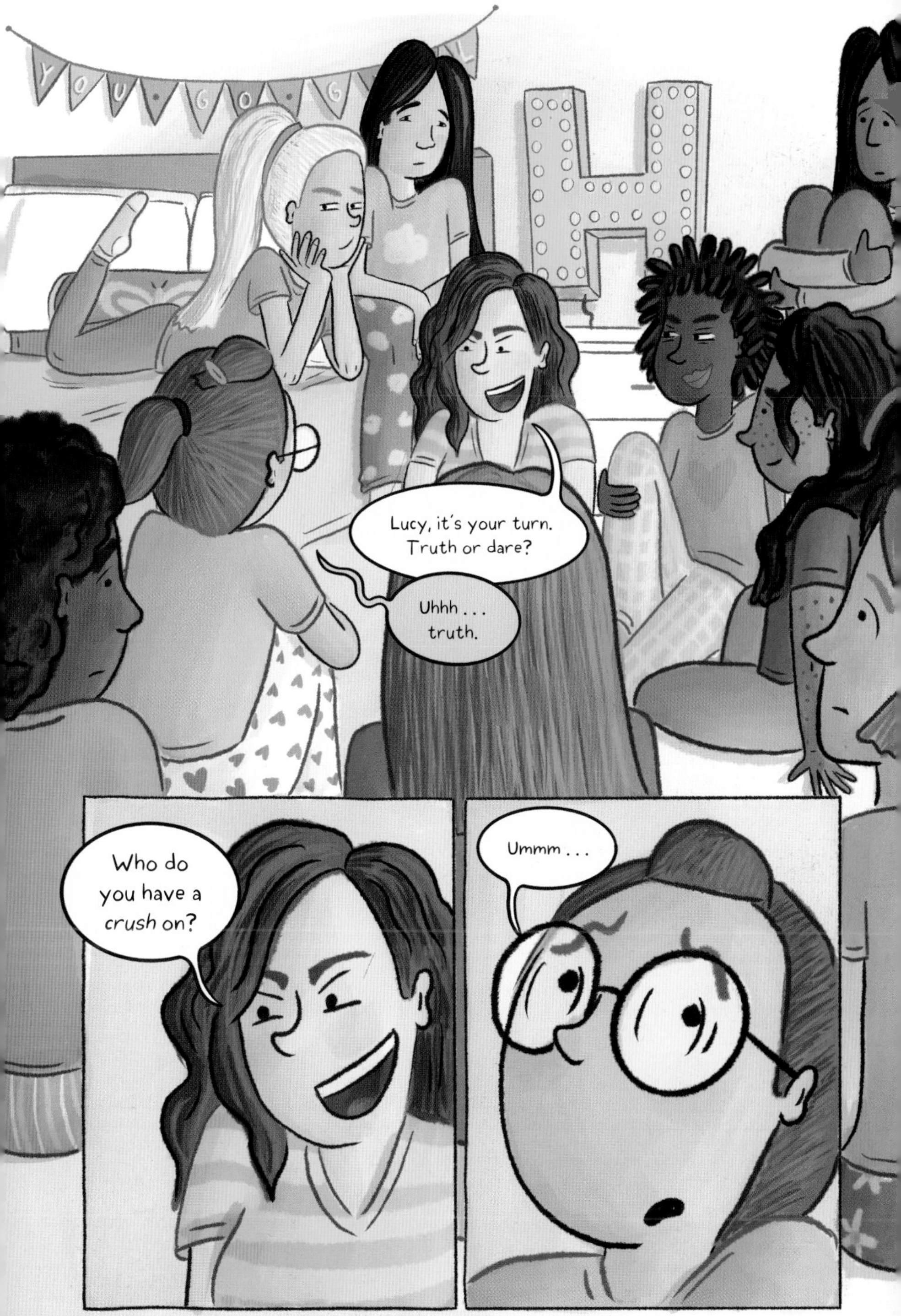
YOU GO G L
Lucy, it's your turn. Truth or dare?
Uhhh . . . truth.
Who do you have a *crush* on?
Ummm . . .

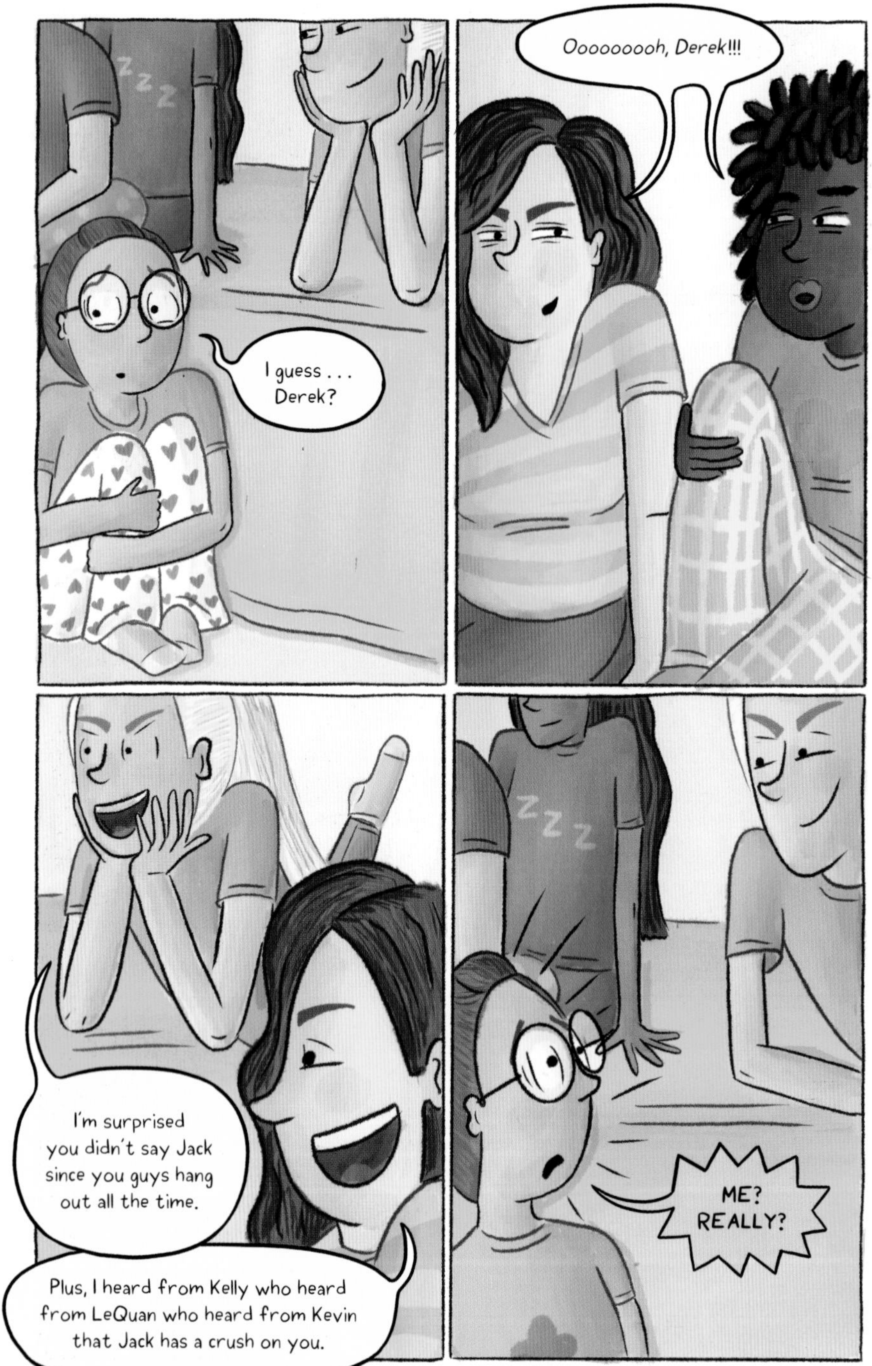
I guess . . . Derek?
Oooooooooh, Derek!!!
I'm surprised you didn't say Jack since you guys hang out all the time.
Plus, I heard from Kelly who heard from LeQuan who heard from Kevin that Jack has a crush on you.
ME? REALLY?

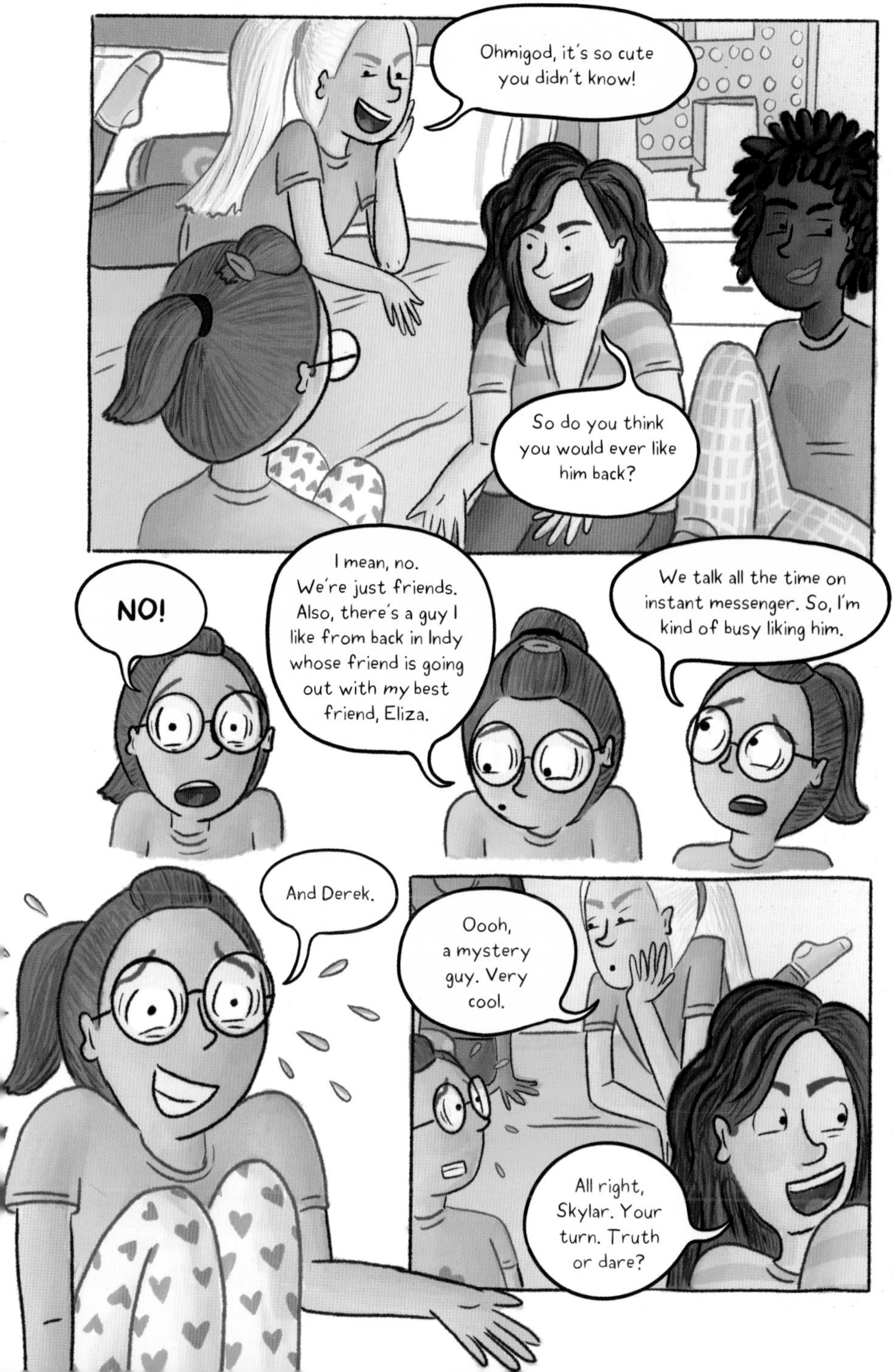
Ohmigod, it's so cute you didn't know!
So do you think you would ever like him back?
NO!
I mean, no. We're just friends. Also, there's a guy I like from back in Indy whose friend is going out with *my* best friend, Eliza.
We talk all the time on instant messenger. So, I'm kind of busy liking him.
And Derek.
Oooh, a mystery guy. Very cool.
All right, Skylar. Your turn. Truth or dare?

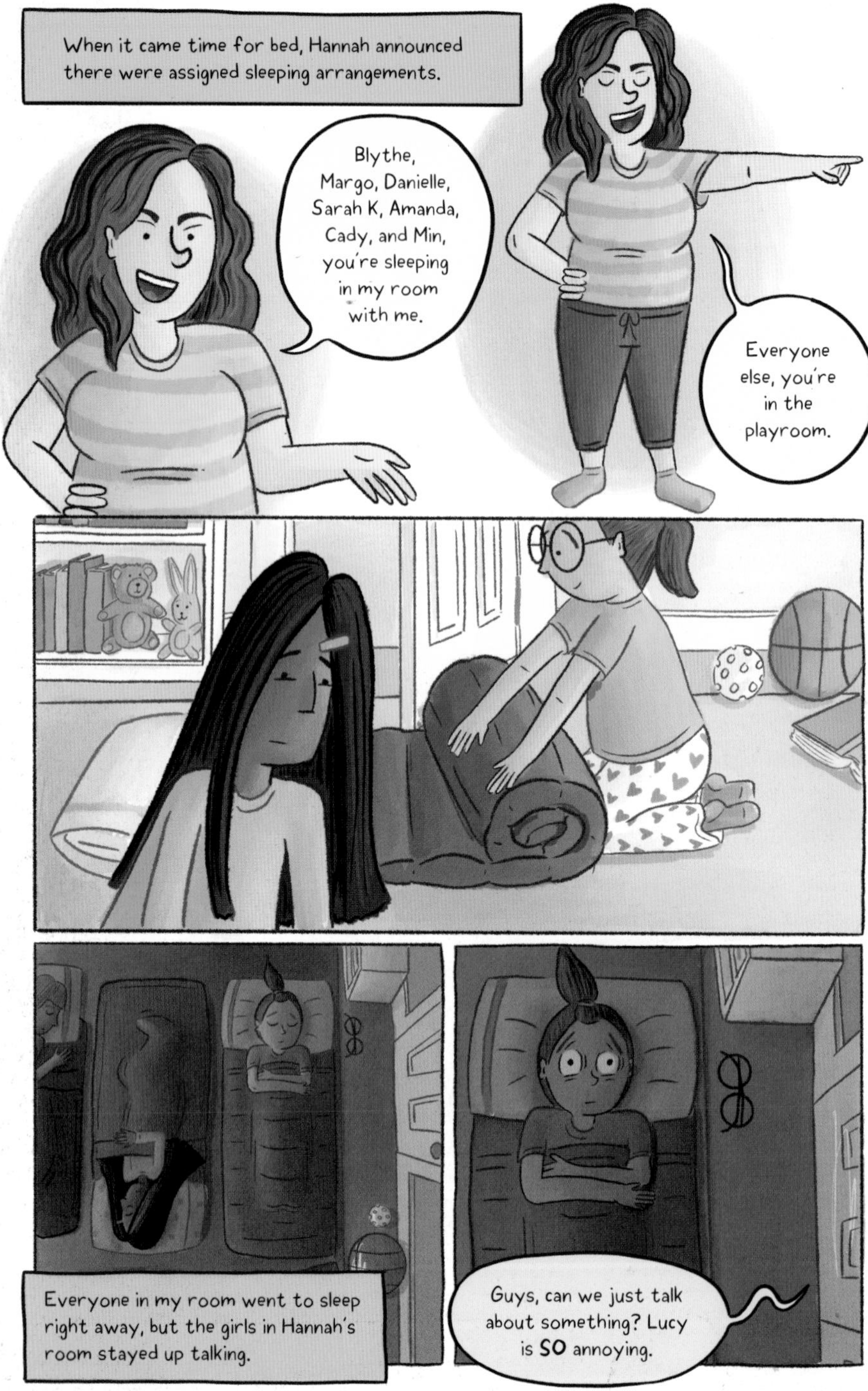
When it came time for bed, Hannah announced there were assigned sleeping arrangements.
Blythe, Margo, Danielle, Sarah K, Amanda, Cady, and Min, you're sleeping in my room with me.
Everyone else, you're in the playroom.
Everyone in my room went to sleep right away, but the girls in Hannah's room stayed up talking.
Guys, can we just talk about something? Lucy is **SO** annoying.

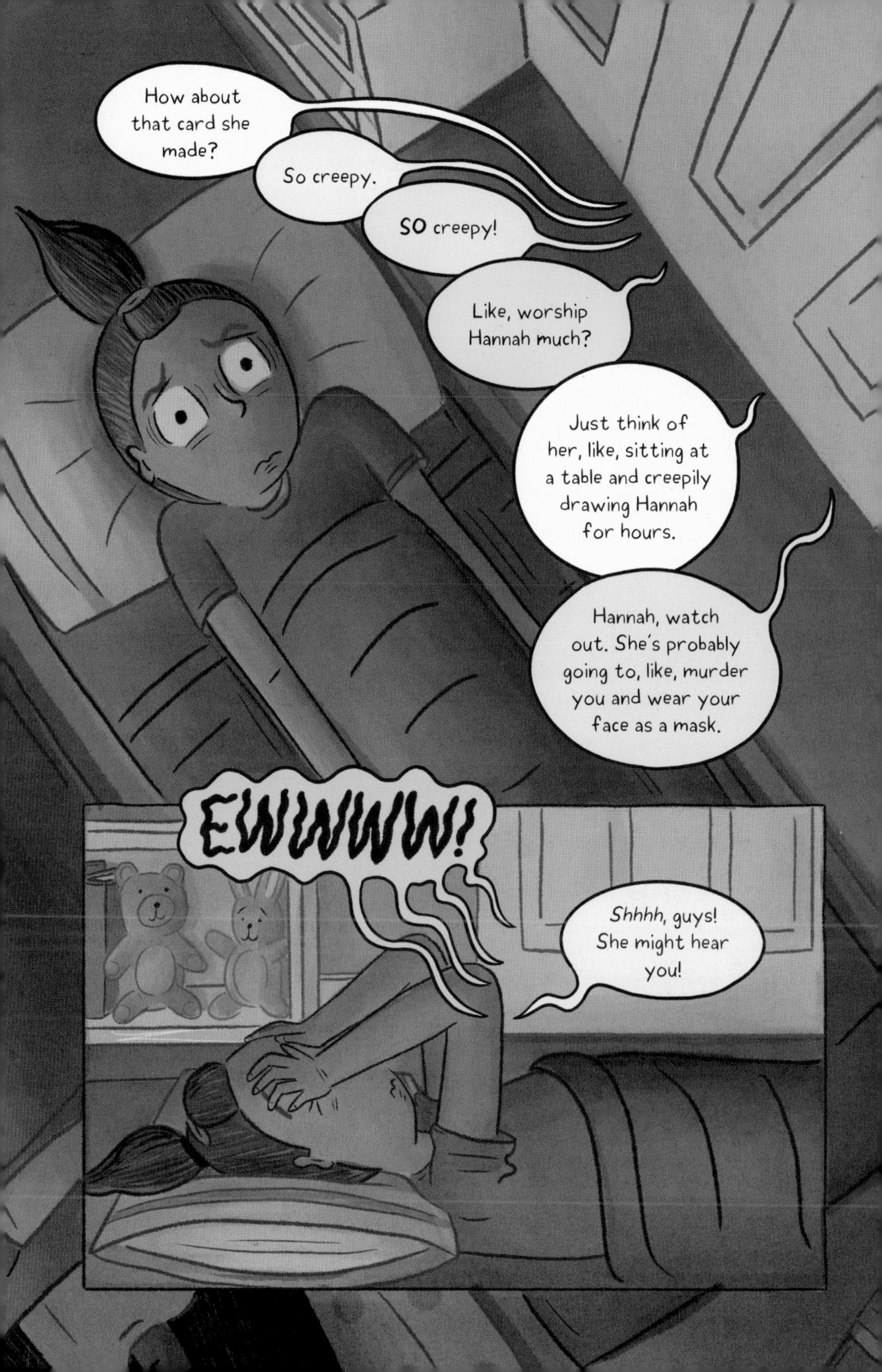
How about that card she made?
So creepy.
SO creepy!
Like, worship Hannah much?
Just think of her, like, sitting at a table and creepily drawing Hannah for hours.
Hannah, watch out. She's probably going to, like, murder you and wear your face as a mask.
EWWWW!
Shhhh, guys! She might hear you!

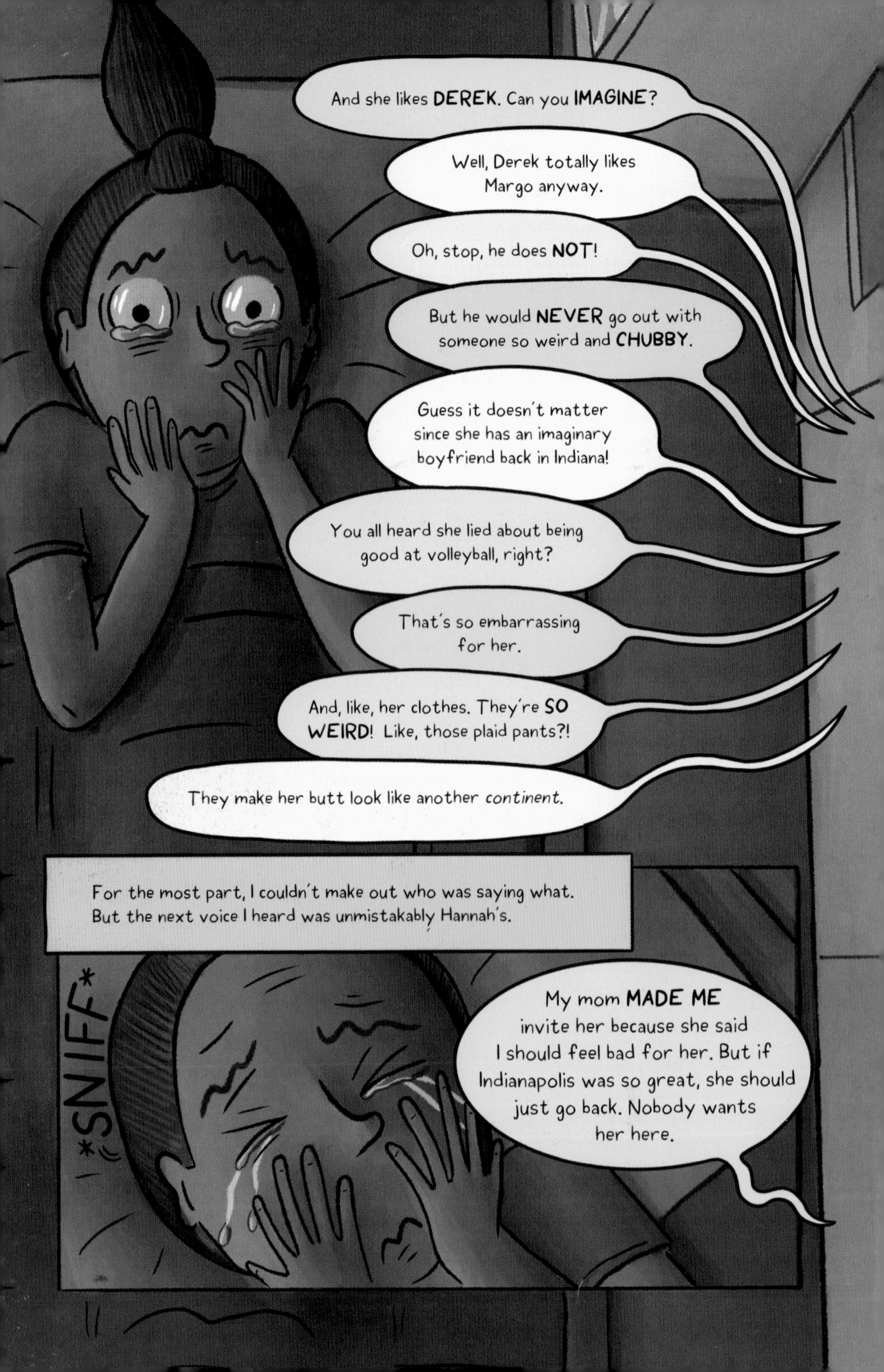
And she likes DEREK. Can you IMAGINE?
Well, Derek totally likes Margo anyway.
Oh, stop, he does NOT!
But he would NEVER go out with someone so weird and CHUBBY.
Guess it doesn't matter since she has an imaginary boyfriend back in Indiana!
You all heard she lied about being good at volleyball, right?
That's so embarrassing for her.
And, like, her clothes. They're SO WEIRD! Like, those plaid pants?!
They make her butt look like another continent.
For the most part, I couldn't make out who was saying what. But the next voice I heard was unmistakably Hannah's.
SNIFF
My mom MADE ME invite her because she said I should feel bad for her. But if Indianapolis was so great, she should just go back. Nobody wants her here.

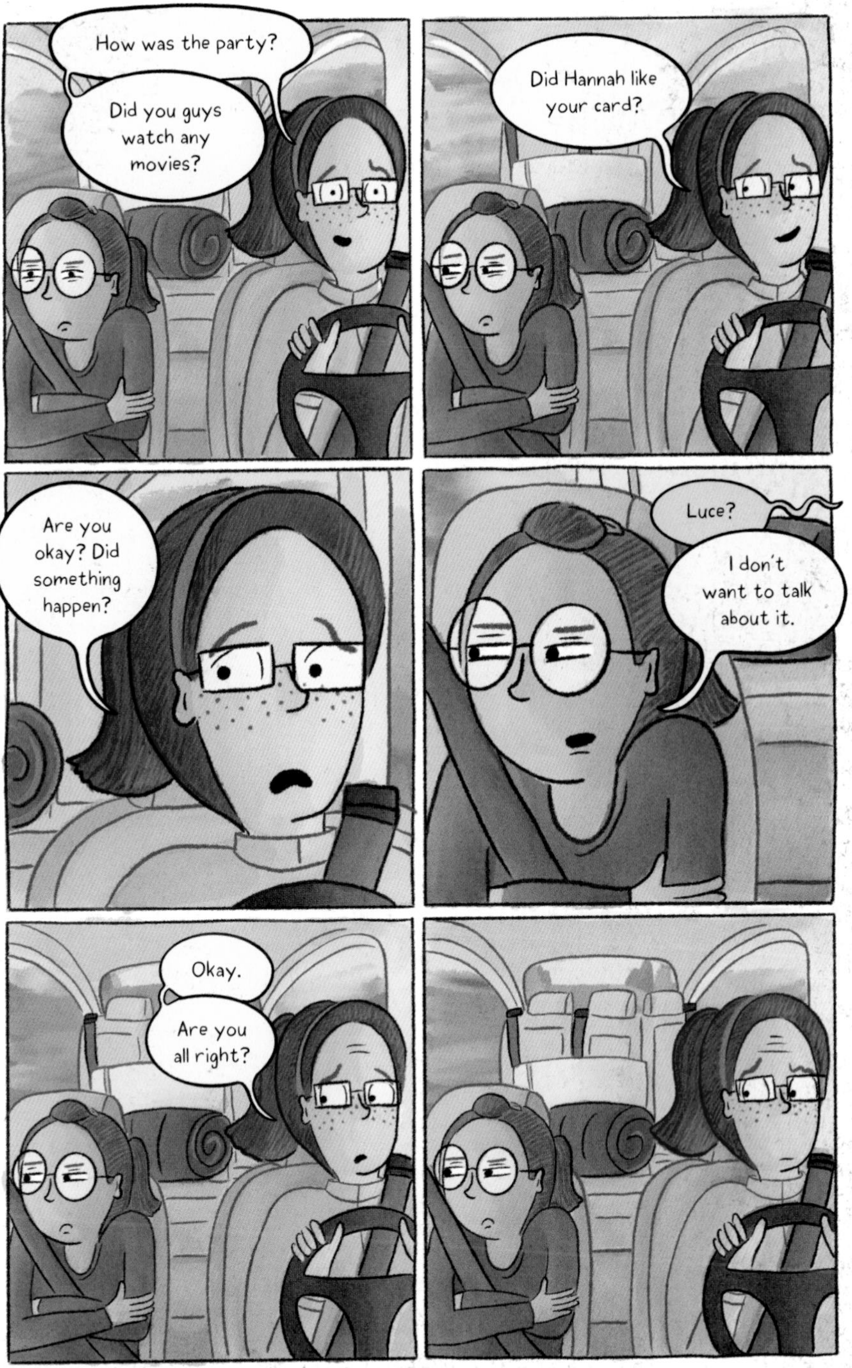
How was the party?
Did you guys watch any movies?
Did Hannah like your card?
Are you okay? Did something happen?
Luce?
I don't want to talk about it.
Okay.
Are you all right?

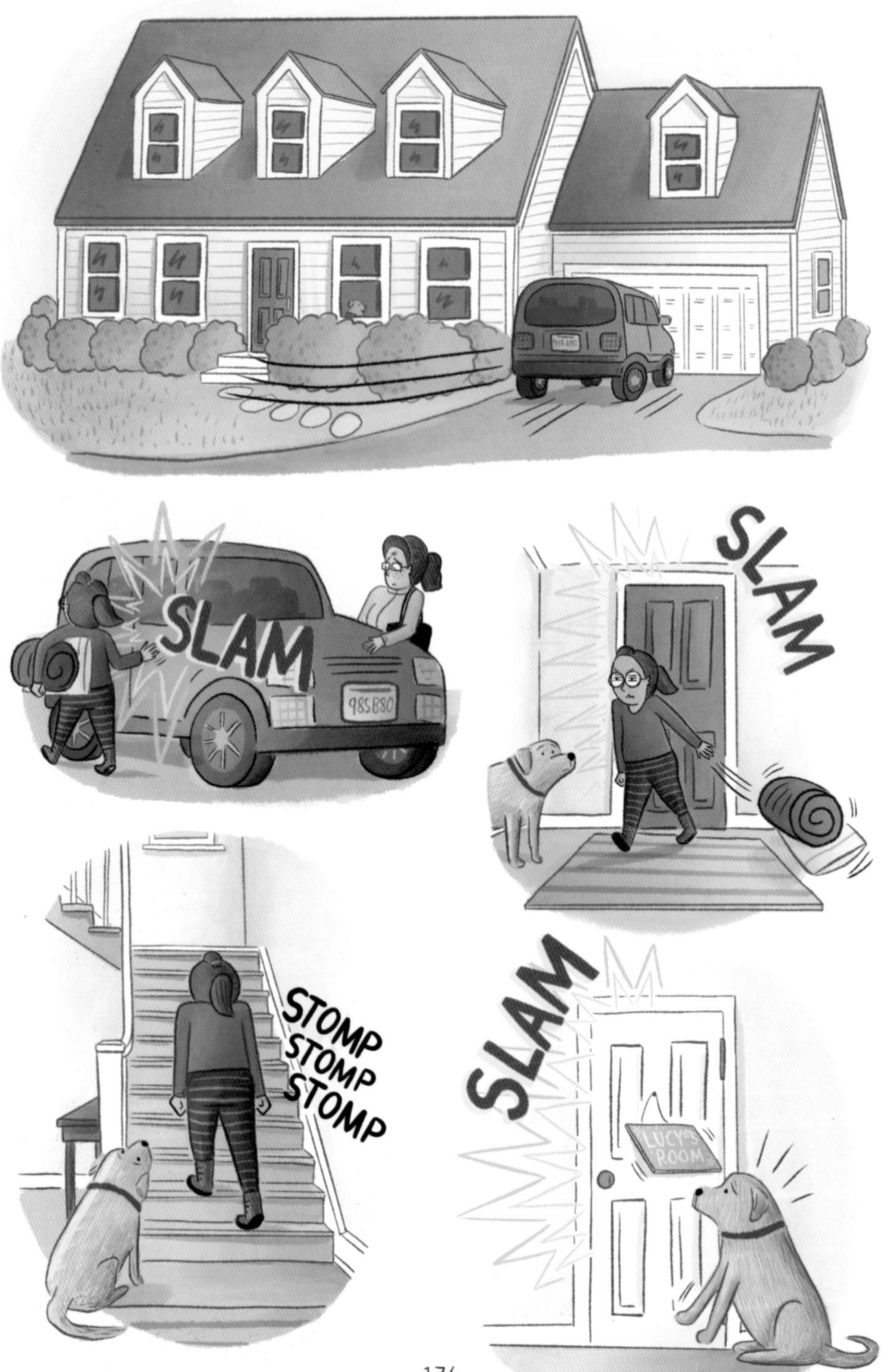
985B80
SLAM
985B80
SLAM
STOMP
STOMP
STOMP
SLAM
LUCY'S ROOM

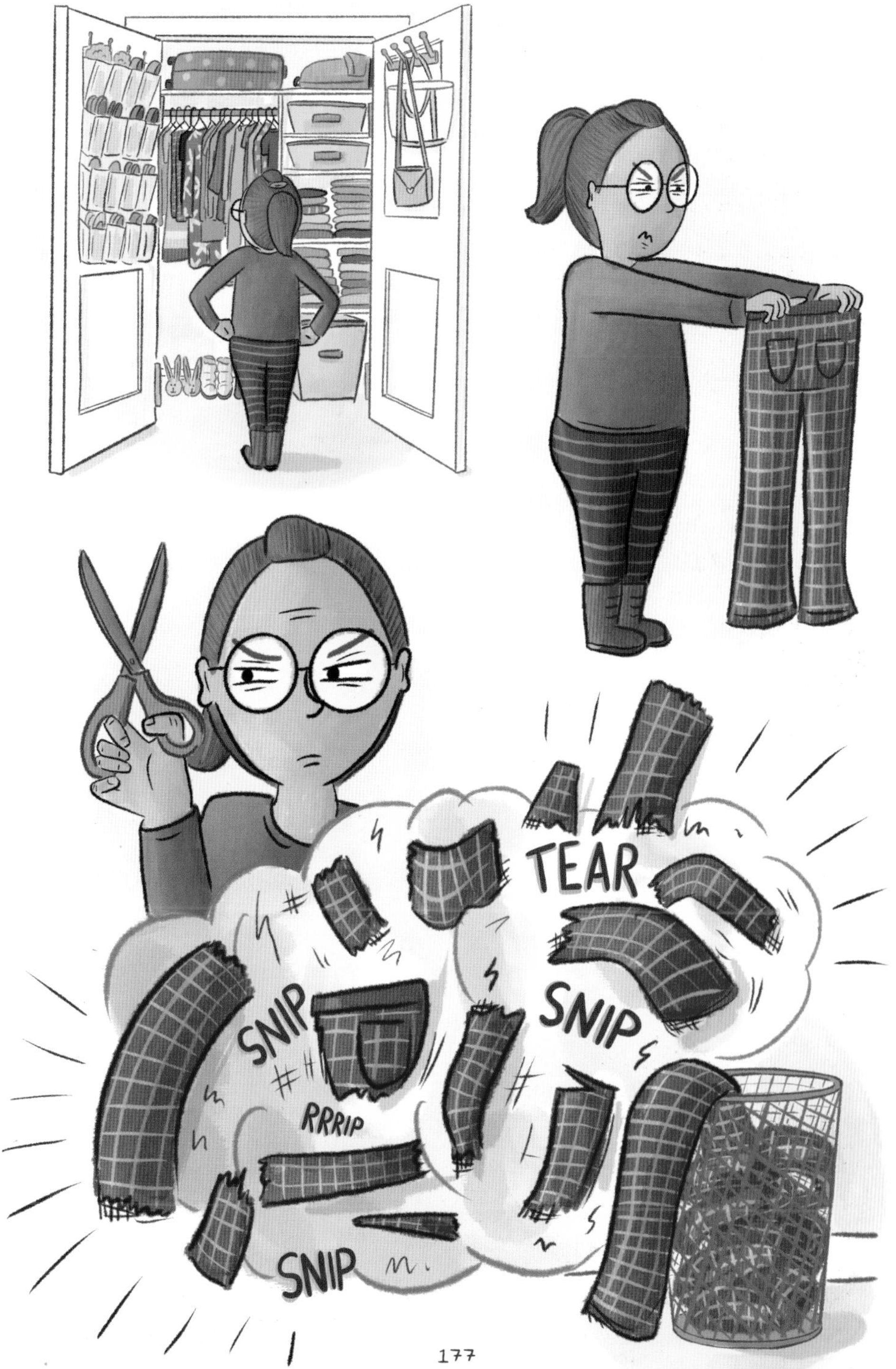
TEAR
SNIP
SNIP
RRRIP
SNIP

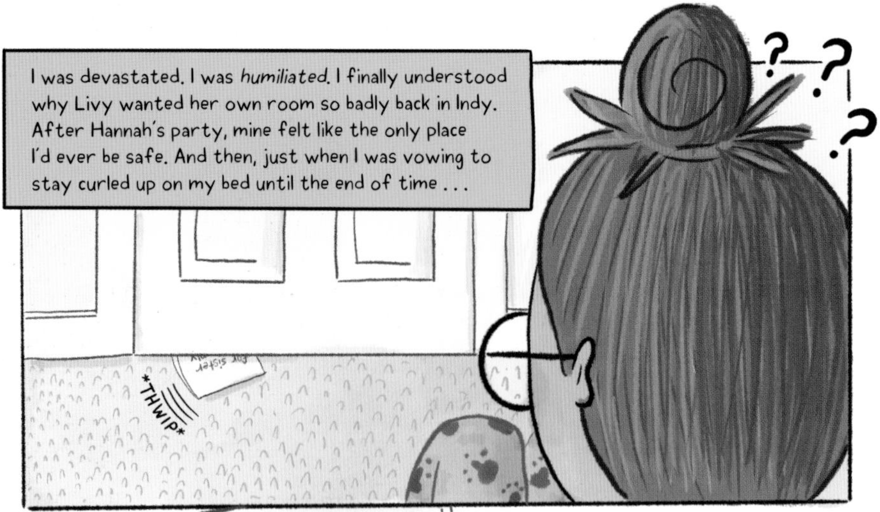
I was devastated. I was *humiliated*. I finally understood why Livy wanted her own room so badly back in Indy. After Hannah's party, mine felt like the only place I'd ever be safe. And then, just when I was vowing to stay curled up on my bed until the end of time . . .
? ? ?
THWIP

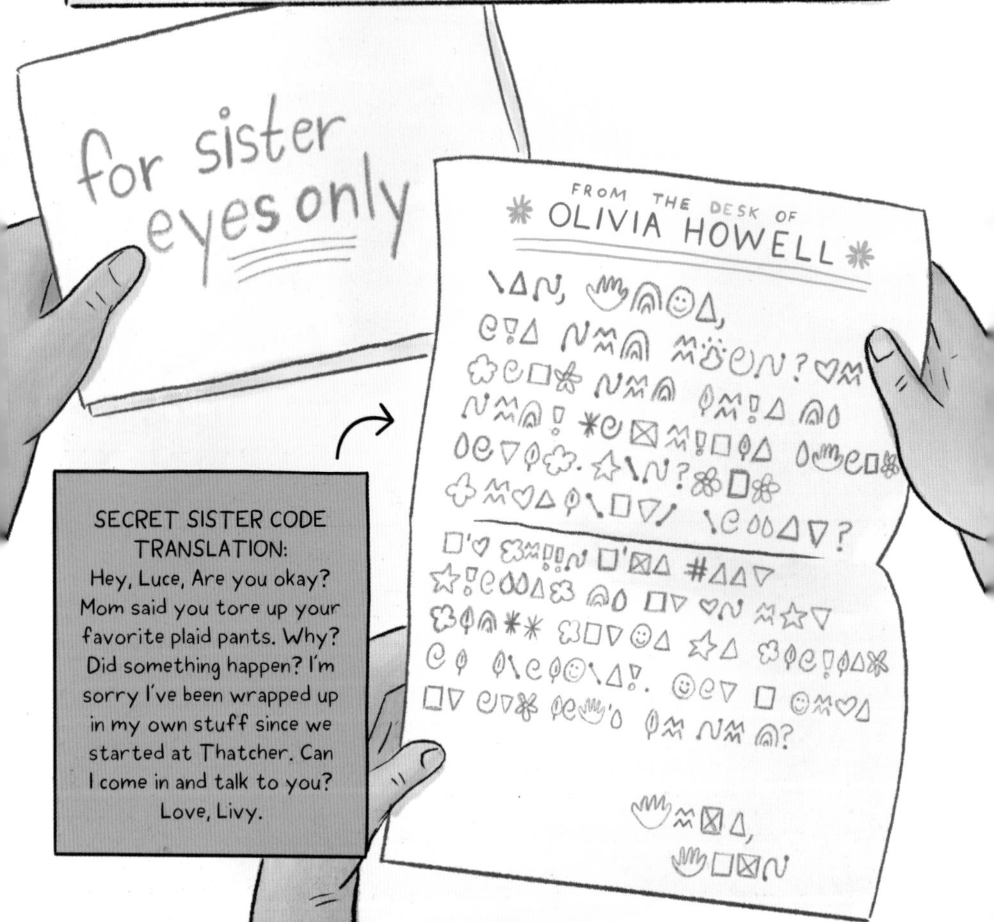
for sister eyes only
FROM THE DESK OF OLIVIA HOWELL
SECRET SISTER CODE TRANSLATION:
Hey, Luce, Are you okay? Mom said you tore up your favorite plaid pants. Why? Did something happen? I'm sorry I've been wrapped up in my own stuff since we started at Thatcher. Can I come in and talk to you? Love, Livy.

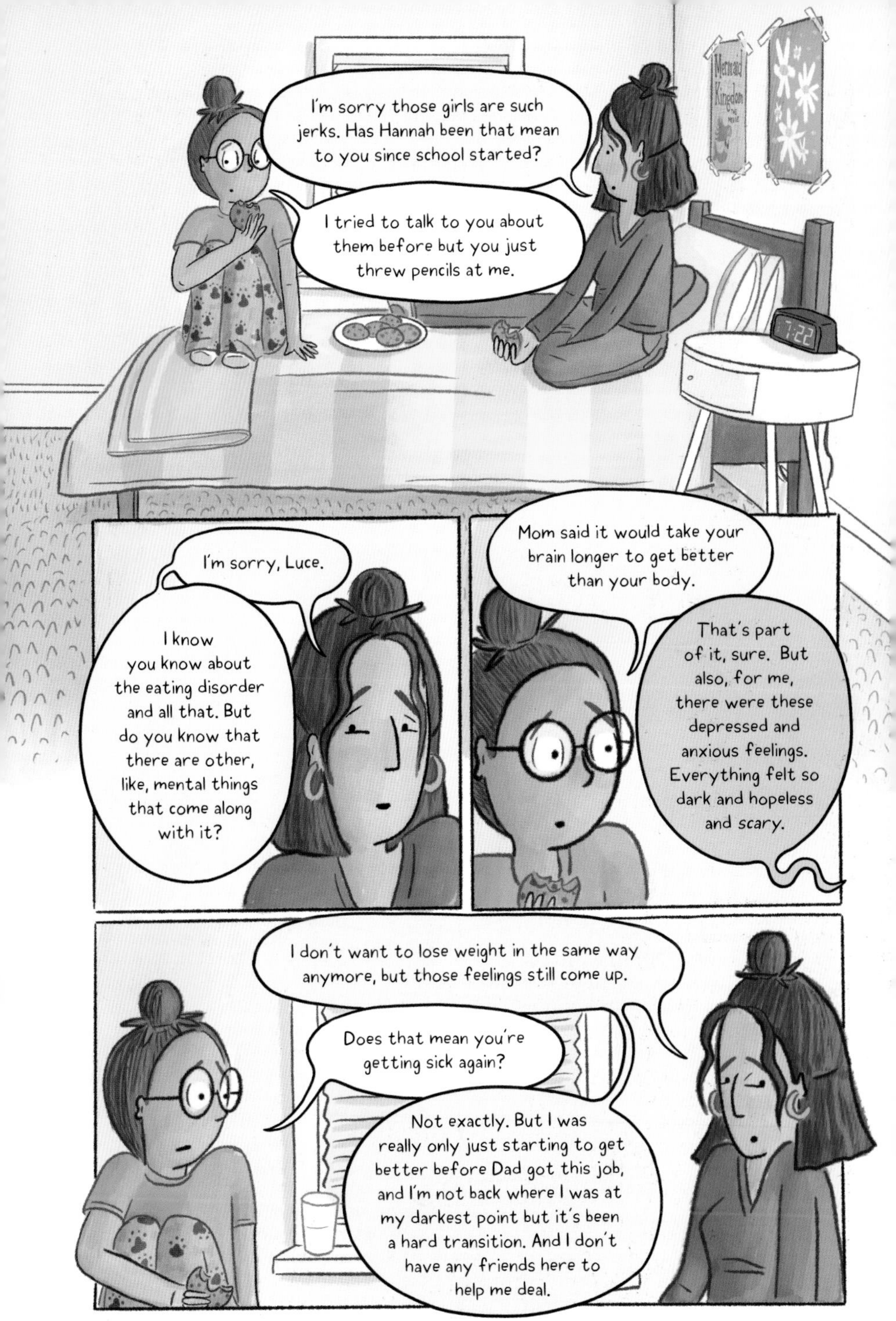

I'm sorry those girls are such jerks. Has Hannah been that mean to you since school started?
I tried to talk to you about them before but you just threw pencils at me.
I'm sorry, Luce.
I know you know about the eating disorder and all that. But do you know that there are other, like, mental things that come along with it?
Mom said it would take your brain longer to get better than your body.
That's part of it, sure. But also, for me, there were these depressed and anxious feelings. Everything felt so dark and hopeless and *scary*.
I don't want to lose weight in the same way anymore, but those feelings still come up.
Does that mean you're getting sick again?
Not exactly. But I was really only just starting to get better before Dad got this job, and I'm not back where I was at my darkest point but it's been a hard transition. And I don't have any friends here to help me deal.

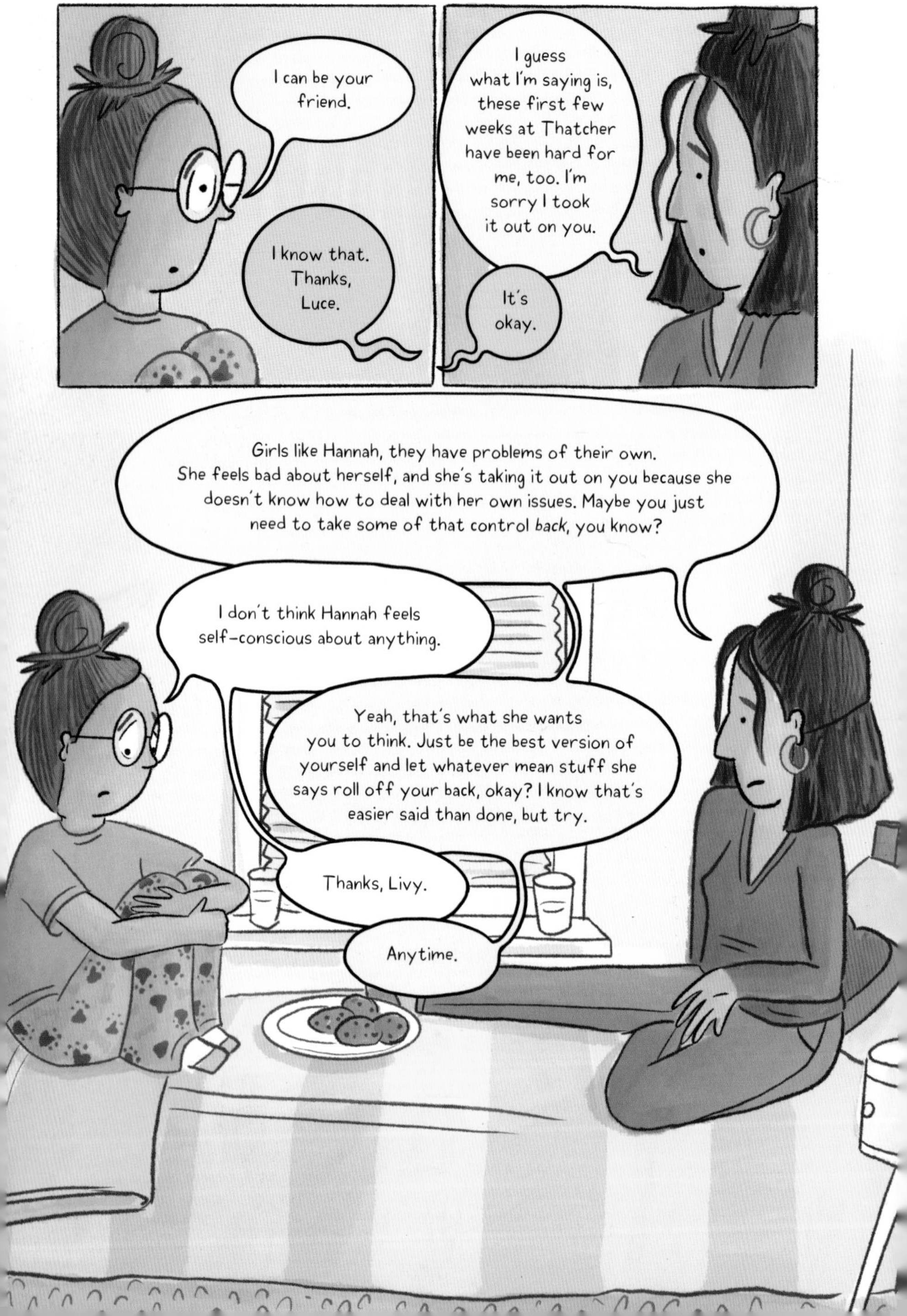
I can be your friend.
I know that. Thanks, Luce.
I guess what I'm saying is, these first few weeks at Thatcher have been hard for me, too. I'm sorry I took it out on you.
It's okay.
Girls like Hannah, they have problems of their own. She feels bad about herself, and she's taking it out on you because she doesn't know how to deal with her own issues. Maybe you just need to take some of that control *back*, you know?
I don't think Hannah feels self-conscious about anything.
Yeah, that's what she wants you to think. Just be the best version of yourself and let whatever mean stuff she says roll off your back, okay? I know that's easier said than done, but try.
Thanks, Livy.
Anytime.

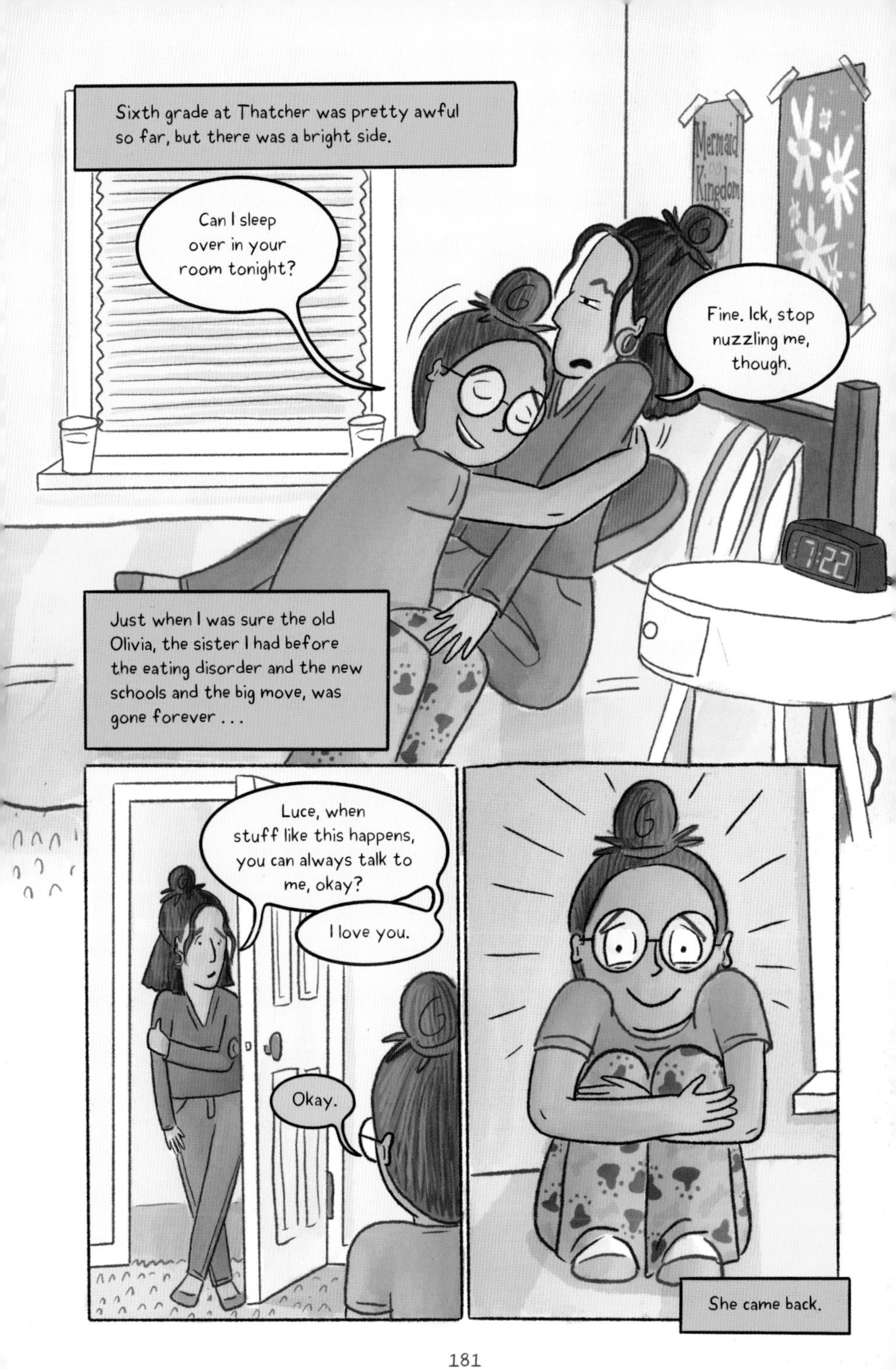

Sixth grade at Thatcher was pretty awful so far, but there was a bright side.
Can I sleep over in your room tonight?
Fine. Ick, stop nuzzling me, though.
Mermaid Kingdom
7:22
Just when I was sure the old Olivia, the sister I had before the eating disorder and the new schools and the big move, was gone forever . . .
Luce, when stuff like this happens, you can always talk to me, okay?
I love you.
Okay.
She came back.

CHAPTER 5

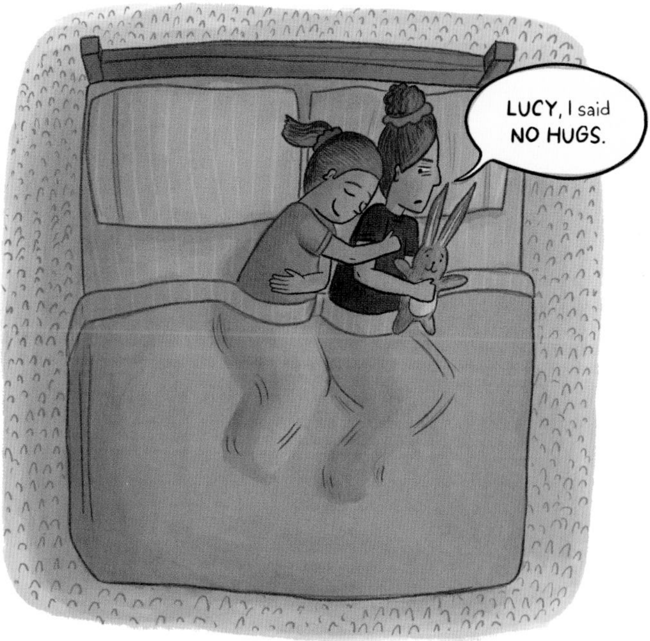
LUCY, I said NO HUGS.

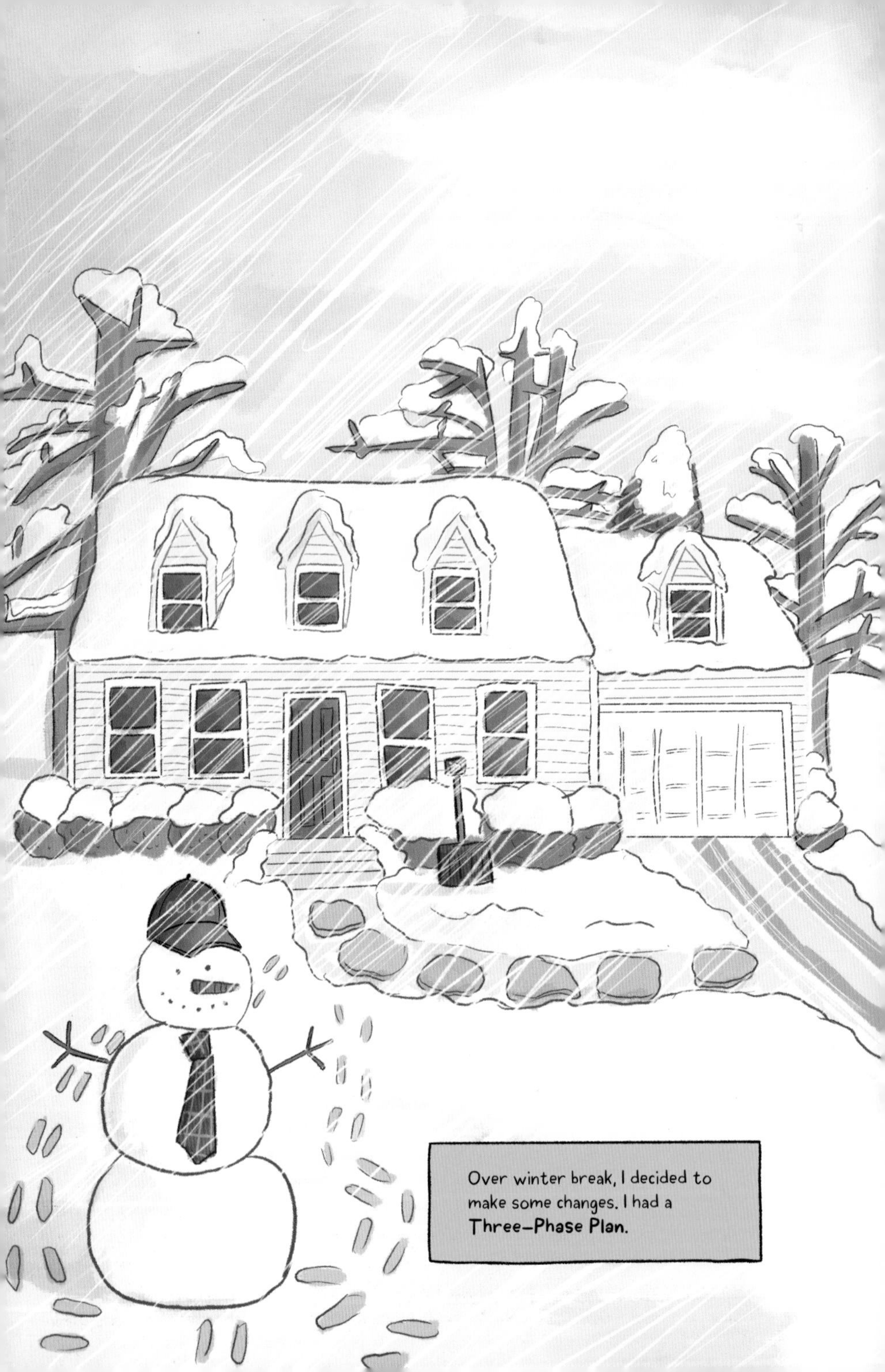
Over winter break, I decided to make some changes. I had a **Three-Phase Plan.**

Phase One required using my Christmas money to get some clothes that were more like the ones the popular girls wore. They weren't designer brands like theirs, but they weren't loud and obvious either.

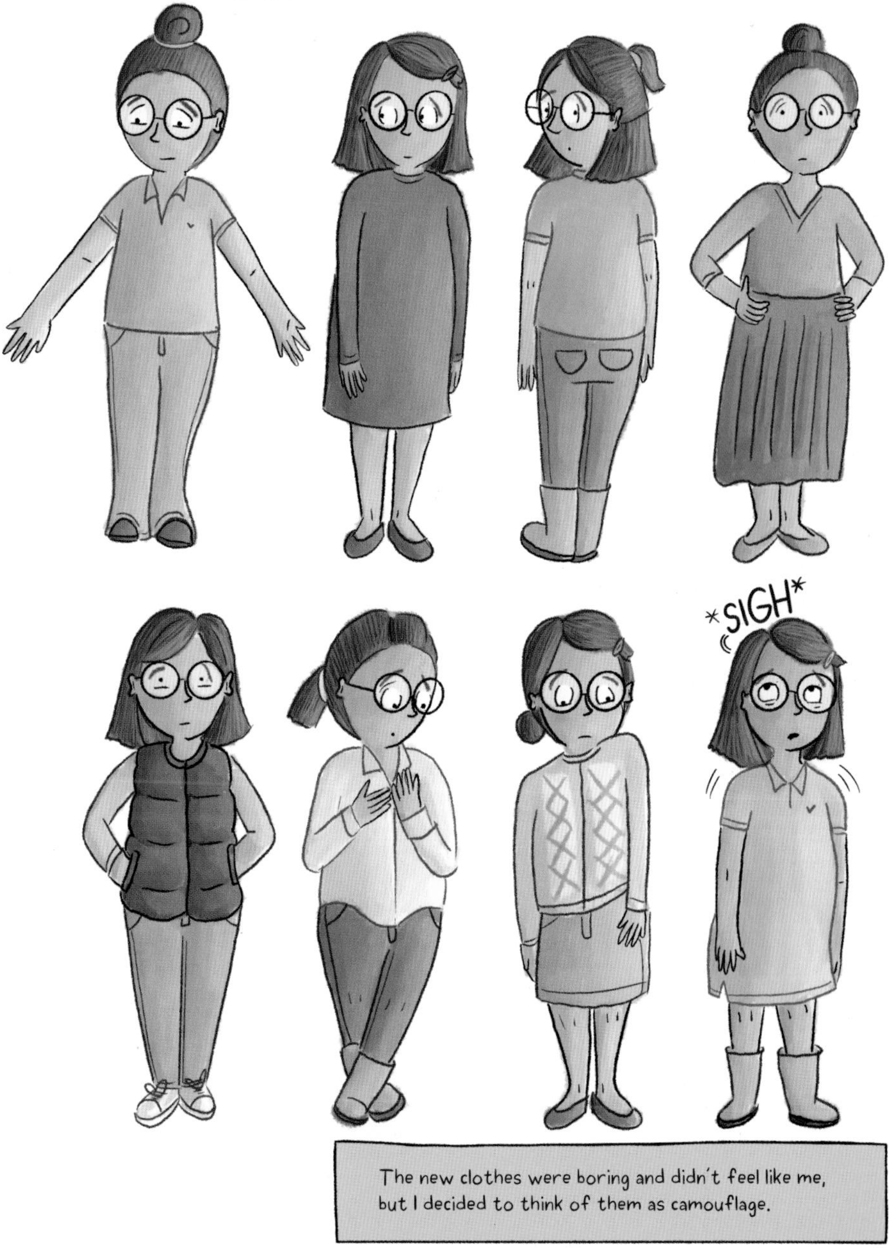
SIGH

The new clothes were boring and didn't feel like me, but I decided to think of them as camouflage.

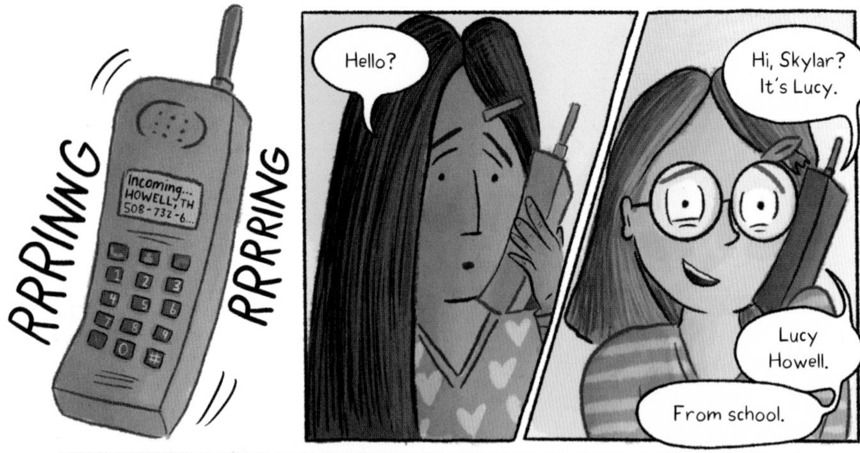
RRRINNG
Incoming... HOWELL, TH 508-732-6...
RRRRING
Hello?
Hi, Skylar? It's Lucy.
Lucy Howell.
From school.

Phase Two was simple. I needed to make a friend—specifically, a friend who was a *girl.* I knew *just one girlfriend* would make everything easier.

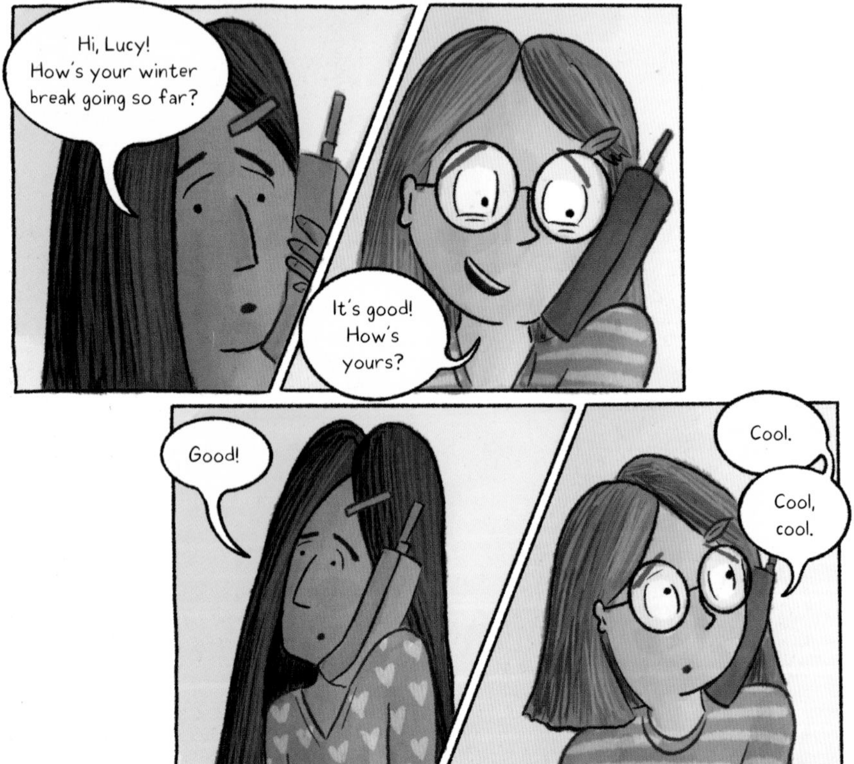
Hi, Lucy! How's your winter break going so far?
It's good! How's yours?
Good!
Cool.
Cool, cool.

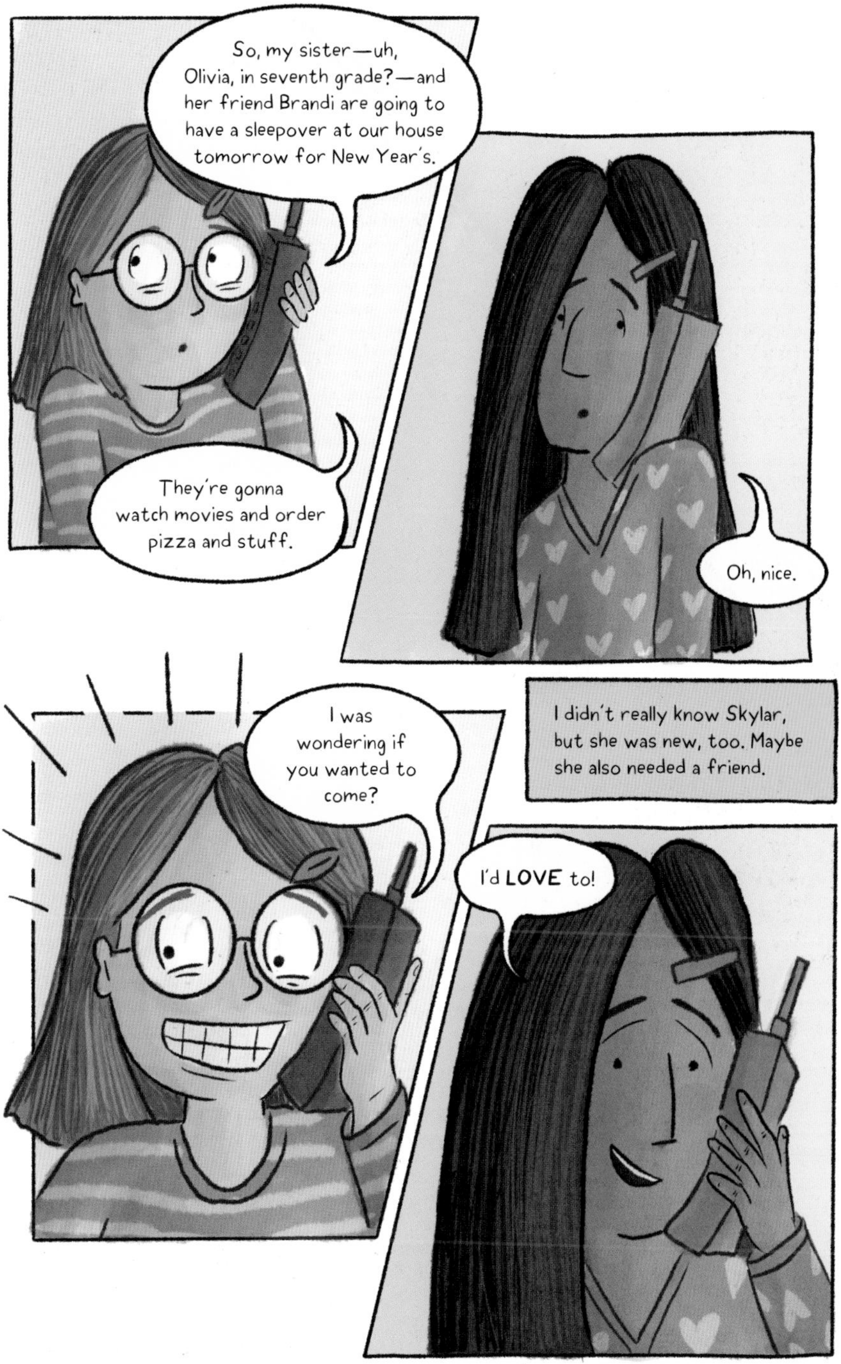
So, my sister—uh, Olivia, in seventh grade?—and her friend Brandi are going to have a sleepover at our house tomorrow for New Year's.
They're gonna watch movies and order pizza and stuff.
Oh, nice.
I was wondering if you wanted to come?
I didn't really know Skylar, but she was new, too. Maybe she also needed a friend.
I'd **LOVE** to!

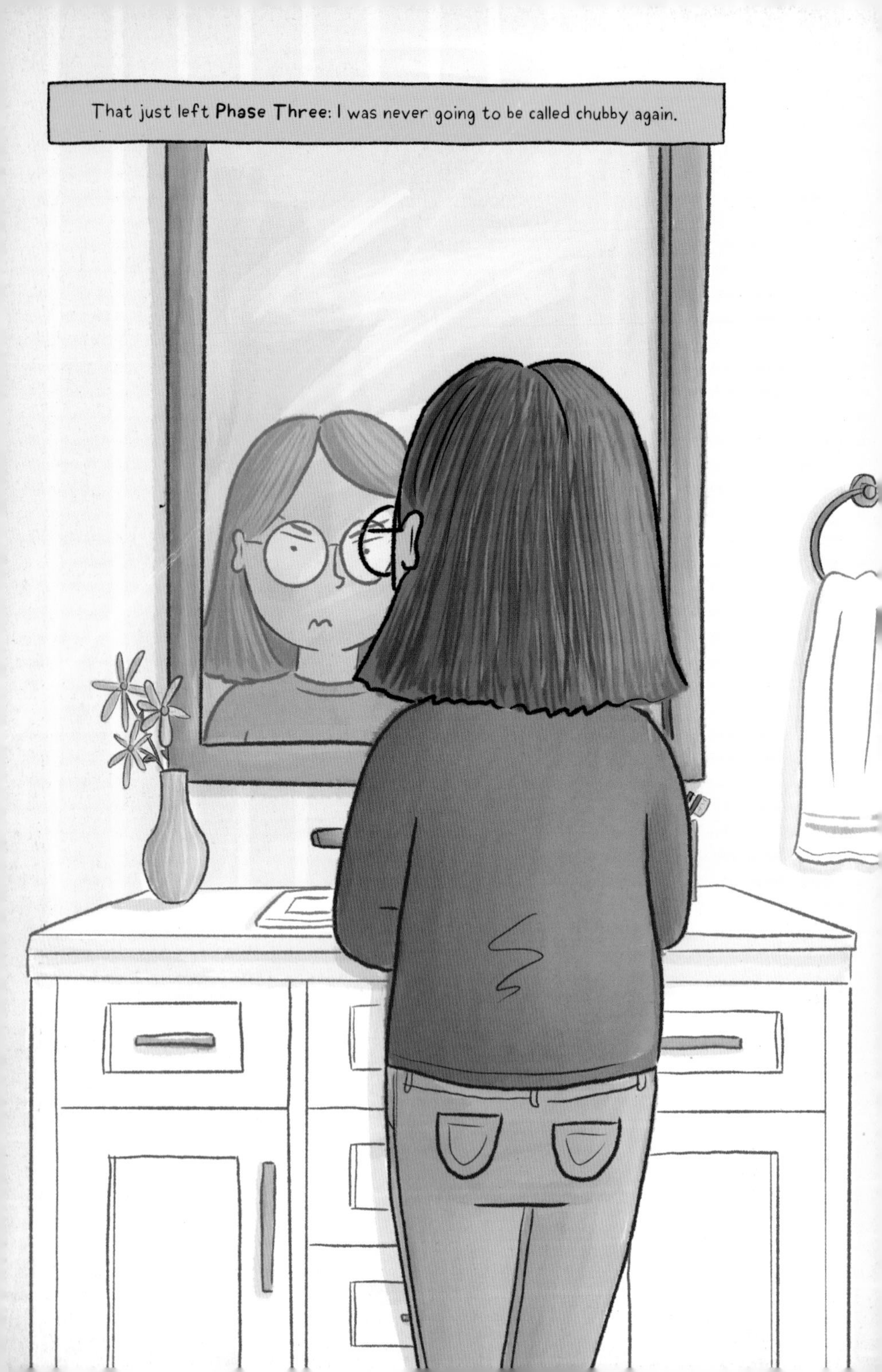
That just left **Phase Three**: I was never going to be called chubby again.

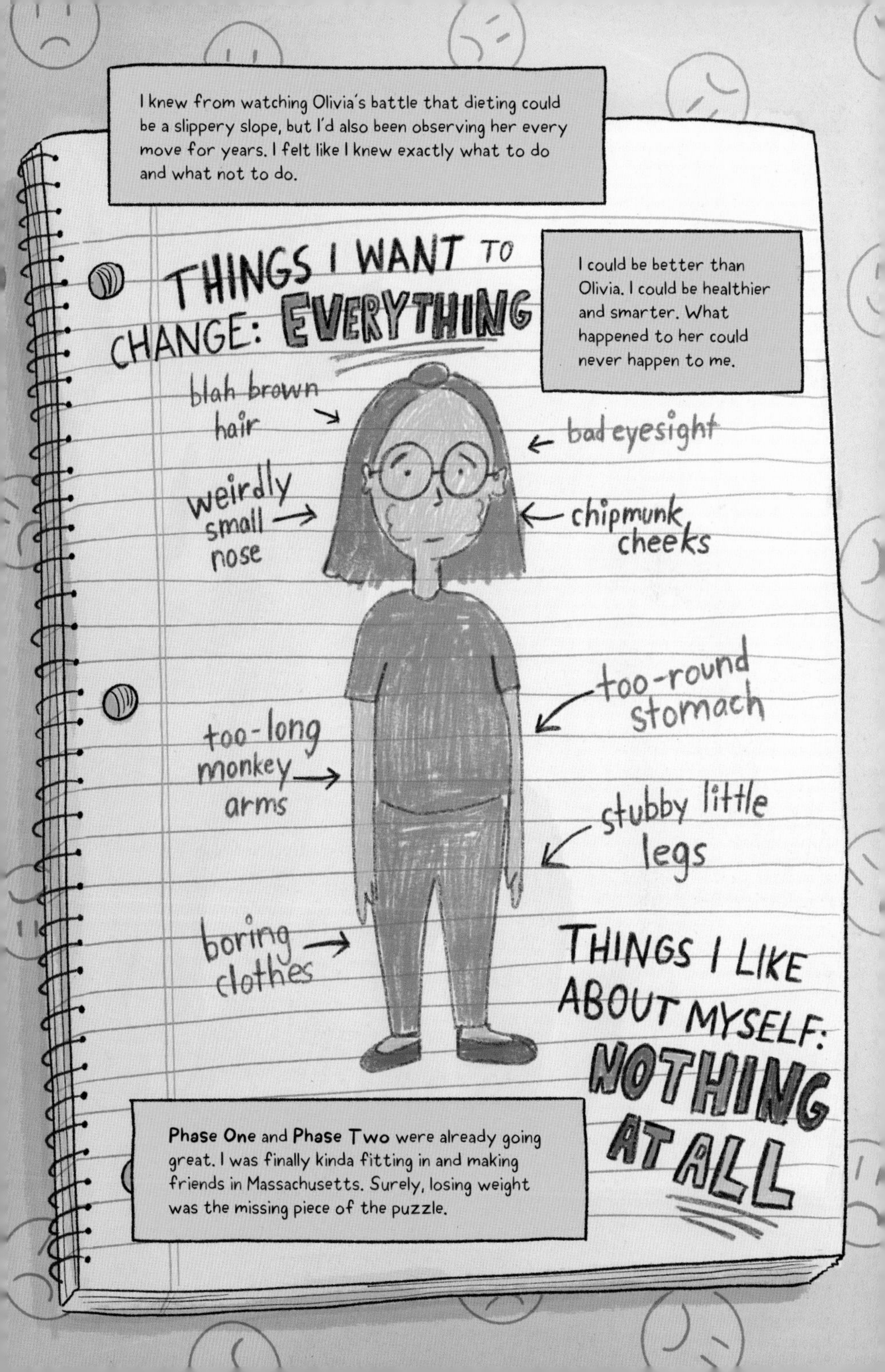
I knew from watching Olivia's battle that dieting could be a slippery slope, but I'd also been observing her every move for years. I felt like I knew exactly what to do and what not to do.
THINGS I WANT TO CHANGE: EVERYTHING
I could be better than Olivia. I could be healthier and smarter. What happened to her could never happen to me.
blah brown hair
bad eyesight
weirdly small nose
chipmunk cheeks
too-round stomach
too-long monkey arms
stubby little legs
boring clothes
THINGS I LIKE ABOUT MYSELF: NOTHING AT ALL
Phase One and Phase Two were already going great. I was finally kinda fitting in and making friends in Massachusetts. Surely, losing weight was the missing piece of the puzzle.

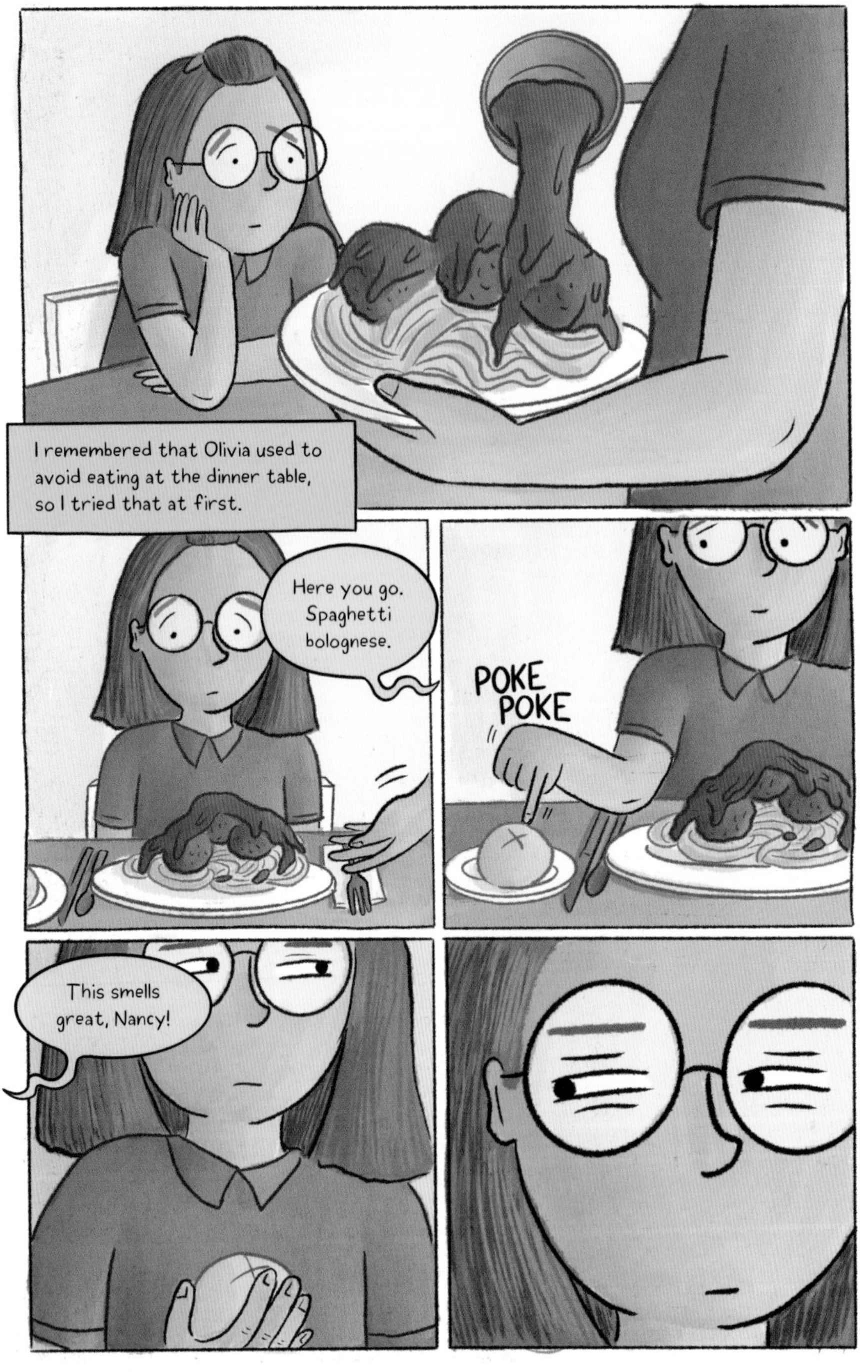

I remembered that Olivia used to avoid eating at the dinner table, so I tried that at first.
Here you go. Spaghetti bolognese.
POKE POKE
This smells great, Nancy!

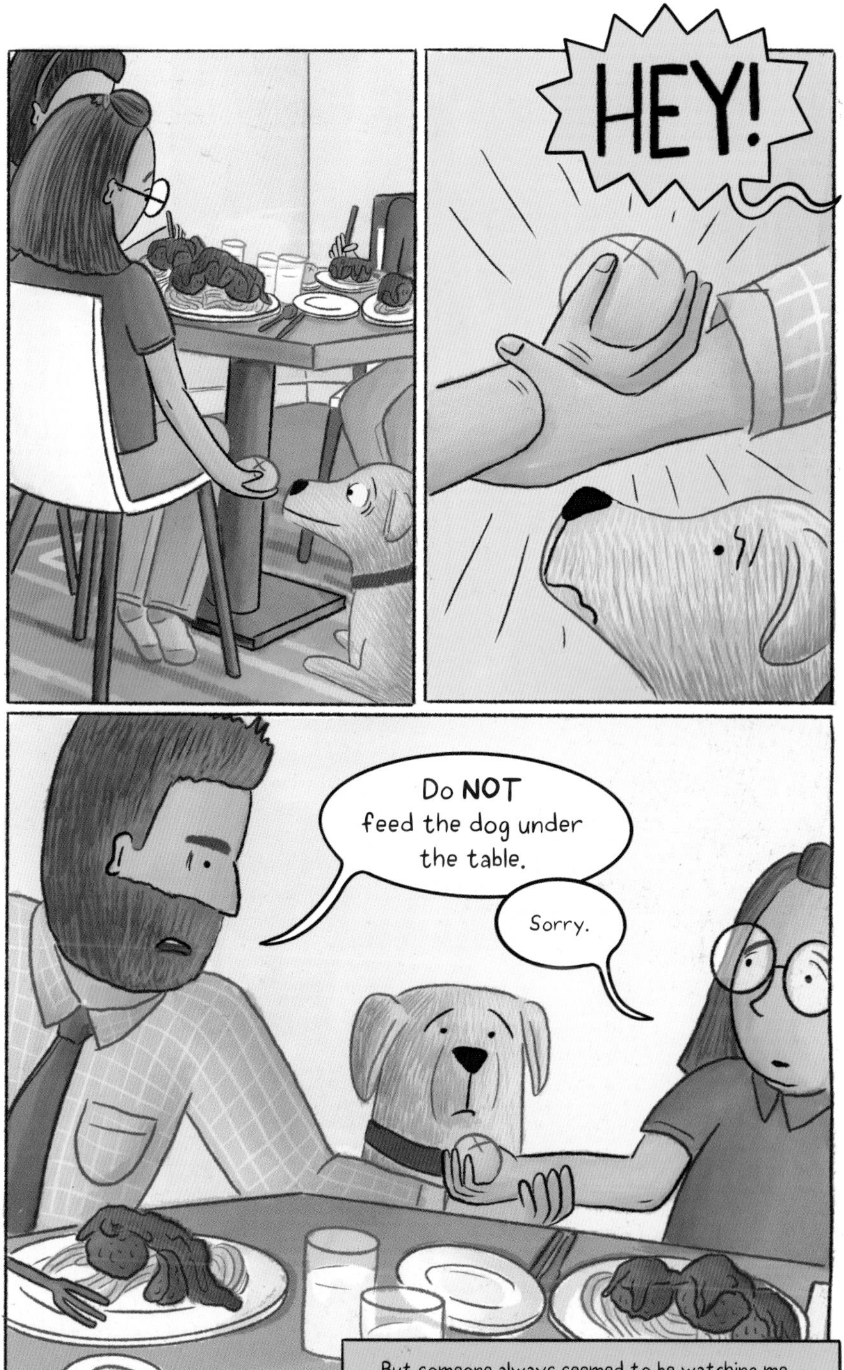
HEY!
Do NOT feed the dog under the table.
Sorry.
But someone always seemed to be watching me.

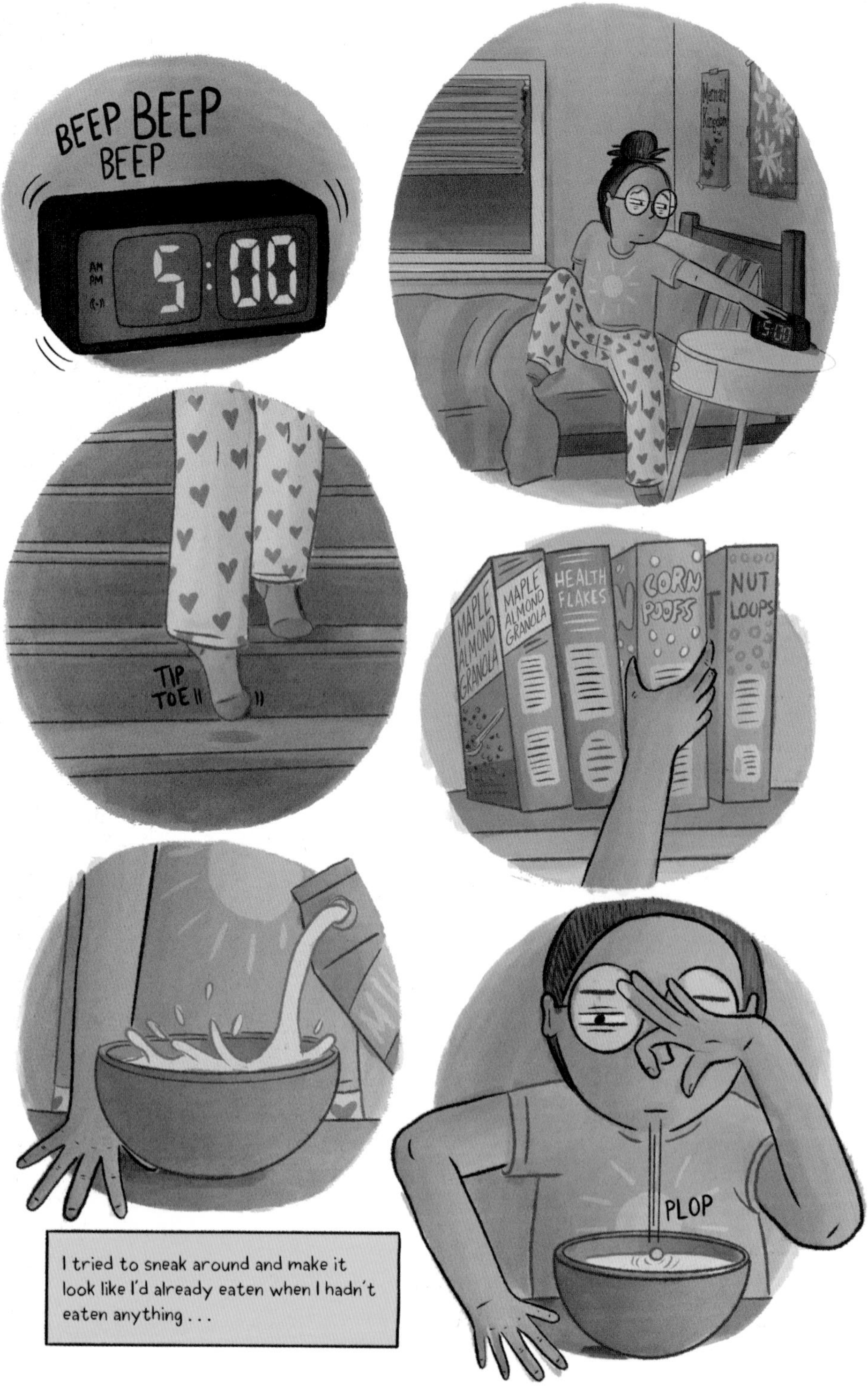
BEEP BEEP
BEEP
AM
PM
5:00
TIP
TOE
MAPLE ALMOND GRANOLA
MAPLE ALMOND GRANOLA
HEALTH FLAKES
CORN POOFS
NUT LOOPS
I tried to sneak around and make it look like I'd already eaten when I hadn't eaten anything . . .
PLOP

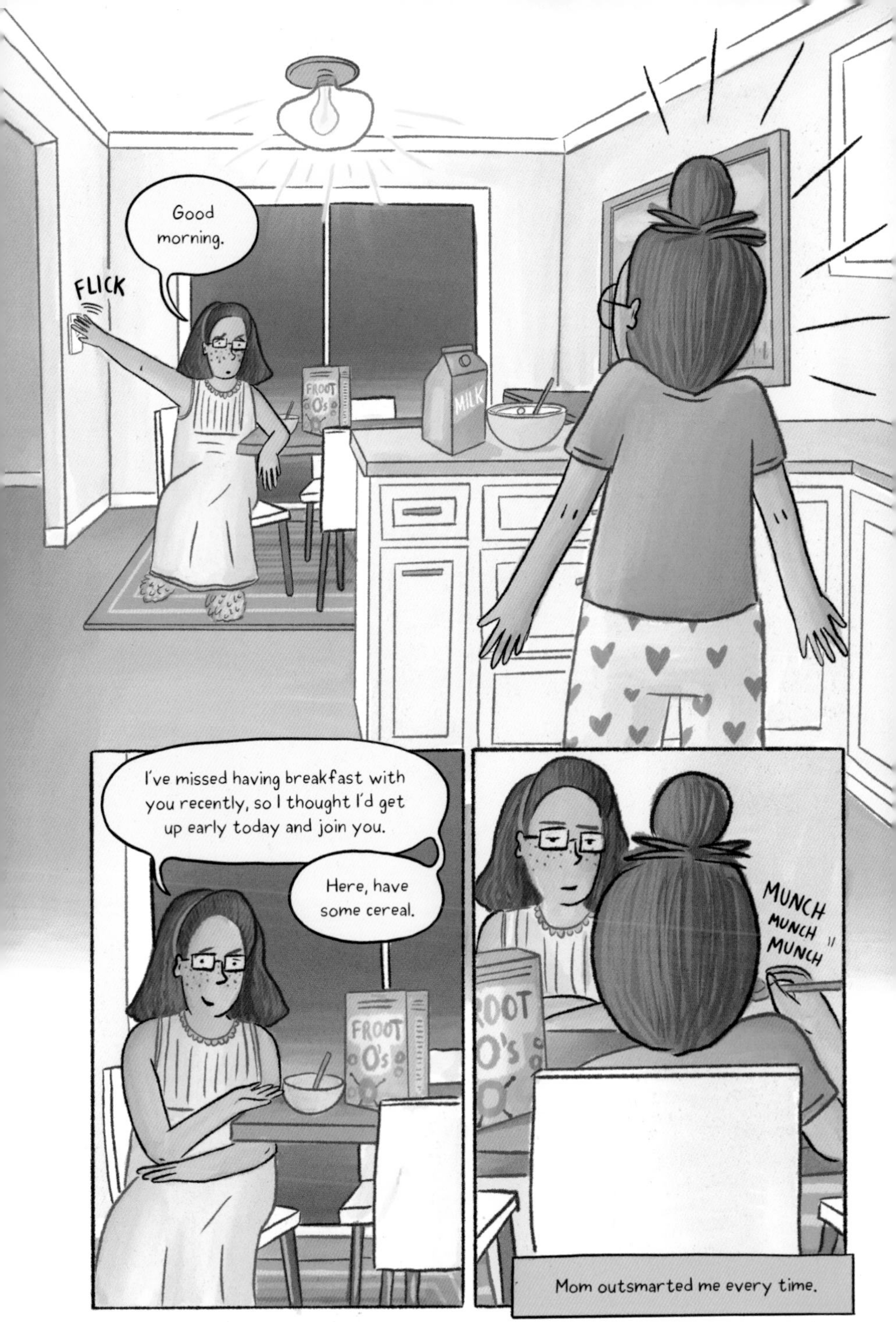
FLICK
Good morning.
FROOT O's
MILK
I've missed having breakfast with you recently, so I thought I'd get up early today and join you.
Here, have some cereal.
FROOT O's
MUNCH
MUNCH
MUNCH
Mom outsmarted me every time.

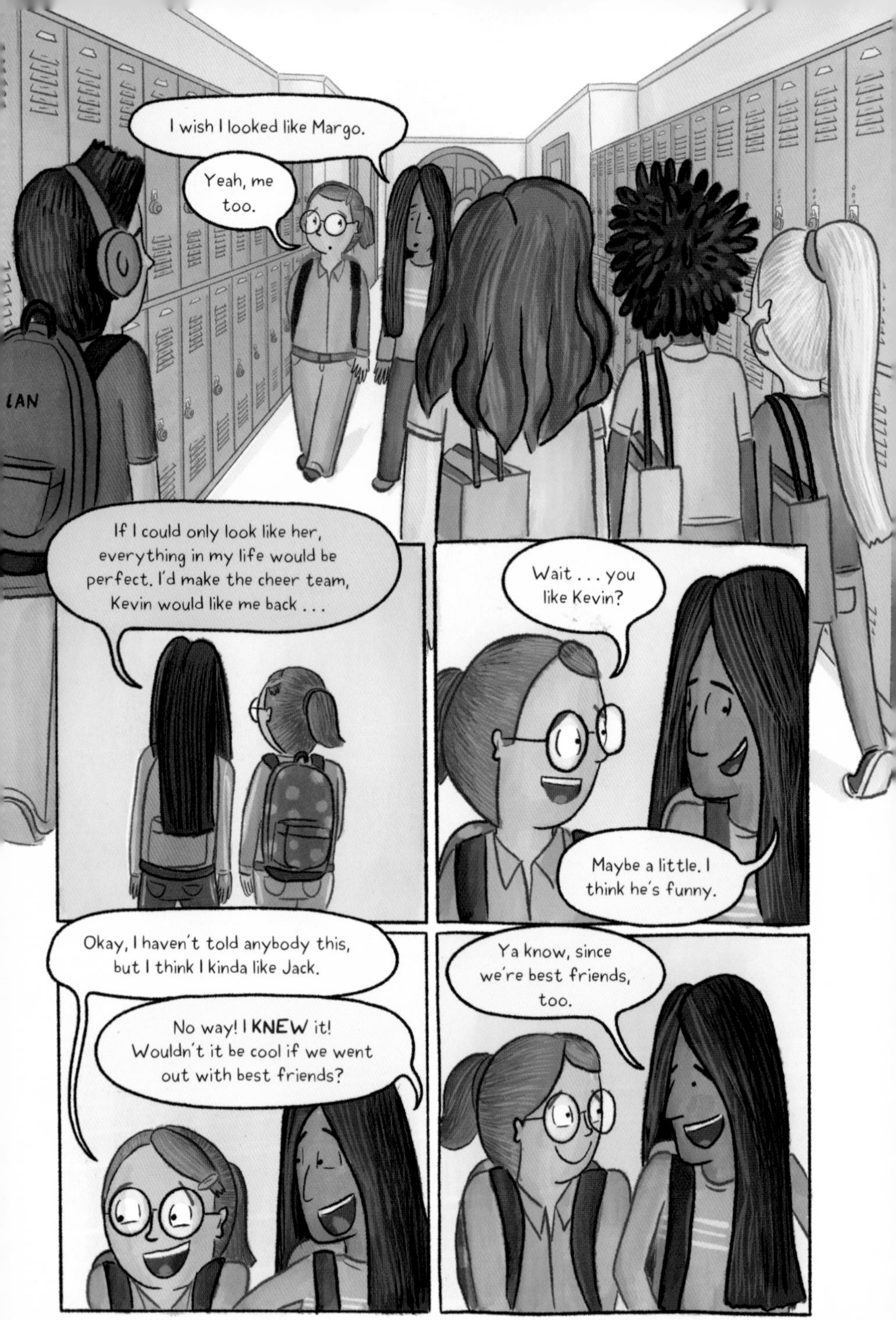
I wish I looked like Margo.
Yeah, me too.
LAN
If I could only look like her, everything in my life would be perfect. I'd make the cheer team, Kevin would like me back . . .
Wait . . . you like Kevin?
Maybe a little. I think he's funny.
Okay, I haven't told anybody this, but I think I kinda like Jack.
No way! I **KNEW** it! Wouldn't it be cool if we went out with best friends?
Ya know, since we're best friends, too.

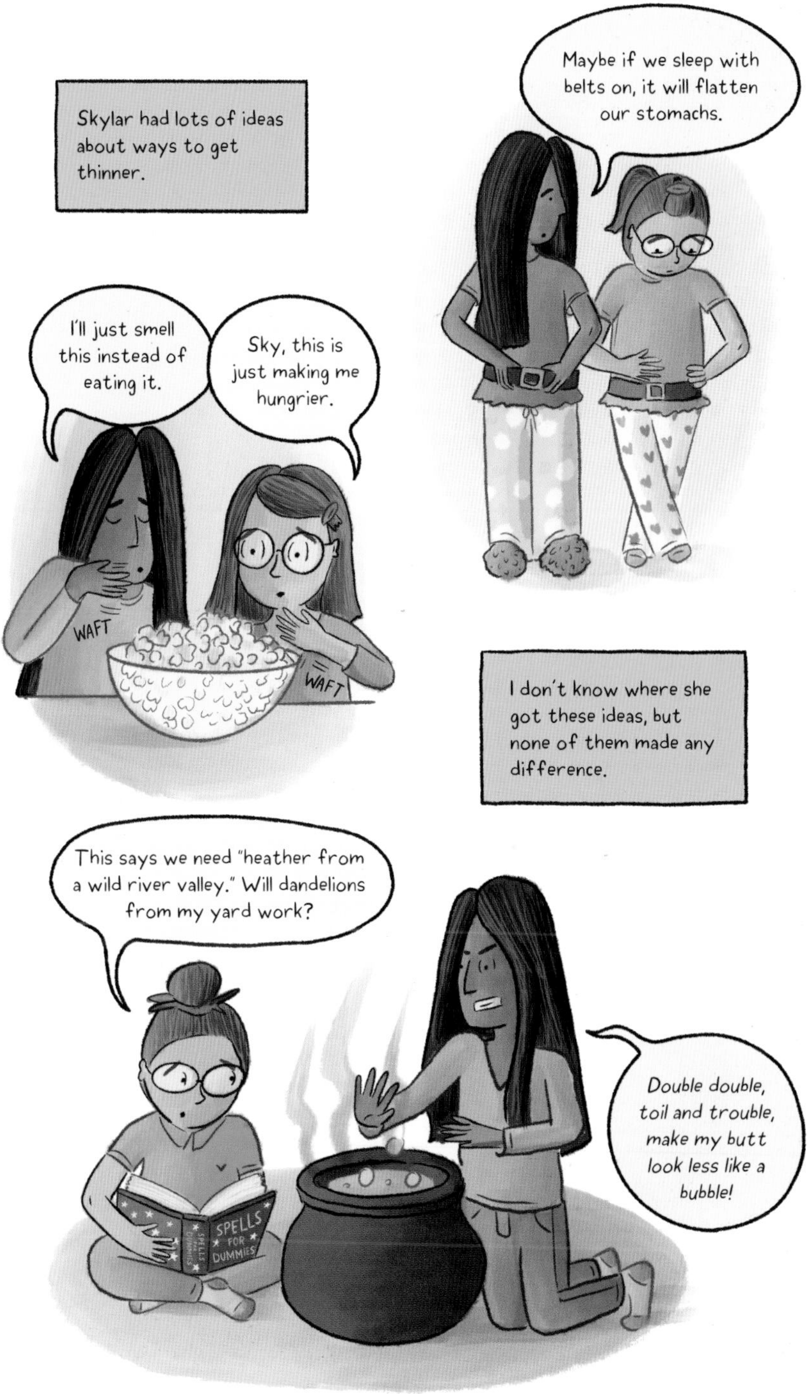
Skylar had lots of ideas about ways to get thinner.
Maybe if we sleep with belts on, it will flatten our stomachs.
I'll just smell this instead of eating it.
Sky, this is just making me hungrier.
WAFT
WAFT
I don't know where she got these ideas, but none of them made any difference.
This says we need "heather from a wild river valley." Will dandelions from my yard work?
SPELLS FOR DUMMIES
Double double, toil and trouble, make my butt look less like a bubble!

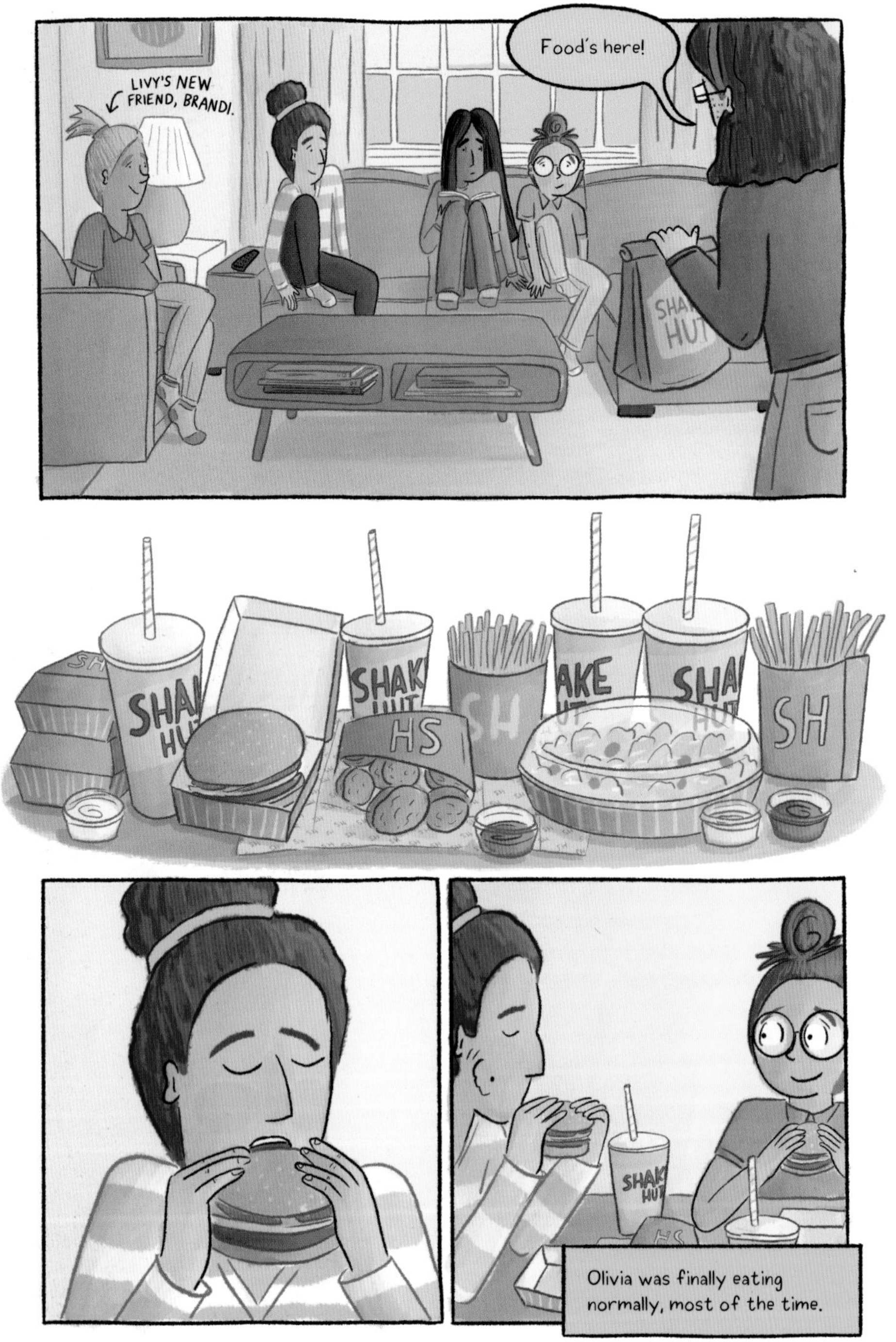
LIVY'S NEW FRIEND, BRANDI.
Food's here!
SHAKE HUT
SHAKE HUT
SHAKE HUT
SH
AKE
SHAKE HUT
SH
HS
SHAKE HUT
Olivia was finally eating normally, most of the time.

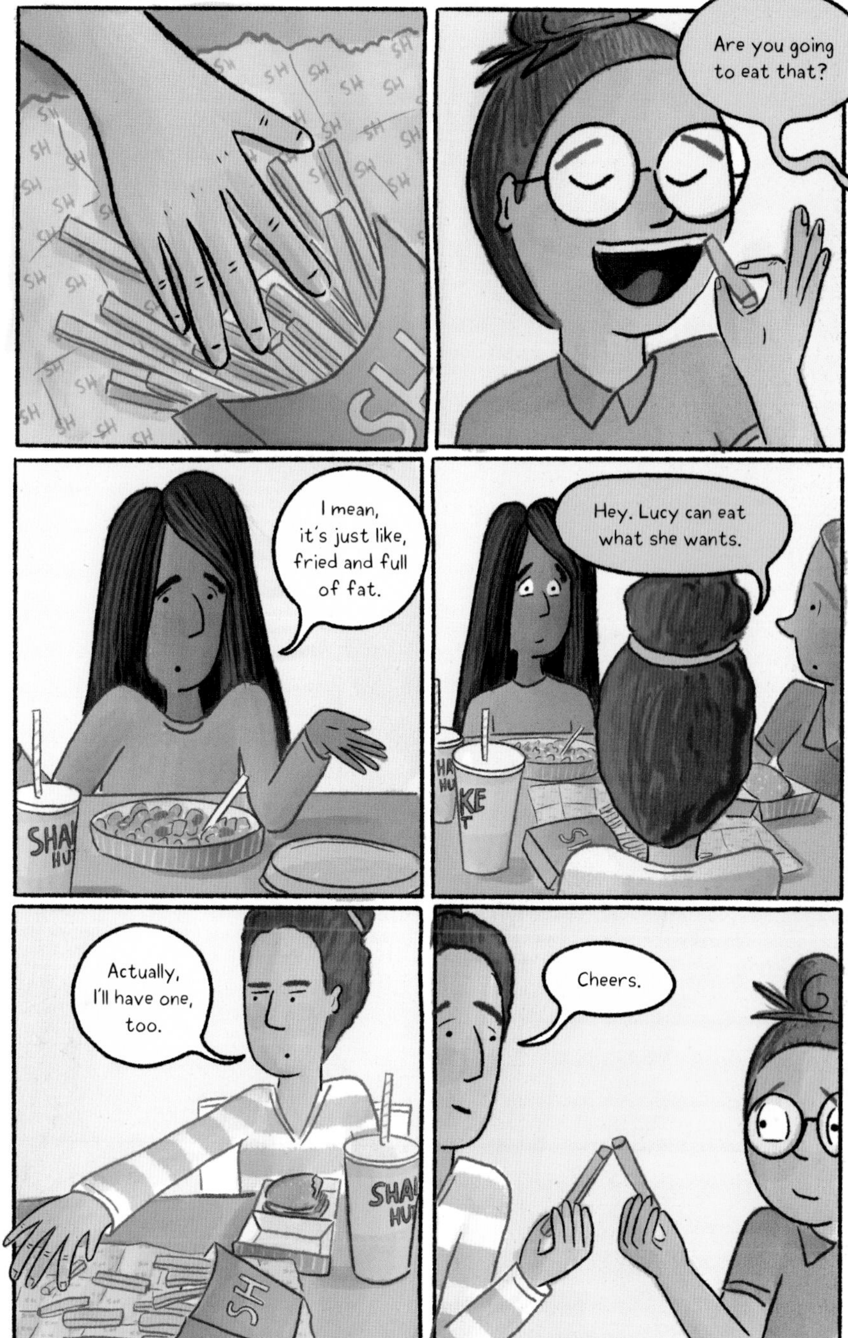
Are you going to eat that?
I mean, it's just like, fried and full of fat.
Hey. Lucy can eat what she wants.
Actually, I'll have one, too.
Cheers.

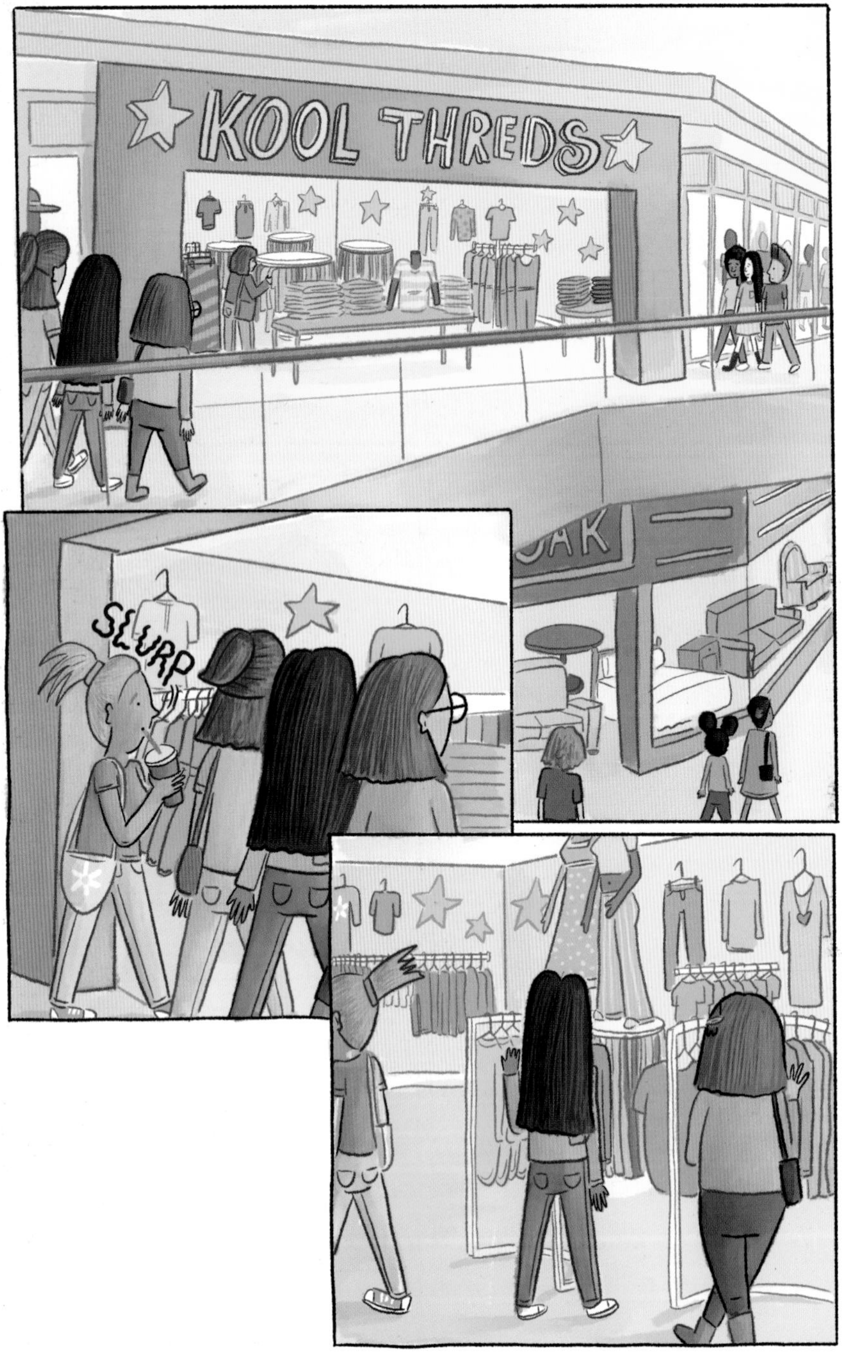
KOOL THREDS
OAK
SLURP

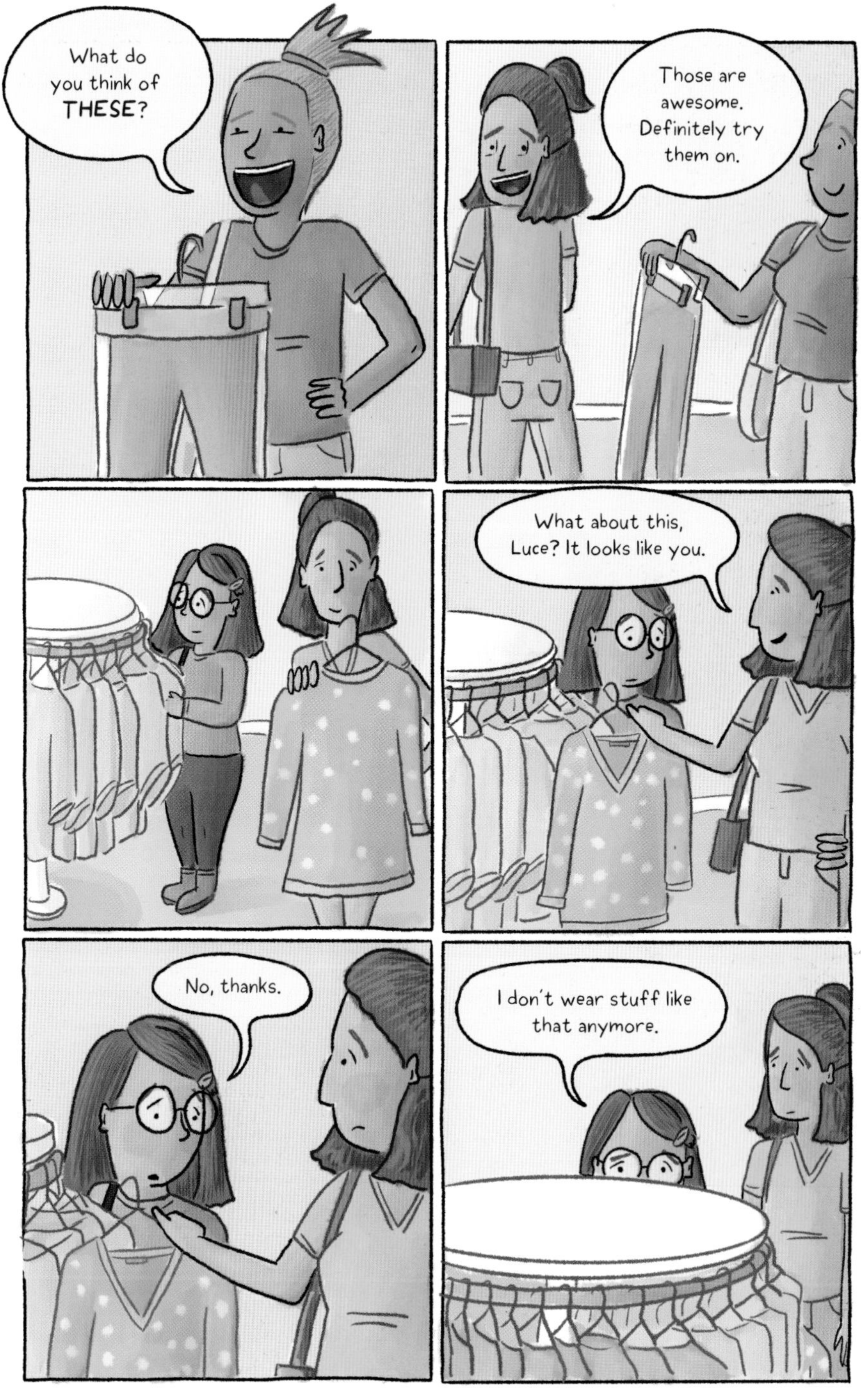
What do you think of THESE?
Those are awesome. Definitely try them on.
What about this, Luce? It looks like you.
No, thanks.
I don't wear stuff like that anymore.

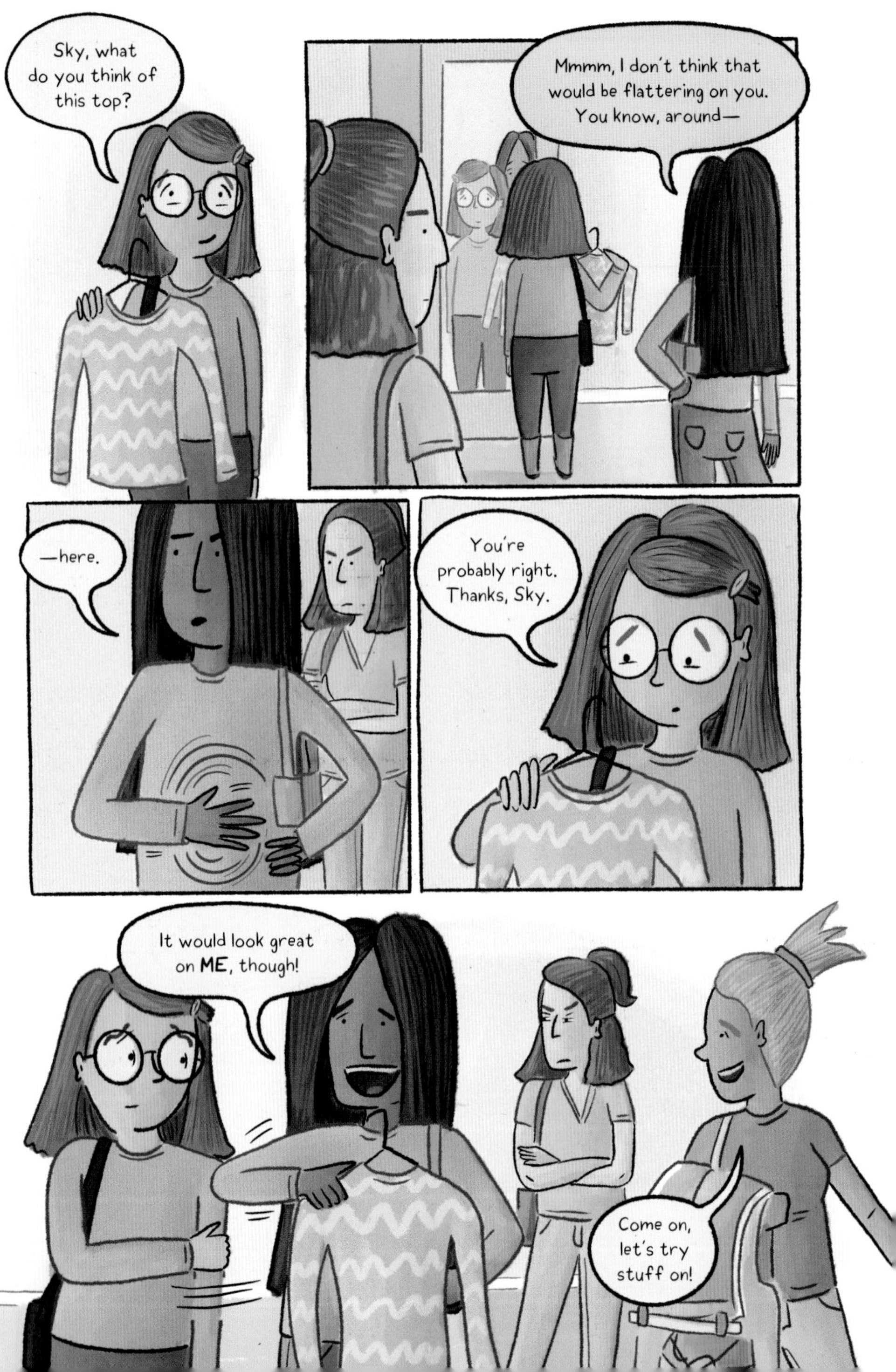
Sky, what do you think of this top?
Mmmm, I don't think that would be flattering on you. You know, around—
—here.
You're probably right. Thanks, Sky.
It would look great on ME, though!
Come on, let's try stuff on!

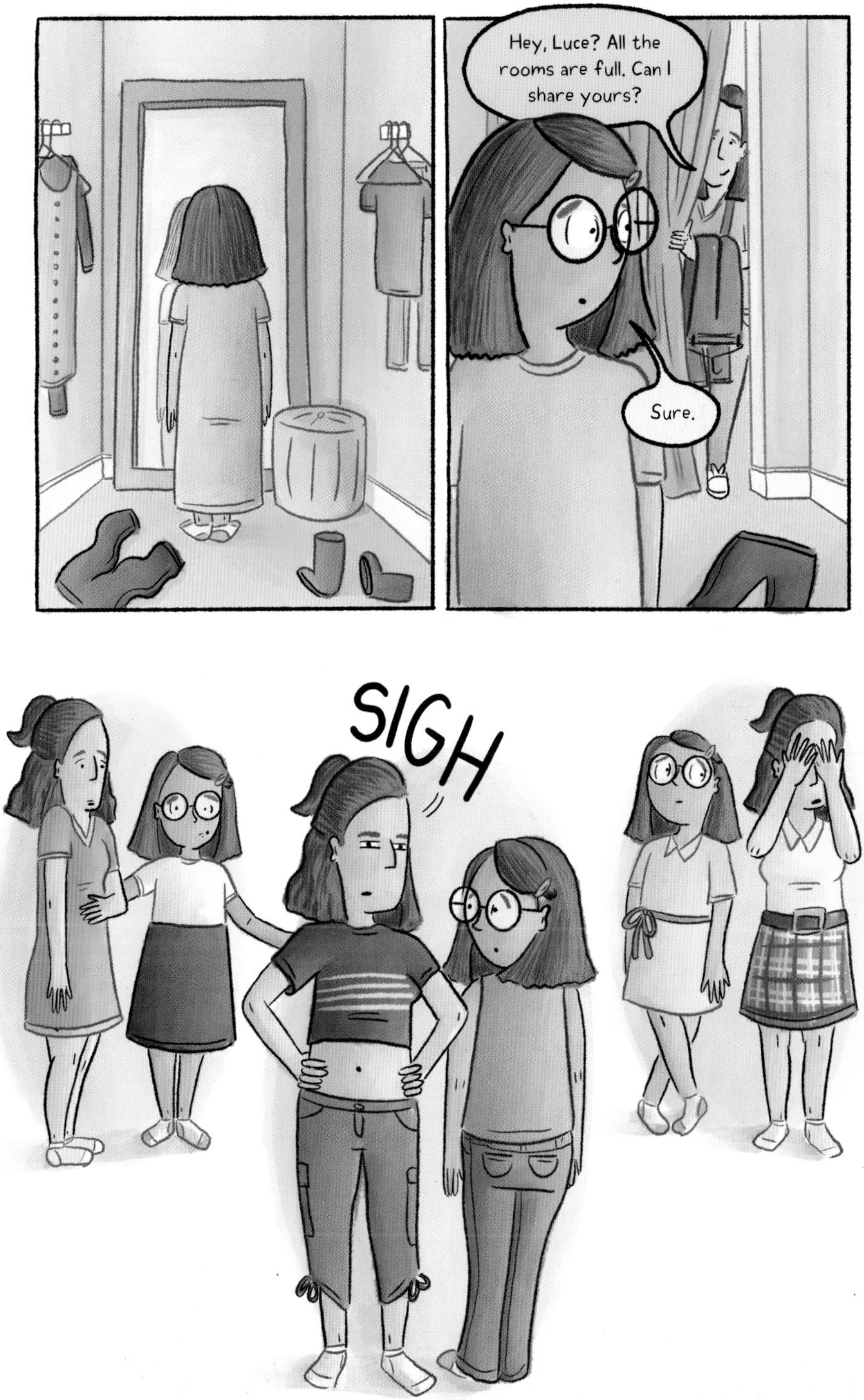
Hey, Luce? All the rooms are full. Can I share yours?
Sure.
SIGH

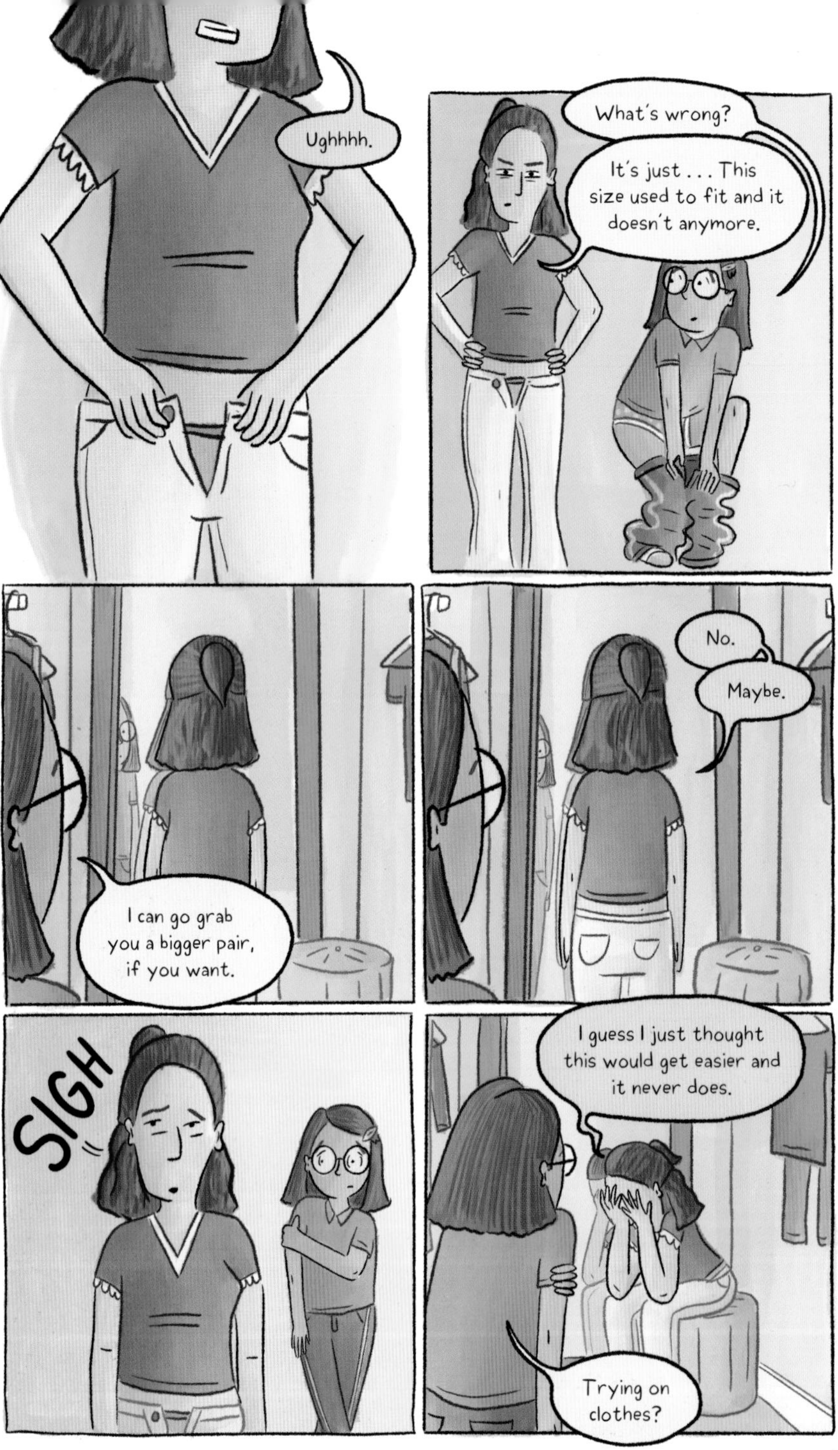
Ughhhh.
What's wrong?
It's just . . . This size used to fit and it doesn't anymore.
I can go grab you a bigger pair, if you want.
No.
Maybe.
SIGH
I guess I just thought this would get easier and it never does.
Trying on clothes?

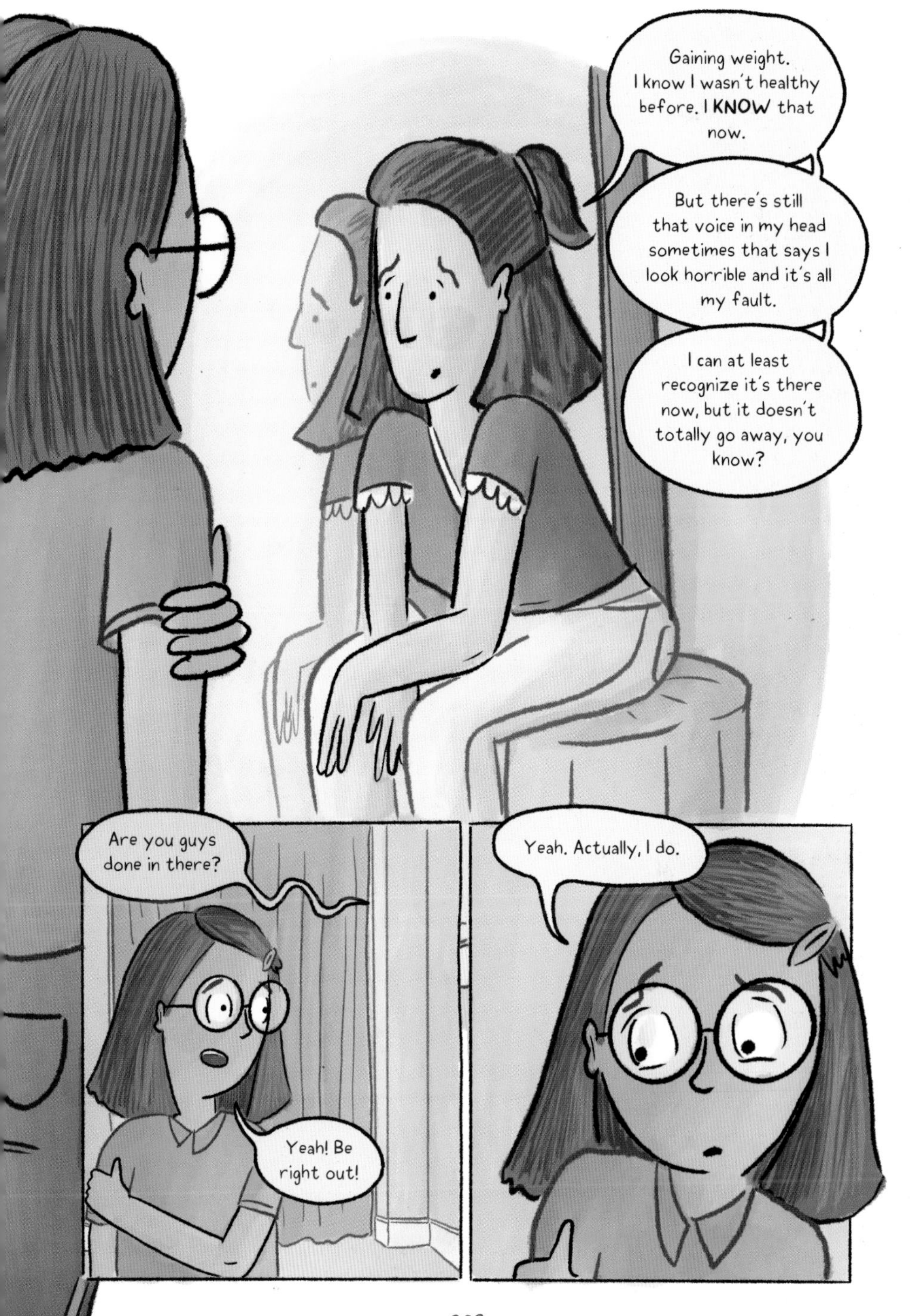
Gaining weight. I know I wasn't healthy before. I KNOW that now.
But there's still that voice in my head sometimes that says I look horrible and it's all my fault.
I can at least recognize it's there now, but it doesn't totally go away, you know?
Are you guys done in there?
Yeah! Be right out!
Yeah. Actually, I do.

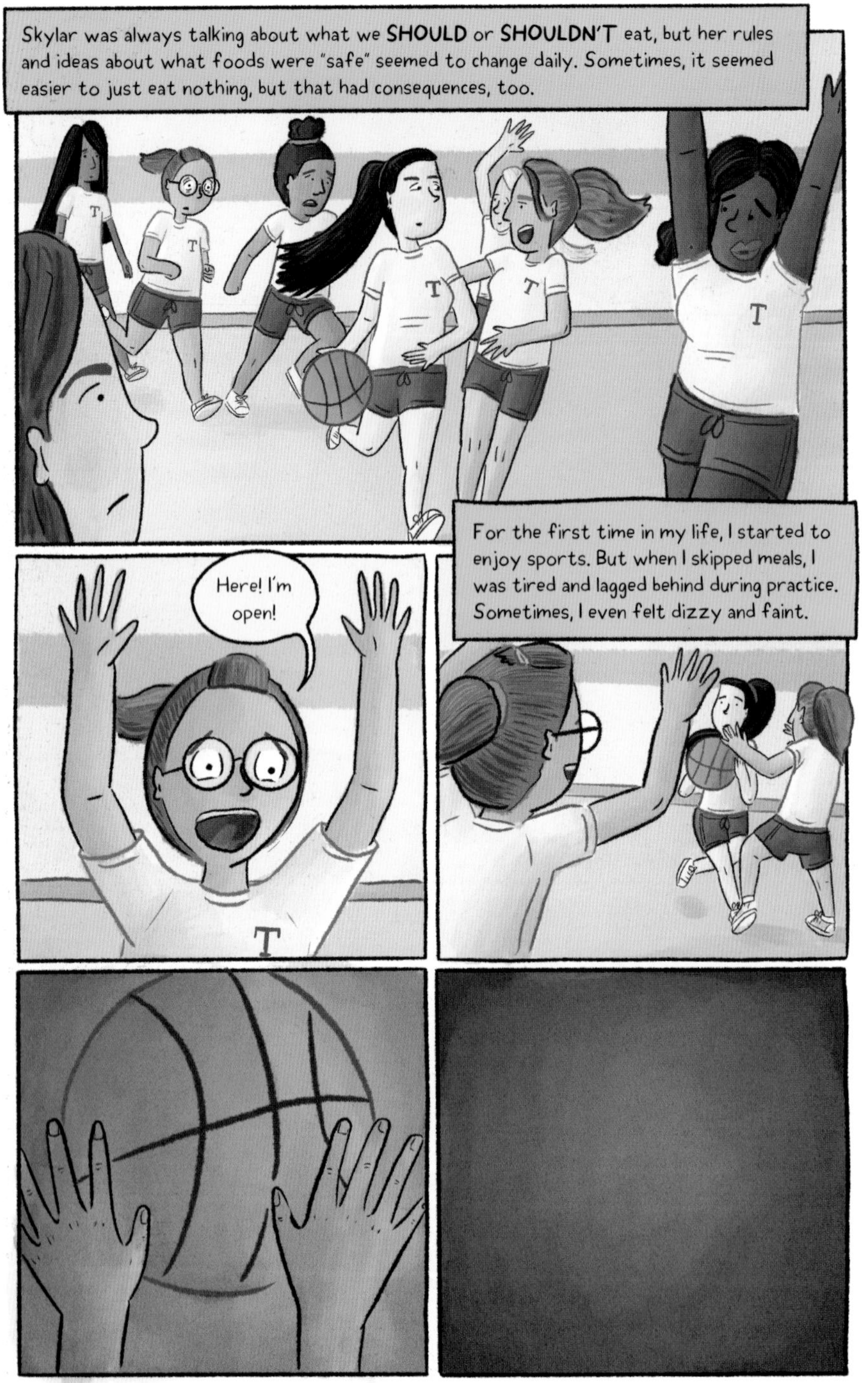
Skylar was always talking about what we SHOULD or SHOULDN'T eat, but her rules and ideas about what foods were "safe" seemed to change daily. Sometimes, it seemed easier to just eat nothing, but that had consequences, too.
For the first time in my life, I started to enjoy sports. But when I skipped meals, I was tired and lagged behind during practice. Sometimes, I even felt dizzy and faint.
Here! I'm open!

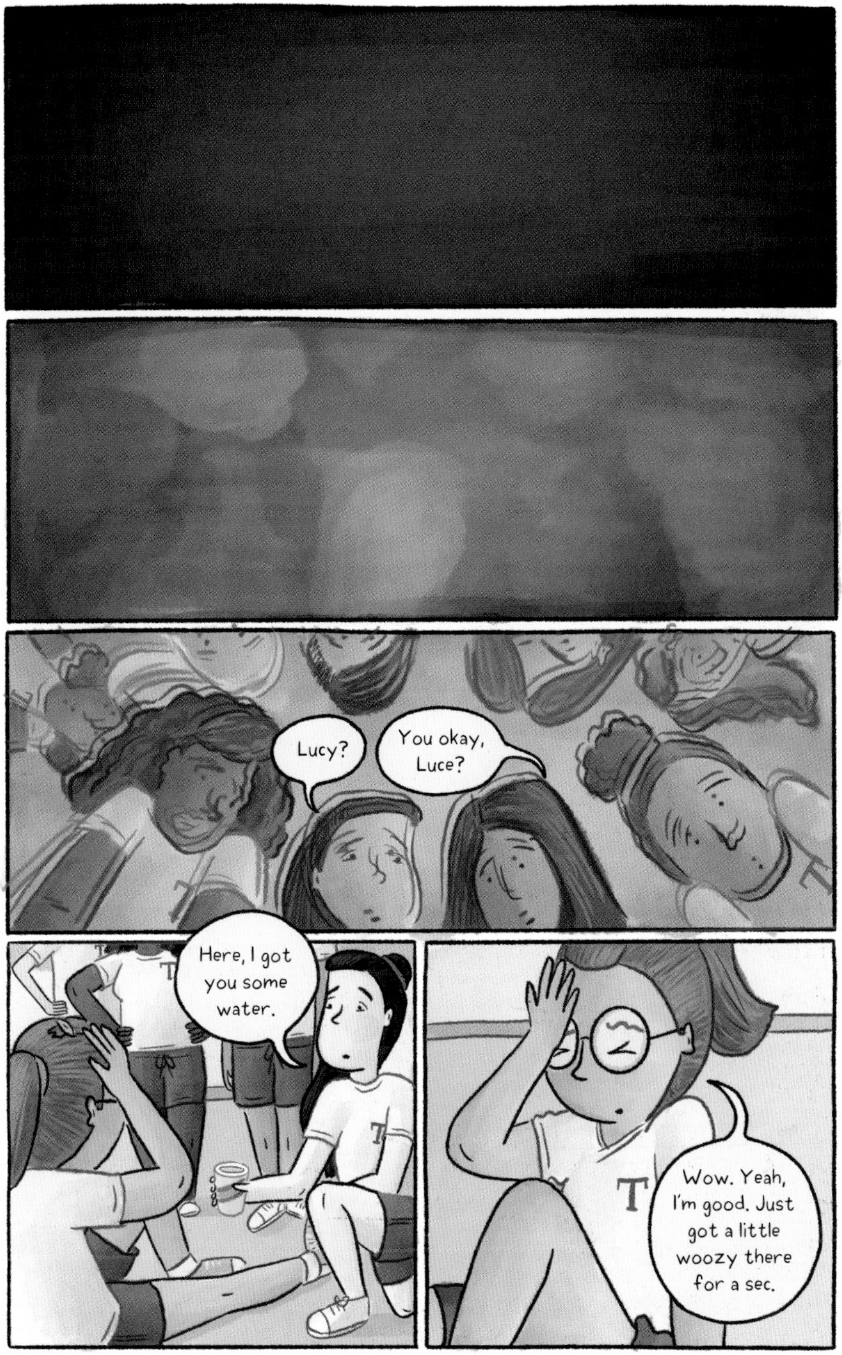
Lucy?
You okay, Luce?
Here, I got you some water.
Wow. Yeah, I'm good. Just got a little woozy there for a sec.

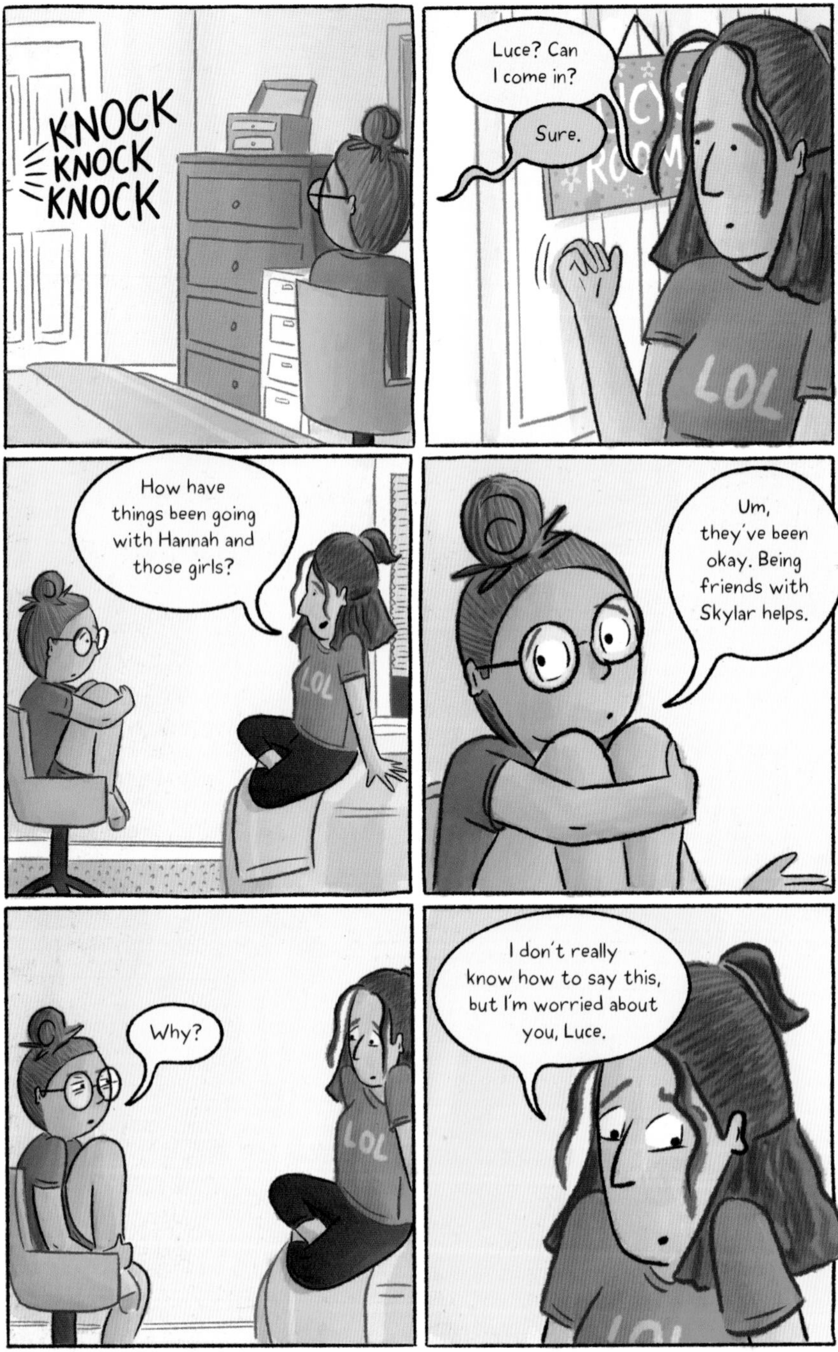
KNOCK
KNOCK
KNOCK
Luce? Can I come in?
Sure.
LOL
How have things been going with Hannah and those girls?
LOL
Um, they've been okay. Being friends with Skylar helps.
Why?
LOL
I don't really know how to say this, but I'm worried about you, Luce.

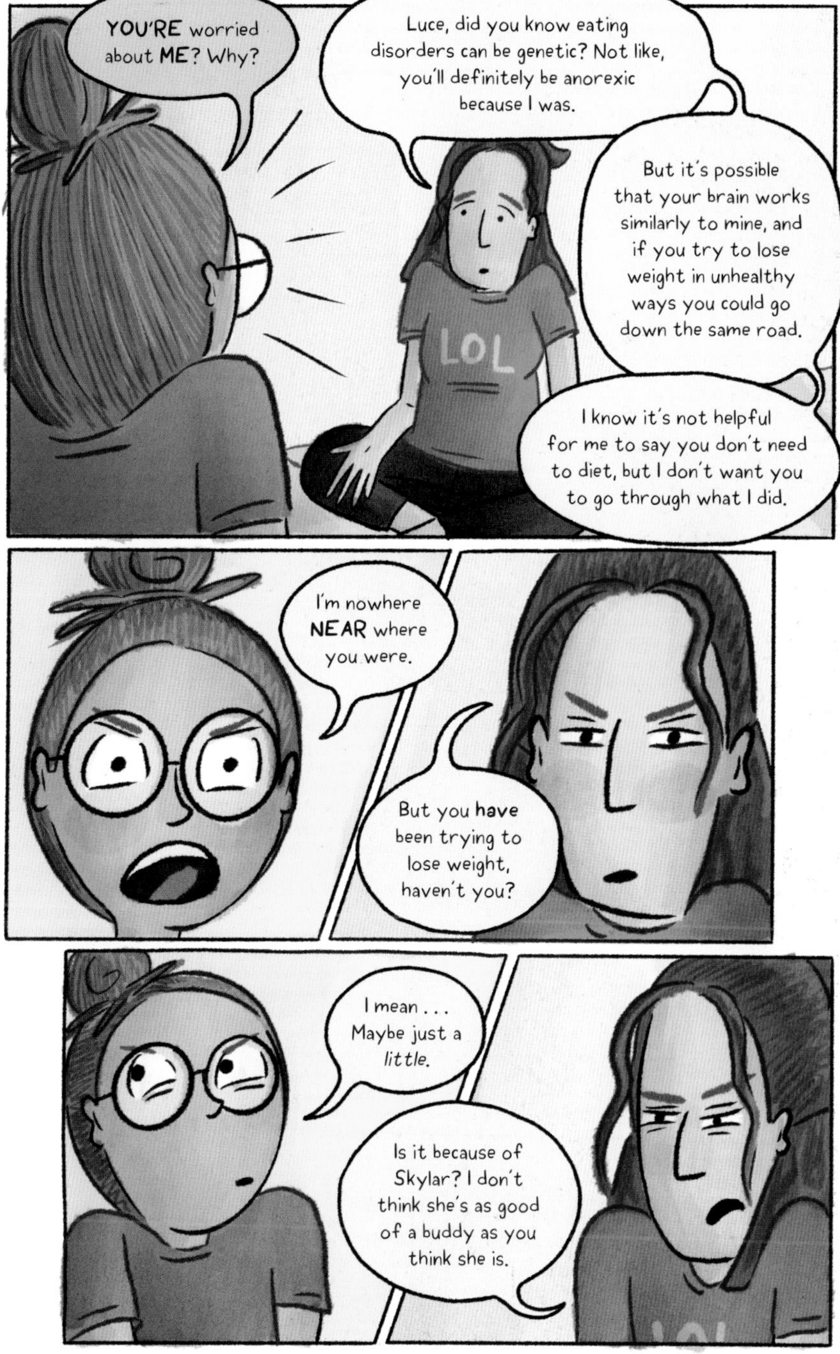
YOU'RE worried about ME? Why?
Luce, did you know eating disorders can be genetic? Not like, you'll definitely be anorexic because I was.
But it's possible that your brain works similarly to mine, and if you try to lose weight in unhealthy ways you could go down the same road.
I know it's not helpful for me to say you don't need to diet, but I don't want you to go through what I did.
LOL
I'm nowhere NEAR where you were.
But you have been trying to lose weight, haven't you?
I mean . . . Maybe just a *little*.
Is it because of Skylar? I don't think she's as good of a buddy as you think she is.

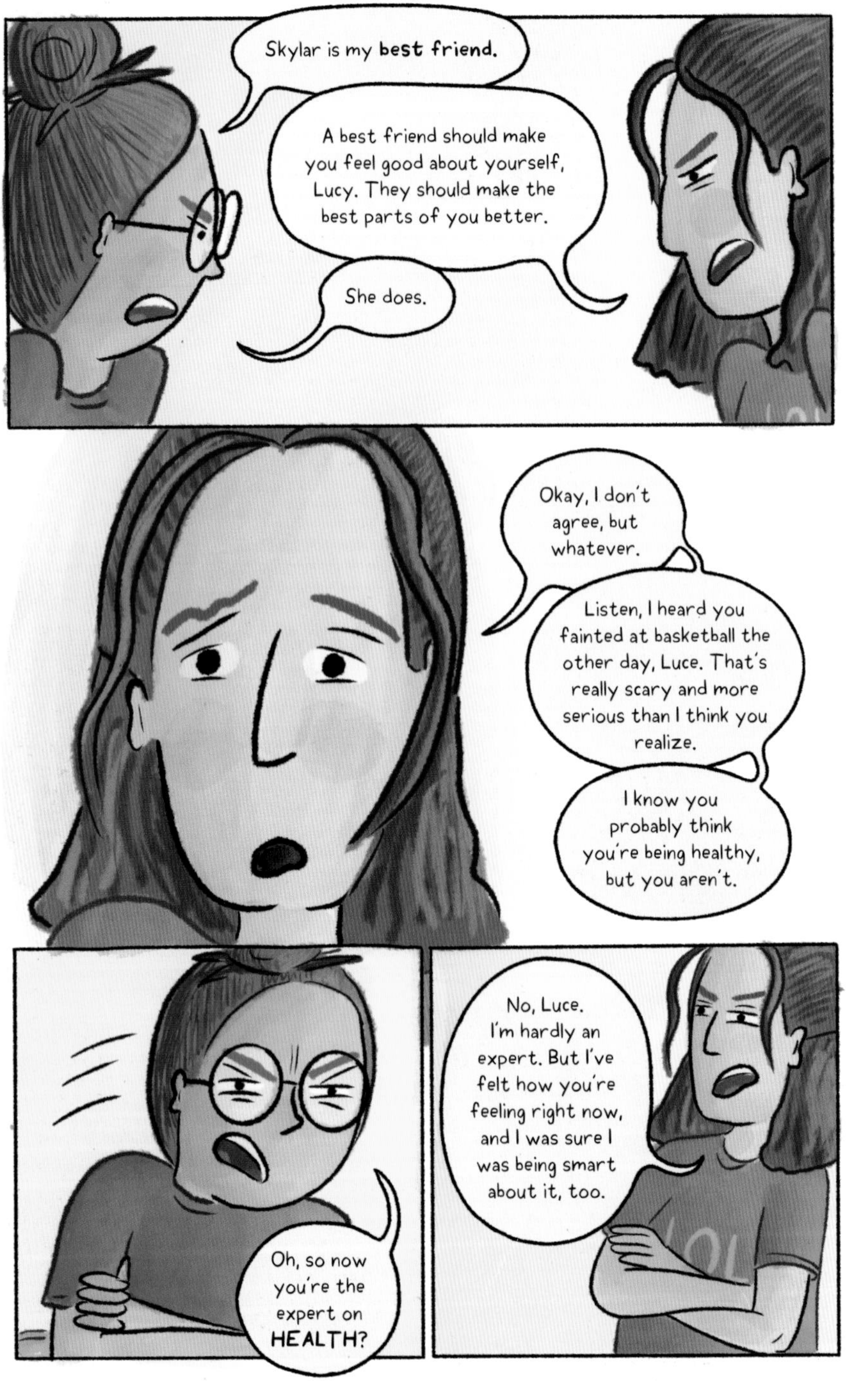
Skylar is my **best friend.**
A best friend should make you feel good about yourself, Lucy. They should make the best parts of you better.
She does.
Okay, I don't agree, but whatever.
Listen, I heard you fainted at basketball the other day, Luce. That's really scary and more serious than I think you realize.
I know you probably think you're being healthy, but you aren't.
Oh, so now you're the expert on **HEALTH?**
No, Luce. I'm hardly an expert. But I've felt how you're feeling right now, and I was sure I was being smart about it, too.

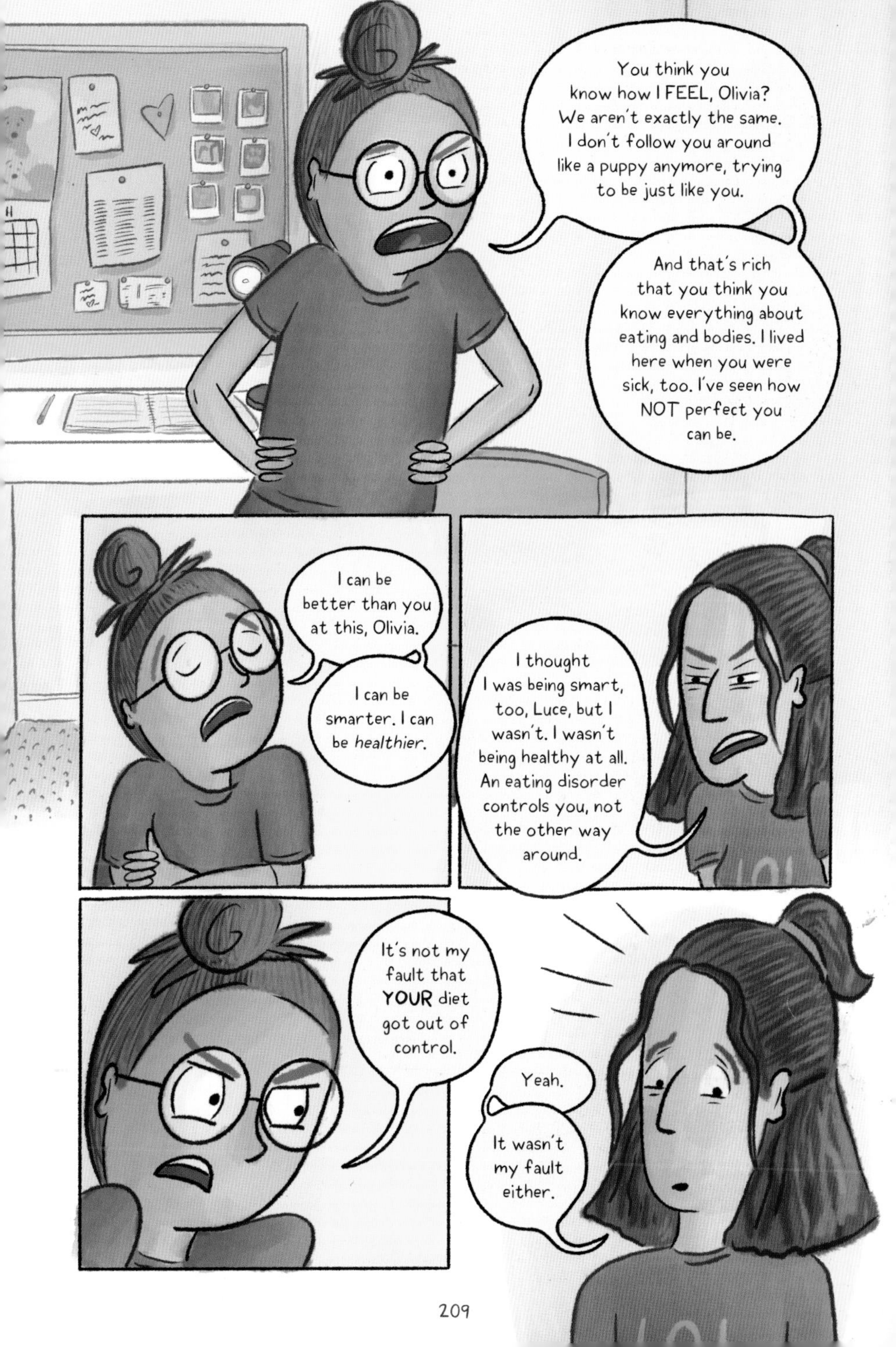
You think you know how I FEEL, Olivia? We aren't exactly the same. I don't follow you around like a puppy anymore, trying to be just like you.
And that's rich that you think you know everything about eating and bodies. I lived here when you were sick, too. I've seen how NOT perfect you can be.
I can be better than you at this, Olivia.
I can be smarter. I can be *healthier*.
I thought I was being smart, too, Luce, but I wasn't. I wasn't being healthy at all. An eating disorder controls you, not the other way around.
It's not my fault that **YOUR** diet got out of control.
Yeah.
It wasn't my fault either.

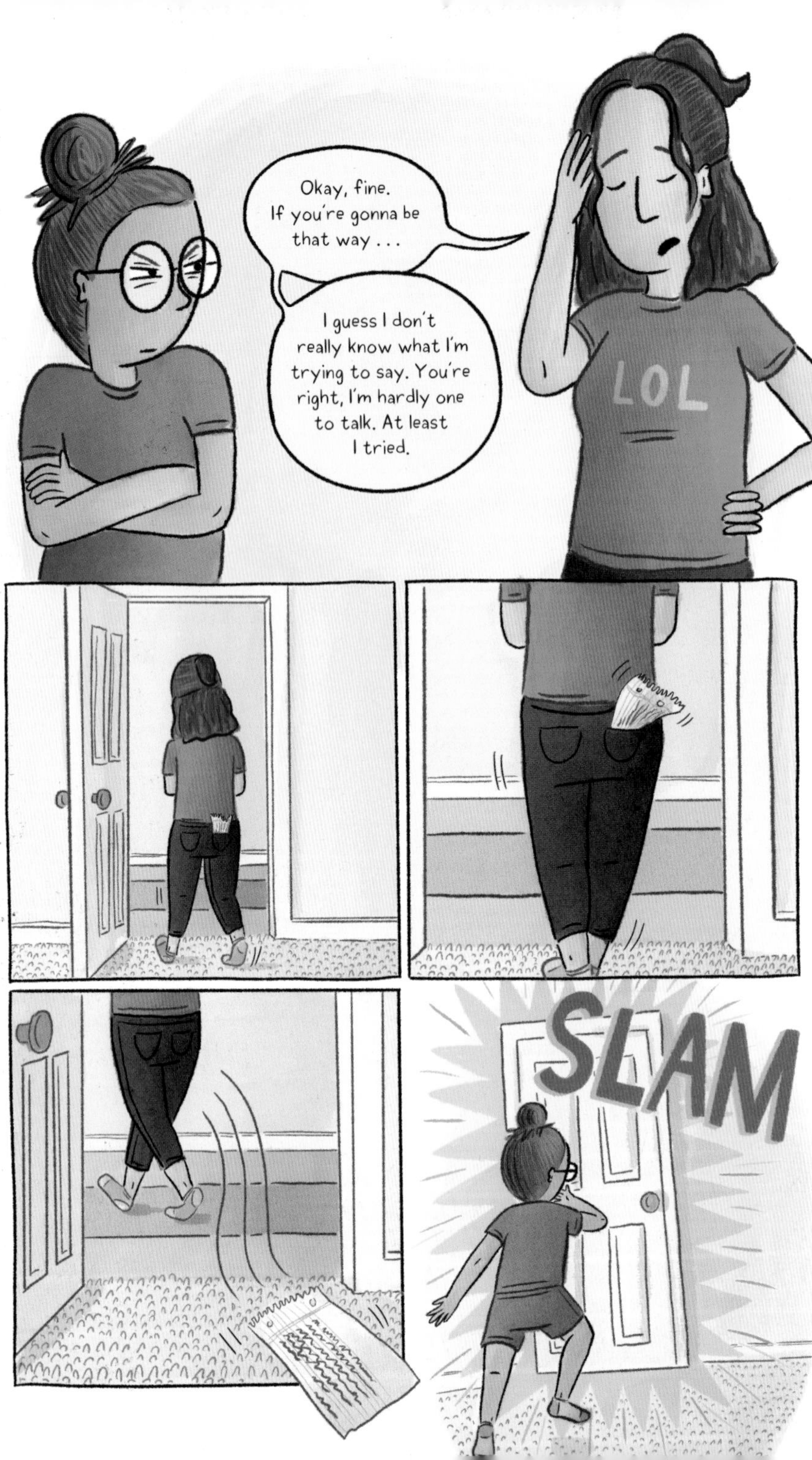
Okay, fine. If you're gonna be that way . . .
I guess I don't really know what I'm trying to say. You're right, I'm hardly one to talk. At least I tried.
LOL
SLAM

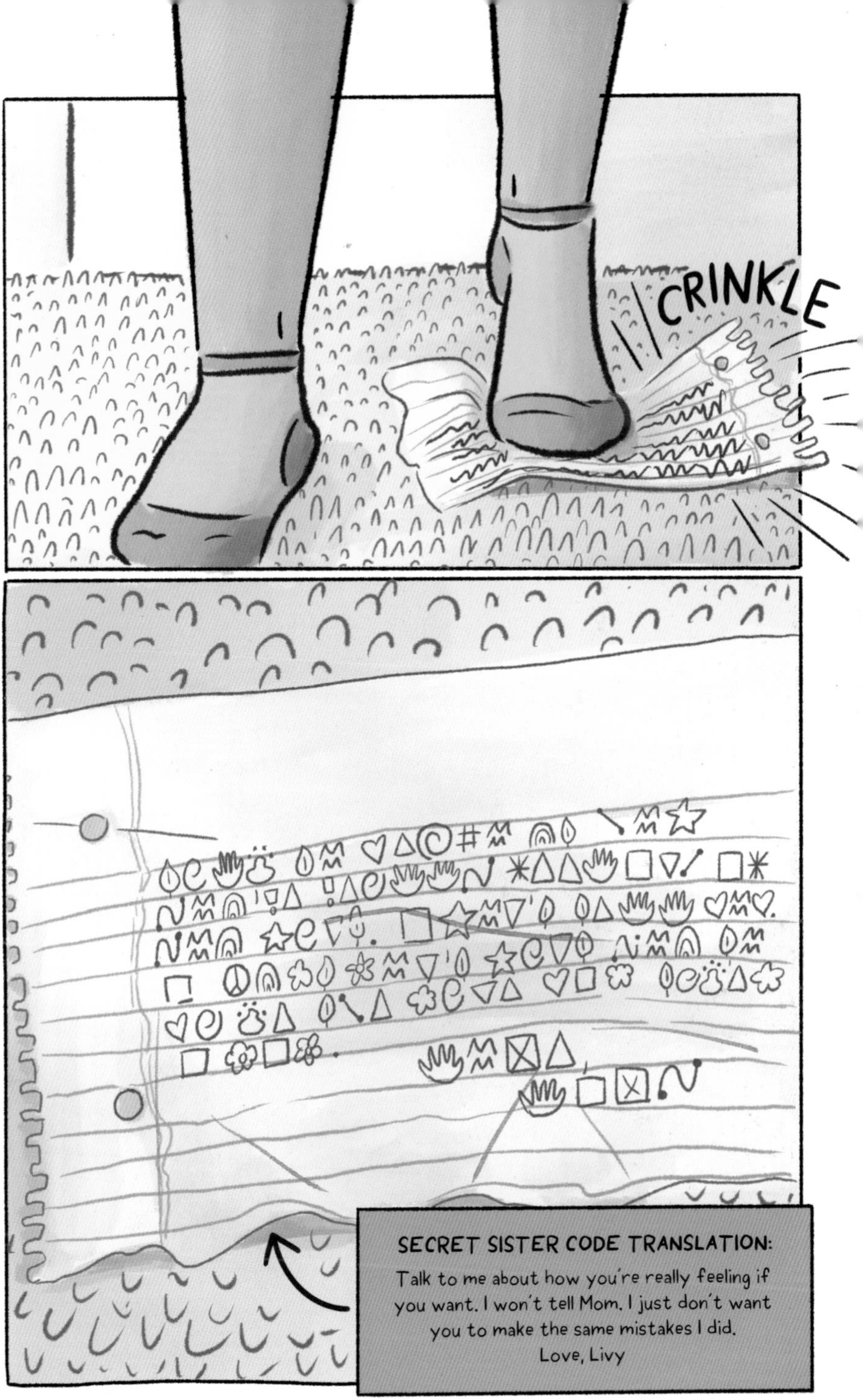
CRINKLE
SECRET SISTER CODE TRANSLATION:
Talk to me about how you're really feeling if you want. I won't tell Mom. I just don't want you to make the same mistakes I did.
Love, Livy

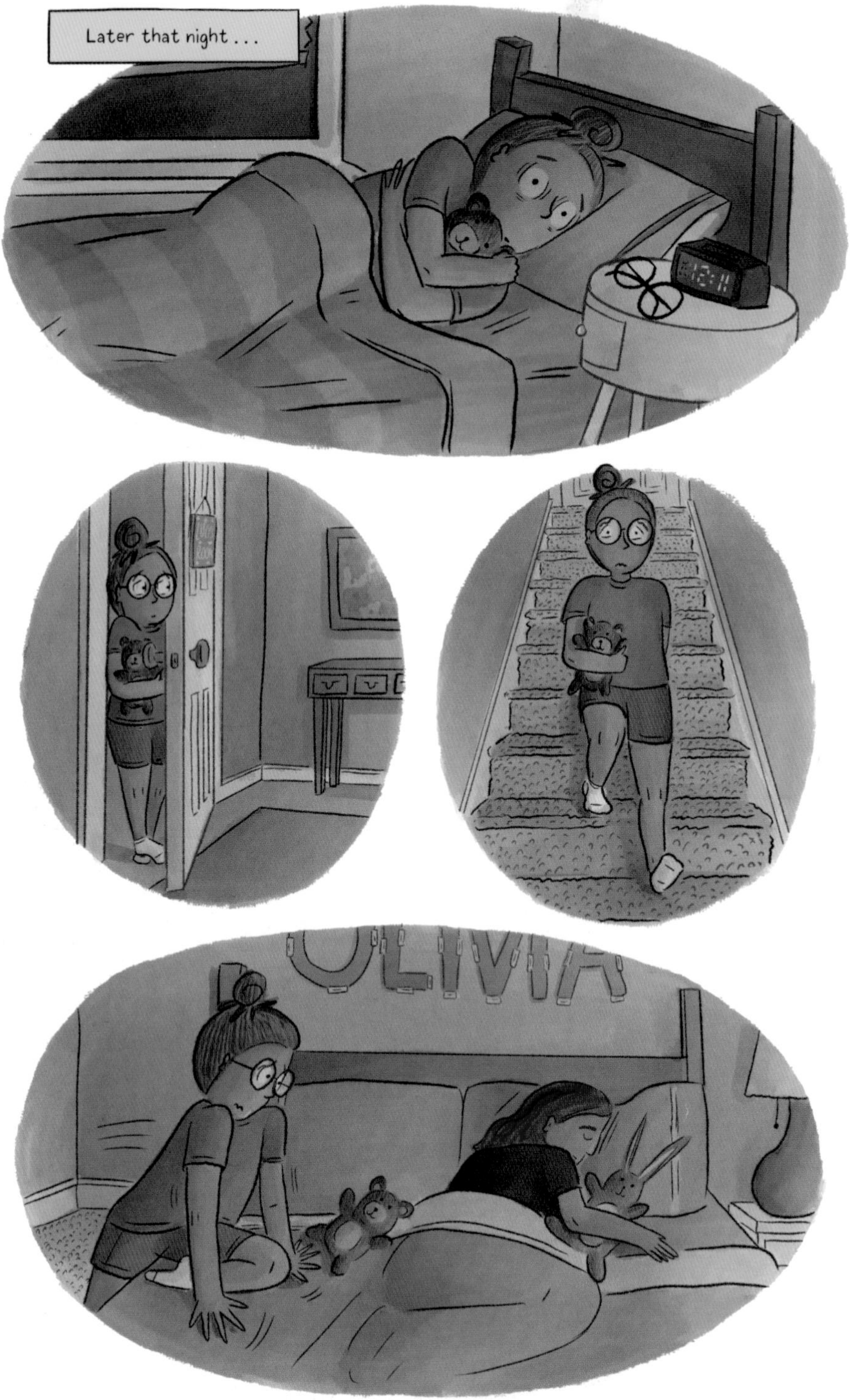
Later that night . . .
12:11
OLIVIA

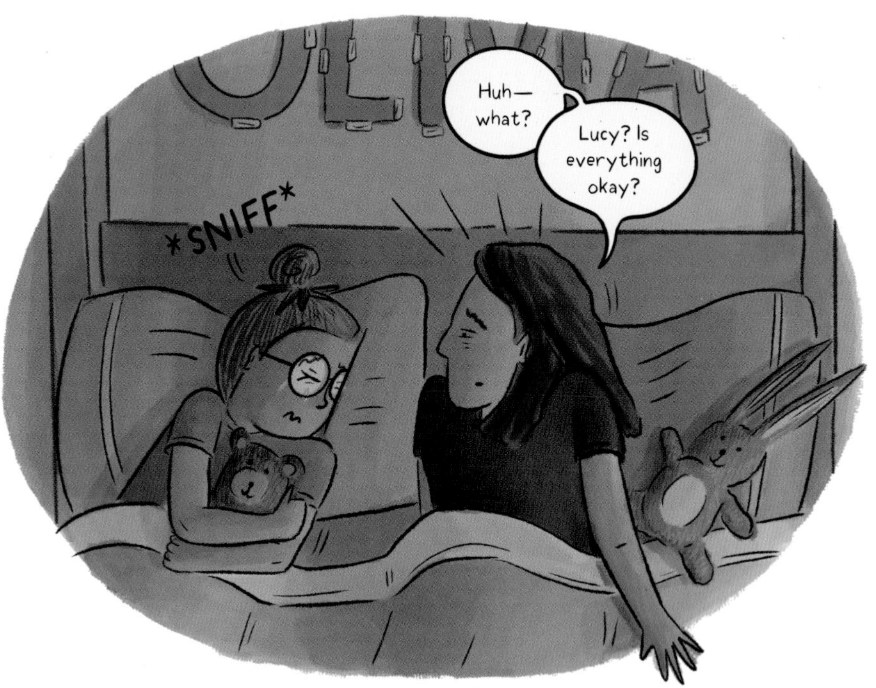
SNIFF
Huh—
what?
Lucy? Is
everything
okay?

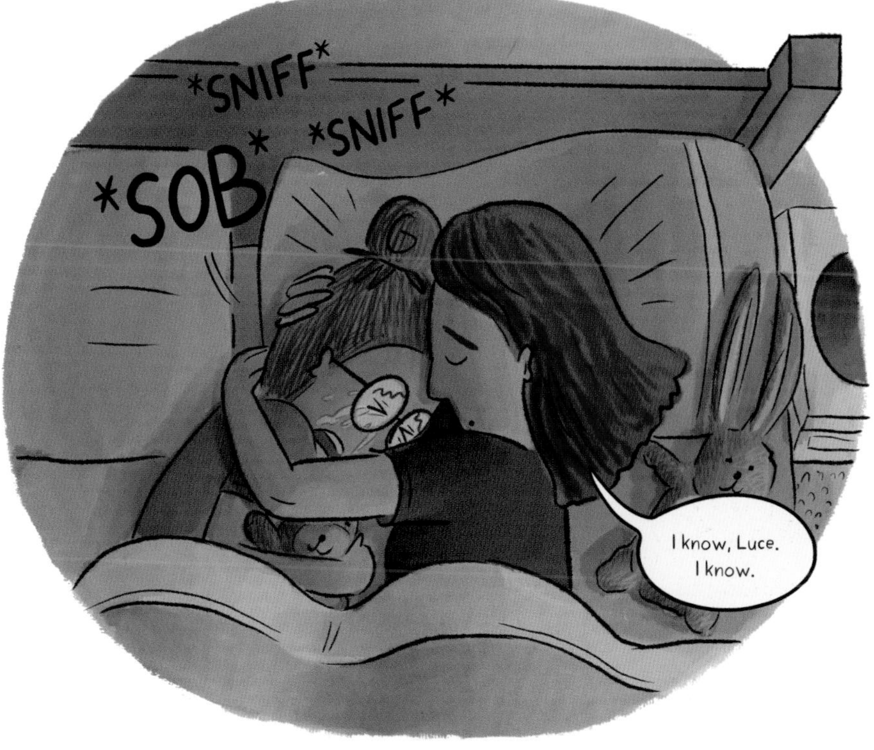
SNIFF
SOB
SNIFF
I know, Luce.
I know.

CHAPTER 6

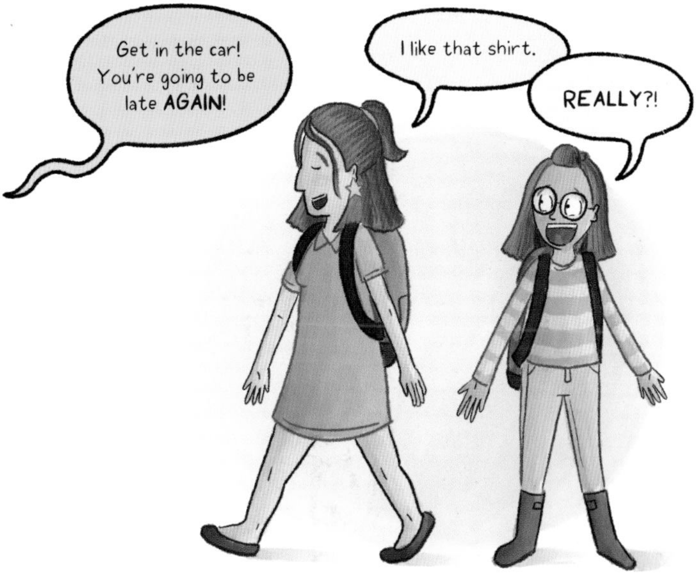

Get in the car! You're going to be late AGAIN!
I like that shirt.
REALLY?!

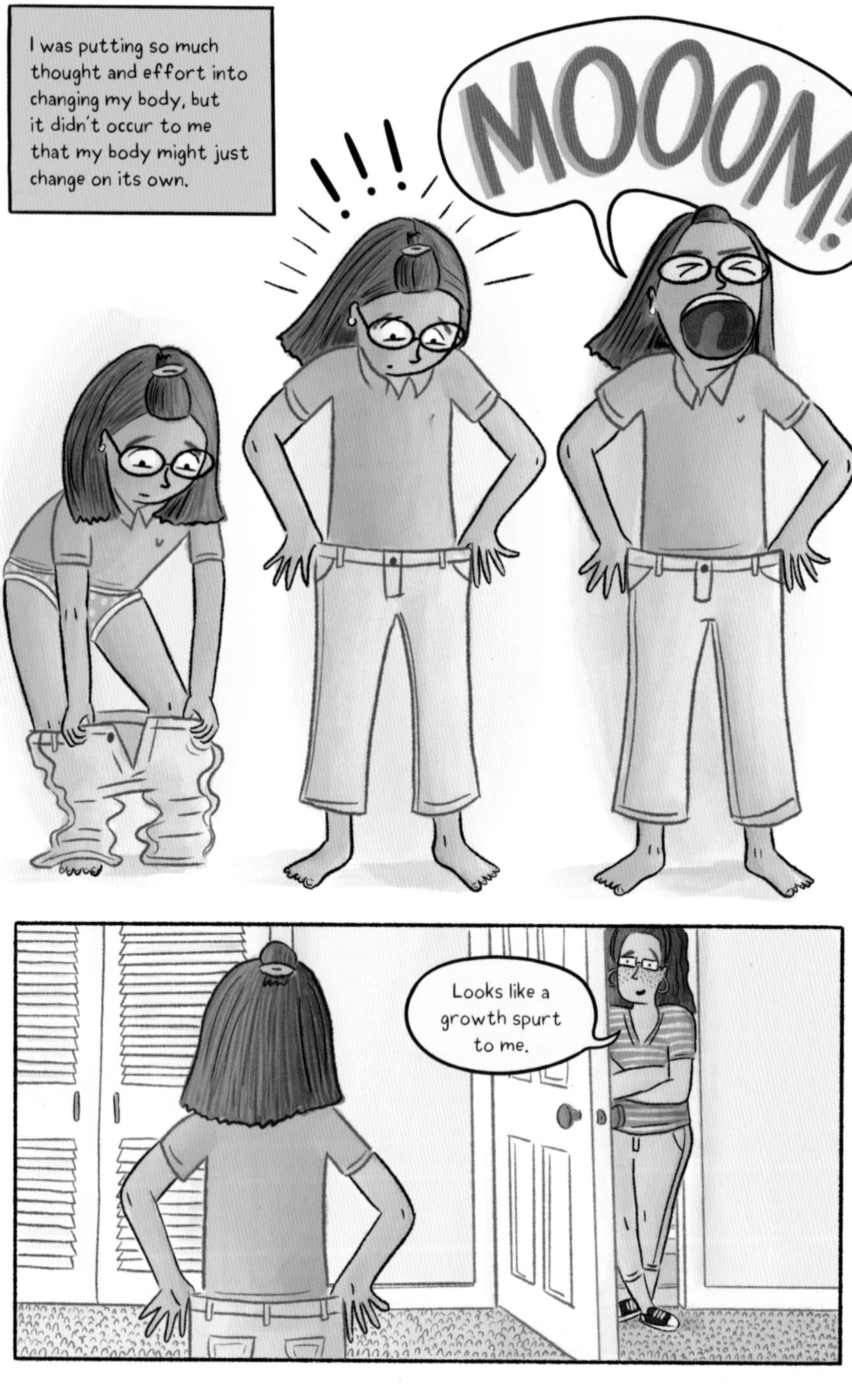
I was putting so much thought and effort into changing my body, but it didn't occur to me that my body might just change on its own.
!!!
MOOOM!
Looks like a growth spurt to me.

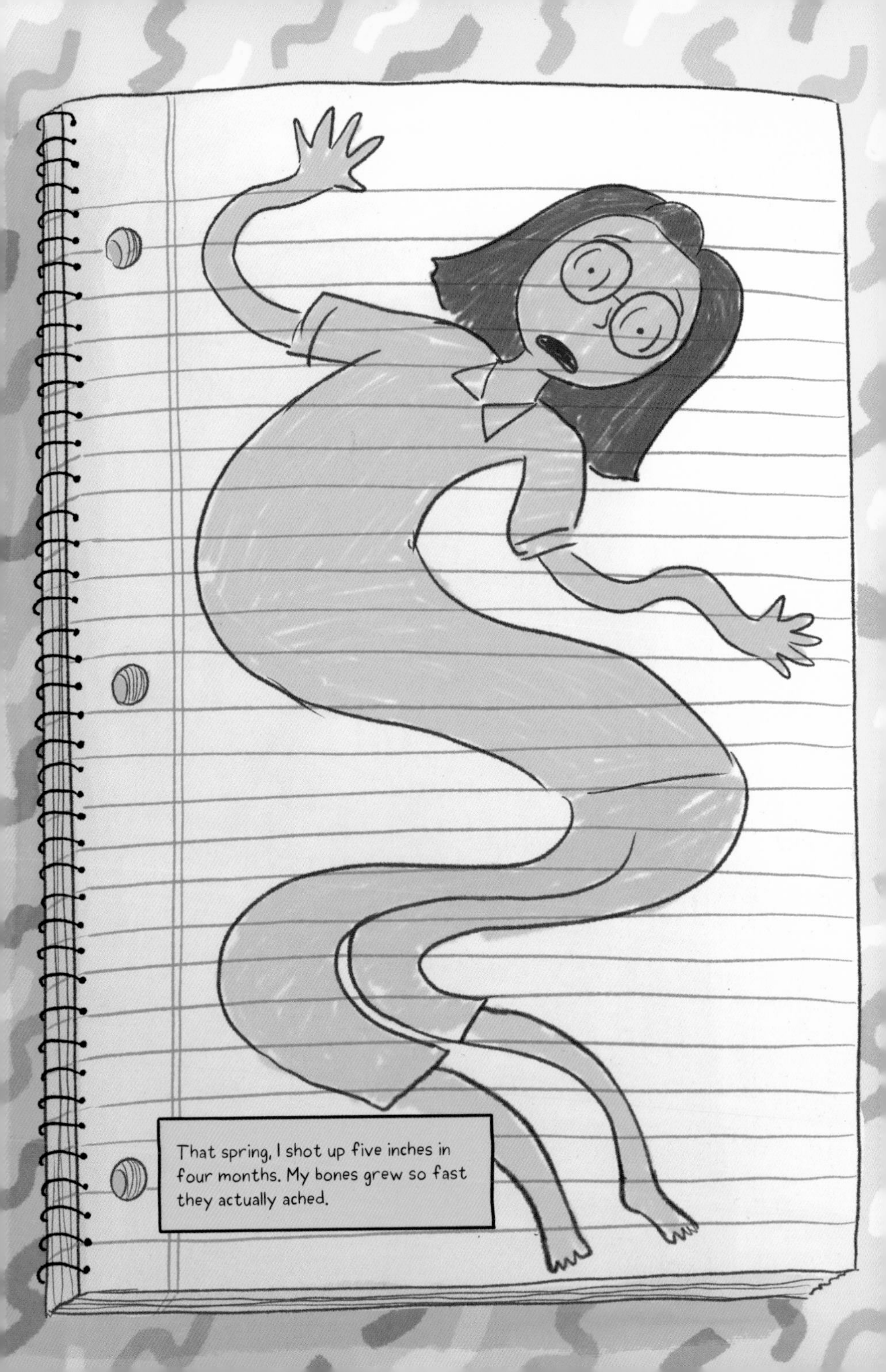
That spring, I shot up five inches in four months. My bones grew so fast they actually ached.

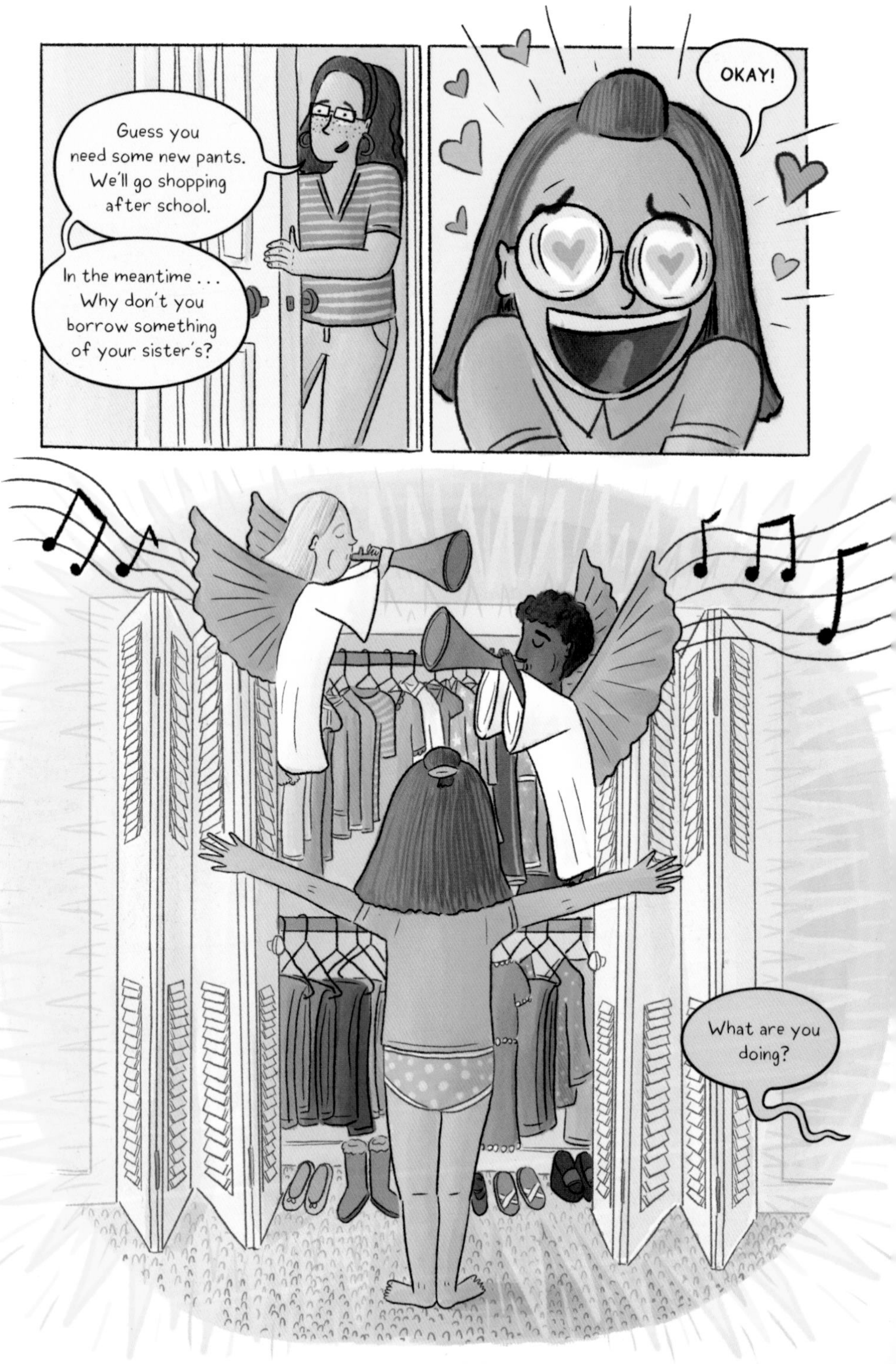
Guess you need some new pants. We'll go shopping after school.
In the meantime . . . Why don't you borrow something of your sister's?
OKAY!
What are you doing?

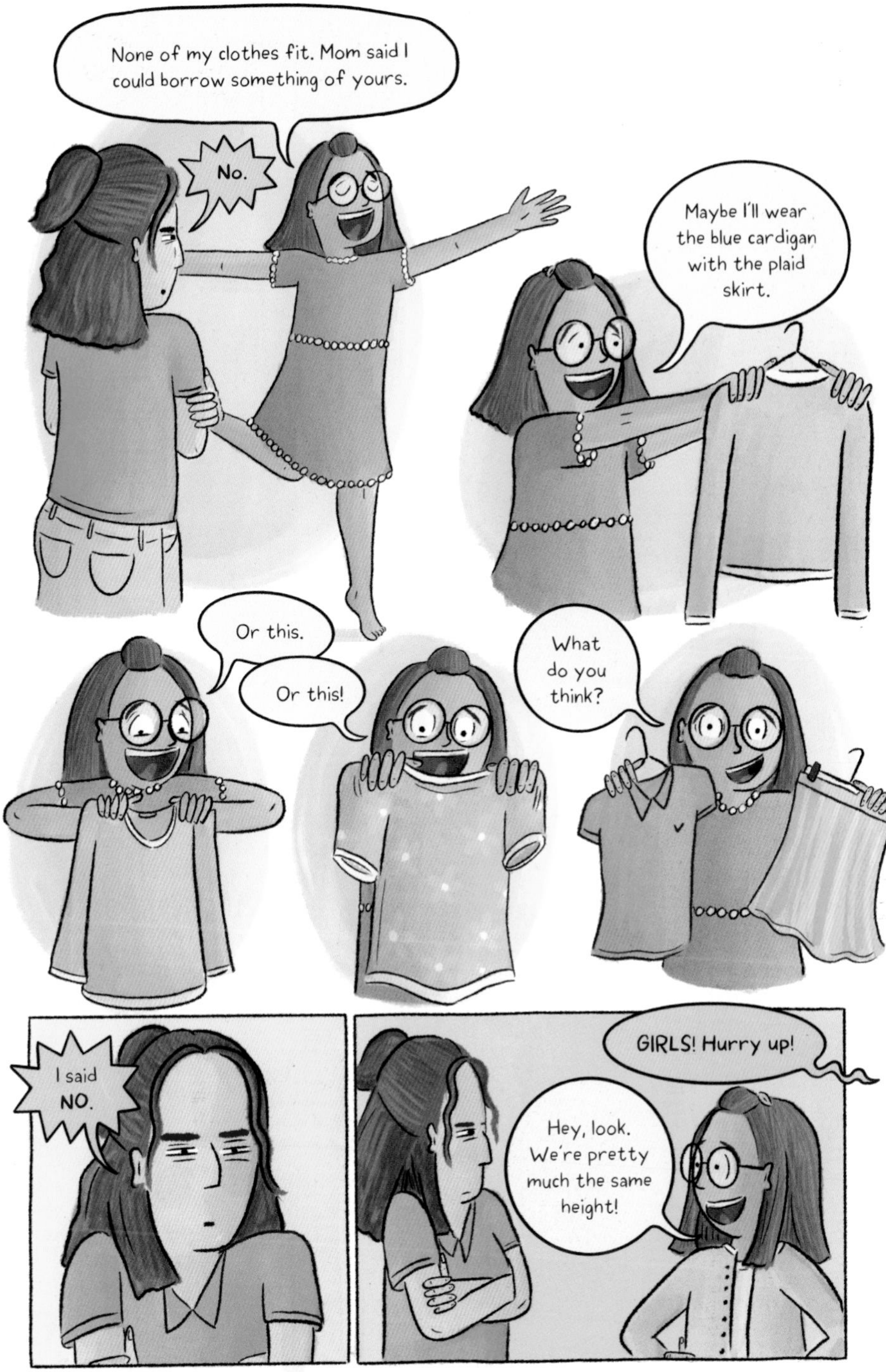
None of my clothes fit. Mom said I could borrow something of yours.
No.
Maybe I'll wear the blue cardigan with the plaid skirt.
Or this.
Or this!
What do you think?
I said NO.
GIRLS! Hurry up!
Hey, look. We're pretty much the same height!

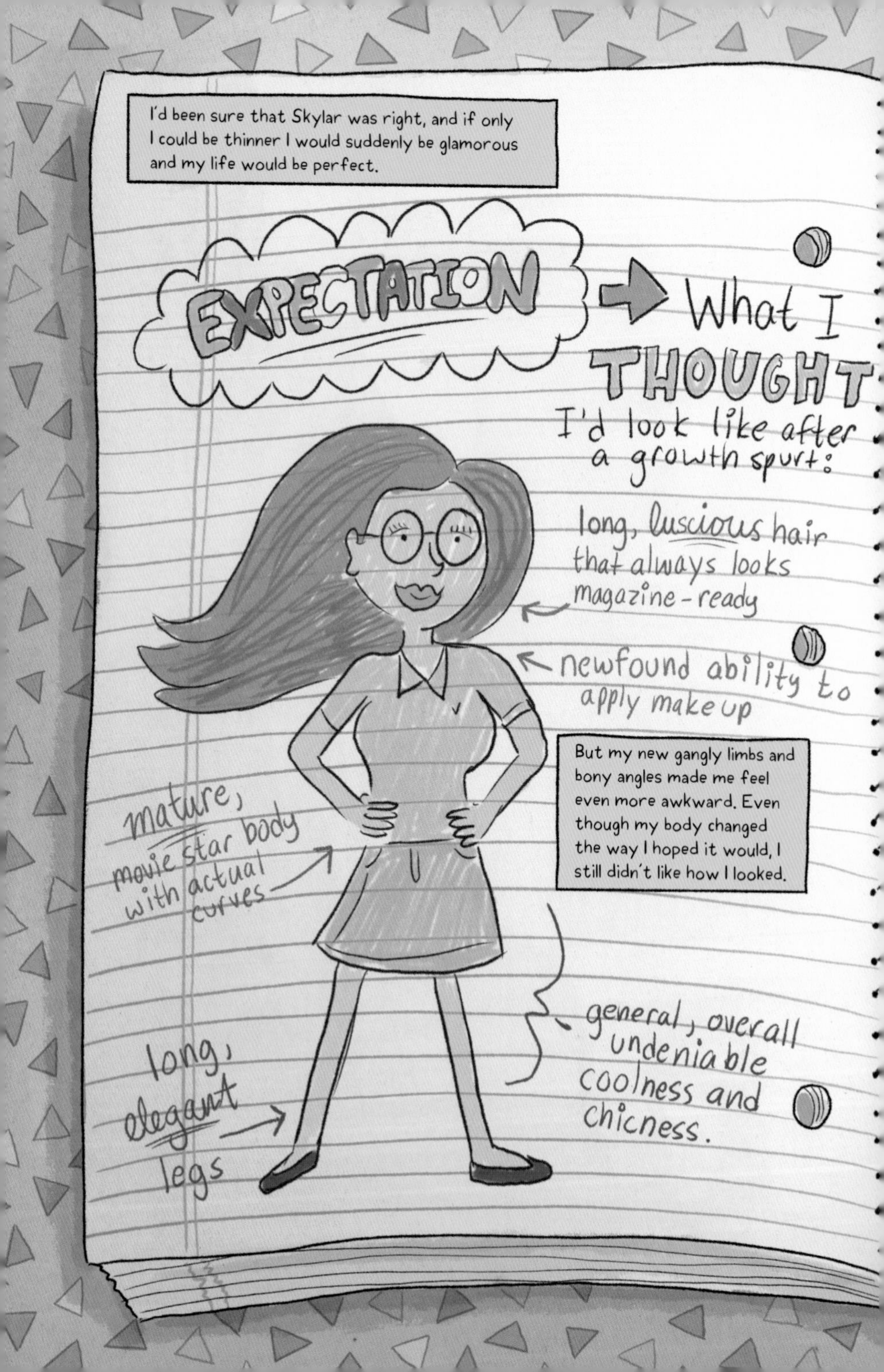

I'd been sure that Skylar was right, and if only I could be thinner I would suddenly be glamorous and my life would be perfect.
EXPECTATION → What I THOUGHT I'd look like after a growth spurt:
long, luscious hair that always looks magazine-ready
newfound ability to apply makeup
But my new gangly limbs and bony angles made me feel even more awkward. Even though my body changed the way I hoped it would, I still didn't like how I looked.
mature, movie star body with actual curves
general, overall undeniable coolness and chicness.
long, elegant legs

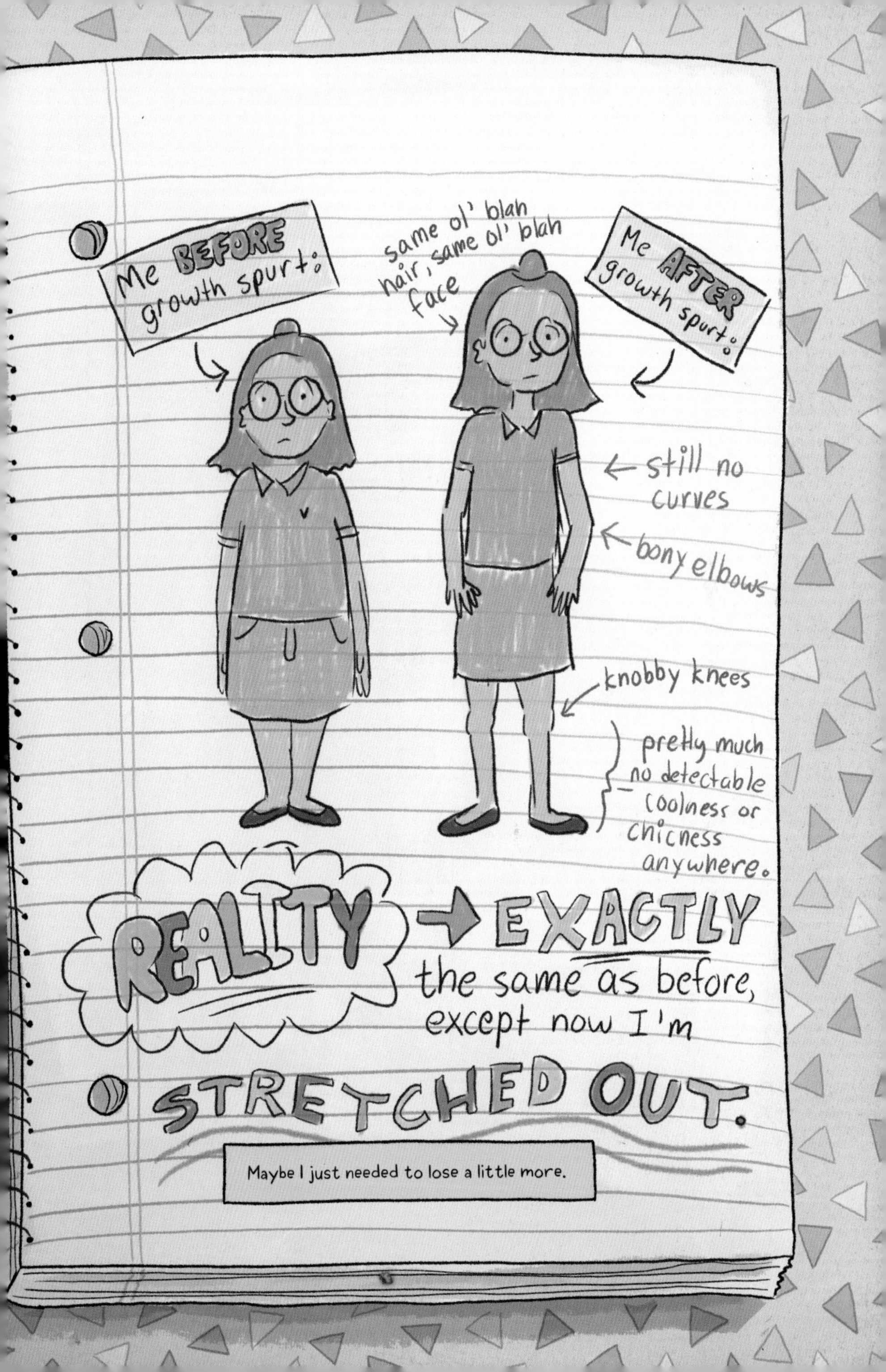
Me BEFORE growth spurt:
same ol' blah hair, same ol' blah face
Me AFTER growth spurt:
still no curves
bony elbows
knobby knees
pretty much no detectable coolness or chicness anywhere.
REALITY → EXACTLY the same as before, except now I'm
STRETCHED OUT.
Maybe I just needed to lose a little more.

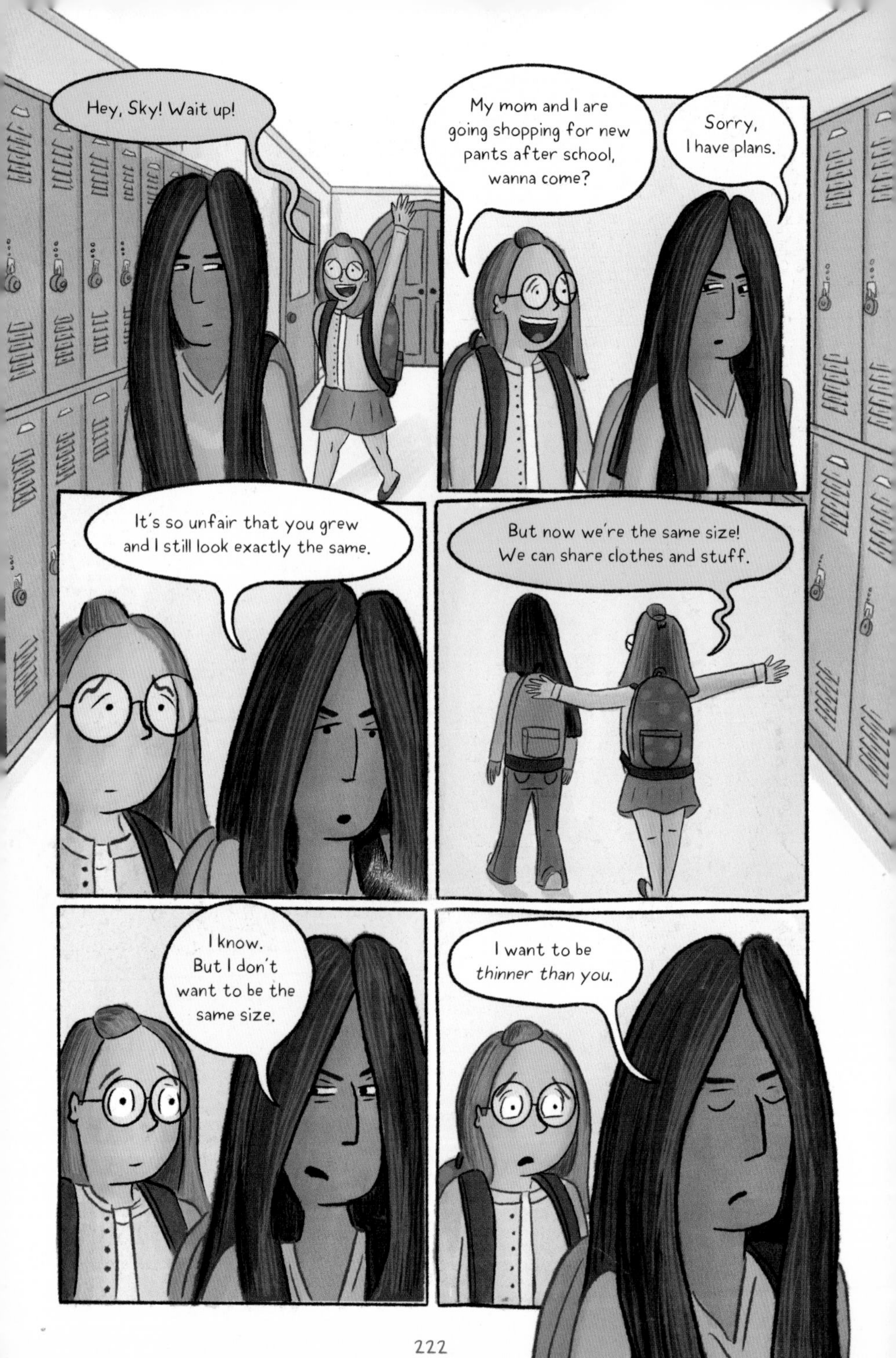
Hey, Sky! Wait up!
My mom and I are going shopping for new pants after school, wanna come?
Sorry, I have plans.
It's so unfair that you grew and I still look exactly the same.
But now we're the same size! We can share clothes and stuff.
I know. But I don't want to be the same size.
I want to be *thinner than you.*

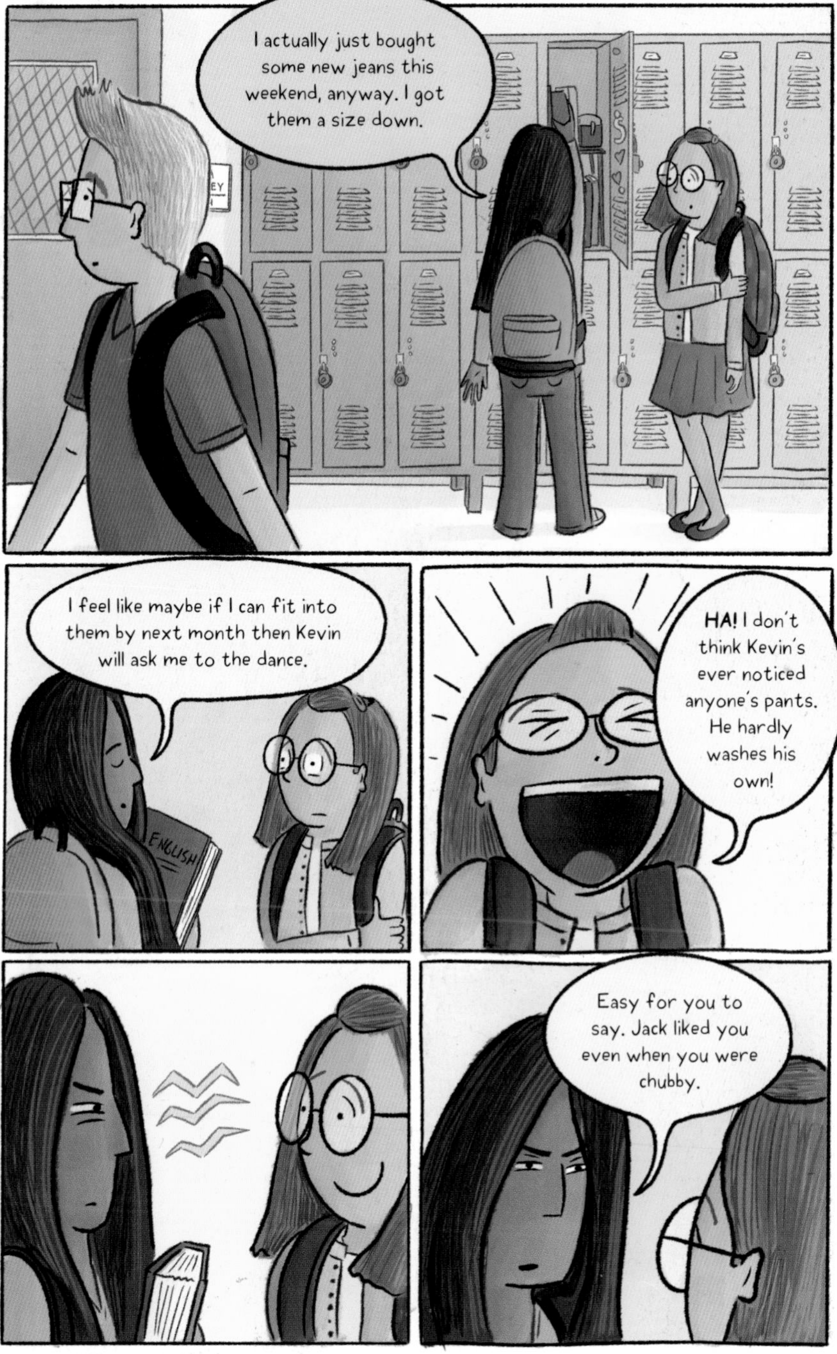
I actually just bought some new jeans this weekend, anyway. I got them a size down.
I feel like maybe if I can fit into them by next month then Kevin will ask me to the dance.
ENGLISH
HA! I don't think Kevin's ever noticed anyone's pants. He hardly washes his own!
Easy for you to say. Jack liked you even when you were chubby.

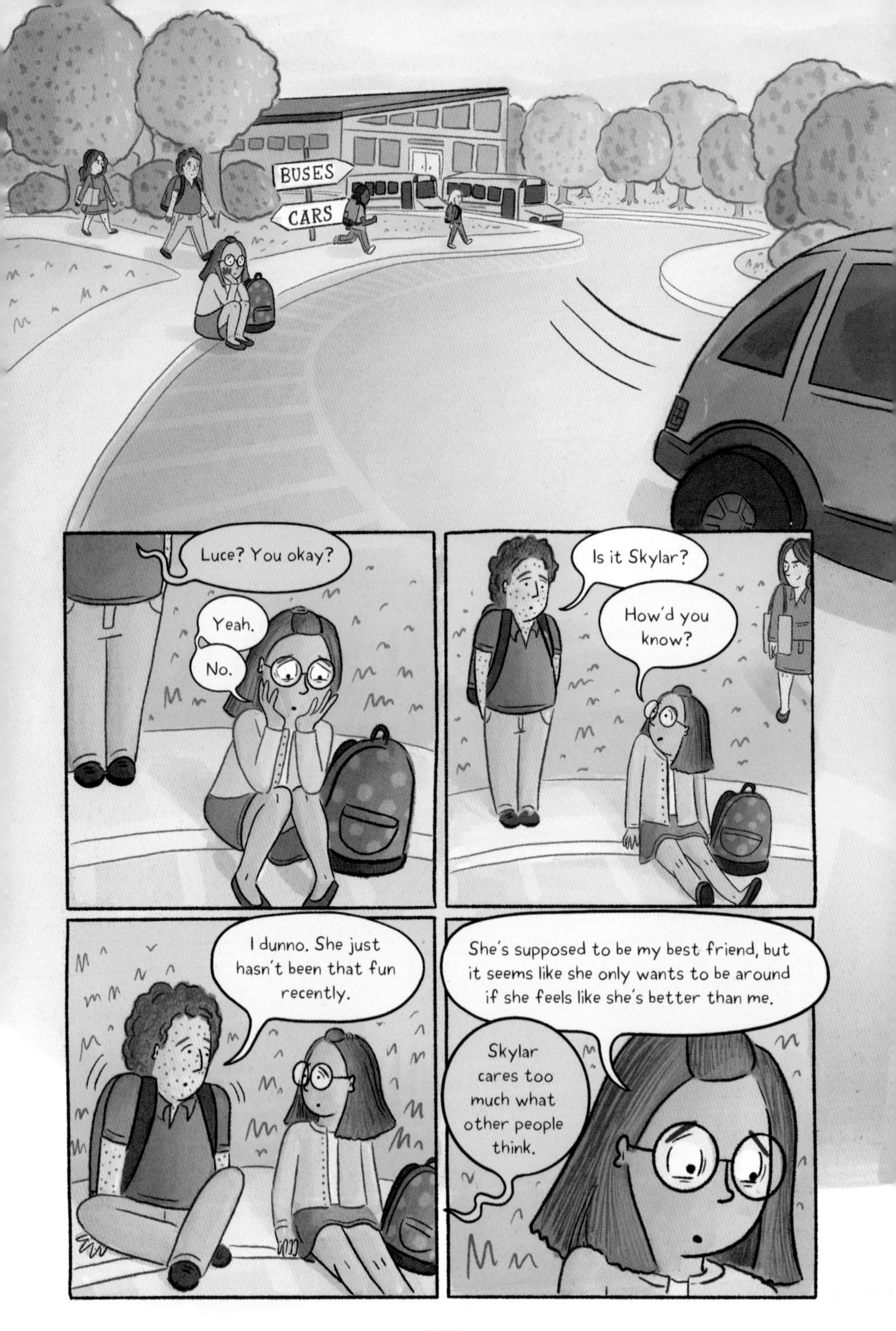
BUSES
CARS
Luce? You okay?
Yeah.
No.
Is it Skylar?
How'd you know?
I dunno. She just hasn't been that fun recently.
She's supposed to be my best friend, but it seems like she only wants to be around if she feels like she's better than me.
Skylar cares too much what other people think.

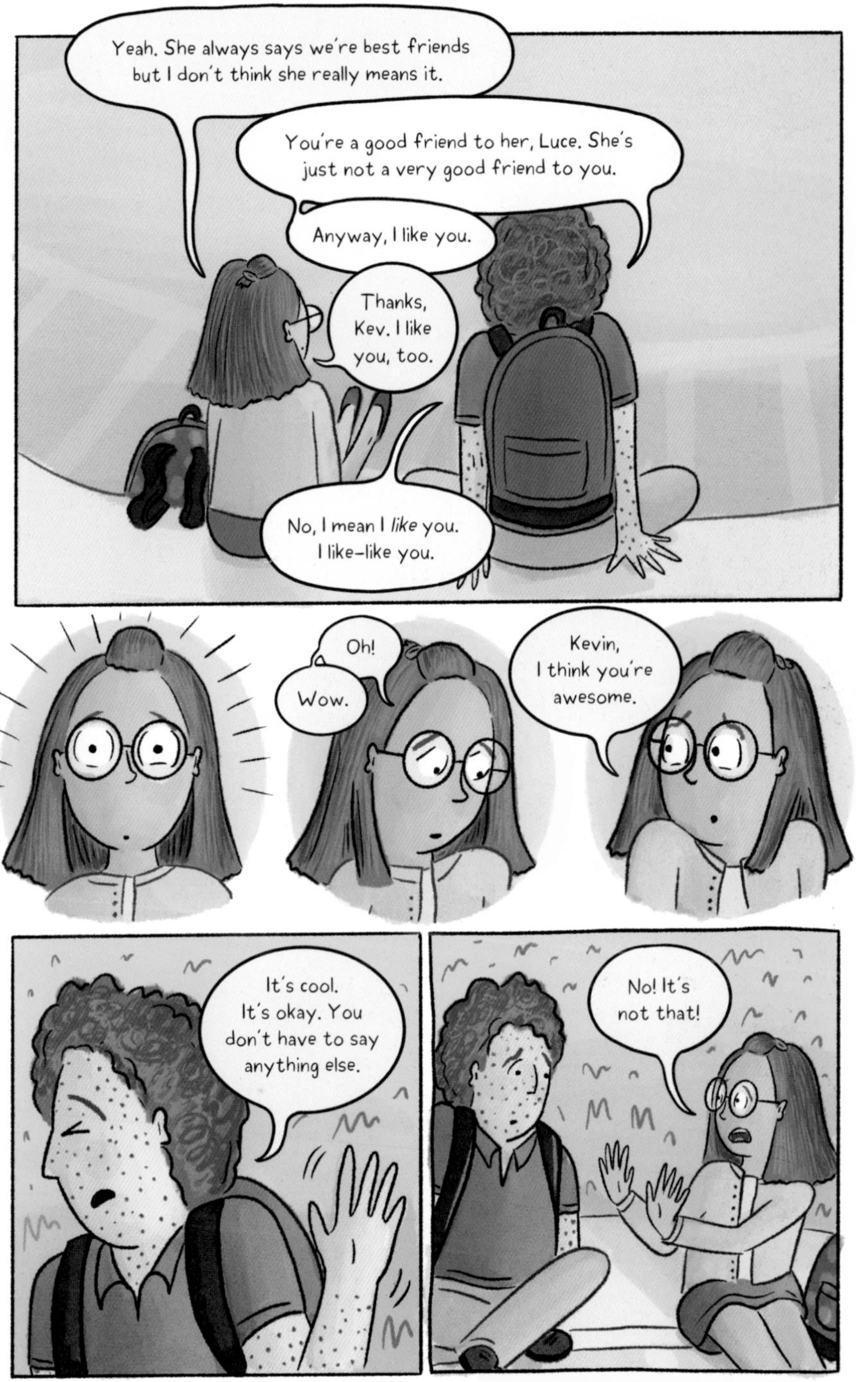
Yeah. She always says we're best friends but I don't think she really means it.
You're a good friend to her, Luce. She's just not a very good friend to you.
Anyway, I like you.
Thanks, Kev. I like you, too.
No, I mean I *like* you. I like-like you.
Oh!
Wow.
Kevin, I think you're awesome.
It's cool. It's okay. You don't have to say anything else.
No! It's not that!

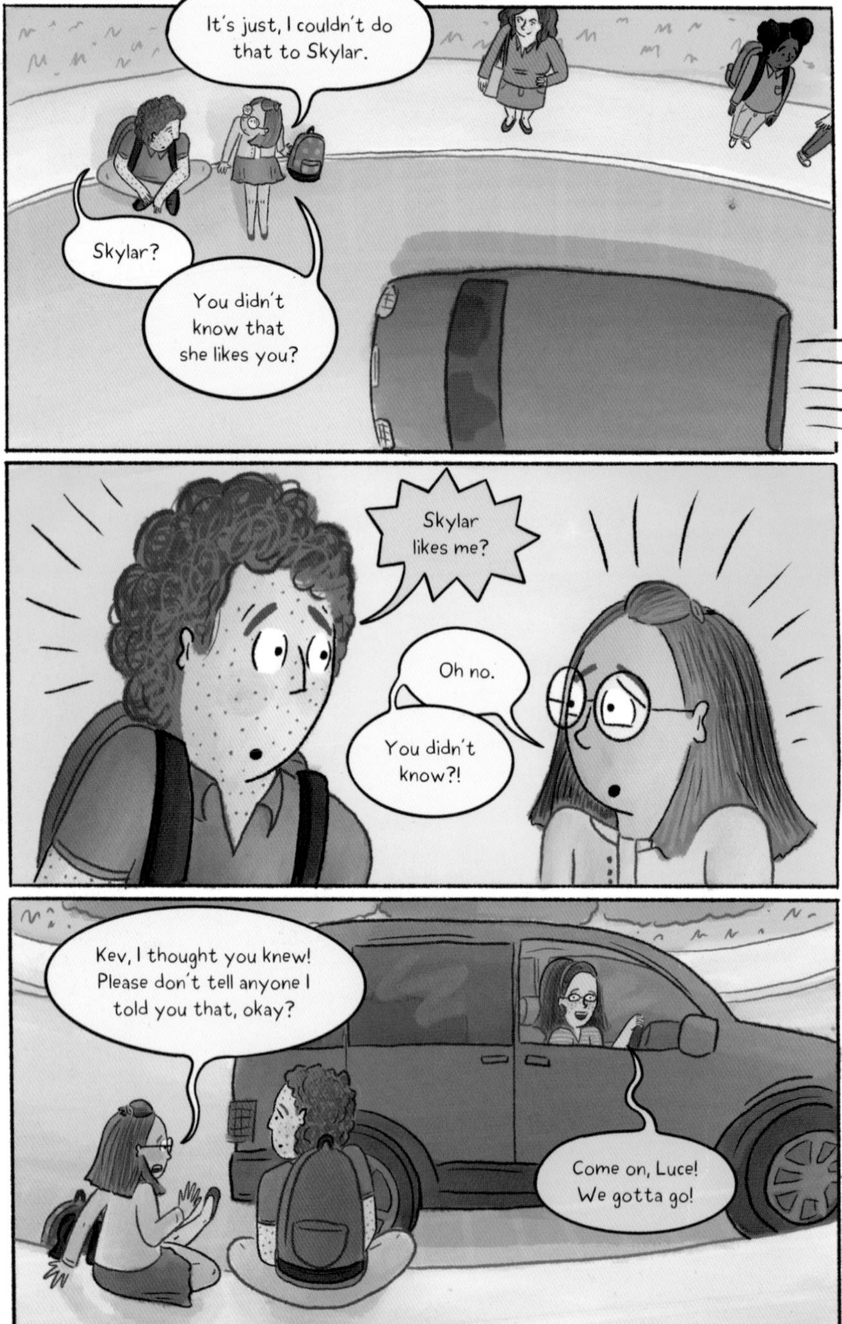
It's just, I couldn't do that to Skylar.
Skylar?
You didn't know that she likes you?
Skylar likes me?
Oh no.
You didn't know?!
Kev, I thought you knew! Please don't tell anyone I told you that, okay?
Come on, Luce! We gotta go!

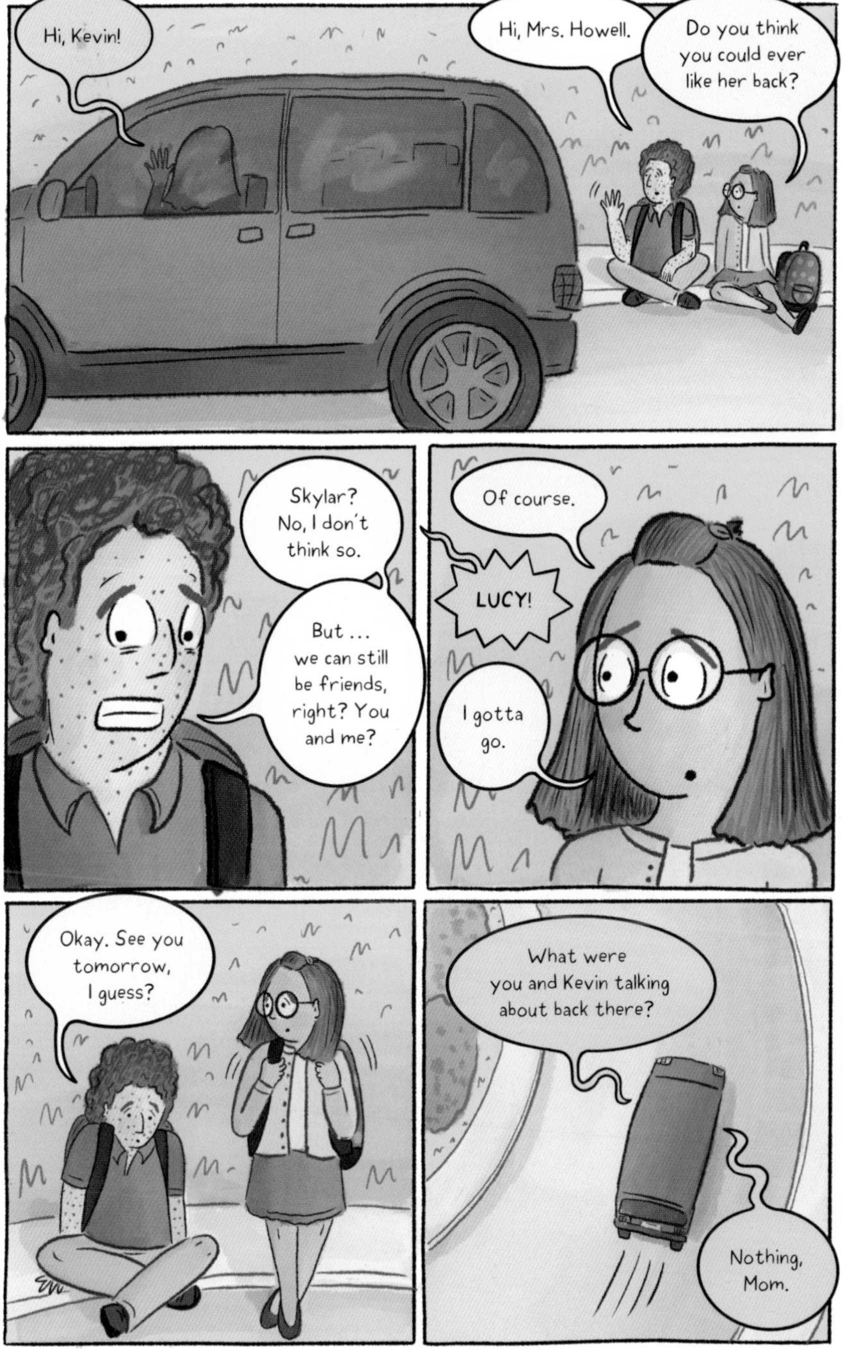
Hi, Kevin!
Hi, Mrs. Howell.
Do you think you could ever like her back?
Skylar? No, I don't think so.
But ... we can still be friends, right? You and me?
Of course.
LUCY!
I gotta go.
Okay. See you tomorrow, I guess?
What were you and Kevin talking about back there?
Nothing, Mom.

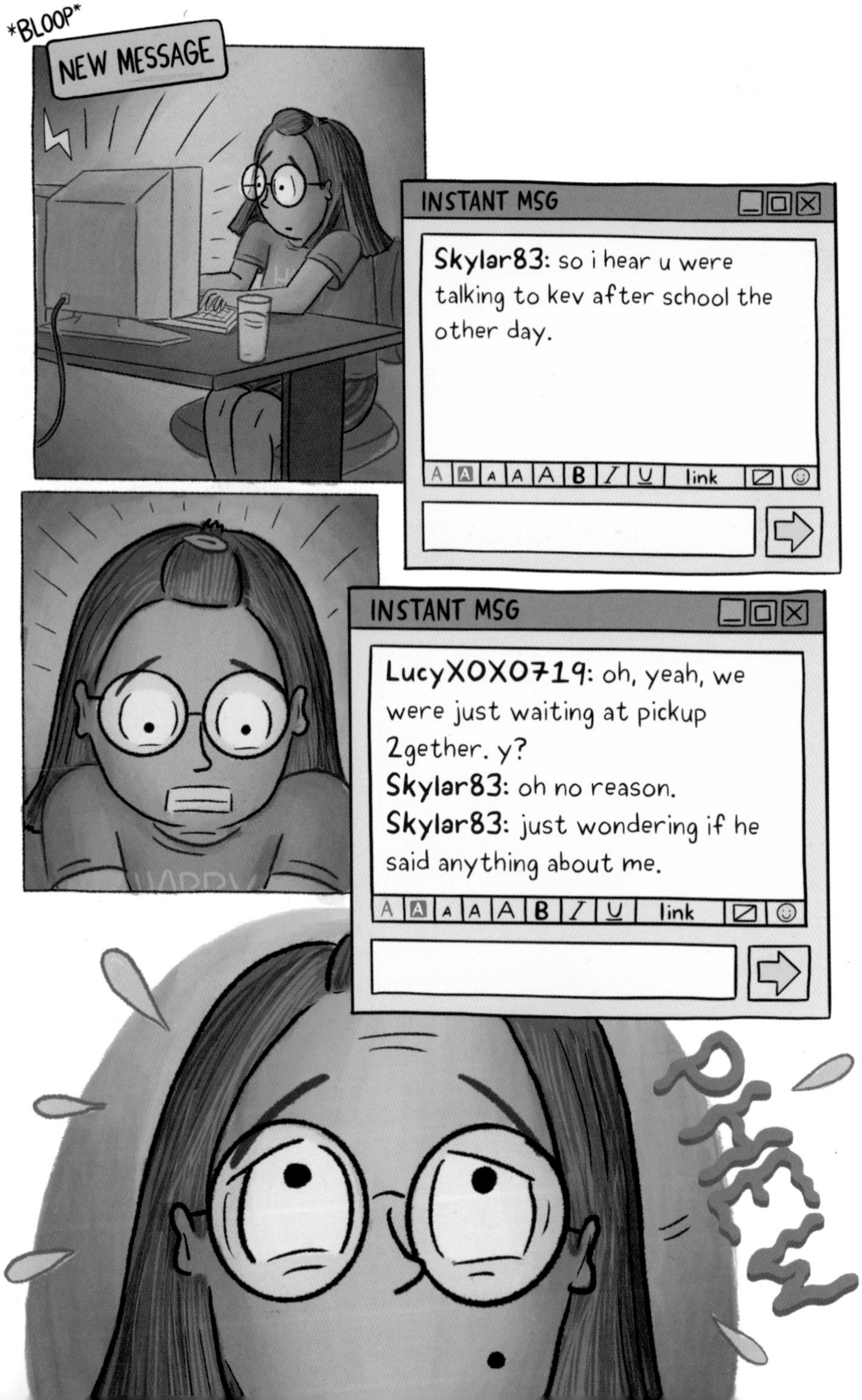
BLOOP
NEW MESSAGE
INSTANT MSG
Skylar83: so i hear u were talking to kev after school the other day.
A A A A A B I U link
INSTANT MSG
LucyXOXO719: oh, yeah, we were just waiting at pickup 2gether. y?
Skylar83: oh no reason.
Skylar83: just wondering if he said anything about me.
A A A A A B I U link
PHEW

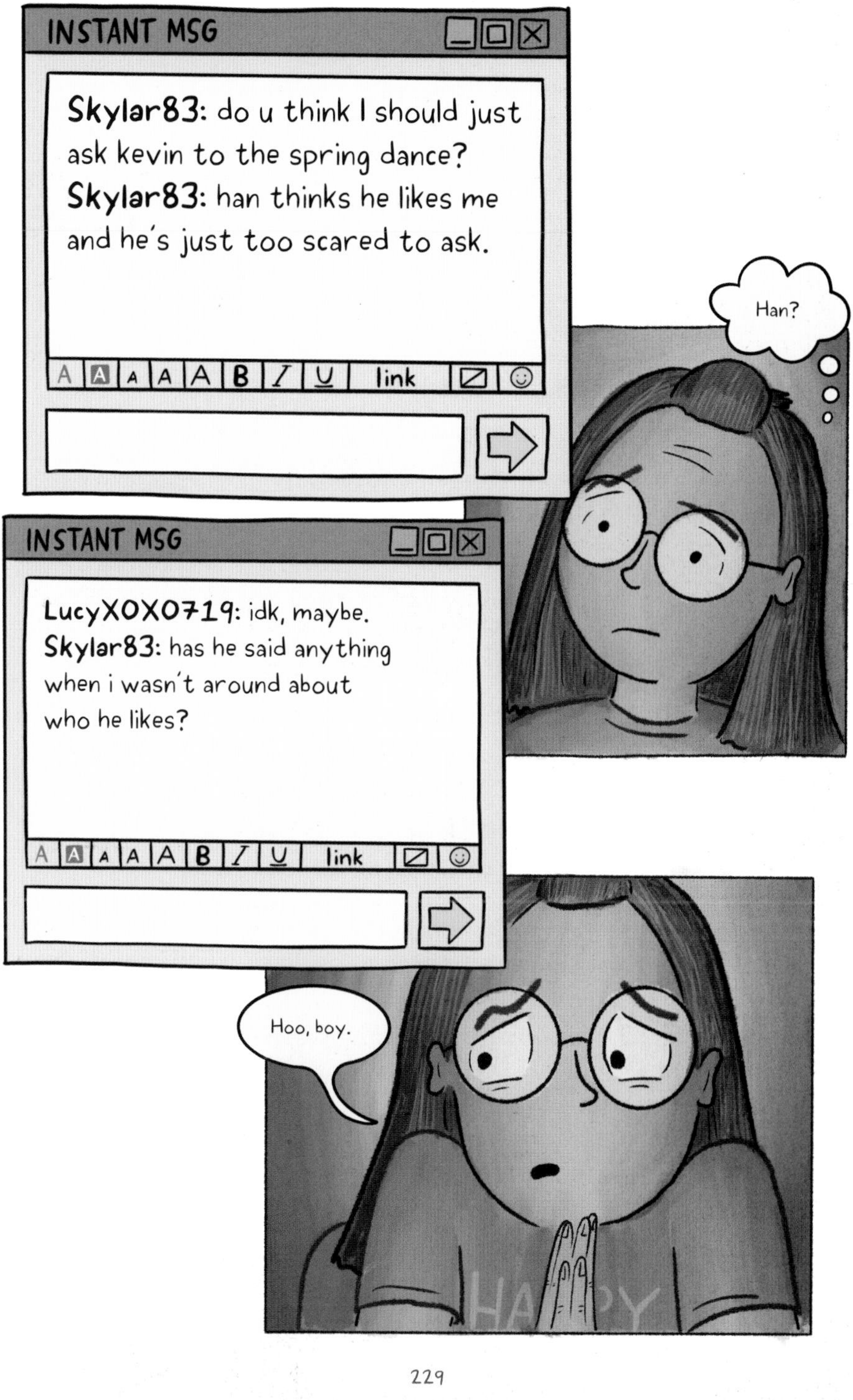
INSTANT MSG
Skylar83: do u think I should just ask kevin to the spring dance?
Skylar83: han thinks he likes me and he's just too scared to ask.
Han?
INSTANT MSG
LucyXOXO719: idk, maybe.
Skylar83: has he said anything when i wasn't around about who he likes?
Hoo, boy.

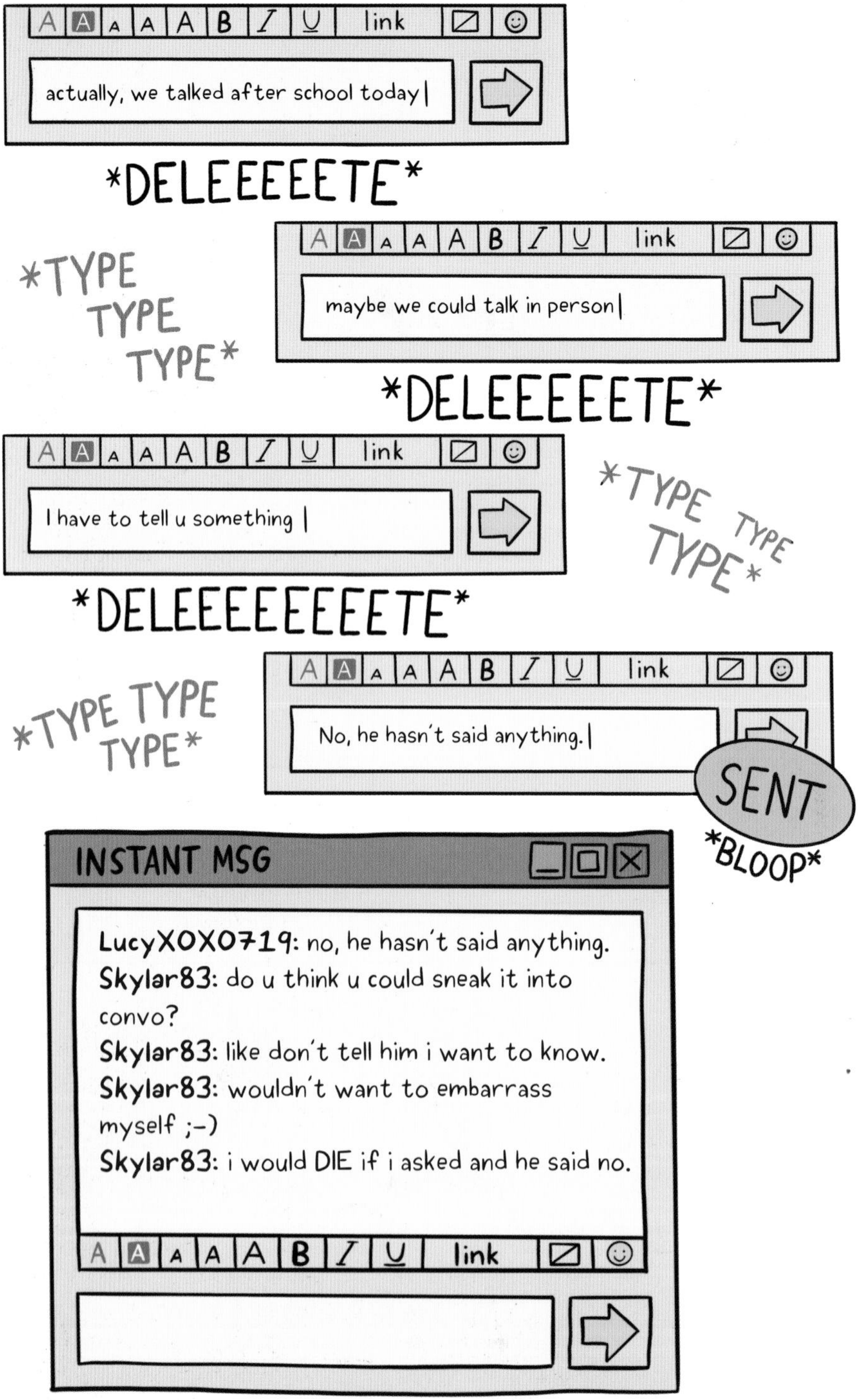
A A A A A B I U link
actually, we talked after school today
DELEEEEETE
TYPE TYPE TYPE
maybe we could talk in person
DELEEEEETE
I have to tell u something
TYPE TYPE TYPE
DELEEEEEEEETE
TYPE TYPE TYPE
No, he hasn't said anything.
SENT
BLOOP
INSTANT MSG
LucyXOXO719: no, he hasn't said anything.
Skylar83: do u think u could sneak it into convo?
Skylar83: like don't tell him i want to know.
Skylar83: wouldn't want to embarrass myself ;-)
Skylar83: i would DIE if i asked and he said no.

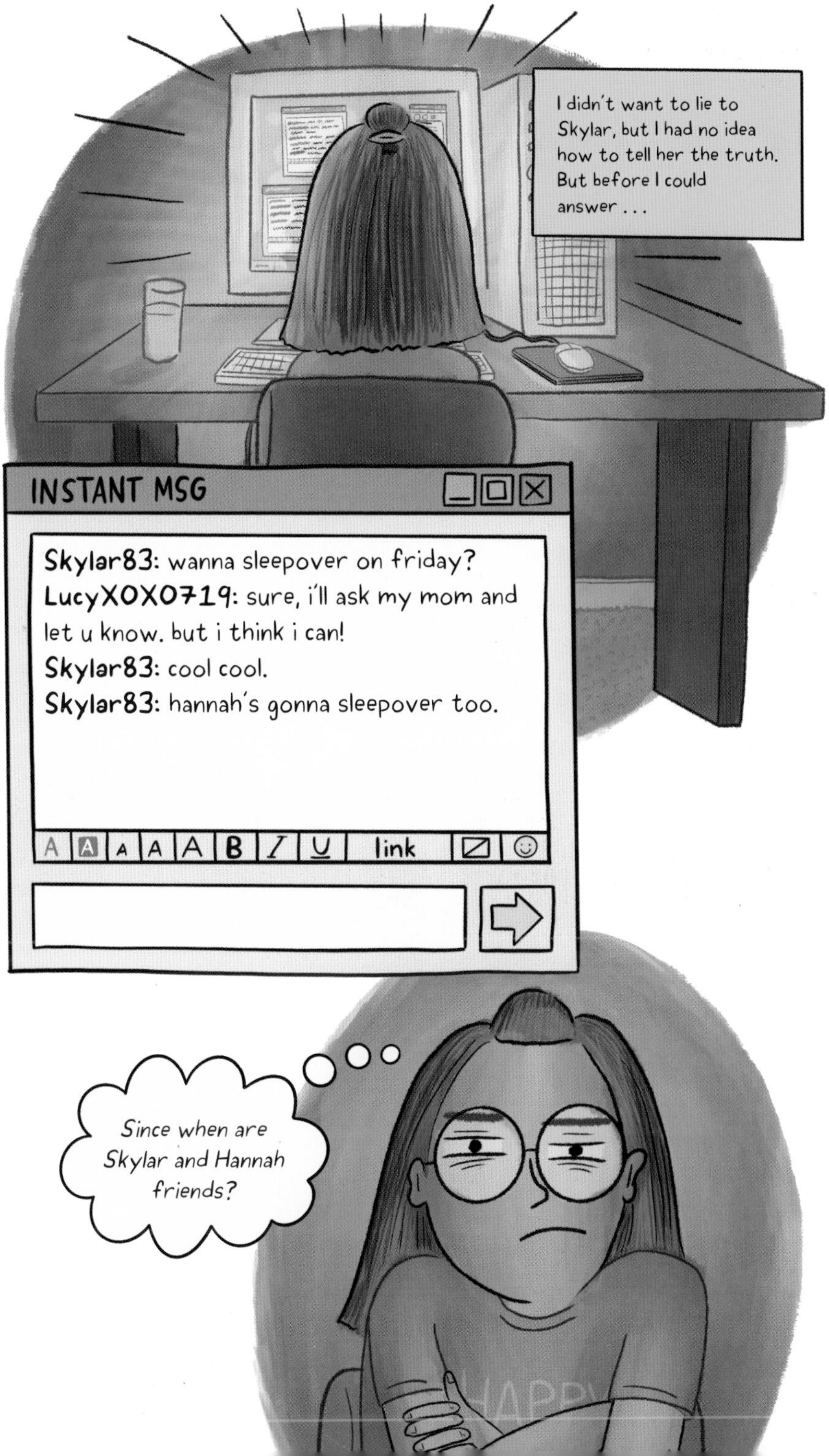
I didn't want to lie to Skylar, but I had no idea how to tell her the truth. But before I could answer . . .
INSTANT MSG
Skylar83: wanna sleepover on friday?
LucyXOXO719: sure, i'll ask my mom and let u know. but i think i can!
Skylar83: cool cool.
Skylar83: hannah's gonna sleepover too.
link
Since when are Skylar and Hannah friends?

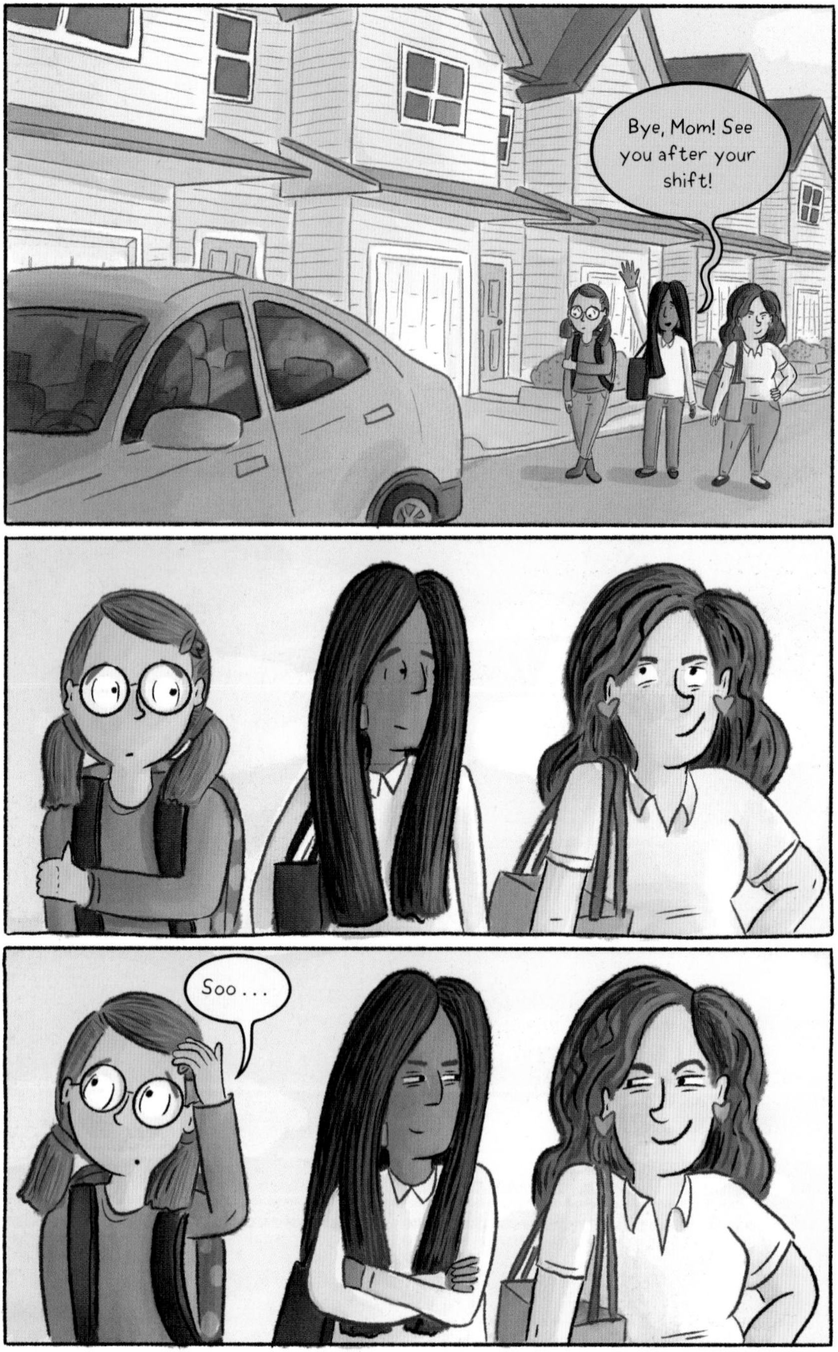
Bye, Mom! See you after your shift!
Soo . . .

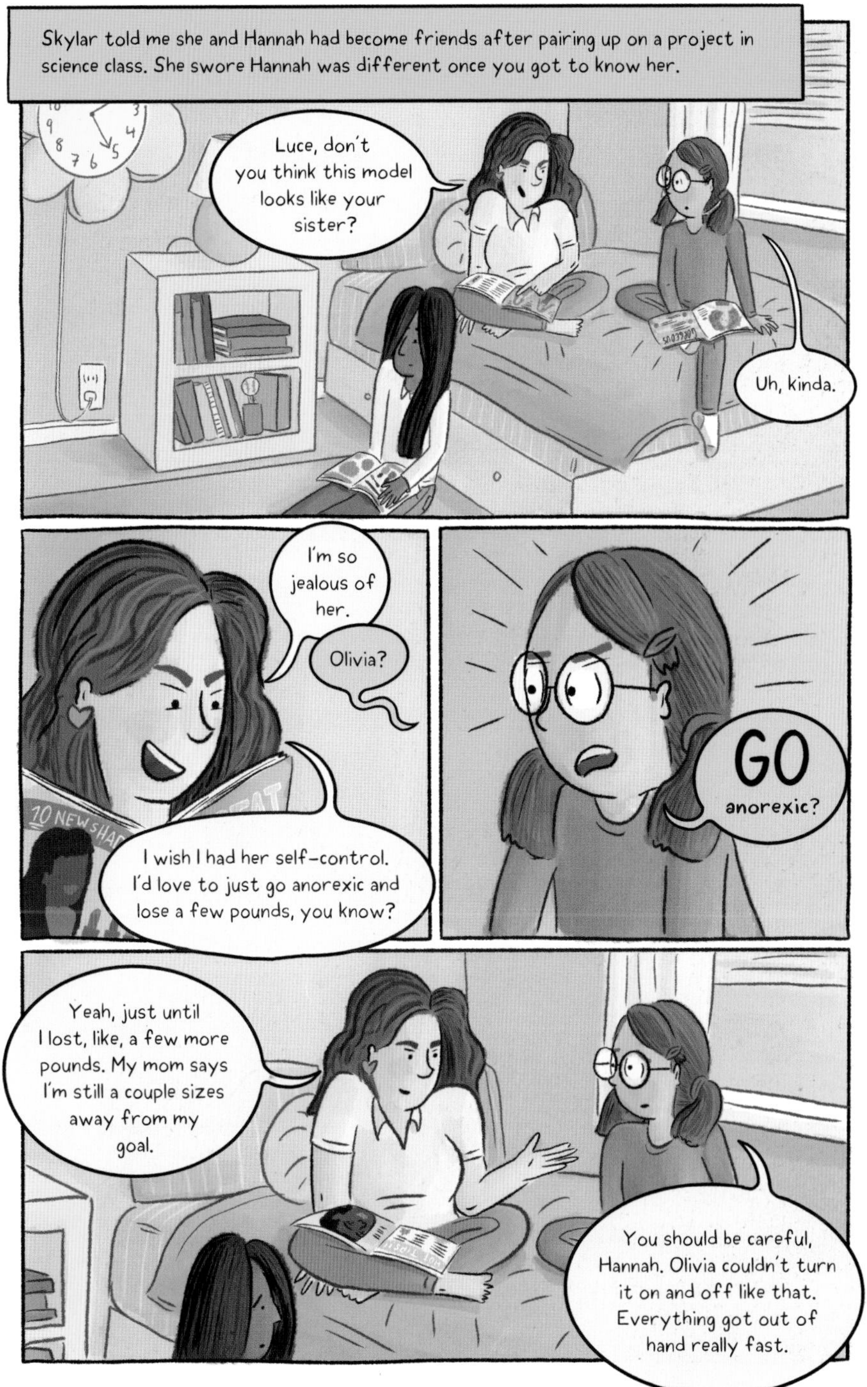
Skylar told me she and Hannah had become friends after pairing up on a project in science class. She swore Hannah was different once you got to know her.
Luce, don't you think this model looks like your sister?
Uh, kinda.
I'm so jealous of her.
Olivia?
I wish I had her self-control. I'd love to just go anorexic and lose a few pounds, you know?
GO anorexic?
Yeah, just until I lost, like, a few more pounds. My mom says I'm still a couple sizes away from my goal.
You should be careful, Hannah. Olivia couldn't turn it on and off like that. Everything got out of hand really fast.

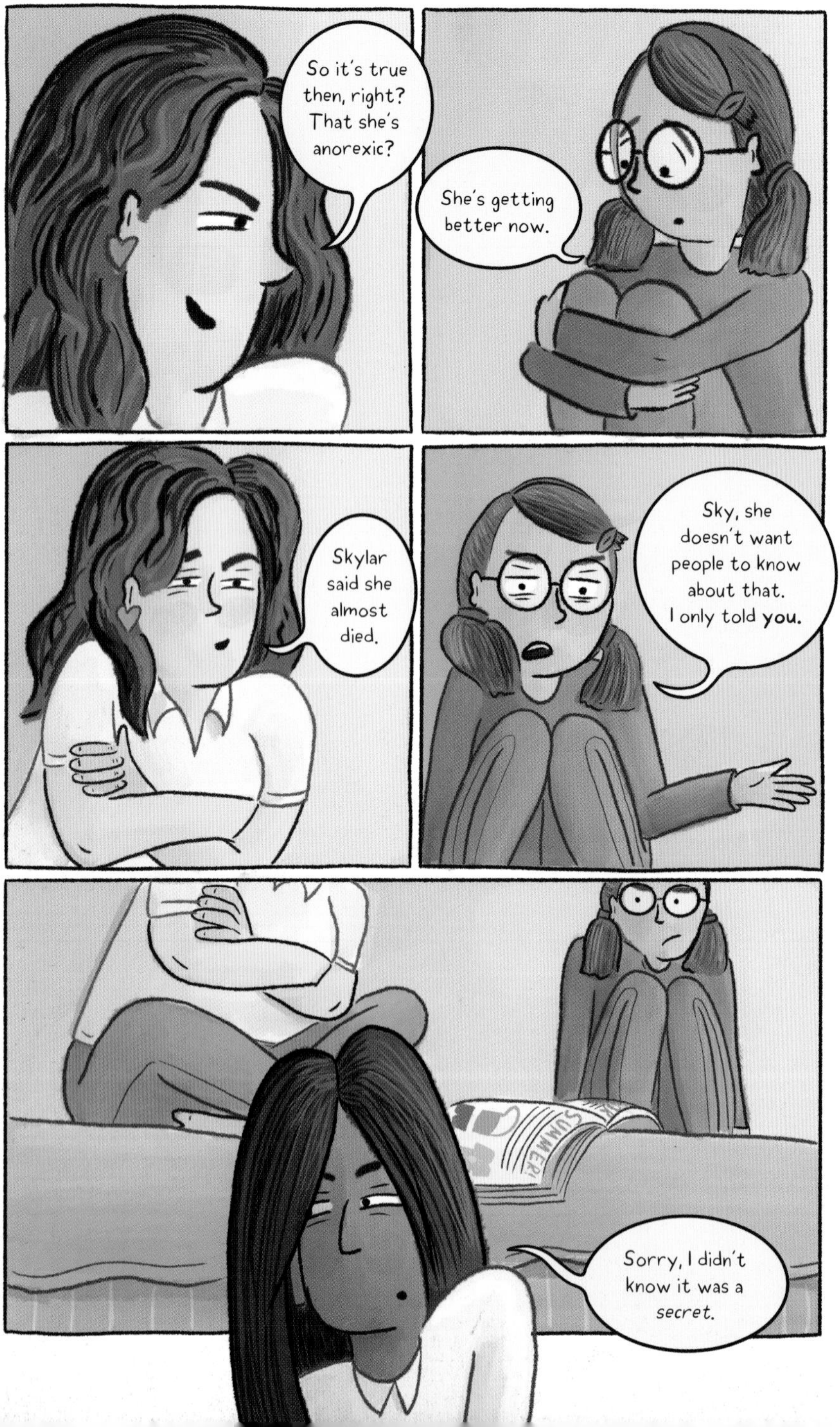
So it's true then, right? That she's anorexic?
She's getting better now.
Skylar said she almost died.
Sky, she doesn't want people to know about that. I only told **you.**
SUMMER!
Sorry, I didn't know it was a *secret.*

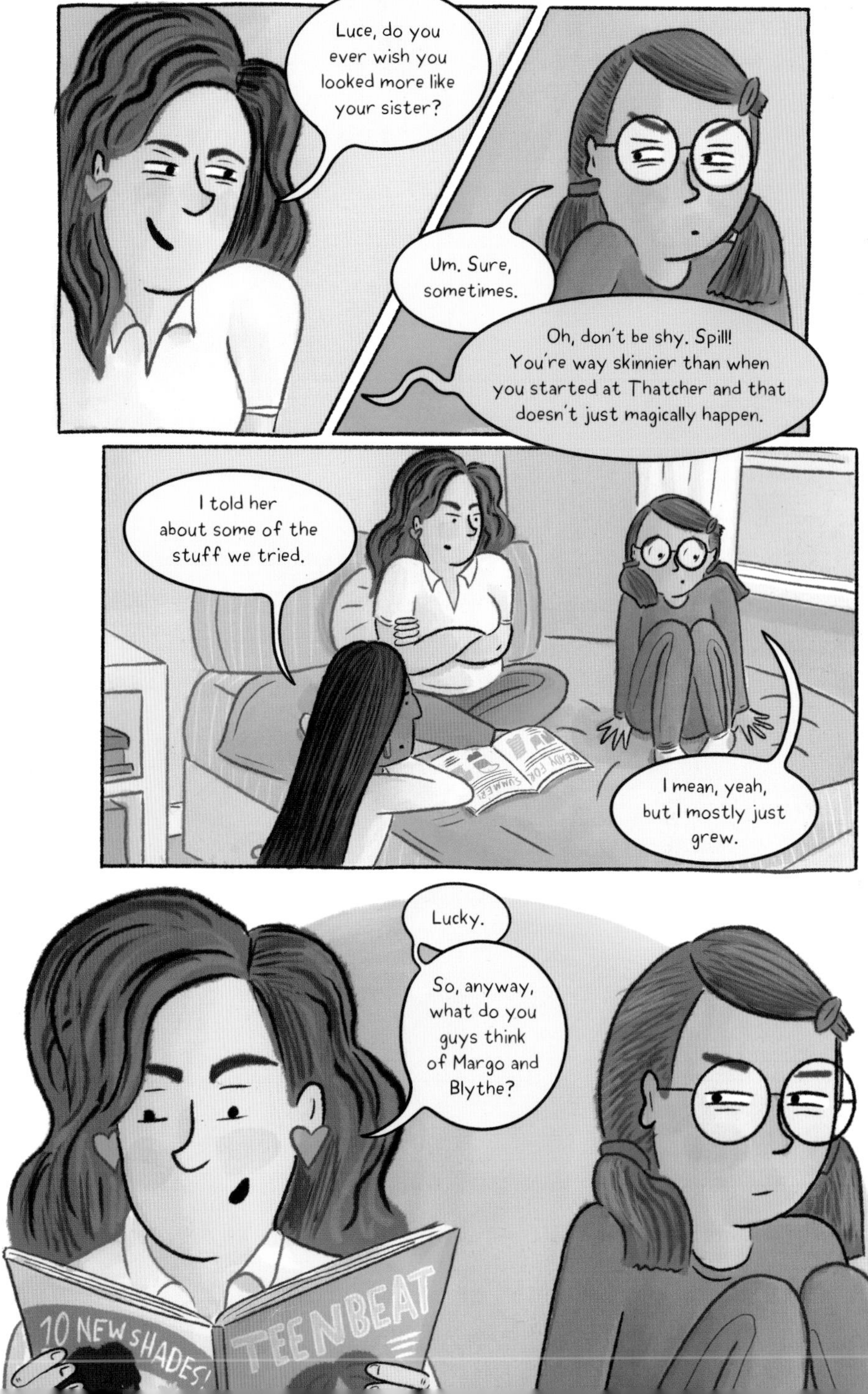
Luce, do you ever wish you looked more like your sister?
Um. Sure, sometimes.
Oh, don't be shy. Spill! You're way skinnier than when you started at Thatcher and that doesn't just magically happen.
I told her about some of the stuff we tried.
READY FOR SUMMER!
I mean, yeah, but I mostly just grew.
Lucky.
So, anyway, what do you guys think of Margo and Blythe?
10 NEW SHADES!
TEENBEAT

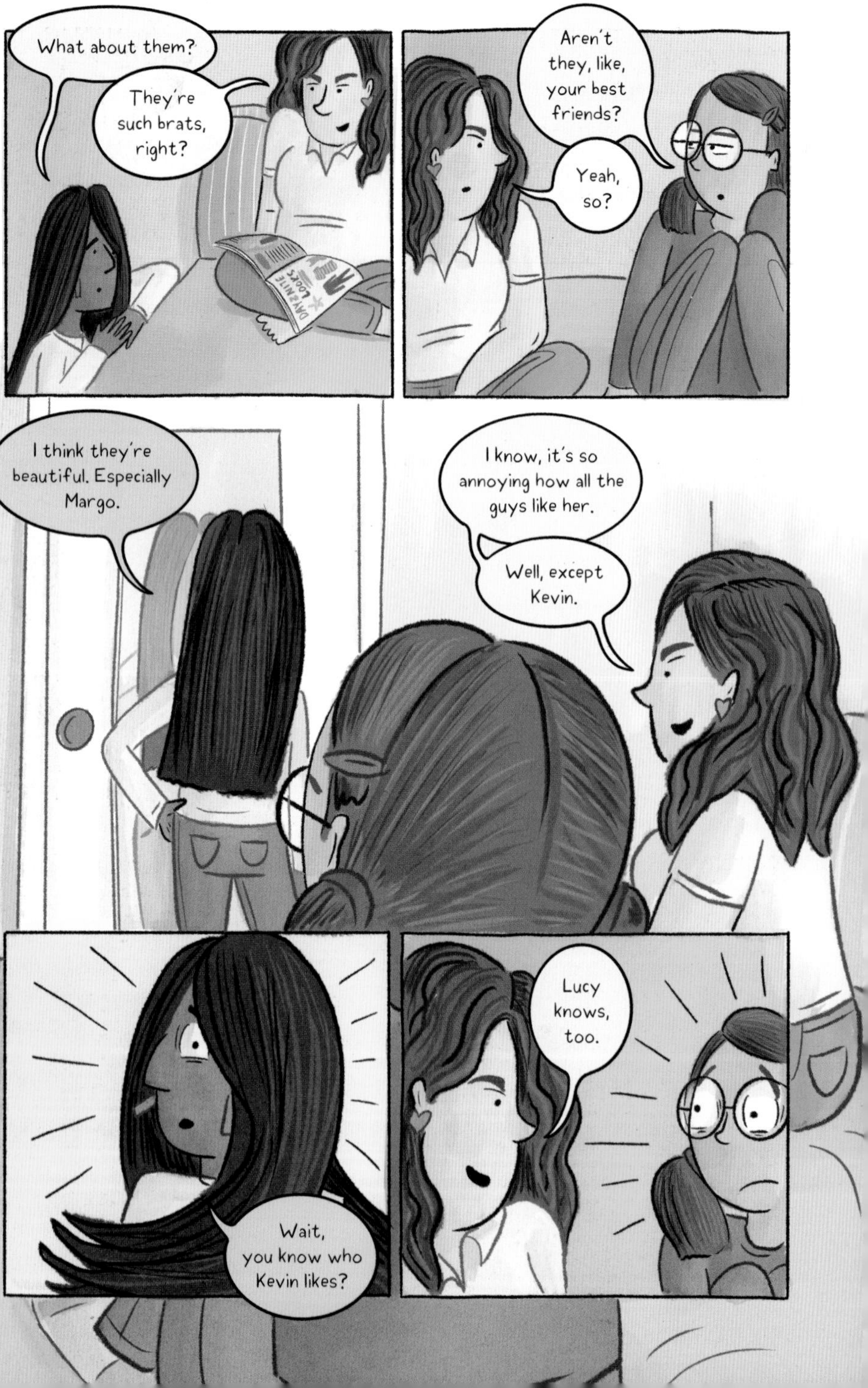
What about them?
They're such brats, right?
Aren't they, like, your best friends?
Yeah, so?
I think they're beautiful. Especially Margo.
I know, it's so annoying how all the guys like her.
Well, except Kevin.
Wait, you know who Kevin likes?
Lucy knows, too.

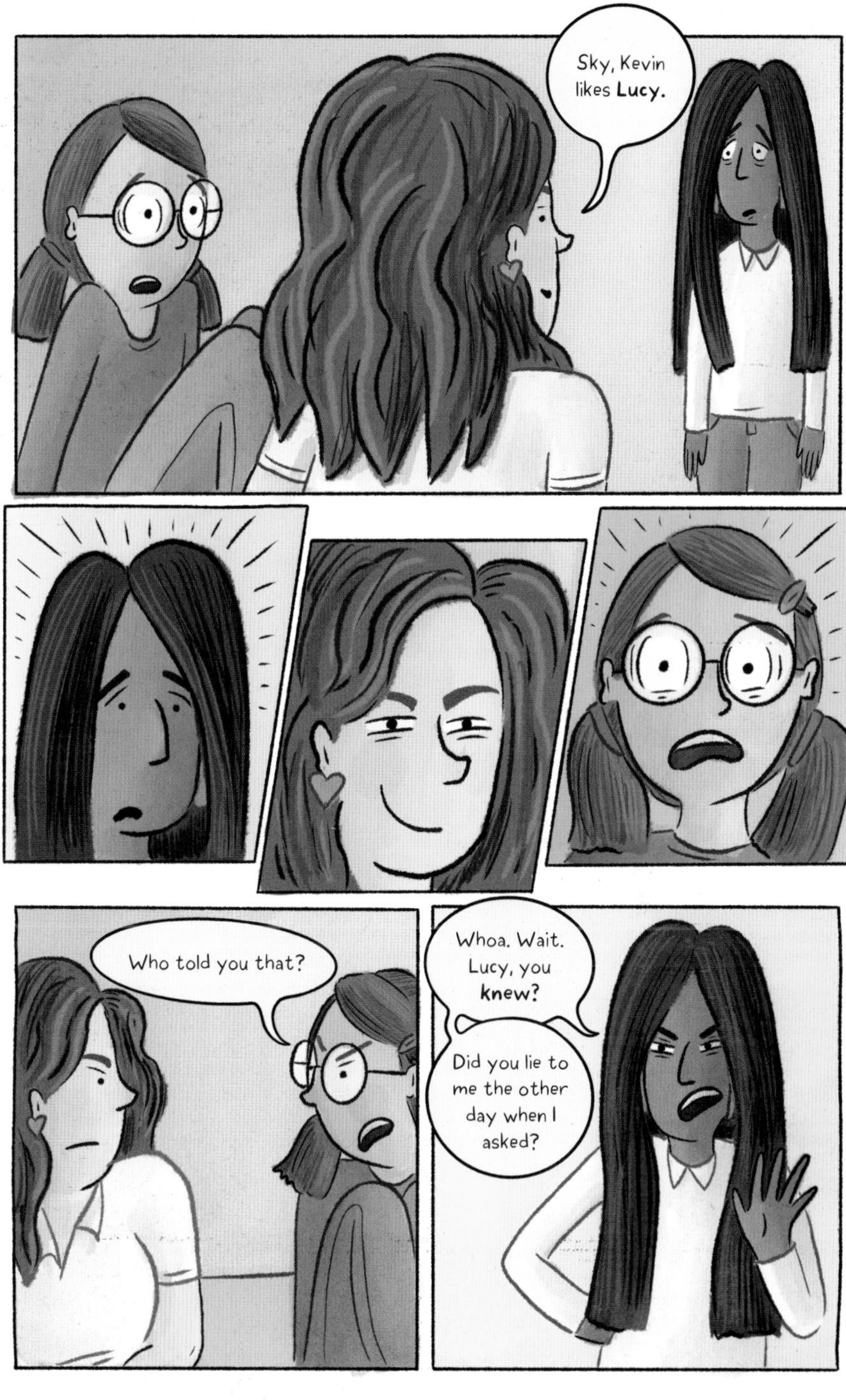
Sky, Kevin likes **Lucy.**
Who told you that?
Whoa. Wait. Lucy, you **knew?**
Did you lie to me the other day when I asked?

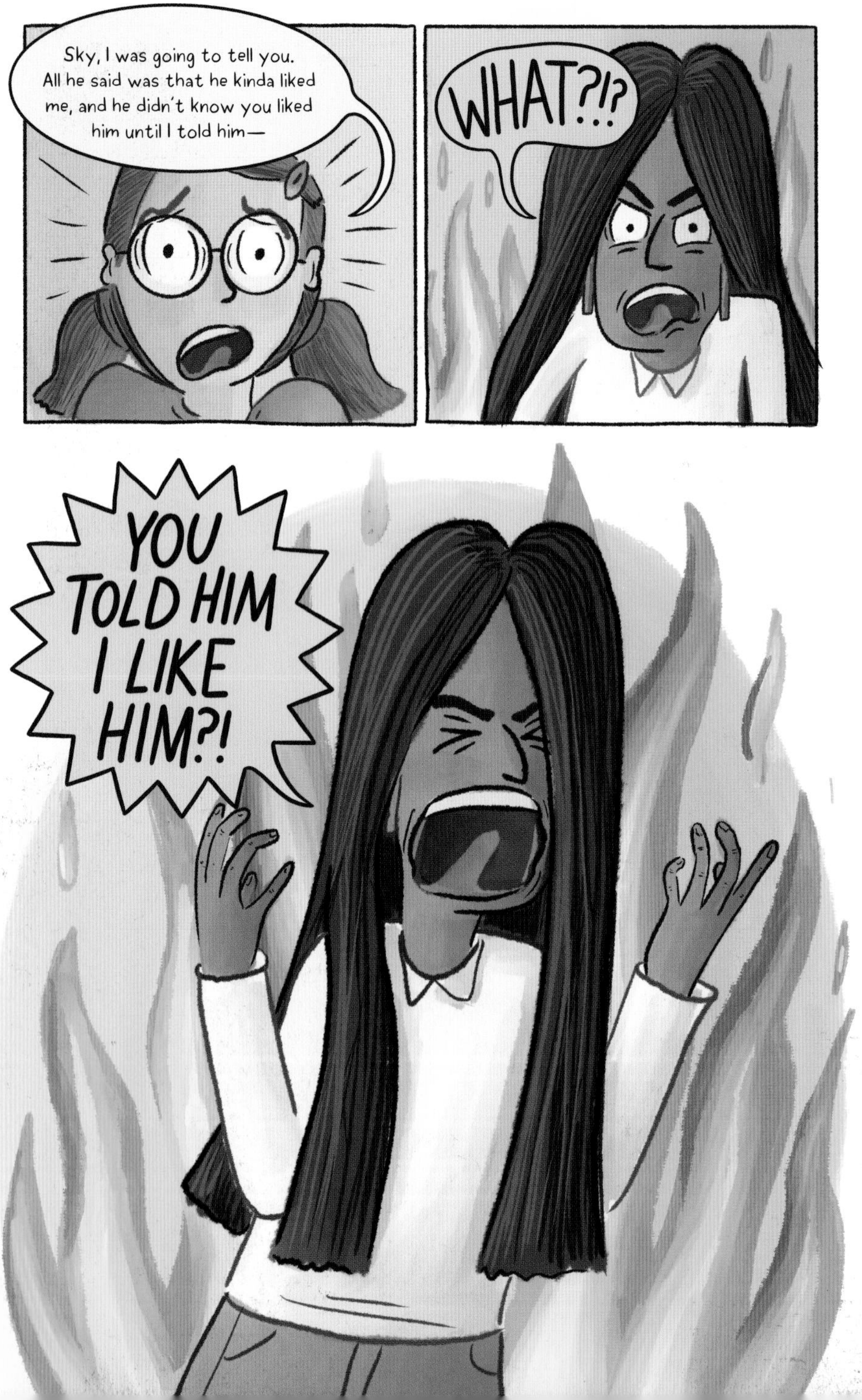
Sky, I was going to tell you. All he said was that he kinda liked me, and he didn't know you liked him until I told him—
WHAT?!?
YOU TOLD HIM I LIKE HIM?!

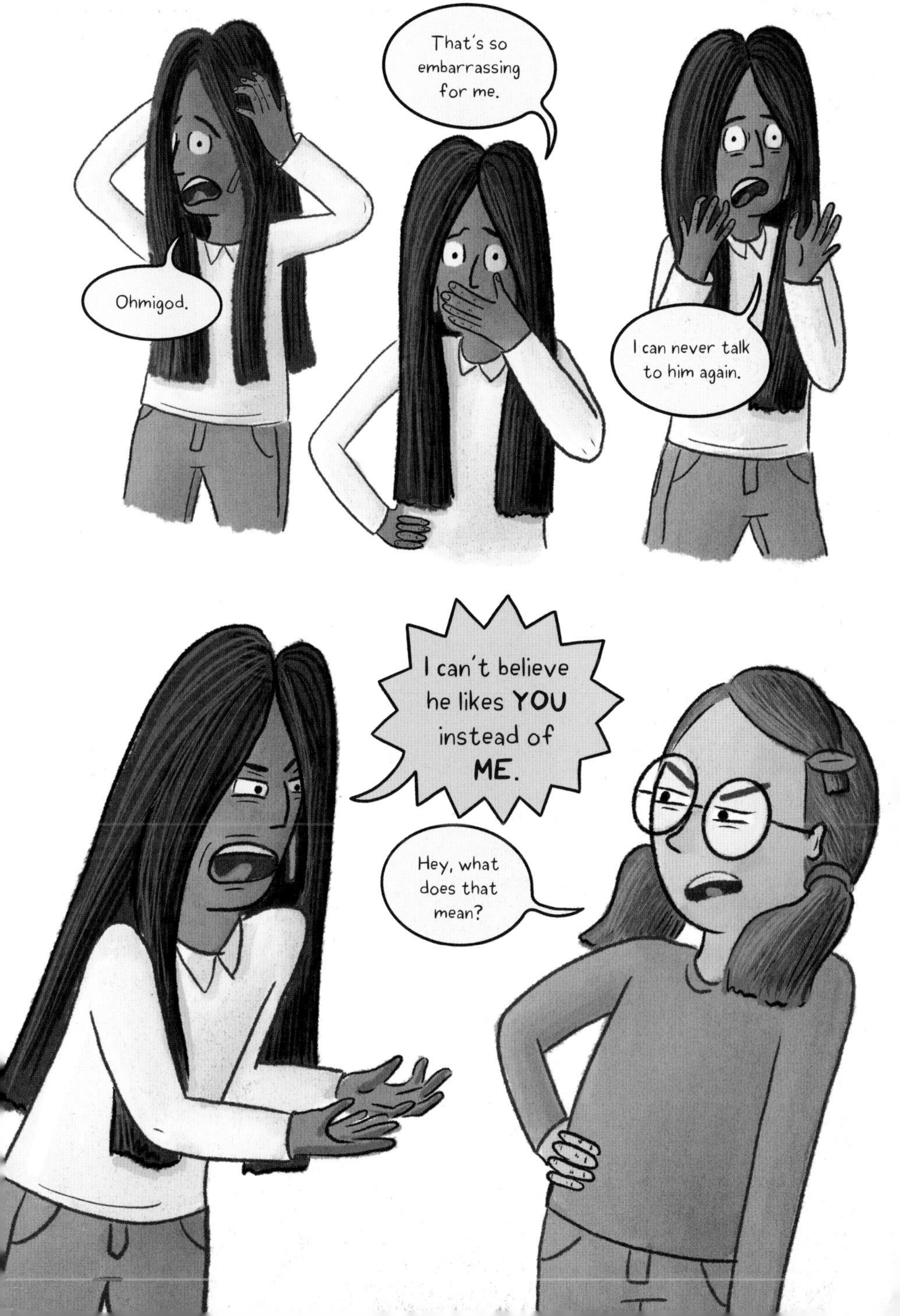
Ohmigod.
That's so embarrassing for me.
I can never talk to him again.
I can't believe he likes **YOU** instead of **ME**.
Hey, what does that mean?

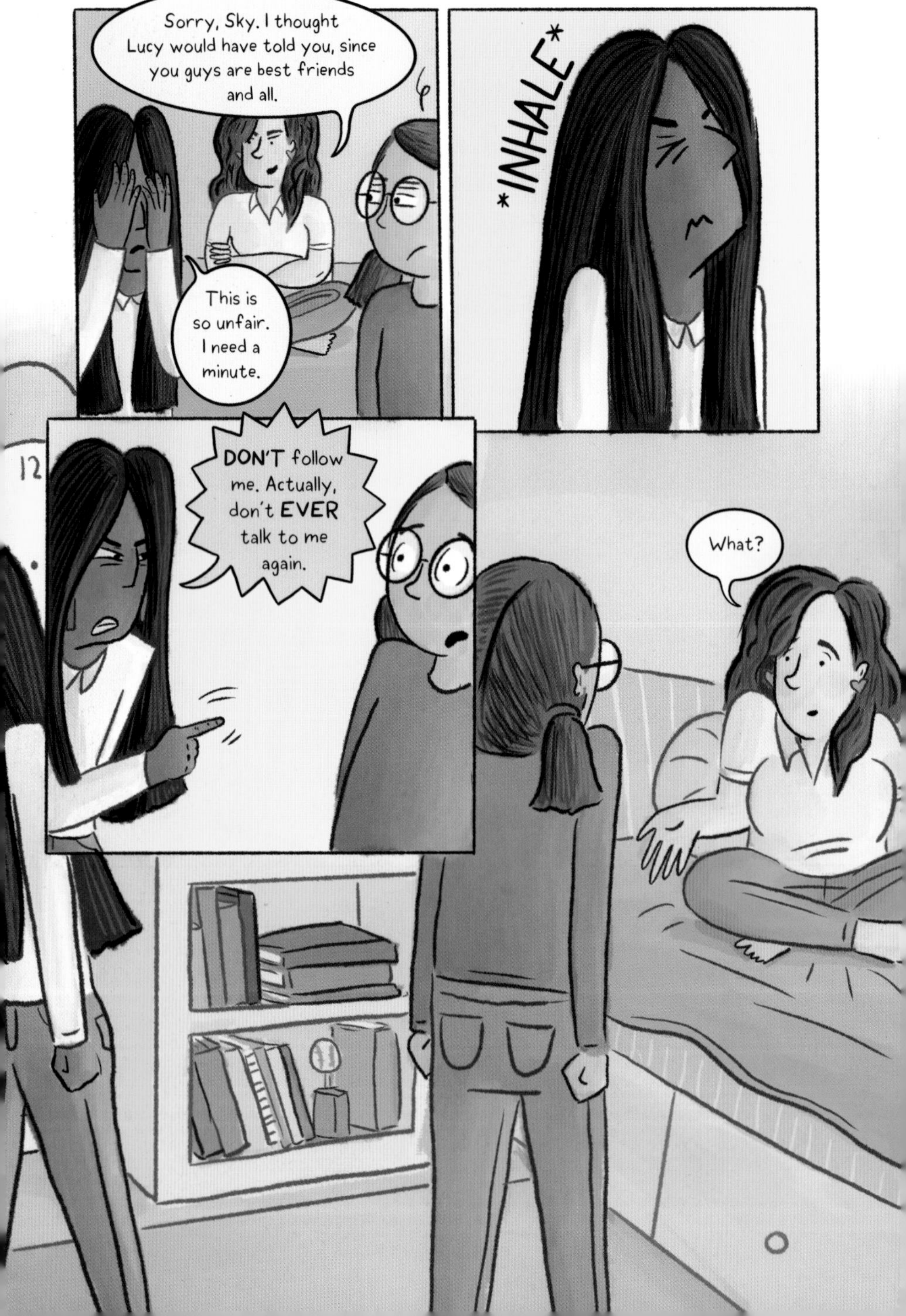
Sorry, Sky. I thought Lucy would have told you, since you guys are best friends and all.
This is so unfair. I need a minute.
INHALE
DON'T follow me. Actually, don't EVER talk to me again.
What?

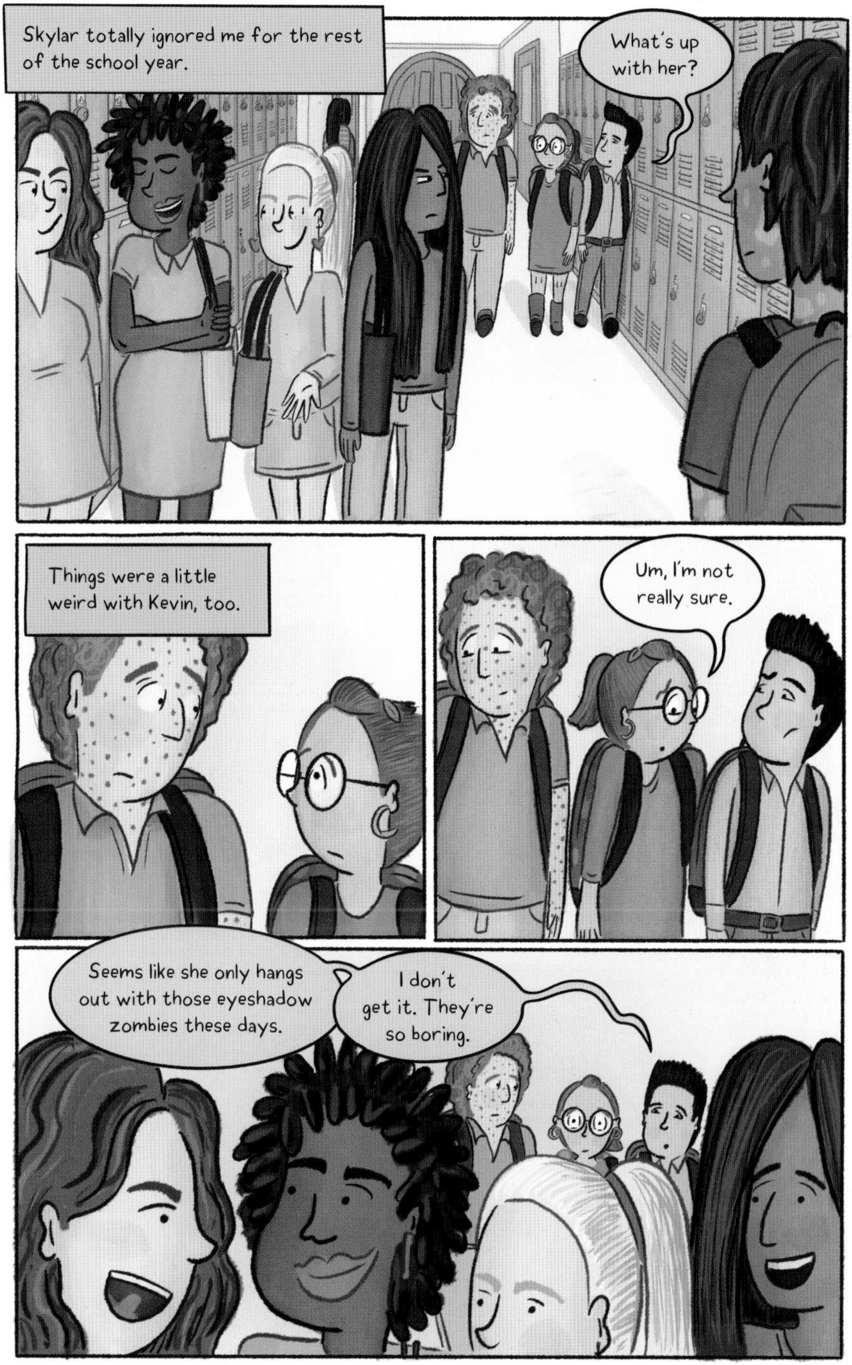
Skylar totally ignored me for the rest of the school year.
What's up with her?
Things were a little weird with Kevin, too.
Um, I'm not really sure.
Seems like she only hangs out with those eyeshadow zombies these days.
I don't get it. They're so boring.

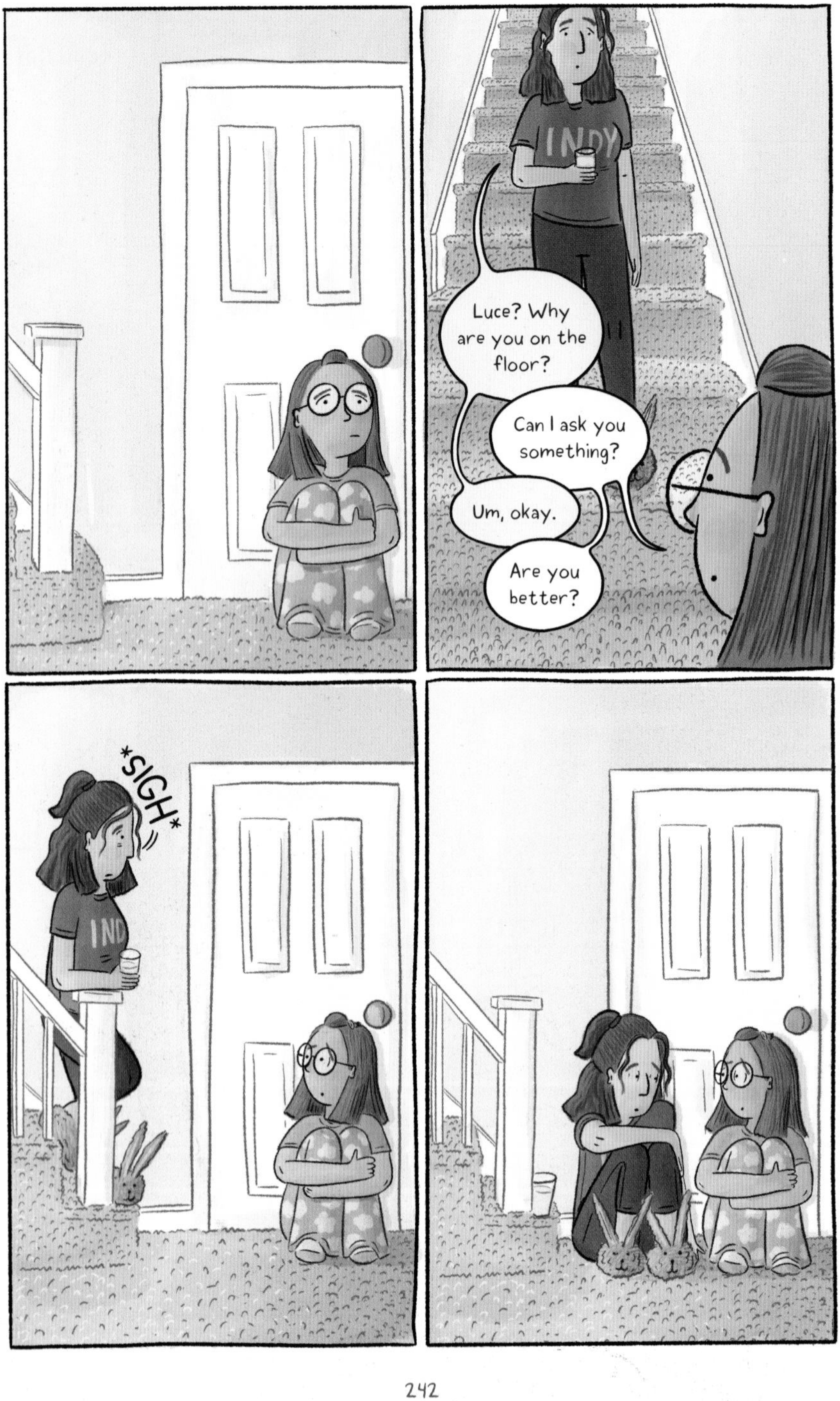
Luce? Why are you on the floor?
Can I ask you something?
Um, okay.
Are you better?
SIGH

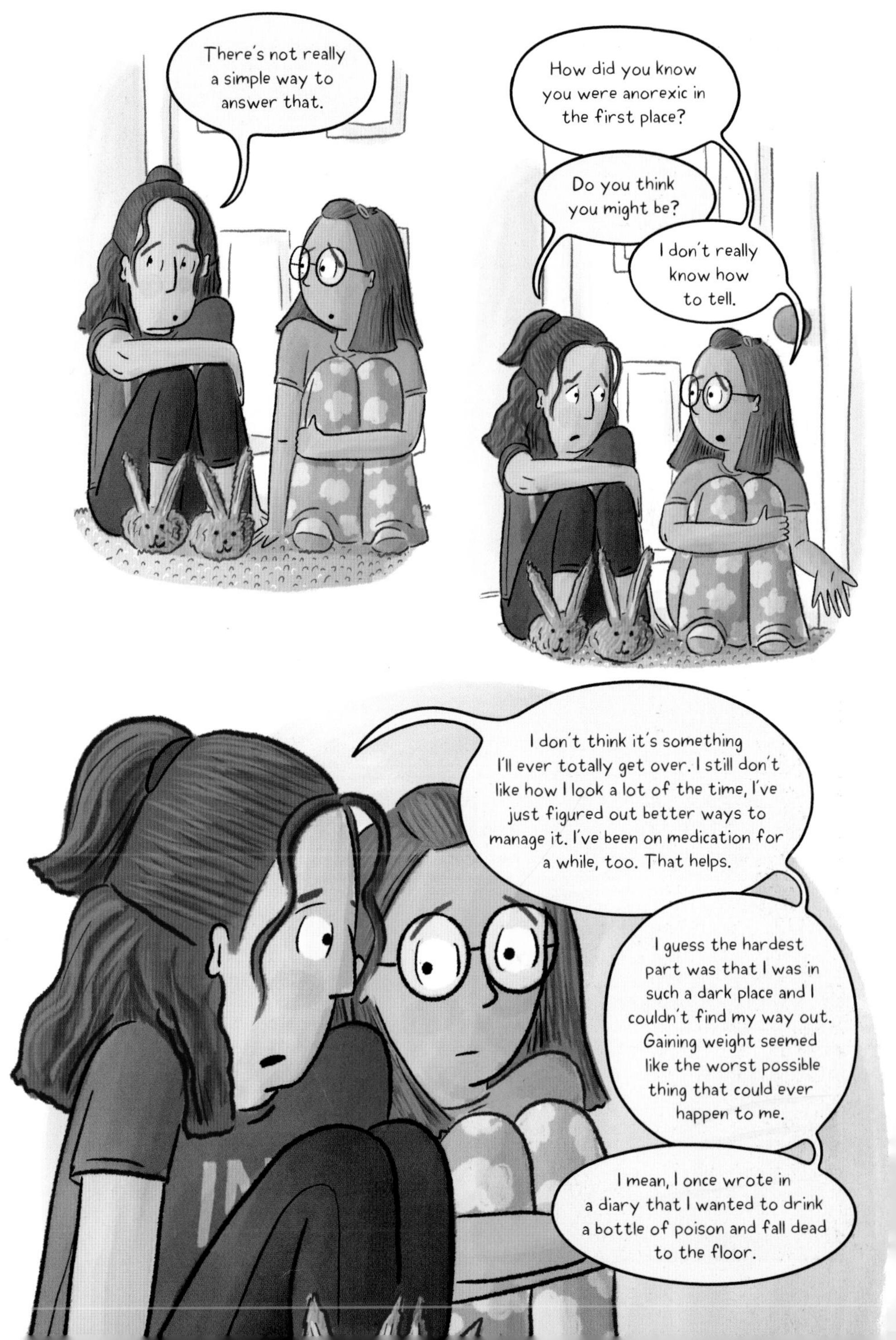
There's not really a simple way to answer that.
How did you know you were anorexic in the first place?
Do you think you might be?
I don't really know how to tell.
I don't think it's something I'll ever totally get over. I still don't like how I look a lot of the time, I've just figured out better ways to manage it. I've been on medication for a while, too. That helps.
I guess the hardest part was that I was in such a dark place and I couldn't find my way out. Gaining weight seemed like the worst possible thing that could ever happen to me.
I mean, I once wrote in a diary that I wanted to drink a bottle of poison and fall dead to the floor.

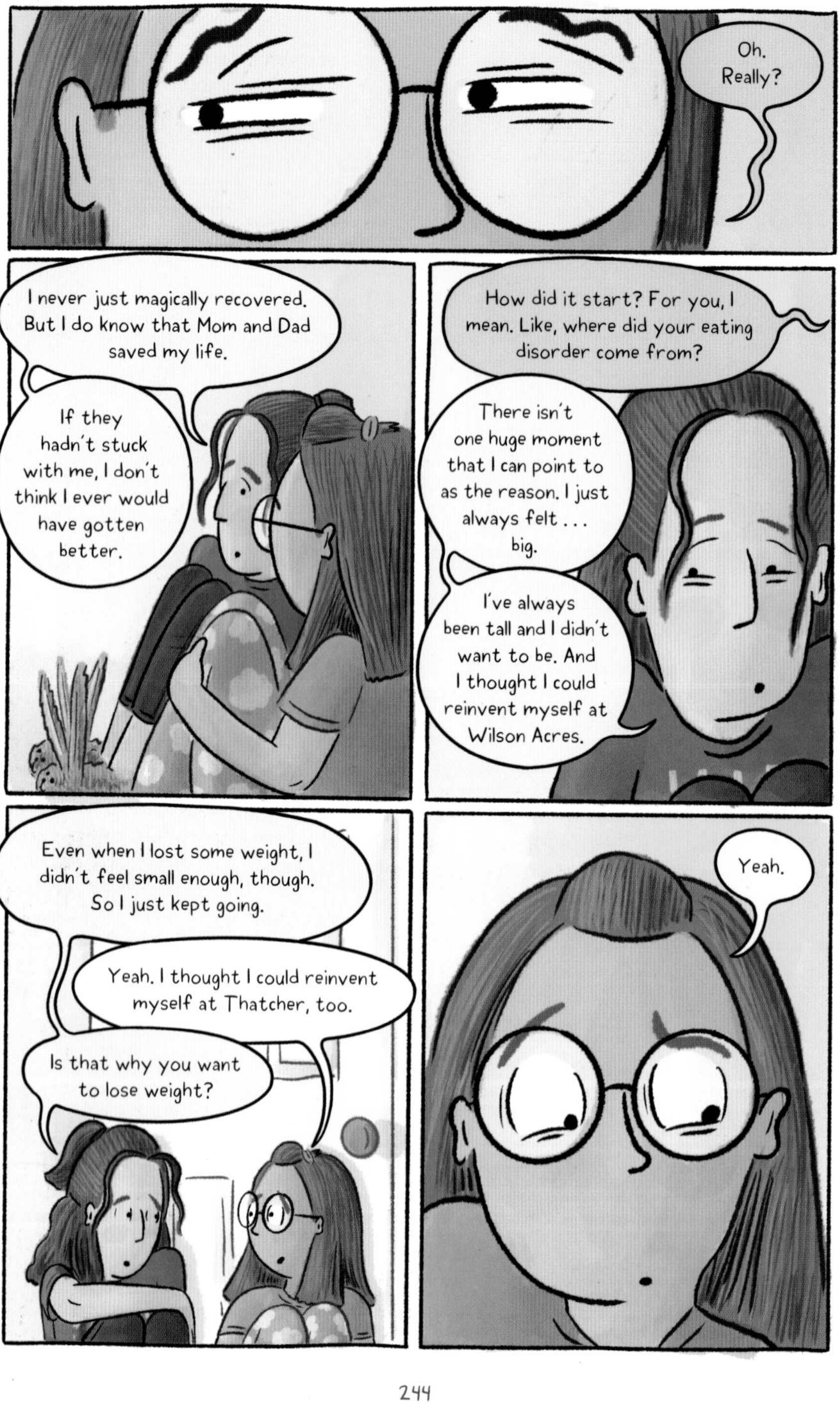
Oh. Really?
I never just magically recovered. But I do know that Mom and Dad saved my life.
If they hadn't stuck with me, I don't think I ever would have gotten better.
How did it start? For you, I mean. Like, where did your eating disorder come from?
There isn't one huge moment that I can point to as the reason. I just always felt . . . big.
I've always been tall and I didn't want to be. And I thought I could reinvent myself at Wilson Acres.
Even when I lost some weight, I didn't feel small enough, though. So I just kept going.
Yeah. I thought I could reinvent myself at Thatcher, too.
Is that why you want to lose weight?
Yeah.

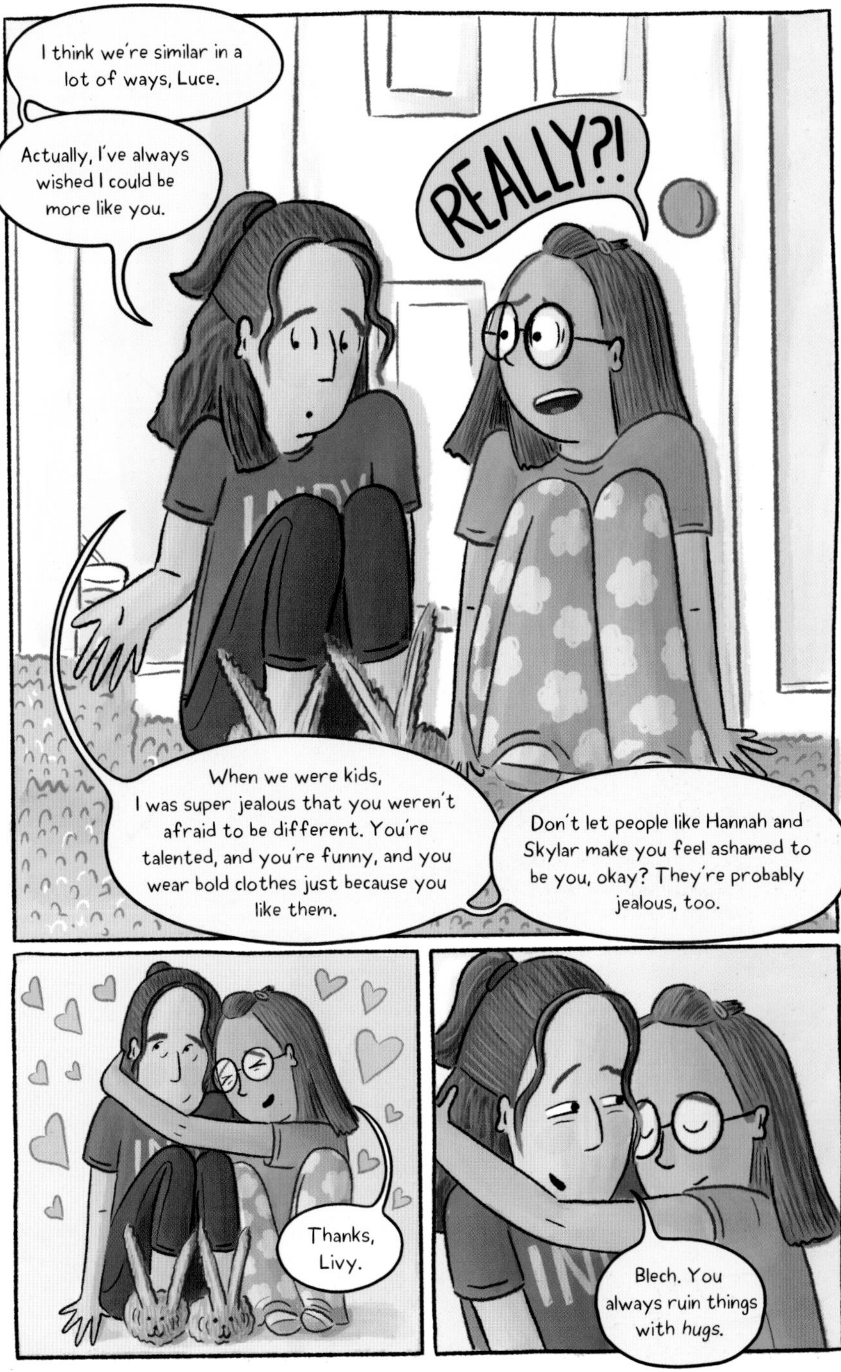
I think we're similar in a lot of ways, Luce.
Actually, I've always wished I could be more like you.
REALLY?!
When we were kids, I was super jealous that you weren't afraid to be different. You're talented, and you're funny, and you wear bold clothes just because you like them.
Don't let people like Hannah and Skylar make you feel ashamed to be you, okay? They're probably jealous, too.
Thanks, Livy.
Blech. You always ruin things with *hugs*.

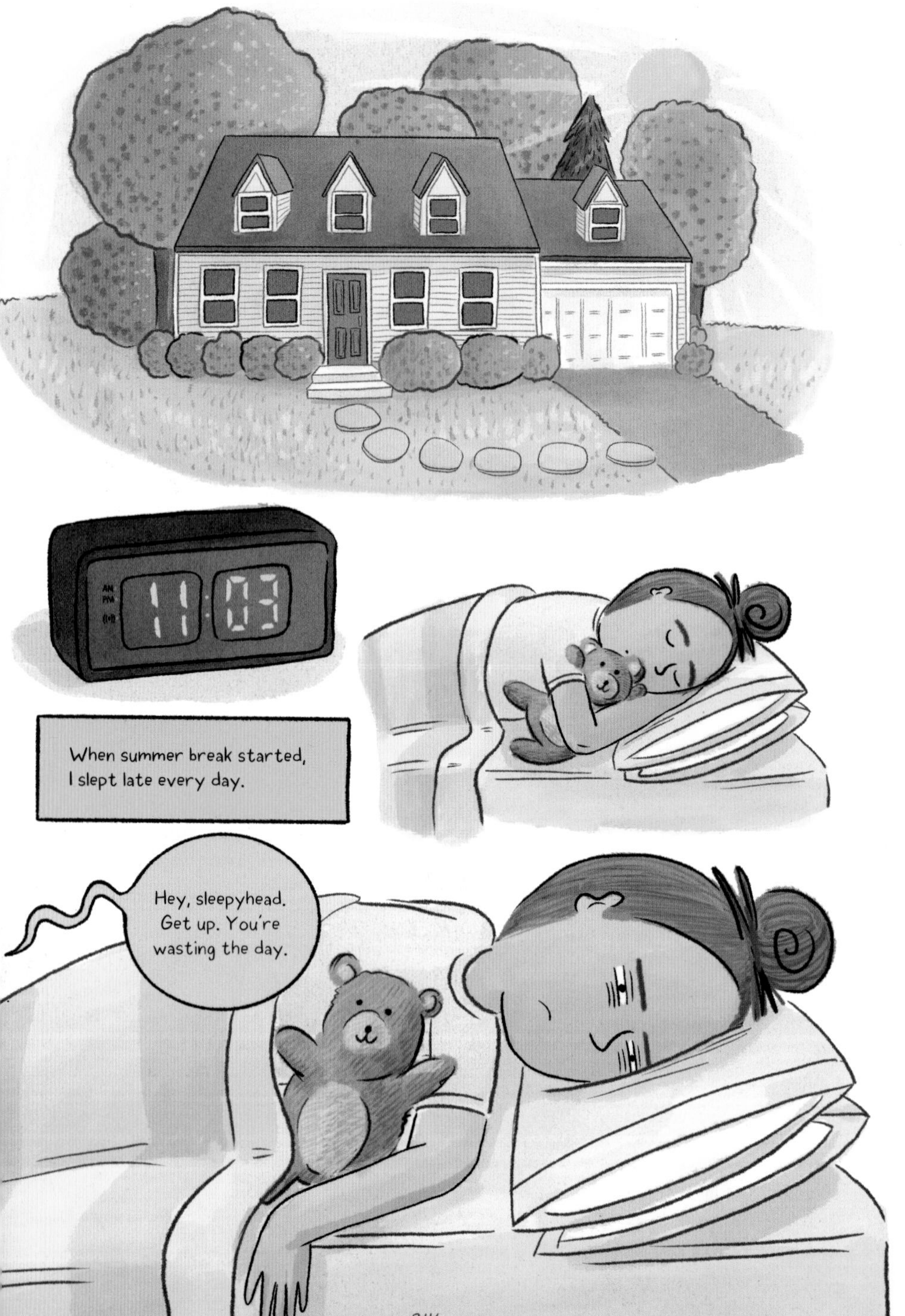

11:03
When summer break started,
I slept late every day.
Hey, sleepyhead. Get up. You're wasting the day.

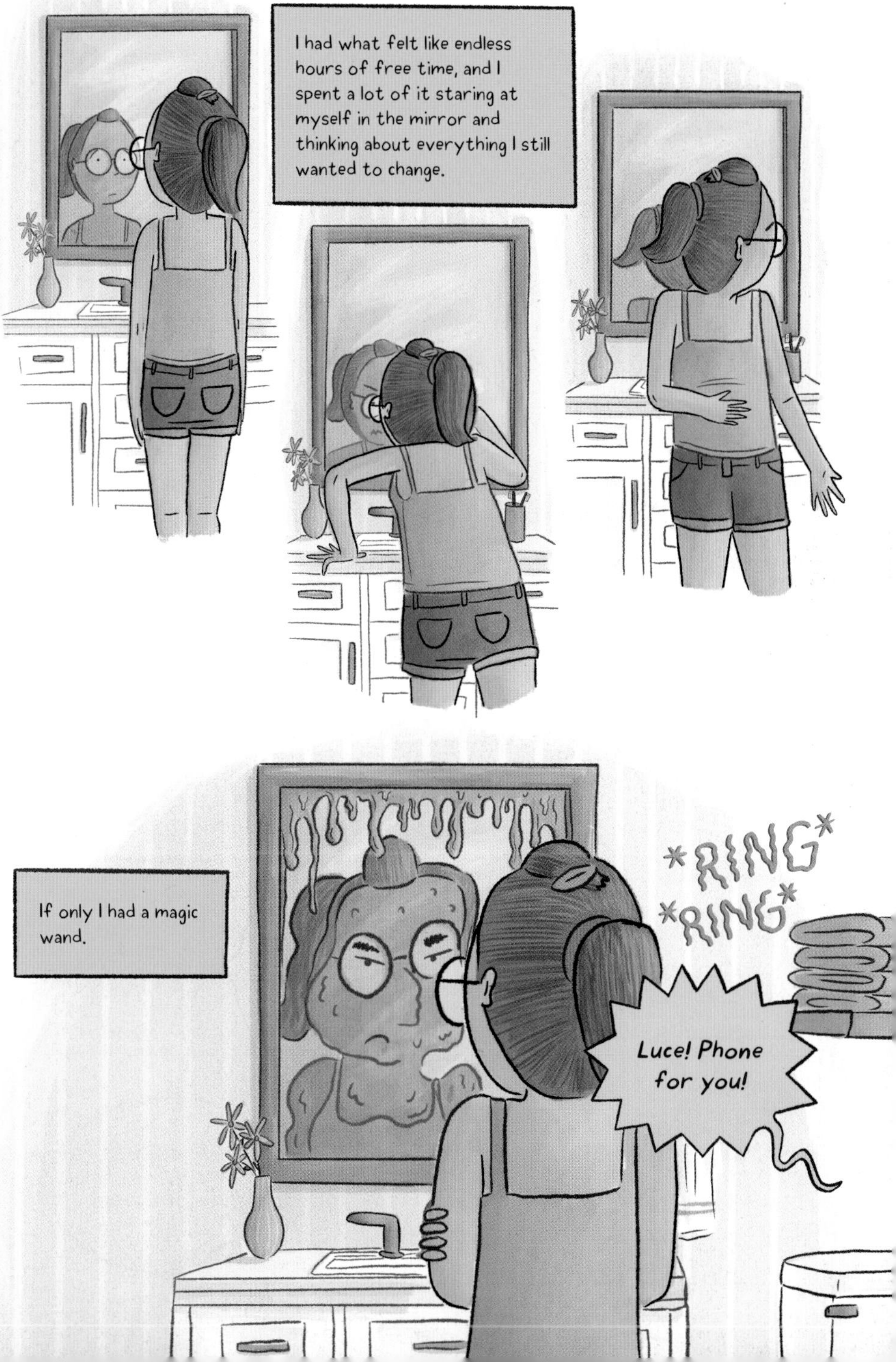
I had what felt like endless hours of free time, and I spent a lot of it staring at myself in the mirror and thinking about everything I still wanted to change.
If only I had a magic wand.
RING
RING
Luce! Phone for you!

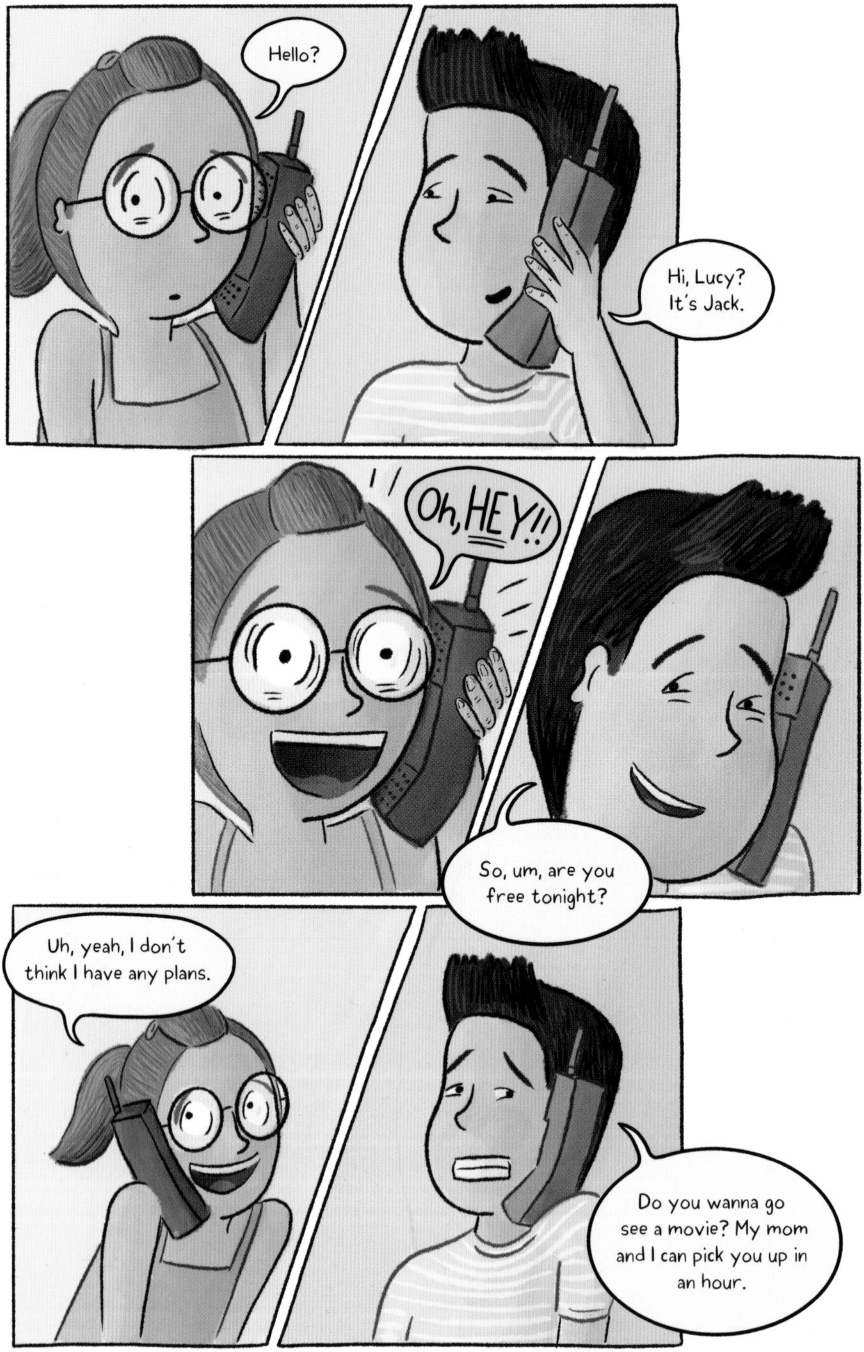
Hello?
Hi, Lucy? It's Jack.
Oh, HEY!!
So, um, are you free tonight?
Uh, yeah, I don't think I have any plans.
Do you wanna go see a movie? My mom and I can pick you up in an hour.

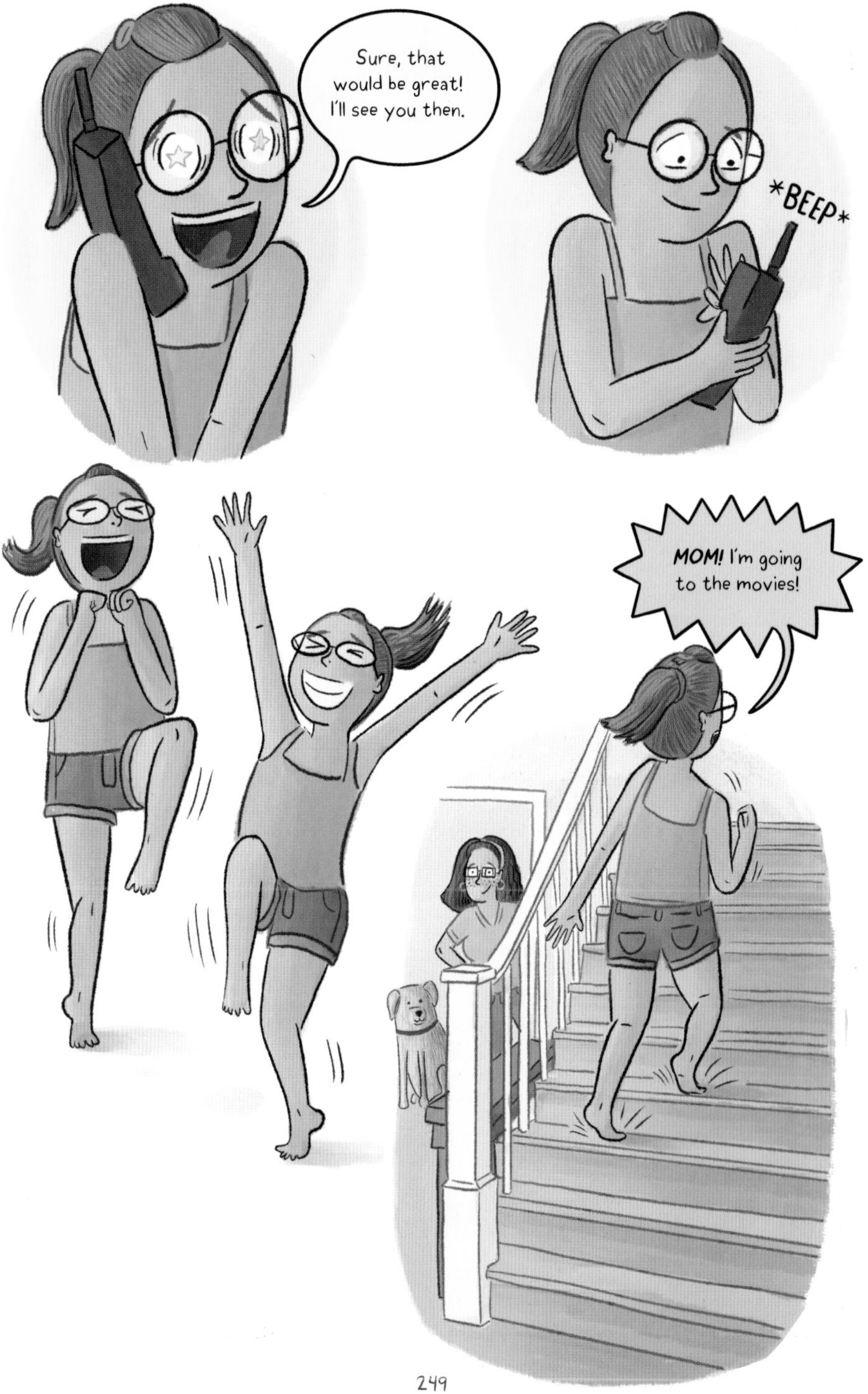
Sure, that would be great! I'll see you then.
BEEP
MOM! I'm going to the movies!

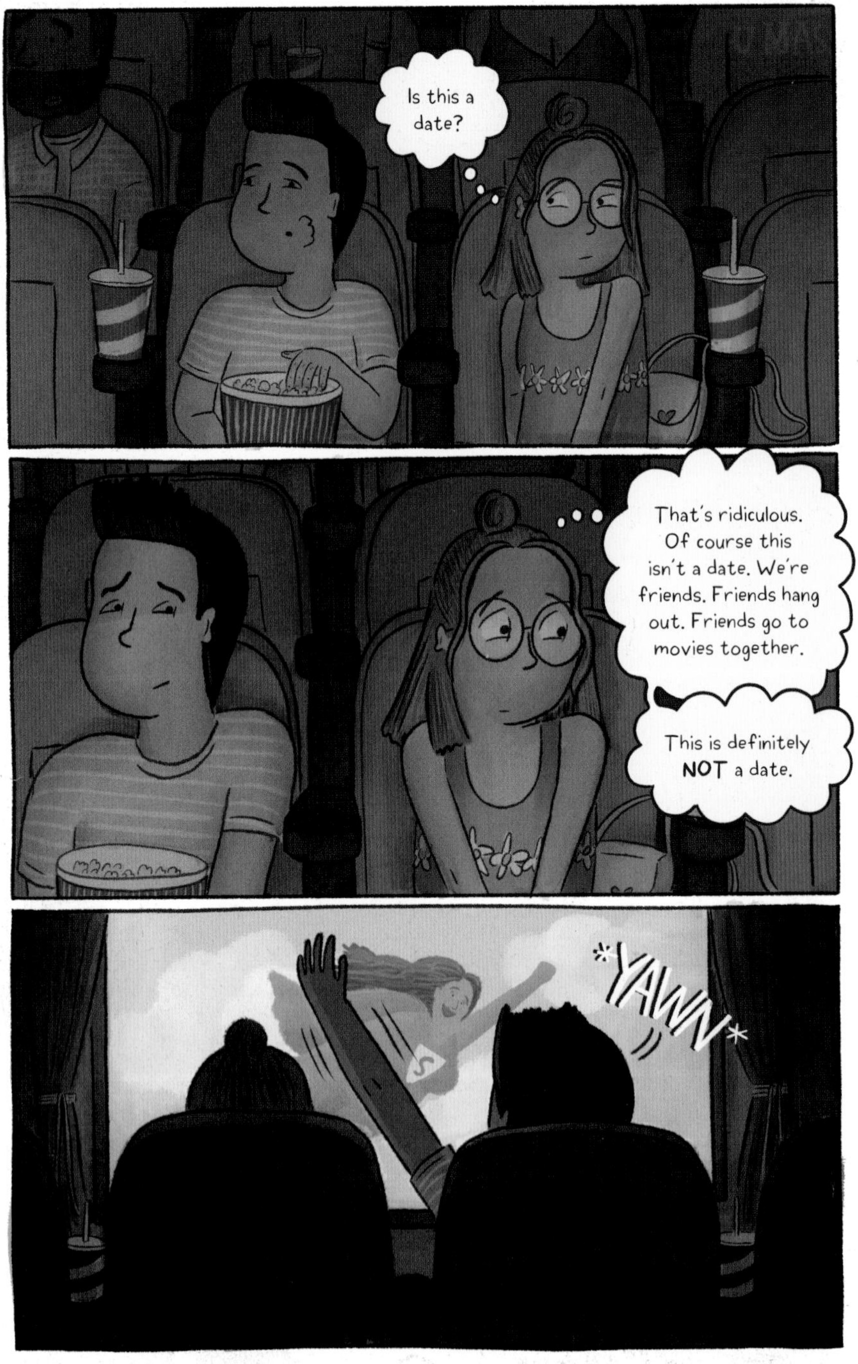
Is this a date?
That's ridiculous. Of course this isn't a date. We're friends. Friends hang out. Friends go to movies together.
This is definitely NOT a date.
YAWN

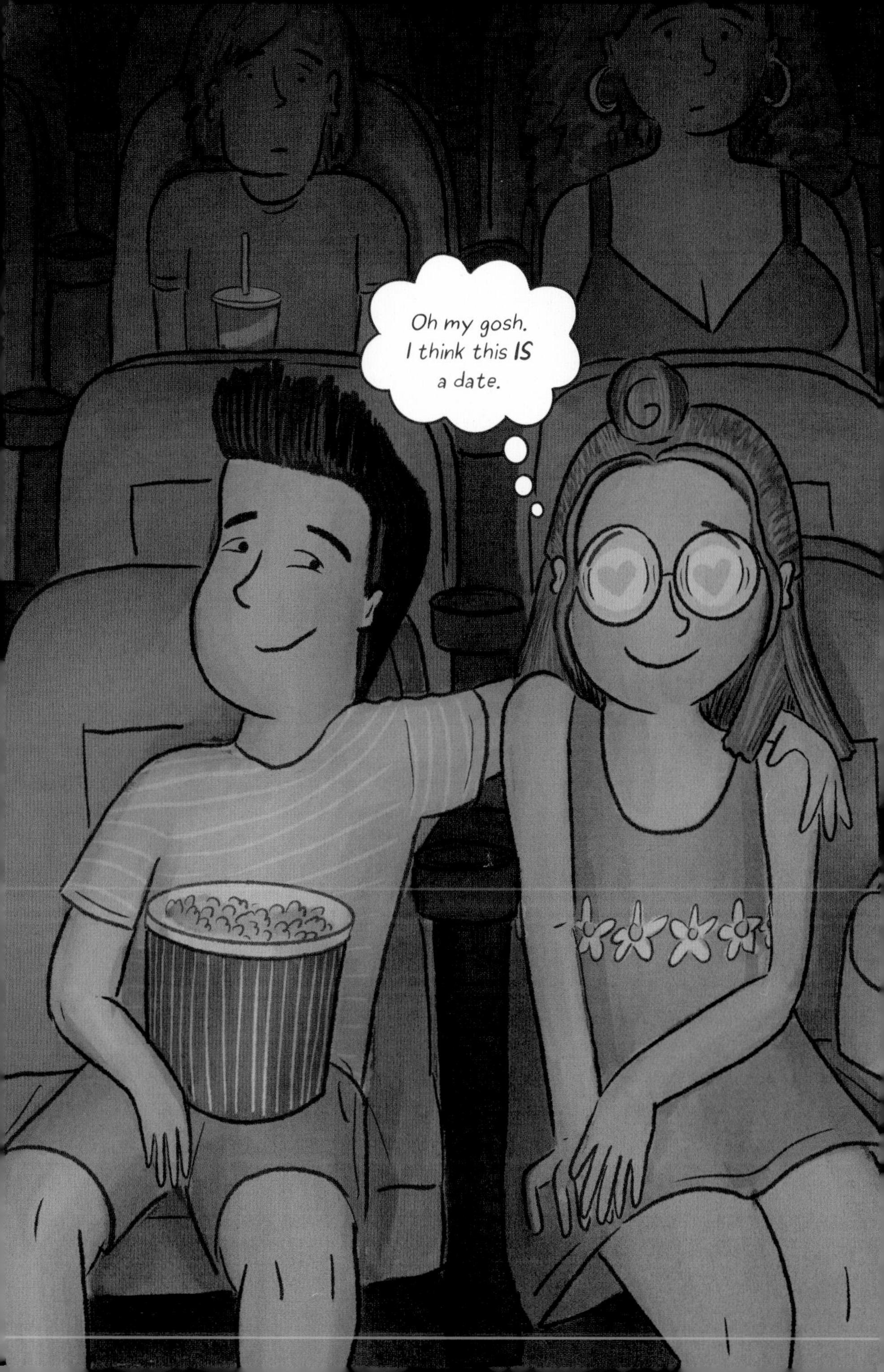
Oh my gosh. I think this **IS** a date.

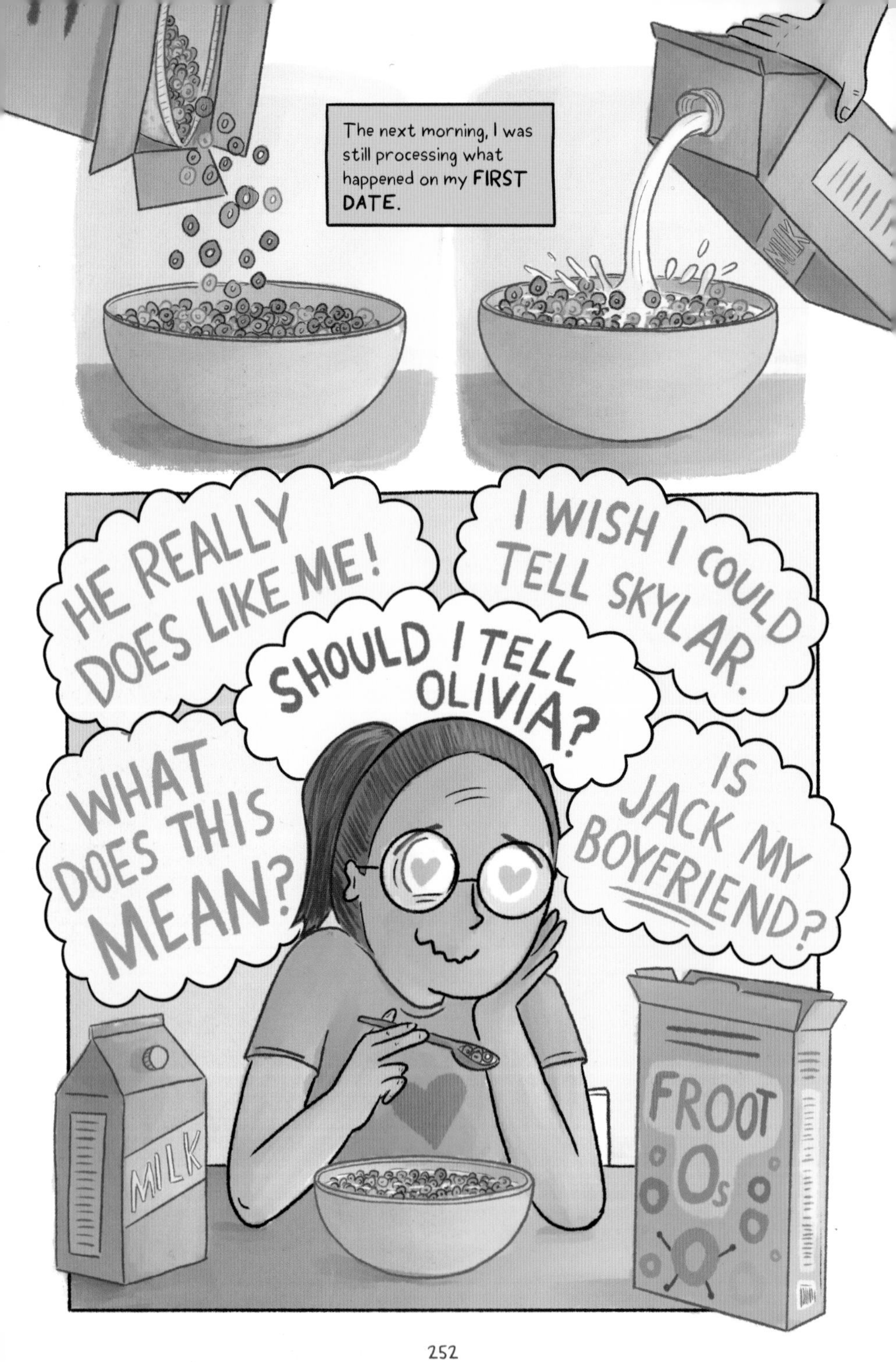
The next morning, I was still processing what happened on my FIRST DATE.
MILK
HE REALLY DOES LIKE ME!
I WISH I COULD TELL SKYLAR.
SHOULD I TELL OLIVIA?
WHAT DOES THIS MEAN?
IS JACK MY BOYFRIEND?
MILK
FROOT Os

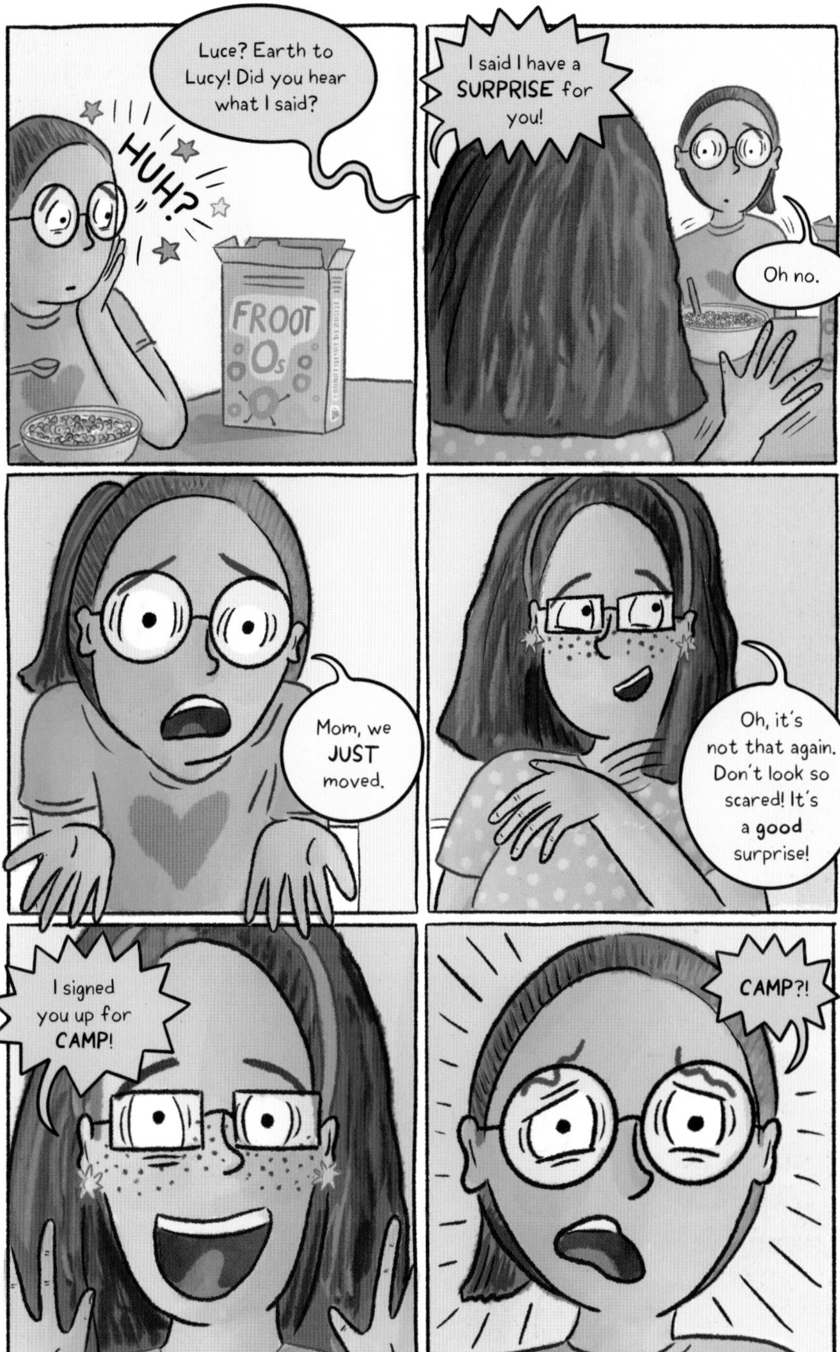
Luce? Earth to Lucy! Did you hear what I said?
HUH?
FROOT Os
I said I have a SURPRISE for you!
Oh no.
Mom, we JUST moved.
Oh, it's not that again. Don't look so scared! It's a good surprise!
I signed you up for CAMP!
CAMP?!

CHAPTER 7

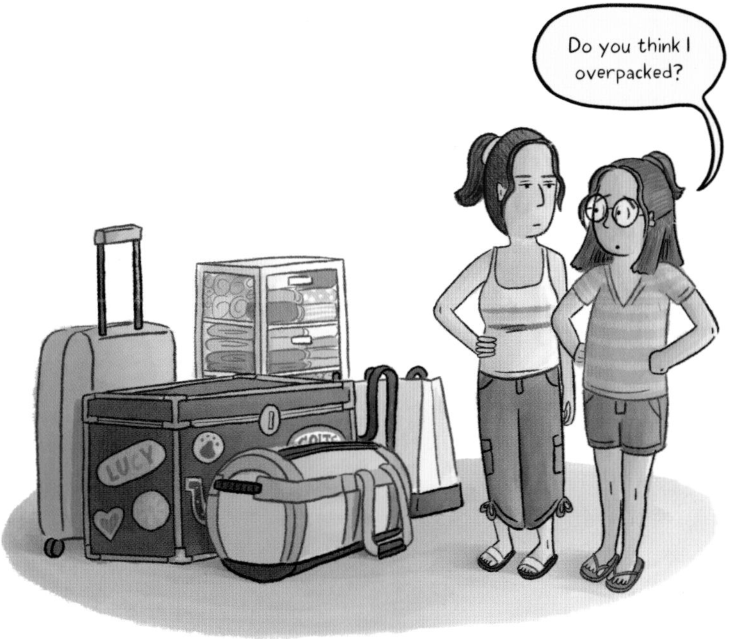
Do you think I overpacked?
LUCY

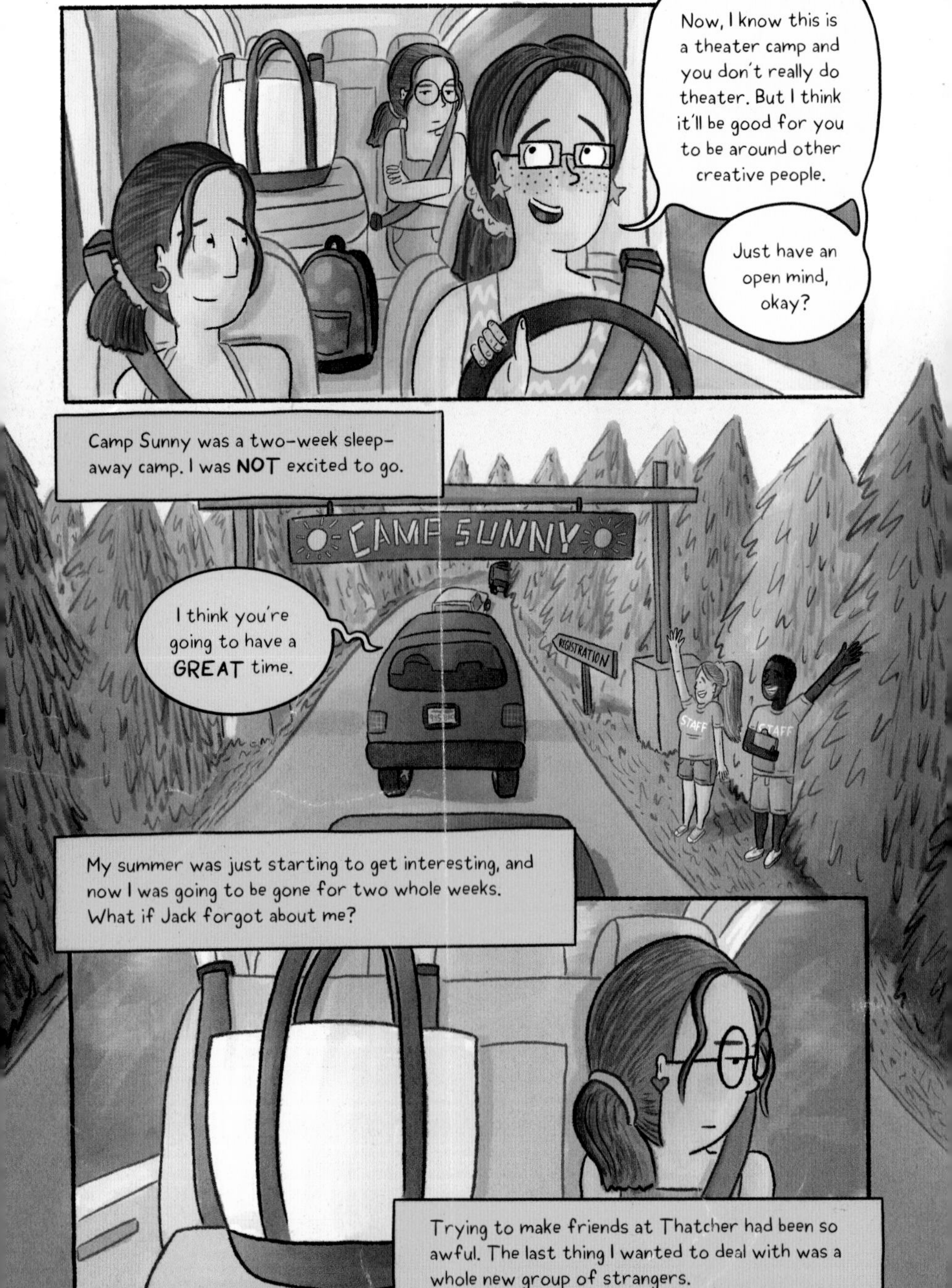

Now, I know this is a theater camp and you don't really do theater. But I think it'll be good for you to be around other creative people.
Just have an open mind, okay?
Camp Sunny was a two-week sleep-away camp. I was **NOT** excited to go.
CAMP SUNNY
REGISTRATION
I think you're going to have a **GREAT** time.
STAFF
STAFF
My summer was just starting to get interesting, and now I was going to be gone for two whole weeks. What if Jack forgot about me?
Trying to make friends at Thatcher had been so awful. The last thing I wanted to deal with was a whole new group of strangers.

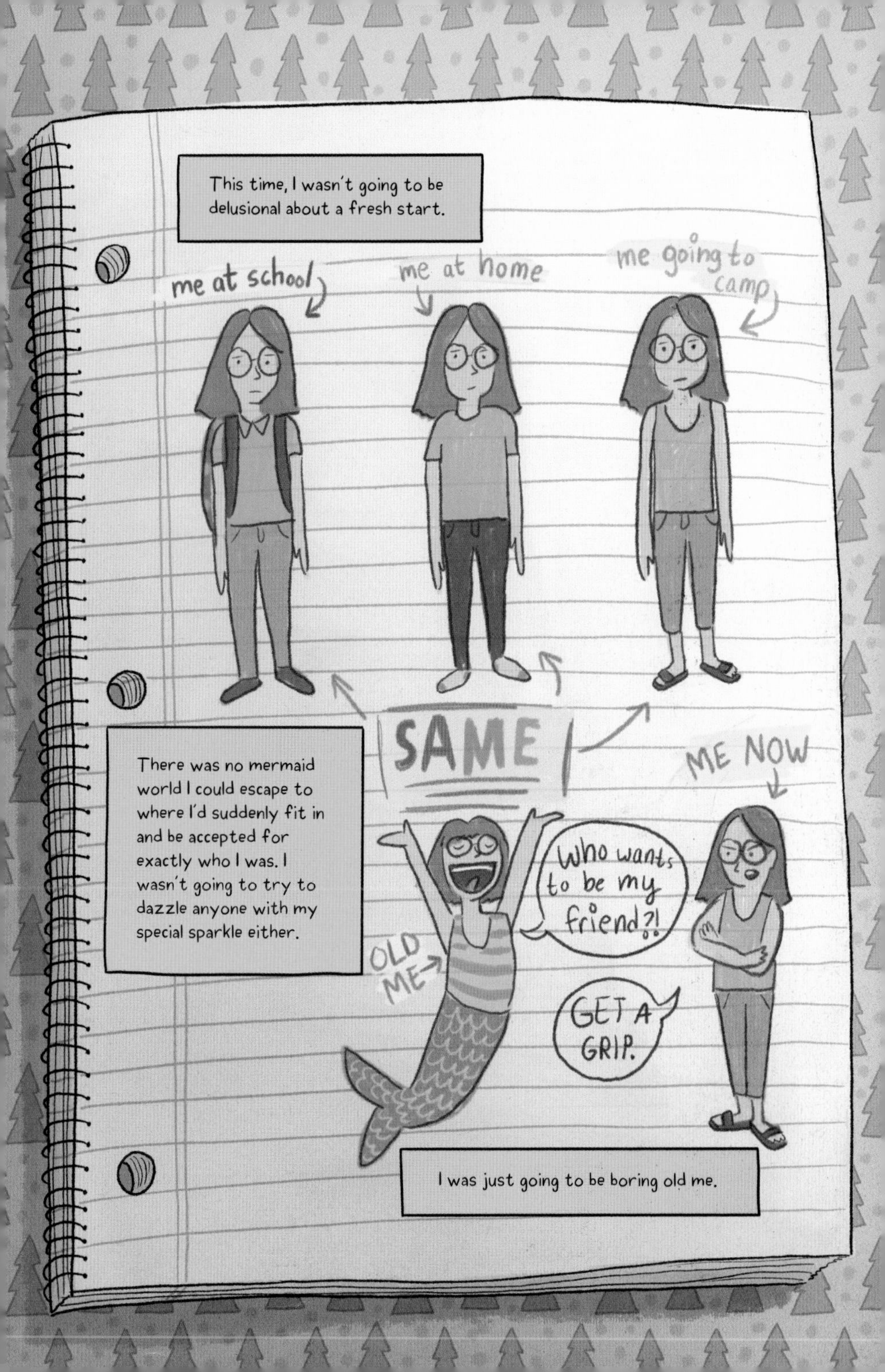
This time, I wasn't going to be delusional about a fresh start.
me at school
me at home
me going to camp
SAME
ME NOW
There was no mermaid world I could escape to where I'd suddenly fit in and be accepted for exactly who I was. I wasn't going to try to dazzle anyone with my special sparkle either.
OLD ME
Who wants to be my friend?!
GET A GRIP.
I was just going to be boring old me.

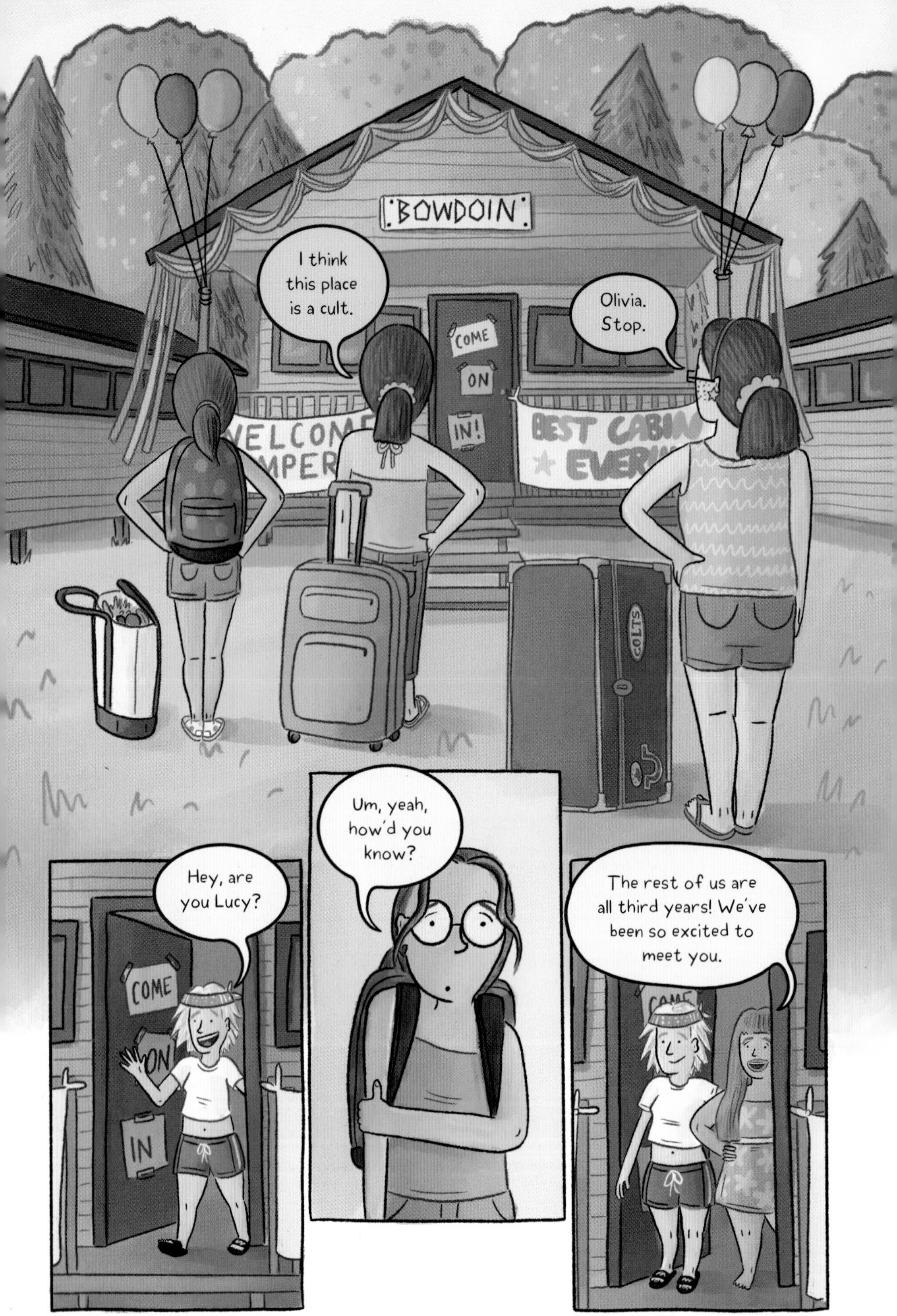
BOWDOIN
WELCOME CAMPERS
COME ON IN!
BEST CABIN EVER
COLTS
I think this place is a cult.
Olivia. Stop.
Hey, are you Lucy?
COME ON IN
Um, yeah, how'd you know?
The rest of us are all third years! We've been so excited to meet you.

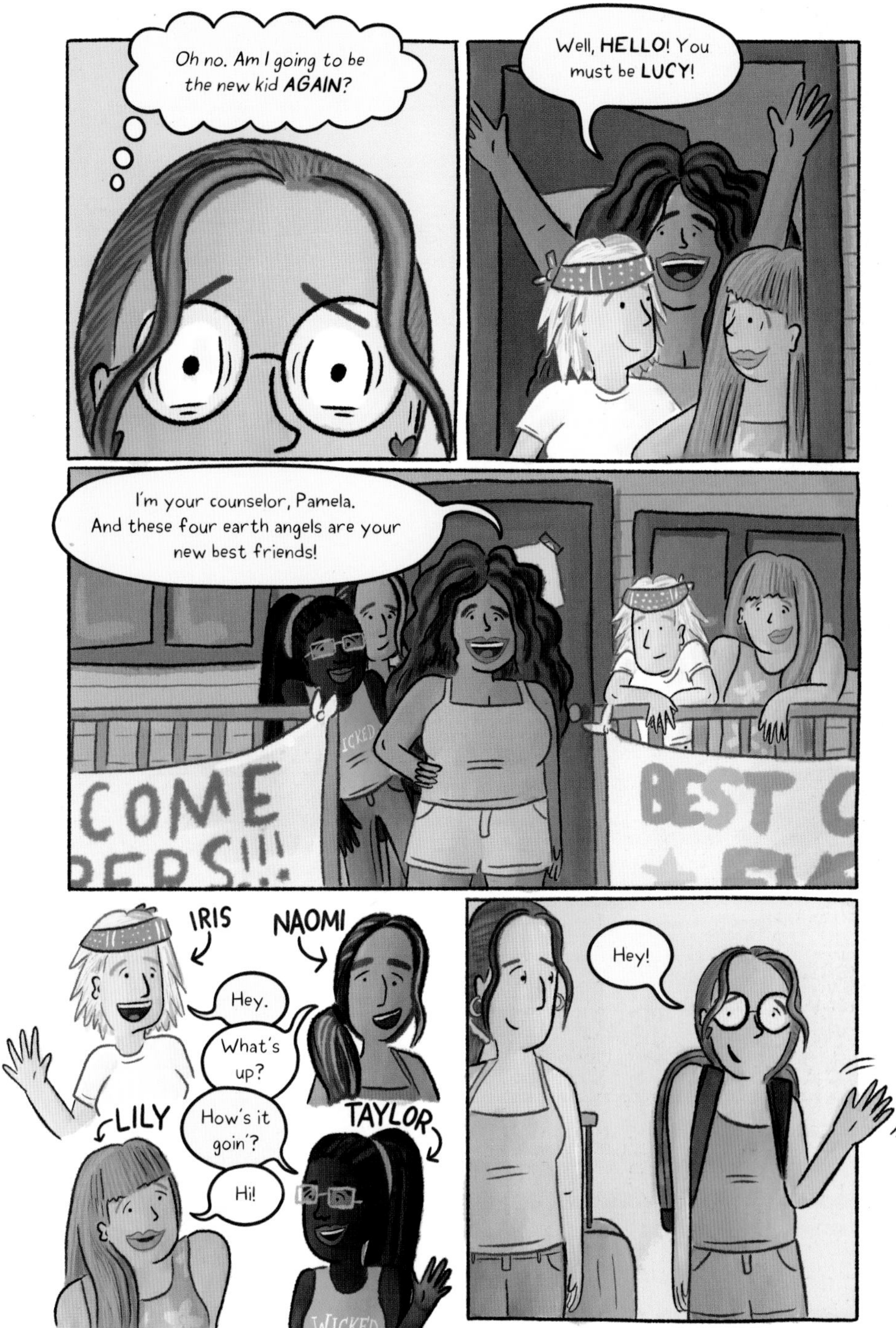

Oh no. Am I going to be the new kid AGAIN?
Well, HELLO! You must be LUCY!
I'm your counselor, Pamela. And these four earth angels are your new best friends!
COME
ERS!!!
BEST O
ICKED
IRIS
NAOMI
Hey.
What's up?
LILY
How's it goin'?
TAYLOR
Hi!
WICKED
Hey!

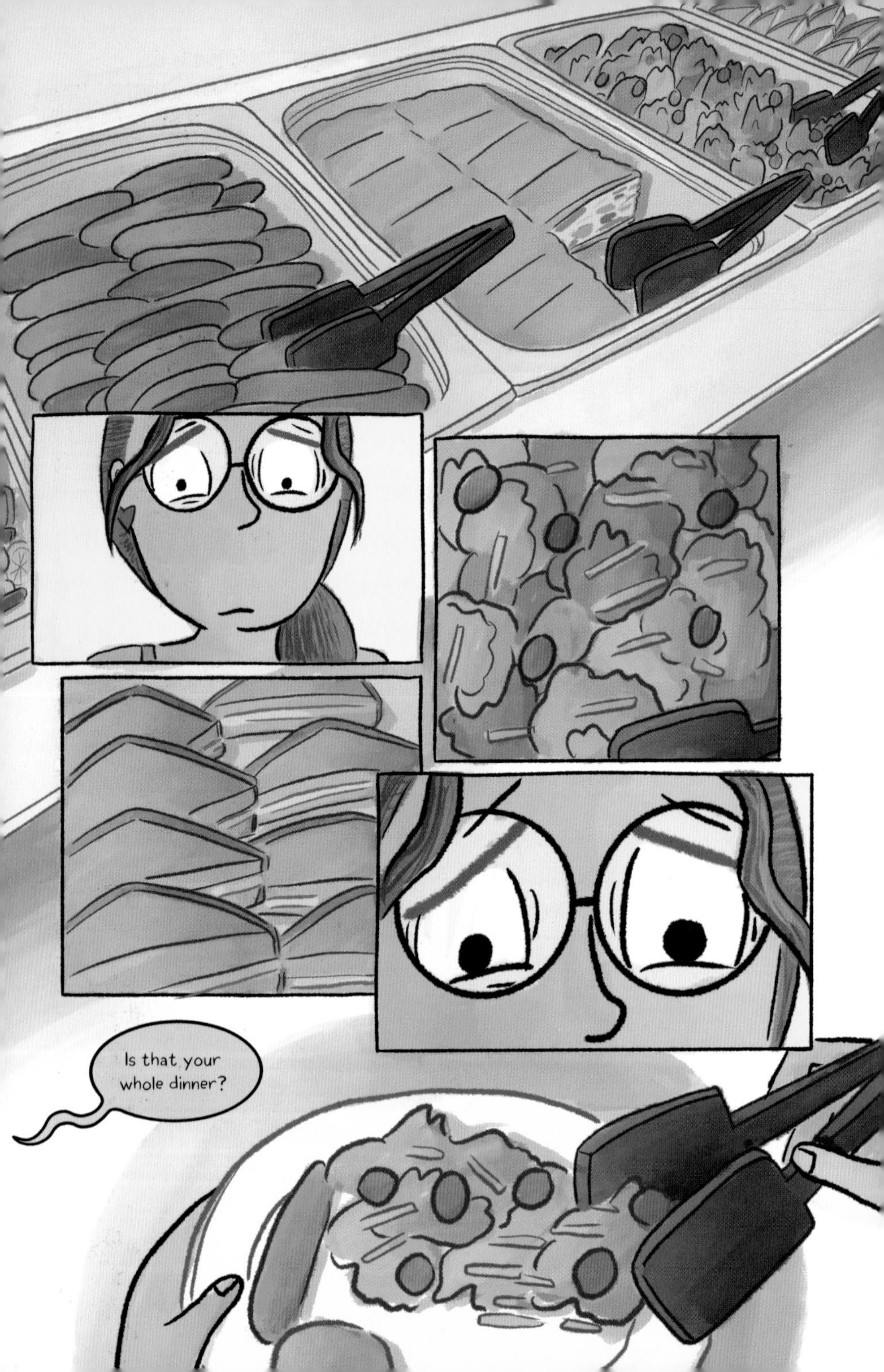
Is that your whole dinner?

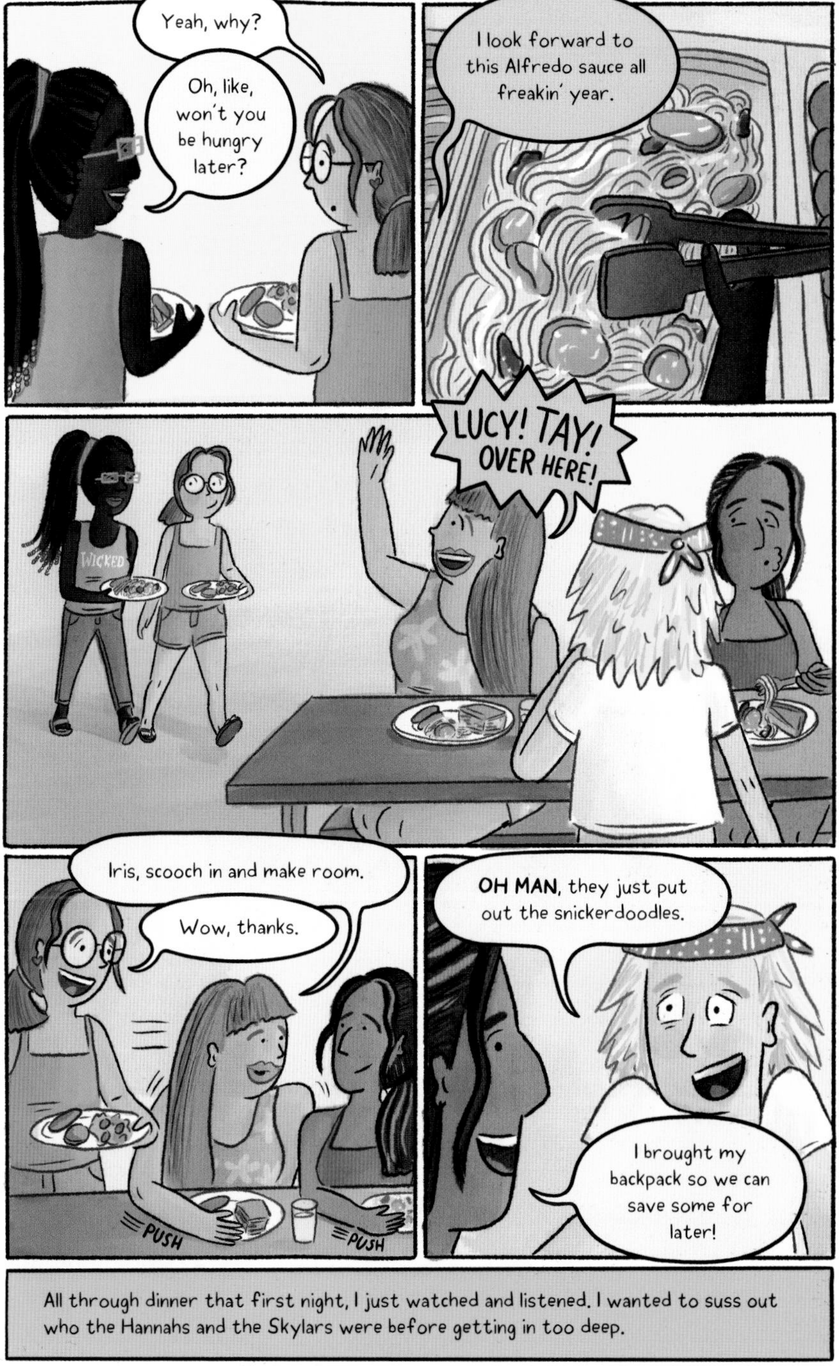
Yeah, why?
Oh, like, won't you be hungry later?
I look forward to this Alfredo sauce all freakin' year.
WICKED
LUCY! TAY! OVER HERE!
Iris, scooch in and make room.
Wow, thanks.
PUSH
PUSH
OH MAN, they just put out the snickerdoodles.
I brought my backpack so we can save some for later!
All through dinner that first night, I just watched and listened. I wanted to suss out who the Hannahs and the Skylars were before getting in too deep.

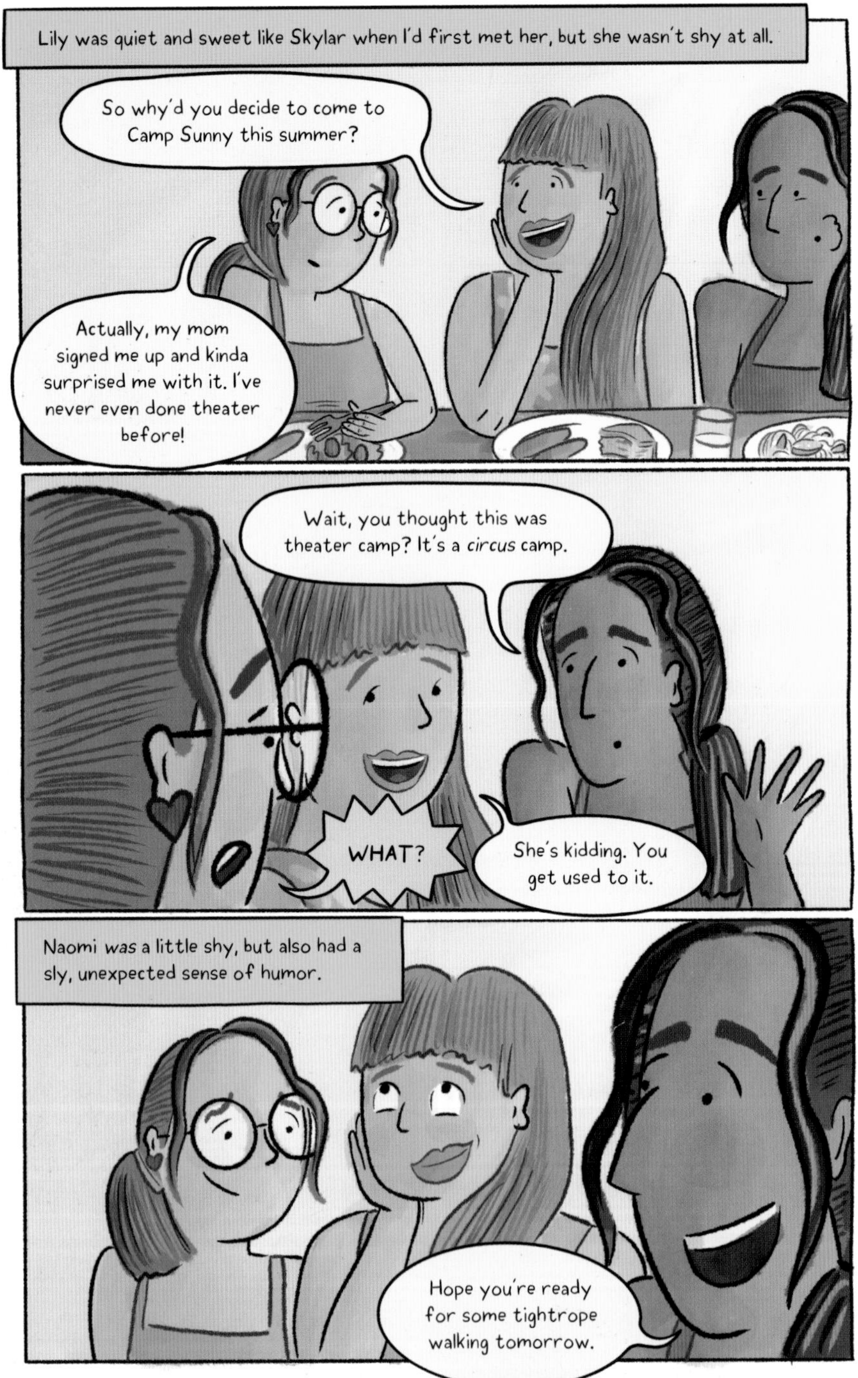
Lily was quiet and sweet like Skylar when I'd first met her, but she wasn't shy at all.
So why'd you decide to come to Camp Sunny this summer?
Actually, my mom signed me up and kinda surprised me with it. I've never even done theater before!
Wait, you thought this was theater camp? It's a *circus* camp.
WHAT?
She's kidding. You get used to it.
Naomi *was* a little shy, but also had a sly, unexpected sense of humor.
Hope you're ready for some tightrope walking tomorrow.

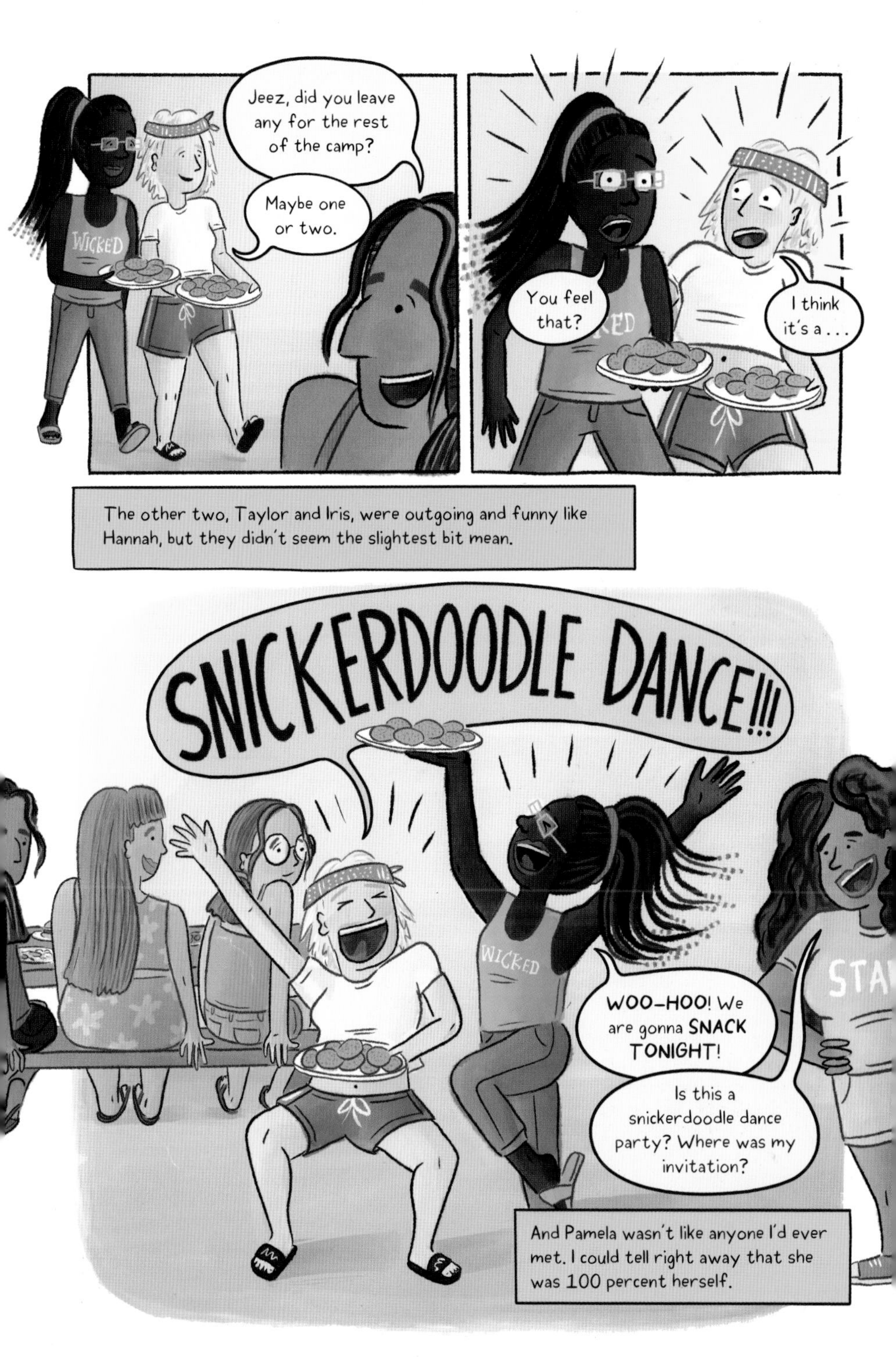
Jeez, did you leave any for the rest of the camp?
Maybe one or two.
You feel that?
I think it's a . . .
The other two, Taylor and Iris, were outgoing and funny like Hannah, but they didn't seem the slightest bit mean.
SNICKERDOODLE DANCE!!!
WOO-HOO! We are gonna SNACK TONIGHT!
Is this a snickerdoodle dance party? Where was my invitation?
And Pamela wasn't like anyone I'd ever met. I could tell right away that she was 100 percent herself.

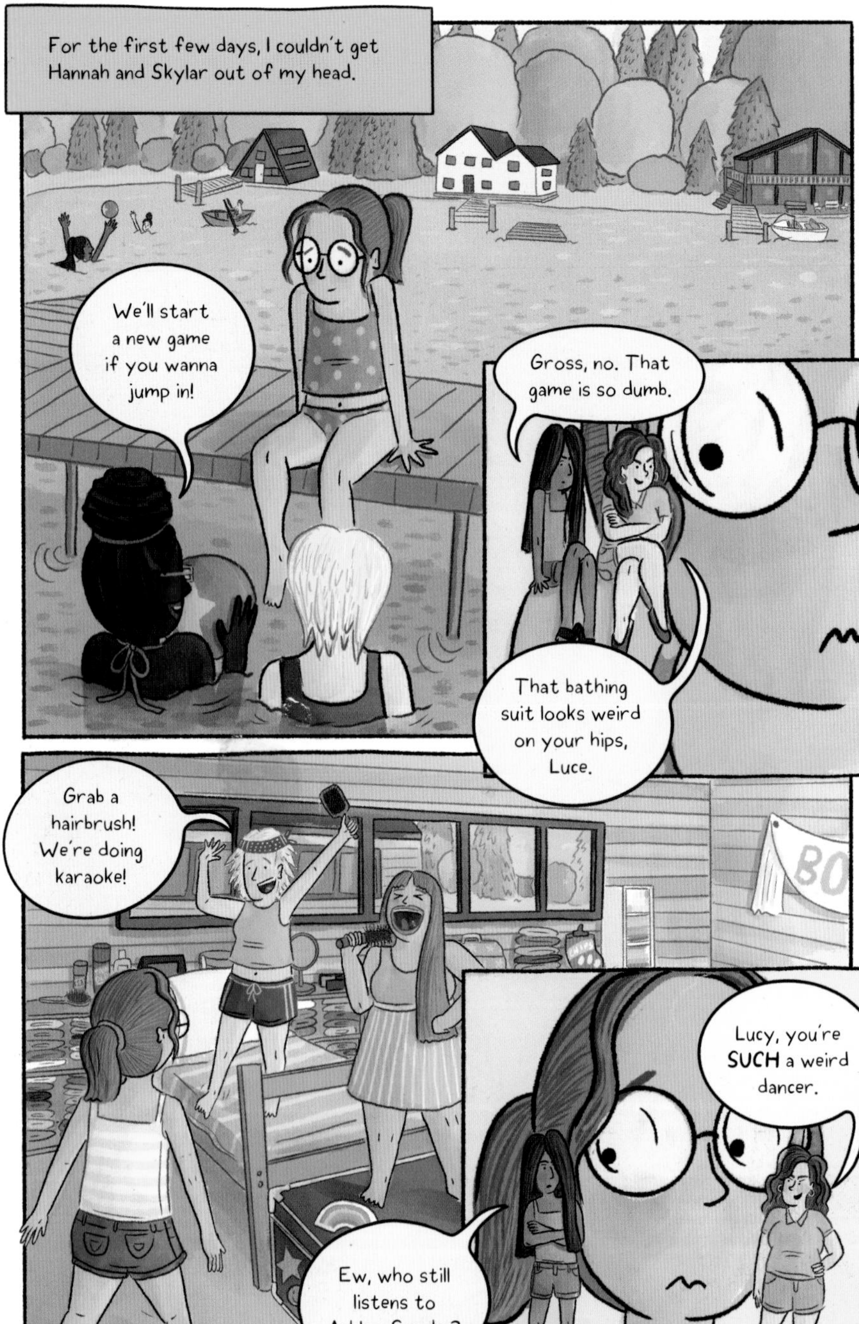
For the first few days, I couldn't get Hannah and Skylar out of my head.
We'll start a new game if you wanna jump in!
Gross, no. That game is so dumb.
That bathing suit looks weird on your hips, Luce.
Grab a hairbrush! We're doing karaoke!
Ew, who still listens to Ashley Sparks?
Lucy, you're **SUCH** a weird dancer.

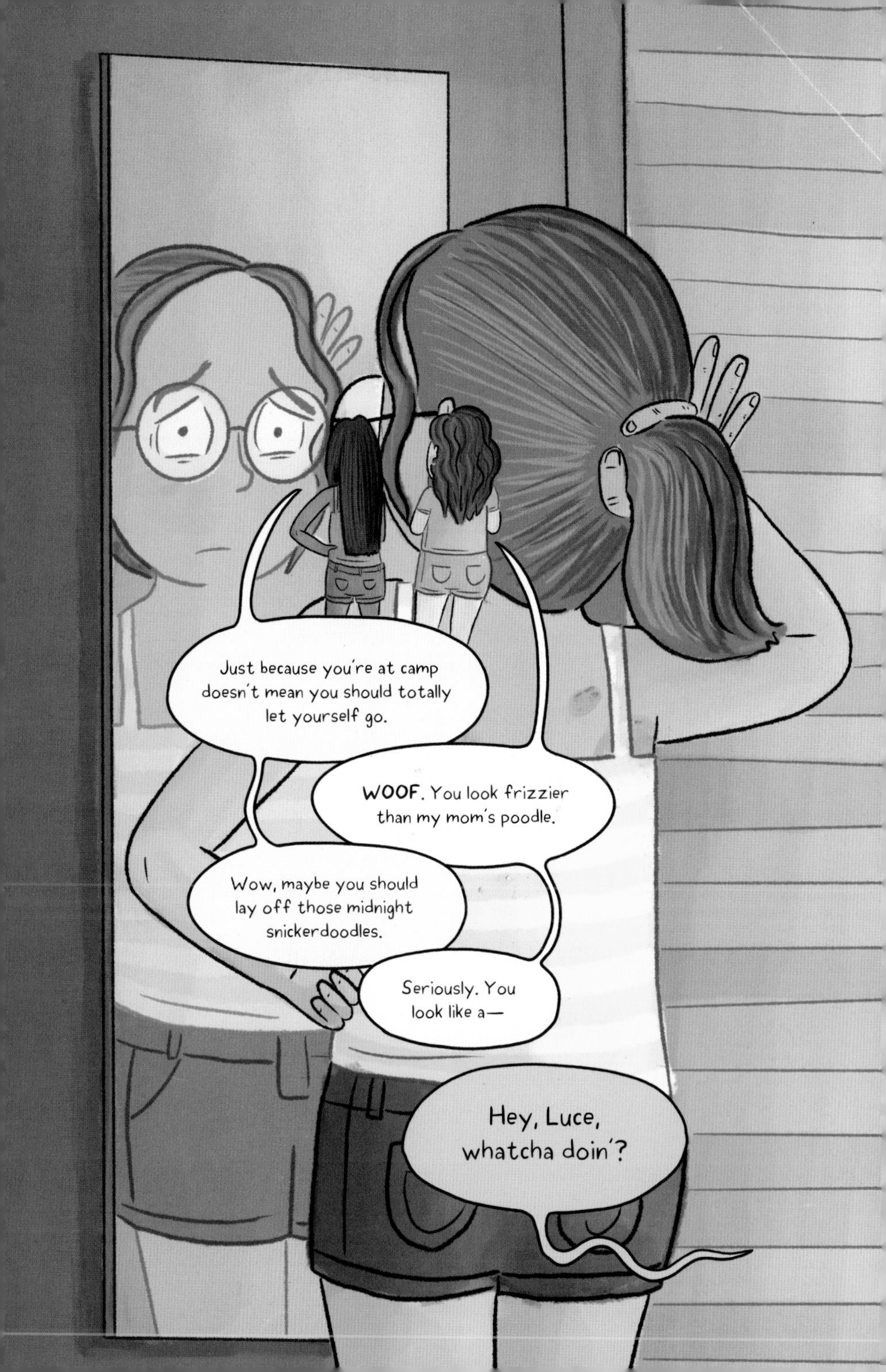
Just because you're at camp doesn't mean you should totally let yourself go.
WOOF. You look frizzier than my mom's poodle.
Wow, maybe you should lay off those midnight snickerdoodles.
Seriously. You look like a—
Hey, Luce, whatcha doin'?

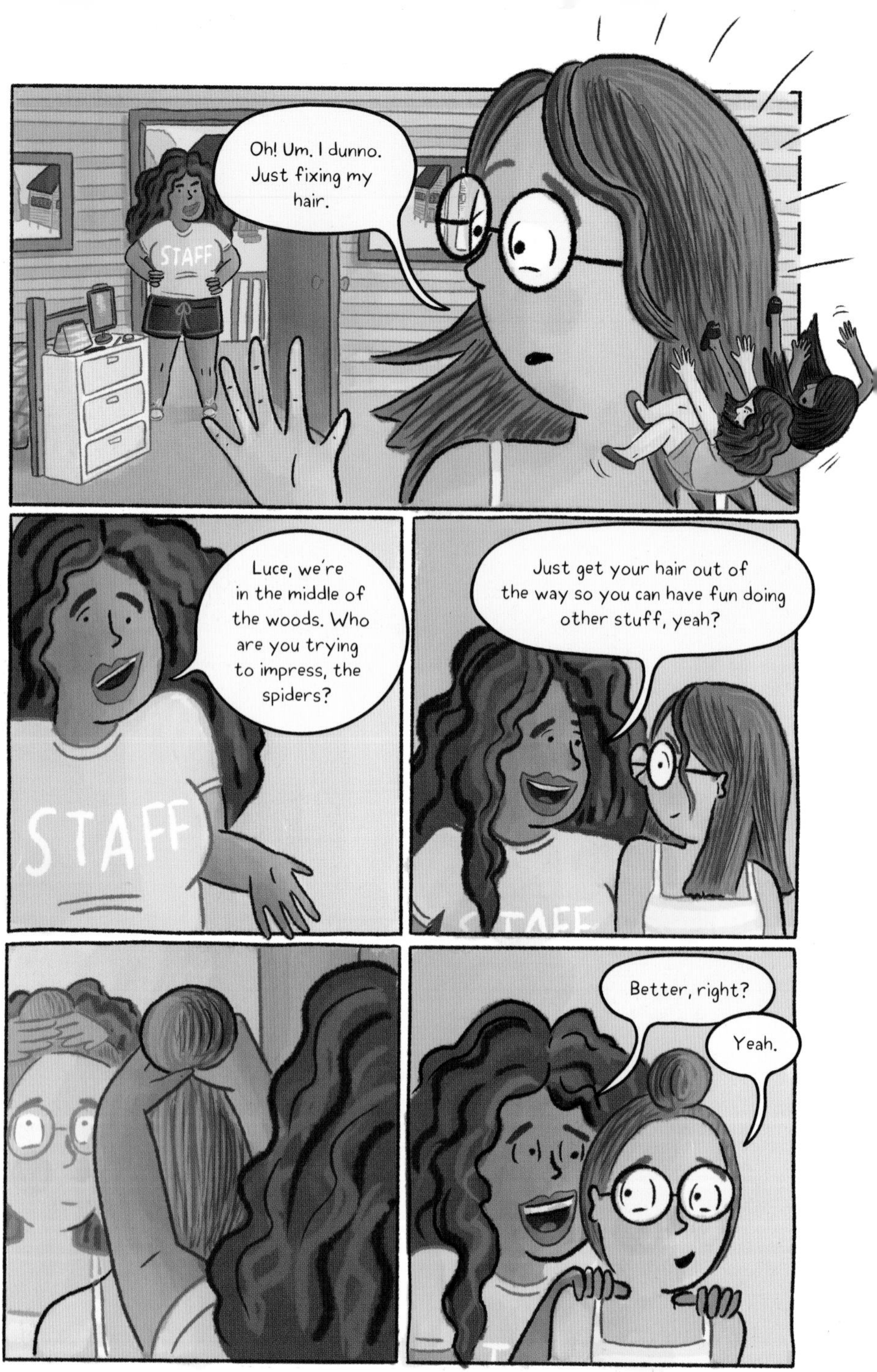
Oh! Um. I dunno. Just fixing my hair.
Luce, we're in the middle of the woods. Who are you trying to impress, the spiders?
Just get your hair out of the way so you can have fun doing other stuff, yeah?
Better, right?
Yeah.

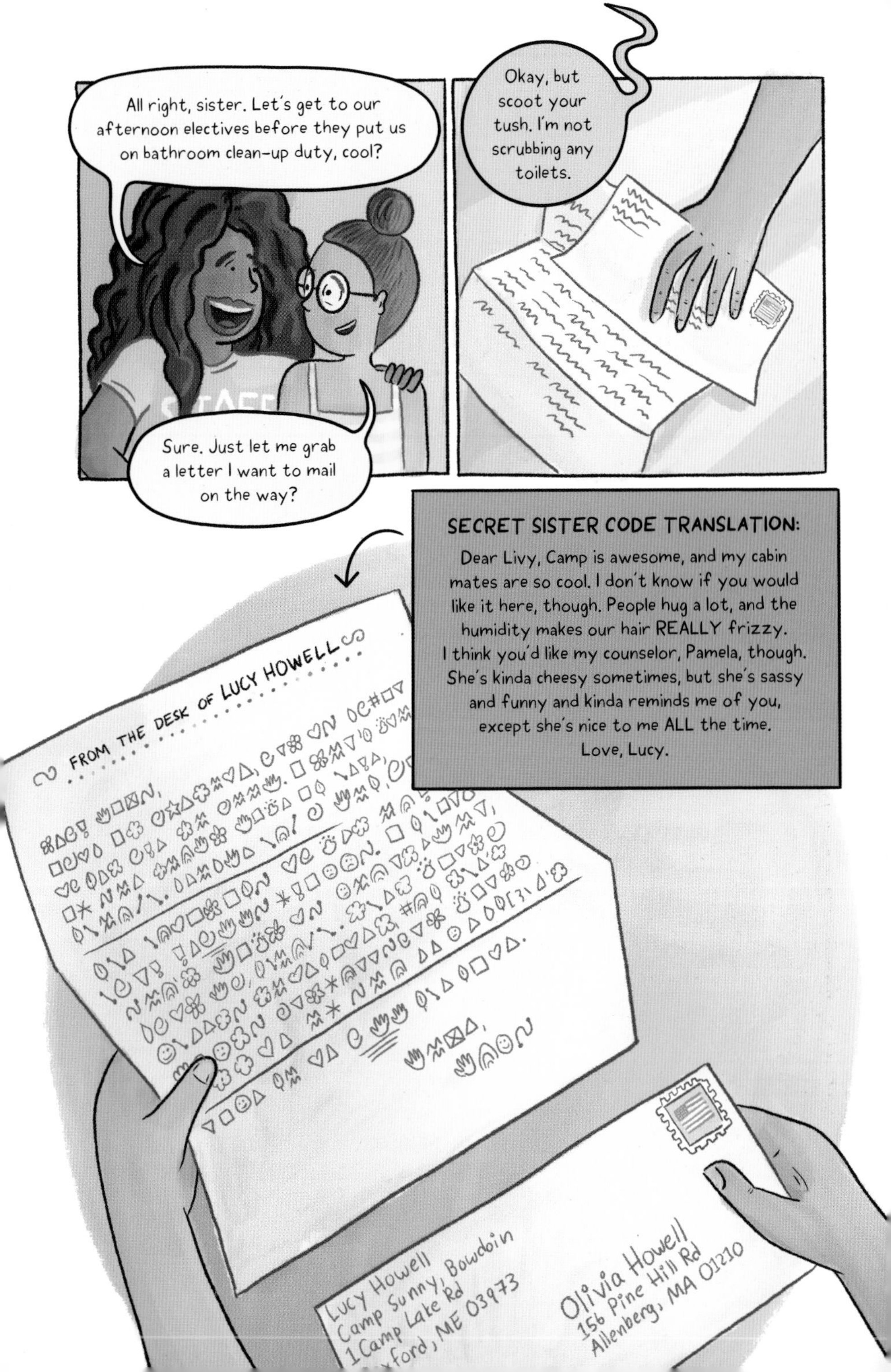
All right, sister. Let's get to our afternoon electives before they put us on bathroom clean-up duty, cool?
Sure. Just let me grab a letter I want to mail on the way?
Okay, but scoot your tush. I'm not scrubbing any toilets.
SECRET SISTER CODE TRANSLATION:
Dear Livy, Camp is awesome, and my cabin mates are so cool. I don't know if you would like it here, though. People hug a lot, and the humidity makes our hair REALLY frizzy.
I think you'd like my counselor, Pamela, though. She's kinda cheesy sometimes, but she's sassy and funny and kinda reminds me of you, except she's nice to me ALL the time.
Love, Lucy.
FROM THE DESK OF LUCY HOWELL
Lucy Howell
Camp Sunny, Bowdoin
1 Camp Lake Rd
xford, ME 03973
Olivia Howell
156 Pine Hill Rd
Allenberg, MA 01210

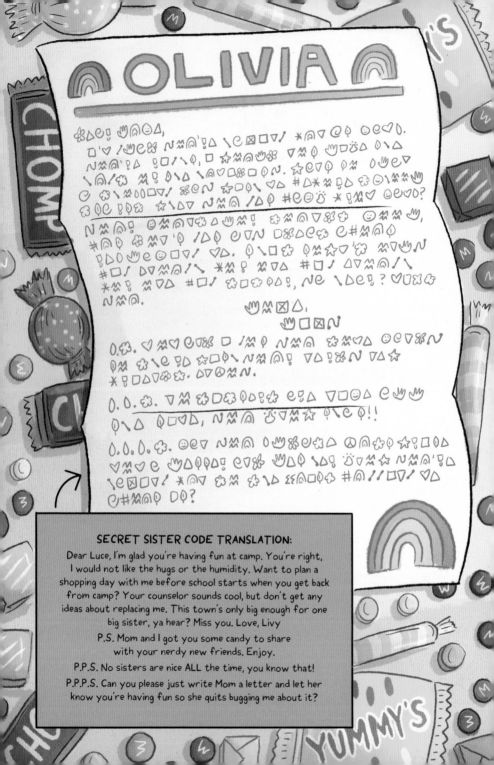

SECRET SISTER CODE TRANSLATION:

Dear Luce, I'm glad you're having fun at camp. You're right, I would not like the hugs or the humidity. Want to plan a shopping day with me before school starts when you get back from camp? Your counselor sounds cool, but don't get any ideas about replacing me. This town's only big enough for one big sister, ya hear? Miss you. Love, Livy

P.S. Mom and I got you some candy to share with your nerdy new friends. Enjoy.

P.P.S. No sisters are nice ALL the time, you know that!

P.P.P.S. Can you please just write Mom a letter and let her know you're having fun so she quits bugging me about it?

Dear Lucy,

Haven't ~~heard~~ heard from you, so I hope that means you're having a blast!!!! Sending candy for you to share with your new camp friends, and a few new magazines for you to enjoy as well.

We all miss you so much. Please write back ~~soon~~ soon!

Love,
Mom ♡

FROM THE DESK OF LUCY HOWELL

Dear Mom,
Camp is awesome! Thanks for the candy and magazines. Really busy today but will write more soon. Love you!

♡ L y

FROM THE DESK OF LUCY HOWELL

[coded symbols]

SECRET SISTER CODE TRANSLATION:

Dear Livy, A shopping day sounds great. And don't worry, there's no replacing the real thing. Love, Lucy

owell
nny, Bowdoin
ake Rd
d, ME 03973

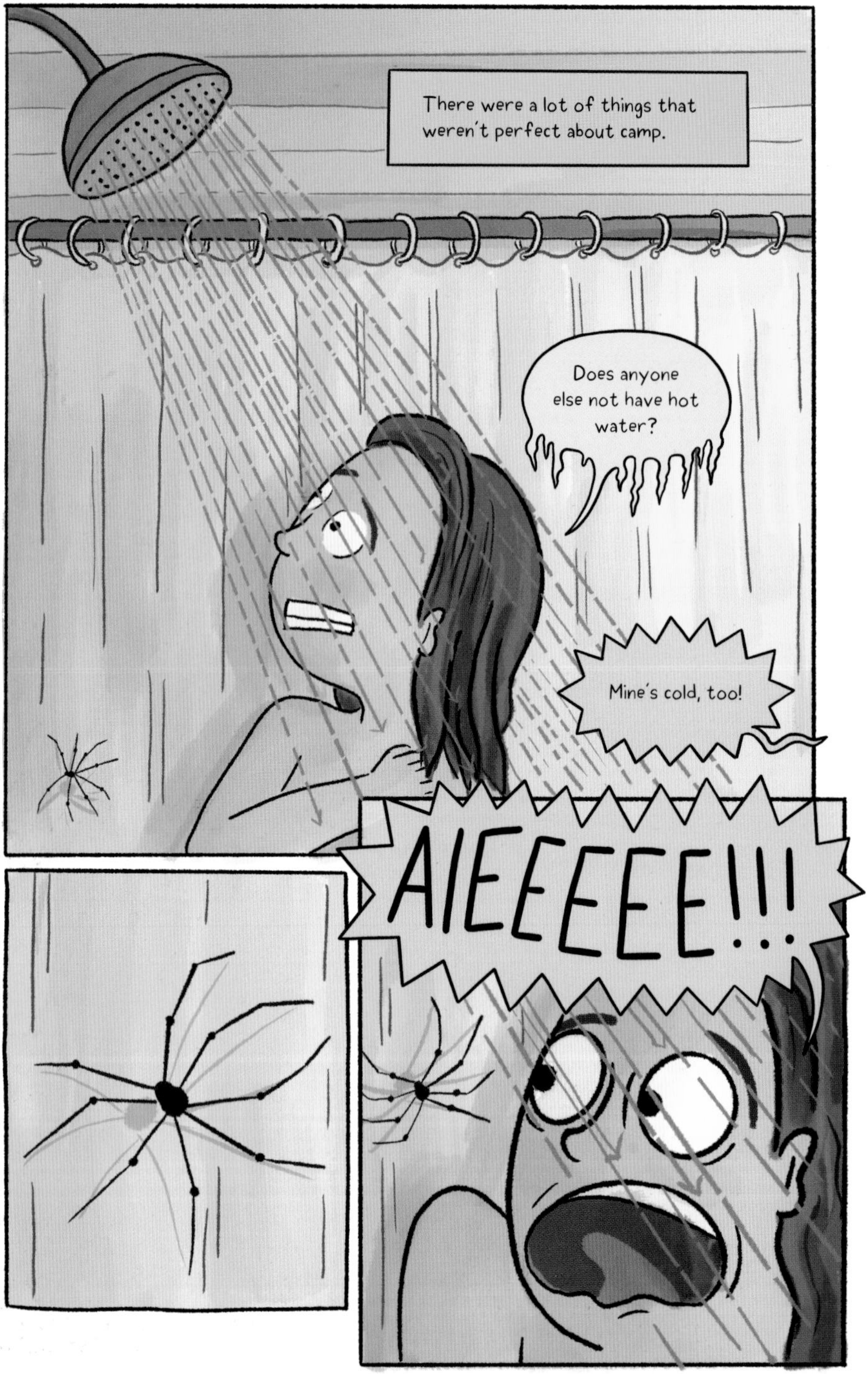
There were a lot of things that weren't perfect about camp.
Does anyone else not have hot water?
Mine's cold, too!
AIEEEEE!!!

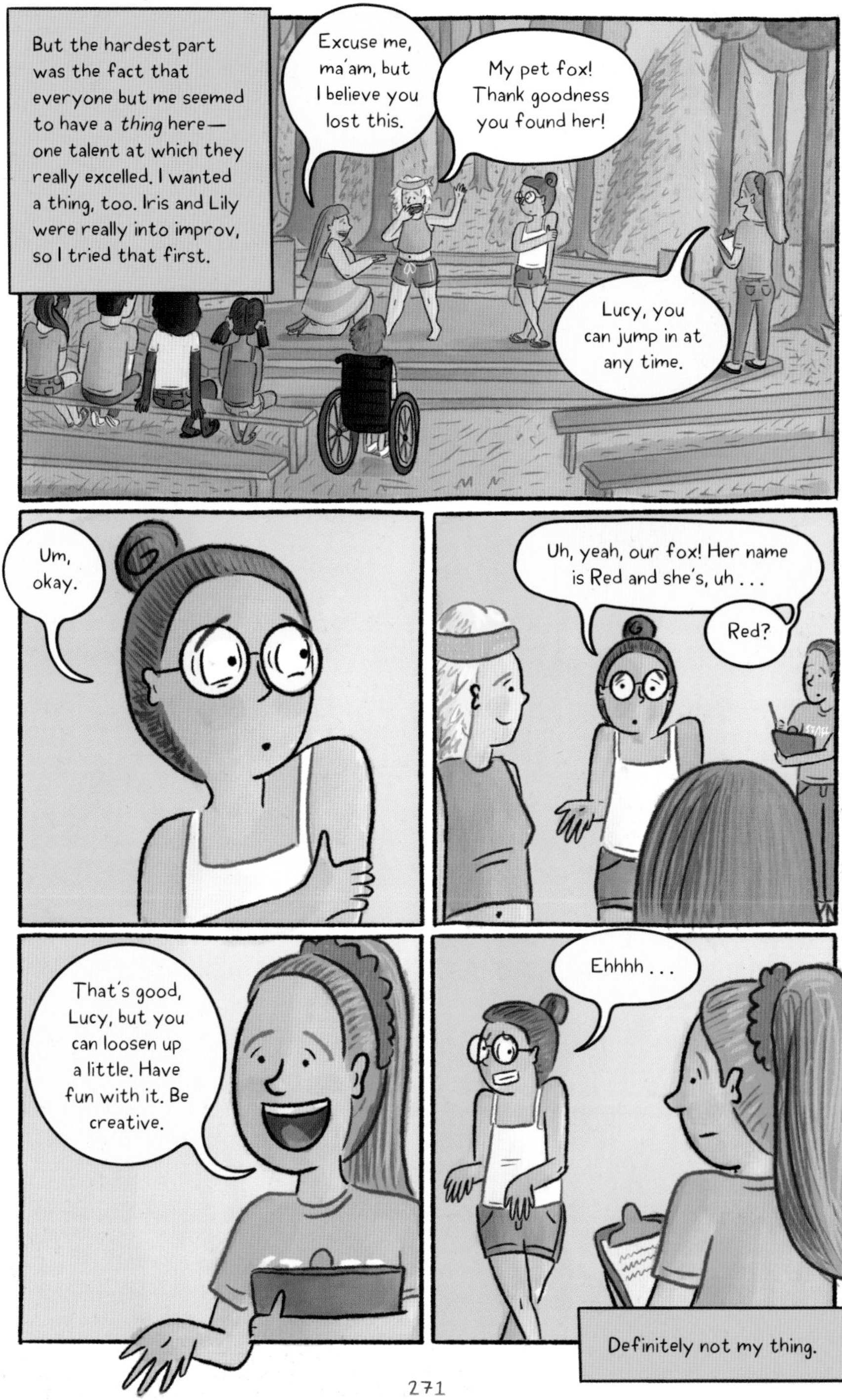

But the hardest part was the fact that everyone but me seemed to have a *thing* here—one talent at which they really excelled. I wanted a thing, too. Iris and Lily were really into improv, so I tried that first.
Excuse me, ma'am, but I believe you lost this.
My pet fox! Thank goodness you found her!
Lucy, you can jump in at any time.
Um, okay.
Uh, yeah, our fox! Her name is Red and she's, uh . . .
Red?
That's good, Lucy, but you can loosen up a little. Have fun with it. Be creative.
Ehhhh . . .
Definitely not my thing.

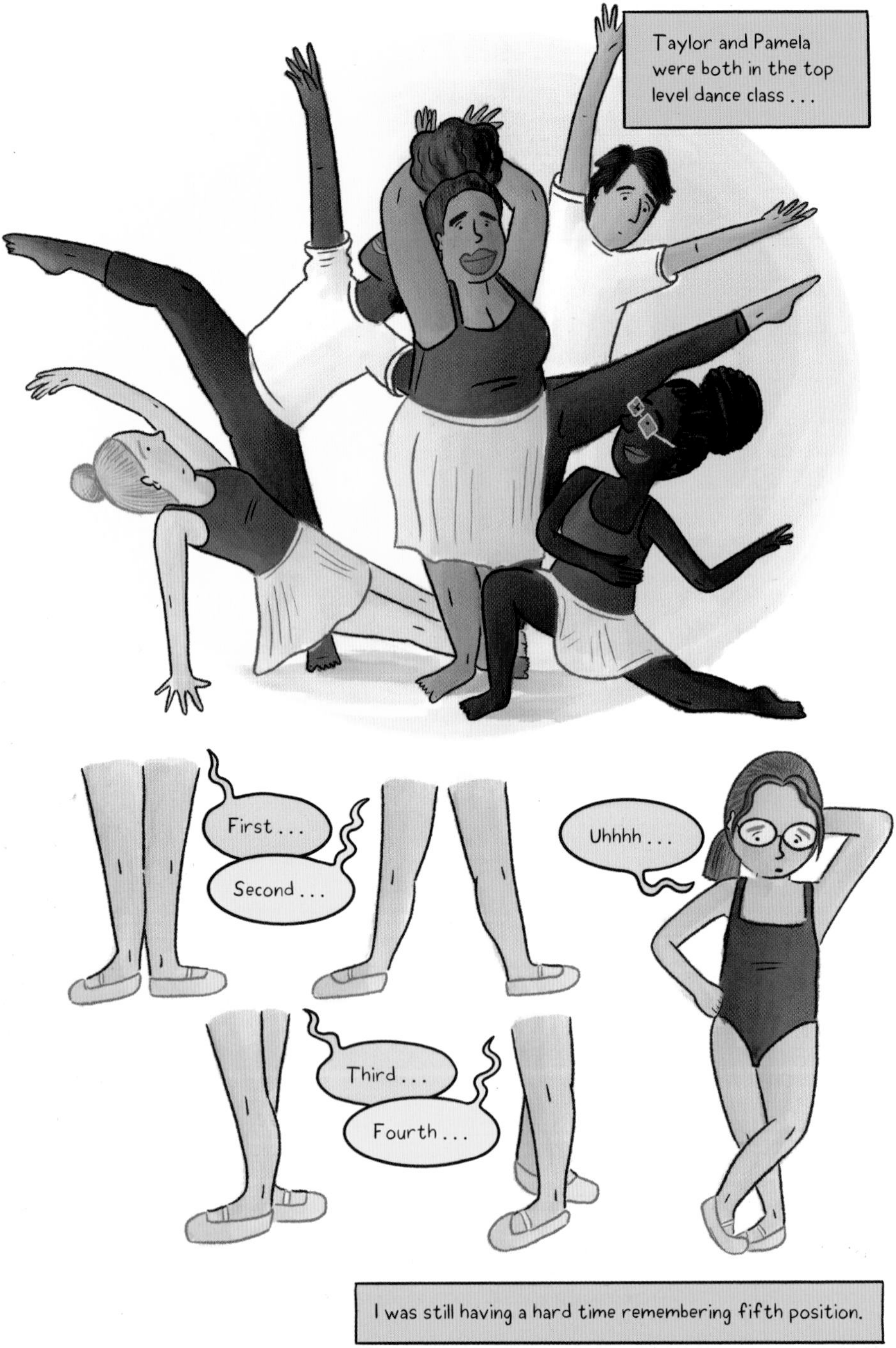
Taylor and Pamela were both in the top level dance class . . .
First . . .
Second . . .
Uhhhh . . .
Third . . .
Fourth . . .
I was still having a hard time remembering fifth position.

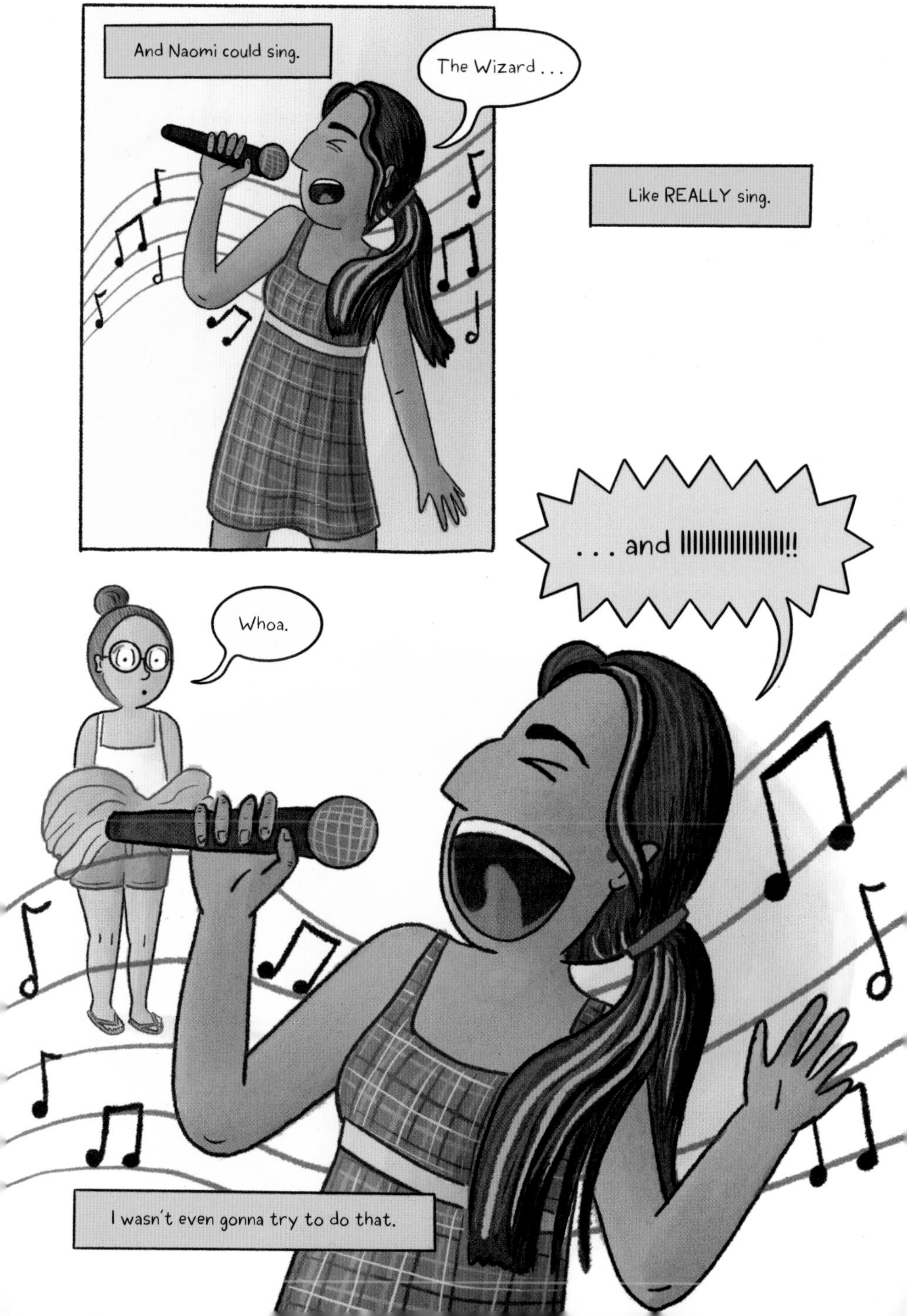
And Naomi could sing.
The Wizard . . .
Like REALLY sing.
. . . and IIIIIIIIIIIIIIIII!!
Whoa.
I wasn't even gonna try to do that.

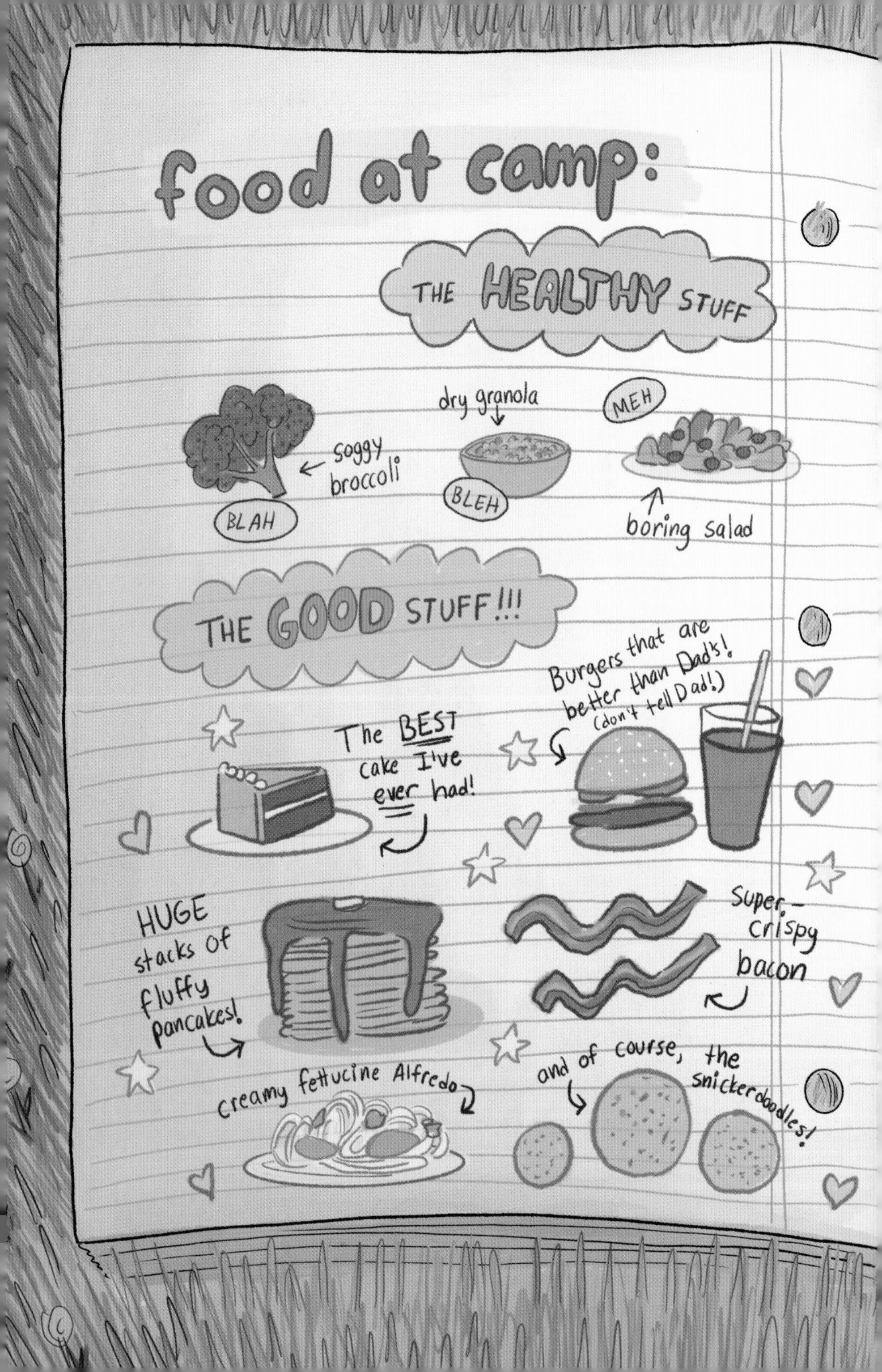
food at camp:
THE HEALTHY STUFF
soggy broccoli
BLAH
dry granola
BLEH
MEH
boring salad
THE GOOD STUFF!!!
The BEST cake I've ever had!
Burgers that are better than Dad's! (don't tell Dad!)
HUGE stacks of fluffy pancakes!
Super-crispy bacon
creamy fettucine Alfredo
and of course, the snickerdoodles!

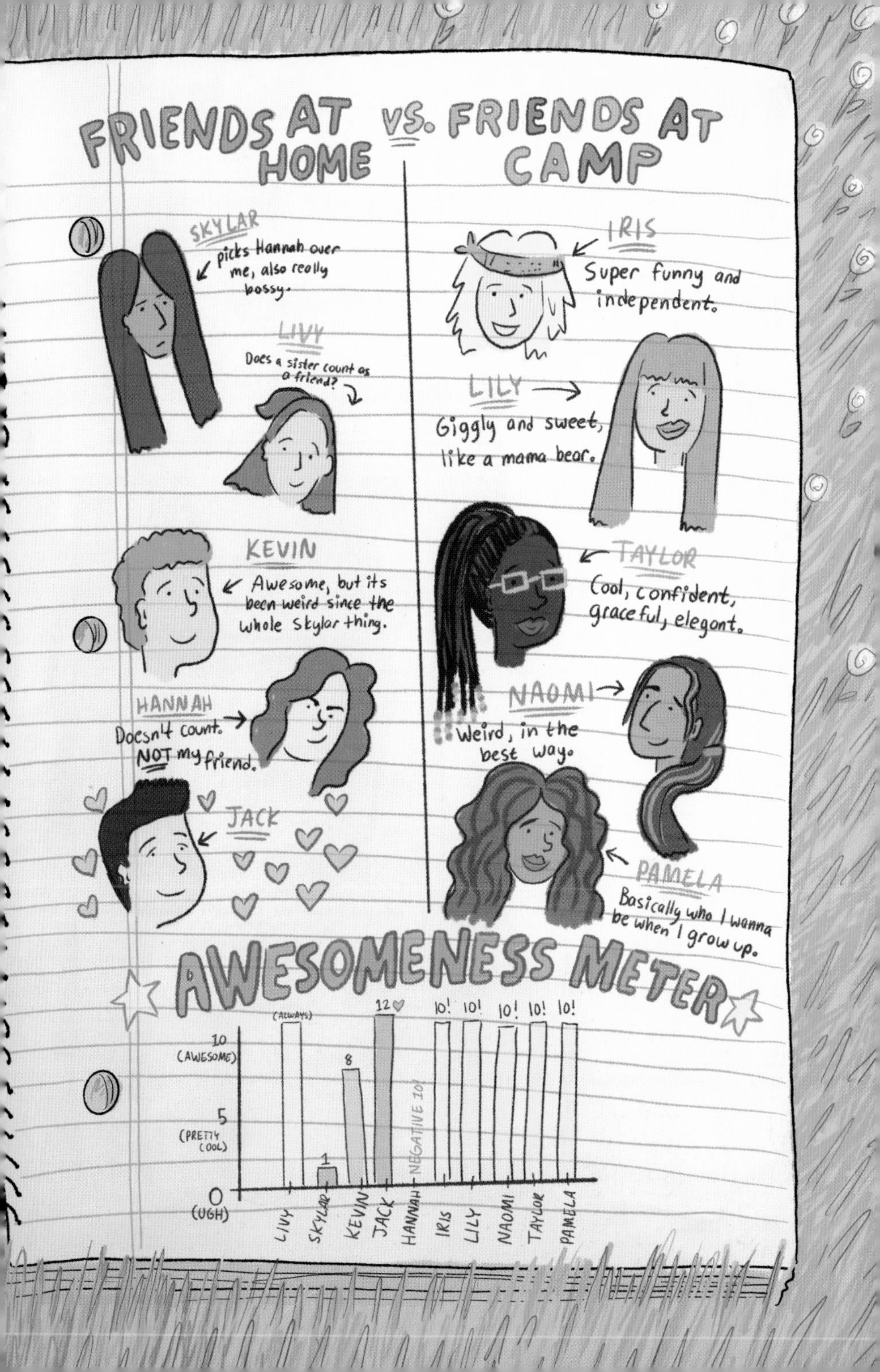

FRIENDS AT HOME vs. FRIENDS AT CAMP
SKYLAR
picks Hannah over me, also really bossy.
LIVY
Does a sister count as a friend?
KEVIN
Awesome, but its been weird since the whole Skylar thing.
HANNAH
Doesn't count. NOT my friend.
JACK
IRIS
Super funny and independent.
LILY
Giggly and sweet, like a mama bear.
TAYLOR
Cool, confident, graceful, elegant.
NAOMI
Weird, in the best way.
PAMELA
Basically who I wanna be when I grow up.
AWESOMENESS METER
10 (AWESOME)
5 (PRETTY COOL)
0 (UGH)
(ALWAYS)
1
8
12♥
NEGATIVE 10!
10!
10!
10!
10!
10!
LIVY
SKYLAR
KEVIN
JACK
HANNAH
IRIS
LILY
NAOMI
TAYLOR
PAMELA

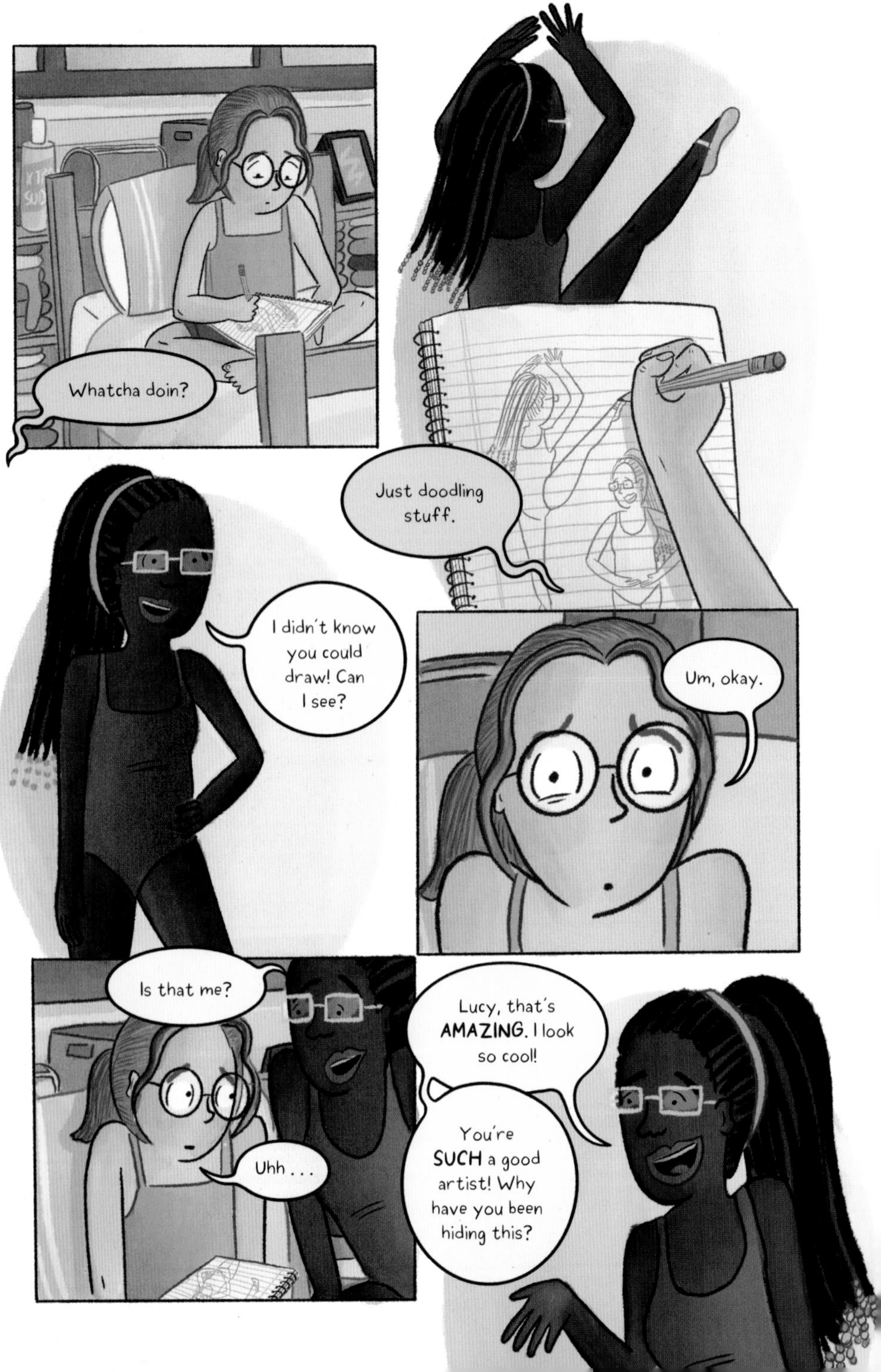
Whatcha doin?
Just doodling stuff.
I didn't know you could draw! Can I see?
Um, okay.
Is that me?
Uhh . . .
Lucy, that's **AMAZING.** I look so cool!
You're **SUCH** a good artist! Why have you been hiding this?

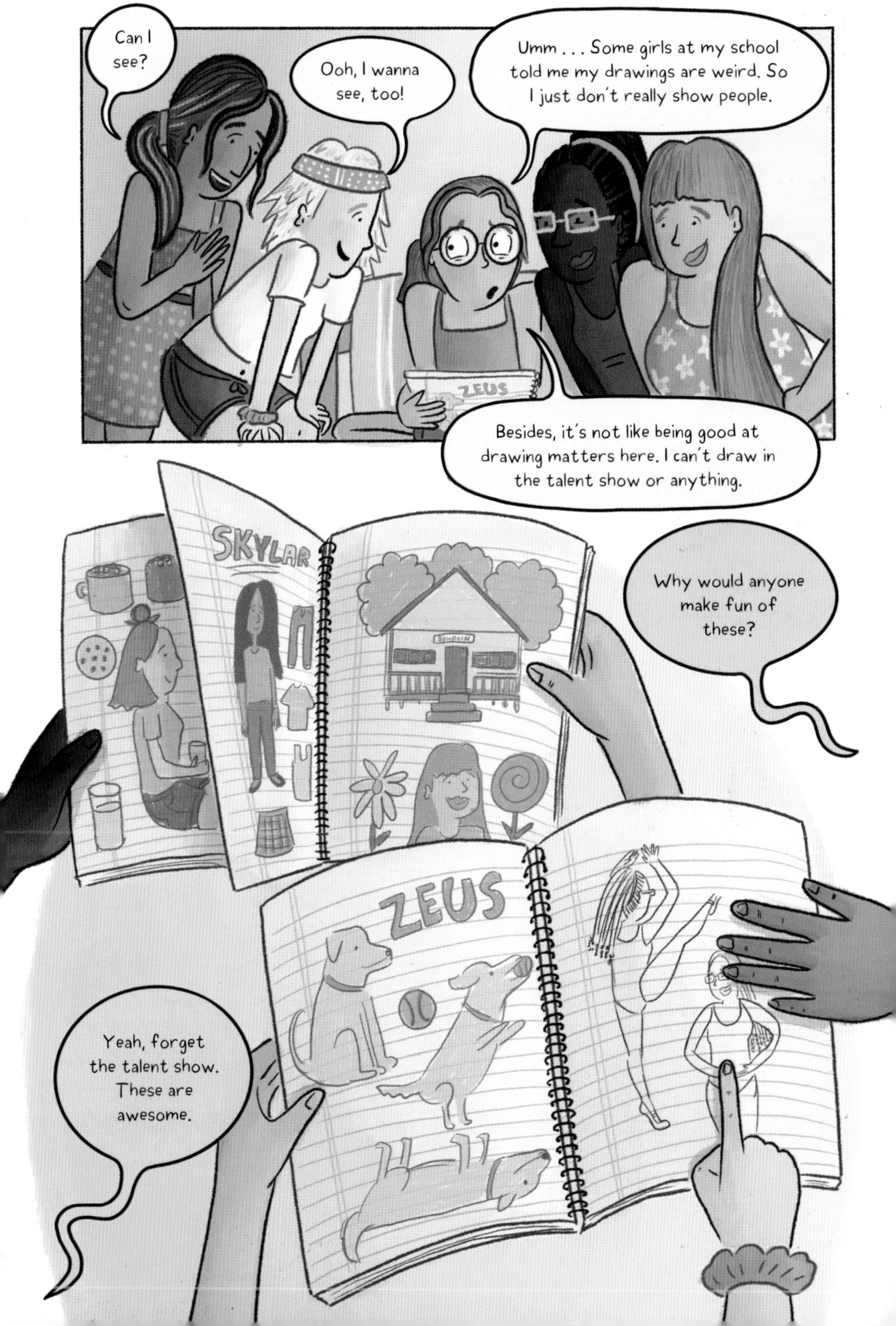
Can I see?
Ooh, I wanna see, too!
Umm . . . Some girls at my school told me my drawings are weird. So I just don't really show people.
Besides, it's not like being good at drawing matters here. I can't draw in the talent show or anything.
SKYLAR
Why would anyone make fun of these?
ZEUS
Yeah, forget the talent show. These are awesome.

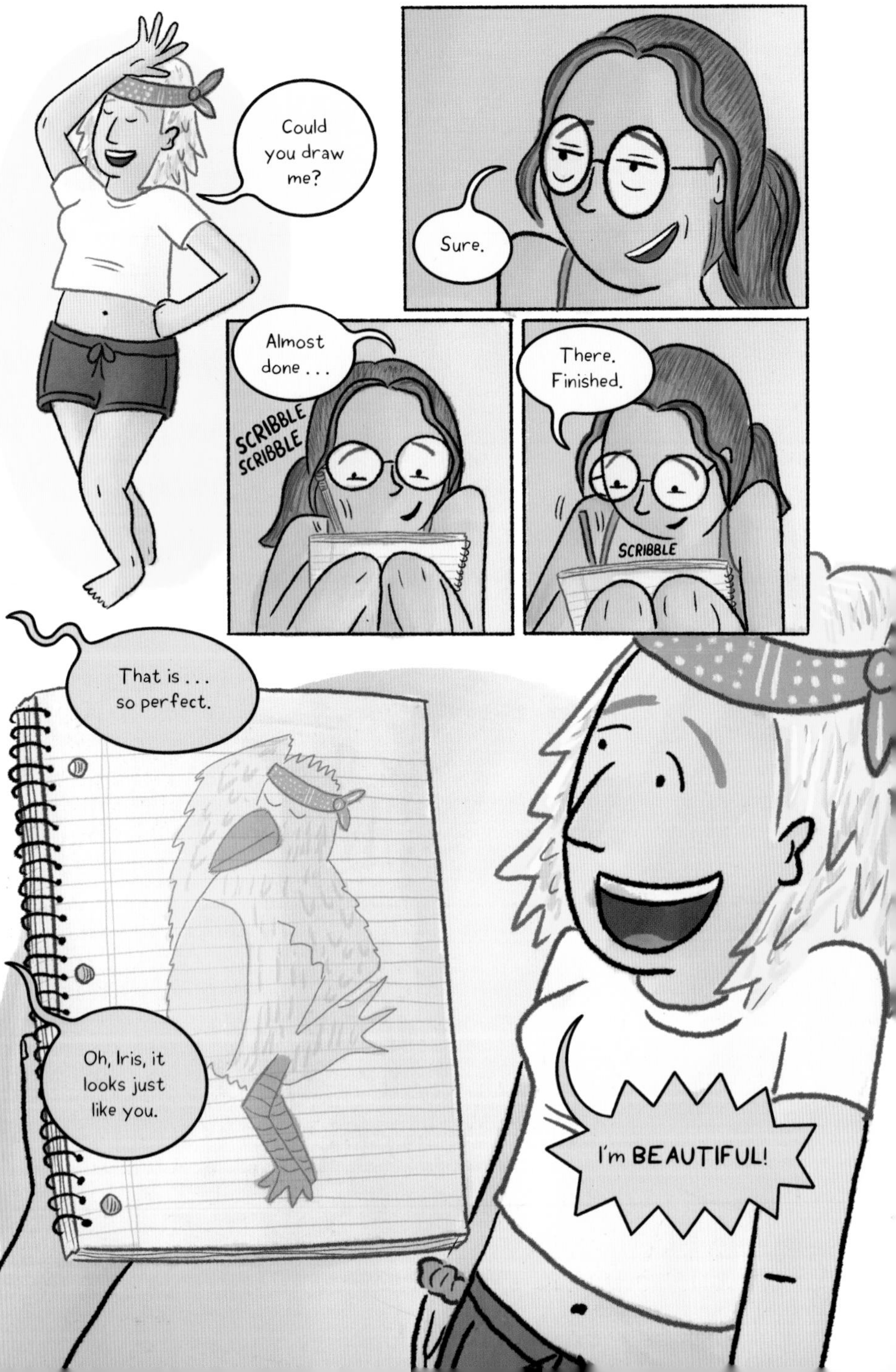
Could you draw me?
Sure.
Almost done . . .
SCRIBBLE SCRIBBLE
There. Finished.
SCRIBBLE
That is . . . so perfect.
Oh, Iris, it looks just like you.
I'm **BEAUTIFUL!**

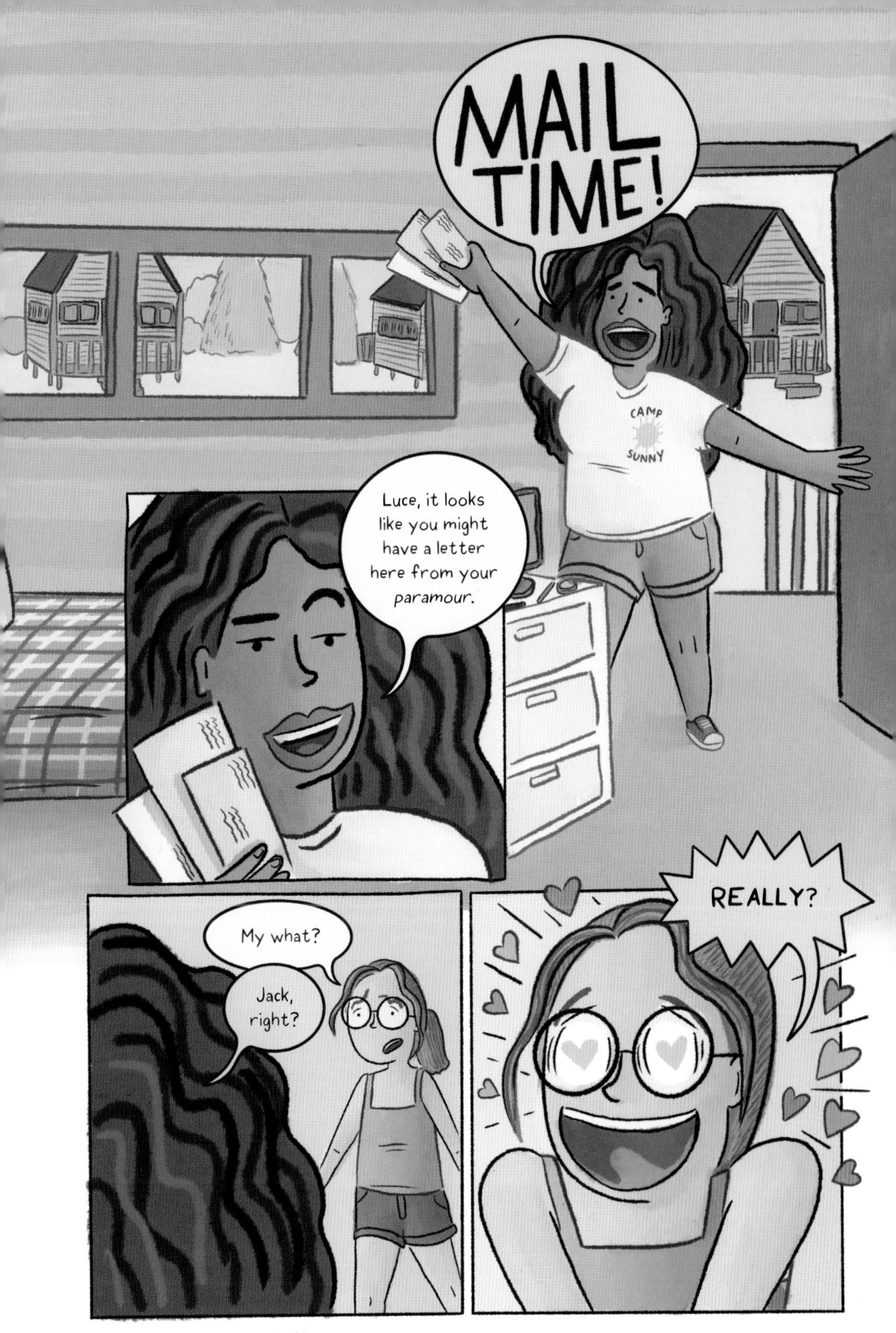
MAIL TIME!
Luce, it looks like you might have a letter here from your *paramour*.
My what?
Jack, right?
REALLY?
CAMP SUNNY

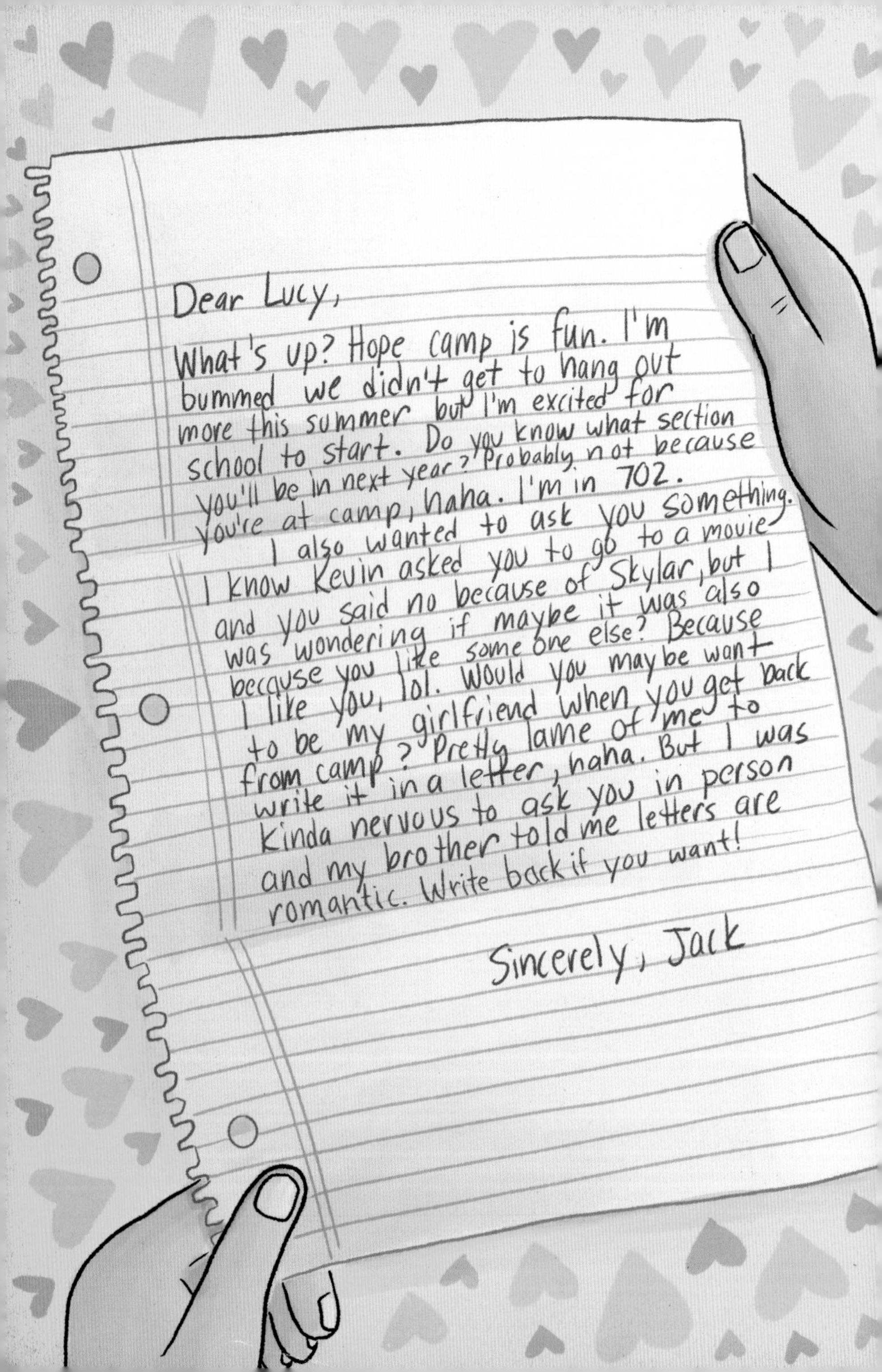
Dear Lucy,

What's up? Hope camp is fun. I'm
bummed we didn't get to hang out
more this summer but I'm excited for
school to start. Do you know what section
you'll be in next year? Probably not because
you're at camp, haha. I'm in 702.
I also wanted to ask you something.
I know Kevin asked you to go to a movie
and you said no because of Skylar, but I
was wondering if maybe it was also
because you like some one else? Because
I like you, lol. Would you maybe want
to be my girlfriend when you get back
from camp? Pretty lame of me to
write it in a letter, haha. But I was
kinda nervous to ask you in person
and my brother told me letters are
romantic. Write back if you want!

Sincerely, Jack

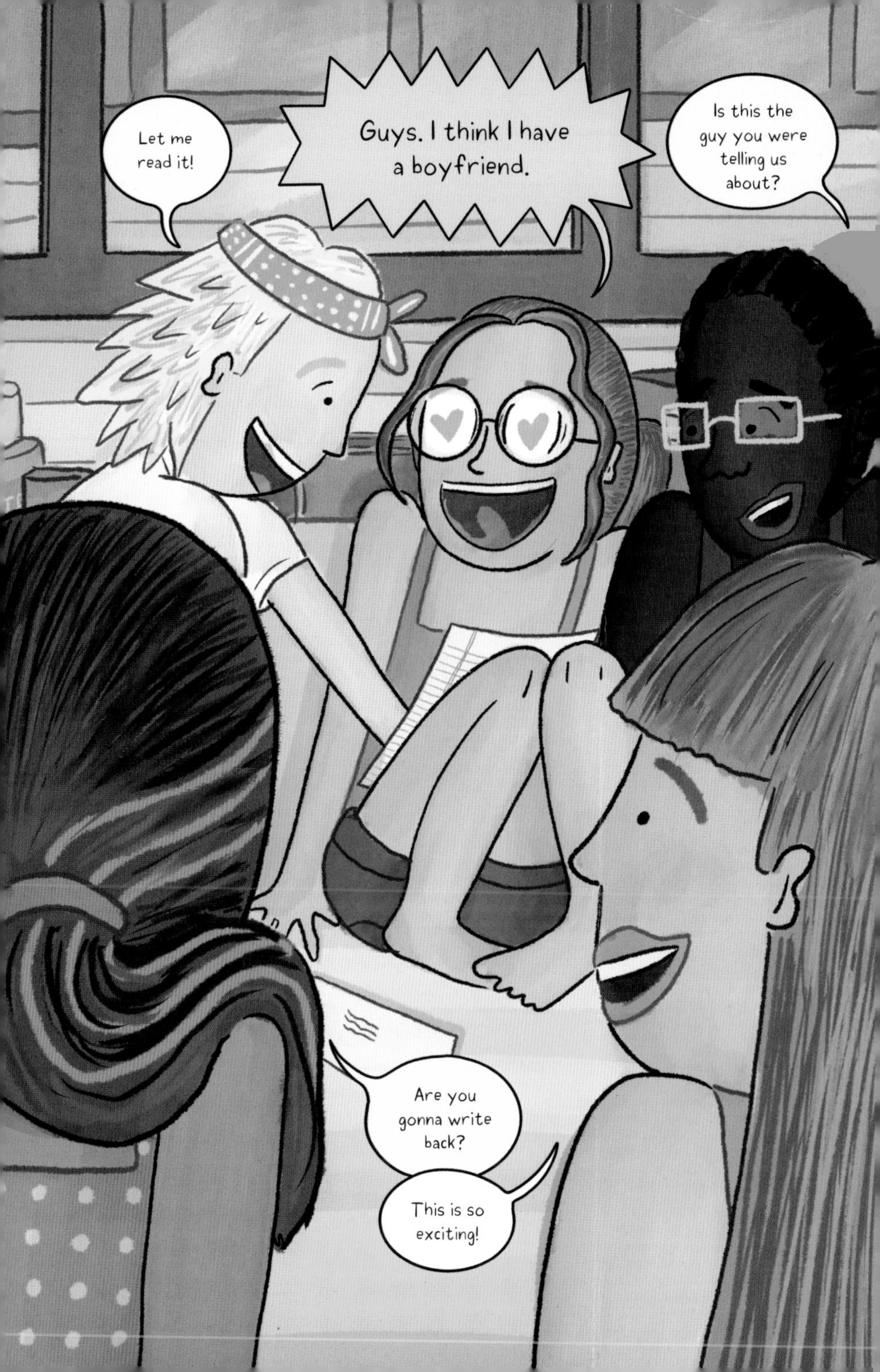
Let me read it!
Guys. I think I have a boyfriend.
Is this the guy you were telling us about?
Are you gonna write back?
This is so exciting!

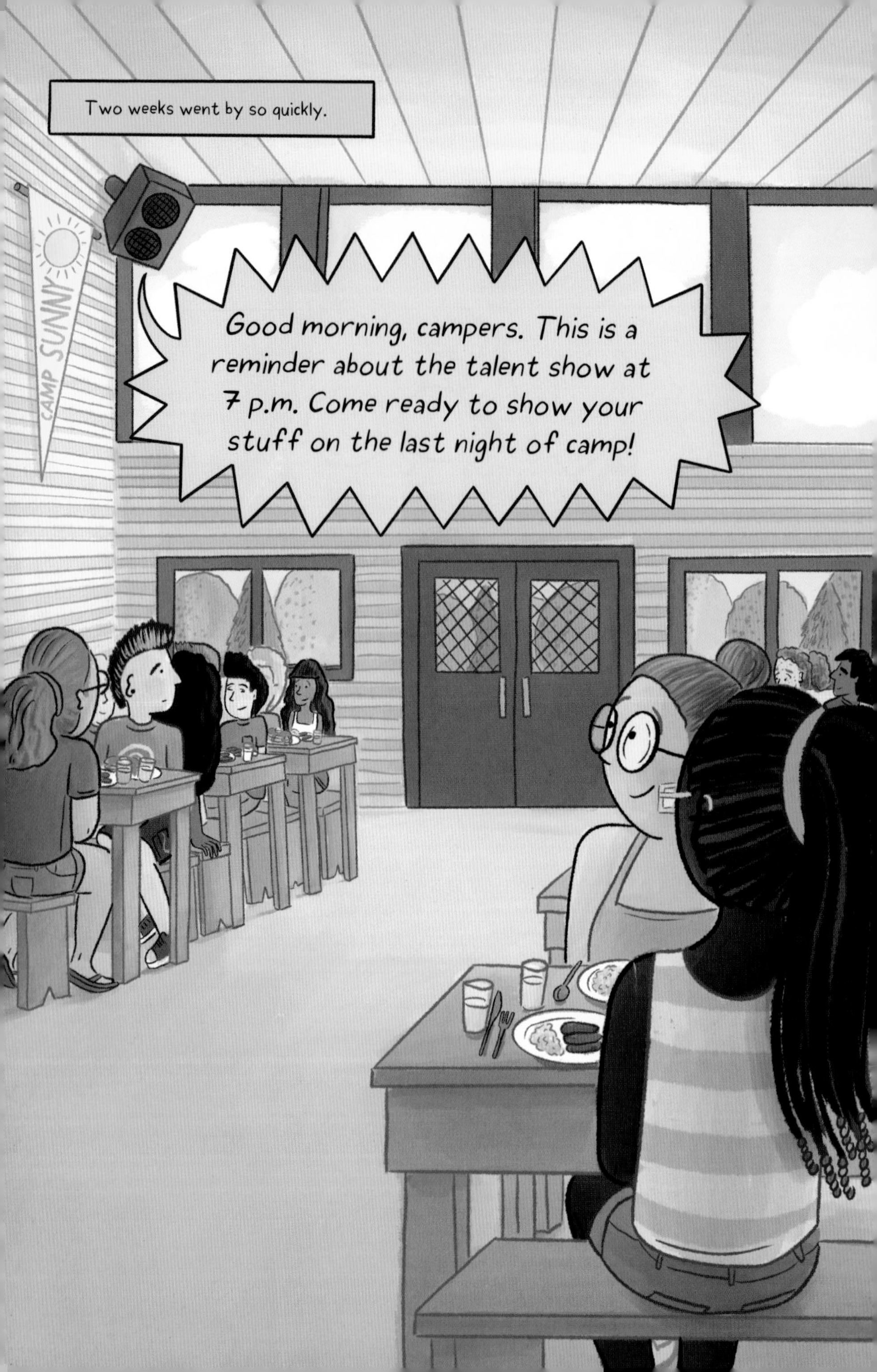
Two weeks went by so quickly.
CAMP SUNNY
Good morning, campers. This is a reminder about the talent show at 7 p.m. Come ready to show your stuff on the last night of camp!

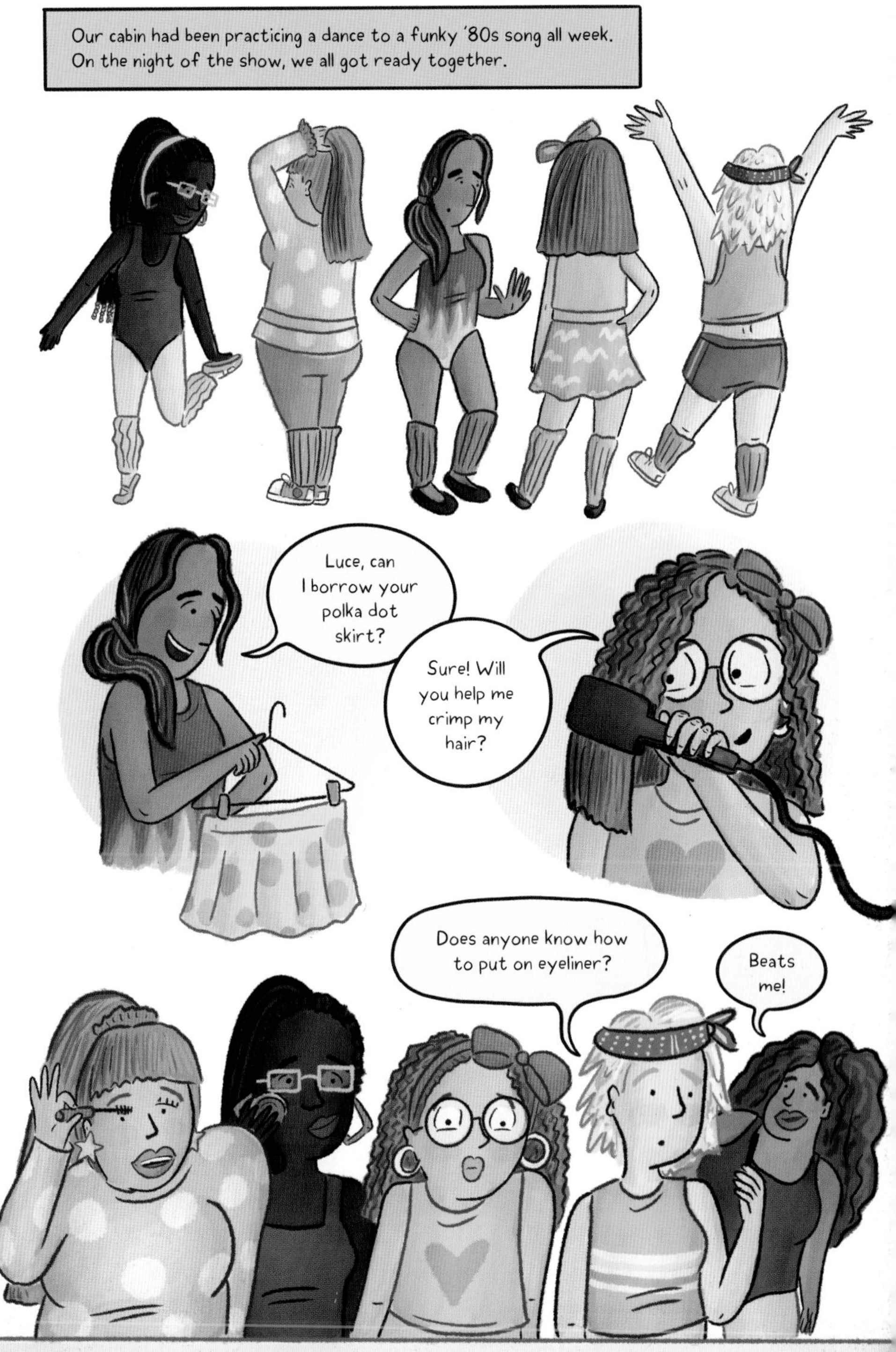

Our cabin had been practicing a dance to a funky '80s song all week. On the night of the show, we all got ready together.
Luce, can I borrow your polka dot skirt?
Sure! Will you help me crimp my hair?
Does anyone know how to put on eyeliner?
Beats me!

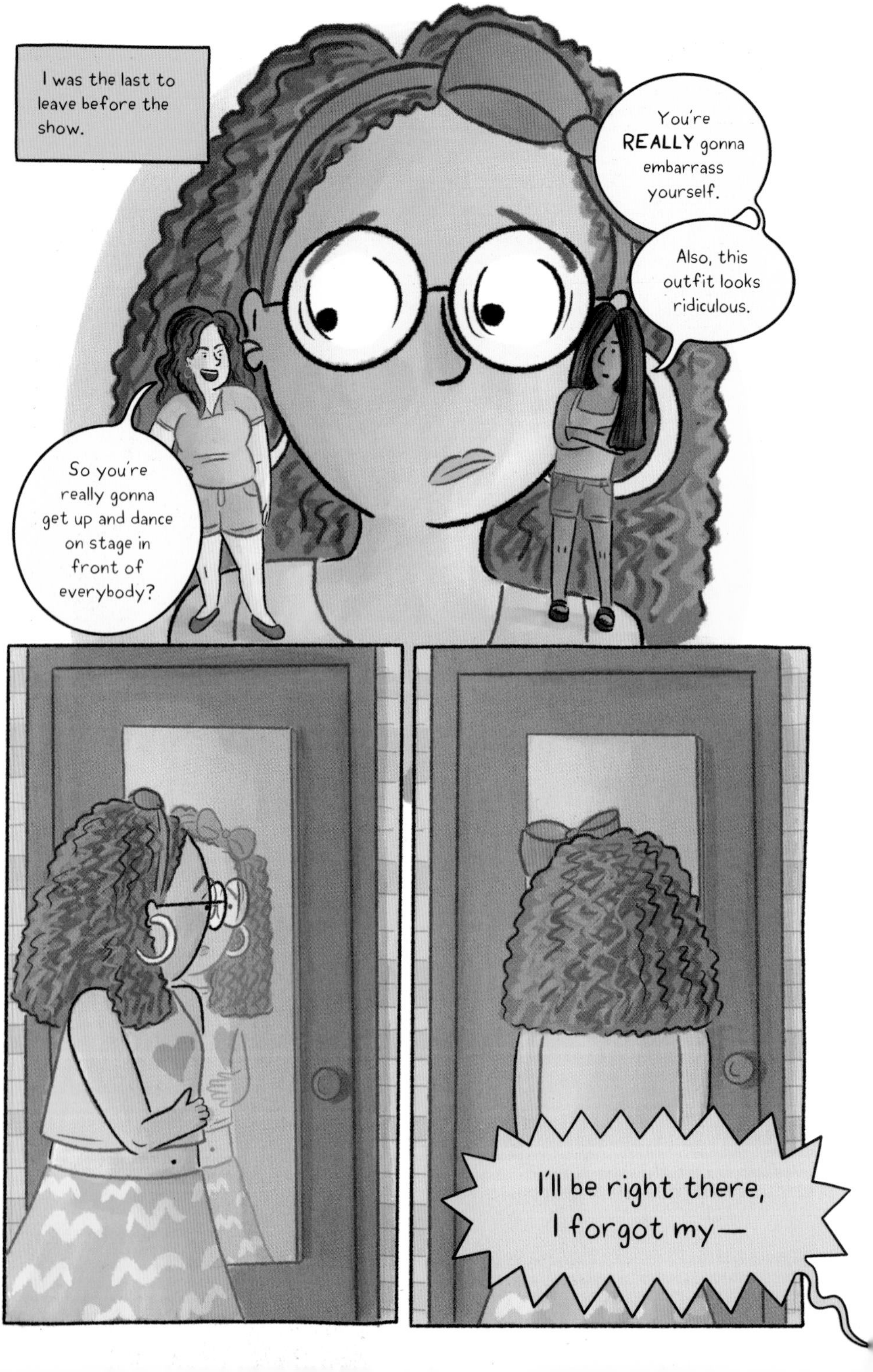
I was the last to leave before the show.
So you're really gonna get up and dance on stage in front of everybody?
You're **REALLY** gonna embarrass yourself.
Also, this outfit looks ridiculous.
I'll be right there, I forgot my—

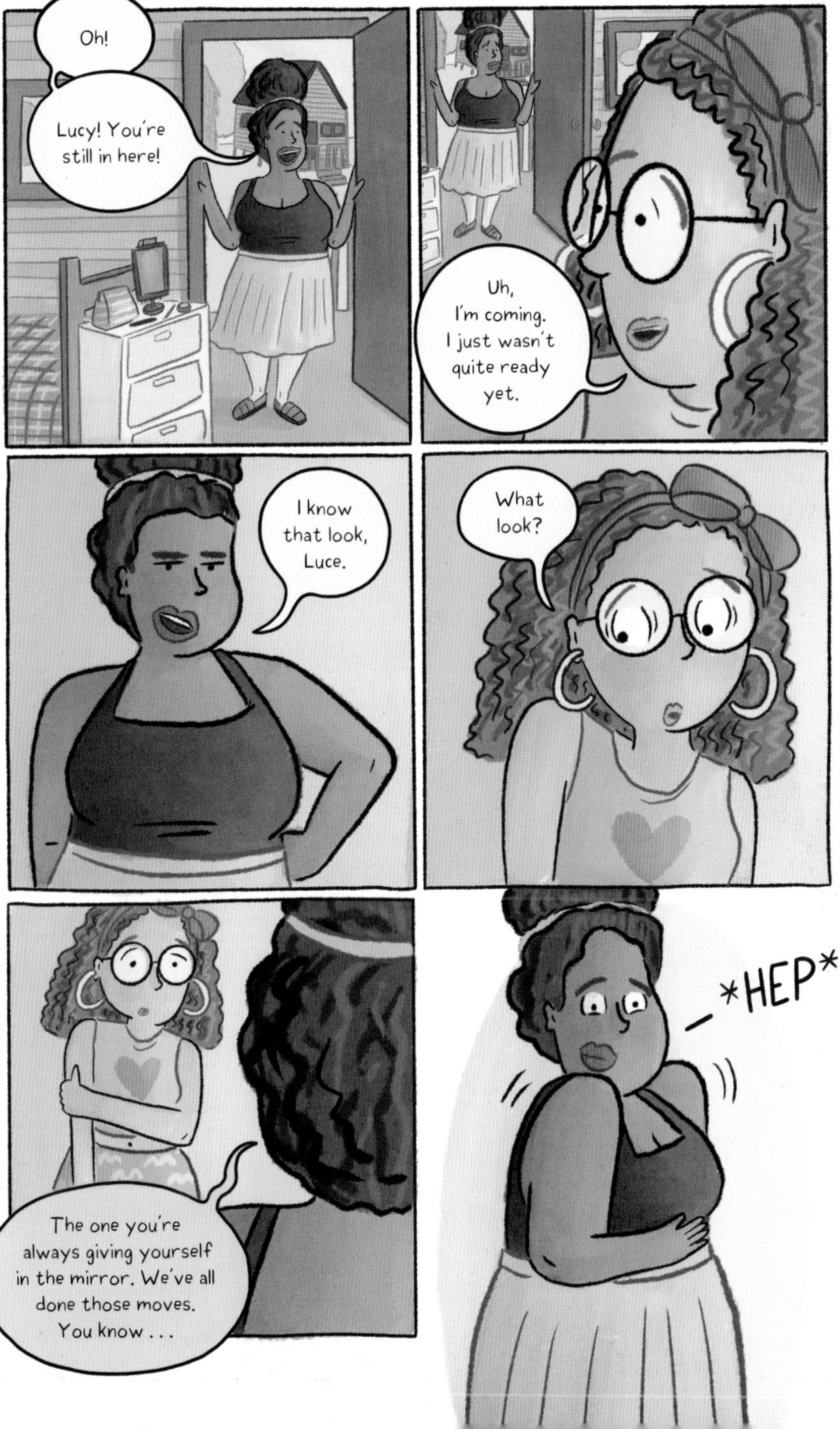
Oh!
Lucy! You're still in here!
Uh, I'm coming. I just wasn't quite ready yet.
I know that look, Luce.
What look?
The one you're always giving yourself in the mirror. We've all done those moves. You know . . .
HEP

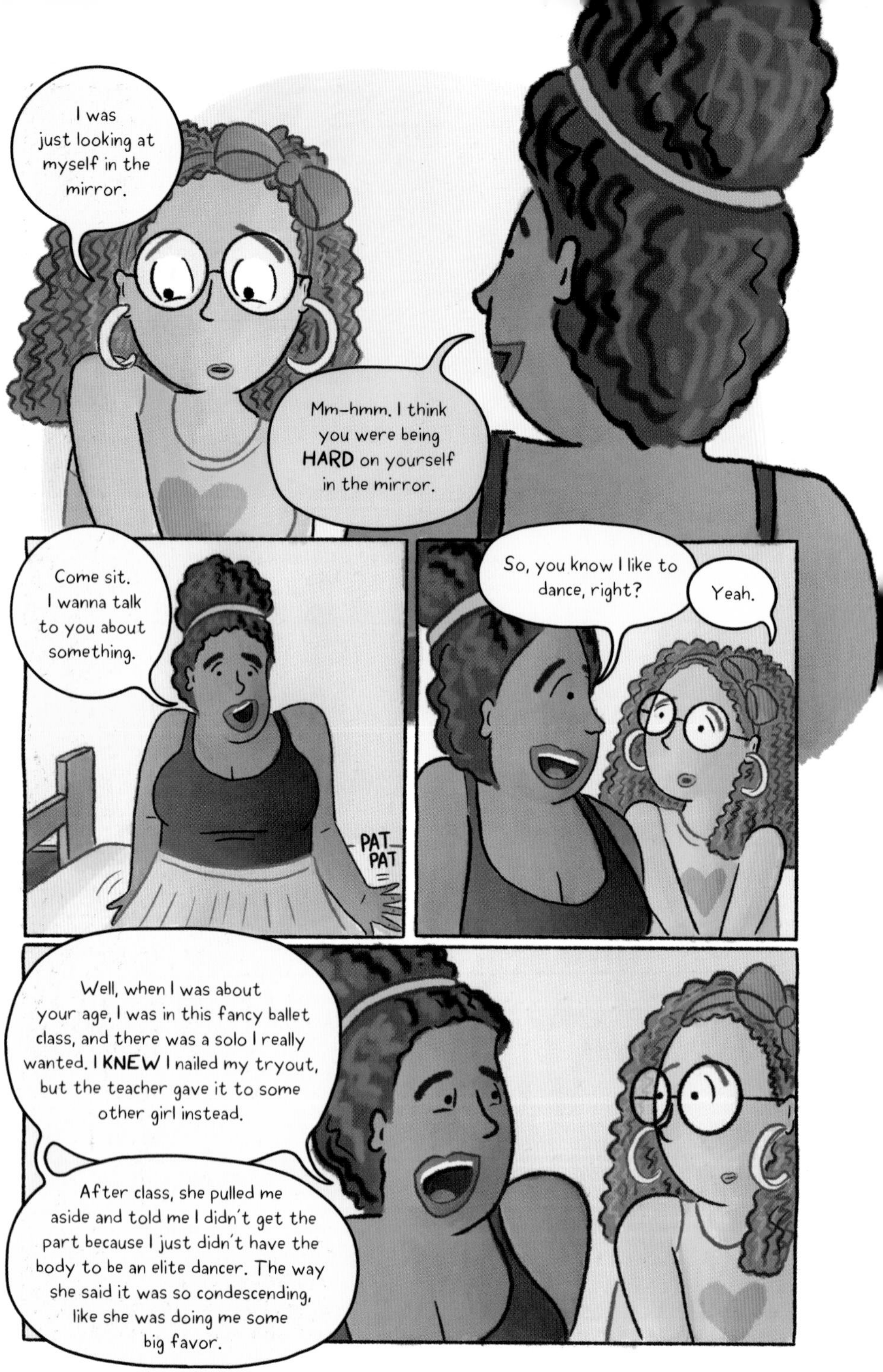
I was just looking at myself in the mirror.
Mm-hmm. I think you were being HARD on yourself in the mirror.
Come sit. I wanna talk to you about something.
PAT PAT
So, you know I like to dance, right?
Yeah.
Well, when I was about your age, I was in this fancy ballet class, and there was a solo I really wanted. I KNEW I nailed my tryout, but the teacher gave it to some other girl instead.
After class, she pulled me aside and told me I didn't get the part because I just didn't have the body to be an elite dancer. The way she said it was so condescending, like she was doing me some big favor.

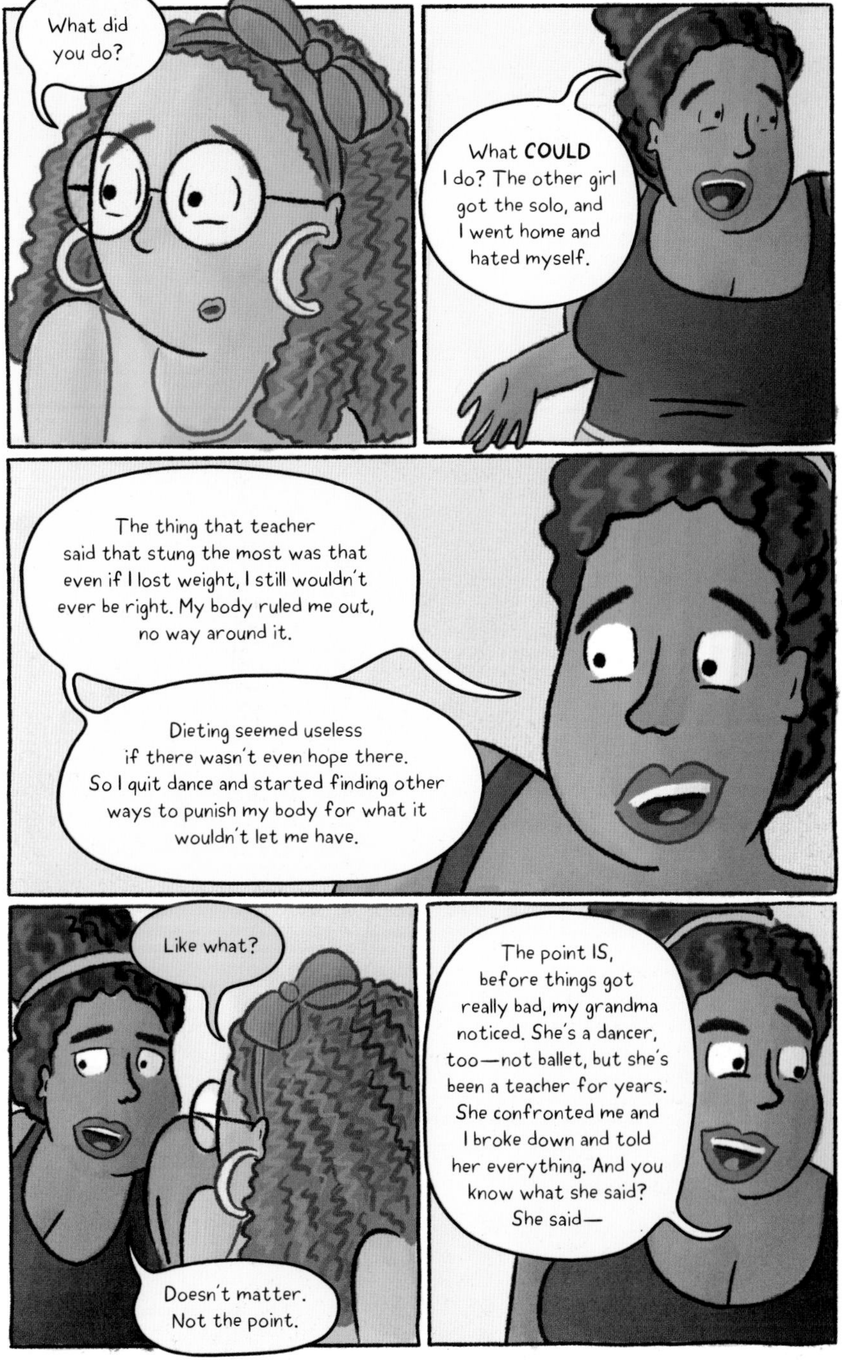
What did you do?
What **COULD** I do? The other girl got the solo, and I went home and hated myself.
The thing that teacher said that stung the most was that even if I lost weight, I still wouldn't ever be right. My body ruled me out, no way around it.
Dieting seemed useless if there wasn't even hope there. So I quit dance and started finding other ways to punish my body for what it wouldn't let me have.
Like what?
Doesn't matter. Not the point.
The point IS, before things got really bad, my grandma noticed. She's a dancer, too—not ballet, but she's been a teacher for years. She confronted me and I broke down and told her everything. And you know what she said? She said—

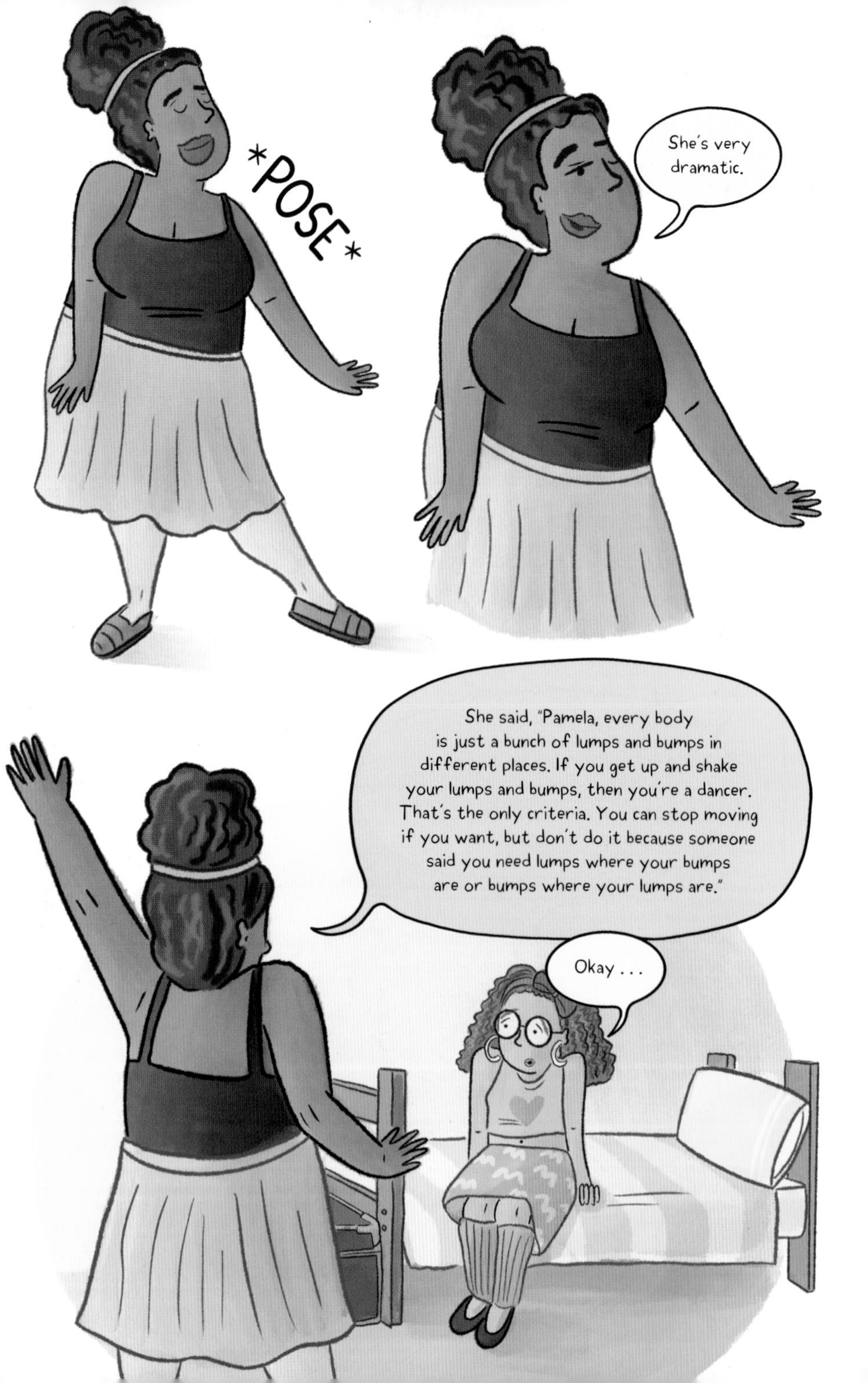
POSE
She's very dramatic.
She said, "Pamela, every body is just a bunch of lumps and bumps in different places. If you get up and shake your lumps and bumps, then you're a dancer. That's the only criteria. You can stop moving if you want, but don't do it because someone said you need lumps where your bumps are or bumps where your lumps are."
Okay . . .

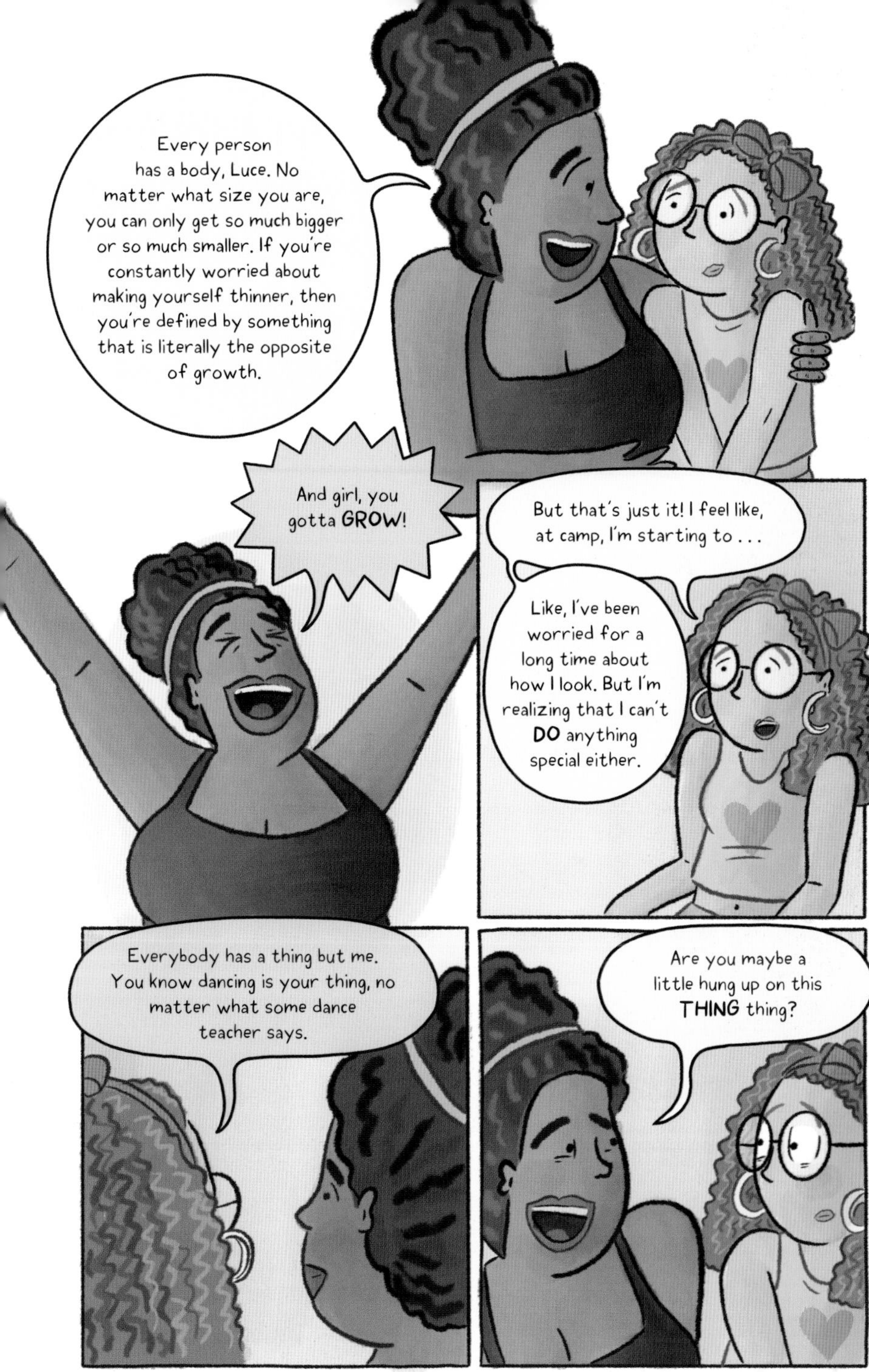
Every person has a body, Luce. No matter what size you are, you can only get so much bigger or so much smaller. If you're constantly worried about making yourself thinner, then you're defined by something that is literally the opposite of growth.
And girl, you gotta GROW!
But that's just it! I feel like, at camp, I'm starting to . . .
Like, I've been worried for a long time about how I look. But I'm realizing that I can't DO anything special either.
Everybody has a thing but me. You know dancing is your thing, no matter what some dance teacher says.
Are you maybe a little hung up on this THING thing?

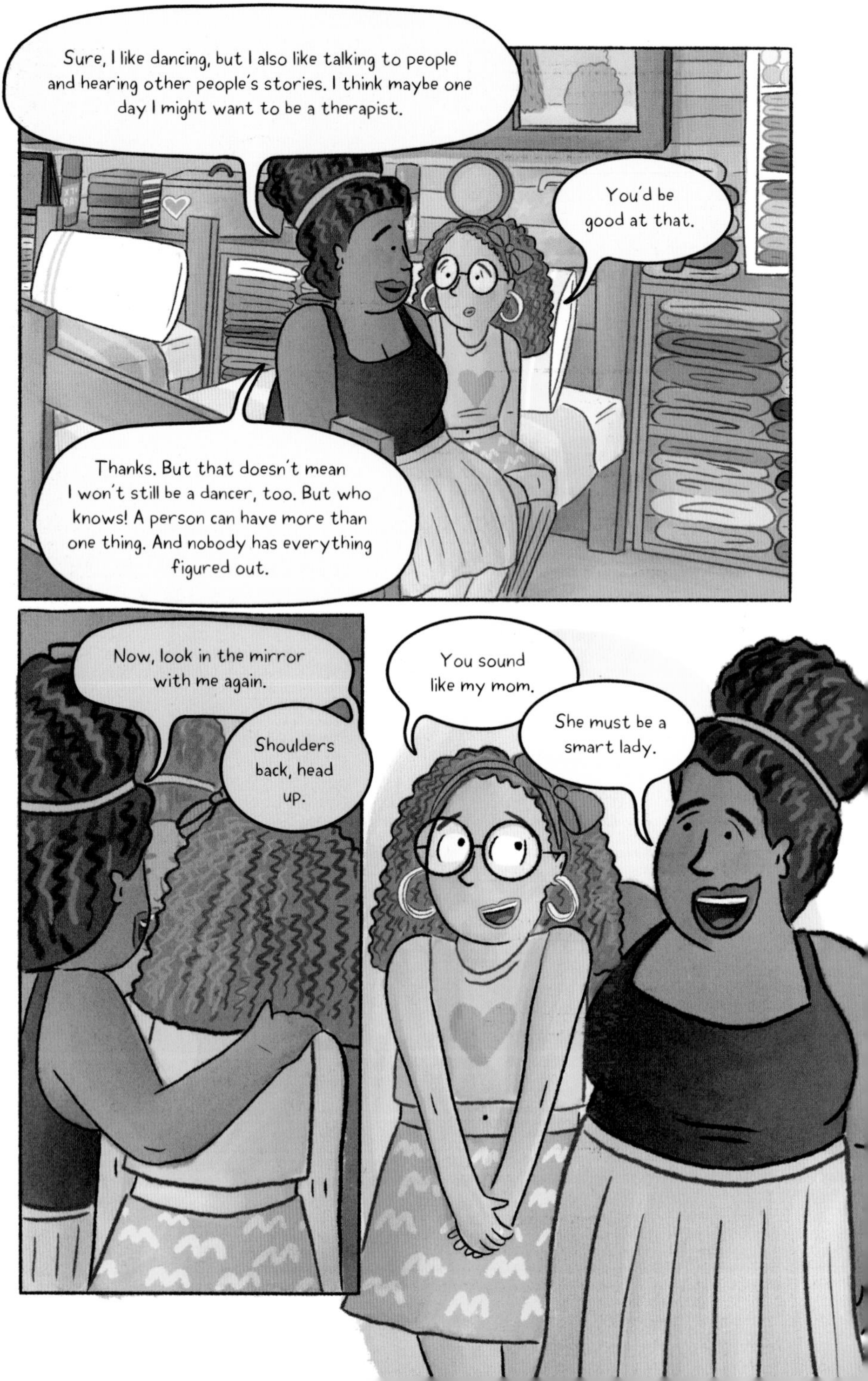
Sure, I like dancing, but I also like talking to people and hearing other people's stories. I think maybe one day I might want to be a therapist.
You'd be good at that.
Thanks. But that doesn't mean I won't still be a dancer, too. But who knows! A person can have more than one thing. And nobody has everything figured out.
Now, look in the mirror with me again.
Shoulders back, head up.
You sound like my mom.
She must be a smart lady.

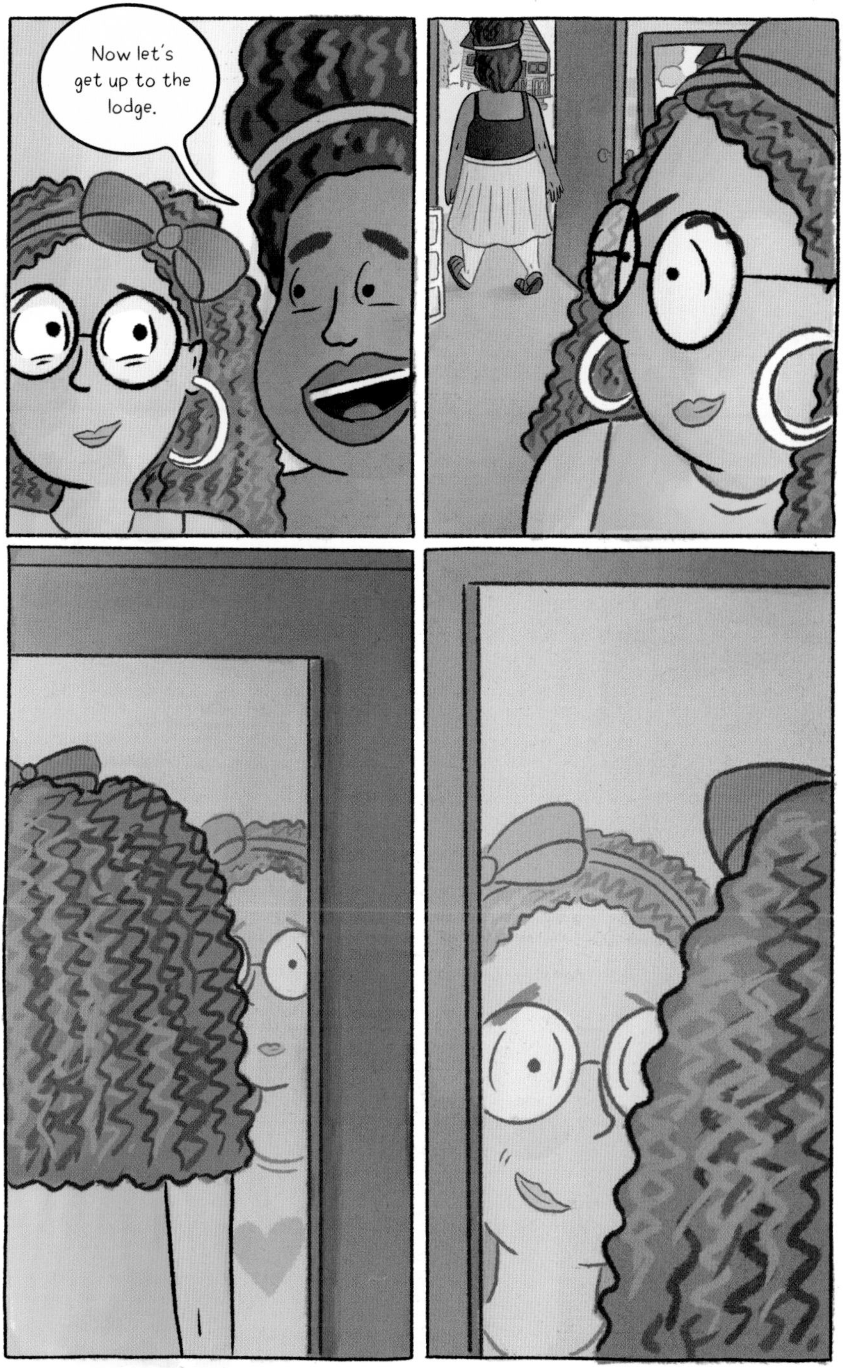
Now let's get up to the lodge.

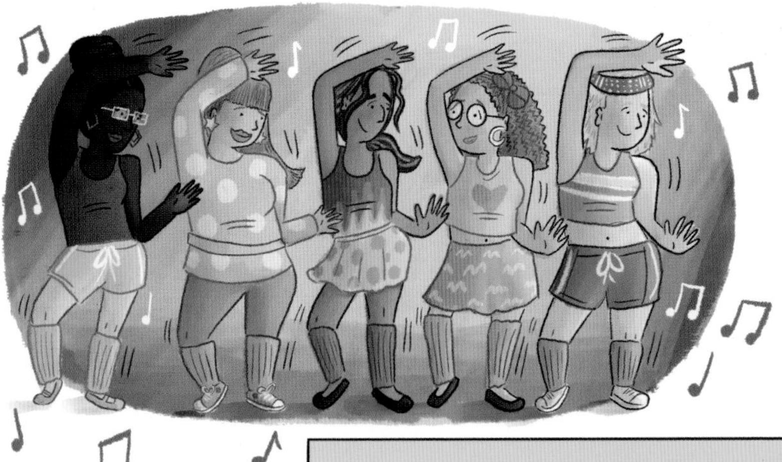

Our cabin's act was up first. My dancing **WAS** totally off beat, but I had so much fun, it didn't matter.

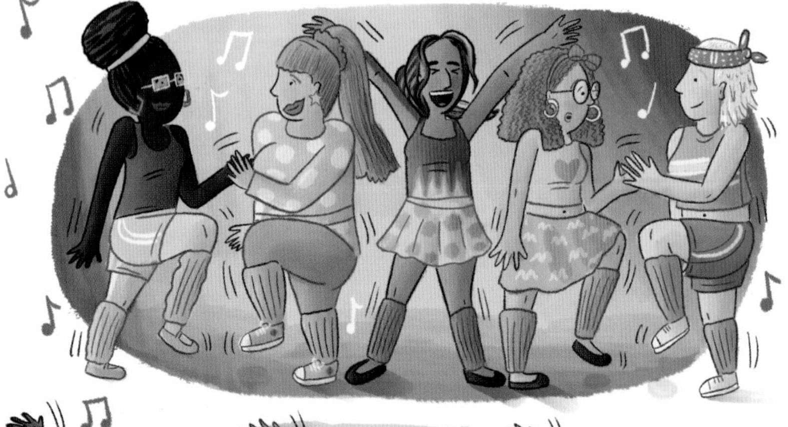

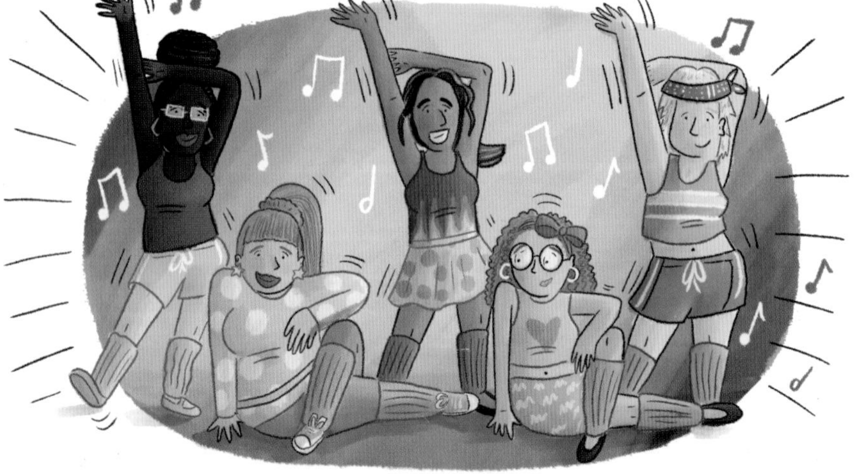

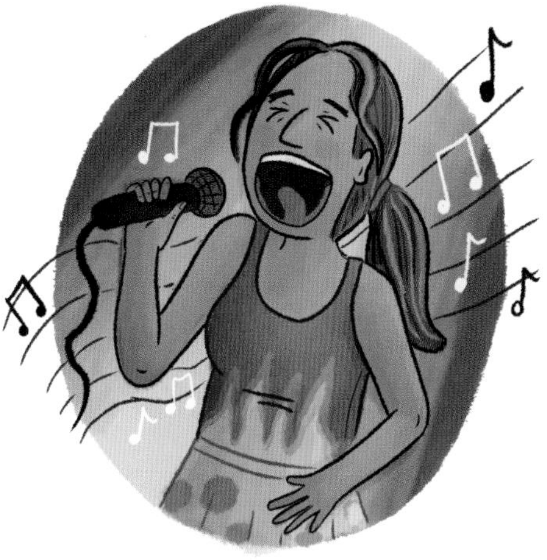

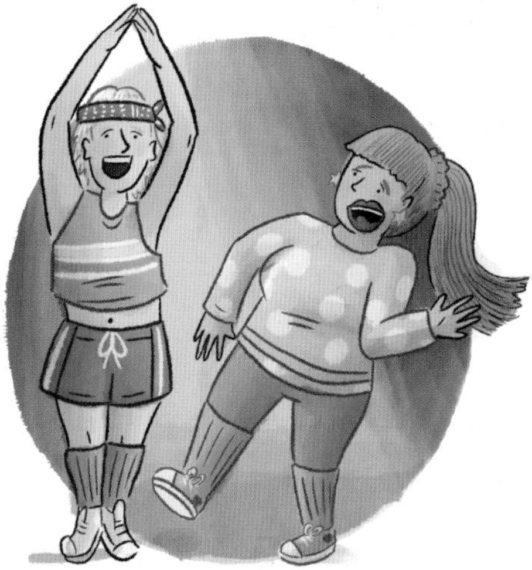

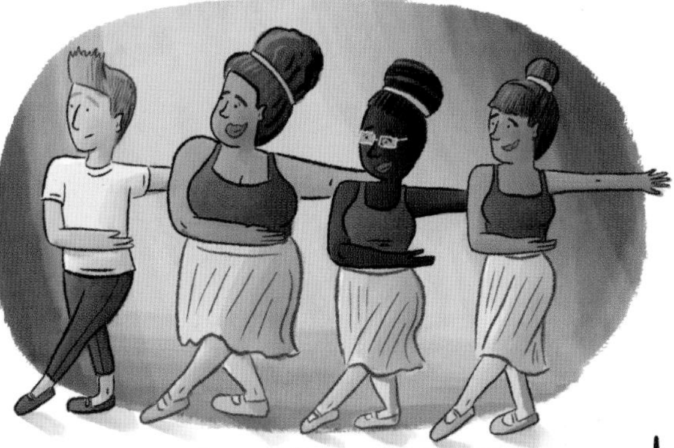

Some of my friends also had their own solo acts in the show, but I didn't. I took my seat in the audience and just watched.

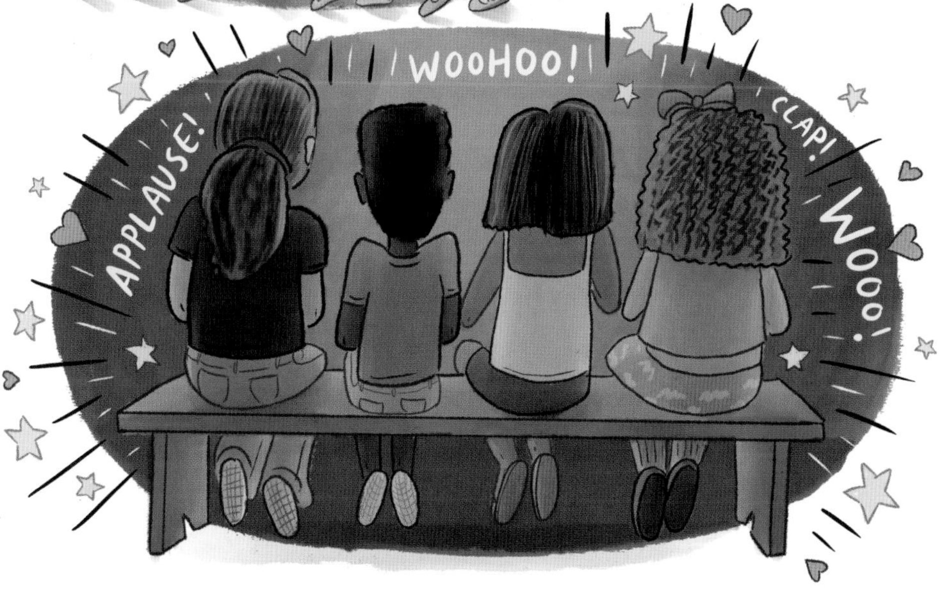
WOOHOO!
APPLAUSE!
CLAP!
WOOO!

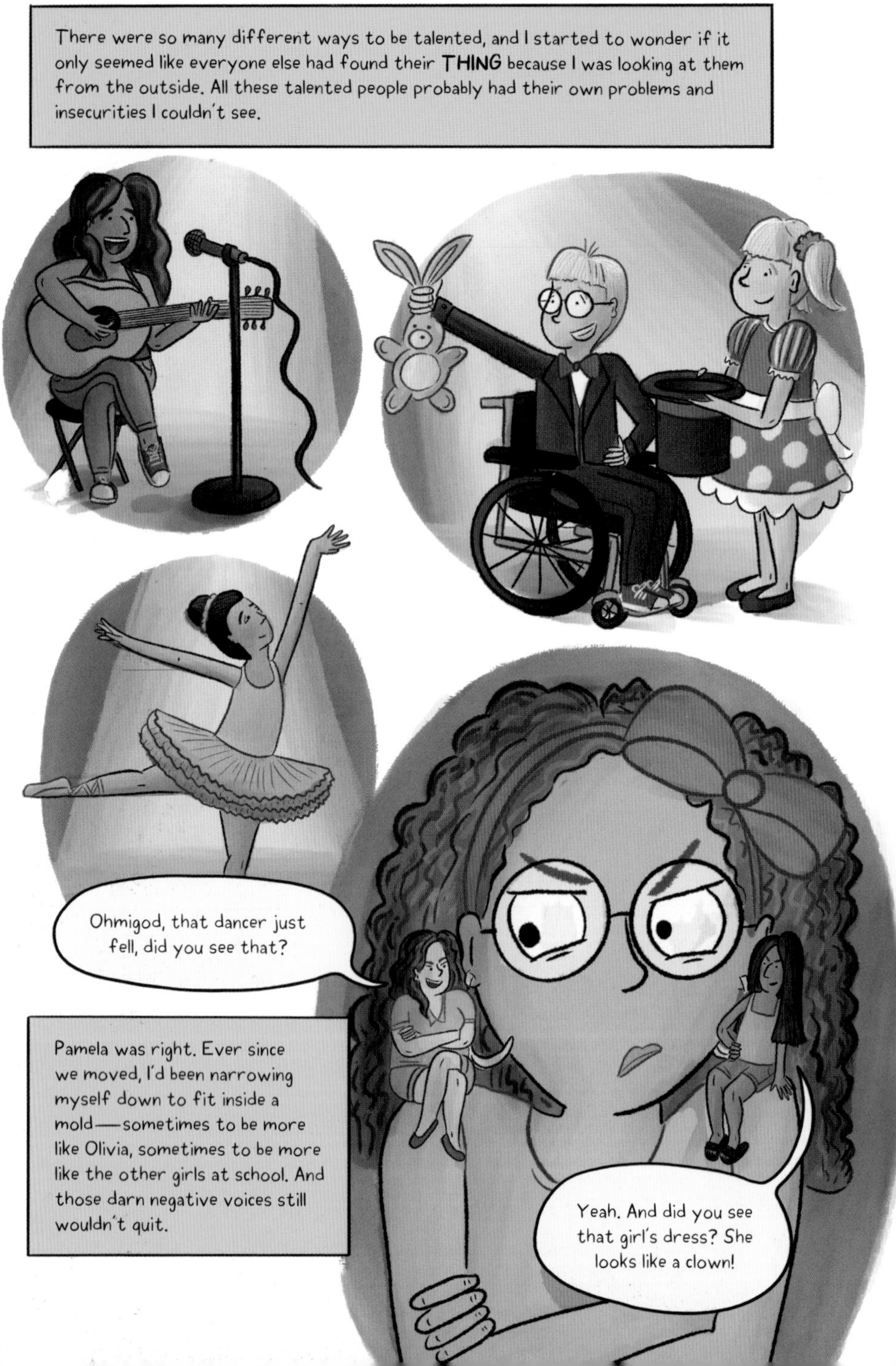
There were so many different ways to be talented, and I started to wonder if it only seemed like everyone else had found their THING because I was looking at them from the outside. All these talented people probably had their own problems and insecurities I couldn't see.
Ohmigod, that dancer just fell, did you see that?
Pamela was right. Ever since we moved, I'd been narrowing myself down to fit inside a mold—sometimes to be more like Olivia, sometimes to be more like the other girls at school. And those darn negative voices still wouldn't quit.
Yeah. And did you see that girl's dress? She looks like a clown!

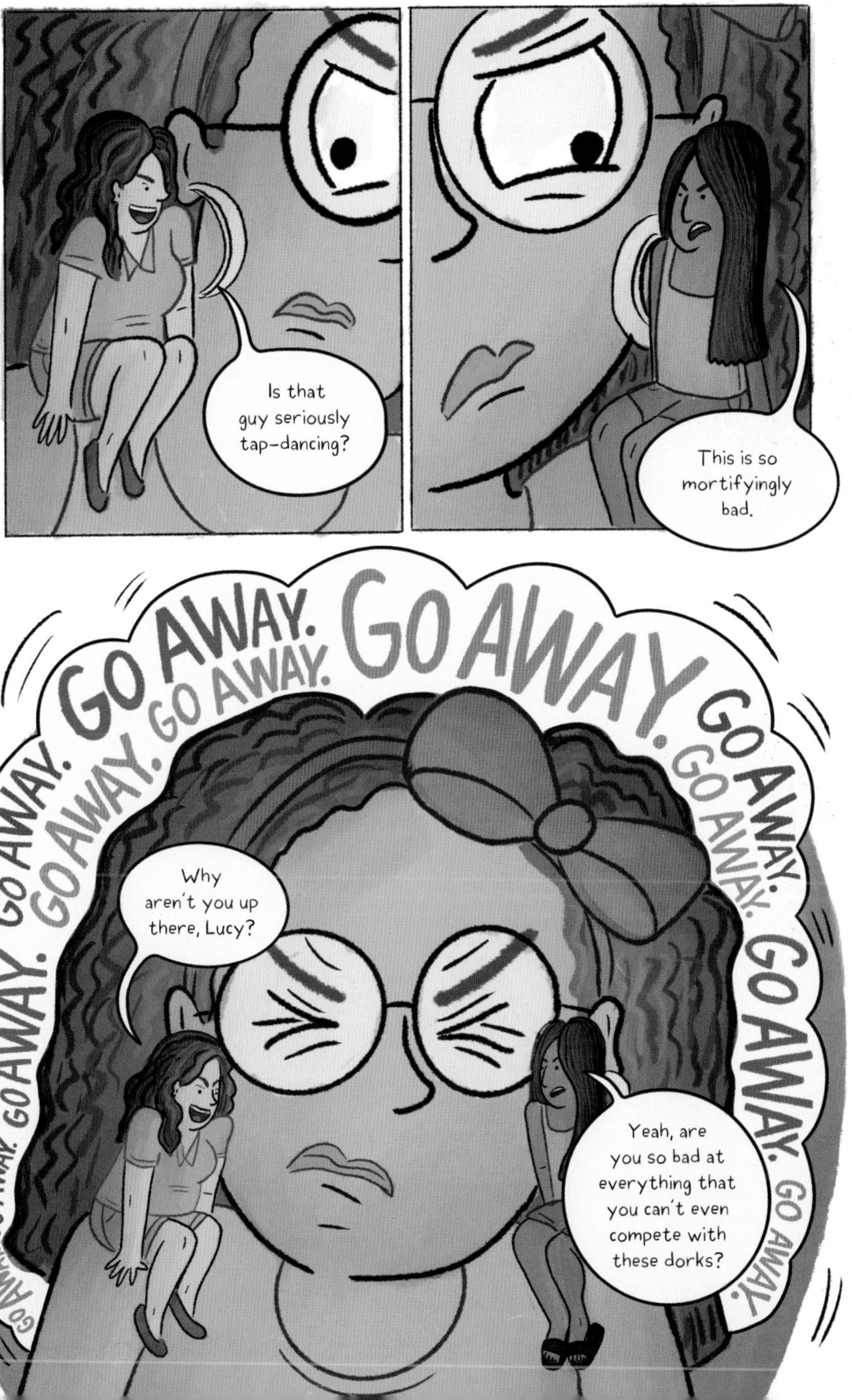

Is that guy seriously tap-dancing?
This is so mortifyingly bad.
GO AWAY. GO AWAY. GO AWAY. GO AWAY. GO AWAY. GO AWAY. GO AWAY. GO AWAY. GO AWAY.
GO AWAY. GO AWAY. GO AWAY. GO AWAY.
Why aren't you up there, Lucy?
Yeah, are you so bad at everything that you can't even compete with these dorks?

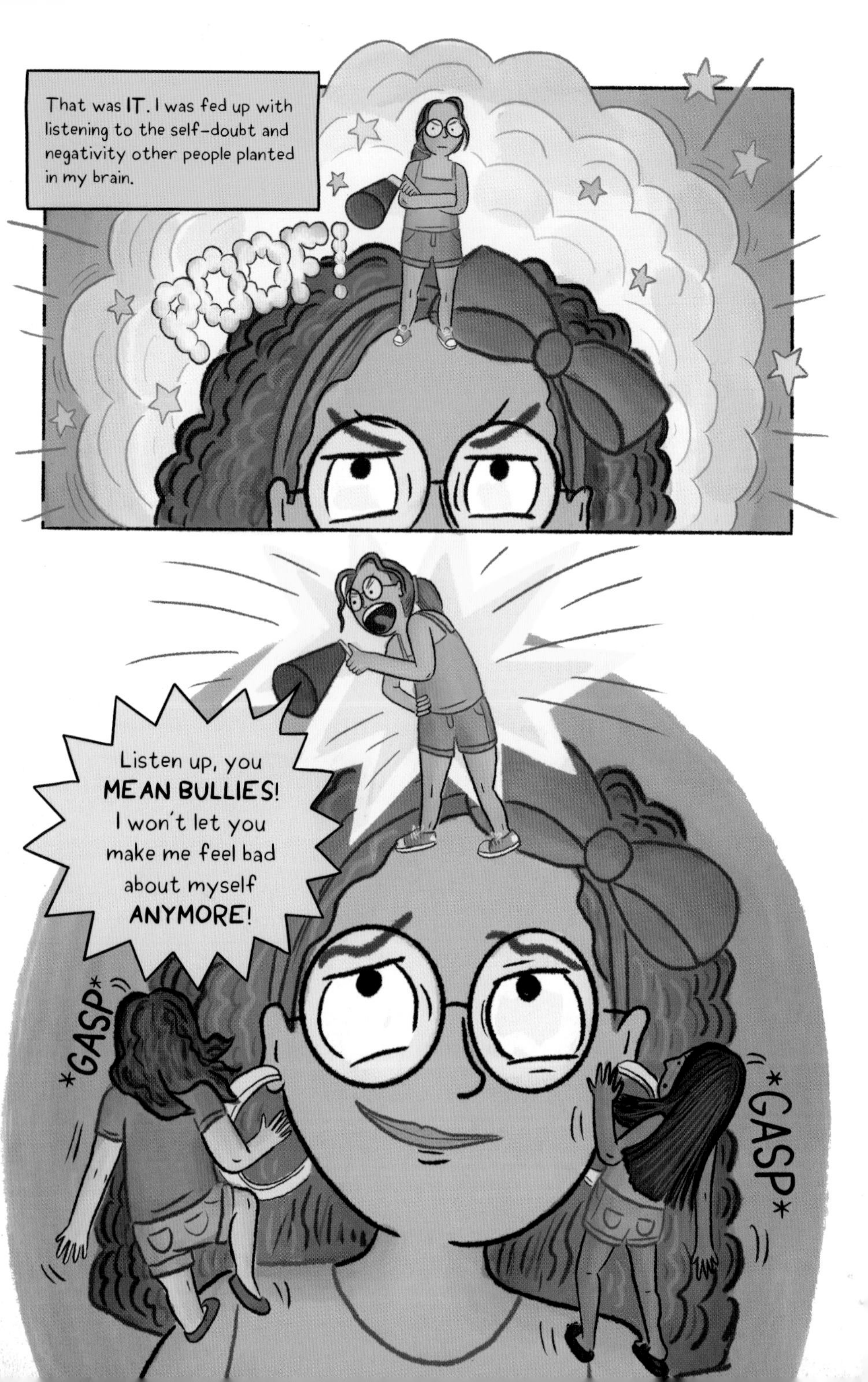
That was IT. I was fed up with listening to the self-doubt and negativity other people planted in my brain.
POOF!
Listen up, you MEAN BULLIES! I won't let you make me feel bad about myself ANYMORE!
GASP
GASP

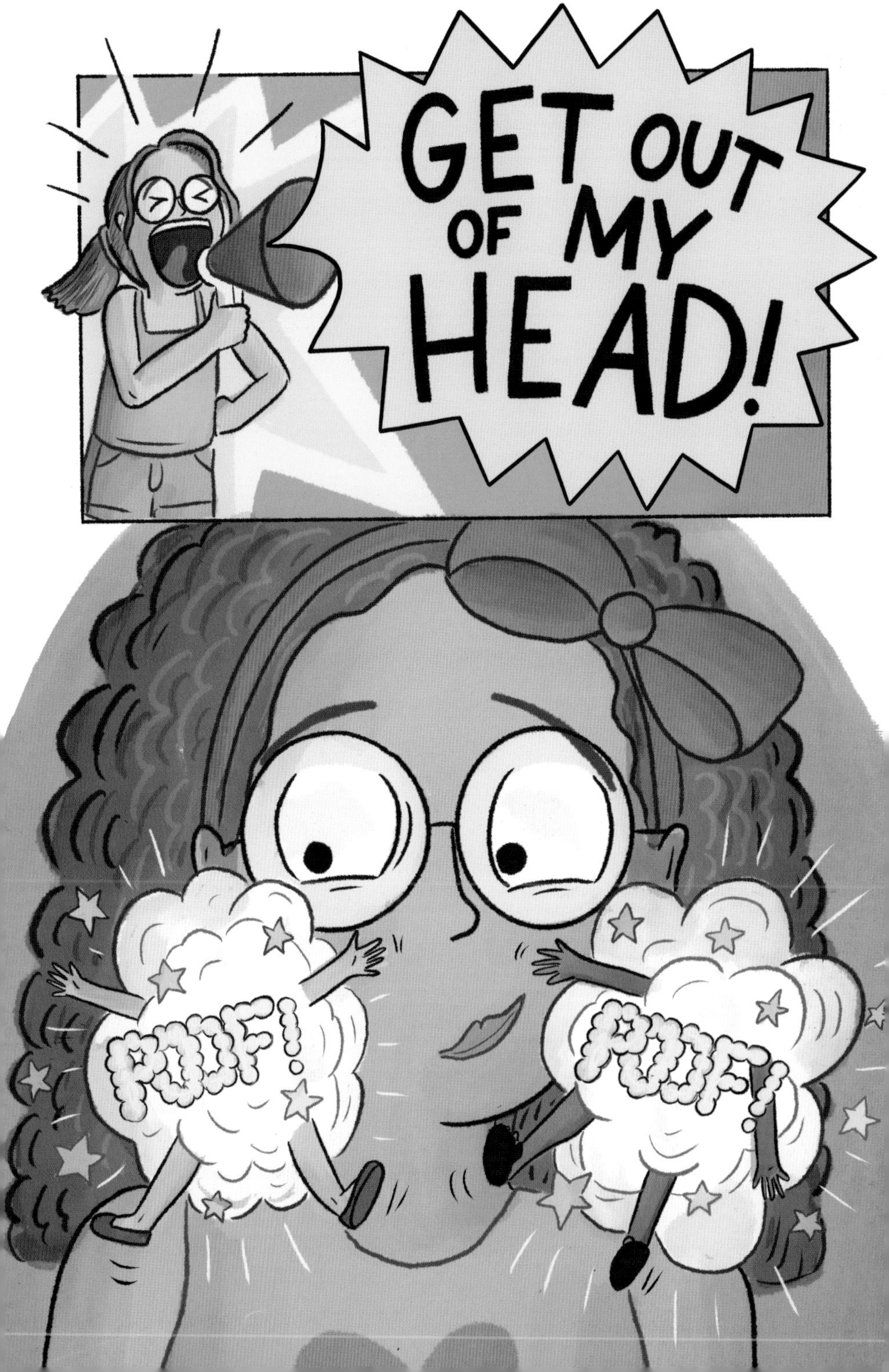
GET OUT OF MY HEAD!
POOF!
POOF!

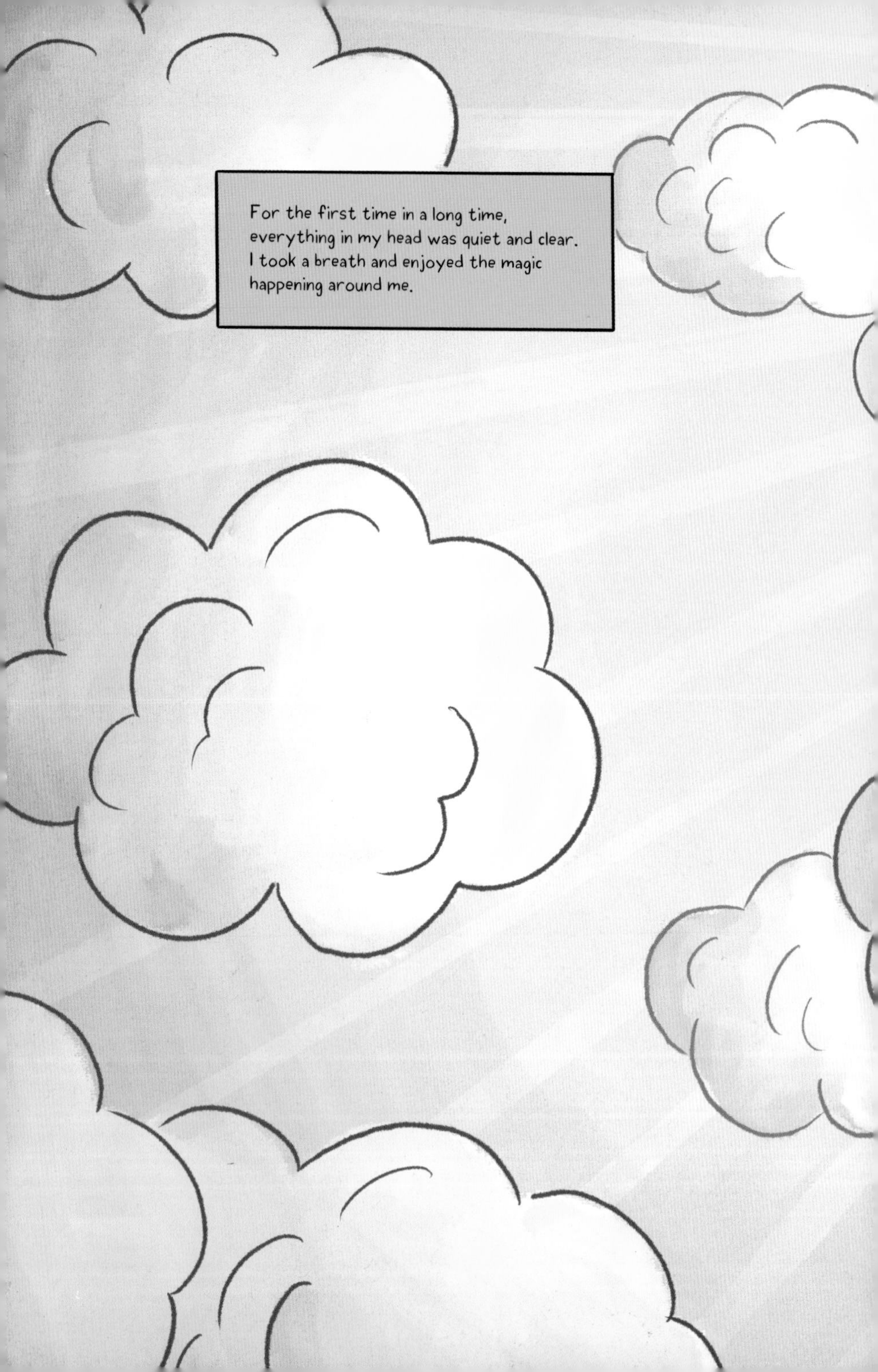
For the first time in a long time, everything in my head was quiet and clear. I took a breath and enjoyed the magic happening around me.

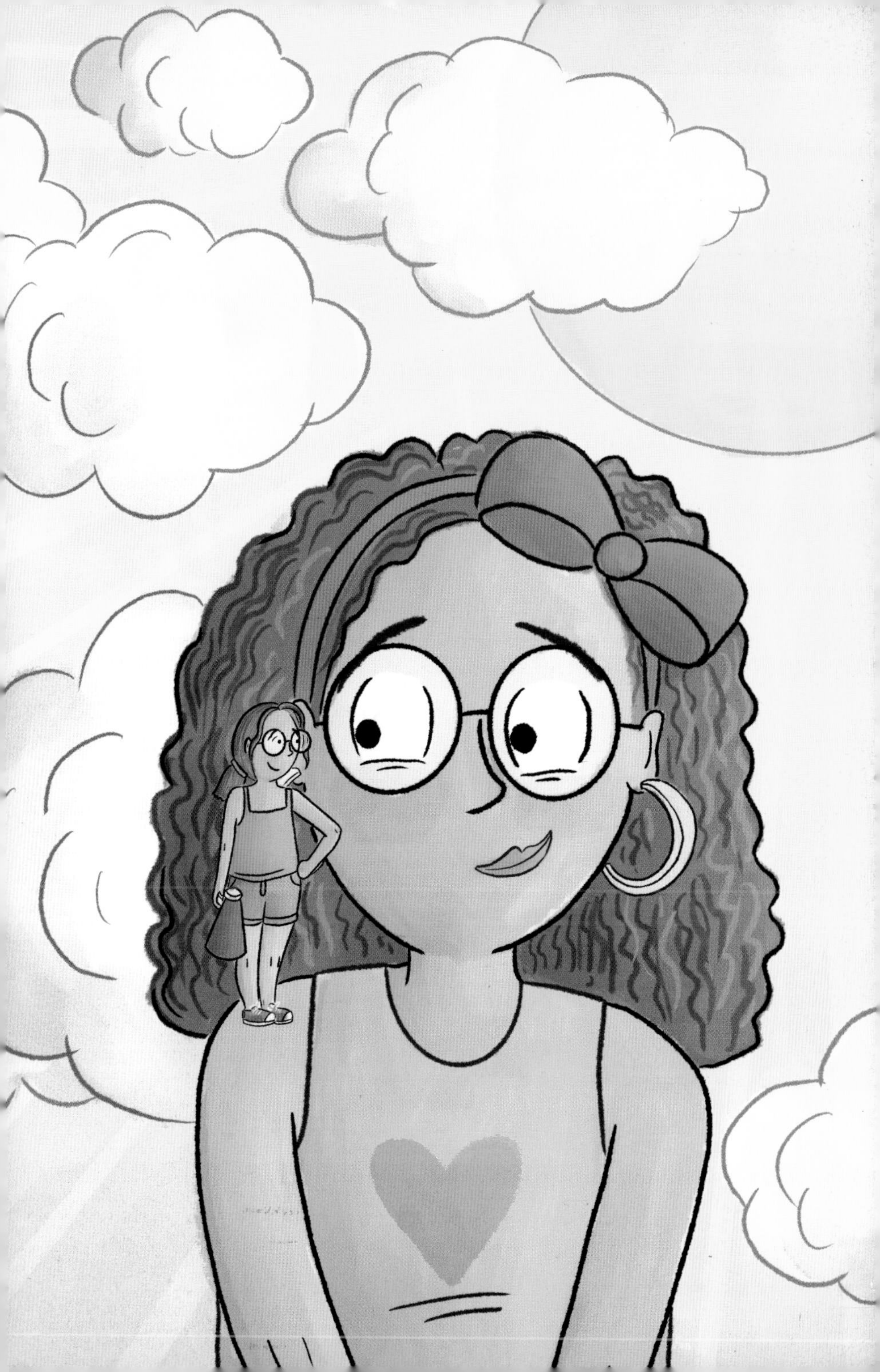

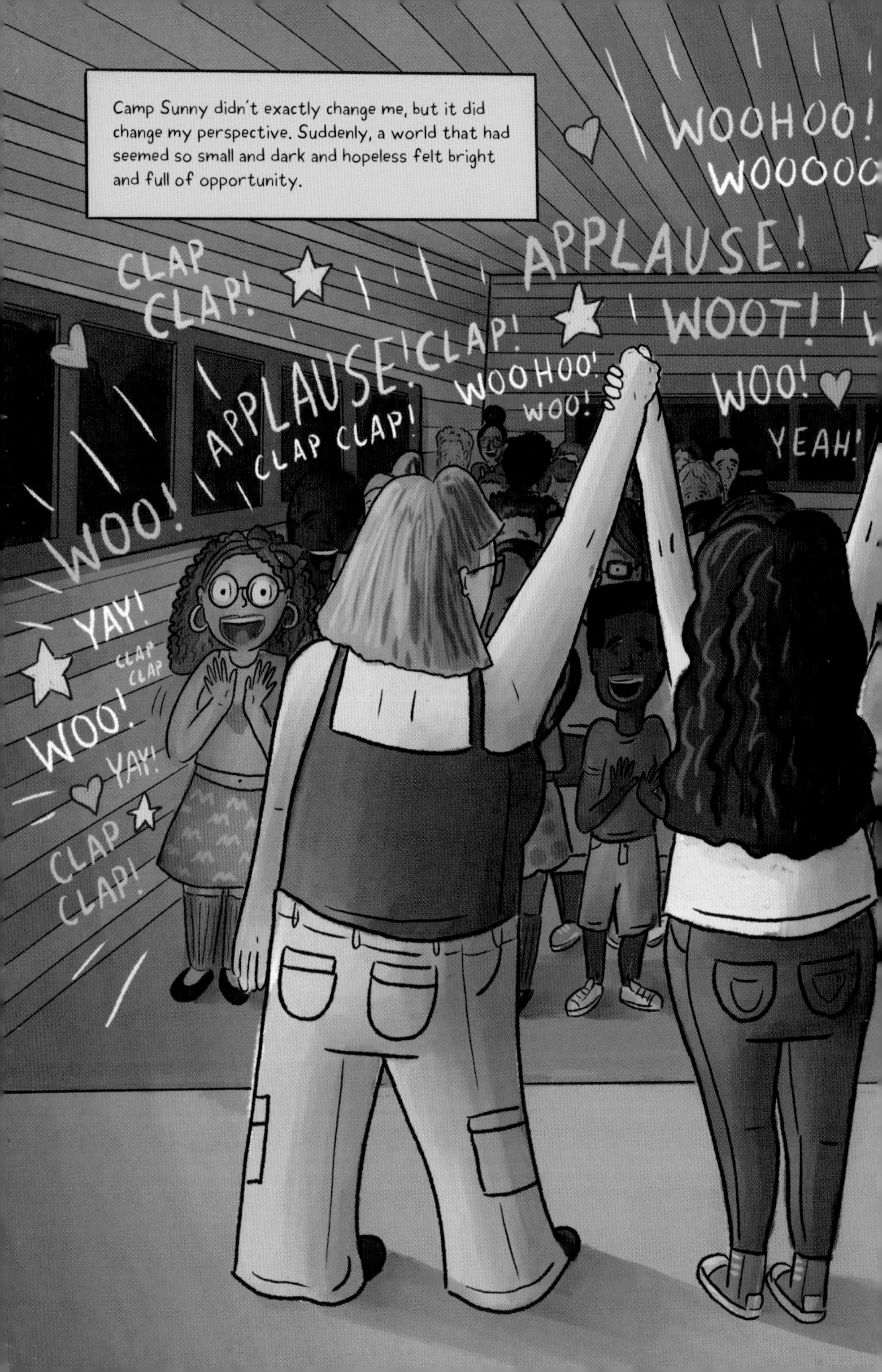
Camp Sunny didn't exactly change me, but it did change my perspective. Suddenly, a world that had seemed so small and dark and hopeless felt bright and full of opportunity.
WOOHOO!
CLAP CLAP!
APPLAUSE!
WOOT!
APPLAUSE!
CLAP!
WOOHOO!
WOO!
WOO!
YEAH!
CLAP CLAP!
WOO!
YAY!
CLAP CLAP
WOO!
YAY!
CLAP CLAP!

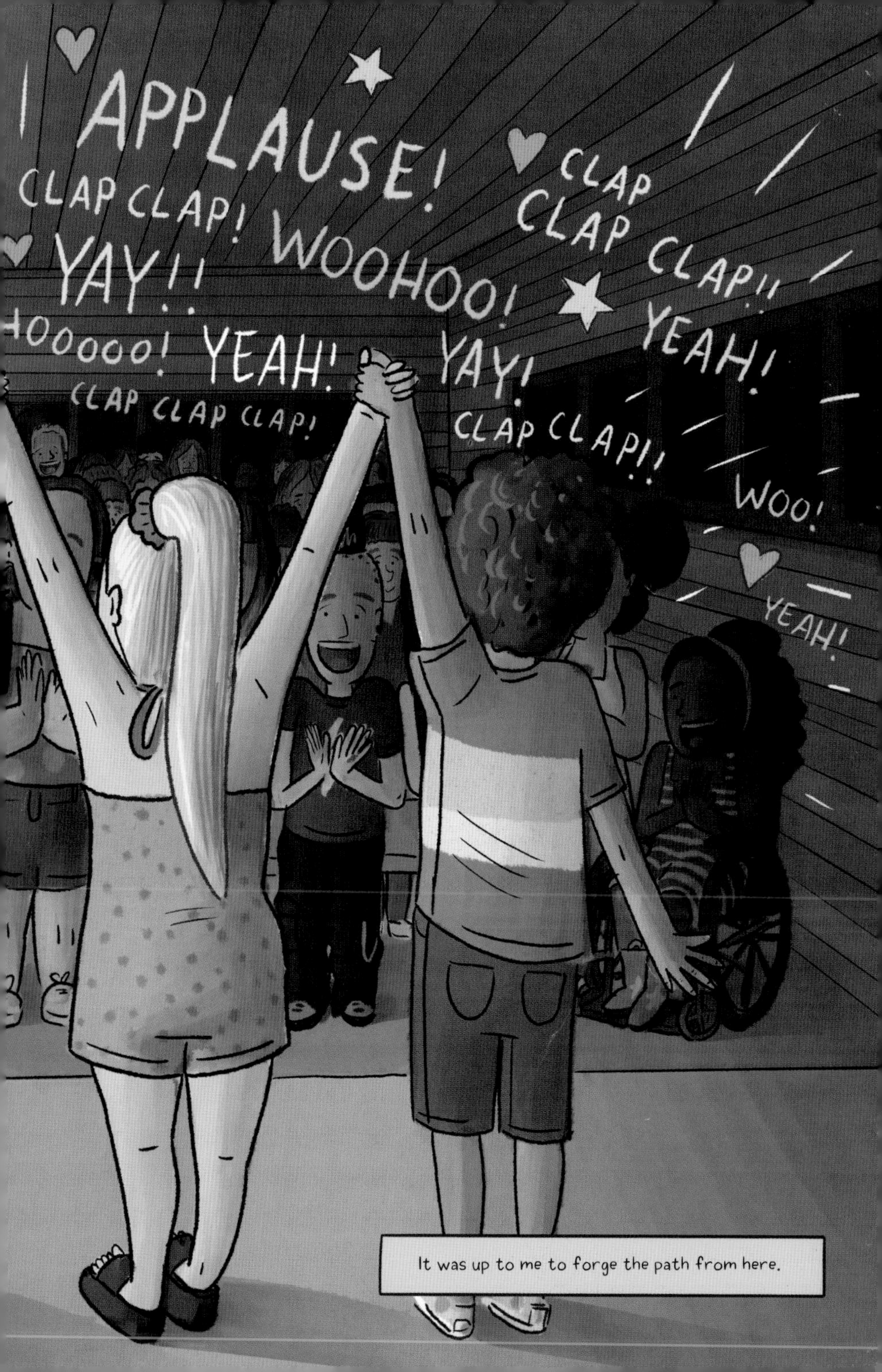
APPLAUSE!
CLAP CLAP!
YAY!!
WOOHOO!
CLAP CLAP CLAP CLAP!!
YEAH!
YAY!
CLAP CLAP CLAP!
CLAP CLAP!!
YEAH!
WOO!
YEAH!
It was up to me to forge the path from here.

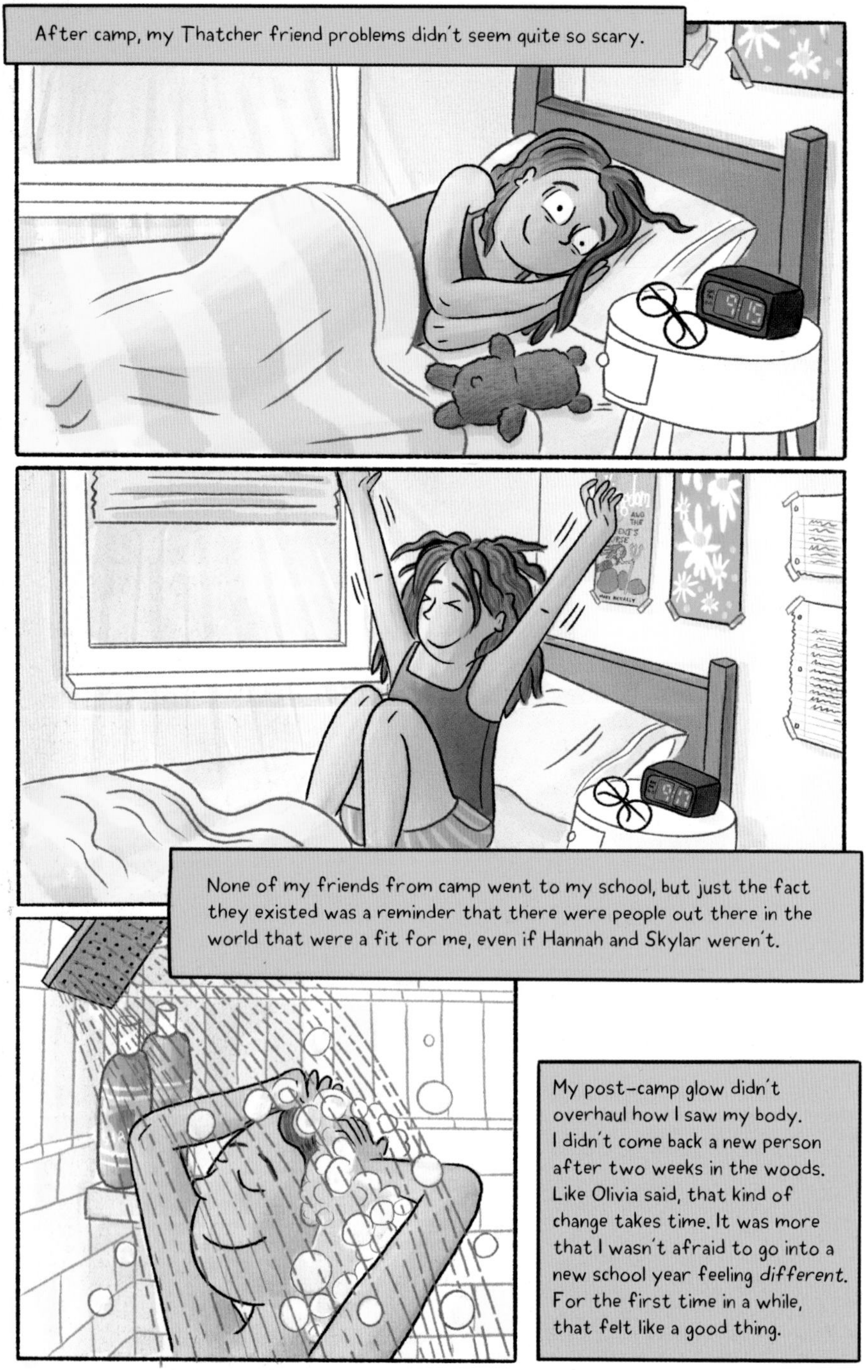
After camp, my Thatcher friend problems didn't seem quite so scary.
None of my friends from camp went to my school, but just the fact they existed was a reminder that there were people out there in the world that were a fit for me, even if Hannah and Skylar weren't.
My post-camp glow didn't overhaul how I saw my body. I didn't come back a new person after two weeks in the woods. Like Olivia said, that kind of change takes time. It was more that I wasn't afraid to go into a new school year feeling *different*. For the first time in a while, that felt like a good thing.

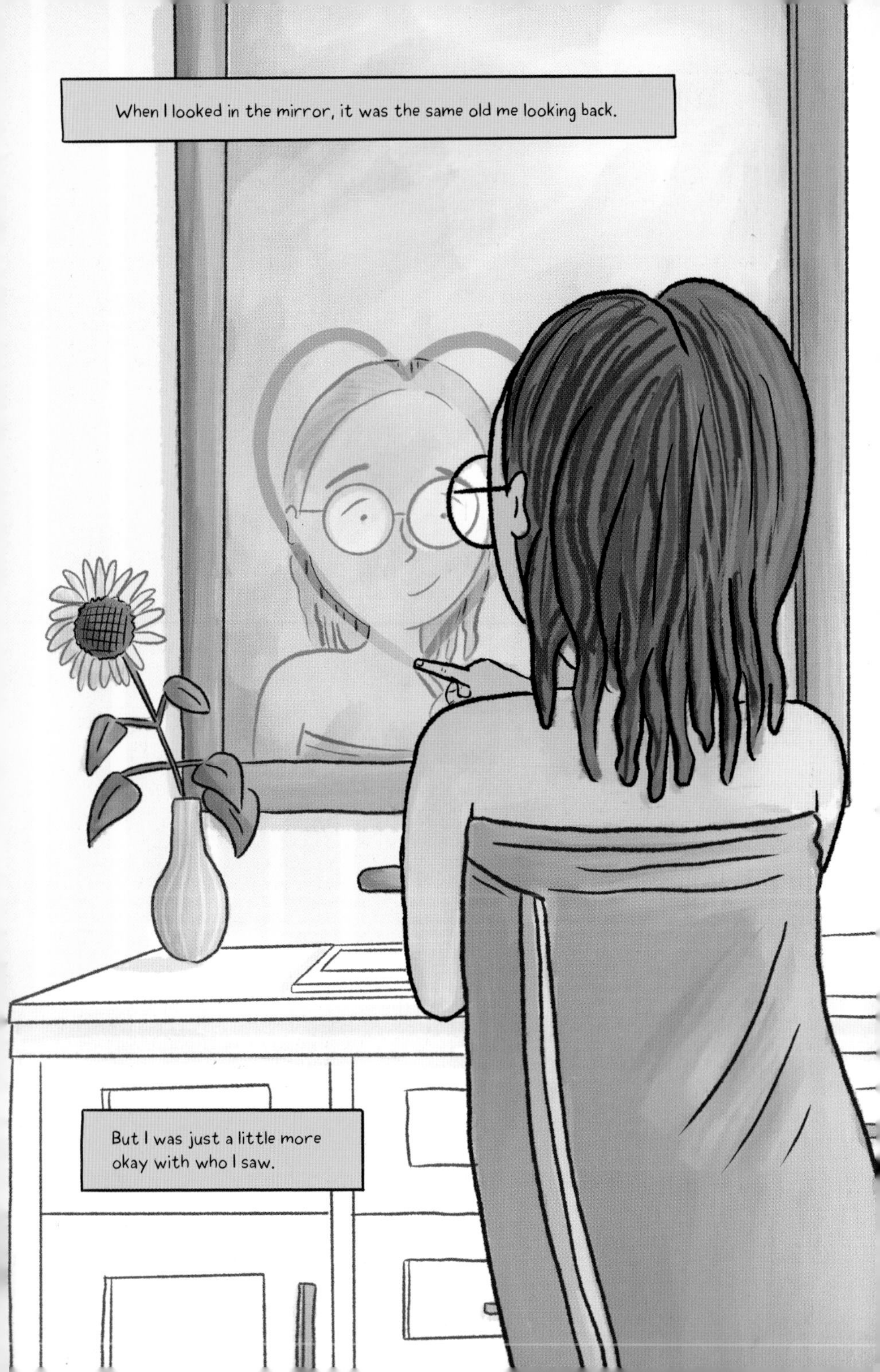
When I looked in the mirror, it was the same old me looking back.
But I was just a little more okay with who I saw.

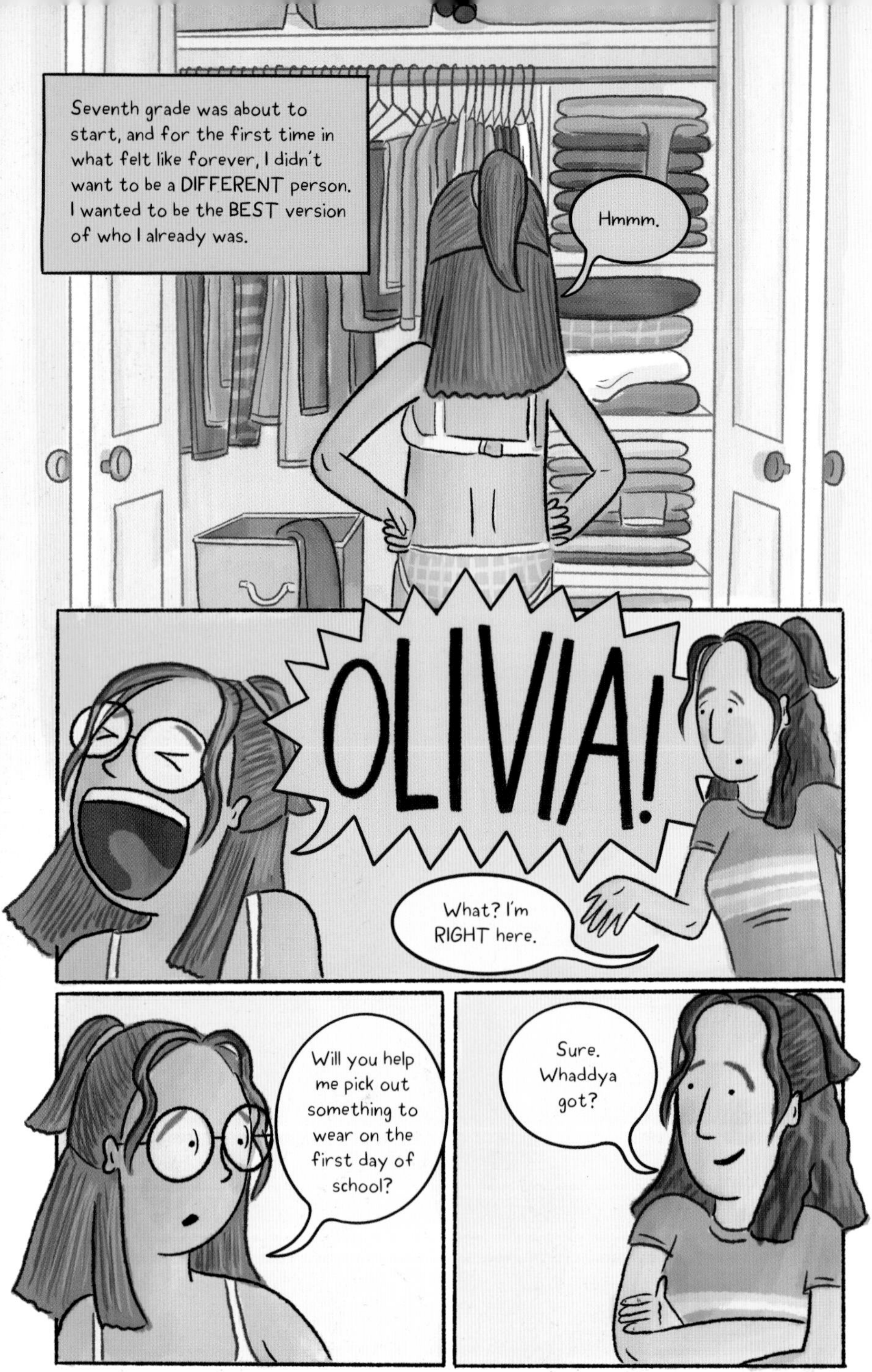
Seventh grade was about to start, and for the first time in what felt like forever, I didn't want to be a DIFFERENT person. I wanted to be the BEST version of who I already was.
Hmmm.
OLIVIA!
What? I'm RIGHT here.
Will you help me pick out something to wear on the first day of school?
Sure. Whaddya got?

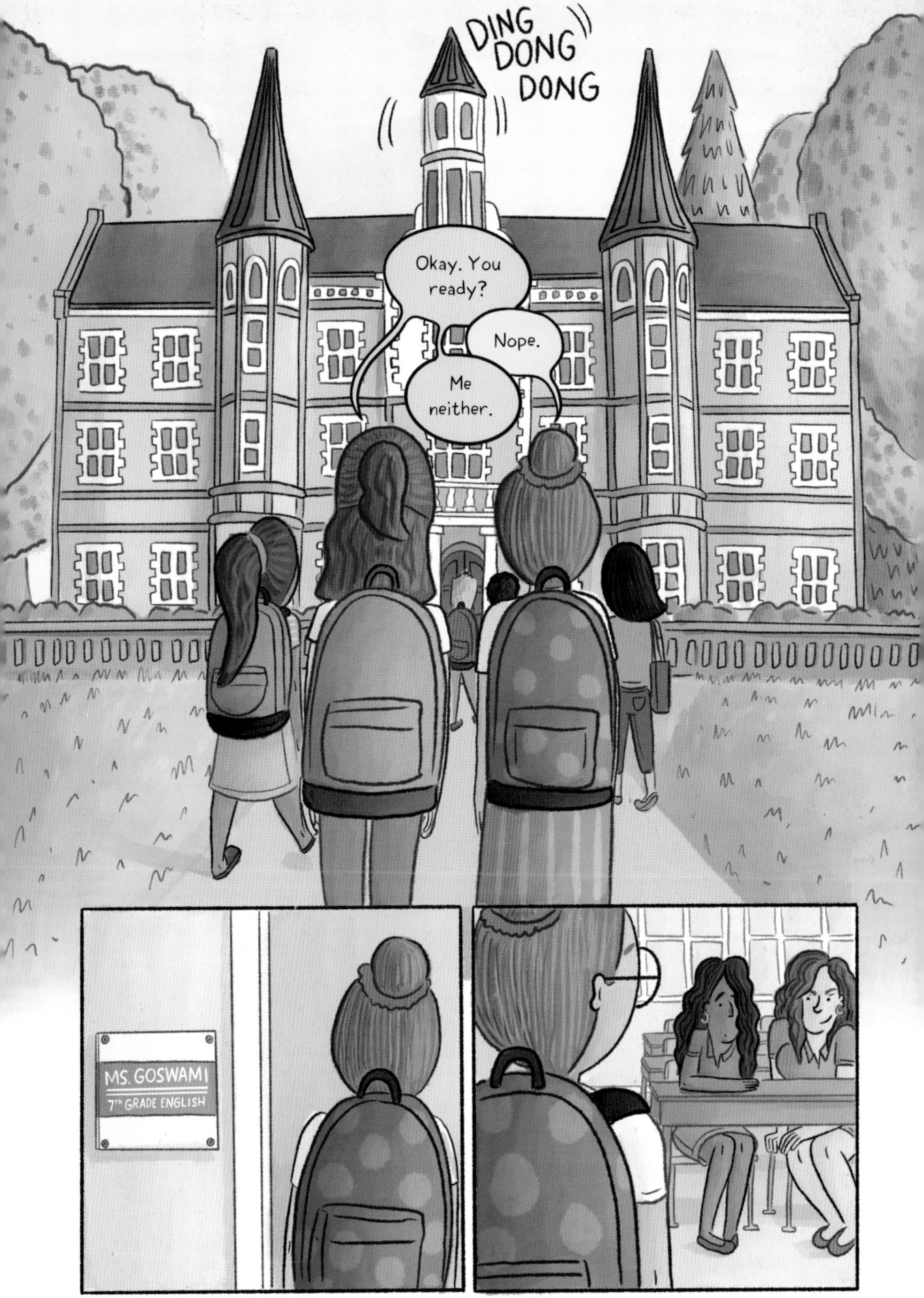
DING DONG DONG
Okay. You ready?
Nope.
Me neither.
MS. GOSWAMI
7TH GRADE ENGLISH

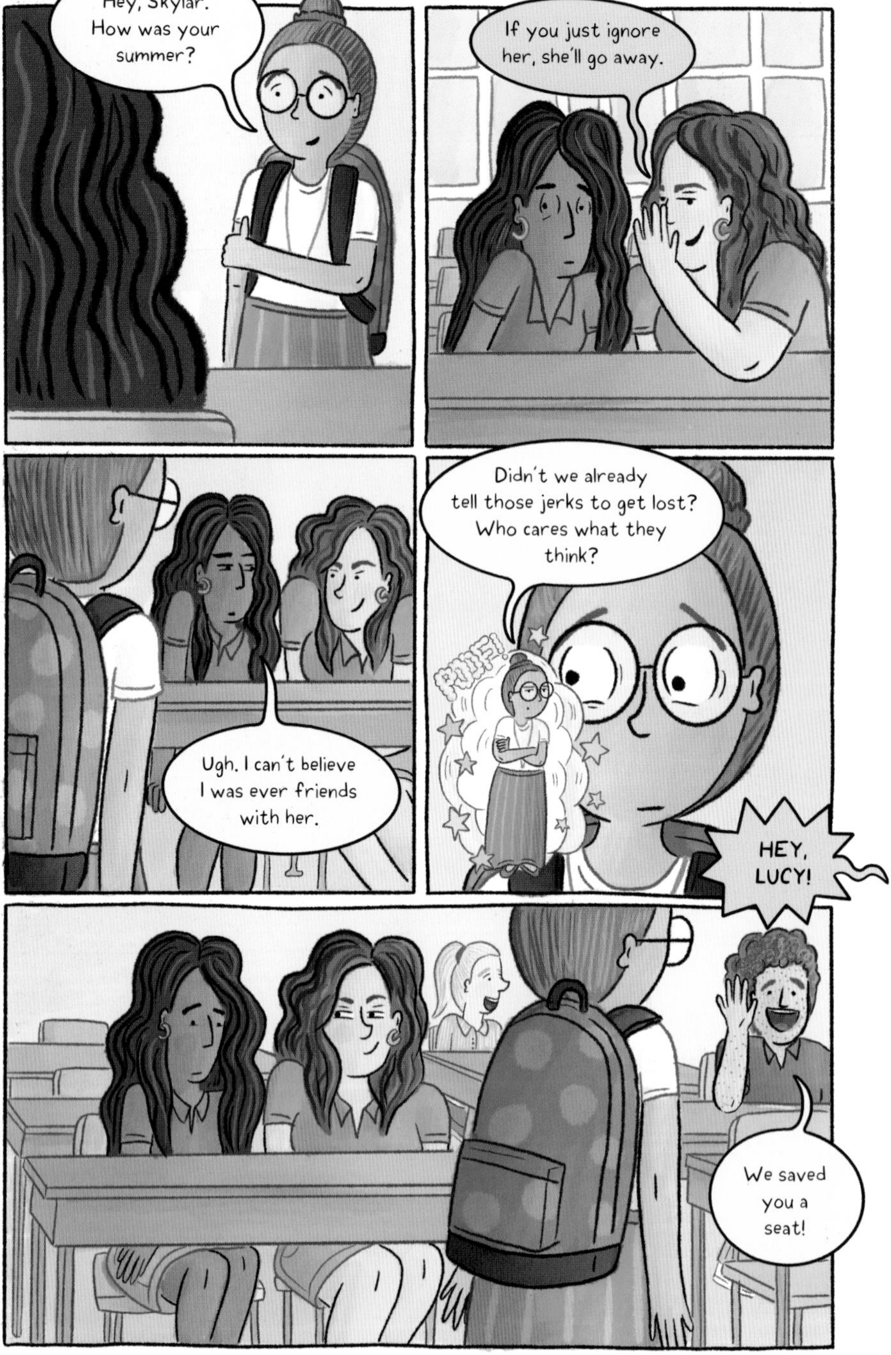
Hey, Skylar. How was your summer?
If you just ignore her, she'll go away.
Ugh. I can't believe I was ever friends with her.
Didn't we already tell those jerks to get lost? Who cares what they think?
HEY, LUCY!
We saved you a seat!

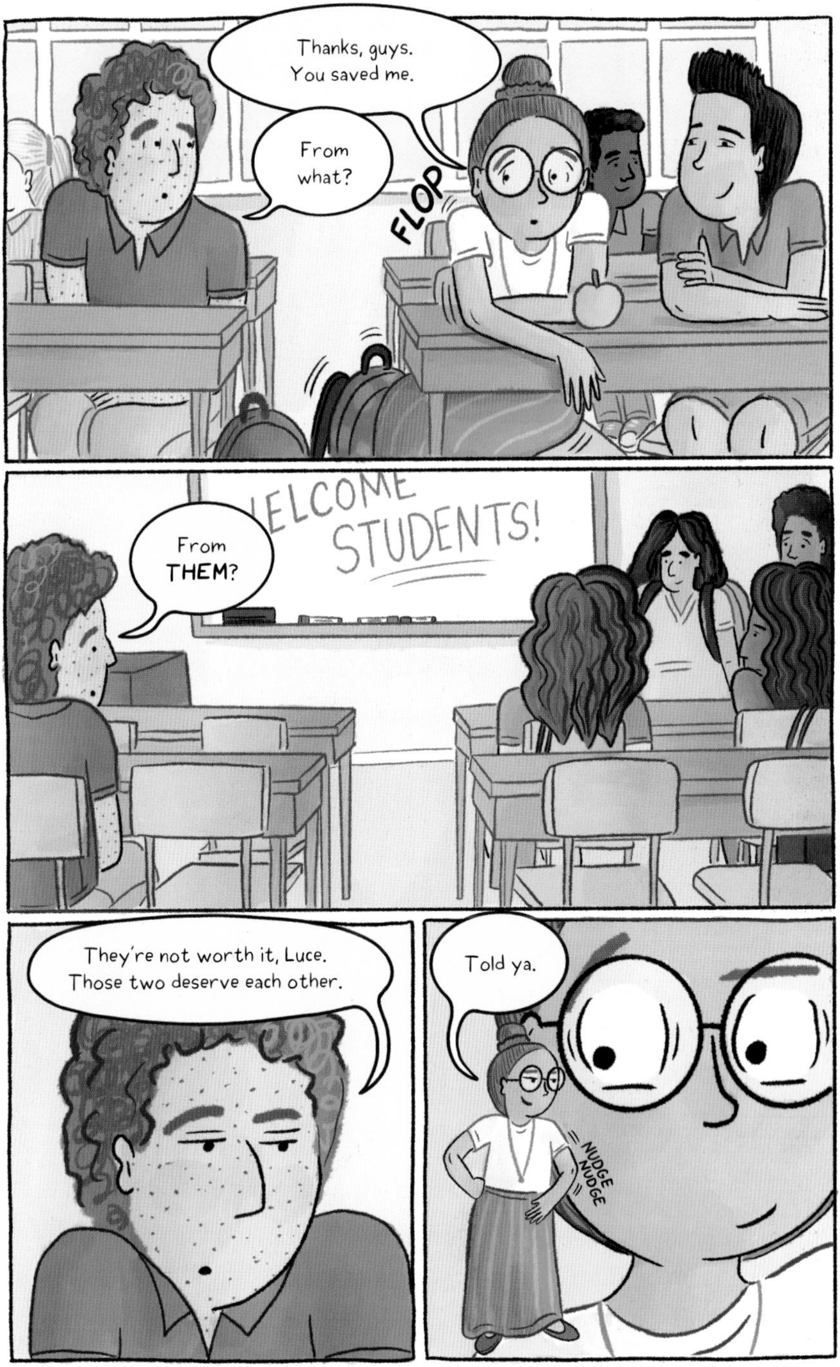
Thanks, guys. You saved me.
From what?
FLOP
ELCOME STUDENTS!
From THEM?
They're not worth it, Luce. Those two deserve each other.
Told ya.
NUDGE NUDGE

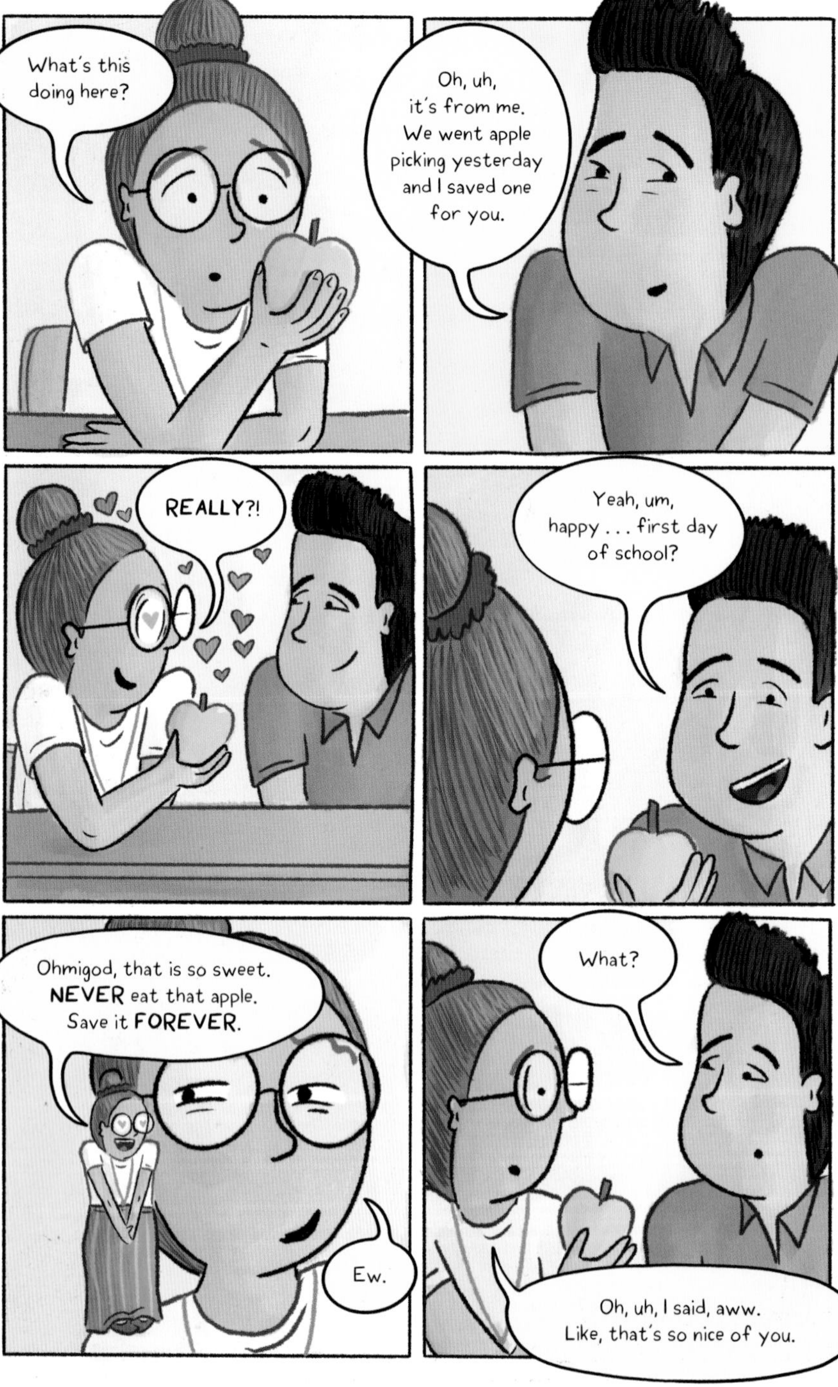
What's this doing here?
Oh, uh, it's from me. We went apple picking yesterday and I saved one for you.
REALLY?!
Yeah, um, happy . . . first day of school?
Ohmigod, that is so sweet. **NEVER** eat that apple. Save it **FOREVER**.
Ew.
What?
Oh, uh, I said, aww. Like, that's so nice of you.

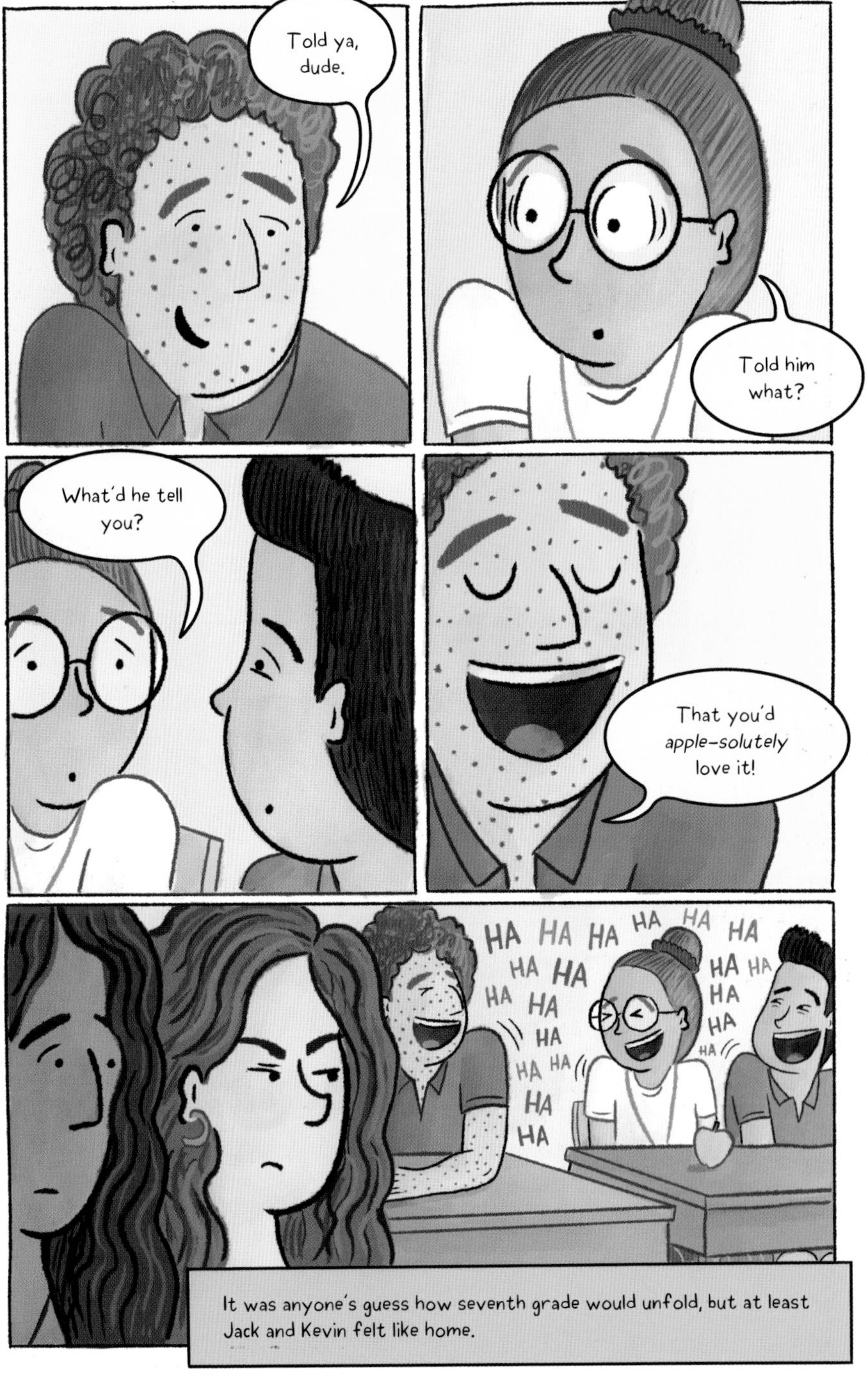
Told ya, dude.
Told him what?
What'd he tell you?
That you'd *apple-solutely* love it!
HA HA HA HA HA HA HA HA HA HA HA HA HA HA HA HA HA HA HA HA HA HA
It was anyone's guess how seventh grade would unfold, but at least Jack and Kevin felt like home.

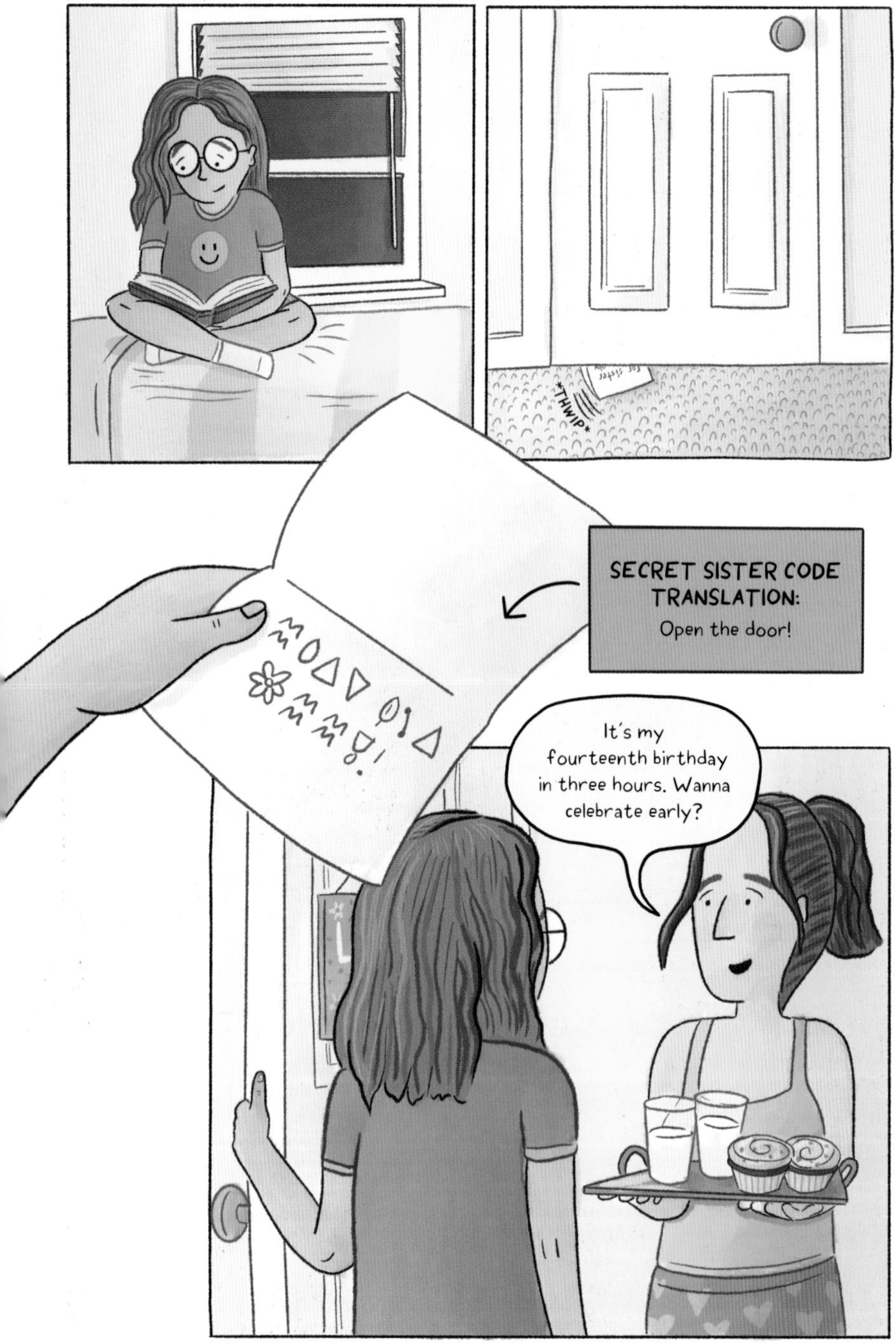
THWIP
SECRET SISTER CODE TRANSLATION:
Open the door!
It's my fourteenth birthday in three hours. Wanna celebrate early?

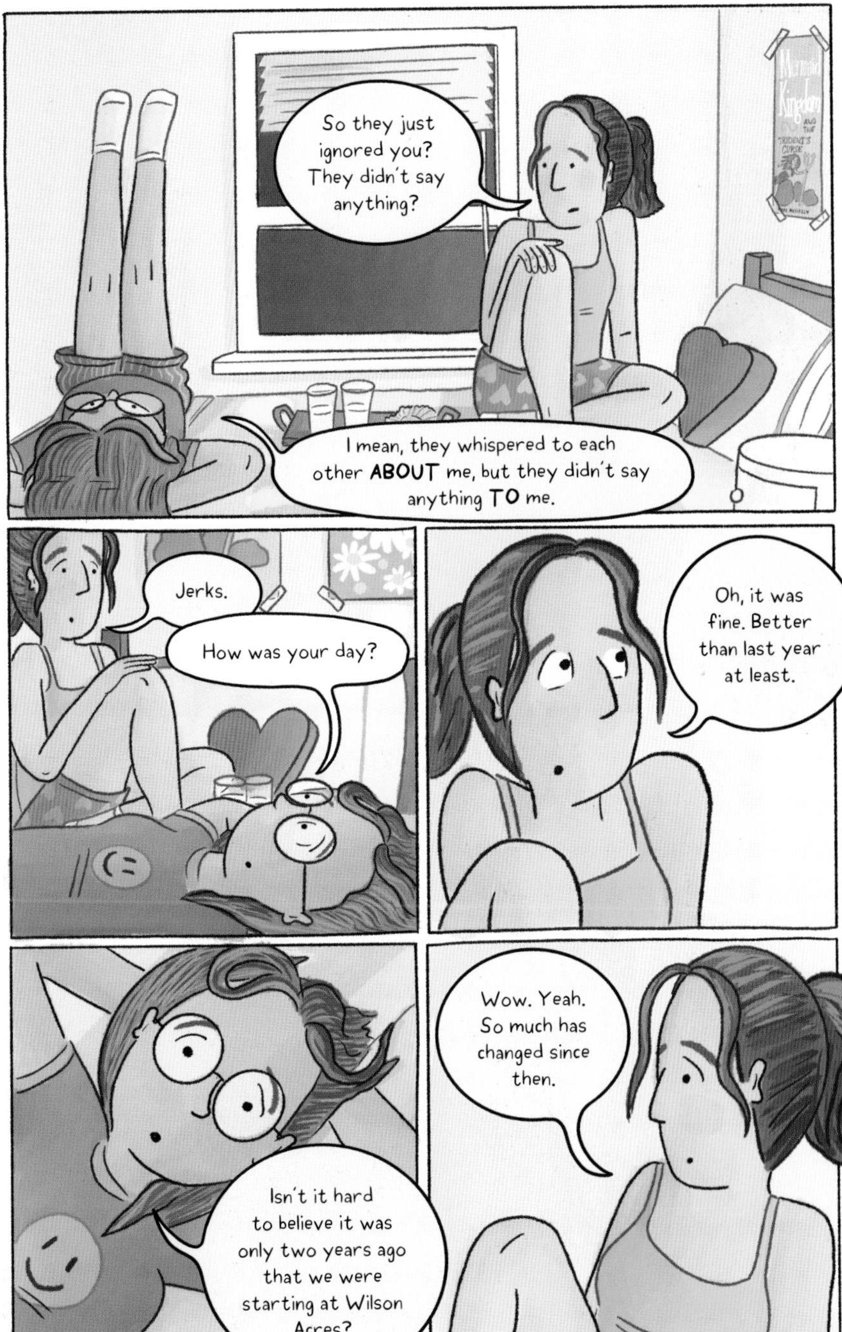
So they just ignored you? They didn't say anything?
I mean, they whispered to each other ABOUT me, but they didn't say anything TO me.
Jerks.
How was your day?
Oh, it was fine. Better than last year at least.
Wow. Yeah. So much has changed since then.
Isn't it hard to believe it was only two years ago that we were starting at Wilson Acres?

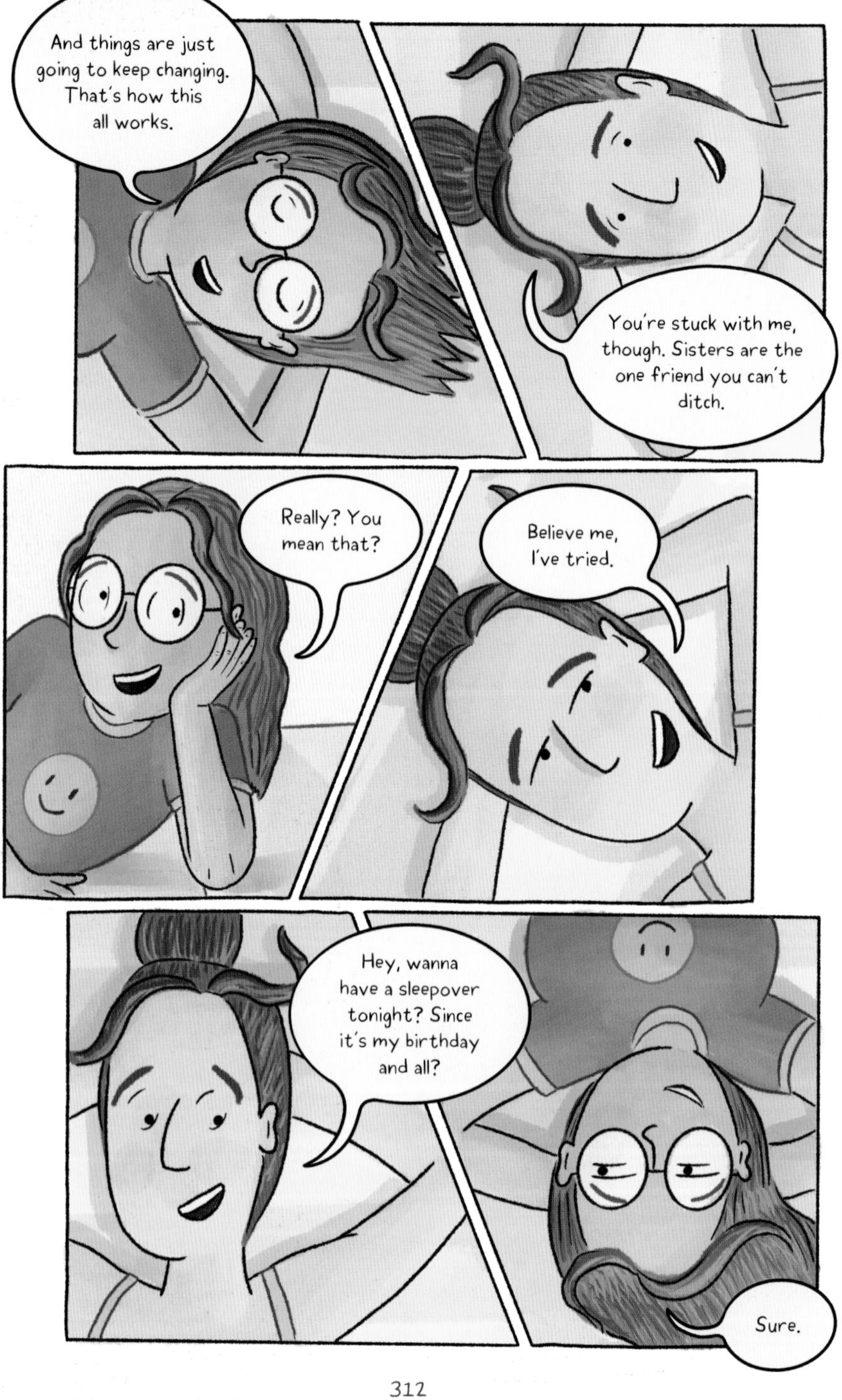
And things are just going to keep changing. That's how this all works.
You're stuck with me, though. Sisters are the one friend you can't ditch.
Really? You mean that?
Believe me, I've tried.
Hey, wanna have a sleepover tonight? Since it's my birthday and all?
Sure.

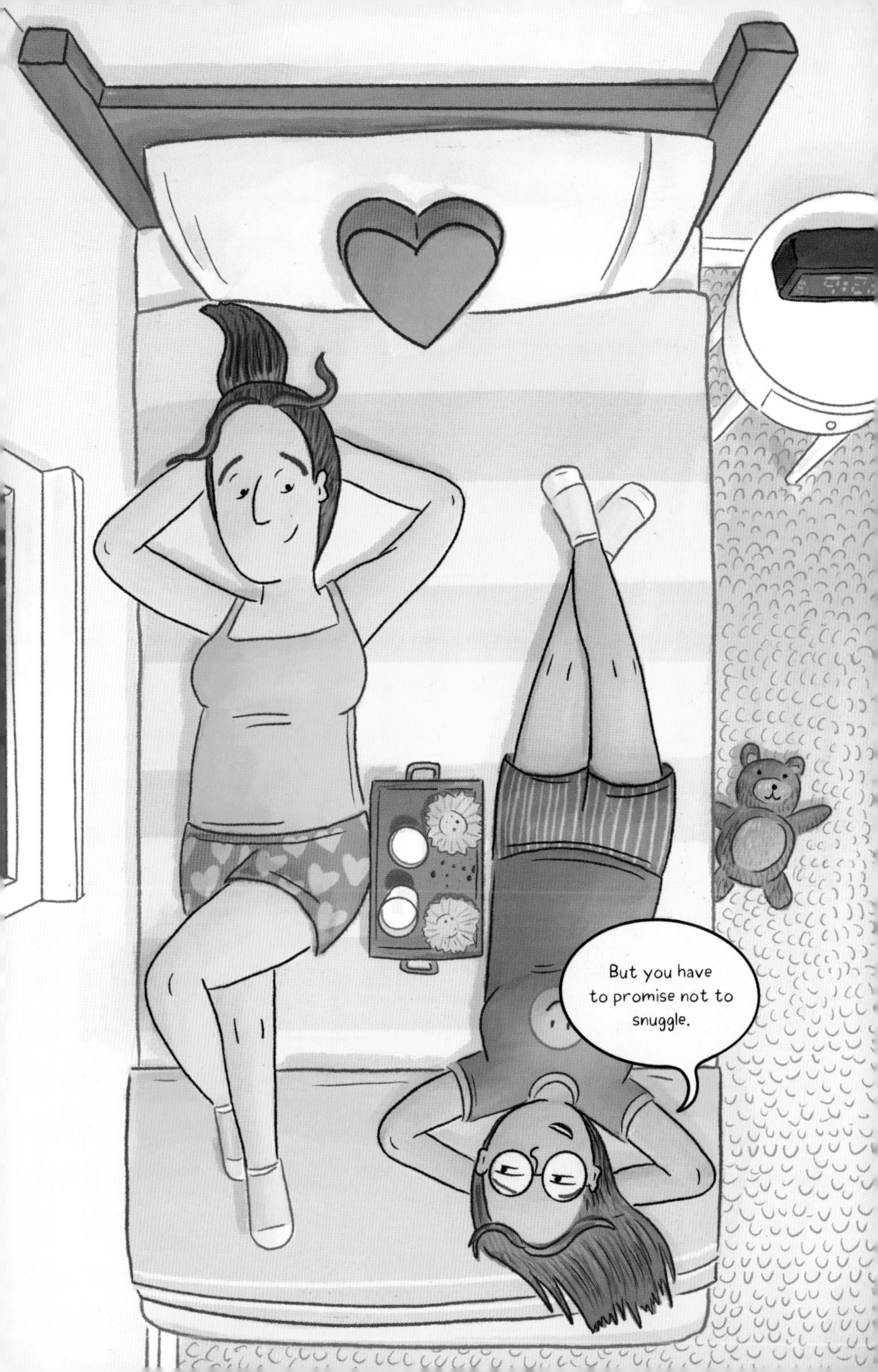
But you have to promise not to snuggle.

AUTHOR'S NOTE

Dear Reader,

Smaller Sister is not a memoir, but it is inspired by real events. My older sister, Katie, was diagnosed with an eating disorder when I was ten and she was twelve. At the time, I struggled to understand why my best friend changed seemingly overnight into someone I didn't know, and I found the complexities of this cruel disease that upended my family as I knew it hard to understand. I loved her and I was scared for her, but I was also mad at her. I was jealous of the attention she received and envious of the way she looked even when I knew it was unhealthy. I looked up to her, and yet I didn't want to be anything like her. But most of all, I wanted my REAL sister to come back, and I wanted my family to go back to the cohesive unit it was before.

But it was by moving forward, not backward, that I eventually got my sister back. Today, Katie is a great writer who runs half marathons, is an expert at doing makeup, and very irritatingly picks all the good parts out of every box of cereal. She is much, much more than a disease.

Like Lucy, I also developed disordered eating in the wake of my sister's eating disorder, and real change didn't happen in the way I saw myself until I started accepting myself as valuable for more than just what I looked like. These days, as a grown-up, my habits are a lot healthier, but those critical voices are still there. I try not to give them too much say, but it isn't easy, and every day is a new conversation.

The thing about bodies is that you only get one. Much like a pesky sister, you have to live with it every single day even when you'd rather trade it in for one you might like better. But it's also just one part of you and, as Pamela says, "no matter what size you are, you can only get so much bigger or so much smaller." And you gotta GROW.

If you or someone you love is struggling with disordered eating, anxiety, or depression, you're not alone. There are great resources available to you, including:

Active Minds: activeminds.org

National Alliance on Mental Illness (NAMI): nami.org

National Eating Disorder Association:
nationaleatingdisorders.org

Multi-Service Eating Disorder Association:
medainc.org

♡ Maggie

SECRET SISTER CODE TRANSLATOR

SHHH!

Write your own secret notes with this handy key!

A	B	C	D	E	F	G	H	I	J
ℭ	#	☺	✿	△	✳	⚲	⌐	□	☮

K	L	M	N	O	P	Q	R	S	T
☺	♙	♡	▽	∞	◖	ξξ	!	✿	◊

U	V	W	X	Y	Z
⋒	⊠	☆	△	∿	☹

SOME FUN EXTRA STUFF!

These are the annual First Day of School photos with my sister, Katie, that my mom took on our front steps in St. Louis, MO, that inspired the cover!

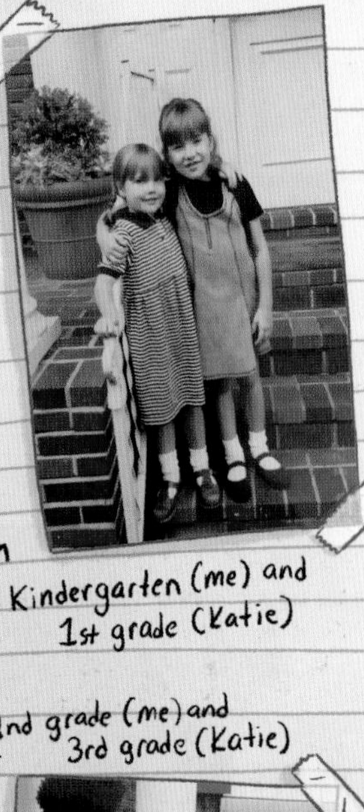

Kindergarten (me) and 1st grade (Katie)

5th grade (me) and 6th grade (Katie)

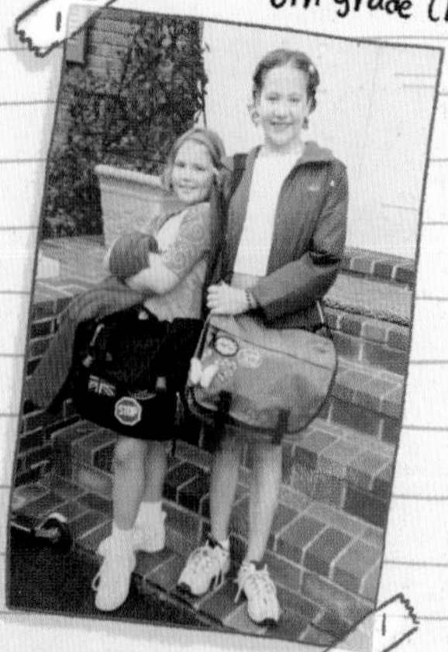

2nd grade (me) and 3rd grade (Katie)

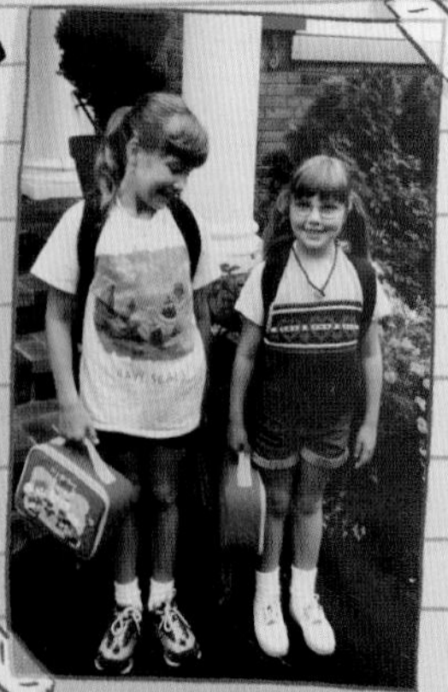

A real diary entry of mine from 5th grade that shows how true to life the sister feelings in this book are!

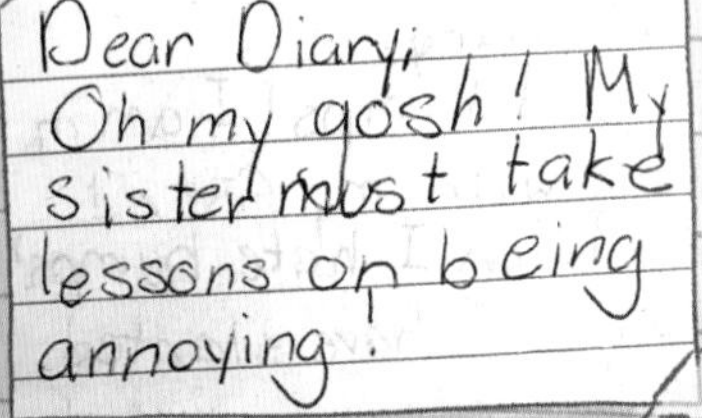

Dear Diary,
Oh my gosh! My sister must take lessons on being annoying!

ACKNOWLEDGMENTS

THANK YOU SO MUCH!

First of all, thank you to my sister, Katie, and to my mom, Laurie, for letting me spin a fictional version of our story. To the rest of my Edkins family—Dad, Jess, Grandma Margie, Ryan, Tim, Viola, Fritz, Penny, and Ruby. To Sue, Tim, and my lil bro, Brian—I am so lucky to be a Willis. To the extended Campbell, Callahan, Willis, and Campilii clans for all your love and support.

To my superhero agent, Jennifer Rofé of Andrea Brown Literary Agency, and to her assistants, Kayla and Adah, for not flinching when I dropped a graphic novel script on you out of nowhere. You somehow always say exactly the right thing to shepherd me where I need to go, and I'm so happy to be on this wild ride of publishing with you. To my brilliant editors, Megan Abbate and Connie Hsu, for championing this story and for helping me shape it into something far better. To the rest of Team *Smaller Sister* at Roaring Brook/Macmillan: Nicolás Oré-Girón, Kirk Benshoff, Molly Johanson, Jen Besser, Allison Verost, Mary Van Akin, Kristen Luby, Elysse Villalobos, Jen Healey, Taylor Pitts, Allene Cassagnol, Molly Ellis, and Mariel Dawson for your tireless work to make this book the best it can be and to get it in the hands of readers.

To my critique group—Kristin Standley, Samira Iravani, Krista Ahlberg, Helen Seachrist, and Ashley Christiano—for sharing your words and wise feedback. To Jen Keenan, my publishing buddy. To all my colleagues and mentors at Penguin Young Readers and Little, Brown for teaching me so much about books and art over the last decade. To Amanda and Barbara Bakowski, Joy Allen, Liz Ballantyne, Justin Moore, Ashley Weyl, Courtney Strickland, Maya Callender, and Kate Carroll for always being there with a hug and a dog pic. To the Princeton Tiger community, and to all my Penn friends and teachers.

Thank you to my readers, and especially to all the Lucys out there. Your plaid pants ARE cool.

And most of all, thank you to my best friend and soulmate, Mike, for reading all those drafts, for narrating the action on TV when I was too busy drawing to pay attention, and for picking up Tico's on your way home. You and Mutzy are my heart. Thank you for lovin' me.

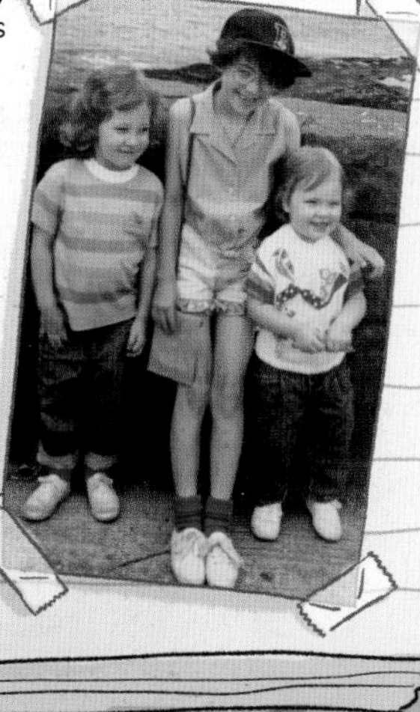

Me and my two REAL-LIFE older sisters, Katie (left) and Jess (middle).

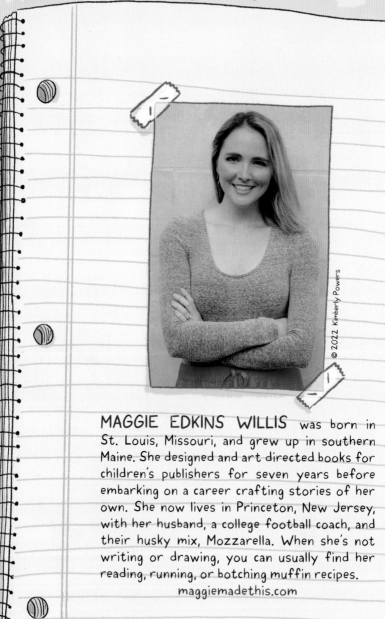

© 2022 Kimberly Powers

MAGGIE EDKINS WILLIS was born in St. Louis, Missouri, and grew up in southern Maine. She designed and art directed books for children's publishers for seven years before embarking on a career crafting stories of her own. She now lives in Princeton, New Jersey, with her husband, a college football coach, and their husky mix, Mozzarella. When she's not writing or drawing, you can usually find her reading, running, or botching muffin recipes.

maggiemadethis.com